The Best Western Stories

The Best Western Stories

Authors Include

MAX BRAND

ZANE GREY

BRET HARTE

O. HENRY

JACK LONDON

JACK SCHAEFER

MALLARD PRESS

An Imprint of BDD Promotional Book Company, Inc.
666 Fifth Avenue
New York, NY 10103

Manufactured in Great Britain

This edition first published in the United States of America in 1990
by The Mallard Press

By arrangement with The Octopus Group Limited

'Mallard Press and its accompanying design and logo are trademarks of BDD Promotional Book Company, Inc.'

ISBN 0 792 45248 8

Printed in Great Britain at The Bath Press, Avon

CONTENTS

FRANCIS BRET HARTE	*The Outcasts of Poker Flat*	7
	Johnson's Old Woman	16
	Left Out on Lone Star Mountain	28
STEPHEN CRANE	*The Bride Comes to Yellow Sky*	49
O. HENRY	*A Chaparral Prince*	59
	The Caballero's Way	67
	The Higher Abdication	77
JACK LONDON	*To Build a Fire*	94
	In a Far Country	107
ZANE GREY	*Siena Waits*	120
	Yaqui	134
	Tappan's Burro	160
FRANK C. ROBERTSON	*Three Little Calves*	196
WILL JENKINS	*Thief*	212
HENRY SINCLAIR DRAGO	*The Ghost of the Cimarron*	225
GEORGE BRYDGES RODNEY	*The Killers*	259
MAX BRAND	*Battle's End*	272
D.M. JOHNSON	*A Man Called Horse*	337
JOHN O'REILLY	*The Sound of Gunfire*	350
T.V. OLSEN	*The Man We Called Jones*	358
JACK SCHAEFER	*One Man's Honor*	368
	Sergeant Houck	383
	Acknowledgements	400

Francis Bret Harte

The Outcasts of Poker Flat

AS Mr John Oakhurst, gambler, stepped into the main street of Poker Flat on the morning of the twenty-third of November, 1850, he was conscious of a change in its moral atmosphere since the preceding night. Two or three men, conversing earnestly together, ceased as he approached, and exchanged significant glances. There was a Sabbath lull in the air, which, in a settlement unused to Sabbath influences, looked ominous.

Mr Oakhurst's calm, handsome face betrayed small concern in these indications. Whether he was conscious of any predisposing cause was another question. 'I reckon they're after somebody,' he reflected; 'likely it's me.' He returned to his pocket the handkerchief with which he had been whipping away the red dust of Poker Flat from his neat boots, and quietly discharged his mind of any further conjecture.

In point of fact, Poker Flat was 'after somebody'. It had lately suffered the loss of several thousand dollars, two valuable horses, and a prominent citizen. It was experiencing a spasm of virtuous reaction, quite as lawless and ungovernable as any of the acts that had provoked it. A secret committee had determined to rid the town of all improper persons. This was done permanently in regard of two men who were then hanging from the boughs of a sycamore in the gulch, and temporarily in the banishment of certain other objectionable characters. I regret to say that some of these were ladies. It is but due to the sex, however, to state that their impropriety was professional, and it was only in such easily established standards of evil that Poker Flat ventured to sit in judgement.

Mr Oakhurst was right in supposing that he was included in this category. A few of the committee had urged hanging him as a possible example, and a sure method of reimbursing themselves from his pockets of the sums he had won from them. 'It's agin justice,' said Jim Wheeler, 'to let this yer young man from Roaring Camp – an entire stranger – carry away our money.' But a crude sentiment of equity residing in the breasts of those who had been fortunate enough to win from Mr Oakhurst overruled this narrower local prejudice.

Mr Oakhurst received his sentence with philosophic calmness, none the less coolly that he was aware of the hesitation of his judges. He was too much of a gambler not to accept Fate. With him life was at best an uncertain game, and he recognized the usual percentage in favour of the dealer.

A body of armed men accompanied the deported wickedness of Poker Flat to the outskirts of the settlement. Besides Mr Oakhurst, who was known to be a coolly desperate man, and for whose intimidation the armed escort was intended, the expatriated party consisted of a young woman familiarly known as 'The Duchess'; another, who had won the title of 'Mother Shipton'; and 'Uncle Billy', a suspected sluice-robber and confirmed drunkard. The cavalcade provoked no comments from the spectators, nor was any word uttered by the escort. Only when the gulch which marked the uttermost limit of Poker Flat was reached, the leader spoke briefly and to the point. The exiles were forbidden to return at the peril of their lives.

As the escort disappeared, their pent-up feelings found vent in a few hysterical tears from the Duchess, some bad language from Mother Shipton, and a Parthian volley of expletives from Uncle Billy. The philosophic Oakhurst alone remained silent. He listened calmly to Mother Shipton's desire to cut somebody's heart out, to the repeated statements of the Duchess that she would die in the road, and to the alarming oaths that seemed to be bumped out of Uncle Billy as he rode forward. With the easy good-humour characteristic of his class, he insisted upon exchanging his own riding-horse, 'Five Spot', for the sorry mule which the Duchess rode. But even this act did not draw the party into any closer sympathy. The young woman readjusted her somewhat draggled plumes with a feeble, faded coquetry; Mother Shipton eyed the possessor of 'Five Spot' with malevolence; and Uncle Billy included the whole party in one sweeping anathema.

The road to Sandy Bar – a camp that, not having as yet experienced the regenerating influences of Poker Flat, consequently seemed to offer some invitation to the emigrants – lay over a steep mountain range. It was distant a day's severe travel. In that advanced season, the party soon passed out of the moist, temperate regions of the foot-hills into the dry, cold, bracing air of the Sierras. The trail was narrow and difficult. At noon the Duchess, rolling out of her saddle upon the ground, declared her intention of going no farther, and the party halted.

The spot was singularly wild and impressive. A wooded amphitheatre, surrounded on three sides by precipitous cliffs of naked granite, sloped gently toward the crest of another precipice that overlooked the valley. It was, undoubtedly, the most suitable spot for a camp, had camping been advisable. But Mr Oakhurst knew that scarcely half the journey to Sandy Bar was accomplished, and the party were not equipped or provisioned for delay. This fact he pointed out to his companions curtly, with a philosophic commentary on the folly of 'throwing up their hand before the game was played out'. But they were furnished with liquor, which in this emergency stood them in place of food, fuel, rest, and prescience. In spite of his remonstrances, it was not long before they were more or less under its influence. Uncle Billy passed rapidly from a bellicose state into one of stupor, the Duchess became maudlin, and Mother Shipton snored. Mr Oakhurst alone remained erect, leaning against a rock, calmly surveying them.

Mr Oakhurst did not drink. It interfered with a profession which required coolness, impassiveness, and presence of mind, and, in his own language, he 'couldn't afford it'. As he gazed at his recumbent fellow-exiles, the loneliness begotten of his pariah-trade, his habits of life, his very vices, for the first time seriously oppressed him. He bestirred himself in dusting his black clothes, washing his hands and face, and other acts characteristic of his studiously neat habits, and for a moment forgot his annoyance. The thought of deserting his weaker and more pitiable companions never perhaps occurred to him. Yet he could not help feeling the want of that excitement which, singularly enough, was most conducive to that calm equanimity for which he was notorious. He looked at the gloomy walls that rose a thousand feet sheer above the circling pines around him; at the sky, ominously clouded; at the valley below, already deepening into shadow. And, doing so, suddenly he heard his own name called.

A horseman slowly ascended the trail. In the fresh, open face of the newcomer Mr Oakhurst recognized Tom Simson, otherwise known as 'The Innocent' of Sandy Bar. He had met him some months before over a 'little game', and had, with perfect equanimity, won the entire fortune – amounting to some forty dollars – of that guileless youth. After the game was finished, Mr Oakhurst drew the youthful speculator behind the door, and thus addressed him: 'Tommy, you're a good little man, but you can't gamble worth a cent. Don't try it over again.' He then handed him his money back, pushed him gently from the room, and so made a devoted slave of Tom Simson.

There was a remembrance of this in his boyish and enthusiastic greeting of Mr Oakhurst. He had started, he said, to go to Poker Flat to seek his fortune. 'Alone?' No, not exactly alone; in fact (a giggle), he had run away with Piney Woods. Didn't Mr Oakhurst remember Piney? She had used to wait on the table at the Temperance House? They had been engaged a long time, but old Jake Woods had objected, and so they had run away, and were going to Poker Flat to be married, and here they were. And they were tired out, and how lucky it was they had found a place to camp and company. All this the Innocent delivered rapidly, while Piney, a stout, comely damsel of fifteen, emerged from behind the pine-tree, where she had been blushing unseen, and rode to the side of her lover.

Mr Oakhurst seldom troubled himself with sentiment, still less with propriety; but he had a vague idea that the situation was not fortunate. He retained, however, his presence of mind sufficiently to kick Uncle Billy, who was about to say something, and Uncle Billy was sober enough to recognize in Mr Oakhurst's kick a superior power that would not bear trifling. He then endeavoured to dissuade Tom Simson from delaying further, but in vain. He even pointed out the fact that there was no provision, nor means of making a camp. But, unluckily, the Innocent met this objection by assuring the party that he was provided with an extra mule loaded with provisions, and by the discovery of a rude attempt at a log-house near the trail. 'Piney can stay with Mrs Oakhurst,' said the Innocent, pointing to the Duchess, 'and I can shift for myself.'

Nothing but Mr Oakhurst's admonishing foot saved Uncle Billy from bursting into a roar of laughter. As it was, he felt compelled to retire up the cañon until he could recover his gravity. There he confided the joke to the tall pine-trees, with many slaps of his leg, contortions of his face, and the usual profanity. But when he returned to the party, he found them seated by a fire – for the air had grown strangely chill and the sky overcast – in apparently amicable conversation. Piney was actually talking in an impulsive, girlish fashion to the Duchess, who was listening with an interest and animation she had not shown for many days. The Innocent was holding forth, apparently with equal effect, to Mr Oakhurst and Mother Shipton, who was actually relaxing into amiability. 'Is this yer a d—d picnic?' said Uncle Billy, with inward scorn, as he surveyed the sylvan group, the glancing firelight, and the tethered animals in the foreground. Suddenly an idea mingled with the alcoholic fumes that disturbed his brain. It was apparently of a jocular nature, for he felt impelled to slap his leg again and cram his fist into his mouth.

As the shadows crept slowly up the mountain, a slight breeze rocked the tops of the pine-trees, and moaned through their long and gloomy aisles. The ruined cabin, patched and covered with pine-boughs, was set apart for the ladies. As the lovers parted, they unaffectedly exchanged a kiss, so honest and sincere that it might have been heard above the swaying pines. The frail Duchess and the malevolent Mother Shipton were probably too stunned to remark upon this last evidence of simplicity, and so turned without a word to the hut. The fire was replenished, the men lay down before the door, and in a few minutes were asleep.

Mr Oakhurst was a light sleeper. Toward morning he awoke benumbed and cold. As he stirred the dying fire, the wind, which was now blowing strongly, brought to his cheek that which caused the blood to leave it – snow!

He started to his feet with the intention of awakening the sleepers, for there was no time to lose. But turning to where Uncle Billy had been lying, he found him gone. A suspicion leaped to his brain and a curse to his lips. He ran to the spot where the mules had been tethered; they were no longer there. The tracks were already rapidly disappearing in the snow.

The momentary excitement brought Mr Oakhurst back to the fire with his usual calm. He did not waken the sleepers. The Innocent slumbered peacefully, with a smile on his good-humoured, freckled face; the virgin Piney slept beside her frailer sisters as sweetly as though attended by celestial guardians, and Mr Oakhurst, drawing his blanket over his shoulders, stroked his moustaches and waited for the dawn. It came slowly in a whirling mist of snow-flakes, that dazzled and confused the eye. What could be seen of the landscape appeared magically changed. He looked over the valley, and summed up the present and future in two words – 'snowed in!'

A careful inventory of the provisions, which, fortunately for the party, had been stored within the hut, and so escaped the felonious fingers of Uncle Billy, disclosed the fact that with care and prudence they might last ten days longer. 'That is,' said Mr Oakhurst, *sotto voce* to the Innocent, 'if you're willing to board us. If you ain't – and perhaps you'd better not – you can wait till Uncle Billy gets back with provisions.' For some occult reason, Mr Oakhurst could not bring himself to disclose Uncle Billy's rascality, and so offered the hypothesis that he had wandered from the camp and had accidentally stampeded the animals. He dropped a warning to the Duchess and Mother Shipton, who of course knew the facts of their associate's defection. 'They'll find out the truth about us *all* when they find out anything,' he added, significantly, 'and there's no good frightening them now.'

Tom Simson not only put all his worldly store at the disposal of Mr Oakhurst, but seemed to enjoy the prospect of their enforced seclusion. 'We'll have a good camp for a week, and then the snow'll melt, and we'll all go back together.' The cheerful gaiety of the young man and Mr Oakhurst's calm infected the others. The Innocent, with the aid of pine-boughs, extemporized a thatch for the roofless cabin, and the Duchess directed Piney in the rearrangement of the interior with a taste and tact that opened the blue eyes of that provincial maiden to their fullest extent. 'I reckon now you're used to fine things at Poker Flat,' said Piney. The Duchess turned away sharply to conceal something that reddened her cheeks through its professional tint, and Mother Shipton requested Piney not to 'chatter'. But when Mr Oakhurst returned from a weary search for the trail, he heard the sound of happy laughter echoed from the rocks. He stopped in some alarm, and his thoughts first naturally reverted to the whisky, which he had prudently cachéd. 'And yet it don't somehow sound like whisky,' said the gambler. It was not until he caught sight of the blazing fire through the still blinding storm and the group around it, that he settled to the conviction that it was 'square fun'.

Whether Mr Oakhurst had cachéd his cards with the whisky as something debarred the free access of the community, I cannot say. It was certain that, in Mother Shipton's words, he 'didn't say cards once' during that evening. Haply the time was beguiled by an accordion, produced somewhat ostentatiously by Tom Simson from his pack. Notwithstanding some difficulties attending the manipulation of this instrument, Piney Woods managed to pluck several reluctant melodies from its keys, to an accompaniment by the Innocent on a pair of bone castinets. But the crowning festivity of the evening was reached in a rude camp-meeting hymn, which the lovers, joining hands, sang with great earnestness and vociferation. I fear that a certain defiant tone and Covenanter's swing to its chorus, rather than any devotional quality, caused it speedily to infect the others, who at last joined in the refrain:

'I'm proud to live in the service of the Lord,
And I'm bound to die in His army.'

The pines rocked, the storm eddied and whirled above the miserable group, and the flames of their altar leaped heavenward, as if in token of the vow.

At midnight the storm abated, the rolling clouds parted, and the stars glittered keenly above the sleeping camp. Mr Oakhurst, whose professional habits had enabled him to live on the smallest possible amount of sleep, in dividing the watch with Tom Simson, somehow managed to take upon himself the greater part of that duty. He excused himself to the Innocent by saying that he had 'often been a week without sleep'. 'Doing what?' asked Tom. 'Poker!' replied Oakhurst, sententiously; 'when a man gets a streak of luck – nigger-luck – he don't get tired. The luck gives in first. Luck,' continued the gambler, reflectively, 'is a mighty queer thing. All you know about it for certain is that it's bound to change. And it's finding out when it's going to change that makes you. We've had a streak of bad luck since we left Poker Flat – you come along, and slap you get into it, too. If you can hold your cards right along you're all right. For,' added the gambler, with cheerful irrelevance

'I'm proud to live in the service of the Lord,
And I'm bound to die in His army.'

The third day came, and the sun, looking through the white-curtained valley, saw the outcasts divide their slowly decreasing store of provisions for the morning meal. It was one of the peculiarities of that mountain climate that its rays diffused a kindly warmth over the wintry landscape, as if in regretful commiseration of the past. But it revealed drift on drift of snow piled high around the hut – a hopeless, unchartered, trackless sea of white lying below the rocky shores to which the castaways still clung. Through the marvellously clear air the smoke of the pastoral village of Poker Flat rose miles away. Mother Shipton saw it, and from a remote pinnacle of her rocky fastness, hurled in that direction a final malediction. It was her last vituperative attempt, and perhaps for that reason was invested with a certain degree of sublimity. It did her good, she privately informed the Duchess. 'Just you go out there and cuss, and see.' She then set herself to the task of amusing 'the child', as she and the Duchess were pleased to call Piney. Piney was no chicken, but it was a soothing and original theory of the pair thus to account for the fact that she didn't swear and wasn't improper.

When night crept up again through the gorges, the reedy notes of the accordion rose and fell in fitful spasms and long-drawn gasps by the flickering camp-fire. But music failed to fill entirely the aching void left by insufficient food, and a new diversion was proposed by Piney – story-telling. Neither Mr Oakhurst nor his female companions caring to relate their personal experiences, this plan would have failed, too, but for the Innocent. Some months before he had chanced upon a stray copy of Mr Pope's ingenious translation of the *Iliad*. He now proposed to narrate the principal incidents of that poem – having thoroughly mastered the argument and fairly forgotten the words – in the current vernacular of Sandy Bar. And so for the rest of that night the Homeric demigods again walked the earth. Trojan bully and wily Greek wrestled in the winds, and the great pines in the cañon seemed to bow to the wrath of the son of Peleus. Mr Oakhurst listened with quiet satisfaction. Most especially was he interested in the fate of 'Ash-heels', as the Innocent persisted in denominating the 'swift-footed Achilles'.

So with small food and much of Homer and the accordion, a week passed over the heads of the outcasts. The sun again forsook them, and again from leaden skies the snowflakes were sifted over the land. Day by day closer around them drew the snowy circle, until at last they looked from their prison over drifted walls of dazzling white, that towered twenty feet above their heads. It became more and more difficult to replenish their fires, even from the fallen trees beside them, now half hidden in the drifts. And yet no one complained. The lovers turned from the dreary prospect and looked into each other's eyes, and were happy. Mr Oakhurst settled himself coolly to the losing game before him. The Duchess, more cheerful than she had been, assumed the care of Piney. Only Mother Shipton – once the strongest of the party – seemed to sicken and fade. At midnight on the tenth day she called Oakhurst to her side. 'I'm going,' she said, in a voice of querulous weakness, 'but don't say anything about it. Don't waken the kids. Take the bundle from under my head and open it.' Mr Oakhurst did so. It contained Mother Shipton's rations for the last week, untouched. 'Give 'em to the child,' she said, pointing to the sleeping Piney. 'You've starved yourself,' said the gambler. 'That's what they call it,' said the woman, querulously, and she lay down again, and, turning her face to the wall, passed quietly away.

The accordion and the bones were put aside that day, and Homer was forgotten. When the body of Mother Shipton had been committed to the snow, Mr Oakhurst took the Innocent aside, and showed him a pair of snow-shoes, which he had fashioned from the old pack-saddle. 'There's one chance in a hundred to save her yet,' he said, pointing to Piney, 'but it's there,' he added, pointing toward Poker Flat. 'If you can reach there in two days she's safe.' 'And you?' asked Tom Simson. 'I'll stay here,' was the curt reply.

The lovers parted with a long embrace. 'You are not going, too?' said the Duchess, as she saw Mr Oakhurst apparently waiting to accompany him. 'As far as the canyon,' he replied. He turned suddenly, and kissed the Duchess, leaving her pallid face aflame, and her trembling limbs rigid with amazement.

Night came, but not Mr Oakhurst. It brought the storm again and the whirling snow. Then the Duchess, feeding the fire, found that some one had quietly piled beside the hut enough fuel to last a few days longer. The tears rose to her eyes, but she hid them from Piney.

The woman slept but little. In the morning, looking into each other's faces, they read their fate. Neither spoke; but Piney, accepting the position of the stronger, drew near and placed her arm around the Duchess's waist. They kept this attitude for the rest of the day. That night the storm reached its greatest fury, and, rending asunder the protecting pines, invaded the very hut.

Toward morning they found themselves unable to feed the fire, which gradually died away. As the embers slowly blackened, the Duchess crept closer to Piney, and broke the silence of many hours: 'Piney, can you pray?' 'No, dear,' said Piney, simply. The Duchess, without knowing exactly why, felt relieved, and, putting her head upon Piney's shoulder, spoke no more. And so reclining, the younger and purer pillowing the head of her soiled sister upon her virgin breast, they fell asleep.

The wind lulled as if it feared to waken them. Feathery drifts of snow, shaken from the long pine-boughs, flew like white-winged birds, and settled about them as they slept. The moon through the rifted clouds looked down upon what had been the camp. But all human stain, all trace of earthly travail, was hidden beneath the spotless mantle mercifully flung from above.

They slept all that day and the next, nor did they waken when voices and footsteps broke the silence of the camp. And when pitying fingers brushed the snow from their wan faces, you could scarcely have told, from the equal peace that dwelt upon them, which was she that had sinned. Even the law of Poker Flat recognized this, and turned away, leaving them still locked in each other's arms.

But at the head of the gulch, on one of the largest pine-trees, they found the deuce of clubs pinned to the bark with a bowie-knife. It bore the following, written in pencil, in a firm hand:

BENEATH THIS TREE LIES THE BODY OF
JOHN OAKHURST
WHO STRUCK A STREAK OF BAD LUCK
ON THE 23RD OF NOVEMBER, 1850,
AND HANDED IN HIS CHECKS
ON THE 7TH DECEMBER, 1850.

And pulseless and cold, with a Derringer by his side and a bullet in his heart, though still calm as in life, beneath the snow lay he who was at once the strongest and yet the weakest of the outcasts of Poker Flat.

Francis Bret Harte

Johnson's 'Old Woman'

IT was growing dark, and the Sonora trail was becoming more indistinct before me at every step. The difficulty had increased over the grassy slope, where the overflow from some smaller watercourse above had worn a number of diverging gullies so like the trail as to be undistinguishable from it. Unable to determine which was the right one, I threw the reins over the mule's neck and resolved to trust to that superior animal's sagacity, of which I had heard so much. But I had not taken into account the equally well-known weaknesses of sex and species, and Chu Chu had already shown uncontrollable signs of wanting her own way. Without a moment's hesitation, feeling the relaxed bridle, she laid down and rolled over.

In this perplexity the sound of horse's hoofs ringing out of the rocky canyon beyond was a relief, even if momentarily embarrassing. An instant afterwards a horse and rider appeared cantering round the hill on what was evidently the lost trail, and pulled up as I succeeded in forcing Chu Chu to her legs again.

'Is that the trail from Sonora?' I asked.

'Yes;' but with a critical glance at the mule, 'I reckon you ain't going thar to-night.'

'Why not?'

'It's a matter of eighteen miles, and most of it a blind trail through the woods after you take the valley.'

'Is it worse than this?'

'What's the matter with this trail? Ye ain't expecting a racecourse or a shell road over the foot-hills – are ye?'

'No. Is there any hotel where I can stop?'

'Nary.'

'Nor any house?'

'No.'

'Thank you. Good night.'

He had already passed on, when he halted again and turned in his saddle. 'Look yer. Just a spell over yon canyon ye'll find a patch o' buckeyes; turn to the right and ye'll see a trail. That'll take ye to a shanty. You ask if it's Johnson's.'

'Who's Johnson?'

'I am. You ain't lookin' for Vanderbilt or God Almighty up here, are you? Well then, you hark to me, will you? You say to my old woman to give you supper and a shake-down somewhar tonight. Say *I* sent you. So long.'

He was gone before I could accept or decline. An extraordinary noise proceeded from Chu Chu, not unlike a suppressed chuckle. I looked sharply at her; she coughed affectedly, and, with her head and neck stretched to their greatest length, appeared to contemplate her neat little off fore shoe with admiring abstraction. But as soon as I had mounted she set off abruptly, crossed the rocky canyon, apparently sighted the patch of buckeyes of her own volition, and without the slightest hesitation found the trail to the right, and in half an hour stood before the shanty.

It was a log cabin, with an additional 'lean-to' of the same material, roofed with bark, and on the other side a larger and more ambitious 'extension' built of rough, unplaned, and unpainted redwood boards, lightly shingled. The 'lean-to' was evidently used as a kitchen, and the central cabin as a living-room. The barking of a dog as I approached called four children of different sizes to the open door, where already an enterprising baby was feebly essaying to crawl over a bar of wood laid across the threshold to restrain it.

'Is this Johnson's house?'

My remark was really addressed to the eldest, a boy of apparently nine or ten, but I felt that my attention was unduly fascinated by the baby, who at that moment had toppled over the bar, and was calmly eyeing me upside down, while silently and heroically suffocating in its petticoats. The boy disappeared without replying, but presently returned with a taller girl of fourteen or fifteen. I was struck with the way that, as she reached the door, she passed her hands rapidly over the heads of the others as if counting them, picked up the baby, reversed it, shook out its clothes, and returned it to the inside without even looking at it. The act was evidently automatic and habitual.

I repeated my question timidly.

Yes, it *was* Johnson's, but he had just gone to King's Mills. I replied hurriedly that I knew it – that I had met him beyond the canyon. As I had lost my way and couldn't get to Sonora tonight, he had been good enough to say that I might stay until morning. My voice was slightly raised for the benefit of Mr Johnson's 'old woman', who, I had no doubt, was inspecting me furtively from some corner.

The girl drew the children away, except the boy. To him she said simply, 'Show the stranger whar to stake out his mule, 'Dolphus,' and disappeared in the 'extension' without another word. I followed my little guide, who was perhaps more actively curious, but equally unresponsive. To my various questions he simply returned a smile of exasperating vacuity. But he never took his eager eyes from me, and I was satisfied that not a detail of my appearance escaped him. Leading the way behind the house to a little wood, whose only 'clearing' had been effected by decay or storm, he stood silently apart while I picketed Chu Chu, neither offering to assist me nor opposing any interruption to my survey of the locality. There was no trace of human cultivation in the surroundings of the cabin; the wilderness still trod sharply on the heels of the pioneer's fresh footprints, and even seemed to obliterate them. For a few yards around the actual dwelling there was an unsavoury fringe of civilization in the shape of cast-off clothes, empty bottles, and tin cans, and the adjacent thorn and elder bushes blossomed unwholesomely with bits of torn white paper and bleaching dish-cloths. This hideous circle never widened; Nature always appeared to roll back the intruding débris; no bird nor beast carried it away; no animal ever forced the uncleanly barrier; civilization remained grimly trenched in its own exuvia. The old terrifying girdle of fire around the hunters' camp was not more deterring to curious night prowlers than this coarse and accidental outwork.

When I regained the cabin I found it empty, the doors of the lean-to and extension closed, but there was a stool set before a rude table, upon which smoked a tin cup of coffee, a tin dish of hot saleratus biscuit, and a plate of fried beef. There was something odd and depressing in this silent exclusion of my presence. Had Johnson's 'old woman' from some dark post of observation taken a dislike to my appearance, or was this churlish withdrawal a peculiarity of Sierran hospitality? Or was Mrs Johnson young and pretty, and hidden under the restricting ban of Johnson's jealousy, or was she a deformed cripple, or even a bed-ridden crone? From the extension at times came a murmur of voices, but never the accents of adult womanhood. The gathering darkness, relieved only by a dull glow from the smouldering logs in the adobe chimney, added to my loneliness. In the circumstances I knew I ought to have put aside the repast and given myself up to gloomy and pessimistic reflection; but Nature is often inconsistent, and in that keen mountain air, I grieve to say, my physical and moral condition was not in that perfect accord always indicated by romancers. I had an appetite, and I gratified it; dyspepsia and ethical reflections might come later. I ate the saleratus biscuit cheerfully, and was meditatively finishing my coffee when a gurgling sound from the rafters above attracted my attention. I looked up; under the overhang of the bark roof three pairs of round eyes were fixed upon me. They belonged to the children I had previously seen, who, in the attitude of Raphael's cherubs, had evidently been deeply interested spectators of my repast. As our eyes met an inarticulate giggle escaped the lips of the youngest.

I never could understand why the shy amusement of children over their elders is not accepted as philosophically by its object as when it proceeds from an equal. We fondly believe that when Jones or Brown laughs at us it is from malice, ignorance, or a desire to show his superiority, but there is always a haunting suspicion in our minds that these little critics *really* see something in us to laugh at. I, however, smiled affably in return, ignoring any possible grotesqueness in my manner of eating in private.

'Come here, Johnny,' I said blandly.

The two elder ones, a girl and a boy, disappeared instantly, as if the crowning joke of this remark was too much for them. From a scraping and kicking against the log wall I judged that they had quickly dropped to the ground outside. The younger one, the giggler, remained fascinated, but ready to fly at a moment's warning.

'Come here, Johnny, boy,' I repeated gently. 'I want you to go to your mother, please, and tell her – '

But here the child, who had been working its face convulsively, suddenly uttered a lugubrious howl and disappeared also. I ran to the front door and looked out in time to see the tallest girl, who had received me, walking away with it under her arm, pushing the boy ahead of her and looking back over her shoulder, not unlike a youthful she-bear conducting her cubs from danger. She disappeared at the end of the extension, where there was evidently another door.

It was very extraordinary. It was not strange that I turned back to the cabin with a chagrin and mortification which for a moment made me entertain the wild idea of saddling Chu Chu and shaking the dust of that taciturn house from my feet. But the ridiculousness of such an act, to say nothing of its ingratitude, as quickly presented itself to me. Johnson had offered me only food and shelter; I could have claimed no more from the inn I had asked him to direct me to. I did not re-enter the house, but, lighting my last cigar, began to walk gloomily up and down the trail. With the outcoming of the stars it had grown lighter; through a wind opening in the trees I could see the heavy bulk of the opposite mountain, and beyond it a superior crest defined by a red line of forest fire, which, however, cast no reflection on the surrounding earth or sky. Faint woodland currents of air, still warm from the afternoon sun, stirred the leaves around me with long-drawn aromatic breaths. But these in time gave way to the steady Sierran night wind sweeping down from the higher summits, and rocking the tops of the tallest pines, yet leaving the tranquillity of the dark lower aisles unshaken. It was very quiet; there was no cry nor call of beast or bird in the darkness; the long rustle of the tree-tops sounded as faint as the far-off wash of distant seas. Nor did the resemblance cease there; the close-set files of the pines and cedars, stretching in illimitable ranks to the horizon, were filled with the immeasurable loneliness of an ocean shore. In this vast silence I began to think I understood the taciturnity of the dwellers in the solitary cabin.

When I returned, however, I was surprised to find the tallest girl standing by the door. As I approached she retreated before me, and, pointing to the corner where a common cot bed had been evidently just put up, said, 'Ye can turn in thar, only ye'll have to rouse out early when 'Dolphus does the chores,' and was turning towards the extension again, when I stopped her almost appealingly.

'One moment, please. Can I see your mother?'

She stopped and looked at me with a singular expression. Then she said sharply

'You know, fust rate, she's dead.'

She was turning away again, but I think she must have seen my concern in my face, for she hesitated. 'But,' I said quickly, 'I certainly understood your father, that is, Mr Johnson,' I added interrogatively, 'to say that – that I was to speak to' – I didn't like to repeat the exact phrase – 'his *wife*'.

'I don't know what he was playin' ye for,' she said shortly. 'Mar has been dead mor'n a year.'

'But,' I persisted, 'is there no grown-up woman here?'

'No.'

'Then who takes care of you and the children?'

'I do.'

'Yourself and your father – eh?'

'Dad ain't here two days running, and then on'y to sleep.'

'And you take the entire charge of the house?'

'Yes, and the log tallies.'

'The log tallies?'

'Yes; keep count and measure the logs that go by the slide.'

It flashed upon me that I had passed the slide or declivity on the hill-side, where logs were slipped down into the valley, and I inferred that Johnson's business was cutting timber for the mill.

'But you're rather young for all this work,' I suggested.

'I'm goin' on sixteen,' she said gravely.

Indeed, for the matter of that, she might have been any age. Her face, on which sunburn took the place of complexion, was already hard and set. But on a nearer view I was struck with the fact that her eyes, which were not large, were almost indistinguishable from the presence of the most singular eyelashes I had ever seen. Intensely black, intensely thick, and even tangled in their profusion, they bristled rather than fringed her eyelids, obliterating everything but the shining black pupils beneath, which were like certain lustrous hairy mountain berries. It was this woodland suggestion that seemed to uncannily connect her with the locality. I went on playfully –

'That's not *very* old; but tell me – does your father, or *did* your father, ever speak of you as "his old woman"?'

She nodded. 'Then you thought I was mar?' she said, smiling.

It was such a relief to see her worn face relax its expression of pathetic gravity – although this operation quite buried her eyes in their black thick-set hedge again – that I continued cheerfully, 'It wasn't much of a mistake, considering all you do for the house and family.'

'Then you didn't tell Billy "to go and be dead in the ground with mar," as he 'lows you did?' she said half suspiciously, yet trembling on the edge of a smile.

No, I had not; but I admitted that my asking him to go to his mother might have been open to this dismal construction by a sensitive infant mind. She seemed mollified, and again turned to go.

'Good night, Miss – ; you know your father didn't tell me your real name,' I said.

'Karline!'

'Good night, Miss Karline.'

I held out my hand.

She looked at it and then at me through her intricate eyelashes. Then she struck it aside briskly, but not unkindly, said 'Quit foolin' now,' as she might have said to one of the children, and disappeared through the inner door. Not knowing whether to be amused or indignant, I remained silent a moment. Then I took a turn outside in the increasing darkness, listened to the now hurrying wind over the treetops, re-entered the cabin, closed the door, and went to bed.

But not to sleep. Perhaps the responsibility towards these solitary children, which Johnson had so lightly shaken off, devolved upon me as I lay there, for I found myself imagining a dozen emergencies of their unprotected state with which the elder girl could scarcely grapple. There was little to fear from depredatory man or beast – desperadoes of the mountain trail never stooped to ignoble burglary, bear or panther seldom approached a cabin – but there was the chance of sudden illness, fire, the accidents that beset childhood, to say nothing of the narrowing moral and mental effect of their isolation at that tender age. It was scandalous in Johnson to leave them alone.

In the silence I found I could hear quite distinctly the sound of their voices in the extension, and it was evident that Caroline was putting them to bed. Suddenly a voice was uplifted – her own! She began to sing and the others to join her. It was the repetition of a single verse of a well-known lugubrious negro melody. 'All the world am sad and dreary,' wailed Caroline, in a high head-note, 'everywhere I roam.' 'O, darkieth,' lisped the younger girl in response, 'how my heart growth weary, far from the old folkth at h-o-o-me.' This was repeated two or three times before the others seemed to get the full swing of it, and then the lines rose and fell sadly and monotonously in the darkness. I don't know why, but I at once got the impression that those motherless little creatures were under a vague belief that their performance was devotional, and was really filling the place of an evening hymn. A brief and indistinct kind of recitation, followed by a dead silence, broken only by the slow creaking of new timber, as if the house were stretching itself to sleep too, confirmed my impression. Then all became quiet again.

But I was more wide awake than before. Finally I rose, dressed myself, and dragging my stool to the fire, took a book from my knapsack, and by the light of a guttering candle, which I discovered in a bottle in the corner of the hearth, began to read. Presently I fell into a doze. How long I slept I could not tell, for it seemed to me that a dreamy consciousness of a dog barking at last forced itself upon me so strongly that I awoke. The barking appeared to come from behind the cabin, in the direction of the clearing where I had tethered Chu Chu. I opened the door hurriedly, ran round the cabin towards the hollow, and was almost at once met by the bulk of the frightened Chu Chu, plunging out of the darkness towards me, kept only in check by her riata in the hand of a blanketed shape slowly advancing with a gun over its shoulder out of the hollow. Before I had time to recover from my astonishment I was thrown into greater confusion by recognizing the shape as none other than Caroline!

Without the least embarrassment or even self-consciousness of her appearance, she tossed the end of the riata to me with the curtest explanation as she passed by. Some prowling bear or catamount had frightened the mule. I had better tether it before the cabin away from the wind.

'But I thought wild beasts never came so near,' I said quickly.

'Mule meat's mighty temptin',' said the girl sententiously and passed on. I wanted to thank her; I wanted to say how sorry I was that she had been disturbed; I wanted to compliment her on her quiet midnight courage, and yet warn her against recklessness; I wanted to know whether she had been accustomed to such alarms; and if the gun she carried was really a necessity. But I could only respect her reticence, and I was turning away when I was struck by a more inexplicable spectacle. As she neared the end of the extension I distinctly saw the tall figure of a man, moving with a certain diffidence and hesitation that did not, however, suggest any intention of concealment, among the trees; the girl apparently saw him at the same moment, and slightly slackened her pace. Not more than a dozen feet separated them. He said something that was inaudible to my ears – but whether from his hesitation or the distance, I could not determine. There was no such uncertainty in her reply, however, which was given in her usual curt fashion – 'All right. You kin traipse along home now and turn in.'

She turned the corner of the extension and disappeared. The tall figure of the man wavered hesitatingly for a moment, and then vanished also. But I was too much excited by curiosity to accept this unsatisfactory conclusion, and, hastily picketing Chu Chu a few rods from the front door, I ran after him, with an instinctive feeling that he had not gone far. I was right. A few paces distant he had halted in the same dubious, lingering way. 'Hallo!' I said.

He turned towards me in the like awkward fashion, but with neither astonishment nor concern.

'Come up and take a drink with me before you go,' I said, 'if you're not in a hurry. I'm alone here, and since I *have* turned out I don't see why we mightn't have a smoke and a talk together.'

'I dursn't.'

I looked up at the six feet of strength before me and repeated wonderingly, 'Dare not?'

'*She* wouldn't like it.' He made a movement with his right shoulder towards the extension.

'Who?'

'Miss Karline.'

'Nonsense!' I said. 'She isn't in the cabin – you won't see *her*. Come along.' He hesitated, although from what I could discern of his bearded face it was weakly smiling.

'Come.'

He obeyed, following me not unlike Chu Chu, I fancied, with the same sense of superior size and strength and a slight whitening of the eye, as if ready to shy at any moment. At the door he 'backed'. Then he entered sideways. I noticed that he cleared the doorway at the top and the sides only by a hair's-breadth.

By the light of the fire I could see that, in spite of his full first growth of beard, he was young – even younger than myself, and that he was by no means bad-looking. As he still showed signs of retreating at any moment, I took my flask and tobacco from my saddle-bags, handed them to him, pointed to the stool, and sat down myself upon the bed.

'You live near here?'

'Yes,' he said a little abstractedly, as if listening for some interruption, 'at Ten Mile Crossing.'

'Why, that's two miles away.'

'I reckon.'

'Then you don't live here – on the clearing?'

'No. I b'long to the mill at "Ten Mile".'

'You were on your way home?'

'No,' he hesitated, looking at his pipe; 'I kinder meander round here at this time, when Johnson's away, to see if everything's goin' straight.'

'I see – you're a friend of the family.'

' 'Deed no!' He stopped, laughed, looked confused, and added, apparently to his pipe, 'That is, a sorter friend. Not much. *She*' – he lowered his voice, as if that potential personality filled the whole cabin – 'wouldn't like it.'

'Then at night, when Johnson's away, you do sentry duty round the house?'

'Yes, "sentry dooty", that's it' – he seemed impressed with the suggestion – 'that's it! Sentry dooty. You've struck it, pardner.'

'And how often is Johnson away?'

' 'Bout two or three times a week on an average.'

'But Miss Caroline appears to be able to take care of herself. She has no fear.'

'Fear! Fear wasn't hangin' round when *she* was born!' He paused. 'No, sir. Did ye ever look into them eyes?'

I hadn't, on account of the lashes. But I didn't care to say this, and only nodded.

'There ain't the created thing livin' or dead that she can't stand straight up to and look at.'

I wondered if he had fancied she experienced any difficulty in standing up before that innocently good-humoured face, but I could not resist saying –

'Then I don't see the use of your walking four miles to look after her.'

I was sorry for it the next minute, for he seemed to have awkwardly broken his pipe, and had to bend down for a long time afterwards to laboriously pick up the smallest fragments of it. At last he said cautiously –

'Ye noticed them bits o' flannin' round the children's throats?'

I remembered that I had, but was uncertain whether it was intended as a preventive of cold or a child's idea of decoration. I nodded.

'That's their trouble. One night, when old Johnson had been off for three days to Coulterville, I was prowling round here and I didn't git to see no one, though there was a light burnin' in the shanty all night. The next night I was here again – the same light twinklin', but no one about. I reckoned that was mighty queer, and I jess crep' up to the house an' listened. I heard suthin' like a little cough onest in a while, and times suthin' like a little moan. I didn't durst to sing out, for I knew *she* wouldn't like it, but I whistled keerless like, to let the chillern know I was there. But it didn't seem to take. I was jess goin' off, when – darn my skin! – if I didn't come across the bucket of water I'd fetched up from the spring *that mornin'*, standin' there full, and *never taken in!* When I saw that I reckoned I'd jess wade in, anyhow, and I knocked. Pooty soon the door was half opened, and I saw her eyes blazin' at me like them coals. Then *she* 'lowed I'd better "git up and get", and shet the door to! Then I 'lowed she might tell me what was up – through the door. Then she said – through the door – as how the chillern lay all sick with that hoss-distemper, diphthery. Then she 'lowed she'd use a doctor ef I'd fetch him. Then she 'lowed again I'd better take the baby, that hadn't ketched it yet, along with me, and leave it where it was safe. Then she passed out the baby through the door all wrapped up in a blankit like a papoose, and you bet I made tracks with it. I knowed thar wasn't no good going to the mill, so I let out for White's, four miles beyond, whar there was White's old mother. I told her how things were pointin', and she lent me a hoss, and I jess rounded on Doctor Green at Mountain Jim's, and had him back here afore sun up! And then I heard she wilted – regularly played out, you see – for she had it all along wuss than the lot, and never let on or whimpered!'

'It was well you persisted in seeing her that night,' I said, watching the rapt expression of his face. He looked up quickly, became conscious of my scrutiny, and dropped his eyes again, smiled feebly, and drawing a circle in the ashes with the broken pipe-stem, said –

'But *she* didn't like it, though.'

I suggested, a little warmly, that if she allowed her father to leave her alone at night with delicate children, she had no right to choose *who* should assist her in an emergency. It struck me afterwards that this was not very complimentary to him, and I added hastily that I wondered if she expected some young lady to be passing along the trail at midnight! But this reminded me of Johnson's style of argument, and I stopped.

'Yes,' he said meekly; 'and ef she didn't keer enough for herself and her brothers and sisters, she orter remember them Beazeley chillern.'

'Beazeley children?' I repeated wonderingly.

'Yes; them two little ones, the size of Mirandy; they're Beazeley's.'

'Who is Beazeley, and what are his children doing here?'

'Beazeley up and died at the mill, and she bedevilled her father to let her take his two young 'uns here.'

'You don't mean to say that with her other work she's taking care of other people's children too?'

'Yes, and eddicatin' them.'

'Educating them?'

'Yes; teachin' them to read and write and do sums. One of our loggers ketched her at it when she was keepin' tally.'

We were both silent for some moments.

'I suppose you know Johnson?' I said finally.

'Not much.'

'But you call here at other times than when you're helping her?'

'Never been in the house before.'

He looked slowly around him as he spoke, raising his eyes to the bare rafters above, and drawing a few long breaths, as if he were inhaling the aura of some unseen presence. He appeared so perfectly gratified and contented, and I was so impressed with this humble and silent absorption of the sacred interior, that I felt vaguely conscious that any interruption of it was a profanation, and I sat still, gazing at the dying fire. Presently he arose, stretched out his hand, shook mine warmly, said, 'I reckon I'll meander along,' took another long breath, this time secretly, as if conscious of my eyes, and then slouched sideways out of the house into the darkness again, where he seemed suddenly to attain his full height, and so looming, disappeared. I shut the door, went to bed, and slept soundly.

So soundly that when I awoke the sun was streaming on my bed from the open door. On the table before me my breakfast was already laid. When I had dressed and eaten it, struck by the silence, I went to the door and looked out. 'Dolphus was holding Chu Chu by the riata a few paces from the cabin.

'Where's Caroline?' I asked.

He pointed to the woods and said, 'Over yon; keeping tally.'

'Did she leave any message?'

'Said I was to git your mule for you.'

'Anything else?'

'Yes; said you was to go.'

I went, but not until I had scrawled a few words of thanks on a leaf of my notebook, which I wrapped about my last Spanish dollar, addressed it to 'Miss Johnson', and laid it upon the table.

It was more than a year later that in the bar-room of the Mariposas Hotel a hand was laid upon my sleeve. I looked up. It was Johnson.

He drew from his pocket a Spanish dollar. 'I reckoned,' he said cheerfully, 'I'd run again ye somewhar some time. My old woman told me to give ye that when I did, and say that she "didn't keep no hotel". But she allowed she'd keep the letter, and has spelled it out to the chillern.'

Here was the opportunity I had longed for to touch Johnson's pride and affection in the brave but unprotected girl. 'I want to talk to you about Miss Johnson,' I said eagerly.

'I reckon so,' he said, with an exasperating smile. 'Most fellers do. But she ain't *Miss* Johnson no more. She's married.'

'Not to that big chap over from Ten Mile Mills?' I said breathlessly.

'What's the matter with *him*?' said Johnson. 'Ye didn't expect her to marry a nobleman, did ye?'

I said I didn't see why she shouldn't – and believed that she *had*.

Francis Bret Harte

Left out on Lone Star Mountain

I

THERE was little doubt that the 'Lone Star' claim was 'played out'. Not dug out, worked out, washed out – but *played* out. For two years its five sanguine proprietors had gone through the various stages of mining enthusiasm; had prospected and planned, dug and doubted. They had borrowed money with hearty, but unredeeming, frankness; established a credit with unselfish agnegation of all responsibility; and had borne the disappointment of their creditors with a cheerful resignation which only the consciousness of some deep Compensating Future could give. Giving little else, however, a singular dissatisfaction obtained with the traders, and, being accompanied with a reluctance to make further advances, at last touched the gentle stoicism of the proprietors themselves. The youthful enthusiasm which had at first lifted the most ineffectual trial – the most useless essay – to the plane of actual achievement, died out, leaving them only the dull, prosaic record of half-finished ditches, purposeless shafts, untenable pits, abandoned engines, and meaningless disruptions of the soil upon the 'Lone Star' claim, and empty flour sacks and pork barrels in the 'Lone Star' cabin.

They had borne their poverty – if that term could be applied to a light renunciation of all superfluities in food, dress, or ornament, ameliorated by the gentle depredations already alluded to – with unassuming levity. More than that: having segregated themselves from their fellow miners of Red Gulch, and entered upon the possession of the little manzanita-thicketed valley five miles away, the failure of their enterprise had assumed in their eyes only the vague significance of the decline and fall of a general community, and to that extent relieved them of individual responsibility. It was easier for them to admit that the 'Lone Star' claim was 'played out' than confess to a personal bankruptcy. Moreover, they still retained the sacred right of criticism of Government, and rose superior in their private opinions to their own collective wisdom. Each one experienced a grateful sense of the entire responsibility of the other four in the fate of their enterprise.

LEFT OUT ON LONE STAR MOUNTAIN

On December 24, 1863, a gentle rain was still falling over the length and breadth of the 'Lone Star' claim. It had been falling for several days, had already called a faint spring colour to the wan landscape, repairing with tender touches the ravages wrought by the proprietors, or charitably covering their faults. The ragged seams in gulch and cañon lost their harsh outlines, a thin green mantle faintly clothed the torn and abraded hill-side. A few weeks more, and a veil of forgetfulness would be drawn over the feeble failures of the 'Lone Star' claim. The charming derelicts themselves, listening to the rain-drops on the roofs of their little cabin, gazed philosophically from the open door, and accepted the prospect as a moral discharge from their obligations. Four of the five partners were present: the 'Right' and 'Left Bowers', 'Union Mills', and the 'Judge'.

It is scarcely necessary to say that not one of these titles was the genuine name of its possessor. The Right and Left Bowers were two brothers; their *sobriquets* a cheerful adaptation from the favourite game of euchre, expressing their relative value in the camp. The mere fact that 'Union Mills' had at one time patched his trousers with an old flour sack legibly bearing that brand of its fabrication, was a tempting baptismal suggestion that the other partners could not forgo. 'The Judge', a singularly inequitable Missourian, with no knowledge whatever of the law, was an inspiration of gratuitous irony.

Union Mills, who had been for some time sitting placidly on the threshold with one leg exposed to the rain, from a sheer indolent inability to change his position, finally withdrew that weather-beaten member, and stood up. The movement more or less deranged the attitudes of the other partners, and was received with cynical disfavour. It was somewhat remarkable that, although generally giving the appearance of healthy youth and perfect physical condition, they one and all simulated the decrepitude of age and invalidism, and after limping about for a few moments, settled back again upon their bunks and stools in their former positions. The Left Bower lazily replaced a bandage that he had worn around his ankle for weeks without any apparent necessity; and the Judge scrutinized with tender solicitude the faded cicatrix of a scratch upon his arm. A passive hypochondria, borne of their isolation, was the last ludicrously pathetic touch to their situation.

The immediate cause of this commotion felt the necessity of an explanation.

'It would have been just as easy for you to have stayed outside with your business leg, instead of dragging it into private life in that obtrusive way,' retorted the Right Bower; 'but that exhaustive effort isn't going to fill the pork barrel. The grocery man at Dalton says – what's that he said?' – he appealed lazily to the Judge.

'Said he reckoned the Lone Star was about played out, and he didn't want any more in his – thank you!' repeated the Judge with a mechanical effort of memory utterly devoid of personal or present interest.

'I always suspected that man, after Grimshaw begun to deal with him,' said the Left Bower. 'They're just mean enough to join hands against us.' It was a fixed belief of the Lone Star partners that they were pursued by personal enmities.

'More than likely those new strangers over in the Fork have been paying cash and filled him up with conceit,' said Union Mills, trying to dry his leg by alternately beating it or rubbing it against the cabin wall. 'Once begin wrong with that kind of snipe and you drag everybody down with you.'

This vague conclusion was received with dead silence. Everybody had become interested in the speaker's peculiar method of drying his leg, to the exclusion of the previous topic. A few offered criticism – no one assistance.

'Who did the grocery man say that to?' asked the Right Bower, finally returning to the question.

'The Old Man,' answered the Judge.

'Of course,' ejaculated the Right Bower sarcastically.

'Of course,' echoed the other partners together. 'That's like him. The Old Man all over!'

It did not appear exactly what was like the Old Man, or why it was like him, but generally that he alone was responsible for the grocery man's defection. It was put more concisely by Union Mills:

'That comes of letting him go there! It's just a fair provocation to any man to have the Old Man sent to him. They can't – sorter – restrain themselves at him. He's enough to spoil the credit of the Rothschilds.'

'That's so,' chimed in the Judge. 'And look at his prospecting. Why, he was out two nights last week – all night – prospecting in the moonlight for blind leads – just out of sheer foolishness.'

'It was quite enough for me,' broke in the Left Bower, 'when the other day – you remember when – he proposed to us white men to settle down to plain ground sluicing – making "grub" wages just like any Chinaman. It just showed his idea of the Lone Star claim.'

'Well, I never said it afore,' added Union Mills, 'but when that one of the Mattison boys came over here to examine the claim with an eye to purchasin', it was the Old Man that took the conceit out of him. He just as good as admitted that a lot of work had got to be done afore any pay ore could be realized. Never even asked him over to the shanty here to jine us in a friendly game – just kept him, so to speak, to himself. And naturally the Mattisons didn't see it.'

A silence followed, broken only by the rain monotonously falling on the roof, and occasionally through the broad adobe chimney, where it provoked a retaliating hiss and splutter from the dying embers of the hearth. The Right Bower, with a sudden access of energy, drew the empty barrel before him, and taking a pack of well-worn cards from his pocket, began to make a 'solitaire' upon the lid. The others gazed at him with languid interest.

'Makin' it for anythin'?' asked Mills.

The Right Bower nodded.

The Judge and Left Bower, who were partly lying in their respective bunks, sat up to get a better view of the game. Union Mills slowly disengaged himself from the wall, and leaned over the 'solitaire' player. The Right Bower turned the last card in a pause of almost thrilling suspense, and clapped it down on the lid with fateful emphasis.

'It went!' said the Judge in a voice of hushed respect. 'What did you make it for?' he almost whispered.

'To know if we'd make the break we talked about and vamose the ranch. It's the *fifth* time today,' continued the Right Bower in a voice of gloomy significance. 'And it went agin bad cards too.'

'I ain't superstitious,' said the Judge, with awe and fatuity beaming from every line of his credulous face, 'but it's flyin' in the face of Providence to go agin such signs as that.'

'Make it again to see if the Old Man must go,' suggested the Left Bower.

The suggestion was received with favour, the three men gathering breathlessly around the player. Again the fateful cards were shuffled deliberately, placed in their mysterious combination, with the same ominous result. Yet everybody seemed to breathe more freely, as if relieved from some responsibility, the Judge accepting this manifest expression of Providence with resigned self-righteousness.

'Yes, gentlemen,' resumed the Left Bower serenely, as if a calm legal decision had just been recorded, 'we must not let any foolishness or sentiment get mixed up with this thing, but look at it like business men. The only sensible move is to get up and get out of the camp.'

'And the Old Man?' queried the Judge.

'The Old Man – hush! – he's coming.'

The doorway was darkened by a slight lissome shadow. It was the absent partner, otherwise known as the 'Old Man'. Need it be added that he was a *boy* of nineteen with a slight down just clothing his upper lip!

'The creek is up over the ford, and I had to "shin" up a willow on the bank and swing myself across,' he said, with a quick, frank laugh; 'but all the same, boys, it's going to clear up in about an hour – you bet. It's breaking away over Bald Mountain, and there's a sun flash on a bit of snow on Lone Peak. Look! You can see it from here. It's for all the world like Noah's dove just landed on Mount Ararat. It's a good omen.'

From sheer force of habit the men had momentarily brightened up at the Old Man's entrance. But the unblushing exhibition of degrading superstition shown in the last sentence recalled their just severity. They exchanged meaning glances. Union Mills uttered hopelessly to himself: 'Hell's full of such omens.'

Too occupied with his subject to notice this ominous reception, the Old Man continued: 'I reckon I struck a fresh lead in the new grocery man at the Crossing. He says he'll let the Judge have a pair of boots on credit, but he can't send them over here; and considering that the Judge has got to try them anyway, it don't seem to be asking too much for the Judge to go over there. He says he'll give us a barrel of pork and a bag of flour if we'll give him the right of using our tail-race and clean out the lower end of it.'

'It's the work of a Chinaman, and a four days' job,' broke in the Left Bower.

'It took one white man only two hours to clean out a third of it,' retorted the Old Man triumphantly, 'for *I* pitched in at once with a pick he let me have on credit, and did that amount of work this morning, and told him the rest of you boys would finish it this afternoon.'

A slight gesture from the Right Bower checked an angry exclamation from the Left. The Old Man did not notice either, but, knitting his smooth young brow in a paternally reflective fashion, went on: 'You'll have to get a new pair of trousers, Mills, but as he doesn't keep clothing, we'll have to get some canvas and cut you out a pair. I traded off the beans he let me have for some tobacco for the Right Bower at the other shop, and got them to throw in a new pack of cards. These are about played out. We'll be wanting some brushwood for the fire; there's a heap in the hollow. Who's going to bring it in? It's the Judge's turn, isn't it? Why – what's the matter with you all?'

The restraint and evident uneasiness of his companions had at last touched him. He turned his frank young eyes upon them; they glanced helplessly at each other. Yet his first concern was for them – his first instinct paternal and protecting. He ran his eyes quickly over them, they were all there and apparently in their usual condition. 'Anything wrong with the claim?' he suggested.

Without looking at him the Right Bower rose, leaned against the open door with his hands behind him and his face towards the landscape, and said – apparently to the distant prospect: 'The claim's played out – the partnership's played out – and the sooner we skedaddle out of this the better. If,' he added, turning to the Old Man, 'if *you* want to stay – if you want to do Chinaman's work at Chinaman's wages – if you want to hang on to the charity of the traders at the Crossing – you can do it, and enjoy the prospects and the Noah's doves alone. But we're calculatin' to step out of it.'

'But I haven't said I wanted to do it *alone*,' protested the Old Man, with a gesture of bewilderment.

'If these are your general ideas of the partnership,' continued the Right Bower, clinging to the established hypothesis of the other partners for support, 'it ain't ours, and the only way we can prove it is to stop the foolishness right here. We calculated to dissolve the partnership and strike out for ourselves elsewhere. You're no longer responsible for us, nor we for you. And we reckon it's the square thing to leave you the claim and the cabin, and all it contains. To prevent any trouble with the traders, we've drawn up a paper here.'

'With a bonus of fifty thousand dollars each down, and the rest to be settled on my children,' interrupted the Old Man, with a half-uneasy laugh. 'Of course. But–' he stopped suddenly, the blood dropped from his fresh cheek, and he again glanced quickly round the group. 'I don't think – I – I – quite *sabe*, boys,' he added, with a slight tremor of voice and lip. 'If it's a conundrum, ask me an easier one.'

Any lingering doubt he might have had of their meaning was dispelled by the Judge. 'It's about the softest thing you kin drop into, Old Man,' he said confidentially; 'if *I* hadn't promised the other boys to go with them, and if I didn't need the best medical advice in Sacramento for my lungs, I'd just enjoy staying with you.'

'It gives a sorter freedom to a young fellow like you, Old Man – like goin' into the world on your own capital – that every Californian boy hasn't got,' said Union Mills patronizingly.

'Of course it's rather hard papers on us, you know, givin' up everything, so to speak; but it's for your good, and we ain't goin' back on you,' said the Left Bower, 'are we, boys?'

The colour had returned to the Old Man's face a little more quickly and freely than usual. He picked up the hat he had cast down, put it on carefully over his brown curls, drew the flap down on the side towards his companions, and put his hands in his pockets. 'All right,' he said, in a slightly altered voice. 'When do you go?'

'Today,' answered the Left Bower. 'We calculate to take a moonlight *pasear* over the Cross Roads and meet the down stage at about twelve tonight. There's plenty of time yet,' he added, with a slight laugh; 'it's only three o'clock now.'

There was a dead silence. Even the rain withheld its continuous patter; a dumb, grey film covered the ashes of the hushed hearth. For the first time the Right Bower exhibited some slight embarrassment.

'I reckon it's held up for a spell,' he said, ostentatiously examining the weather, 'and we might as well take a run round the claim to see if we've forgotten nothing. Of course, we'll be back again,' he added hastily, without looking at the Old Man, 'before we go, you know.'

The others began to look for their hats, but so awkwardly and with such evident preoccupation of mind that it was not at first discovered that the Judge had his already on. This raised a laugh, as did also a clumsy stumble of Union Mills against the pork barrel, although that gentleman took refuge from his confusion and secured a decent retreat by a gross exaggeration of his lameness, as he limped after the Right Bower. The Judge whistled feebly. The Left Bower, in a more ambitious effort to impart a certain gaiety to his exit, stopped on the threshold and said, as if in arch confidence to his companions: 'Darned if the Old Man don't look two inches higher, since he became a proprietor,' laughed patronizingly, and vanished.

If the newly-made proprietor had increased in stature, he had not otherwise changed his demeanour. He remained in the same attitude until the last figure disappeared behind the fringe of buckeye that hid the distant highway. Then he walked slowly to the fire-place, and, leaning against the chimney, kicked the dying embers together with his foot. Something dropped and spattered in the film of hot ashes. Surely the rain had not yet ceased!

His high colour had already fled except for a spot on either cheekbone that lent a brightness to his eyes. He glanced around the cabin. It looked familiar and yet strange. Rather, it looked strange *because* still familiar, and therefore incongruous with the new atmosphere that surrounded it – discordant with the echo of their last meeting and painfully accenting the change. There were the four 'bunks', or sleeping berths, of his companions, each still bearing some traces of the individuality of its late occupant with a dumb loyalty that seemed to make their light-hearted defection monstrous. In the dead ashes of the Judge's pipe scattered on his shelf still lived his old fire; in the whittled and carved edges of the Left Bower's bunk still were the memories of by-gone days of delicious indolence; in the bullet-holes clustered round a knot of one of the beans there was still the record of the Right Bower's old-time skill and practice; in the few engravings of female loveliness stuck upon each headboard there were the proofs of their old extravagant devotion – all a mute protest to the change.

He remembered how, a fatherless, truant schoolboy, he had drifted into their adventurous nomadic life – itself a life of grown-up truancy like his own – and became one of that gipsy family. How they had taken the place of relations and household in his boyish fancy – filling it with the unsubstantial pageantry of a child's play at grown-up existence – he knew only too well. But how, from being a pet and protégé, he had gradually and unconsciously asserted his own individuality and taken upon his younger shoulders not only a poet's keen appreciation of that life, but its actual responsibilities and half-childish burdens, he never suspected. He had fondly believed that he was a neophyte in their ways – a novice in their charming faith and indolent creed – and they had encouraged it; now their renunciation of that faith could only be an excuse for a renunciation of *him*. The poetry that had for two years invested the material and sometimes even mean details of their existence was too much a part of himself to be lightly dispelled. The lesson of those ingenuous moralists failed, as such lessons are apt to fail: their discipline provoked but did not subdue; a rising indignation, stirred by a sense of injury, mounted to his cheek and eyes. It was slow to come, but was none the less violent that it had been preceded by the benumbing shock of shame and pride.

I hope I shall not prejudice the reader's sympathies if my duty as a simple chronicler compels me to state, therefore, that the sober second thought of this gentle poet was to burn down the cabin on the spot with all its contents. This yielded to a milder counsel – waiting for the return of the party, challenging the Right Bower, a duel to the death, perhaps himself the victim, with the crushing explanation *in extremis*: 'It seems we are *one* too many. No matter; it is settled now. Farewell!' Dimly remembering, however, that there was something of this in the last well-worn novel they had read together, and that his antagonist might recognize it – or even worse, anticipate it – himself, the idea was quickly rejected. Besides, the opportunity for an apotheosis of self-sacrifice was past. Nothing remained now but to refuse the proffered bribe of claim and cabin by letter, for he must not wait their return. He tore a leaf from a blotted diary, begun and abandoned long since, and essayed to write. Scrawl after scrawl was torn up until his fury had cooled down to a frigid third personality. 'Mr John Ford regrets to inform his late partners that their tender of house of furniture,' however, seemed too inconsistent with the pork-barrel table he was writing on; a more eloquent renunciation of their offer became frivolous and idiotic from a caricature of Union Mills, label and all, that appeared suddenly on the other side of the leaf; and when he at last indited a satisfactory and impassioned exposition of his feelings, the legible *addendum* of 'Oh, ain't you glad you're out of the wilderness!' – the forgotten first line of a popular song, which no scratching would erase, seemed too like an ironical postscript to be thought of for a moment. He threw aside his pen and cast the discordant record of past foolish pastime into the dead ashes of the hearth.

How quiet it was! With the cessation of the rain, the wind, too, had gone down, and scarcely a breath of air came through the open door. He walked to the threshold and gazed on the hushed prospect. In this listless attitude he was faintly conscious of a distant reverberation, a mere phantom of sound – perhaps the explosion of a distant blast in the hills – that left the silence more marked and oppressive. As he turned again into the cabin a change seemed to have come over it. It already looked old and decayed. The loneliness of years of desertion seemed to have taken possession of it; the atmosphere of dry rot was in the beams and rafters. To his excited fancy the few disordered blankets and articles of clothing seemed dropping to pieces; in one of the bunks there was a hideous resemblance in the longitudinal heap of clothing to a withered and mummied corpse. So it might look in years, when some passing stranger – but he stopped. A dread of the place was beginning to creep over him; a dread of the days to come, when the monotonous sunshine should lay bare the loneliness of these walls: the long, long days of endless blue and cloudless overhanging solitude; summer days when the wearying, incessant trade-winds should sing around that empty shell and voice its desolation. He gathered together hastily a few articles that were especially his own – rather that the free communion of the camp, from indifference or accident, had left wholly to him. He hesitated for a moment over his rifle, but, scrupulous in his wounded pride, turned away and left the familiar weapon that in the dark days had so often provided the dinner or breakfast of the little household. Candour compels me to state that his equipment was not large nor eminently practical. His scant pack was a light weight for even his young shoulders, but I fear he thought more of getting away from the Past than providing for the Future.

With this vague but sole puprose he left the cabin, and almost mechanically turned his steps towards the creek he had crossed that morning. He knew that by this route he would avoid meeting his companions; its difficulties and circuitousness would exercise his feverish limbs and give him time for reflection. He had determined to leave the claim, but whence he had not yet considered. He reached the bank of the creek where he had stood two hours before; it seemed to him two years. He looked curiously at his reflection in one of the broad pools of overflow and fancied he looked older. He watched the rush and outset of the turbid current hurrying to meet the South Fork, and to eventually lose itself in the yellow Sacramento. Even in his preoccupation he was impressed with a likeness to himself and his companions in this flood that had burst its peaceful boundaries. In the drifting fragments of one of their forgotten flumes washed from the bank, he fancied he saw an omen of the disintegration and decay of the 'Lone Star' claim.

The strange hush in the air that he had noticed before – a calm so inconsistent with that hour and the season as to seem portentous – became more marked in contrast to the feverish rush of the turbulent watercourse. A few clouds lazily huddled in the west apparently had gone to rest with the sun on beds of somnolent poppies. There was a gleam as of golden water everywhere along the horizon, washing out the cold snow peaks, and drowning even the rising moon. The creek caught it here and there, until, in grim irony, it seemed to bear their broken sluiceboxes and useless engines on the very Pactolian stream they had been hopefully created to direct and carry. But by some peculiar trick of the atmosphere, the perfect plenitude of that golden sunset glory was lavished on the rugged sides and tangled crest of the Lone Star Mountain. That isolated peak – the landmark of their claim, the gaunt monument of their folly – transfigured in the evening splendour, kept its radiance unquenched, long after the glow had fallen from the encompassing skies, and when at last the rising moon, step by step, put out the fires along the winding valley and plains, and crept up the bosky sides of the canyon, the vanishing sunset was lost only to reappear as a golden crown.

The eyes of the young man were fixed upon it with more than a momentary picturesque interest. It had been the favourite ground of his prospecting exploits, its lowest flank had been scarred in the old enthusiastic days with hydraulic engines, or pierced with shafts, but its central position in the claim and its superior height had always given it a commanding view of the extent of their valley and its approaches, and it was this practical pre-eminence that alone attracted him at that moment. He knew that from its crest he would be able to distinguish the figures of his companions, as they crossed the valley near the cabin, in the growing moonlight. Thus he could avoid encountering them on his way to the high road, and yet see them, perhaps, for the last time. Even in his sense of injury there was a strange satisfaction in the thought.

The ascent was toilsome, but familiar. All along the dim trail he was accompanied by gentler memories of the past, that seemed like the faint odour of spiced leaves and fragrant grasses wet with the rain and crushed beneath his ascending tread, to exhale the sweeter perfume in his effort to subdue or rise above them. There was the thicket of manzanita, where they had broken noonday bread together; here was the rock beside their maiden shaft, where they had poured a wild libation in boyish enthusiasm of success; and here the ledge where their first flat – a red shirt heroically sacrificed – was displayed from a long-handled shovel to the gaze of admirers below. When he at last reached the summit, the mysterious hush was still in the air, as if in breathless sympathy with his expedition. In the west, the plain was faintly illuminated, but disclosed no moving figures. He turned towards the rising moon, and moved slowly to the eastern edge. Suddenly he stopped. Another step would have been his last! He stood upon the crumbling edge of a precipice. A landslip had taken place on the eastern flank, leaving the gaunt ribs and fleshless bones of Lone Star Mountain bare in the moonlight. He understood now the strange rumble and reverberation he had heard; he understood now the strange hush of bird and beast in break and thicket.

Although a single rapid glance convinced him that the slide had taken place in an unfrequented part of the mountain, above an inaccessible canyon, and reflection assured him his companions could not have reached that distance when it took place, a feverish impulse led him to descend a few rods in the track of the avalanche. The frequent recurrence of outcrop and angle made this comparatively easy. Here he called aloud; the feeble echo of his own voice seemed only a dull impertinence to the significant silence. He turned to reascend: the furrowed flank of the mountain before him lay full in the moonlight. To his excited fancy, a dozen luminous star-like points in the rocky crevices started into life as he faced them. Throwing his arm over the ledge above him, he supported himself for a moment by what appeared to be a projection of the solid rock. It trembled slightly. As he raised himself to its level, his heart stopped beating. It was simply a fragment detached from the outcrop lying loosely on the ledge, but upholding him by *its own weight only.*He examined it with trembling fingers; the encumbering soil fell from its sides and left its smoothed and worn protuberances glistening in the moonlight. It was virgin gold!

Looking back upon that moment afterwards, he remembered that he was not dazed, dazzled, or startled. It did not come to him as a discovery or an accident, a stroke of chance or a caprice of fortune. He saw it all in that supreme moment; Nature had worked out their poor deduction. What their feeble engines had essayed spasmodically and helplessly against the curtain of soil that hid the treasure, the elements had achieved with mightier but more patient forces. The slow sapping of the winter rains had loosened the soil from the auriferous rock, even while the swollen stream was carrying their impotent and shattered engines to the sea. What mattered that his single arm could not lift the treasure he had found; what mattered that to unfix those glittering stars would still tax both skill and patience! The work was done – the goal was reached! Even his boyish impatience was content with that. He rose slowly to his feet, unstrapped his long-handled shovel from his back, secured it in the crevice, and quietly regained the summit.

It was all his own! His own by right of discovery under the law of the land, and without accepting a favour from *them*. He recalled even the fact that it was *his* prospecting on the mountains that first suggested the existence of gold in the outcrop and the use of the hydraulic. *He* had never abandoned that belief, whatever the others had done. He dwelt somewhat indignantly to himself on this circumstance, and half-unconsciously faced defiantly towards the plain below. But it was sleeping peacefully in full sight of the moon, without life or motion. He looked at the stars; it was still far from midnight. His companions had no doubt long since returned to the cabin to prepare for their midnight journey. They were discussing him – perhaps laughing at him, or worse, pitying him and his bargain. Yet here was his bargain! A slight laugh he gave vent to here startled him a little, it sounded so hard and so unmirthful, and so unlike, as he oddly fancied, what he really *thought*. But *what* did he think?

Nothing mean or revengeful; no, they never would say *that*. When he had taken out all the surface gold and put the mine in working order, he would send them each a draft for a thousand dollars. Of course, if they were ever ill or poor he would do more. One of the first, the very first, things he should do would be to send them each a handsome gun and tell them that he only asked in return the old-fashioned rifle that once was his. Looking back at the moment in after years, he wondered that, with this exception, he made no plans for his own future, or the way he should dispose of his newly-acquired wealth. This was the more singular as it had been the custom of the five partners to lie awake at night, audibly comparing with each other what they would do in case they made a strike. He remembered how, Alnaschar-like, they nearly separated once over a difference in the disposal of a hundred thousand dollars that they never had nor expected to have. He remembered how Union Mills always began his career as a millionaire by a 'square meal' at Delmonico's; how the Right Bower's initial step was always a trip home 'to see his mother'; how the Left Bower would immediately placate the parents of his beloved with priceless gifts – (it may be parenthetically remarked that the parents and the beloved one were as hypothetical as the fortune) – and how the Judge would make his first start as a capitalist by breaking a certain faro bank in Sacramento. He himself had been equally eloquent in extravagant fancy in these penniless days – he who now was quite cold and impassive beside the more extravagant reality.

How different it might have been! If they had only waited a day longer! If they had only broken their resolves to him kindly and parted in good-will! How he would long ere this have rushed to greet them with the joyful news! How they would have danced around it, sung themselves hoarse, laughed down their enemies, and run up the flat triumphantly on the summit of the Lone Star Mountain! How they would have crowned him, 'the Old Man', 'the hero of the camp'! How he would have told them the old story; how some strange instinct had impelled him to ascend the summit, and how another step on that summit would have precipitated him into the canyon! And how – but what if somebody else – Union Mills or the Judge – had been the first discoverer? Might they not have meanly kept the secret from him; have selfishly helped themselves and done –

'What *you* are doing now.'

The hot blood rushed to his cheek, as if a strange voice were at his ear. For a moment he could not believe that it came from his own pale lips until he found himself speaking. He rose to his feet, tingling with shame, and began hurriedly to descend the mountain.

He would go to them, tell them of his discovery, let them give him his share, and leave them for ever. It was the only thing to be done – strange that he had not thought of it at once. Yet it was hard, very hard and cruel to be forced to meet them again. What had he done to suffer this mortification? For a moment he actually hated this vulgar treasure that had forever buried under its gross ponderability the light and careless past, and utterly crushed out the poetry of their old indolent happy existence.

He was sure to find them waiting at the cross roads where the coach came past. It was three miles away, yet he could get there in time if he hastened. It was a wise and practical conclusion of his evening's work – a lame and impotent conclusion to his evening's indignation. No matter! They would perhaps at first think he had come to weakly follow them – perhaps they would at first doubt his story. No matter! He bit his lips to keep down the foolish rising tears, but still went blindly forward.

He saw not the beautiful night, cradled in the dark hills, swathed in luminous mists, and hushed in the awe of its own loveliness! Here and there the moon had laid her calm face on lake and overflow, and gone to sleep embracing them, until the whole plain seemed to be lifted into infinite quiet. Walking on as in a dream, the black impenetrable barriers of skirting thickets opened and gave way to vague distances that it appeared impossible to reach – dim vistas that seemed unapproachable. Gradually he seemed himself to become a part of the mysterious night. He was becoming as pulseless, as calm, as passionless.

What was that? A shot in the direction of the cabin! yet so faint, so echoless, so ineffective in the vast silence, that he would have thought it his fancy but for the strange instinctive jar upon his sensitive nerves. Was it an accident, or was it an intentional signal to him? He stopped; it was not repeated – the silence reasserted itself, but this time with an ominous death-like suggestion. A sudden and terrible thought crossed his mind. He cast aside his pack and all encumbering weight, took a deep breath, lowered his head and darted like a deer in the direction of the challenge.

II

THE exodus of the seceding partners of the Lone Star claim had been scarcely an imposing one. For the first five minutes after quitting the cabin, the procession was straggling and vagabond. Unwonted exertion had exaggerated the lameness of some, and feebleness of moral purpose had predisposed the others to obtrusive musical exhibition. Union Mills limped and whistled with affected abstraction; the Judge whistled and limped with affected earnestness. The Right Bower led the way with some show of definite design; the Left Bower followed with his hands in his pockets. The two feebler natures, drawn together in unconscious sympathy, looked vaguely at each other for support.

'You see,' said the Judge suddenly, as if triumphantly concluding an argument, 'there ain't anything better for a young fellow than independence. Nature, so to speak, point the way. Look at the animals.'

'There's a skunk hereabouts,' said Union Mills, who was supposed to be gifted with aristocratically sensitive nostrils, 'within ten miles of this place; like as not crossing the Ridge. It's always my luck to happen out just at such times. I don't see the necessity anyhow of traipesing round the claim now, if we calculate to leave it tonight.'

Both men waited to observe if the suggestion was taken up by the Right and Left Bower moodily plodding ahead. No response following, the Judge shamelessly abandoned his companion.

'You wouldn't stand snoopin' round instead of lettin' the Old Man get used to the idea alone? No; I could see all along that he was takin' it in – takin' it in – kindly, but slowly, and I reckoned the best thing for us to do was to git up and git until he'd got round it.' The Judge's voice was slightly raised for the benefit of the two before him.

'Didn't he say,' remarked the Right Bower, stopping suddenly and facing the others – 'didn't he say that that new trader was goin' to let him have some provisions anyway?'

Union Mills turned appealingly to the Judge; that gentleman was forced to reply: 'Yes; I remember distinctly he said it. It was one of the things I was particular about on his account,' responded the Judge, with the air of having arranged it all himself with the new trader. 'I remember I was easier in my mind about it.'

'But didn't he say,' queried the Left Bower, also stopping short, 'suthin' about its being contingent on our doing some work on the race?'

The Judge turned for support to Union Mills, who, however, under the hollow pretence of preparing for a long conference, had luxuriously seated himself on a stump. The Judge sat down also, and replied hesitatingly: 'Well, yes! Us or him.'

'Us or him,' repeated the Right Bower, with gloomy irony. 'And you ain't quite clear in your mind, are you, if *you* haven't done the work already? You're just killing yourself with this spontaneous, promiscuous, and premature overwork; that's what's the matter with you.'

'I reckon I heard somebody say suthin' about its being a Chinaman's three-day job,' interpolated the Left Bower, with equal irony, 'but I ain't quite clear in my mind about that.'

'It'll be a sorter distraction for the Old Man,' said Union Mills feebly – 'kinder take his mind off his loneliness.'

Nobody taking the least notice of the remark, Union Mills stretched out his legs more comfortably and took out his pipe. He had scarcely done so when the Right Bower, wheeling suddenly, set off in the direction of the creek. The Left Bower, after a slight pause, followed without a word. The Judge, wisely conceiving it better to join the stronger party, ran feebly after him, and left Union Mills to bring up a weak and vacillating rear.

Their course, diverging from Lone Star Mountain, led them now directly to the bend of the creek – the base of their old ineffectual operations. Here was the beginning of the famous tail-race that skirted the new trader's claim, and then lost its way in a swampy hollow. It was choked with débris; a thin, yellow stream that once ran through it seemed to have stopped work when they did, and gone into greenish liquidation.

They had scarcely spoken during this brief journey, and had received no other explanation from the Right Bower, who led them, than that afforded by his mute example when he reached the race. Leaping into it without a word, he at once began to clear away the broken timbers and driftwood. Fired by the spectacle of what appeared to be a new and utterly frivolous game, the men gaily leaped after him, and were soon engaged in a fascinating struggle with the impeded race. The Judge forgot his lameness in springing over a broken sluice-box; Union Mills forgot his whistle in a happy imitation of a Chinese coolie's song. Nevertheless, after ten minutes of this mild dissipation, the pastime flagged. Union Mills was beginning to rub his leg when a distant rumble shook the earth. The men looked at each other; the diversion was complete; a languid discussion of the probabilities of its being an earthquake or a blast followed, in the midst of which the Right Bower, who was working a little in advance of the others, uttered a warning cry and leaped from the race. His companions had barely time to follow before a sudden and inexplicable rise in the waters of the creek sent a swift irruption of the flood through the race. In an instant its choked and impeded channel was cleared, the race was free, and the scattered débris of logs and timber floated upon its easy current. Quick to take advantage of this labour-saving phenomenon, the Lone Star partners sprang into the water, and by disentangling and directing the eddying fragments completed their work.

'The Old Man oughter been here to see this,' said the Left Bower; 'it's just one o' them climaxes of poetic justice he's always huntin' up. It's easy to see what's happened. One o' them high-toned shrimps over in the Excelsior claim has put a blast in too near the creek. He's tumbled the bank into the creek, and sent the back water down here just to wash out our race. That's what I call poetical retribution.'

'And who was it advised us to dam the creek below the race, and make it do the same thing?' asked the Right Bower moodily.

'That was one of the Old Man's ideas, I reckon,' said the Left Bower dubiously.

'And you remember,' broke in the Judge with animation, 'I allus said: "Go slow, go slow. You just hold on and suthin' will happen." And,' he added triumphantly, 'you see suthin' *has* happened. I don't want to take credit to myself, but I reckoned on them Excelsior boys bein' fools, and took the chances.'

'And what if I happen to know that the Excelsior boys ain't blastin' today?' said the Right Bower sarcastically.

As the Judge had evidently based his hypothesis on the alleged fact of a blast, he deftly evaded the point. 'I ain't saying the Old Man's head ain't level on some things; he wants a little more *sabe* of the world. He's improved a good deal in euchre lately, and in poker – well! He's got that sorter dreamy, listenin'-to-the-angels kind o' way, that you can't exactly tell whether he's bluffin' or has got a full hand. Hasn't he?' he asked, appealing to Union Mills.

But that gentleman, who had been watching the dark face of the Right Bower, preferred to take what he believed to be his cue from him. 'That ain't the question,' he said virtuously; 'we ain't takin' this step to make a card-sharp of him. We're not doin' Chinamen's work in this race today for that! No, sir! We're teachin' him to paddle his own canoe.' Not finding the sympathetic response he looked for in the Right Bower's face, he turned to the Left.

'I reckon we were teaching him our canoe was too full,' was the Left Bower's unexpected reply. 'That's about the size of it.'

The Right Bower shot a rapid glance under his brows at his brother. The latter, with his hands in his pockets, stared unconsciously at the rushing water, and then quietly turned away. The Right Bower followed him. 'Are you going back on us?' he asked.

'Are you?' responded the other.

'*No*, then it is,' returned the Left Bower quietly. The elder brother hesitated in half-angry embarrassment.

'Then what did you mean by saying we reckoned our canoe was too full?'

'Wasn't that our idea?' returned the Left Bower indifferently. Confounded by this practical expression of his own unformulated good intentions, the Right Bower was staggered.

'Speakin' of the Old Man,' broke in the Judge with characteristic infelicity, 'I reckon he'll sort o' miss us, times like these. We were allers runnin' him and bedevillin' him after work, just to get him excited and amusin', and he'll kinder miss that sorter stimulatin'. I reckon we'll miss it too – somewhat. Don't you remember, boys, the night we put up that little sell on him and made him believe we'd struck it rich in the bank of the creek, and got him so conceited he wanted to go off and settle all our debts at once?'

'And how I came bustin' into the cabin with a panful of iron pyrites and black sand,' chuckled Union Mills, continuing the reminiscences, 'and how them big grey eyes of his nearly bulged out of his head. Well, it's some satisfaction to know we did our duty by the young fellow even in those little things.' He turned for confirmation of their general disinterestedness to the Right Bower, but he was already striding away, uneasily conscious of the lazy following of the Left Bower, like a laggard conscience at his back. This movement again threw Union Mills and the Judge into feeble complicity in the rear, as the procession slowly straggled homeward from the creek.

Night had fallen. Their way lay through the shadow of Lone Star Mountain, deepened here and there by the slight bosky ridges that, starting from its base, crept across the plain like vast roots of its swelling trunk. The shadows were growing blacker as the moon began to assert itself over the rest of the valley, when the Right Bower halted suddenly on one of these ridges. The Left Bower lounged up to him, and stopped also, while the two others came up and completed the group. 'There's no light in the shanty,' said the Right Bower in a low voice, half to himself and half in answer to their inquiring attitude. The men followed the direction of his finger. In the distance the black outline of the Lone Star cabin stood out distinctly in the illuminated space. There was the blank, sightless, external glitter of moonlight on its two windows that seemed to reflect its dim vacancy – empty alike of light, and warmth, and motion.

'That's sing'lar,' said the Judge, in an awed whisper.

The Left Bower, by simply altering the position of his hands in his trousers' pockets, managed to suggest that he knew perfectly the meaning of it – had always known it – but that being now, so to speak, in the hands of Fate, he was callous to it. This much, at least, the elder brother read in his attitude. But anxiety at that moment was the controlling impulse of the Right Bower, as a certain superstitious remorse was the instinct of the two others, and without heeding the cynic, the three started at a rapid pace for the cabin.

They reached it silently, as the moon, now riding high in the heavens, seemed to touch it with the tender grace and hushed repose of a tomb. It was with something of this feeling that the Right Bower softly pushed open the door; it was with something of this dread that the two others lingered on the threshold, until the Right Bower, after vainly trying to stir the dead embers on the hearth into life with his foot, struck a match and lit their solitary candle. Its flickering light revealed the familiar interior unchanged in aught but one thing. The bunk that the Old Man had occupied was stripped of its blankets; the few cheap ornaments and photographs were gone; the rude poverty of the bare boards and scant pallet looked up at them unrelieved by the bright face and gracious youth that had once made them tolerable. In the grim irony of that exposure, their own penury was doubly conscious. The little knapsack, the tea-cup and coffee-pot that had hung near his bed, were gone also. The most indignant protest, the most pathetic of the letters he had composed and rejected, whose torn fragments still littered the floor, could never have spoken with the eloquence of this empty space! The men exchanged no words; the solitude of the cabin, instead of drawing them together, seemed to isolate each one in selfish distrust of the others. Even the unthinking garrulity of Union Mills and the Judge was checked. A moment later, when the Left Bower entered the cabin, his presence was scarcely noticed.

The silence was broken by a joyous exclamation from the Judge. He had discovered the Old Man's rifle in the corner, where it had been at first overlooked. 'He ain't gone yet, gentlemen – for yer's his rifle,' he broke in, with a feverish return of volubility, and a high excited falsetto. 'He wouldn't have left this behind. No! I knowed it from the first. He's just outside a bit, foraging for wood and water. No, sir! Coming along here I said to Union Mills – didn't I? – "Bet your life the Old Man's not far off, even if he ain't in the cabin." Why, the moment I stepped foot –'

'And I said coming along,' interrupted Union Mills, with equally reviving mendacity, ' "Like as not he's hangin' round yer, and lyin' low just to give us a surprise." He! ho!'

'He's gone for good, and he left that rifle here on purpose,' said the Left Bower in a low voice, taking the weapon almost tenderly in his hands.

'Drop it then!' said the Right Bower. The voice was that of his brother, but suddenly changed with passion. The two other partners instinctively drew back in alarm.

'I'll not leave it here for the first comer,' said the Left Bower calmly, 'because we've been fools and he too. It's too good a weapon for that.'

'Drop it, I say!' said the Right Bower, with a savage stride towards him.

The young brother brought the rifle to a half charge, with a white face but a steady eye.

'Stop where you are!' he said collectedly. 'Don't row with *me*, because you haven't either the grit to stick to your ideas or the heart to confess them wrong. We've followed your lead, and here we are! The camp's broken up – the Old Man's gone – and we're going. And as for the d—d rifle –'

'Drop it, do you hear!' shouted the Right Bower, clinging to that one idea with the blind pertinacity of rage and a losing cause. 'Drop it!'

The Left Bower drew back, but his brother had seized the barrel with both hands. There was a momentary struggle, a flash through the half-lighted cabin, and a shattering report. The two men fell back from each other; the rifle dropped on the floor between them.

The whole thing was over so quickly that the other two partners had not had time to obey their common impulse to separate them, and consequently even now could scarcely understand what had passed. It was over so quickly that the two actors themselves walked back to their places, scarcely realizing their own act.

A dead silence followed. The Judge and Union Mills looked at each other in dazed astonishment, and then nervously set about their former habits, apparently in that fatuous belief common to such natures, that they were ignoring a painful situation. The Judge drew the barrel towards him, picked up the cards and began mechanically to 'make a patience', on which Union Mills gazed with ostentatious interest, but with eyes furtively conscious of the rigid figure of the Right Bower by the chimney and the abstracted face of the Left Bower at the door. Ten minutes had passed in this occupation, the Judge and Union Mills conversing in the furtive whispers of children unavoidably but fascinatedly present at a family quarrel, when a light step was heard upon the crackling brushwood outside, and the bright panting face of the Old Man appeared upon the threshold. There was a shout of joy; in another moment he was half-buried in the bosom of the Right Bower's shirt, half-dragged into the lap of the Judge, upsetting the barrel, and completely encompassed by the Left Bower and Union Mills. With the enthusiastic utterance of his name the spell was broken.

Happily unconscious of the previous excitement that had provoked this spontaneous unanimity of greeting, the Old Man, equally relieved, at once broke into a feverish announcement of his discovery. He painted the details with, I fear, a slight exaggeration of colouring, due partly to his own excitement, and partly to justify their own. But he was strangely conscious that these bankrupt men appeared less elated with their personal interest in their stroke of fortune than with his own success. 'I told you he'd do it,' said the Judge, with a reckless unscrupulousness of statement that carried everybody with it. 'Look at him! the game little pup.' 'O no! he ain't the right breed – is he?' echoed Union Mills with arch irony, while the Right and Left Bower, grasping either hand, pressed a proud but silent greeting that was half new to him, but wholly delicious. It was not without difficulty that he could at last prevail upon them to return with him to the scene of his discovery, or even then restrain them from attempting to carry him thither on their shoulders on the plea of his previous prolonged exertions. Once only there was a momentary embarrassment. 'Then you fired that shot to bring me back?' said the Old Man gratefully. In the awkward silence that followed, the hands of the two brothers sought and grasped each other, penitently. 'Yes,' interposed the Judge, with delicate tact, 'ye see the Right and Left Bower almost quarrelled to see which should be the first to fire for ye. I disremember which did –' 'I never touched the trigger,' said the Left Bower hastily. With a hurried backward kick, the Judge resumed: 'It went off sorter spontaneous.'

The difference in the sentiment of the procession that once more issued from the Lone Star cabin did not fail to show itself in each individual partner according to his temperament. The subtle tact of Union Mills, however, in expressing an awakened respect for their fortunate partner by addressing him, as if unconsciously, as 'Mr Ford', was at first discomposing, but even this was forgotten in their breathless excitement as they neared the base of the mountain. When they had crossed the creek the Right Bower stopped reflectively.

'You say you heard the slide come down before you left the cabin?' he said, turning to the Old Man.

'Yes; but I did not know then what it was. It was about an hour and a half after you left,' was the reply.

'Then look here, boys,' continued the Right Bower with superstitious exultation, 'it was the *slide* that tumbled into the creek, overflowed it, and helped *us* clear out the race!'

It seemed so clearly that Providence had taken the partners of the Lone Star directly in hand that they faced the toilsome ascent of the mountain with the assurance of conquerors. They paused only on the summit to allow the Old Man to lead the way to the slope that held their treasure. He advanced cautiously to the edge of the crumbling cliff, stopped, looked bewildered, advanced again, and then remained white and immovable. In an instant the Right Bower was at his side.

'Is anything the matter? Don't – don't look so, Old Man, for God's sake!'

The Old Man pointed to the dull, smooth, black side of the mountain, without a crag, break, or protuberance, and said with ashen lips:

'It's gone!'

And it was gone! A *second* slide had taken place, stripping the flank of the mountain, and burying the treasure and the weak implement that had marked its side deep under a chaos of rock and débris at its base.

'Thank God!' The blank faces of his companions turned quickly to the Right Bower. 'Thank God!' he repeated, with his arm around the neck of the Old Man. 'Had he stayed behind he would have been buried too.' He paused, and, pointing solemnly to the depths below, said: 'And thank God for showing us where we may yet labour for it in hope and patience like honest men.'

The men silently bowed their heads and slowly descended the mountain. But when they had reached the plain one of them called out to the others to watch a star that seemed to be rising and moving towards them over the hushed and sleeping valley.

'It's only the stage coach, boys,' said the Left Bower, smiling; 'the coach that was to take us away.'

In the security of their new-found fraternity they resolved to wait and see it pass. As it swept by with flash of light, beat of hoofs, and jingle of harness, the only real presence in the dreamy landscape, the driver shouted a hoarse greeting to the phantom partners, audible only to the Judge, who was nearest the vehicle.

'Did you hear – *did* you hear what he said, boys?' he gasped, turning to his companions. 'No! Shake hands all round, boys! God bless you all, boys! To think we didn't know it all this while!'

'Know what?'

'Merry Christmas!'

Stephen Crane

The Bride Comes to Yellow Sky

I

THE great Pullman was whirling onward with such dignity of motion that a glance from the window seemed simply to prove that the plains of Texas were pouring eastward. Vast flats of green grass, dull-hued spaces of mesquit and cactus, little groups of frame houses, woods of light and tender trees, all were sweeping into the east, sweeping over the horizon, a precipice.

A newly-married pair had boarded this train at San Antonio. The man's face was reddened from many days in the wind and sun, and a direct result of his new black clothes was that his brick-coloured hands were constantly performing in a most conscious fashion. From time to time he looked down respectfully at his attire. He sat with a hand on each knee, like a man waiting in a barber's shop. The glances he devoted to other passengers were furtive and shy.

The bride was not pretty, nor was she very young. She wore a dress of blue cashmere, with small reservations of velvet here and there, and with steel buttons abounding. She continually twisted her head to regard her puff-sleeves, very stiff, straight, and high. They embarrassed her. It was quite apparent that she had cooked, and that she expected to cook, dutifully. The blushes caused by the careless scrutiny of some passengers as she had entered the car were strange to see upon this plain, under-class countenance, which was drawn in placid, almost emotionless lines.

They were evidently very happy. 'Ever been in a parlour-car before?' he asked, smiling with delight.

'No,' she answered; 'I never was. It's fine, ain't it?'

'Great. And then, after a while, we'll go forward to the diner, and get a big lay-out. Finest meal in the world. Charge, a dollar.'

'Oh, do they?' cried the bride. 'Charge a dollar? Why, that's too much – for us – ain't it, Jack?'

'Not this trip, anyhow,' he answered bravely. 'We're going to go the whole thing.'

Later, he explained to her about the train. 'You see, it's a thousand miles from one end of Texas to the other, and this train runs right across it, and never stops but four times.'

He had the pride of an owner. He pointed out to her the dazzling fittings of the coach, and, in truth, her eyes opened wider as she contemplated the sea-green figured velvet, the shining brass, silver, and glass, the wood that gleamed as darkly brilliant as the surface of a pool of oil. At one end a bronze figure sturdily held a support for a separated chamber, and at convenient places on the ceiling were frescoes in olive and silver.

To the minds of the pair, their surroundings reflected the glory of their marriage that morning in San Antonio. This was the environment of their new estate, and the man's face, in particular, beamed with an elation that made him appear ridiculous to the negro porter. This individual at times surveyed them from afar with an amused and superior grin. On other occasions he bullied them with skill in ways that did not make it exactly plain to them that they were being bullied. He subtly used all the manners of the most unconquerable kind of snobbery. He oppressed them, but of this oppression they had small knowledge, and they speedily forgot that unfrequently a number of travellers covered them with stares of derisive enjoyment. Historically there was supposed to be something infinitely humorous in their situation.

'We are due in Yellow Sky at 3.42,' he said, looking tenderly into her eyes.

'Oh, are we?' she said, as if she had not been aware of it.

To evince surprise at her husband's statement was part of her wifely amiability. She took from a pocket a little silver watch, and as she held it before her, and stared at it with a frown of attention, the new husband's face shone.

'I bought it in San Anton' from a friend of mine,' he told her gleefully.

'It's seventeen minutes past twelve,' she said, looking at him with a kind of shy and clumsy coquetry.

A passenger, noting this play, grew excessively sardonic, and winked at himself in one of the numerous mirrors.

At last they went to the dining-car. Two rows of negro waiters in dazzling white suits surveyed their entrance with the interest, and also the equanimity, of men who had been forewarned. The pair fell to the lot of a waiter who happened to feel pleasure in steering them through their meal. He viewed them with the manner of a fatherly pilot, his countenance radiant with benevolence. The patronage entwined with the ordinary deference was not palpable to them. And yet as they returned to their coach they showed in their faces a sense of escape.

To the left, miles down a long purple slope, was a little ribbon of mist, where moved the keening Rio Grande. The train was approaching it at an angle, and the apex was Yellow Sky. Presently it was apparent that as the distance from Yellow Sky grew shorter, the husband became commensurately restless. His brick-red hands were more insistent in their prominence. Occasionally he was even rather absent-minded and far away when the bride leaned forward and addressed him.

As a matter of truth, Jack Potter was beginning to find the shadow of a deed weigh upon him like a leaden slab. He, the town-marshal of Yellow Sky, a man known, liked, and feared in his corner, a prominent person, had gone to San Antonio to meet a girl he believed he loved, and there, after the usual prayers, had actually induced her to marry him without consulting Yellow Sky for any part of the transaction. He was now bringing his bride before an innocent and unsuspecting community.

Of course, people in Yellow Sky married as it pleased them in accordance with a general custom, but such was Potter's thought of his duty to his friends, or of their idea of his duty, or of an unspoken form which does not control men in these matters, that he felt he was heinous. He had committed an extraordinary crime. Face to face with this girl in San Antonio, and spurred by his sharp impulse, he had gone headlong over all the social hedges. At San Antonio he was like a man hidden in the dark. A knife to sever any friendly duty, any form, was easy to his hand in that remote city. But the hour of Yellow Sky, the hour of daylight, was approaching.

He knew full well that his marriage was an important thing to his town. It could only be exceeded by the burning of the new hotel. His friends would not forgive him. Frequently he had reflected upon the advisability of telling them by telegraph, but a new cowardice had been upon him. He feared to do it. And now the train was hurrying him toward a scene of amazement, glee, reproach. He glanced out of the window at the line of haze swinging slowly in toward the train.

Yellow Sky had a kind of brass band which played painfully to the delight of the populace. He laughed without heart as he thought of it. If the citizens could dream of his prospective arrival with his bride, they would parade the band at the station, and escort them, amid cheers and laughing congratulations, to his adobe home.

He resolved that he would use all the devices of speed and plainscraft in making the journey from the station to his house. Once within that safe citadel, he could issue some sort of vocal bulletin, and then not go among the citizens until they had time to wear off a little of their enthusiasm.

The bride looked anxiously at him. 'What's worrying you, Jack?'

He laughed again. 'I'm not worrying, girl. I'm only thinking of Yellow Sky.'

She flushed in comprehension.

A sense of mutual guilt invaded their minds, and developed a finer tenderness. They looked at each other with eyes softly aglow. But Potter often laughed the same nervous laugh. The flush upon the bride's face seemed quite permanent.

The traitor to the feelings of Yellow Sky narrowly watched the speeding landscape.

'We're nearly there,' he said.

Presently the porter came and announced the proximity of Potter's home. He held a brush in his hand, and, with all his airy superiority gone, he brushed Potter's new clothes, as the latter slowly turned this way and that way. Potter fumbled out a coin, and gave it to the porter as he had seen others do. It was a heavy and muscle-bound business, as that of a man shoeing his first horse.

The porter took their bag, and, as the train began to slow, they moved forward to the hooded platform of the car. Presently the two engines and their long string of coaches rushed into the station of Yellow Sky.

'They have to take water here,' said Potter, from a constricted throat, and in mournful cadence as one announcing death. Before the train stopped his eye had swept the length of the platform, and he was glad and astonished to see there was no one upon it but the station-agent, who, with a slightly hurried and anxious air, was walking toward the water-tanks. When the train had halted, the porter alighted first and placed in position a little temporary step.

'Come on, girl,' said Potter, hoarsely.

As he helped her down, they each laughed on a false note. He took the bag from the negro, and bade his wife cling to his arm. As they slunk rapidly away, his hang-dog glance perceived that they were unloading the two trunks, and also that the station-agent, far ahead, near the baggage-car, had turned, and was running toward him, making gestures. He laughed, and groaned as he laughed, when he noted the first effect of his marital bliss upon Yellow Sky. He gripped his wife's arm firmly to his side, and they fled. Behind them the porter stood chuckling fatuously.

II

THE California Express on the Southern Railway was due at Yellow Sky in twenty-one minutes. There were six men at the bar of the Weary Gentleman saloon. One was a drummer, who talked a great deal and rapidly; three were Texans, who did not care to talk at that time; and two were Mexican sheep-herders, who did not talk as a general practice in the Weary Gentleman saloon. The bar-keeper's dog lay on the board-walk that crossed in front of the door. His head was on his paws, and he glanced drowsily here and there with the constant vigilance of a dog that is kicked on occasion. Across the sandy street were some vivid green grass plots, so wonderful in appearance amid the sands that burned near them in a blazing sun, that they caused a doubt in the mind. They exactly resembled the grass-mats used to represent lawns on the stage. At the cooler end of the railway-station a man without a coat sat in a tilted chair and smoked his pipe. The fresh-cut bank of the Rio Grande circled near the town, and there could be seen beyond it a great plum-coloured plain of mesquit.

Save for the busy drummer and his companions in the saloon, Yellow Sky was dozing. The newcomer leaned gracefully upon the bar, and recited many tales with the confidence of a bard who has come upon a new field.

'And at the moment that the old man fell downstairs, with the bureau in his arms, the old woman was coming up with two scuttles of coal, and, of course –'

The drummer's tale was interrupted by a young man who suddenly appeared in the front door. He cried –

'Scratchy Wilson's drunk, and has turned loose with both hands.'

The two Mexicans at once set down their glasses, and faded out of the rear entrance of the saloon.

The drummer, innocent and jocular, answered –

'All right, old man. S'pose he has. Come and have a drink, anyhow.'

But the information had made such an obvious cleft in every skull in the room, that the drummer was obliged to see its importance. All had become instantly morose.

'Say,' said he, mystified, 'what is this?'

His three companions made the introductory gesture of eloquent speech, but the young man at the door forestalled them.

'It means, my friend,' he answered, as he came into the saloon, 'that for the next two hours this town won't be a health resort.'

The bar-keeper went to the door, and locked and barred it. Reaching out of the window, he pulled in heavy wooden shutters and barred them. Immediately a solemn, chapel-like gloom was upon the place. The drummer was looking from one to another.

'But say,' he cried, 'what is this, anyhow? You don't mean there is going to be a gun-fight?'

'Don't know whether there'll be a fight or not,' answered one man grimly. 'But there'll be some shootin' – some good shootin'.'

The young man who had warned them waved his hand. 'Oh, there'll be a fight, fast enough, if any one wants it. Anybody can get a fight out there in the street. There's a fight just waiting.'

The drummer seemed to be swayed between the interest of a foreigner, and a perception of personal danger.

'What did you say his name was?' he asked.

'Scratchy Wilson,' they answered in chorus.

'And will he kill anybody? What are you going to do? Does this happen often? Does he rampage round like this once a week or so? Can he break in that door?'

'No, he can't break down that door,' replied the bar-keeper. 'He's tried it three times. But when he comes you'd better lay down on the floor, stranger. He's dead sure to shoot at it, and a bullet may come through.'

Thereafter the drummer kept a strict eye on the door. The time had not yet been called for him to hug the floor, but as a minor precaution he sidled near to the wall.

'Will he kill anybody?' he said again.

The men laughed low and scornfully at the question.

'He's out to shoot, and he's out for trouble. Don't see any good in experimentin' with him.'

'But what do you do in a case like this? What do you do?'

A man responded – 'Why, he and Jack Potter –'

But, in chorus, the other men interrupted – 'Jack Potters in San Anton'.'

'Well, who is he? What's he got to do with it?'

'Oh, he's the town-marshal. He goes out and fights Scratchy when he gets on one of these tears.'

'Whow!' said the drummer, mopping his brow. 'Nice job he's got.'

The voices had toned away to mere whisperings. The drummer wished to ask further questions, which were born of an increasing anxiety and bewilderment, but when he attempted them, the men merely looked at him in irritation, and motioned him to remain silent. A tense waiting hush was upon them. In the deep shadows of the room their eyes shone as they listened for sounds from the street. One man made three gestures at the bar-keeper, and the latter, moving like a ghost, handed him a glass and a bottle. The man poured a full glass of whisky, and set down the bottle noiselessly. He gulped the whisky in a swallow, and turned again toward the door in immovable silence. The drummer saw that the bar-keeper, without a sound, had taken a Winchester from beneath the bar. Later, he saw this individual beckoning to him, so he tip-toed across the room.

'You better come with me back of the bar.'

'No, thanks,' said the drummer, perspiring. 'I'd rather be where I can make a break for the back-door.'

Whereupon the man of bottles made a kindly but peremptory gesture. The drummer obeyed it, and finding himself seated on a box, with his head below the level of the bar, balm was laid upon his soul at sight of various zinc and copper fittings that bore a resemblance to plate armour. The bar-keeper took a seat comfortably upon an adjacent box.

'You see,' he whispered, 'this here Scratchy Wilson is a wonder with a gun – a perfect wonder – and when he goes on the war-trail, we hunt our holes – naturally. He's about the last one of the old gang that used to hang out along the river here. He's a terror when he's drunk. When he's sober, he's all right – kind of simple – wouldn't hurt a fly – nicest fellow in town. But when he's drunk – whoo!'

There were periods of stillness.

'I wish Jack Potter was back from San Anton',' said the bar-keeper. 'He shot Wilson up once – in the leg – and he would sail in and pull out the kinks in this thing.'

Presently they heard from a distance the sound of a shot, followed by three wild yells. It instantly removed a bond from the men in the darkened saloon. There was a shuffling of feet. They looked at each other.

'Here he comes,' they said.

III

A MAN in a maroon-coloured flannel shirt, which had been purchased for purposes of decoration, and made, principally, by some Jewish women on the east side of New York, rounded a corner and walked into the middle of the main street of Yellow Sky. In either hand the man held a long, heavy blue-black revolver. Often he yelled, and these cries rang through a semblance of a deserted village, shrilly flying over the roofs in a volume that seemed to have no relation to the ordinary vocal strength of a man. It was as if the surrounding stillness formed the arch of a tomb over him. These cries of ferocious challenge rang against walls of silence. And his boots had red tops with gilded imprints, of the kind beloved in winter by little sledging boys on the hillsides of New England.

The man's face flamed in a rage begot of whisky. His eyes, rolling and yet keen for ambush, hunted the still doorways and windows. He walked with the creeping movement of the midnight cat. As it occurred to him, he roared menacing information. The long revolvers in his hands were as easy as straws; they were moved with an electric swiftness. The little fingers of each hand played sometimes in a musician's way. Plain from the low collar of the shirt, the cords of his neck straightened and sank as passion moved in. The only sounds were his terrible invitations. The calm adobes preserved their demeanour at the passing of this small thing in the middle of the street.

There was no offer of fight – no offer of fight. The man called to the sky. There were no attractions. He bellowed and fumed and swayed his revolver here and everywhere.

The dog of the bar-keeper of the Weary Gentleman saloon had not appreciated the advance of events. He yet lay dozing in front of his master's door. At sight of the dog, the man paused and raised his revolver humorously. At sight of the man, the dog sprang up and walked diagonally away, with a sullen head and growling. The man yelled, and the dog broke into a gallop. As it was about to enter an alley, there was a loud noise, a whistling, and something spat the ground directly before it. The dog screamed, and, wheeling in terror, galloped headlong in a new direction. Again there was a noise, a whistling, and sand was kicked viciously before it. Fear-stricken, the dog turned and flurried like an animal in a pen. The man stood laughing, his weapons at his hips.

Ultimately the man was attracted by the closed door of the Weary Gentleman saloon. He went to it, and, hammering with a revolver, demanded drink.

The door remaining imperturbable, he picked a bit of paper from the walk, and nailed it to the framework with a knife. He then turned his back contemptuously upon this popular resort, and, walking to the opposite side of the street and spinning there on his heel quickly and lithely, fired at the bit of paper. He missed it by a half-inch. He swore at himself, and went away. Later, he comfortably fusilladed the windows of his most intimate friend. The man was playing with this town. It was a toy for him.

But still there was no offer of fight. The name of Jack Potter, his ancient antagonist, entered his mind, and he concluded that it would be a glad thing if he should go to Potter's house, and, by bombardment, induce him to come out and fight. He moved in the direction of his desire, chanting Apache scalp music.

When he arrived at it, Potter's house presented the same still, calm front as had the other adobes. Taking up a strategic position, the man howled a challenge. But this house regarded him as might a great stone god. It gave no sign. After a decent wait, the man howled further challenges, mingling with them wonderful epithets.

Presently there came the spectacle of a man churning himself into deepest rage over the immobility of a house. He fumed at it as the winter wind attacks a prairie cabin in the north. To the distance there should have gone the sound of a tumult like the fighting of two hundred Mexicans. As necessity bade him, he paused for breath or to reload his revolvers.

IV

POTTER and his bride walked sheepishly and with speed. Sometimes they laughed together shamefacedly and low.

'Next corner, dear,' he said finally.

They put forth the efforts of a pair walking bowed against a strong wind. Potter was about to raise a finger to point the first appearance of the new home, when, as they circled the corner, they came face to face with a man in a maroon-coloured shirt, who was feverishly pushing cartridges into a large revolver. Upon the instant the man dropped this revolver to the ground, and, like lightning, whipped another from its holster. The second weapon was aimed at the bridegroom's chest.

There was a silence. Potter's mouth seemed to be merely a grave for his tongue. He exhibited an instinct to at once loosen his arm from the woman's grip, and he dropped the bag to the sand. As for the bride, her face had gone as yellow as old cloth. She was a slave to hideous rites, gazing at the apparitional snake.

The two men faced each other at a distance of three paces. He of the revolver smiled with a new and quiet ferocity. 'Tried to sneak up on me!' he said. 'Tried to sneak up on me!' His eyes grew more baleful. As Potter made a slight movement, the man thrust his revolver venomously forward. 'No; don't you do it, Jack Potter. Don't you move a finger towards a gun just yet. Don't you move an eyelash. The time has come for me to settle with you, and I'm going to do it my own way, and loaf along with no interferin'. So if you don't want a gun bent on you, just mind what I tell you.'

Potter looked at his enemy. 'I ain't got a gun on me, Scratchy,' he said. 'Honest, I ain't.' He was stiffening and steadying, but yet somewhere at the back of his mind a vision of the Pullman floated – the sea-green figured velvet, the shining brass, silver, and glass, the wood that gleamed as darkly brilliant as the surface of a pool of oil – all the glory of their marriage, the environment of the new estate.

'You know I fight when it comes to fighting, Scratchy Wilson, but I ain't got a gun on me. You'll have to do all the shootin' yourself.'

His enemy's face went livid. He stepped forward, and lashed his weapon to and fro before Potter's chest.

'Don't you tell me you ain't got no gun on you, you whelp. Don't tell me no lie like that. There ain't a man in Texas ever seen you without no gun. Don't take me for no kid.'

His eyes blazed with light and his throat worked like a pump.

'I ain't takin' you for no kid,' answered Potter. His heels had not moved an inch backward. 'I'm takin' you for a fool. I tell you I ain't got a gun, and I ain't. If you're goin' to shoot me up, you'd better begin now. You'll never get a chance like this again.'

So much enforced reasoning had told on Wilson's rage. He was calmer.

'If you ain't got a gun, why ain't you got a gun?' he sneered. 'Been to Sunday school?'

'I ain't got a gun because I've just come from San Anton' with my wife. I'm married,' said Potter. 'And if I'd thought there was going to be any galoots like you prowling around when I brought my wife home, I'd had a gun, and don't you forget it.'

'Married!' said Scratchy, not at all comprehending.

'Yes, married! I'm married,' said Potter, distinctly.

'Married!' said Scratchy; seeming for the first time he saw the drooping drowning woman at the other man's side. 'No!' he said. He was like a creature allowed a glimpse of another world. He moved a pace backward, and his arm with the revolver dropped to his side. 'Is – this – is this the lady?' he asked.

'Yes, this is the lady,' answered Potter.

There was another period of silence.

'Well,' said Wilson at last, slowly, 'I s'pose it's all off now?'

'It's all off if you say so, Scratchy. You know I didn't make the trouble.'

Potter lifted his valise.

'Well, I 'low it's off, Jack,' said Wilson. He was looking at the ground. 'Married!' He was not a student of chivalry; it was merely that in the presence of this foreign condition he was a simple child of the earlier plains. He picked up his starboard revolver, and placing both weapons in their holsters, he went away. His feet made funnel-shaped tracks in the heavy sand.

O. Henry

A Chaparral Prince

NINE o'clock at last, and the drudging toil of the day was ended. Lena climbed to her room in the third half-storey of the Quarrymen's Hotel. Since daylight she had slaved, doing the work of a full-grown woman, scrubbing the floors, washing the heavy ironstone plates and cups, making the beds, and supplying the insatiate demands for wood and water in that turbulent and depressing hostelry.

The din of the day's quarrying was over – the blasting and drilling, the creaking of the great cranes, the shouts of the foremen, the backing and shifting of the flat-cars hauling the heavy blocks of limestone. Down in the hotel office three or four of the labourers were growling and swearing over a belated game of checkers. Heavy odours of stewed meat, hot grease, and cheap coffee hung like a depressing fog about the house.

Lena lit the stump of a candle and sat limply upon her wooden chair. She was eleven years old, thin and ill-nourished. Her back and limbs were sore and aching. But the ache in her heart made the biggest trouble. The last straw had been added to the burden upon her small shoulders. They had taken away Grimm. Always at night, however tired she might be, she had turned to Grimm for comfort and hope. Each time had Grimm whispered to her that the prince or the fairy would come and deliver her out of the wicked enchantment. Every night she had taken fresh courage and strength from Grimm.

To whatever tale she read she found an analogy in her own condition. The woodcutter's lost child, the unhappy goose girl, the persecuted stepdaughter, the little maiden imprisoned in the witch's hut – all these were but transparent disguises for Lena, the overworked kitchenmaid in the Quarrymen's Hotel. And always when the extremity was direct came the good fairy or the gallant prince to the rescue.

So, here in the ogre's castle, enslaved by a wicked spell, Lena had leaned upon Grimm and waited, longing for the powers of goodness to prevail. But on the day before Mrs Maloney had found the book in her room and had carried it away, declaring sharply that it would not do for servants to read at night; they lost sleep and did not work briskly the next day. Can one only eleven years old, living away from one's mamma, and never having any time to play, live entirely deprived of Grimm? Just try it once and you will see what a difficult thing it is.

Lena's home was in Texas, away up among the little mountains on the Pedernales River, in a little town called Fredericksburg. They are all German people who live in Fredericksburg. Of evenings they sit at little tables along the sidewalk and drink beer and play pinochle and scat. They are very thrifty people.

Thriftiest among them was Peter Hildesmuller, Lena's father. And that is why Lena was sent to work in the hotel at the quarries, thirty miles away. She earned three dollars every week there, and Peter added her wages to his well-guarded store. Peter had an ambition to become as rich as his neighbour, Hugo Heffelbauer, who smoked a meerschaum pipe three feet long and had wiener schnitzel and hassenpfeffer for dinner every day in the week. And now Lena was quite old enough to work and assist in the accumulation of riches. But conjecture if you can, what it means to be sentenced at eleven years of age from a home in the pleasant little Rhine village to hard labour in the ogre's castle, where you must fly to serve the ogres, while they devour cattle and sheep, growling fiercely as they stamp white limestone dust from their great shoes for you to sweep and scour with your weak, aching fingers. And then – to have Grimm taken away from you!

Lena raised the lid of an old empty case that had once contained canned corn and got out a sheet of paper and a piece of pencil. She was going to write a letter to her mamma. Tommy Ryan was going to post it for her at Ballinger's. Tommy was seventeen, worked in the quarries, went home to Ballinger's every night, and was now waiting in the shadows under Lena's window for her to throw the letter out to him. That was the only way she could send a letter to Fredericksburg. Mrs Maloney did not like for her to write letters.

The stump of candle was burning low, so Lena hastily bit the wood from around the lead of her pencil and began. This is the letter she wrote:

DEAREST MAMMA: I want so much to see you. And Gretel and Claus and Heinrich and little Adolf. I am so tired. I want to see you. Today I was slapped by Mrs Maloney and had no supper. I could not bring in enough wood, for my hand hurt. She took my book yesterday. I mean 'Grimms's Fairy Tales', which Uncle Leo gave me. It did not hurt anyone for me to read the book. I try to work as well as I can, but there is so much to do. I read only a little bit every night. Dear mamma, I shall tell you what I am going to do. Unless you send for me tomorrow to bring me home I shall go to a deep place I know in the river and drown. It is wicked to drown, I suppose, but I wanted to see you, and there is no one else. I am very tired, and Tommy is waiting for the letter. You will excuse me, mamma, if I do it.

Your respectful and loving daughter,
LENA.

Tommy was still waiting faithfully when the letter was concluded, and when Lena dropped it out she saw him pick it up and start up the steep hillside. Without undressing she blew out the candle and curled herself upon the mattress on the floor.

At 10.30 o'clock old man Ballinger came out of his house in his stocking feet and leaned over the gate, smoking his pipe. He looked down the big road, white in the moonshine, and rubbed one ankle with the toe of his other foot. It was time for the Fredericksburg mail to come pattering up the road.

Old man Ballinger had waited only a few minutes when he heard the lively hoofbeats of Fritz's team of little black mules, and very soon afterward his covered spring wagon stood in front of the gate. Fritz's big spectacles flashed in the moonlight and his tremendous voice shouted a greeting to the postmaster of Ballinger's. The mail-carrier jumped out and took the bridles from the mules, for he always fed them oats at Ballinger's.

While the mules were eating from their feed bags old man Ballinger brought out the mail sack and threw it into the wagon.

Fritz Bergmann was a man of three sentiments – or to be more accurate – four, the pair of mules deserving to be reckoned individually. Those mules were the chief interest and joy of his existence. Next came the Emperor of Germany and Lena Hildesmuller.

'Tell me,' said Fritz, when he was ready to start, 'contains the sack a letter to Frau Hildesmuller from the little Lena at the quarries? One came in the last mail to say that she is a little sick, already. Her mamma is very anxious to hear again.'

'Yes,' said old man Ballinger, 'thar's a letter for Mrs Helterskelter, or some sich name. Tommy Ryan brung it over when he come. Her little gal workin' over thar, you say?'

'In the hotel,' shouted Fritz, as he gathered up the lines; 'eleven years old and not bigger as a frankfurter. The close-fist of a Peter Hildesmuller! – some day shall I with a big club pound that man's dummkopf – all in and out the town. Perhaps in this letter Lena will say that she is yet feeling better. So, her mamma will be glad. *Auf wiedersehen*, Herr Ballinger – your feets will take cold out in the night air.'

'So long, Fritzy,' said old man Ballinger. 'You got a nice cool night for your drive.'

Up the road went the little black mules at their steady trot, while Fritz thundered at them occasional words of endearment and cheer.

These fancies occupied the mind of the mail-carrier until he reached the big post oak forest, eight miles from Ballinger's. Here his ruminations were scattered by the sudden flash and report of pistols and a whooping as if from a whole tribe of Indians. A band of galloping centaurs closed in around the mail wagon. One of them leaned over the front wheel, covered the driver with his revolver, and ordered him to stop. Others caught at the bridles of Donder and Blitzen.

'Donnerwetter!' shouted Fritz, with all his tremendous voice – 'wass ist? Release your hands from dose mules. Ve vas der United States mail!'

'Hurry up, Dutch!' drawled a melancholy voice. 'Don't you know when you're in a stick-up? Reverse your mules and climb out of the cart.'

It is due to the breadth of Hondo Bill's demerit and the largeness of his achievements to state that the holding up of the Fredericksburg mail was not perpetrated by way of an exploit. As the lion while in the pursuit of prey commensurate to his prowess might set a frivolous foot upon a casual rabbit in his path, so Hondo Bill and his gang had swooped sportively upon the pacific transport of Meinherr Fritz.

The real work of their sinister night ride was over. Fritz and his mail bag and his mules came as a gentle relaxation, grateful after the arduous duties of their profession. Twenty miles to the southeast stood a train with a killed engine, hysterical passengers and a looted express and mail car. That represented the serious occupation of Hondo Bill and his gang. With a fairly rich prize of currency and silver the robbers were making a wide detour to the west through the less populous country, intending to seek safety in Mexico by means of some fordable spot on the Rio Grande. The booty from the train had melted the desperate bushrangers to jovial and happy skylarkers.

Trembling with outraged dignity and no little personal apprehension, Fritz climbed out to the road after replacing his suddenly removed spectacles. The band had dismounted and were singing, capering, and whooping, thus expressing their satisfied delight in the life of a jolly outlaw. Rattlesnake Rogers, who stood at the heads of the mules, jerked a little too vigorously at the rein of the tender-mouthed Donder, who reared and emitted a loud, protesting snort of pain. Instantly Fritz, with a scream of anger, flew at the bulky Rogers and began to assiduously pommel that surprised freebooter with his fists.

'Villain!' shouted Fritz, 'dog, bigstiff! Dot mule he has a soreness by his mouth. I vill knock off your shoulders mit your head – robbermans!'

'Yi-yi!' howled Rattlesnake, roaring with laughter and ducking his head, 'somebody git this here sourkrout off'n me!'

One of the band yanked Fritz back by the coat-tail, and the woods rang with Rattlesnake's vociferous comments.

'The dog-goned little wienerwurst,' he yelled, amiably. 'He's not so much of a skunk, for a Dutchman. Took up for his animile plum quick, didn't he? I like to see a man like his hoss, even if it is a mule. The dad-blamed little Limburger he went for me, didn't he! Whoa, now, muley – I ain't a-goin' to hurt your mouth agin any more.'

Perhaps the mail would not have been tampered with had not Ben Moody, the lieutenant, possessed certain wisdom that seemed to promise more spoils.

'Say, Cap,' he said, addressing Hondo Bill, 'there's liable to be good pickings in these mail sacks. I've done some hoss tradin' with these Dutchmen around Fredericksburg, and I know the style of the varmints. There's big money goes through the mails to that town. Them Dutch risk a thousand dollars sent wrapped in a piece of paper before they'd pay the banks to handle the money.'

Hondo Bill, six feet two, gentle of voice and impulsive in action, was dragging the sacks from the rear of the wagon before Moody had finished his speech. A knife shone in his hand, and they heard the ripping sound as it bit through the tough canvas. The outlaws crowded around and began tearing open letters and packages, enlivening their labours by swearing affably at the writers, who seemed to have conspired to confute the prediction of Ben Moody. Not a dollar was found in the Fredericksburg mail.

'You ought to be ashamed of yourself,' said Hondo Bill to the mail-carrier in solemn tones, 'to be packing around such a lot of old, trashy paper as this. What d'you mean by it, anyhow? Where do you Dutchers keep your money at?'

The Ballinger mail sack opened like a cocoon under Hondo's knife. It contained but a handful of mail. Fritz had been fuming with terror and excitement until this sack was reached. He now remembered Lena's letter. He addressed the leader of the band, asking that that particular missive be spared.

'Much obliged, Dutch,' he said to the disturbed carrier. 'I guess that's the letter we want. Got spondulicks in it, ain't it? Here she is. Make a light, boys.'

Hondo found and tore open the letter to Mrs Hildesmuller. The others stood about, lighting twisted-up letters one from another. Hondo gazed with mute disapproval at the single sheet of paper covered with the angular German script.

'Whatever is this you've humbugged us with, Dutchy? You call this here a valuable letter? That's a mighty low-down trick to play on your friends what come along to help you distribute your mail.'

'That's Chiny writin',' said Sandy Grundy, peering over Hondo's shoulder.

'You're off your kazip,' declared another of the gang, an effective youth, covered with silk handkerchiefs and nickel plating. 'That's shorthand. I seen 'em do it once in court.'

'Ach, no, no, no – dot is German,' said Fritz. 'It is no more as a little girl writing a letter to her mamma. One poor little girl, sick and vorking hard avay from home. Ach! it is a shame. Good Mr Robberman, you vill please let me have dot letter?'

'What the devil do you take us for, old Pretzels?' said Hondo with sudden and surprising severity. 'You ain't presumin' to insinuate that we gents ain't possessed of sufficient politeness for to take an interest in the miss's health, are you? Now, you go on, and you read that scratchin' out loud and in plain United States language to this here company of educated society.'

Hondo twirled his six-shooter by its trigger guard and stood towering above the little German, who at once began to read the letter, translating the simple words into English. The gang of rovers stood in absolute silence, listening intently.

'How old is that kid?' asked Hondo when the letter was done.

'Eleven,' said Fritz.

'And where is she at?'

'At dose rock quarries – working. Ach, mein Gott – little Lena, she speak of drowning. I do not know if she vill do it, but if she shall I schwear I vill dot Peter Hildesmuller shoot mit a gun.'

'You Dutchers,' said Hondo Bill, his voice swelling with fine contempt, 'make me plenty tired. Hirin' out your kids to work when they ought to be playin' dolls in the sand. You're a hell of a sect of people. I reckon we'll fix your clock for a while just to show what we think of your old cheesy nation. Here, boys!'

Hondo Bill parleyed aside briefly with his band, and then they seized Fritz and conveyed him off the road to one side. Here they bound him fast to a tree with a couple of lariats. His team they tied to another tree near by.

'We aint going to hurt you bad,' said Hondo reassuringly. ' 'Twon't hurt you to be tied up for a while. We will now pass you the time of day, as it is up to us to depart. Ausgespielt – nixcumrous, Dutchy. Don't get any more impatience.'

Fritz heard a great squeaking of saddles as the men mounted their horses. Then a loud yell and a great clatter of hoofs as they galloped pell-mell back along the Fredericksburg road.

For more than two hours Fritz sat against his tree, tightly but not painfully bound. Then from the reaction after his exciting adventure he sank into slumber. How long he slept he knew not, but he was at last awakened by a rough shake. Hands were untying his ropes. He was lifted to his feet, dazed, confused in mind, and weary of body. Rubbing his eyes, he looked and saw that he was again in the midst of the same band of terrible bandits. They shoved him up to the seat of his wagon and placed the lines in his hands.

'Hit it out for home, Dutch,' said Hondo Bill's voice commandingly. 'You've given us lots of trouble and we're pleased to see the back of your neck. Spiel! Zwei bier! Vamoose!'

Hondo reached out and gave Blitzen a smart cut with his quirt.

The little mules sprang ahead, glad to be moving again. Fritz urged them along, himself dizzy and muddled over his fearful adventure.

According to schedule time, he should have reached Fredericksburg at daylight. As it was, he drove down the long street of the town at eleven o'clock am. He had to pass Peter Hildesmuller's house on his way to the post-office. He stopped his team at the gate and called. But Frau Hildesmuller was watching for him. Out rushed the whole family of Hildesmullers.

Frau Hildesmuller, fat and flushed, inquired if he had a letter from Lena, and then Fritz raised his voice and told the tale of his adventure. He told the contents of the letter that the robber had made him read, and then Frau Hildesmuller broke into wild weeping. Her little Lena drown herself! Why had they sent her from home? What could be done? Perhaps it would be too late by the time they could send for her now. Peter Hildesmuller dropped his meerschaum on the walk and it shivered into pieces.

'Woman!' he roared at his wife, 'why did you let that child go away? It is your fault if she comes home to us no more.'

Every one knew that it was Peter Hildesmuller's fault, so they paid no attention to his words.

A moment afterward a strange, faint voice was heard to call: 'Mamma!' Frau Hildesmuller at first thought it was Lena's spirit calling, and then she rushed to the rear of Fritz's covered wagon, and, with a loud shriek of joy, caught up Lena herself, covering her pale little face with kisses and smothering her with hugs. Lena's eyes were heavy with the deep slumber of exhaustion, but she smiled and lay close to the one she had longed to see. There among the mail sacks, covered in a nest of strange blankets and comforters, she had lain asleep until wakened by the voices around her.

Fritz stared at her with eyes that bulged behind his spectacles.

'Gott in Himmel!' he shouted. 'How did you get in that wagon? Am I going cray as well as to be murdered and hanged by robbers this day?'

'You brought her to us, Fritz,' cried Frau Hildesmuller. 'How can we ever thank you enough?'

'Tell mamma how you came in Fritz's wagon,' said Frau Hildesmuller.

'I don't know,' said Lena. 'But I know how I got away from the hotel. The Prince brought me.'

'By the Emperor's crown!' shouted Fritz, 'we are all going crazy.'

'I always knew he would come,' said Lena, sitting down on her bundle of bedclothes on the sidewalk. 'Last night he came with his armed knights and captured the ogre's castle. They broke the dishes and kicked down the doors. They pitched Mr Maloney into a barrel of rain water and threw flour all over Mrs Maloney. The workmen in the hotel jumped out of the windows and ran into the woods when the knights began firing their guns. They wakened me up and I peeped down the stair. And then the Prince came up and wrapped me in the bedclothes and carried me out. He was so tall and strong and fine. His face was as rough as a scrubbing brush, and he talked soft and kind and smelled of schnapps. He took me on his horse before him and we rode away among the knights. He held me close and I went to sleep that way, and didn't wake up till I got home.'

'Rubbish!' cried Fritz Bergmann. 'Fairy tales! How did you come from the quarries to my wagon?'

'The Prince brought me,' said Lena, confidently.

And to this day the good people of Fredericksburg haven't been able to make her give any other explanation.

O. Henry

The Caballero's Way

THE Cisco Kid had killed six men in more or less fair scrimmages, had murdered twice as many (mostly Mexicans), and had winged a larger number whom he modestly forbore to count. Therefore a woman loved him.

The Kid was twenty-five, looked twenty; and a careful insurance company would have estimated the probable time of his demise at, say, twenty-six. His habitat was anywhere between the Frio and the Rio Grande. He killed for the love of it – because he was quick-tempered – to avoid arrest – for his own amusement – any reason that came to his mind would suffice. He had escaped capture because he could shoot five-sixths of a second sooner than any sheriff or ranger in the service, and because he rode a speckled roan horse that knew every cow-path in the mesquite and pear thickets from San Antonio to Matamoras.

Tonia Perez, the girl who loved the Cisco Kid, was half Carmen, half Madonna, and the rest – oh, yes, a woman who is half Carmen and half Madonna can always be something more – the rest, let us say, was humming-bird. She lived in a grass-roofed *jacal* near a little Mexican settlement at the Lone Wolf Crossing of the Frio. With her lived a father or grandfather, a lineal Aztec, somewhat less than a thousand years old, who herded a hundred goats and lived in a continuous drunken dream from drinking *mescal*. Back of the *jacal* a tremendous forest of bristling pear, twenty feet high at its worst, crowded almost to its door. It was along the bewildering maze of this spinous thicket that the speckled roan would bring the Kid to see his girl. And once, clinging like a lizard to the ridge-pole, high up under the peaked grass roof, he had heard Tonia, with her Madonna face and Carmen beauty and humming-bird soul, parley with the sheriff's posse, denying knowledge of her man in her soft *mélange* of Spanish and English.

One day the adjutant-general of the State, who is, *ex officio*, commander of the ranger forces, wrote some sarcastic lines to Captain Duval of Company X, stationed at Laredo, relative to the serene and undisturbed existence led by murderers and desperadoes in the said captain's territory.

The captain turned the colour of brick dust under his tan, and forwarded the letter, after adding a few comments, per ranger Private Bill Adamson, to ranger Lieutenant Sandridge, camped at a water hole on the Nueces with a squad of five men in preservation of law and order.

Lieutenant Sandridge turned a beautiful *couleur de rose* through his ordinary strawberry complexion, tucked the letter in his hip pocket, and chewed off the ends of his gamboge moustache.

The next morning he saddled his horse and rode alone to the Mexican settlement at the Lone Wolf Crossing of the Frio, twenty miles away.

Six feet two, blond as a Viking, quiet as a deacon, dangerous as a machine gun, Sandridge moved among the *Jacales*, patiently seeking news of the Cisco Kid.

Far more than the law, the Mexicans dreaded the cold and certain vengeance of the lone rider that the ranger sought. It had been one of the Kid's pastimes to shoot Mexicans 'to see them kick': if he demanded from them moribund Terpsichorean feats, simply that he might be entertained, what terrible and extreme penalties would be certain to follow should they anger him! One and all they lounged with upturned palms and shrugging shoulders, filling the air with '*quien sabes*' and denials of the Kid's acquaintance.

But there was a man named Fink who kept a store at the Crossing – a man of many nationalities, tongues, interests, and ways of thinking.

'No use to ask them Mexicans,' he said to Sandridge. 'They're afraid to tell. This *hombre* they call the Kid – Goodall is his name, ain't it? – he's been in my store once or twice. I have an idea you might run across him at – but I guess I don't keer to say, myself. I'm two seconds later in pulling a gun than I used to be, and the difference is worth thinking about. But this Kid's got a half-Mexican girl at the Crossing that he comes to see. She lives in that *jacal* a hundred yards down the arroyo at the edge of the pear. Maybe she – no, I don't suppose she would, but that *jacal* would be a good place to watch, anyway.'

Sandridge rode down to the *jacal* of Perez. The sun was low, and the broad shade of the great pear thicket already covered the grass-thatched hut. The goats were enclosed for the night in a brush corral near by. A few kids walked the top of it, nibbling the chaparral leaves. The old Mexican lay upon a blanket on the grass, already in a stupor from his mescal, and dreaming, perhaps, of the nights when he and Pizarro touched glasses to their New World fortunes – so old his wrinkled face seemed to proclaim him to be. And in the door of the *jacal* stood Tonia. And Lieutenant Sandridge sat in his saddle staring at her like a gannet agape at a sailorman.

The Cisco Kid was a vain person, as all eminent and successful assassins are, and his bosom would have been ruffled had he known that at a simple exchange of glances two persons, in whose minds he had been looming large, suddenly abandoned (at least for the time) all thought of him.

Never before had Tonia seen such a man as this. He seemed to be made of sunshine and blood-red tissue and clear weather. He seemed to illuminate the shadow of the pear when he smiled, as though the sun were rising again. The men she had known had been small and dark. Even the Kid, in spite of his achievements, was a stripling no larger than herself, with black, straight hair and a cold, marble face that chilled the noonday.

As for Tonia, though she sends description to the poorhouse, let her make a millionaire of your fancy. Her blue-black hair, smoothly divided in the middle and bound close to her head, and her large eyes full of the Latin melancholy, gave her the Madonna touch. Her motions and air spoke of the concealed fire and the desire to charm that she had inherited from the *gitanas* of the Basque province. As for the humming-bird part of her, that dwelt in her heart; you could not perceive it unless her bright red skirt and dark blue blouse gave you a symbolic hint of the vagarious bird.

The newly lighted sun-god asked for a drink of water. Tonia brought it from the red jar hanging under the brush shelter. Sandridge considered it necessary to dismount so as to lessen the trouble of her ministrations.

I play no spy; nor do I assume to master the thoughts of any human heart; but I assert, by the chronicler's right, that before a quarter of an hour had sped, Sandridge was teaching her how to plait a six-strand rawhide stake-rope, and Tonia had explained to him that were it not for her little English book that the peripatetic *padre* had given her and the little crippled *chivo*, that she fed from a bottle, she would be very, very lonely indeed.

Which leads to a suspicion that the Kid's fences needed repairing, and that the adjutant-general's sarcasm had fallen upon unproductive soil.

In his camp by the water hole Lieutenant Sandridge announced and reiterated his intention of either causing the Cisco Kid to nibble the black loam of the Frio country prairies or of hauling him before a judge and jury. That sounded business-like. Twice a week he rode over to the Lone Wolf Crossing of the Frio, and directed Tonia's slim, slightly lemon-tinted fingers among the intricacies of the slowly growing lariata. A six-strand plait is hard to learn and easy to teach.

The ranger knew that he might find the Kid there at any visit. He kept his armament ready, and had a frequent eye for the pear thicket at the rear of the *jacal*. Thus he might bring down the kite and the humming-bird with one stone.

While the sunny-haired ornithologist was pursuing his studies the Cisco Kid was also attending to his professional duties. He moodily shot up a saloon in a small cow village on Quintana Creek, killed the town marshal (plugging him neatly in the centre of his tin badge), and then rode away, morose and unsatisfied. No true artist is uplifted by shooting an aged man carrying an old-style .38 bulldog.

On his way the Kid suddenly experienced the yearning that all men feel when wrong-doing loses its keen edge of delight. He yearned for the woman he loved to reassure him that she was his in spite of it. He wanted her to call his bloodthirstiness bravery and his cruelty devotion. He wanted Tonia to bring him water from the red jar under the brush shelter, and tell him how the *chivo* was thriving on the bottle.

The Kid turned the speckled roan's head up the ten-mile pear flat that stretches along the Arroyo Hondo until it ends at the Lone Wolf Crossing of the Frio. The roan whickered; for he had a sense of locality and direction equal to that of a belt-line street-car horse; and he knew he would soon be nibbling the rich mesquite grass at the end of a forty-foot stake-rope while Ulysses rested his head in Circe's straw-roofed hut.

More weird and lonesome than the journey of an Amazonian explorer is the ride of one through a Texas pear flat. With dismal monotony and startling variety the uncanny and multiform shapes of the cacti lift their twisted trunks, and fat, bristly hands to encumber the way. The demon plant, appearing to live without soil or rain, seems to taunt the parched traveller with its lush grey greenness. It warps itself a thousand times about what look to be open and inviting paths, only to lure the rider into blind and impassable spine-defended 'bottoms of the bag', leaving him to retreat, if he can, with the points of the compass whirling in his head.

To be lost in the pear is to die almost the death of the thief on the cross, pierced by nails and with grotesque shapes of all the fiends hovering about.

But it was not so with the Kid and his mount. Winding, twisting, circling, tracing the most fantastic and bewildering trail ever picked out, the good roan lessened the distance to the Lone Wolf Crossing with every coil and turn that he made.

While they fared the Kid sang. He knew but one tune and sang it, as he knew but one code and lived it, and but one girl and loved her. He was a single-minded man of conventional ideas. He had a voice like a coyote with bronchitis, but whenever he chose to sing his song he sang it. It was a conventional song of the camps and trail, running at its beginning as near as may be to these words:

Don't you monkey with my Lulu girl
Or I'll tell you what I'll do

and so on. The roan was inured to it, and did not mind.

But even the poorest singer will, after a certain time, gain his own consent to refrain from contributing to the world's noises. So the Kid, by the time he was within a mile or two of Tonia's *jacal*, had reluctantly allowed his song to die away – not because his vocal performance had become less charming to his own ears, but because his laryngeal muscles were aweary.

As though he were in a circus ring the speckled roan wheeled and danced through the labyrinth of pear until at length his rider knew by certain landmarks that the Lone Wolf Crossing was close at hand. Then, where the pear was thinner, he caught sight of the grass roof of the *jacal* and the hackberry tree on the edge of the arroyo. A few yards farther the Kid stopped the roan and gazed intently through the prickly openings. Then he dismounted, dropped the roan's reins, and proceeded on foot, stooping and silent, like an Indian. The roan, knowing his part, stood still, making no sound.

The Kid crept noiselessly to the very edge of the pear thicket and reconnoitred between the leaves of a clump of cactus.

Ten yards from his hiding-place, in the shade of the *jacal*, sat his Tonia calmly plaiting a rawhide lariat. So far she might surely escape condemnation; women have been known, from time to time, to engage in more mischievous occupations. But if all must be told, there is to be added that her head reposed against the broad and comfortable chest of a tall red-and-yellow man, and that his arm was about her, guiding her nimble small fingers that required so many lessons at the intricate six-strand plait.

Sandridge glanced quickly at the dark mass of pear when he heard a slight squeaking sound that was not altogether unfamiliar. A gun-scabbard will make that sound when one grasps the handle of a six-shooter suddenly. But the sound was not repeated; and Tonia's fingers needed close attention.

And then, in the shadow of death, they began to talk of their love; and in the still July afternoon every word they uttered reached the ears of the Kid.

'Remember, then,' said Tonia, 'you must not come again until I send for you. Soon he will be here. A *vaquero* at the *tienda* said to-day he saw him on the Guadalupe three days ago. When he is that near he always comes. If he comes and finds you here he will kill you. So, for my sake, you must come no more until I send you the word.'

'All right,' said the ranger. 'And then what?'

'And then,' said the girl, 'you must bring your men here and kill him. If not, he will kill you.'

'He ain't a man to surrender, that's sure,' said Sandridge. 'It's kill or be killed for the officer that goes up against Mr Cisco Kid.'

'He must die,' said the girl. 'Otherwise there will not be any peace in the world for thee and me. He has killed many. Let him so die. Bring your men, and give him no chance to escape.'

'You used to think right much of him,' said Sandridge.

Tonia dropped the lariat, twisted herself around, and curved a lemon-tinted arm over the ranger's shoulder.

'But then,' she murmured in liquid Spanish, 'I had not beheld thee, thou great, red mountain of a man! And thou art kind and good, as well as strong. Could one choose him, knowing thee? Let him die; for then I will not be filled with fear by day and night lest he hurt thee or me.'

'How can I know when he comes?' asked Sandridge.

'When he comes,' said Tonia, 'he remains two days, sometimes three. Gregorio, the small son of old Luisa, the *lavandera*, has a swift pony. I will write a letter to thee and send it by him, saying how it will be best to come upon him. By Gregorio will the letter come. And bring many men with thee, and have much care, oh, dear red one, for the rattlesnake is not quicker to strike than is *El Chivato*, as they call him, to send a ball from his *pistola*.'

'The Kid's handy with his gun, sure enough,' admitted Sandridge, 'but when I come for him I shall come alone. I'll get him by myself or not at all. The Cap wrote one or two things to me that make me want to do the trick without any help. You let me know when Mr Kid arrives, and I'll do the rest.'

'I will send you the message by the boy Gregorio,' said the girl. 'I knew you were braver than that small slayer of men who never smiles. How could I ever have thought I cared for him?'

It was time for the ranger to ride back to his camp on the water hole. Before he mounted his horse he raised the slight form of Tonia with one arm high from the earth for a parting salute. The drowsy stillness of the torpid summer air still lay thick upon the dreaming afternoon. The smoke from the fire in the *jacal*, where the *frijoles* blubbered in the iron pot, rose straight as a plumb-line above the clay-daubed chimney. No sound or movement disturbed the serenity of the dense pear thicket ten yards away.

When the form of Sandridge had disappeared, loping his big dun down the steep banks of the Frio crossing, the Kid crept back to his own horse, mounted him, and rode back along the tortuous trail he had come.

But not far. He stopped and waited in the silent depths of the pear until half an hour had passed. And then Tonia heard the high, untrue notes of his unmusical singing coming nearer and nearer; and she ran to the edge of the pear to meet him.

The Kid seldom smiled; but he smiled and waved his hat when he saw her. He dismounted, and his girl sprang into his arms. The Kid looked at her fondly. His thick, black hair clung to his head like a wrinkled mat. The meeting brought a slight ripple of some undercurrent of feeling to his smooth, dark face that was usually as motionless as a clay mask.

'How's my girl?' he asked, holding her close.

'Sick of waiting so long for you, dear one,' she answered. 'My eyes are dim with always gazing into that devil's pincushion through which you come. And I can see into it such a little way, too. But you are here, beloved one, and I will not scold. *Que mal muchacho!* not to come to see your *alma* more often. Go in and rest, and let me water your horse and stake him with the long rope. There is cool water in the jar for you.'

The Kid kissed her affectionately.

'Not if the court knows itself do I let a lady stake my horse for me,' said he. 'But if you'll run in, *chica*, and throw a pot of coffee together while I attend to the *caballo*, I'll be a good deal obliged.'

Besides his marksmanship the Kid had another attribute for which he admired himself greatly. He was *muy caballero*, as the Mexicans express it, where the ladies were concerned. For them he had always gentle words and consideration. He could not have spoken a harsh word to a woman. He might ruthlessly slay their husbands and brothers, but he could not have laid the weight of a finger in anger upon a woman. Wherefore many of that interesting division of humanity who had come under the spell of his politeness declared their disbelief in the stories circulated about Mr Kid. One shouldn't believe everything one heard, they said. When confronted by their indignant men folk with proof of the *caballero's* deeds of infamy, they said maybe he had been driven to it, and that he knew how to treat a lady, anyhow.

Considering this extremely courteous idiosyncrasy of the Kid and the pride that he took in it, one can perceive that the solution of the problem that was presented to him by what he saw and heard from his hiding-place in the pear that afternoon (at least as to one of the actors) must have been obscured by difficulties. And yet one could not think of the Kid overlooking little matters of that kind.

At the end of the short twilight they gathered around a supper of *frijoles*, goat steaks, canned peaches, and coffee, by the light of a lantern in the *jacal*. Afterward, the ancestor, his flock corralled, smoked a cigarette and became a mummy in a grey blanket. Tonia washed the few dishes while the Kid dried them with the flour-sacking towel. Her eyes shone; she chatted volubly of the inconsequent happenings of her small world since the Kid's last visit; it was as all his other homecomings had been.

Then outside Tonia swung in a grass hammock with her guitar and sang sad *canciones de amor*.

'Do you love me just the same, old girl?' asked the Kid, hunting for his cigarette papers.

'Always the same, little one,' said Tonia, her dark eyes lingering upon him.

'I must go over to Fink's,' said the Kid, rising, 'for some tobacco. I thought I had another sack in my coat. I'll be back in a quarter of an hour.'

'Hasten,' said Tonia, 'and tell me – how long shall I call you my own this time? Will you be gone again tomorrow, leaving me to grieve, or will you be longer with your Tonia?'

'Oh, I might stay two or three days this trip,' said the Kid, yawning. 'I've been on the dodge for a month, and I'd like to rest up.'

He was gone half an hour for his tobacco. When he returned Tonia was still lying in the hammock.

'It's funny,' said the Kid, 'how I feel. I feel like there was somebody lying behind every bush and tree waiting to shoot me. I never had mullygrubs like them before. Maybe it's one of them presumptions. I've got half a notion to light out in the morning before day. The Guadalupe country is burning up about that old Dutchman I plugged down there.'

'You are not afraid – no one could make my brave little one fear.'

'Well, I haven't been usually regarded as a jackrabbit when it comes to scrapping; but I don't want a posse smoking me out when I'm in your *jacal*. Somebody might get hurt that oughtn't to.'

'Remain with your Tonia; no one will find you here.'

The Kid looked keenly into the shadows up and down the arroyo and toward the dim lights of the Mexican village.

'I'll see how it looks later on,' was his decision.

At midnight a horseman rode into the rangers' camp, blazing his way by noisy 'halloes' to indicate a pacific mission. Sandridge and one or two others turned out to investigate the row. The rider announced himself to be Domingo Sales, from the Lone Wold Crossing. He bore a letter for Señor Sandridge. Old Luisa, the *lavendero*, had persuaded him to bring it, he said, her son Gregorio being too ill of a fever to ride.

Sandridge lighted the camp lantern and read the letter. These were its words:

Dear One: He has come. Hardly had you ridden away when he came out of the pear. When he first talked he said he would stay three days or more. Then as it grew later he was like a wolf or a fox, and walked about without rest, looking and listening. Soon he said he must leave before daylight when it is dark and stillest. And then he seemed to suspect that I be not true to him. He looked at me so strange that I am frightened. I swear to him that I love him, his own Tonia. Last of all he said I must prove to him I am true. He thinks that even now men are waiting to kill him as he rides from my house. To escape he says he will dress in my clothes, my red skirt and the blue waist I wear and the brown mantilla over the head, and thus ride away. But before that he says that I must put on his clothes, his *pantalones* and *camisa* and hat, and ride away on his horse from the *jacal* as far as the big road beyond the crossing and back again. This before he goes, so he can tell if I am true and if men are hidden to shoot him. It is a terrible thing. An hour before daybreak this is to be. Come, my dear one, and kill this man and take me for your Tonia. Do not try to take hold of him alive, but kill him quickly. Knowing all, you should do that. You must come long before the time and hide yourself in the little shed near the *jacal* where the wagon and saddles are kept. It is dark in there. He will wear my red skirt and blue waist and brown mantilla. I send you a hundred kisses. Come surely and shoot quickly and straight.

THINE OWN TONIA.

Sandridge quickly explained to his men the official part of the missive. The rangers protested against his going alone.

'I'll get him easy enough,' said the lieutenant. 'The girl's got him trapped. And don't even think he'll get the drop on me.'

Sandridge saddled his horse and rode to the Lone Wolf Crossing. He tied his big dun in a clump of brush on the arroyo, took his Winchester from its scabbard, and carefully approached the Perez *jacal*. There was only the half of a high moon drifted over by ragged, milk-white gulf clouds.

The wagon-shed was an excellent place for ambush; and the ranger got inside it safely. In the black shadow of the brush shelter in front of the *jacal* he could see a horse tied and hear him impatiently pawing the hard-trodden earth.

He waited almost an hour before two figures came out of the *jacal*. One, in man's clothes, quickly mounted the horse and galloped past the wagon-shed toward the crossing and village. And then the other figure, in skirt, waist, and mantilla over its head, stepped out into the faint moonlight, gazing after the rider. Sandridge thought he would take his chance then before Tonia rode back. He fancied she might not care to see it.

'Throw up your hands,' he ordered loudly, stepping out of the wagon-shed with his Winchester at his shoulder.

There was a quick turn of the figure, but no movement to obey, so the ranger pumped in the bullets – one – two – three – and then twice more; for you never could be too sure of bringing down the Cisco Kid. There was no danger of missing at ten paces, even in that half moonlight.

The old ancestor, asleep on his blanket, was awakened by the shots. Listening further, he heard a great cry from some man in mortal distress or anguish, and rose up grumbling at the disturbing ways of moderns.

The tall, red ghost of a man burst into the *jacal*, reaching one hand, shaking like a *tule* reed, for the lantern hanging on its nail. The other spread a letter on the table.

'Look at this letter, Perez,' cried the man. 'Who wrote it?'

'*Ah Dios!* it is Señor Sandridge,' mumbled the old man, approaching. '*Pues, señor*, that letter was written by *El Chivato*, as he is called – by the man of Tonia. They say he is a bad man; I do not know. While Tonia slept he wrote the letter and sent it by this old hand of mine to Domingo Sales to be brought to you. Is there anything wrong in the letter? I am very old; and I did not know. *Valgame Dios!* it is a very foolish world; and there is nothing in the house to drink – nothing to drink.'

Just then all that Sandridge could think of to do was to go outside and throw himself face downward in the dust by the side of his humming-bird, of whom not a feather fluttered. He was not a *caballero* by instinct, and he could not understand the niceties of revenge.

A mile away the rider who had ridden past the wagon-shed struck up a harsh, untuneful song, the words of which began:

Don't you monkey with my Lulu girl
Or I'll tell you what I'll do –

O. Henry

The Higher Abdication

CURLY the tramp sidled toward the free-lunch counter. He caught a fleeting glance from the bartender's eye, and stood still, trying to look like a business man who had just dined at the Menger and was waiting for a friend who had promised to pick him up in his motor car. Curly's histrionic powers were equal to the impersonation; but his make-up was wanting.

The bartender rounded the bar in a casual way, looking up at the ceiling as though he was pondering some intricate problem of kalsomining, and then fell upon Curly so suddenly that the roadster had no excuses ready. Irresistibly, but so composedly that it seemed almost absentmindedness on his part, the dispenser of drinks pushed Curly to the swinging doors and kicked him out, with a nonchalance that almost amounted to sadness. That was the way of the Southwest.

Curly arose from the gutter leisurely. He felt no anger or resentment toward his ejector. Fifteen years of tramphood spent out of the twenty-two years of his life had hardened the fibres of his spirit. The slings and arrows of outrageous fortune fell blunted from the buckler of his armoured pride. With especial resignation did he suffer contumely and injury at the hands of bartenders. Naturally, they were his enemies; and unnaturally, they were often his friends. He had to take his chances with them. But he had not yet learned to estimate these cool, languid, Southwestern knights of the bungstarter, who had the manners of an Earl of Pawtucket, and who, when they disapproved of your presence, moved you with the silence and despatch of a chess automaton advancing a pawn.

Curly stood for a few moments in the narrow, mesquite-paved street. San Antonio puzzled and disturbed him. Three days he had been a non-paying guest of the town, having dropped off there from a box car of an I. & G. N. freight, because Greaser Johnny had told him in Des Moines that the Alamo City was manna fallen, gathered, cooked, and served free with cream and sugar. Curly had found the tip partly a good one. There was hospitality in plenty of a careless, liberal, irregular sort. But the town itself was a weight upon his spirits after his experience with the rushing, business-like, systematized cities of the North and East. Here he was often flung a dollar, but too frequently a good-natured kick would follow it. Once a band of hilarious cowboys had roped him on Military Plaza and dragged him across the black soil until no respectable rag-bag would have stood sponsor for his clothes. The winding, doubling streets, leading nowhere, bewildered him. And then there was a little river, crooked as a pot-hook, that crawled through the middle of the town, crossed by a hundred little bridges so nearly alike that they got on Curly's nerves. And the last bartender wore a number nine shoe.

The saloon stood on a corner. The hour was eight o'clock. Home-farers and outgoers jostled Curly on the narrow stone sidewalk. Between the buildings to his left he looked down a cleft that proclaimed itself another thoroughfare. The alley was dark except for one patch of light. Where there was light there were sure to be human beings. Where there were human beings after nightfall in San Antonio there might be food, and there was sure to be drink. So Curly headed for the light.

The illumination came from Schwegel's Café. On the sidewalk in front of it Curly picked up an old envelope. It might have contained a cheque for a million. It was empty; but the wanderer read the address, 'Mr Otto Schwegel'. And the name of the town and State. The post-mark was Detroit.

Curly entered the saloon. And now in the light it could be perceived that he bore the stamp of many years of vagabondage. He had none of the tidiness of the calculating and shrewd professional tramp. His wardrobe represented the cast-off specimens of half a dozen fashions and eras. Two factories had combined their efforts in providing shoes for his feet. As you gazed at him there passed through your mind vague impressions of mummies, wax figures, Russian exiles, and men lost on desert islands. His face was covered almost to his eyes with a curly brown beard that he kept trimmed short with a pocket-knife, and that had furnished him with his *nom de route*. Light-blue eyes, full of sullen-ness, fear, cunning, impudence, and fawning, witnessed the stress that had been laid upon his soul.

The saloon was small, and in its atmosphere the odours of meat and drink struggled for the ascendency. The pig and the cabbage wrestled with hydrogen and oxygen. Behind the bar Schwegel laboured with an assistant whose epidermal pores showed no signs of being obstructed. Hot wienerwurst and sauerkraut were being served to purchasers of beer. Curly shuffled to the end of the bar, coughed hollowly, and told Schwegel that he was a Detroit cabinet-maker out of a job.

It followed as the night the day that he got his schooner and lunch.

'Was you acquainted maybe mit Heinrich Strauss in Detroit?' asked Schwegel.

'Did I know Heinrich Strauss?' repeated Curly, affectionately. 'Why, say, 'Bo, I wish I had a dollar for every game of pinocle me and Heine has played on Sunday afternoons.'

More beer and a second plate of steaming food was set before the diplomat. And then Curly, knowing to a fluid-drachm how far a 'con' game would go, shuffled out into the unpromising street.

And now he began to perceive the inconveniences of this stony Southern town. There was none of the outdoor gaiety and brilliancy and music that provided distraction even to the poorest in the cities of the North. Here, even so early, the gloomy, rock-walled houses were closed and barred against the murky dampness of the night. The streets were mere fissures through which flowed grey wreaths of river mist. As he walked he heard laughter and the chink of coin and chips behind darkened windows, and music coming from every chink of wood and stone. But the diversions were selfish; the day of popular pastimes had not yet come to San Antonio.

But at length Curly, as he strayed, turned the sharp angle of another lost street and came upon a rollicking band of stockmen from the outlying ranches celebrating in the open in front of an ancient wooden hotel. One great roisterer from the sheep country who had just instigated a movement toward the bar, swept Curly in like a stray goat with the rest of his flock. The princes of kine and wool hailed him as a new zoological discovery, and uproariously strove to preserve him in the diluted alcohol of their compliments and regards.

An hour afterward Curly staggered from the hotel barroom dismissed by his fickle friends, whose interest in him had subsided as quickly as it had risen. Full – stoked with alcoholic fuel and cargoed with food, the only question remaining to disturb him was that of shelter and bed.

A drizzling, cold Texas rain had begun to fall – an endless, lazy, unintermittent downfall that lowered the spirits of men and raised a reluctant steam from the warm stones of the streets and houses. Thus comes the 'norther' dousing gentle spring and amiable autumn with the chilling salutes and adieux of coming and departing winter.

Curly followed his nose down the first tortuous street into which his irresponsible feet conducted him. At the lower end of it, on the bank of the serpentine stream, he perceived an open gate in a cemented rock wall. Inside he saw camp fires and a row of low wooden sheds built against three sides of the enclosing wall. He entered the enclosure. Under the sheds many horses were champing at their oats and corn. Many wagons and buckboards stood about with their teams' harness thrown carelessly upon the shafts and doubletrees. Curly recognized the place as a wagon-yard, such as is provided by merchants for their out-of-town friends and customers. No one was in sight. No doubt the drivers of those wagons were scattered about the town 'seeing the elephant and hearing the owl'. In their haste to become patrons of the town's dispensaries of mirth and good cheer the last ones to depart must have left the great wooden gate swinging open.

Curly had satisfied the hunger of an anaconda and the thirst of a camel, so he was neither in the mood nor the condition of an explorer. He zigzagged his way to the first wagon that his eyesight distinguished in the semi-darkness under the shed. It was a two-horse wagon with a top of white canvas. The wagon was half filled with loose piles of wool sacks, two or three great bundles of grey blankets, and a number of bales, bundles, and boxes. A reasoning eye would have estimated the load at once as ranch supplies, bound on the morrow for some outlying hacienda. But to the drowsy intelligence of Curly they represented only warmth and softness and protection against the cold humidity of the night. After several unlucky efforts, at last he conquered gravity so far as to climb over a wheel and pitch forward upon the best and warmest bed he had fallen upon in many a day. Then he became instinctively a burrowing animal, and dug his way like a prairie-dog down among the sacks and blankets, hiding himself from the cold air as snug and safe as a bear in his den. For three nights sleep had visited Curly only in broken and shivering doses. So now, when Morpheus condescended to pay him a call, Curly got such a stranglehold on the mythological old gentleman that it was a wonder that anyone else in the whole world got a wink of sleep that night.

Six cowpunchers of the Cibolo Ranch were waiting around the door of the ranch store. Their ponies cropped grass near by, tied in the Texas fashion – which is not tied at all. Their bridle reins had been dropped to the earth, which is a more effectual way of securing them (such is the power of habit and imagination) than you could devise out of a half-inch rope and a live-oak tree.

These guardians of the cow lounged about, each with a brown cigarette paper in his hand, and gently but unceasingly cursed Sam Revell, the storekeeper. Sam stood in the door, snapping the red elastic bands on his pink madras shirtsleeves and looking down affectionately at the only pair of tan shoes within a forty-mile radius. His offence had been serious, and he was divided between humble apology and admiration for the beauty of his raiment. He had allowed the ranch stock of 'smoking' to become exhausted.

'I thought sure there was another case of it under the counter, boys,' he explained. 'But it happened to be catterdges.'

'You've sure got a case of happenedicitis,' said Poky Rodgers, a fence rider of the Largo Verde *potrero*. 'Somebody ought to happen to give you a knock on the head with the butt end of a quirt. I've rode in nine miles for some tobacco; and it don't appear natural and seemly that you ought to be allowed to live.'

'The boys was smokin' cut plug and dried mesquite leaves mixed when I left,' sighed Mustang Taylor, horse wrangler of the Three Elm camp. 'They'll be lookin' for me back by nine. They'll be settin' up, with their papers ready to roll a whiff of the real thing before bedtime. And I've got to tell 'em that this pink-eyed, sheep-headed, sulphur-footed, shirt-waisted son of a calico broncho, Sam Revell, hasn't got no tobacco on hand.'

Gregorio Falcon, Mexican vaquero and best thrower of the rope on the Cibolo, pushed his heavy, silver-embroidered straw sombrero back upon his thicket of jet black curls, and scraped the bottoms of his pockets for a few crumbs of the precious weed.

'Ah, Don Samuel,' he said, reproachfully, but with his touch of Castilian manners, 'excuse me. Dthey say dthe jackrabbeet and dthe sheep have dthe most leetle *sesos* – how you call dthem – brain-es? Ah don' believe dthat, Don Samuel – escuse me. An dthink people w'at don' keep esmokin' tobacco, dthey – bot you weel escuse me, Don Samuel.'

'Now, what's the use of chewin' the rag, boys,' said the untroubled Sam, stooping over to rub the toes of his shoes with a red-and-yellow handkerchief. 'Ranse took the order for some more smokin' to San Antone with him Tuesday. Pancho rode Ranse's hoss back yesterday; and Ranse is goin' to drive the wagon back himself. There wa'n't much of a load – just some woolsacks and blankets and nails and canned peaches and a few things we was out of. I look for Ranse to roll in to-day sure. He's an early starter and a hell-to-split driver, and he ought to be here not far from sundown.'

'What plugs is he drivin'?' asked Mustang Taylor, with a smack of hope in his tones.

'The buckboard greys,' said Sam.

'I'll wait a spell, then,' said the wrangler. 'Them plugs eat up a trail like a road-runner swallowin' a whip snake. And you may bust me open a can of greengage plums, Sam, while I'm waitin' for somethin' better.'

'Open me some yellow clings,' ordered Poky Rodgers. 'I'll wait, too.'

The tobaccoless punchers arranged themselves comfortably on the steps of the store. Inside Sam chopped open with a hatchet the tops of the cans of fruit.

The store, a big, white wooden building like a barn, stood fifty yards from the ranch-house. Beyond it were the horse corrals; and still farther the wool sheds and the brush-topped shearing pens – for the Rancho Cibolo raised both cattle and sheep. Behind the store, at a little distance, were the grass-thatched *jacals* of the Mexicans who bestowed their allegiance upon the Cibolo.

The ranch-house was composed of four large rooms, with plastered adobe walls, and a two-room wooden ell. A twenty-feet-wide 'gallery' circumvented the structure. It was set in a grove of immense live-oaks and water-elms near a lake – a long, not very wide, and tremendously deep lake in which at nightfall, great gars leaped to the surface and plunged with the noise of hippopotamuses frolicking at their bath. From the trees hung garlands and massive pendants of the melancholy grey moss of the South. Indeed, the Cibolo ranch-house seemed more of the South than of the West. It looked as if old 'Kiowa' Truesdell might have brought it with him from the lowlands of Mississippi when he came to Texas with his rifle in the hollow of his arm in '55.

But, though he did not bring the family mansion, Truesdell did bring something in the way of a family inheritance that was more lasting than brick or stone. He brought one end of the Truesdell-Curtis family feud. And when a Curtis bought the Rancho de los Olmos, sixteen miles from the Cibolo, there were lively times on the pear flats and in the chaparral thickets of the Southwest. In those days Truesdell cleaned the brush of many a wolf and tiger cat and Mexican lion; and one or two Curtises fell heirs to notches on his rifle stock. Also he buried a brother with a Curtis bullet in him on the bank of the lake at Cibolo. And then the Kiowa Indians made their last raid upon the ranches between the Frio and the Rio Grande, and Truesdell at the head of his rangers rid the earth of them to the last brave, earning his sobriquet. Then came prosperity in the form of waxing herds and broadening lands. And then old age and bitterness, when he sat, with his great mane of hair as white as the Spanish-dagger blossoms and his fierce, pale-blue eyes, on the shaded gallery at Cibolo, growling like the pumas that he had slain. He snapped his fingers at old age; the bitter taste to life did not come from that. The cup that stuck at his lips was that his only son Ransom wanted to marry a Curtis, the last youthful survivor of the other end of the feud.

For a while the only sounds to be heard at the store were the rattling of the tin spoons and the gurgling intake of the juicy fruits by the cow-punchers, the stamping of the grazing ponies, and the singing of a doleful song by Sam as he contentedly brushed his stiff auburn hair for the twentieth time that day before a crinkly mirror.

From the door of the store could be seen the irregular, sloping stretch of prairie to the south, with its reaches of light-green, billowy mesquite flats in the lower places, and its rises crowned with nearly black masses of short chaparral. Through the mesquite flat wound the ranch road that, five miles away, flowed into the old government trail to San Antonio. The sun was so low that the gentlest elevation cast its grey shadow miles into the green-gold sea of sunshine.

That evening ears were quicker than eyes.

The Mexican held up a tawny finger to still the scraping of tin against tin.

'One waggeen,' said he, 'cross dthe Arroyo Hondo. Ah hear dthe wheel. Verree rockee place, dthe Hondo.'

'You've got good ears, Gregorio,' said Mustang Taylor. 'I never heard nothin' but the song-bird in the bush and the zephyr skallyhootin' across the peaceful dell.'

In ten minutes Taylor remarked: 'I see the dust of a wagon risin' right above the fur end of the flat.'

'You have verree good eyes, señor,' said Gregorio, smiling.

Two miles away they saw a faint cloud dimming the green ripples of the mesquites. In twenty minutes they heard the clatter of the horses' hoofs: in five minutes more the grey plugs dashed out of the thicket, whickering for oats and drawing the light wagon behind them like a toy.

From the *jacals* came a cry of: '*El Amo! El Amo!*' Four Mexican youths raced to unharness the greys. The cowpunchers gave a yell of greeting and delight.

Ranse Truesdell, driving, threw the reins to the ground and laughed.

'It's under the wagon sheet, boys,' he said. 'I know what you're waiting for. If Sam lets it run out again we'll use them yellow shoes of his for a target. There's two cases. Pull 'em out and light up. I know you all want a smoke.'

After striking dry country Ranse had removed the wagon sheet from the bows and thrown it over the goods in the wagon. Six pair of hasty hands dragged it off and grabbed beneath the sacks and blankets for the cases of tobacco.

Long Collins, tobacco messenger from the San Gabriel outfit, who rode with the longest stirrups west of the Mississippi, delved with an arm like the tongue of a wagon. He caught something harder than a blanket and pulled out a fearful thing – a shapeless, muddy bunch of leather tied together with wire and twine. From its ragged end, like the head and claws of a disturbed turtle, protruded human toes.

'Who-ee!' yelled Long Collins. 'Ranse, are you a-packin' around of corpuses? Here's a – howlin' grasshoppers!'

Up from his long slumber popped Curly, like some vile worm from its burrow. He clawed his way out and sat blinking like a disreputable, drunken owl. His face was a bluish-red and puffed and seamed and crosslined as the cheapest round steak of the butcher. His eyes were swollen slits; his nose a pickled beet; his hair would have made the wildest thatch of a Jack-in-the-box look like the satin poll of a Cléo de Mérode. The rest of him was scarecrow done to the life.

Ranse jumped down from his seat and looked at his strange cargo with wide-open eyes.

'Here, you maverick, what are you doing in my wagon? How did you get in there?'

The punchers gathered around in delight. For the time they had forgotten tobacco.

Curly looked around him slowly in every direction. He snarled like a Scotch terrier through his ragged beard.

'Where is this?' he rasped through his parched throat. 'It's a damn farm in an old field. What'd you bring me here for – say? Did I say I wanted to come here? What are you Reubs rubberin' at – hey? G'wan or I'll punch some of yer faces.'

'Drag him out, Collins,' said Ranse.

Curly took a slide and felt the ground rise up and collide with his shoulder blades. He got up and sat on the steps of the store shivering from outraged nerves, hugging his knees and sneering. Taylor lifted out a case of tobacco and wrenched off its top. Six cigarettes began to glow, bringing peace and forgiveness to Sam.

'How'd you come in my wagon?' repeated Ranse, this time in a voice that drew a reply.

Curly recognized the tone. He had heard it used by freight brakemen and large persons in blue carrying clubs.

'Me?' he growled. 'Oh, was you talkin' to me? Why, I was on my way to the Menger, but my valet had forgot to pack my pajamas. So I crawled into that wagon in the wagon-yard – see? I never told you to bring me out to this bloomin' farm – see?'

'What is it, Mustang?' asked Poky Rodgers, almost forgetting to smoke in his ecstasy. 'What do it live on?'

'It's a galliwampus, Poky,' said Mustang. 'It's the thing that hollers "willi-walloo" up in ellum trees in the low grounds of nights. I don't know if it bites.'

'No, it ain't, Mustang,' volunteered Long Collins. 'Them galliwampuses has fins on their backs, and eighteen toes. This here is a hicklesnifter. It lives under the ground and eats cherries. Don't stand so close to it. It wipes out villages with one stroke of its prehensile tail.'

Sam, the cosmopolite, who called bartenders in San Antone by their first name, stood in the door. He was a better zoologist.

'Well, ain't that a Willie for your whiskers?' he commented. 'Where'd you dig up the hobo, Ranse? Goin' to make an auditorium for inbreviates out of the ranch?'

'Say,' said Curly, from whose panoplied breast all shafts of wit fell blunted. 'Any of you kiddin' guys got a drink on you? Have your fun. Say, I've been hittin' the stuff till I don't know straight up.'

He turned to Ranse. 'Say, you shanghaied me on your d—d old prairie schooner – did I tell you to drive me to a farm? I want a drink. I'm goin' all to little pieces. What's doin'?'

Ranse saw that the tramp's nerves were racking him. He despatched one of the Mexican boys to the ranch-house for a glass of whisky. Curly gulped it down; and into his eyes came a brief, grateful glow – as human as the expression in the eye of a faithful setter dog.

'Thanky, boss,' he said, quietly.

'You're thirty miles from a railroad, and forty miles from a saloon,' said Ranse.

Curly fell back weakly against the steps.

'Since you are here,' continued the ranchman, 'come along with me. We can't turn you out on the prairie. A rabbit might tear you to pieces.'

He conducted Curly to a large shed where the ranch vehicles were kept. There he spread out a canvas cot and brought blankets.

'I don't suppose you can sleep,' said Ranse, 'since you've been pounding your ear for twenty-four hours. But you can camp here till morning. I'll have Pedro fetch you up some grub.'

'Sleep!' said Curly. 'I can sleep a week. Say, sport, have you got a coffin nail on you?'

Fifty miles had Ransom Truesdell driven that day. And yet this is what he did.

Old 'Kiowa' Truesdell sat in his great wicker chair reading by the light of an immense oil lamp. Ranse laid a bundle of newspapers fresh from town at his elbow.

'Back, Ranse?' said the old man, looking up.

'Son,' old 'Kiowa' continued, 'I've been thinking all day about a certain matter that we have talked about. I want you to tell me again. I've lived for you. I've fought wolves and Indians and worse white men to protect you. You never had any mother that you can remember. I've taught you to shoot straight, ride hard, and live clean. Later on I've worked to pile up dollars that'll be yours. You'll be a rich man, Ranse, when my chunk goes out. I've made you. I've licked you into shape like a leopard cat licks its cubs. You don't belong to yourself – you've got to be a Truesdell first. Now, is there to be any more nonsense about this Curtis girl?'

'I'll tell you once more,' said Ranse, slowly. 'As I am a Truesdell and as you are my father, I'll never marry a Curtis.'

'Good boy,' said old 'Kiowa'. 'You'd better go get some supper.'

Ranse went to the kitchen at the rear of the house. Pedro, the Mexican cook, sprang up to bring the food he was keeping warm in the stove.

'Just a cup of coffee, Pedro,' he said, and drank it standing. And then:

'There's a tramp on a cot in the wagon-shed. Take him something to eat. Better make it enough for two.'

Ranse walked out toward the *jacals*. A boy came running.

'Manuel, can you catch Vaminos, in the little pasture, for me?'

'Why not, señor? I saw him near the *puerta* but two hours past. He bears a drag-rope.'

'Get him and saddle him as quick as you can.'

'*Prontito, señor.*'

Soon, mounted on Vaminos, Ranse leaned in the saddle, pressed with his knees, and galloped eastward past the store, where sat Sam trying his guitar in the moonlight.

Vaminos shall have a word – Vaminos the good dun horse. The Mexicans, who have a hundred names for the colours of a horse, called him *gruyo*. He was a mouse-coloured, slate-coloured, flea-bitten roan-dun, if you can conceive it. Down his back from his mane to his tail went a line of black. He would live forever; and surveyors have not laid off as many miles in the world as he could travel in a day.

Eight miles east of the Cibolo ranch-house Ranse loosened the pressure of his knees, and Vaminos stopped under a big ratama tree. The yellow ratama blossoms showered fragrance that would have undone the roses of France. The moon made the earth a great concave bowl with a crystal sky for a lid. In a glade five jackrabbits leaped and played together like kittens. Eight miles farther east shone a faint star that appeared to have dropped below the horizon. Night riders, who often steered their course by it, knew it to be the light in the Rancho de los Olmos.

In ten minutes Yenna Curtis galloped to the tree on her sorrel pony Dancer. The two leaned and clasped hands heartily.

'I ought to have ridden nearer your home,' said Ranse. 'But you never will let me.'

Yenna laughed. And in the soft light you could see her strong white teeth and fearless eyes. No sentimentality there, in spite of the moonlight, the odour of the ratamas, and the admirable figure of Ranse Truesdell, the lover. But she was there, eight miles from her home, to meet him.

'How often have I told you, Ranse,' she said, 'that I am your half-way girl? Always half-way.'

'Well?' said Ranse, with a question in his tones.

'I did,' said Yenna, with almost a sigh. 'I told him after dinner when I thought he would be in a good humour. Did you ever wake up a lion, Ranse, with the mistaken idea that he would be a kitten? He almost tore the ranch to pieces. It's all up. I love my daddy, Ranse, and I'm afraid – I'm afraid of him, too. He ordered me to promise that I'd never marry a Truesdell. I promised. That's all. What luck did you have?'

'The same,' said Ranse, slowly. 'I promised him that his son would never marry a Curtis. Somehow I couldn't go against him. He's mighty old. I'm sorry, Yenna.'

The girl leaned in her saddle and laid one hand on Ranse's, on the horn of his saddle.

'I never thought I'd like you better for giving me up,' she said ardently, 'but I do. I must ride back now, Ranse. I slipped out of the house and saddled Dancer myself. Goodnight, neighbour.'

'Goodnight,' said Ranse. 'Ride carefully over them badger holes.'

They wheeled and rode away in opposite directions. Yenna turned in her saddle and called clearly:

'Don't forget I'm your half-way girl, Ranse.'

'Damn all family feuds and inherited scraps,' muttered Ranse vindictively to the breeze as he rode back to the Cibolo.

Ranse turned his horse into the small pasture and went to his own room. He opened the lowest drawer of an old bureau to get out the packet of letters that Yenna had written him one summer when she had gone to Mississippi for a visit. The drawer stuck, and he yanked at it savagely – as a man will. It came out of the bureau, and bruised both his shins – as a drawer will. An old, folded yellow letter without an envelope fell from somewhere – probably from where it had lodged in one of the upper drawers. Ranse took it to the lamp and read it curiously.

Then he took his hat and walked to one of the Mexican *jacals*.

'Tia Juana,' he said, 'I would like to talk with you a while.'

An old, old Mexican woman, white-haired and wonderfully wrinkled, rose from a stool.

'Sit down,' said Ranse, removing his hat and taking the one chair in the *jacal*. 'Who am I, Tia Juana?' he asked, speaking Spanish.

'Don Ransom, our good friend and employer. Why do you ask?' answered the old woman wonderingly.

'Tia Juana, who am I?' he repeated, with his stern eyes looking into hers.

A frightened look came in the old woman's face. She fumbled with her black shawl.

'Who am I, Tia Juana?' said Ranse once more.

'Thirty-two years I have lived on the Rancho Cibolo,' said Tia Juana. 'I thought to be buried under the coma mott beyond the garden before these things should be known. Close the door, Don Ransom, and I will speak. I see in your face that you know.'

An hour Ranse spent behind Tia Juana's closed door. As he was on his way back to the house Curly called to him from the wagon-shed.

The tramp sat on his cot, swinging his feet and smoking.

'Say, sport,' he grumbled. 'This is no way to treat a man after kidnappin' him. I went up to the store and borrowed a razor from that fresh guy and had a shave. But that ain't all a man needs. Say – can't you loosen up for about three fingers more of that booze? I never asked you to bring me to your d—d farm.'

'Stand up out here in the light,' said Ranse, looking at him closely.

Curly got up sullenly and took a step or two.

His face, now shaven smooth, seemed transformed. His hair had been combed, and it fell back from the right side of his forehead with a peculiar wave. The moonlight charitably softened the ravages of drink; and his aquiline, well-shaped nose and small, square cleft chin almost gave distinction to his looks.

Ranse sat on the foot of the cot and looked at him curiously.

'Where did you come from – have you got any home or folks anywhere?'

'Me? Why, I'm a dook,' said Curly. 'I'm Sir Reginald – oh, cheese it. No; I don't know anything about my ancestors. I've been a tramp ever since I can remember. Say, old pal, are you going to set 'em up again tonight or not?'

'You answer my questions and maybe I will. How did you come to be a tramp?'

'Me?' answered Curly. 'Why, I adopted that profession when I was an infant. Case of had to. First thing I can remember, I belonged to a big, lazy hobo called Beefsteak Charley. He sent me around to houses to beg. I wasn't hardly big enough to reach the latch of a gate.'

'Did he ever tell you how he got you?' asked Ranse.

'Once when he was sober he said he bought me for an old six-shooter and six bits from a band of drunken Mexican sheep-shearers. But what's the diff? That's all I know.'

'All right,' said Ranse. 'I reckon you're a maverick for certain. I'm going to put the Rancho Cibolo brand on you. I'll start you to work in one of the camps tomorrow.'

'Work!' sniffed Curly, disdainfully. 'What do you take me for? Do you think I'd chase cows, and hop-skip-and-jump around after crazy sheep like that pink and yellow guy at the store says these Reubs do? Forget it.'

'Oh, you'll like it when you get used to it,' said Ranse. 'Yes, I'll send you up one more drink by Pedro. I think you'll make a first-class cowpuncher before I get through with you.'

'Me?' said Curly. 'I pity the cows you set me to chaperon. They can go chase themselves. Don't forget my nightcap, please, boss.'

Ranse paid a visit to the store before going to the house. Sam Revell was taking off his tan shoes regretfully and preparing for bed.

'Any of the boys from the San Gabriel camp riding in early in the morning?' asked Ranse.

'Long Collins,' said Sam briefly. 'For the mail.'

'Tell him,' said Ranse, 'to take that tramp out to camp with him and keep him till I get there.'

Curly was sitting on his blankets in the San Gabriel camp cursing talentedly when Ranse Truesdell rode up and dismounted on the next afternoon. The cowpunchers were ignoring the stray. He was grimy with dust and black dirt. His clothes were making their last stand in favour of the conventions.

Ranse went up to Buck Rabb, the camp boss, and spoke briefly.

'He's a plumb buzzard,' said Buck. 'He won't work, and he's the low-downest passel of inhumanity I ever see. I didn't know what you wanted done with him, Ranse, so I just let him set. That seems to suit him. He's been condemned to death by the boys a dozen times, but I told 'em maybe you was savin' him for torture.'

Ranse took off his coat.

'I've got a hard job before me, Buck, I reckon, but it has to be done. I've got to make a man out of that thing. That's what I've come to camp for.'

He went up to Curly.

'Brother,' he said, 'don't you think if you had a bath it would allow you to take a seat in the company of your fellow-man with less injustice to the atmosphere.'

'Run away, farmer,' said Curly, sardonically. 'Willie will send for nursery when he feels like having his tub.'

The *charco*, or water hole, was twelve yards away. Ranse took one of Curly's ankles and dragged him like a sack of potatoes to the brink. Then with the strength and sleight of a hammer-thrower he hurled the offending member of society far into the lake.

Curly crawled out and up the bank spluttering like a porpoise.

Ranse met him with a piece of soap and a coarse towel in his hands.

'Go to the other end of the lake and use this,' he said. 'Buck will give you some dry clothes at the wagon.'

The tramp obeyed without protest. By the time supper was ready he had returned to camp. He was hardly to be recognized in his new blue shirt and brown duck clothes. Ranse observed him out of the corner of his eye.

'Lordy, I hope he ain't a coward,' he was saying to himself. 'I hope he won't turn out to be a coward.'

His doubts were soon allayed. Curly walked straight to where he stood. His light-blue eyes were blazing.

'Now I'm clean,' he said meaningly, 'maybe you'll talk to me. Think you've got a picnic here, do you? You clodhoppers think you can run over a man because you know he can't get away. All right. Now, what do you think of that?'

Curly planted a stinging slap against Ranse's left cheek. The print of his hand stood out a dull red against the tan.

Ranse smiled happily.

The cowpunchers talk to his day of the battle that followed.

Somewhere in his restless tour of the cities Curly had acquired the art of self-defence. The ranchman was equipped only with the splendid strength and equilibrium of perfect health and the endurance conferred by decent living. The two attributes nearly matched. There were no formal rounds. At last the fibre of the clean liver prevailed. The last time Curly went down from one of the ranchman's awkward but powerful blows he remained on the grass, but looking up with an unquenched eye.

Ranse went to the water barrel and washed the red from a cut on his chin in the stream from the faucet.

On his face was a grin of satisfaction.

Much benefit might accrue to educators and moralists if they could know the details of the curriculum of reclamation through which Ranse put his waif during the month that he spent in the San Gabriel camp. The ranchman had no fine theories to work out – perhaps his whole stock of pedagogy embraced only a knowledge of horse-breaking and a belief in heredity.

The cowpunchers saw that their boss was trying to make a man out of the strange animal that he had sent among them; and they tacitly organized themselves into a faculty of assistants. But their system was their own.

Curly's first lesson stuck. He became on friendly and then on intimate terms with soap and water. And the thing that pleased Ranse most was that his 'subject' held his ground at each successive higher step. But the steps were sometimes far apart.

Once he got at the quart bottle of whisky kept sacredly in the grub tent for rattlesnake bites, and spent sixteen hours on the grass, magnificently drunk. But when he staggered to his feet his first move was to find his soap and towel and start for the *charco*. And once, when a treat came from the ranch in the form of a basket of fresh tomatoes and young onions, Curly devoured the entire consignment before the punchers reached the camp at supper time.

And then the punchers punished him in their own way. For three days they did not speak to him, except to reply to his own questions or remarks. And they spoke with absolute and unfailing politeness. They played tricks on one another; they pounded one another hurtfully and affectionately; they heaped upon one another's heads friendly curses and obloquy; but they were polite to Curly. He saw it, and it stung him as much as Ranse hoped it would.

Then came a night that brought a cold, wet norther. Wilson, the youngest of the outfit, had lain in camp two days, ill with a fever. When Joe got up at daylight to begin breakfast he found Curly sitting asleep against a wheel of the grub wagon with only a saddle blanket around him, while Curly's blankets were stretched over Wilson to protect him from the rain and wind.

Three nights after that Curly rolled himself in his blanket and went to sleep. Then the other punchers rose up softly and began to make preparations. Ranse saw Long Collins tie a rope to the horn of a saddle. Others were getting out their six-shooters.

'Boys,' said Ranse, 'I'm much obliged. I was hoping you would. But I didn't like to ask.'

Half a dozen six-shooters began to pop – awful yells rent the air – Long Collins galloped wildly across Curly's bed, dragging the saddle after him. That was merely their way of gently awaking their victim. Then they hazed him for an hour, carefully and ridiculously, after the code of cow camps. Whenever he uttered protest they held him stretched over a roll of blankets and thrashed him woefully with a pair of leather leggings.

And all this meant that Curly had won his spurs, that he was receiving the puncher's accolade. Nevermore would they be polite to him. But he would be their 'pardner' and stirrup-brother, foot to foot.

When the fooling was ended all hands made a raid on Joe's big coffee-pot by the fire for a Java nightcap. Ranse watched the new knight carefully to see if he understood and was worthy. Curly limped with his cup of coffee to a log and sat upon it. Long Collins followed and sat by his side. Buck Rabb went and sat at the other. Curly – grinned.

And then Ranse furnished Curly with mounts and saddle and equipment, and turned him over to Buck Rabb, intructing him to finish the job.

Three weeks later Ranse rode from the ranch into Rabb's camp, which was then in Snake Valley. The boys were saddling for the day's ride. He sought out Long Collins among them.

'How about that bronco?' he asked.

Long Collins grinned.

'Reach out your hand, Ranse Truesdell,' he said, 'and you'll touch him. And you can shake his'n, too, if you like, for he's plumb white and there's none better in no camp.'

Ranse looked again at the clear-faced, bronzed, smiling cowpuncher who stood at Collins's side. Could this be Curly? He held out his hand, and Curly grasped it with the muscles of a bronco-buster.

'I want you at the ranch,' said Ranse.

'All right, sport,' said Curly, heartily. 'But I want to come back again. Say, pal, this is a dandy farm. And I don't want any better fun than hustlin' cows with this bunch of guys. They're all to the merry-merry.'

At the Cibolo ranch-house they dismounted. Ranse bade Curly wait at the door of the living room. He walked inside. Old 'Kiowa' Truesdell was reading at a table.

'Good morning, Mr Truesdell,' said Ranse.

The old man turned his white head quickly.

'How is this?' he began. 'Why do you call me "Mr "?'

When he looked at Ranse's face he stopped, and the hand that held his newspaper shook slightly.

'Boy,' he said slowly, 'how did you find it out?'

'It's all right,' said Ranse, with a smile. 'I made Tia Juana tell me. It was kind of by accident, but it's all right.'

'You've been like a son to me,' said old 'Kiowa', trembling.

'Tia Juana told me all about it,' said Ranse. 'She told me how you adopted me when I was knee-high to a puddle duck out of a wagon train of prospectors that was bound West. And she told me how the kid – your own kid, you know – got lost or was run away with. And she said it was the same day that the sheep-shearers got on a bender and left the ranch.'

'Our boy strayed from the house when he was two years old,' said the old man. 'And then along came these emigrant wagons with a youngster they didn't want; and we took you. I never intended you to know, Ranse. We never heard of our boy again.'

'He's right outside, unless I'm mighty mistaken,' said Ranse, opening the door and beckoning.

Curly walked in.

No one could have doubted. The old man and the young had the same sweep of hair, the same nose, chin, line of face, and prominent light-blue eyes.

Old 'Kiowa' rose eagerly.

Curly looked about the room curiously. A puzzled expression came over his face. He pointed to the wall opposite.

'Where's the tick-tock?' he asked, absent-mindedly.

'The clock,' cried old 'Kiowa' loudly. 'The eight-day clock used to stand there. Why '

He turned to Ranse, but Ranse was not there.

Already a hundred yards away, Vaminos, the good flea-bitten dun, was bearing him eastward like a racer through dust and chaparral towards the Rancho de los Olmos.

Jack London

To Build a Fire

DAY had broken cold and grey, exceedingly cold and grey, when the man turned aside from the main Yukon trail and climbed the high earth-bank, where a dim and little-travelled trail led eastward through the fat spruce timberland. It was a steep bank, and he paused for breath at the top, excusing the act to himself by looking at his watch. It was nine o'clock. There was no sun nor hint of sun, though there was not a cloud in the sky. It was a clear day, and yet there seemed an intangible pall over the face of things, a subtle gloom that made the day dark, and that was due to the absence of sun. This fact did not worry the man. He was used to the lack of sun. It had been days since he had seen the sun, and he knew that a few more days must pass before that cheerful orb, due south, would just peep above the skyline and dip immediately from view.

The man flung a look back along the way he had come. The Yukon lay a mile wide and hidden under three feet of ice. On top of this ice were as many feet of snow. It was all pure white, rolling in gentle undulations where the ice jams of the freeze-up had formed. North and south, as far as his eye could see, it was unbroken white, save for a dark hairline that curved and twisted from around the spruce-covered island to the south, and that curved and twisted away into the north, where it disappeared behind another spruce-covered island. This dark hairline was the trail – the main trail – that led south five hundred miles to the Chilcoot Pass, Dyea, and salt water; and that led north seventy miles to Dawson, and still on to the north a thousand miles to Nulato, and finally to St Michael, on Bering Sea, a thousand miles and half a thousand more.

But all this – the mysterious, far-reaching hairline trail, the absence of sun from the sky, the tremendous cold, and the strangeness and weirdness of it all – made no impression on the man. It was not because he was long used to it. He was a newcomer in the land, a *chechaquo*, and this was his first winter. The trouble with him was that he was without imagination. He was quick and alert in the things of life, but only in the things, and not in the significances. Fifty degrees below zero meant eighty-odd degrees of frost. Such fact impressed him as being cold and uncomfortable, and that was all. It did not lead him to meditate upon his frailty as a creature of temperature, and upon man's frailty in general, able only to live within certain narrow limits of heat and cold; and from there on it did not lead him to the conjectural field of immortality and man's place in the universe. Fifty degrees below zero stood for a bite of frost that hurt and that must be guarded against by the use of mittens, ear flaps, warm moccasins, and thick socks. Fifty degrees below zero. That there should be anything more to it than that was a thought that never entered his head.

As he turned to go on, he spat speculatively. There was a sharp explosive crackle that startled him. He spat again. And again, in the air, before it could fall to the snow, the spittle crackled. He knew that at fifty below spittle crackled on the snow, but this spittle had crackled in the air. Undoubtedly it was colder than fifty below – how much colder he did not know. But the temperature did not matter. He was bound for the old claim on the left fork of Henderson Creek, where the boys were already. They had come over across the divide from the Indian Creek country, while he had come the roundabout way to take a look at the possibilities of getting out logs in the spring from the islands in the Yukon. He would be in to camp by six o'clock; a bit after dark, it was true, but the boys would be there, a fire would be going, and a hot supper would be ready. As for lunch, he pressed his hand against the protruding bundle under his jacket. It was also under his shirt, wrapped up in a handkerchief and lying against the naked skin. It was the only way to keep the biscuits from freezing. He smiled agreebly to himself as he thought of those biscuits, each cut open and sopped in bacon grease, and each enclosing a generous slice of fried bacon.

He plunged in among the big spruce trees. The trail was faint. A foot of snow had fallen since the last sled had passed over, and he was glad he was without a sled, travelling light. In fact, he carried nothing but the lunch wrapped in the handkerchief. He was surprised, however, at the cold. It certainly was cold, he concluded, as he rubbed his numb nose and cheekbones with his mittened hand. He was a warm-whiskered man, but the hair on his face did not protect the high cheekbones and the eager nose that thrust itself aggressively into the frosty air.

At the man's heels trotted a dog, a big native husky, the proper wolf-dog, grey-coated and without any visible or temperamental difference from its brother, the wild wolf. The animal was depressed by the tremendous cold. It knew that it was no time for travelling. Its instinct told it a truer tale than was told to the man by the man's judgment. In reality, it was not merely colder than fifty below zero; it was colder than sixty below, than seventy below. It was seventy-five below zero. Since the freezing point is thirty-two above zero, it meant that one hundred and seven degrees of frost obtained. The dog did not know anything about thermometers. Possibly in its brain there was no sharp consciousness of a condition of very cold such as was in the man's brain. But the brute had its instinct. It experienced a vague but menacing apprehension that subdued it and made it slink along at the man's heels, and that made it question eagerly every unwonted movement of the man as if expecting him to go into camp or to seek shelter somewhere and build a fire. The dog had learned fire, and it wanted fire, or else to burrow under the snow and cuddle its warmth away from the air.

The frozen moisture of its breathing had settled on its fur in a fine powder of frost, and especially were its jowls, muzzle, and eyelashes whitened by its crystal breath. The man's red beard and moustache were likewise frosted, but more solidly, the deposit taking the form of ice and increasing with every warm, moist breath he exhaled. Also, the man was chewing tobacco, and the muzzle of ice held his lips so rigidly that he was unable to clear his chin when he expelled the juice. The result was a crystal beard of the colour and solidity of amber was increasing its length on his chin. If he fell down it would shatter itself, like glass, into brittle fragments. But he did not mind the appendage. It was the penalty all tobacco chewers paid in that country, and he had been out before in two cold snaps. They had not been so cold as this, he knew, but by the spirit thermometer at Sixty Mile he knew they had been registered at fifty below and at fifty-five.

He held on through the level stretch of woods for several miles, crossed a wide flat of nigger heads, and dropped down a bank to the frozen bed of a small stream. This was Henderson Creek, and he knew he was ten miles from the forks. He looked at his watch. It was ten o'clock. He was making four miles an hour, and he calculated that he would arrive at the forks at half-past twelve. He decided to celebrate that event by eating his lunch there.

The dog dropped in again at his heels, with a tail drooping discouragement, as the man swung along the creek bed. The furrow of the old sled trail was plainly visible, but a dozen inches of snow covered up the marks of the last runners. In a month no man had come up or down that silent creek. The man held steadily on. He was not much given to thinking, and just then particularly he had nothing to think about save that he would eat lunch at the forks and that at six o'clock he would be in camp with the boys. There was nobody to talk to; and, had there been, speech would have been impossible because of the ice muzzle on his mouth. So he continued monotonously to chew tobacco and to increase the length of his amber beard.

Once in a while the thought reiterated itself that it was very cold and that he had never experienced such cold. As he walked along he rubbed his cheekbones and nose with the back of his mittened hand. He did this automatically, now and again changing hands. But, rub as he would, the instant he stopped his cheekbones went numb, and the following instant the end of his nose went numb. He was sure to frost his cheeks; he knew that, and experienced a pang of regret that he had not devised a nose strap of the sort Bud wore in cold snaps. Such a snap passed across the cheeks, as well, and saved them. But it didn't matter much, after all. What were frosted cheeks? A bit painful, that was all; they were never serious.

Empty as the man's mind was of thoughts, he was keenly observant, and he noticed the changes in the creeks, the curves and bends and timber jams, and always he sharply noted where he placed his feet. Once, coming round a bend, he shied abruptly, like a startled horse, curved away from the place where he had been walking, and retreated several paces back along the trail. The creek he knew was frozen clear to the bottom – no creek could contain water in that arctic winter – but he knew also that there were springs that bubbled out from the hillsides and ran along under the snow and on top of the ice of the creek. He knew that the coldest snaps never froze these springs, and he knew likewise their danger. They were traps. They hid pools of water under the snow that might be three inches deep, or three feet. Sometimes a skin of ice half an inch thick covered them, and in turn was covered by the snow. Sometimes there were alternate layers of water and ice skin, so that when one broke through he kept on breaking through for a while, sometimes wetting himself to the waist.

That was why he had shied in such a panic. He had felt the give under his feet and heard the crackle of a snow-hidden ice skin. And to get his feet wet in such a temperature meant trouble and danger. At the very least it meant delay, for he would be forced to stop and build a fire, and under its protection to bare his feet while he dried his socks and moccasins. He stood and studied the creek bed and its banks, and decided that the flow of water came from the right. He reflected awhile, rubbing his nose and cheeks, then skirted to the left, stepping gingerly and testing the footing for each step. Once clear of the danger, he took a fresh chew of tobacco and swung along at his four-mile gait.

In the course of the next two hours he came upon several similar traps. Usually the snow above the hidden pools had a sunken, candied appearance that advertised the danger. Once again, however, he had a close call; and once, suspecting danger, he compelled the dog to go on in front. The dog did not want to go. It hung back until the man shoved it forward, and then it went quickly across the white, unbroken surface. Suddenly it broke through, floundered to one side, and got away to firmer footing. It had wet its forefeet and legs, and almost immediately the water that clung to it turned to ice. It made quick efforts to lick the ice off its legs, then dropped down in the snow and began to bite out the ice that had formed between the toes. This was a matter of instinct. To permit the ice to remain would mean sore feet. It did not know this. It merely obeyed the mysterious prompting that arose from the deep crypts of its being. But the man knew, having achieved a judgment on the subject, and he removed the mitten from his right hand and helped to tear out the ice particles. He did not expose his fingers more than a minute, and was astonished at the swift numbness that smote them. It certainly was cold. He pulled on the mitten hastily, and beat the hand savagely across his chest.

At twelve o'clock the day was at its brightest. Yet the sun was too far south on its winter journey to clear the horizon. The bulge of the earth intervened between it and Henderson Creek, where the man walked under a clear sky at noon and cast no shadow. At half-past twelve, to the minute, he arrived at the forks of the creek. He was pleased at the speed he had made. If he kept it up, he would certainly be with the boys by six. He unbuttoned his jacket and shirt and drew forth his lunch. The action consumed no more than a quarter of a minute, yet in that brief moment the numbness laid hold of the exposed fingers. He did not put the mitten on, but, instead, struck the fingers a dozen sharp smashes against his leg. Then he sat down on a snow-covered log to eat. The sting that followed upon the striking of his fingers against his leg ceased so quickly that he was startled. He had had no chance to take a bite of biscuit. He struck the fingers repeatedly and returned them to the mitten, baring the other hand for the purpose of eating. He tried to take a mouthful, but the ice muzzle prevented. He had forgotten to build a fire and thaw out. He chuckled at his foolishness, and as he chuckled he noted the numbness creeping into the exposed fingers. Also, he noted that the stinging which had first come to his toes when he sat down was already passing away. He wondered whether the toes were warm or numb. He moved them inside the moccasins and decided that they were numb.

He pulled the mitten on hurriedly and stood up. He was a bit frightened. He stamped up and down until the stinging returned into the feet. It certainly was cold, was his thought. That man from Sulphur Creek had spoken the truth when telling how cold it sometimes got in the country. And he had laughed at him at the time! That showed one must not be too sure of things. There was no mistake about it, it *was* cold. He strode up and down, stamping his feet and threshing his arms, until reassured by the returning warmth. Then he got out matches and proceeded to make a fire. From the undergrowth, where high water of the previous spring had lodged a supply of seasoned twigs, he got his firewood. Working carefully from a small beginning, he soon had a roaring fire, over which he thawed the ice from his face and in the protection of which he ate his biscuits. For the moment the cold of space was outwitted. The dog took satisfaction in the fire, stretching out close enough for warmth and far enough away to escape being singed.

When the man had finished, he filled his pipe and took his comfortable time over a smoke. Then he pulled on his mittens, settled the earflaps of his cap firmly about his ears, and took the creek trail up the left fork. The dog was disappointed and yearned back towards the fire. This man did not know cold. Possibly all the generations of his ancestry had been ignorant of cold, of real cold, of cold one hundred and seven degrees below freezing point. But the dog knew; all its ancestry knew, and it had inherited the knowledge. And it knew that it was not good to walk abroad in such fearful cold. It was the time to lie snug in a hole in the snow and wait for a curtain of cloud to be drawn across the face of outer space whence this cold came. On the other hand, there was no keen intimacy between the dog and the man. The one was the toil slave of the other, and the only caresses it had ever received were the caresses of the whip lash and of harsh and menacing throat sounds that threatened the whip lash. So the dog made no effort to communicate its apprehension to the man. It was not concerned in the welfare of the man; it was for its own sake that it yearned back towards the fire. But the man whistled and spoke to it with the sound of whip lashes, and the dog swung in at the man's heels and followed after.

The man took a chew of tobacco and proceeded to start a new amber beard. Also, his moist breath quickly powdered with white his moustache, eyebrows and lashes. There did not seem to be so many springs on the left fork of the Henderson, and for half an hour the man saw no signs of any. And then it happened. At a place where there were no signs, where the soft, unbroken snow seemed to advertise solidity beneath, the man broke through. It was not deep. He wet himself halfway to the knees before he floundered out to the firm crust.

He was angry, and cursed his luck aloud. He had hoped to get into camp with the boys at six o'clock, and this would delay him an hour, for he would have to build a fire and dry out his footgear. This was imperative at that low temperature – he knew that much; and he turned aside to the bank, which he climbed. On top, tangled in the underbrush about the trunks of several small spruce trees, was a highwater deposit of dry firewood – sticks and twigs, principally, but also larger portions of seasoned branches and fine, dry, last year's grasses. He threw down several large pieces on top of the snow. This served for a foundation and prevented the young flame from drowning itself in the snow it otherwise would melt. The flame he got by touching a match to a small shred of birch bark that he took from his pocket. This burned even more readily than paper. Placing it on the foundation, he fed the young flame with wisps of dry grass and with the tiniest dry twigs.

He worked slowly and carefully, keenly aware of his danger. Gradually, as the flame grew stronger, he increased the size of the twigs with which he fed it. He squatted in the snow pulling the twigs out from their entanglement in the brush and feeding directly to the flame. He knew there must be no failure. When it is seventy-five below zero, a man must not fail in his first attempt to build a fire – that is, if his feet are wet. If his feet are dry, and he fails, he can run along the trail for half a mile and restore his circulation. But the circulation of wet and freezing feet cannot be restored by running when it is seventy-five below. No matter how fast he runs, the wet feet will freeze the harder.

All this the man knew. The old-timer on Sulphur Creek had told him about it the previous fall and now he was appreciating the advice. Already all sensation had gone out of his feet. To build the fire he had been forced to remove his mittens, and the fingers had quickly gone numb. His pace of four miles an hour had kept his heart pumping blood to the surface of his body and to all the extremities. But the instant he stopped, the action of the pump eased down. The cold of space smote the unprotected tip of the planet, and he, being on that unprotected tip, received the full force of the blow. The blood of his body recoiled before it. The blood was alive, like the dog, and like the dog it wanted to hide away and cover itself up and from the fearful cold. So long as he walked four miles an hour, he pumped that blood, willy-nilly, to the surface; but now it ebbed away and sank down into the recesses of his body. The extremities were the first to feel its absence. His wet feet froze the faster, and his exposed fingers numbed the faster, though they had not yet begun to freeze. Nose and cheeks were already freezing, while the skin of all his body chilled as it lost its blood.

But he was safe. Toes and nose and cheeks would be only touched by the frost, for the fire was beginning to burn with strength. He was feeding it with twigs the size of his finger. In another minute he would be able to feed it with branches the size of his wrist, and then he could remove his wet footgear, and, while it dried, he could keep his naked feet warm by the fire, rubbing them at first, of course, with snow. The fire was a success. He was safe. He remembered the advice of the old-timer on Sulphur Creek, and smiled. The old-timer had been very serious in laying down the law that no man must travel alone in the Klondike after fifty below. Well, here he was; he had had the accident; he was alone; and he had saved himself. Those old-timers were rather womanish, some of them, he thought. All a man had to do was to keep his head, and he was all right. Any man who was a man could travel alone. But it was surprising, the rapidity with which his cheeks and nose were freezing. And he had not thought his fingers could go lifeless in so short a time. Lifeless they were, for he could scarcely make them move together to grip a twig, and they seemed remote from his body and from him. When he touched a twig, he had to look and see whether or not he had hold of it. The wires were pretty well down between him and his finger ends.

All of which counted for little. There was the fire, snapping and crackling and promising life with every dancing flame. He started to untie his moccasins. They were coated with ice; the thick German socks were like sheaths of iron halfway to the knees; and the moccasin strings were like rods of steel all twisted and knotted as by some conflagration. For a moment he tugged with his numb fingers, then, realizing the folly of it, he drew his sheath knife.

But before he could cut the strings, it happened. It was his own fault, or rather, his mistake. He should not have built the fire under the spruce tree. He should have built it in the open. But it had been easier to pull the twigs from the brush and drop them directly on the fire. Now the tree under which he had done this carried a weight of snow on its boughs. No wind had blown for weeks, and each bough was fully freighted. Each time he had pulled a twig he had communicated a slight agitation to the tree – an imperceptible agitation, so far as he was concerned, but an agitation sufficient to bring about the disaster. High up in the tree one bough capsized its load of snow. This fell on the boughs beneath, capsizing them. This process continued, spreading out and involving the whole tree. It grew like an avalanche, and it descended without warning upon the man and the fire, and the fire was blotted out! Where it had burned was a mantle of fresh and disordered snow.

The man was shocked. It was as though he had just heard his own sentence of death. For a moment he sat and stared at the spot where the fire had been. Then he grew very calm. Perhaps the old-timer on Sulphur Creek was right. It he had only had a trail mate he would have been in no danger now. The trail mate could have built the fire. Well, it was up to him to build the fire over again, and this second time there must be no failure. Even if he succeeded, he would most likely lose some toes. His feet must be badly frozen by now, and there would be some time before the second fire was ready.

Such were his thoughts, but he did not sit and think them. He was busy all the time they were passing through his mind. He made a new foundation for a fire, this time in the open, where no treacherous tree could blot it out. Next he gathered dry grasses and tiny twigs from the high-water flotsam. He could not bring his fingers together to pull them out, but he was able to gather them by the handful. In this way he got many rotten twigs and bits of green moss that were undesirable, but it was the best he could do. He worked methodically, even collecting an armful of the larger branches to be used later when the fire gathered strength. And all the while the dog sat and watched him, a certain yearning wistfulness in its eyes, for it looked upon him as the fire provider, and the fire was slow in coming.

When all was ready, the man reached in his pocket for a second piece of birch bark. He knew the bark was there, and, though he could not feel it with his fingers, he could hear its crisp rustling as he fumbled for it. Try as he would, he could not clutch hold of it. And all the time, in his consciousness, was the knowledge that each instant his feet were freezing. This thought tended to put him in a panic, but he fought against it and kept calm. He pulled on his mittens with his teeth, and threshed his arms back and forth, beating his hands with all his might against his sides. He did this sitting down, and he stood up to do it; and all the while the dog sat in the snow, its wolf brush of a tail curled around warmly over its forefront, its sharp wolf ears pricked forward intently as it watched the man. And the man, as he beat and threshed with his arms and hands, felt a great surge of envy as he regarded the creature that was warm and secure in its natural covering.

After a time he was aware of the first faraway signals of sensation in his beaten fingers. The faint tingling grew stronger till it evolved into a stinging ache that was excruciating, but which the man hailed with satisfaction. He stripped the mitten from his right hand and fetched forth the birch bark. The exposed fingers were quickly going numb again. Next he brought out his bunch of sulphur matches. But the tremendous cold had already driven the life out of his fingers. In his efforts to separate one match from the others, the whole bunch fell in the snow. He tried to pick it out of the snow, but failed. The dead fingers could neither touch nor clutch. He was very careful. He drove the thought of his freezing feet, and nose, and cheeks, out of his mind, devoting his whole soul to the matches. He watched, using the sense of vision in place of that touch, and when he saw his fingers on each side the bunch, he closed them – that is, he willed to close them, for the wires were down, and the fingers did not obey. He pulled the mitten on the right hand, and beat it fiercely against his knee. Then with both mittened hands, he scooped the bunch of matches, along with much snow, into his lap. Yet he was no better off.

After some manipulation he managed to get the bunch between the heels of his mittened hands. In this fashion he carried it to his mouth. The ice crackled and snapped when by a violent effort he opened his mouth. He drew the lower jaw in, curled the upper lip out of the way, and scraped the bunch with his upper teeth in order to separate a match. He succeeded in getting one, which he dropped on his lap. He was no better off. He could not pick it up. Then he devised a way. He picked it up in his teeth and scratched it on his leg. Twenty times he scratched before he succeeded in lighting it. As it flamed he held it with his teeth to the birch bark. But the burning brimstone went up his nostrils and into his lungs, causing him to cough spasmodically. The match fell into the snow and went out.

The old-timer on Sulphur Creek was right, he thought in the moment of controlled despair that ensued: after fifty below, a man should travel with a partner. He beat his hands, but failed in exciting any sensation. Suddenly he bared both hands, removing the mittens with his teeth. He caught the whole bunch between the heels of his hands. His arm muscles not being frozen enabled him to press the hand heels tightly against the matches. Then he scratched the bunch along his leg. It flared into flame, seventy sulphur matches at once! There was no wind to blow them out. He kept his head to one side to escape the strangling fumes, and held the blazing bunch to the birch bark. As he so held it, he became aware of sensation in his hand. His flesh was burning. He could smell it. Deep down below the surface he could feel it. The sensation developed into pain that grew acute. And still he endured it, holding the flame of the matches clumsily to the bark that would not light readily because his own burning hands were in the way, absorbing most of the flame.

At last, when he could endure no more, he jerked his hands apart. The blazing matches fell sizzling into the snow, but the birch bark was alight. He began laying dry grasses and the tiniest twigs on the flame. He could not pick and choose, for he had to lift the fuel between the heels of his hands. Small pieces of rotten wood and green moss clung to the twigs, and he bit them off as well as he could with his teeth. He cherished the flame carefully and awkwardly. It meant life, and it must not perish. The withdrawal of blood from the surface of his body now made him begin to shiver, and he grew more awkward. A large piece of green moss fell squarely on the little fire. He tried to poke it out with his fingers, but his shivering frame made him poke too far, and he disrupted the nucleus of the little fire, the burning grasses and tiny twigs separating and scattering. He tried to poke them together again, but in spite of the tenseness of the effort, his shivering got away with him, and the twigs were hopelessly scattered. Each twig gushed a puff of smoke and went out. The fire provider had failed. As he looked apathetically about him, his eyes chanced on the dog, sitting across the ruins of the fire from him, in the snow, making restless, hunching movements, slightly lifting one forefoot and then the other, shifting its weight back and forth on them with wistful eagerness.

The sight of the dog put a wild idea into his head. He remembered the tale of the man, caught in a blizzard, who killed a steer and crawled inside the carcass, and so was saved. He would kill the dog and bury his hands in the warm body until the numbness went out of them. Then he could build another fire. He spoke to the dog, calling it to him; but in his voice was a strange note of fear that frightened the animal, who had never known the man to speak in such a way before. Something was the matter, and its suspicious nature sensed danger – it knew not what danger, but somewhere, somehow, in its brain arose an apprehension of the man. It flattened its ears down at the sound of the man's voice, and its restless, hunching movements and the liftings and shiftings of its forefeet became more pronounced; but it would not come to the man. He got on his hands and knees and crawled towards the dog. This unusual posture again excited suspicion, and the animal sidled mincingly away.

The man sat up in the snow for a moment and struggled for calmness. Then he pulled on his mittens, by means of his teeth, and got upon his feet. He glanced down at first in order to assure himself that he was really standing up, for the absence of sensation in his feet left him unrelated to the earth. His erect position in itself started to drive the webs of suspicion from the dog's mind; and when he spoke peremptorily, with the sound of whip lashes in his voice, the dog rendered its customary allegiance and came to him. As it came within reaching distance, the man lost his control. His arms flashed out to the dog, and he experienced genuine surprise when he discovered that his hands could not clutch, that there was neither bend nor feeling in the fingers. He had forgotten for the moment that they were frozen and that they were freezing more and more. All this happened quickly, and before the animal could get away, he encircled its body with his arms. He sat down in the snow, and in this fashion held the dog, while it snarled and whined and struggled.

But it was all he could do, hold its body encircled in his arms and sit there. He realized he could not kill the dog. There was no way to do it. With his helpless hands he could neither draw nor hold his sheath knife nor throttle the animal. He released it, and it plunged wildly away, with tail between its legs, and still snarling. It halted forty feet away and surveyed him curiously, with ears sharply pricked forward.

The man looked down at his hands in order to locate them, and found them hanging on the ends of his arms. It struck him as curious that one should have to use his eyes in order to find out where his hands were. He began threshing his arms back and forth, beating the mittened hands against his sides. He did this for five minutes, violently, and his heart pumped enough blood up to the surface to put a stop to his shivering. But no sensation was aroused in the hands. He had an impression that they hung like weights on the ends of his arms, but when he tried to run the impression down, he could not find it.

A certain fear of death, dull and oppressive, came to him. This fear quickly became poignant as he realized that it was no longer a mere matter of freezing his fingers and toes, or of losing his hands and feet, but that it was a matter of life and death with the chances against him. This threw him into a panic, and he turned and ran up the creek bed along the old, dim trail. The dog joined in behind him and kept up with him. He ran blindly, without intention, in fear such as he had never known in his life. Slowly, as he ploughed and floundered through the snow, he began to see things again – the banks of the creek, the old timber jams, the leafless aspens, and the sky. The running made him feel better. He did not shiver. Maybe, if he ran on, his feet would thaw out; and, anyway, if he ran far enough, he would reach camp and the boys. Without doubt he would lose some fingers and toes and some of his face; but the boys would take care of him, and save the rest of him when he got there. And at the same time there was another thought in his mind that said he would never get to the camp and the boys; that it was too many miles away, that the freezing had too great a start on him, and that he would soon be stiff and dead. This thought he kept in the background and refused to consider. Sometimes it pushed itself forward and demanded to be heard, but he thrust it back and strove to think of other things.

It struck him as curious that he could run at all on feet so frozen that he could not feel them when they struck the earth and took the weight of his body. He seemed to himself to skim along above the surface, and to have no connection with the earth. Somewhere he had once seen a winged Mercury, and he wondered if Mercury felt as he felt when skimming over the earth.

His theory of running until he reached camp and the boys had one flaw in it: he lacked the endurance. Several times he stumbled, and finally he tottered, crumpled up, and fell. When he tried to rise, he failed. He must sit and rest, he decided, and next time he would merely walk and keep on going. As he sat and regained his breath, he noted that he was feeling quite warm and comfortable. He was not shivering, and it even seemed that a warm glow had come to his chest and trunk. And yet, when he touched his nose or cheeks, there was no sensation. Running would not thaw them out. Nor would it thaw out his hands and feet. Then the thought came to him that the frozen portions of his body must be extending. He tried to keep this thought down, to forget it, to think of something else; he was aware of the panicky feeling that it caused, and he was afraid of the panic. But the thought asserted itself, and persisted, until it produced a vision of his body totally frozen. This was too much, and he made another wild run along the trail. Once he slowed down to a walk, but the thought of the freezing extending itself made him run again.

And all the time the dog ran with him, at his heels. When he fell down a second time, it curled its tail over its forefeet and sat in front of him, facing him, curiously eager and intent. The warmth and security of the animal angered him, and he cursed it till it flattened down its ears appeasingly. This time the shivering came more quickly upon the man. He was losing in his battle with the frost. It was creeping into his body from all sides. The thought of it drove him on, but he ran no more than a hundred feet, when he staggered and pitched headlong. It was his last panic. When he had recovered his breath and control, he sat up and entertained in his mind the conception of meeting death with dignity. However, the conception did not come to him in such terms. His idea of it was that he had been making a fool of himself, running around like a chicken with its head cut off – such was the simile that occurred to him. Well, he was bound to freeze anyway, and he might as well take it decently. With this new-found peace of mind came the first glimmerings of drowsiness. A good idea, he thought, to sleep off to death. It was like taking an anaesthetic. Freezing was not so bad as people thought. There were lots worse ways to die.

He pictured the boys finding his body next day. Suddenly he found himself with them, coming along the trail looking for himself. And, still with them, he came around a turn in the trail and found himself lying in the snow. He did not belong with himself any more, for even then he was out of himself, standing with the boys and looking at himself in the snow. It certainly was cold, was his thought. When he got back to the States, he could tell the folks what real cold was. He drifted on from this to a vision of the old-timer on Sulphur Creek. He could see him quite clearly, warm and comfortable, and smoking a pipe.

'You were right, old hoss; you were right,' the man mumbled to the old-timer of Sulphur Creek.

Then the man drowsed off into what seemed to him the most comfortable and satisfying sleep he had ever known. The dog sat facing him and waiting. The brief day drew to a close in a long, slow twilight. There was no signs of a fire to be made, and, besides, never in the dog's experience had it known a man to sit like that in the snow and make no fire. As the twilight drew on, its eager yearning for the fire mastered it, and with a great lifting and shifting of forefeet, it whined softly, then flattened its ears down in anticipation of being chidden by the man. But the man remained silent. Later the dog whined loudly. And still later it crept close to the man and caught the scent of death. This made the animal bristle and back away. A little longer it delayed, howling under the stars that leaped and danced and shone brightly in the cold sky. Then it turned and trotted up the trail in the direction of the camp it knew, where were the other food providers and fire providers.

Jack London

In a Far Country

WHEN a man journeys into a far country, he must be prepared to forget many of the things he has learned, and to acquire such customs as are inherent with existence in the new land; he must abandon the old ideals and the old gods, and often-times he must reverse the very codes by which his conduct has hitherto been shaped. To those who have the protean faculty of adaptability, the novelty of such change may even be a source of pleasure; but to those who happened to be hardened to the ruts in which they were created, the pressure of the altered environment is unbearable, and they chafe in body and in spirit under the new restrictions which they do not understand. This chafing is bound to act and react, producing divers evils and leading to various misfortunes. It were better for the man who cannot fit himself to the new groove to return to his own country; if he delays too long, he will surely die.

The man who turns his back upon the comforts of an elder civilization, to face the savage youth, the primordial simplicity of the North, may estimate success at an inverse ratio to the quantity and quality of his hopelessly fixed habits. He will soon discover, if he be a fit candidate, that the material habits are the less important. The exchange of such things as a dainty menu for rough fare, of the stiff leather shoe for the soft, shapeless moccasin, of the feather bed for a couch in the snow, is after all a very easy matter. But his pinch will come in learning properly to shape his mind's attitude toward all things, and especially toward his fellow man. For the courtesies of ordinary life, he must substitute unselfishness, forbearance, and tolerance. Thus, and thus only, can he gain that pearl of great price – true comradeship. He must not say 'Thank you'; he must mean it without opening his mouth, and prove it by responding in kind. In short, he must substitute the deed for the word, the spirit for the letter.

When the world rang with the tale of Arctic gold, and the lure of the North gripped the heartstrings of men, Carter Weatherbee threw up his snug clerkship, turned the half of his savings over to his wife, and with the remainder bought an outfit. There was no romance in his nature – the bondage of commerce had crushed all that; he was simply tired of the ceaseless grind, and wished to risk great hazards in view of corresponding returns. Like many another fool, disdaining the old trails used by the Northland pioneers for a score of years, he hurried to Edmonton in the spring of the year; and there, unluckily for his soul's welfare, he allied himself with a party of men.

There was nothing unusual about this party, except its plans. Even its goal, like that of all other parties, was the Klondike. But the route it had mapped out to attain the goal took away the breath of the hardiest native, born and bred to the vicissitudes of the north-west. Even Jacques Baptiste, born of a Chippewa woman and a renegade *voyageur* (having raised his first whimpers in a deerskin lodge north of the sixty-fifth parallel, and had the same hushed by blissful sucks of raw tallow), was surprised. Though he sold his services to them and agreed to travel even to the never-opening ice, he shook his head ominously whenever his advice was asked.

Percy Cuthfert's evil star must have been in the ascendant, for he, too, joined this company of argonauts. He was an ordinary man, with a bank account as deep as his culture, which is saying a good deal. He had no reason to embark on such a venture – no reason in the world, save that he suffered from an abnormal development of sentimentality. He mistook this for the true spirit of romance and adventure. Many another man has done the like, and made as fatal a mistake.

The first break-up of spring found the party following the ice-run of Elk River. It was an imposing fleet, for the outfit was large, and they were accompanied by a disreputable contingent of half-breed *voyageurs* with their women and children. Day in and day out, they laboured with the bateaux and canoes, fought mosquitoes and other kindred pests, or sweated and swore at the portages. Severe toil like this lays a man naked to the very roots of his soul, and ere Lake Athabasca was lost in the south, each member of the party had hoisted his true colours.

The two shirks and chronic grumblers were Carter Weatherbee and Percy Cuthfert. The whole party complained less of its aches and pains than did either of them. Not once did they volunteer for the thousand and one petty duties of the camp. A bucket of water to be brought, an extra armful of wood to be chopped, the dishes to be washed and wiped, a search to be made through the outfit for some suddenly indispensable article – and these two effete scions of civilization discovered sprains or blisters requiring instant attention. They were the first to turn in at night, with a score of tasks yet undone; the last to turn out in the morning, when the start should be in readiness before the breakfast was begun. They were the first to fall to at meal-time, the last to have a hand in the cooking; the first to dive for a slim delicacy; the last to discover they had added to their own another man's share. If they toiled at the oars, they slyly cut the water at each stroke and allowed the boat's momentum to float up the blade. They thought nobody noticed; but their comrades swore under their breaths, and grew to hate them, while Jacques Baptiste sneered openly, and damned them from morning till night. But Jacques Baptiste was no gentleman.

At the Great Slave, Hudson Bay dogs were purchased, and the fleet sank to the guards with its added burden of dried fish and pemmican. Then canoe and bateau answered to the swift current of the Mackenzie, and they plunged into the Great Barren Ground. Every likely-looking 'feeder' was prospected, but the elusive 'pay-dirt' danced ever to the north. At the Great Bear, overcome by the common dread of the Unknown Lands, their *voyageurs* began to desert, and Fort of Good Hope saw the last and bravest bending to the tow-lines as they bucked the current down which they had so treacherously glided. Jacques Baptiste alone remained. Had he not sworn to travel even to the never-opening ice?

The lying charts, compiled in main from hearsay, were now constantly consulted. And they felt the need of hurry, for the sun had already passed its northern solstice, and was leading the winter south again. Skirting the shores of the bay, where the Mackenzie disembogues into the Arctic Ocean, they entered the mouth of the Little Peel River. Then began the arduous up-stream toil, and the two Incapables fared worse than ever. Tow-line and pole, paddle and tump-line, rapids and portages – such tortures served to give the one a deep disgust for great hazards, and printed for the other a fiery text on the true romance of adventure. One day they waxed mutinous, and being vilely cursed by Jacques Baptiste, turned, as worms sometimes will. But the half-breed thrashed the twain, and sent them, bruised and bleeding, about their work. It was the first time either had been man-handled.

Abandoning their river craft at the headwaters of the Little Peel, they consumed the rest of the summer in the great portage over the Mackenzie watershed to the West Rat. This little stream fed the Porcupine, which in turn joined the Yukon where that mighty highway of the north countermarches on the Arctic Circle. But they had lost in the race with winter, and one day they tied their rafts to the thick eddy-ice, and hurried their goods ashore. That night the river jammed and broke several times; the following morning it had fallen asleep for good.

'We can't be more'n four hundred miles from the Yukon,' concluded Sloper, multiplying his thumb nails by the scale of the map. The council, in which the two Incapables had whined to excellent disadvantage, was drawing to a close.

'Hudson Bay Post, long time ago. No use um now.' Jacques Baptiste's father had made the trip for the Fur Company in the old days, incidentally marking the trail with a couple of frozen toes.

'Sufferin' cracky!' cried another of the party. 'No whites?'

'Nary white,' Sloper sententiously affirmed; 'but it's only five hundred more up the Yukon to Dawson. Call it a rough thousand from here.'

Weatherbee and Cuthfert groaned in chorus. 'How long'll that take, Baptiste?'

The half-breed figured for a moment. 'Workum like hell, no man play out, ten – twenty-forty-fifty days. Um babies come,' (designating the Incapables) 'no can tell. Mebbe when hell freeze over; mebbe not then.'

The manufacture of snowshoes and moccasins ceased. Somebody called the name of an absent member, who came out of an ancient cabin at the edge of the camp-fire and joined them. The cabin was one of the many mysteries which lurk in the vast recesses of the north. Built when and by whom, no man could tell. Two graves in the open, piled high with stones, perhaps contained the secret of those early wanderers. But whose hand had piled the stones?

The moment had come. Jacques Baptiste paused in the fitting of a harness, and pinned the struggling dog in the snow. The cook made mute protest for delay, threw a handful of bacon into a noisy pot of beans, then came to attention. Sloper rose to his feet. His body was a ludicrous contrast to the healthy physiques of the Incapables. Yellow and weak, fleeing from a South American fever-hole, he had not broken his flight across the zones, and was still able to toil with men. His weight was probably ninety pounds, with the heavy hunting-knife thrown in, and his grizzled hair told of a prime which had ceased to be. The fresh young muscles of either Weatherbee or Cuthfert were equal to ten times the endeavour of his; yet he could walk them into the earth in a day's journey. And all this day he had whipped his stronger comrades into venturing a thousand miles of the stiffest hardship man can conceive. He was the incarnation of the unrest of his race, and the old Teutonic stubbornness, dashed with the quick grasp and action of the Yankee, held the flesh in the bondage of the spirit.

'All those in favour of going on with the dogs as soon as the ice sets, say ay.'

'Ay!' rang out eight voices – voices destined to string a trail of oaths along many a hundred miles of pain.

'Contrary minded?'

'No!' For the first time the Incapables were united without some compromise of personal interests.

'And what are you going to do about it?' Weatherbee added, belligerently.

'Majority rule! Majority rule!' clamoured the rest of the party.

'I know the expedition is liable to fall through if you don't come,' Sloper replied sweetly; 'but I guess, if we try real hard, we can manage to do without you. What do you say, boys?'

The sentiment was cheered to the echo.

'But I say, you know,' Cuthfert ventured apprehensively; 'what's a chap like me to do?'

'Ain't you coming with us?'

'No-o.'

'Then do as you damn well please. We won't have nothing to say.'

'Kind o' calkilate yuh might settle it with that canoodlin' pardner of yourn,' suggested a heavy-going Westerner from the Dakotas, at the same time pointing out Weatherbee. 'He'll be shore to ask yuh what yur a-goin' to do when it comes to cookin' an' gatherin' the wood.'

'Then we'll consider it all arranged,' concluded Sloper. 'We'll pull out tomorrow, if we camp within five miles – just to get everything in running order and remember if we've forgotten anything.'

The sleds groaned by on their steel-shod runners, and the dogs strained low in the harnesses in which they were born to die. Jacques Baptiste paused by the side of Sloper to get a last glimpse of the cabin. The smoke curled up pathetically from the Yukon stove-pipe. The two Incapables were watching them from the doorway.

Sloper laid his hand on the other's shoulder.

'Jacques Baptiste, did you ever hear of the Kilkenny cats?'

The half-breed shook his head.

'Well, my friend and good comrade, the Kilkenny cats fought till neither hide, nor hair, nor yowl, was left. You understand? – till nothing was left. Very good. Now, these two men don't like work. They won't work. We know that. They'll be all alone in that cabin all winter – a mighty long dark winter. Kilkenny cats – well?'

The Frenchman in Baptiste shrugged his shoulders, but the Indian in him was silent. Nevertheless, it was an eloquent shrug, pregnant with prophecy.

Things prospered in the little cabin at first. The rough badinage of their comrades had made Weatherbee and Cuthfert conscious of the mutual responsibility which had devolved upon them; besides, there was not so much work after all for two healthy men. And the removal of the cruel whip-hand, or in other words, the bulldozing half-breed, had brought with it a joyous reaction. At first, each strove to outdo the other, and they performed petty tasks with an unction which would have opened the eyes of their comrades who were now wearing out bodies and souls on the Long Trail.

All care was banished. The forest, which shouldered in upon them from three sides, was an inexhaustible wood-yard. A few yards from their door slept the Porcupine, and a hole through its winter robe formed a bubbling spring of water, crystal clear and painfully cold. But they soon grew to find fault with even that. The hole would persist in freezing up, and thus gave them many a miserable hour of ice-chopping. The unknown builders of the cabin had extended the side-logs so as to support a cache at the rear. In this was stored the bulk of the party's provisions. Food there was, without stint, for three times the men who were fated to live upon it. But the most of it was of the kind which built up brawn and sinew, but did not tickle the palate. True there was sugar in plenty for two ordinary men; but these two were little else than children. They early discovered the virtues of hot water judiciously saturated with sugar, and they prodigally swam their flapjacks and soaked their crusts in the rich, white syrup. Then coffee and tea, and especially the dried fruits, made disastrous inroads upon it. The first words they had were over the sugar question. And it is a really serious thing when two men, wholly dependent upon each other for company, begin to quarrel.

Weatherbee loved to discourse blatantly on politics, while Cuthfert, who had been prone to clip his coupons, and let the commonwealth jog on as best it might, either ignored the subject or delivered himself of startling epigrams. But the clerk was too obtuse to appreciate the clever shaping of thought, and this waste of ammunition irritated Cuthfert. He had been used to blinding people by his brilliancy, and it worked him quite a hardship, this loss of an audience. He felt personally aggrieved, and unconsciously held his mutton-head companion responsible for it.

Save existence, they had nothing in common – came in touch on no single point. Weatherbee was a clerk who had known naught but clerking all his life; Cuthfert was a master of arts, a dabbler in oils, and had written not a little. The one was a lower-class man, who considered himself a gentleman, and the other was a gentleman who knew himself to be such. From this it may be remarked that a man can be a gentleman without possessing the first instinct of true comradeship. The clerk was as sensuous as the other was aesthetic, and his love adventures, told at great length, and chiefly coined from his imagination, affected the super-sensitive master of arts in the same way as so many whiffs of sewer gas. He deemed the clerk a filthy, uncultured brute, whose place was in the muck with the swine, and told him so; and he was reciprocally informed that he was a milk-and-water cissy and a cad. Weatherbee could not have defined 'cad' for his life; but it satisfied its purpose, which after all seems the main point in life.

Weatherbee flatted every third note, and sang such songs as 'The Boston Burglar' and 'The Handsome Cabin Boy', for hours at a time, while Cuthfert wept with rage, till he could stand it no longer, and fled into the outer cold. But there was no escape. The intense frost could not be endured for long at a time, and the little cabin crowded them – beds, stove, table, and all – into a space of ten by twelve. The very presence of either became a personal affront to the other, and they lapsed into sullen silences, which increased in length and strength as the days went by. Occasionally, the flash of an eye or the curl of a lip got the better of them, though they strove to wholly ignore each other during these mute periods. And a great wonder sprang up in the breast of each, as to how God had ever come to create the other.

With little to do, time became an intolerable burden to them. This naturally made them still lazier. They sank into a physical lethargy, which there was no escaping, and which made them rebel at the performance of the smallest chore. One morning when it was his turn to cook the common breakfast, Weatherbee rolled out of his blankets, and to the snoring of his companion, lighted first the slush-lamp and then the fire. The kettles were frozen hard, and there was no water in the cabin with which to wash. But he did not mind that. Waiting for it to thaw, he sliced the bacon and plunged into the hateful task of bread-making. Cuthfert had been slyly watching through his half-closed lids. Consequently there was a scene, in which they fervently blessed each other, and agreed, thenceforth, that each do his own cooking. A week later, Cuthfert neglected his morning ablutions, but none the less complacently ate the meal which he had cooked. Weatherbee grinned. After that the foolish custom of washing passed out of their lives.

As the sugar-pile and other luxuries dwindled, they began to be afraid they were not getting their proper shares, and in order that they might not be robbed, they fell to gorging themselves. The luxuries suffered in this gluttonous contest, as did also the men. In the absence of fresh vegetables and exercise, their blood became impoverished, and a loathsome, purplish rash crept over their bodies. Yet they refused to heed the warning. Next, their muscles and joints began to swell, the flesh turning black, while their mouths, gums and lips took on the colour of rich cream. Instead of being drawn together by their misery, each gloated over the other's symptoms as the scurvy took its course.

They lost all regard for personal appearance, and for that matter, common decency. The cabin became a pigpen, and never once were the beds made or fresh pine boughs laid underneath. Yet they could not keep to their blankets, as they would have wished; for the frost was inexorable, and the fire box consumed much fuel. The hair of their heads and faces grew long and shaggy, while their garments would have disgusted a ragpicker. But they did not care. They were sick, and there was no one to see; besides, it was very painful to move about.

To all this was added a new trouble – the Fear of the North. This Fear was the joint child of the Great Cold and the Great Silence, and was born in the darkness of December, when the sun dipped below the southern horizon for good. It affected them according to their natures. Weatherbee fell prey to the grosser superstitions, and did his best to resurrect the spirits which slept in the forgotten graves. It was a fascinating thing, and in his dreams they came to him from out of the cold, and snuggled into his blankets, and told him of their toils and troubles ere they died. He shrank away from their clammy contact as they drew closer and twined their frozen limbs about him, and when they whispered in his ear of things to come, the cabin rang with his frightened shrieks. Cuthfert did not understand – for they no longer spoke – and when thus awakened he invariably grabbed for his revolver. Then he would sit up in bed, shivering nervously, with the weapon trained on the unconscious dreamer. Cuthfert deemed the man going mad, and so came to fear for his life.

His own malady assumed a less concrete form. The mysterious artisan who had laid the cabin, log by log, had pegged a wind-vane to the ridge-pole. Cuthfert noticed it always pointed south, and one day, irritated by its steadfastness of purpose, he turned it towards the east. He watched eagerly, but never a breath came by to disturb it. Then he turned the vane to the north, swearing never again to touch it till the wind did blow. But the air frightened him with its unearthly calm, and he often rose in the middle of the night to see if the vane had veered – ten degrees would have satisfied him. But no, it poised above him as unchangeable as fate. His imagination ran riot, till it became to him a fetish. Sometimes he followed the path it pointed across the dismal dominions, and allowed his soul to become saturated with the Fear. He dwelt upon the unseen and the unknown till the burden of eternity appeared to be crushing him. Everything in the Northland had that crushing effect – the absence of life and motion; the darkness; the infinite peace of the brooding land; the ghastly silence, which made the echo of each heart-beat a sacrilege; the solemn forest which seemed to guard an awful, inexpressible something, which neither word nor thought could compass.

The world he had so recently left, with its busy nations and great enterprises, seemed very far away. Recollections occasionally obtruded – recollections of marts and galleries and crowded thoroughfares, of evening dress and social functions, of good men and dear women he had known – but they were dim memories of a life he had lived long centuries agone, on some other planet. This phantasm was the Reality. Standing beneath the wind-vane, his eyes fixed on the polar skies, he could not bring himself to realize that the Southland really existed, that at that very moment it was a-roar with life and action. There was no Southland, no men being born of women, no giving and taking in marriage. Beyond his bleak skyline there stretched vast solitudes, and beyond these still vaster solitudes. There were no lands of sunshine, heavy with the perfume of flowers. Such things were only old dreams of paradise. The sunlands of the West and the spice-lands of the East, the smiling Arcadias and blissful Islands of the Blest – ha! ha! His laughter split the void, and shocked him with its unwonted sound. There was no sun. This was the Universe, dead and cold and dark, and he its only citizen. Weatherbee? At such moments Weatherbee did not count. He was a Caliban, a monstrous phantom, fettered to him for untold ages, the penalty of some forgotten crime.

He lived with Death among the dead, emasculated by the sense of his own insignificance, crushed by the passive mastery of the slumbering ages. The magnitude of all things appalled him. Everything partook of the superlative save himself – the perfect cessation of wind and motion, the immensity of the snow-covered wilderness, the height of the sky and the depth of the silence. That wind-vane – if it would only move. If a thunderbolt would fall, or the forest flare up in flame. The rolling up of the heavens as a scroll, the crash of Doom – anything, anything! But no, nothing moved; the Silence crowded in, and the Fear of the North laid icy fingers on his heart.

Once, like another Crusoe, by the edge of the river he came upon a track – the faint tracery of a snowshoe rabbit on the delicate snow-crust. It was a revelation. There was life in the Northland. He would follow it, look upon it, gloat over it. He forgot his swollen muscles, plunging through the deep snow in an ecstasy of anticipation. The forest swallowed him up, and the brief midday twilight vanished; but he pursued his quest till exhausted nature exerted itself and laid him helpless in the snow. There he groaned and cursed his folly, and knew the track to be the fancy of his brain; and late that night he dragged himself into the cabin on hands and knees, his cheeks frozen and a strange numbness about his feet. Weatherbee grinned malevolently, but made no offer to help him. He thrust needles into his toes and thawed them out by the stove. A week later mortification set in.

But the clerk had his own troubles. The dead men came out of their graves more frequently now, and rarely left him, waking or sleeping. He grew to wait and dread their coming, never passing the twin cairns without a shudder. One night they came to him in his sleep and led him forth – to an appointed task. Frightened into inarticulate horror, he awoke between the heaps of stones, and fled wildly to the cabin. But he had laid there for some time, for his feet and cheeks were also frozen.

Sometimes he became frantic at their insistent presence, and danced about the cabin, cutting the empty air with an axe, and smashing everything within reach. During these ghostly encounters, Cuthfert huddled into his blankets and followed the madman about with a cocked revolver, ready to shoot him if he came too near. But, recovering from one of these spells, the clerk noticed the weapon trained upon him. His suspicions were aroused, and thenceforth, he, too, lived in fear of his life. They watched each other closely after that, and faced about in startled fright whenever either passed behind the other's back. This apprehensiveness became a mania which controlled them even in their sleep. Through mutual fear they tacitly let the slush-lamp burn all night, and saw to a plentiful supply of bacon-grease before retiring. The slightest movement on the part of one was sufficient to arouse the other, and many a still watch their gazes countered as they shook beneath their blankets with fingers on the trigger-guards.

What with the Fear of the North, the mental strain, and the ravages of the disease, they lost all semblance of humanity, taking on the appearance of wild beasts, hunted and desperate. Their cheeks and noses, as an aftermath of the freezing, had turned black. Their frozen toes had begun to drop away at the first and second joints. Every movement brought pain, but the fire-box was insatiable, wringing a ransom of torture from their miserable bodies. Day in, day out, it demanded its food – a veritable pound of flesh – and they dragged themselves into the forest to chop wood on their knees. Once, crawling thus in search of dry sticks, unknown to each other they entered a thicket from opposite sides. Suddenly, without warning, two peering death's-heads confronted each other. Suffering had so transformed them that recognition was impossible. They sprang to their feet, shrieking with terror, and dashed away on their mangled stumps; and falling at the cabin door, they clawed and scratched like demons till they discovered their mistake.

Occasionally they lapsed normal, and during one of these sane intervals, the chief bone of contention, the sugar, had been divided equally between them. They guarded their separate sacks, stored up in the cache, with jealous eyes; for there were but a few cupfuls left, and they were totally devoid of faith in each other. But one day Cuthfert made a mistake. Hardly able to move, sick with pain, with his head swimming and eyes blinded, he crept into the cache, sugar canister in hand, and mistook Weatherbee's sack for his own.

January had been born but a few days when this occurred. The sun had some time since passed its lowest southern declination, and at meridian now threw flaunting streaks of yellow light upon the northern sky. On the day following his mistake with the sugar-bag, Cuthfert found himself feeling better, both in body and spirit. As noontime drew near and the day brightened, he dragged himself outside to feast on the evanescent glow, which was to him an earnest of the sun's future intentions. Weatherbee was also feeling somewhat better, crawled out beside him. They propped themselves in the snow beneath the moveless wind-vane, and waited.

The stillness of death was about them. In other climes, when nature falls into such moods, there is a subdued air of expectancy, a waiting for some small voice to take up the broken strain. Not so in the north. The two men had lived seeming aeons in this ghostly peace. They could remember no song of the past; they could conjure no song of the future. This unearthly calm had always been – the tranquil silence of eternity.

Their eyes were fixed upon the north. Unseen, behind their backs, behind the towering mountains to the south, the sun swept towards the zenith of another sky than theirs. Sole spectators of the mighty canvas, they watched the false dawn slowly grow. A faint flame began to glow and smoulder. It deepened in intensity, ringing the changes of reddish-yellow, purple, and saffron. So bright did it become that Cuthfert thought the sun must surely be behind it – a miracle, the sun rising in the north! Suddenly, without warning and without fading, the canvas was swept clean. There was no colour in the sky. The light had gone out of the day. They caught their breaths in half-sobs. But lo! The air was a-glint with particles of scintillating frost, and there, to the north, the wind-vane lay in vague outline on the snow. A shadow! A shadow! It was exactly midday. They jerked their heads hurriedly to the south. A golden rim peeped over the mountain's snowy shoulder, smiled upon them an instant, then dipped from sight again.

There were tears in their eyes as they sought each other. A strange softening came over them. They felt irresistibly drawn toward each other. The sun was coming back again. It would be with them to-morrow, and the next day, and the next. And it would stay longer every visit, and a time would come when it would ride their heaven day and night, never once dropping below the sky-line. There would be no night. The ice-locked winter would be broken; the winds would blow, and the forests answer; the land would bathe in the blessed sunshine, and life renew. Hand in hand, they would quit this horrid dream and journey back to the Southland. They lurched blindly forward, and their hands met – their poor maimed hands, swollen and distorted beneath their mittens.

But the promise was destined to remain unfulfilled. The Northland is the Northland, and men work out their souls by strange rules, which other men, who have not journeyed into far countries, cannot come to understand.

An hour later, Cuthfert put a pan of bread into the oven, and fell to speculating on what the surgeons could do with his feet when he got back. Home did not seem so very far away now. Weatherbee was rummaging in the cache. Of a sudden, he raised a whirlwind of blasphemy, which in turn ceased with startling abruptness. The other man had robbed his sugar-sack. Still, things might have happened differently, had not the two dead men come out from under the stones and hushed the hot words in his throat. They led him quite gently from the cache, which he forgot to close. That consummation was reached; that something they had whispered to him in his dreams was about to happen. They guided him gently, very gently, to the woodpile, where they put the axe in his hands. Then they helped him shove open the cabin door, and he felt sure they shut it after him – at least he heard it slam and the latch fall sharply into place. And he knew they were waiting just without, waiting for him to do his task.

'Carter! I say, Carter!'

Percy Cuthfert was frightened at the look on the clerk's face, and he made haste to put the table between them.

Carter Weatherbee followed, without haste and without enthusiasm. There was neither pity nor passion in his face, but rather the patient, stolid look of one who has certain work to do and goes about it methodically.

'I say, what's the matter?'

The clerk dodged back, cutting off his retreat to the door, but never opening his mouth.

'I say, Carter, I say; let's talk. There's a good chap.'

The master of arts was thinking rapidly, now, shaping a skilful flank movement on the bed where his Smith and Wesson lay. Keeping his eyes on the madman, he rolled backward on the bunk, at the same time clutching the pistol.

'Carter!'

The powder flashed full in Weatherbee's face, but he swung his weapon and leaped forward. The axe bit deeply at the base of the spine, and Percy Cuthfert felt all consciousness of his lower limbs leave him. Then the clerk fell heavily upon him, clutching him by the throat with feeble fingers. The sharp bite of the axe had caused Cuthfert to drop the pistol, and as his lungs panted for release, he fumbled aimlessly for it among the blankets. Then he remembered. He slid a hand up the clerk's belt to the sheath-knife; and they drew very close to each other in that last clinch.

Percy Cuthfert felt his strength leave him. The lower portion of his body was useless. The inert weight of Weatherbee crushed him – crushed him and pinned him there like a bear under a trap. The cabin became filled with a familiar odour, and he knew the bread to be burning. Yet what did it matter? He would never need it. And there were all of six cupfuls of sugar in the cache – if he had foreseen this he would not have been so saving the last several days. Would the wind-vane ever move? It might even be veering now. Why not? Had he not seen the sun to-day? He would go and see. No; it was impossible to move. He had not thought the clerk so heavy a man.

How quickly the cabin cooled! The fire must be out. The cold was forcing in. It must be below zero already, and the ice creeping up the inside of the door. He could not see it, but his past experience enabled him to gauge its progress by the cabin's temperature. The lower hinge must be white ere now. Would the tale of this ever reach the world? How would his friends take it? They would read it over their coffee, most likely, and talk it over at the clubs. He could see them very clearly. 'Poor old Cuthfert,' they murmured; 'not such a bad sort of a chap, after all.' He smiled at the eulogies, and passed on in search of a Turkish bath. It was the same old crowd upon the streets. Strange, they did not notice his moosehide moccasins and tattered German socks. He would take a cab. And after the bath a shave would not be bad. No; he would eat first. Steak, and potatoes, and green things – how fresh it all was! And what was that? Squares of honey, streaming liquid amber! But why did they bring so much? Ha! ha! he could never eat it all. Shine! Why certainly. He put his foot on the box. The bootblack looked curiously up at him, and he remembered his moosehide moccasins, and went away hastily.

Hark! The wind-vane must be surely spinning. No; a mere singing in his ears. That was all – a mere singing. The ice must have passed the latch by now. More likely the upper hinge was covered. Between the moss-chinked roof-poles, little points of frost began to appear. How slowly they grew! No; not so slowly. There was a new one, and there another. Two – three – four; they were coming too fast to count. There were two growing together. And there, a third had joined them. Why, there were no more spots. They had run together and formed a sheet.

Well, he would have company. If Gabriel ever broke the silence of the north, they would stand together, hand in hand, before the great White Throne. And God would judge them, God would judge them!

Then Percy Cuthfert closed his eyes and dropped off to sleep.

Zane Grey

Siena Waits

A VOICE on the wind whispered to Siena the prophecy of his birth. 'A chief is born to save the vanishing tribe of Crows! A hunter to his starving people!' While he listened, at his feet swept swift water, the rushing, green-white, thundering Athabasca, spirit-forsaken river; and it rumbled his name and murmured his fate. 'Siena! Siena! His bride will rise from a wind kiss on the flowers in the moonlight! A new land calls to the last of the Crows! Northward where the wild goose ends its flight Siena will father a great people!'

So Siena, a hunter of the leafy trails, dreamed his dreams, and at sixteen he was the hope of the remnant of a once powerful tribe, a stripling chief, beautiful as a bronzed autumn god, silent, proud, forever listening to voices on the wind.

To Siena the lore of the woodland came as flight comes to the strong-winged wildfowl. The secrets of the forest were his, and of the rocks and rivers.

He knew how to find the nests of the plover, to call the loon, to net the heron, and spear the fish. He understood the language of the whispering pines. Where the deer came down to drink and the caribou browsed on moss and the white rabbit nibbled in the grass and the bear dug in the logs for grubs – all these he learned; and also when the black flies drove the moose into the water and when the honk of the geese meant the approach of the north wind.

He lived in the woods, with his bow, his net, and his spear. The trees were his brothers. The loon laughed for his happiness, the wolf mourned for his sadness. The bold crag above the river, Old Stoneface, heard his step when he climbed there in the twilight. He communed with the stem god of his ancestors and watched the flashing Northern Lights and listened.

From all four corners came his spirit guides with steps of destiny on his trail. On all the four winds breathed voices whispering of his future; loudest of all called the Athabasca, godforsaken river, murmuring of the bride born of a wind kiss on the flowers in the moonlight.

SIENA WAITS

It was autumn, with the flame of leaf fading, the haze rolling out of the hollows, the lull yielding to the moan of coming wind. All the signs of a severe winter were in the hulls of the nuts, in the fur of the foxes, in the flight of waterfowl. Siena was spearing fish for winter store. None so keen of sight as Siena, so swift of arm; and as he was the hope, so he alone was the provider for the starving tribe. Siena stood to his knees in a brook where it flowed over its gravelly bed into the Athabasca. Poised high was his wooden spear. It glinted downward swift as a shaft of sunlight through the leaves. Then Siena lifted a quivering whitefish and tossed it upon the bank where his mother Ema, with other women of the tribe, sun-dried the fish upon a rock.

Again and again, many times, flashed the spear. The young chief seldom missed his aim. Early frosts on the uplands had driven the fish down to deeper water, and as they came darting over the bright pebbles Siena called them by name.

The oldest squaw could not remember such a run of fish. Ema sang the praises of her son; the other women ceased the hunger chant of the tribe.

Suddenly a hoarse shout pealed out over the waters.

Ema fell in a fright; her companions ran away; Siena leaped upon the bank, clutching his spear. A boat in which were men with white faces drifted down towards him.

'Hal-loa!' again sounded the hoarse cry.

Ema cowered in the grass. Siena saw a waving of white hands; his knees knocked together and he felt himself about to flee. But Siena of the Crows, the saviour of a vanishing tribe, must not fly from visible foes.

'Palefaces,' he whispered, trembling, yet stood his ground ready to fight for his mother. He remembered stories of an old Indian who had journeyed far to the south and had crossed the trails of the dreaded white men. There stirred in him vague memories of strange Indian runners telling campfire tales of white hunters with weapons of lightning and thunder.

'Naza! Naza!' Siena cast one fleeting glance to the north and a prayer to his god of gods. He believed his spirit would soon be wandering in the shades of the other Indian world.

As the boat beached on the sand Siena saw men lying with pale faces upward to the sky, and voices in an unknown tongue greeted him. The tone was friendly, and he lowered his threatening spear. Then a man came up the bank, his hungry eyes on the pile of fish, and he began to speak haltingly in mingled Cree and Chippewayan language:

'Boy – we're white friends – starving – let us buy fish – trade for fish – we're starving and we have many moons to travel.'

'Siena's tribe is poor,' replied the lad; 'sometimes they starve too. But Siena will divide his fish and wants no trade.'

His mother, seeing the white men intended no evil, came out of her fright and complained bitterly to Siena of his liberality. She spoke of the menacing winter, of the frozen streams, the snow-bound forest, the long nights of hunger. Siena silenced her and waved the frightened braves and squaws back to their wigwams.

'Siena is young,' he said simply; 'but he is chief here. If we starve – we starve.'

Whereupon he portioned out a half of the fish. The white men built a fire and sat around it feasting like famished wolves around a fallen stag. When they had appeased their hunger they packed the remaining fish in the boat, whistling and singing the while. Then the leader made offer to pay, which Siena refused, though the covetous light in his mother's eyes hurt him sorely.

'Chief,' said the leader, 'the white man understands; now he offers presents as one chief to another.'

Thereupon he proffered bright beads and tinselled trinkets, yards of calico and strips of cloth. Siena accepted with a dignity in marked contrast to the way in which the greedy Ema pounced upon the glittering heap. Next the paleface presented a knife which, drawn from its scabbard, showed a blade that mirrored its brightness in Siena's eyes.

'Chief, your woman complains of a starving tribe?' went on the white man. 'Are there not many moose and reindeer?'

'Yes. But seldom can Siena creep within range of his arrow.'

'A-ha! Siena will starve no more,' replied the man, and from the boat he took a long iron tube with a wooden stock.

'What is that?' asked Siena.

'The wonderful shooting stick. Here, boy, watch! See the bark on the campfire. Watch!'

He raised the stick to his shoulder. Then followed a streak of flame, a puff of smoke, a booming report; and the bark of the campfire flew into bits.

The children dodged into the wigwams with loud cries, the women ran screaming. Ema dropped in the grass wailing that the end of the world had come, while Siena, unable to move hand or foot, breathed another prayer to Naza of the northland.

The white man laughed and, patting Siena's arm, he said: 'No fear.' Then he drew Siena away from the bank, and began to explain the meaning and use of the wonderful shooting stick. He reloaded it and fired again and yet again, until Siena understood and was all aflame at the possibilities of such a weapon.

Patiently the white man taught the Indian how to load it, sight, and shoot, and how to clean it with ramrod and buckskin. Next he placed at Siena's feet a keg of powder, a bag of lead bullets, and boxes full of caps. Then he bade Siena farewell, entered the boat with his men and drifted round a bend of the swift Athabasca.

Siena stood alone upon the bank, the wonderful shooting stick in his hands, and the wail of his frightened mother in his ears. He comforted her, telling her the white men were gone, that he was safe, and that the prophecy of his birth had at last begun its fulfilment. He carried the precious ammunition to a safe hiding place in a hollow log near his wigwam and then he plunged into the forest.

Siena bent his course towards the runways of the moose. He walked in a kind of dream, for he both feared and believed. Soon the glimmer of water, splashes and widening ripples, caused him to crawl stealthily through the ferns and grasses to the border of a pond. The familiar hum of flies told him of the location of his quarry. The moose had taken to the water, driven by the swarms of black flies, and were standing neck deep, lifting their muzzles to feed on the drooping poplar branches. Their wide-spreading antlers, tipped back into the water, made the ripples.

Trembling as never before, Siena sank behind a log. He was within fifty paces of the moose. How often in that very spot had he strung a feathered arrow and shot it vainly! But now he had the white man's weapon, charged with lightning and thunder. Just then the poplars parted above the shore, disclosing a bull in the act of stepping down. He tossed his antlered head at the cloud of humming flies, then stopped, lifting his nose to scent the wind.

'Naza!' whispered Siena in his swelling throat.

He rested the shooting stick on the log and tried to see over the brown barrel. But his eyes were dim. Again he whispered a prayer to Naza. His sight cleared, his shaking arms stilled, and with his soul waiting, hoping, doubting, he aimed and pulled the trigger.

Boom!

High the moose flung his ponderous head, to crash down upon his knees, to roll in the water and churn a bloody foam, and then lie still.

'Siena! Siena!'

Shrill the young chief's exultant yell pealed over the listening waters, piercing the still forest, to ring back in echo from Old Stoneface. It was Siena's triumphant call to his forefathers, watching him from the silence.

The herd of moose ploughed out of the pond and crashed into the woods, where, long after they had disappeared, their antlers could be heard cracking the saplings.

When Siena stood over the dead moose his doubts fled; he was indeed god-chosen. No longer chief of a starving tribe! Reverently and with immutable promise he raised the shooting stick to the north, towards Naza who had remembered him; and to the south, where dwelt the enemies of his tribe, his dark glance brooded wild and proud and savage.

Eight times the shooting stick boomed out in the stillness and eight moose lay dead in the wet grasses. In the twilight Siena wended his way home and placed eight moose tongues before the whimpering squaws.

'Siena is no longer a boy,' he said. 'Siena is a hunter. Let his women go bring in the meat.'

Then to the rejoicing and feasting and dancing of his tribe he turned a deaf ear, and passed the night alone under the shadow of Old Stoneface, where he walked with the spirits of his ancestors and believed the voices on the wind.

Before the ice locked the ponds Siena killed a hundred moose and reindeer. Meat and fat and oil and robes changed the world for the Crow tribe.

Fires burned brightly all the long winter; the braves awoke from their stupor and chanted no more; the women sang of the Siena who had come, and prayed for summer wind and moonlight to bring his bride.

Spring went by, summer grew into blazing autumn, and Siena's fame and the wonder of the shooting stick spread through the length and breadth of the land.

Another year passed, then another, and Siena was the great chief of the rejuvenated Crows. He had grown into a warrior's stature, his face had the beauty of the god-chosen, his eye the falcon flash of the Sienas of old. Long communion in the shadow of Old Stoneface had added wisdom to his other gifts; and now to his worshipping tribe all that was needed to complete the prophecy of his birth was the coming of the alien bride.

It was another autumn, with the wind whipping the tamaracks and moaning in the pines, and Siena stole along a brown, fern-lined trail. The dry smell of fallen leaves filled his nostrils; he tasted snow in the keen breezes. The flowers were dead, and still no dark-eyed bride sat in his wigwam. Siena sorrowed and strengthened his heart to wait. He saw her flitting in the shadows around him, a wraith with dusky eyes veiled by dusky wind-blown hair, and ever she hovered near him, whispering from every dark pine, from every waving tuft of grass.

To her whispers he replied: 'Siena waits.'

He wondered of what alien tribe she would come. He hoped not of the unfriendly Chippewayans or the far-distant Blackfeet; surely not of the hostile Crees, life enemies of his tribe, destroyers of its once puissant strength, jealous now of its resurging power.

Other shadows flitted through the forest, spirits that rose silently from the graves over which he trod, and warned him of double steps on his trail, of unseen foes watching him from the dark coverts. His braves had repeated gossip, filterings from stray Indian wanderers, hinting of plots against the risen Siena. To all these he gave no heed, for was not he Siena, god-chosen, and had he not the wonderful shooting stick?

It was the season that he loved, when dim forest and hazy fernland spoke most impellingly. The tamaracks talked to him, the poplars bowed as he passed, and the pines sang for him alone. The dying vines twined about his feet and clung to him, and the brown ferns, curling sadly, waved him a welcome that was a farewell. A bird twittered a plaintive note and a loon whistled a lonely call. Across the wide grey hollows and meadows of white moss moaned the north wind, bending all before it, blowing full into Siena's face with its bitter promise. The lichen-covered rocks and the rugged-barked trees and the creatures that moved among them – the whole world of earth and air – heard Siena's step on the rustling leaves and a thousand voices hummed in the autumn stillness.

So he passed through the shadowy forest and over the grey muskeg flats to his hunting place. With his birch-bark horn he blew the call of the moose. He alone of hunting Indians had the perfect moose call. There, hidden within a thicket, he waited, calling and listening till an angry reply bellowed from the depths of a hollow, and a bull moose, snorting fight, came cracking the saplings in his rush. When he sprang fierce and bristling into the glade, Siena killed him. Then, laying his shooting stick over a log, he drew his knife and approached the beast.

A snapping of twigs alarmed Siena and he whirled upon the defensive, but too late to save himself. A band of Indians pounced upon him and bore him to the ground. Siena made one wrestling heave, then he was overpowered and bound. Looking upward, he knew his captors, though he had never seen them before; they were the lifelong foes of his people, the fighting Crees.

A sturdy chief, bronze of face and sinister of eye, looked grimly down upon his captive. 'Baroma makes Siena a slave.'

Siena and his tribe were dragged far southward to the land of the Crees. The young chief was bound upon a block in the centre of the village where hundreds of Crees spat upon him, beat him, and outraged him in every way their cunning could devise. Siena's gaze was on the north and his face showed no sign that he felt the torments.

At last Baroma's old advisers stopped the spectacle, saying: 'This is a man!'

Siena and his people became slaves of the Crees. In Baroma's lodge, hung upon caribou antlers, was the wonderful shooting stick with

Siena's powder horn and bullet pouch, objects of intense curiosity and fear.

None knew the mystery of this lightning-flashing, thunder-dealing thing; none dared touch it.

The heart of Siena was broken; not for his shattered dreams or the end of his freedom, but for his people. His fame had been their undoing. Slaves to the murderers of his forefathers! His spirit darkened, his soul sickened; no more did sweet voices sing to him on the wind, and his mind dwelt apart from his body among shadows and dim shapes.

Because of his strength he was worked like a dog at hauling packs and carrying wood; because of his fame he was set to cleaning fish and washing vessels with the squaws. Seldom did he get to speak a word to his mother or any of his people. Always he was driven.

One day, when he lagged almost fainting, a maiden brought him water to drink. Siena looked up, and all about him suddenly brightened, as when sunlight bursts from cloud.

'Who is kind to Siena?' he asked, drinking.

'Baroma's daughter,' replied the maiden.

'What is her name?'

Quickly the maiden bent her head, veiling dusky eyes with dusky hair. 'Emihiyah.'

'Siena has wandered on lonely trails and listened to voices not meant for other ears. He has heard the music of Emihiyah on the winds. Let the daughter of Siena's great foe not fear to tell of her name.'

'Emihiyah means a wind kiss on the flowers in the moonlight,' she whispered shyly and fled.

Love came to the last of the Sienas and it was like a glory. Death shuddered no more in Siena's soul. He saw into the future, and out of his gloom he rose again, god-chosen in his own sight, with such added beauty to his stern face and power to his piercing eye and strength to his lofty frame that the Crees quailed before him and marvelled. Once more sweet voices came to him, and ever on the soft winds were songs of the dewy moorlands to the north, songs of the pines and the laugh of the loon and of the rushing, green-white, thundering Athabasca, godforsaken river.

Siena's people saw him strong and patient, and they toiled on, unbroken, faithful. While he lived, the pride of Baroma was vaunting. 'Siena waits' were the simple words he said to his mother, and she repeated them as wisdom. But the flame of his eye was like the leaping Northern Lights, and it kept alive the fire deep down in their breasts.

In the winter when the Crees lolled in their wigwams, when less labour fell to Siena, he set traps in the snow trails for silver fox and marten. No Cree had ever been such a trapper as Siena. In the long months he captured many furs, with which he wrought a robe the like of which had not before been the delight of a maiden's eye. He kept it by him for seven nights, and always during this time his ear was turned to the wind. The seventh night was the night of the midwinter feast, and when the torches burned bright in front of Baroma's lodge Siena took the robe and, passing slowly and stately till he stood before Emihiyah, he laid it at her feet.

Emihiyah's dusky face paled, her eyes that shone like stars drooped behind her flying hair, and all her slender body trembled.

'Slave!' cried Baroma, leaping erect. 'Come closer that Baroma may see what kind of a dog approaches Emihiyah.'

Siena met Baroma's gaze, but spoke no word. His gift spoke for him. The hated slave had dared to ask in marriage the hand of the proud Baroma's daughter. Siena towered in the firelight with something in his presence that for a moment awed beholders. Then the passionate and untried braves broke the silence with a clamour of the wolf pack.

Tillimanqua, wild son of Baroma, strung an arrow to his bow and shot it into Siena's hip, where it stuck, with feathered shaft quivering.

The spring of the panther was not swifter than Siena; he tossed Tillimanqua into the air and, flinging him down, trod on his neck and wrenched the bow away. Siena pealed out the long-drawn war whoop of his tribe that had not been heard for a hundred years, and the terrible cry stiffened the Crees in their tracks.

Then he plucked the arrow from his hip and, fitting it to the string, pointed the gory flint head at Tillimanqua's eyes and began to bend the bow. He bent the tough wood till the ends almost met, a feat of exceeding great strength, and thus he stood with brawny arms knotted and stretched.

A scream rent the suspense. Emihiyah fell upon her knees. 'Spare Emihiyah's brother!'

Siena cast one glance at the kneeling maiden, then, twanging the bow string, he shot the arrow towards the sky.

'Baroma's slave is Siena,' he said, with scorn like the lash of a whip. 'Let the Cree learn wisdom.'

Then Siena strode away, with a stream of dark blood down his thigh, and went to his brush tepee, where he closed his wound.

In the still watches of the night, when the stars blinked through the leaves and the dew fell, when Siena burned and throbbed in pain, a shadow passed between his weary eyes and the pale light. And a voice that was not one of the spirit voices on the wind called softly over him, 'Siena! Emihiyah comes.'

The maiden bound the hot thigh with a soothing balm and bathed his fevered brow.

Then her hands found his in tender touch, her dark face bent low to his, her hair lay upon his cheek. 'Emihiyah keeps the robe,' she said.

'Siena loves Emihiyah,' he replied.

'Emihiyah loves Siena,' she whispered.

She kissed him and stole away.

On the morrow Siena's wound was as if it had never been; no eye saw his pain. Siena returned to his work and his trapping. The winter melted into spring, spring flowered into summer, summer withered into autumn.

Once in the melancholy days Siena visited Baroma in his wigwam. 'Baroma's hunters are slow. Siena sees a famine in the land.'

'Let Baroma's slave keep his place among the squaws,' was the reply.

That autumn the north wind came a moon before the Crees expected it; the reindeer took their annual march farther south; the moose herded warily in open groves; the whitefish did not run, and the seven-year pest depleted the rabbits.

When the first snow fell Baroma called a council and then sent his hunting braves far and wide.

One by one they straggled back to camp, footsore and hungry, and each with the same story. It was too late.

A few moose were in the forest, but they were wild and kept far out of range of the hunter's arrows, and there was no other game.

A blizzard clapped down upon the camp, and sleet and snow whitened the forest and filled the trails. Then winter froze everything in icy clutch. The old year drew to a close.

The Crees were on the brink of famine. All day and all night they kept up their chanting and incantations and beating of tom-toms to conjure the return of the reindeer. But no reindeer appeared.

It was then that the stubborn Baroma yielded to his advisers and consented to let Siena save them from starvation by means of his wonderful shooting stick. Accordingly Baroma sent word to Siena to appear at his wigwam.

Siena did not go, and said to the medicine man: 'Tell Baroma soon it will be for Siena to demand.'

Then the Cree chieftain stormed and stamped in his wigwam and swore away the life of his slave. Yet again the wise medicine men prevailed. Siena and the wonderful shooting stick would be the salvation of the Crees. Baroma, muttering deep in his throat like distant thunder, gave sentence to starve Siena until he volunteered to go forth to hunt, or let him be the first to die.

The last scraps of meat, except a little hoarded in Baroma's lodge, were devoured, and then began the boiling of bones and skins to make a soup to sustain life. The cold days passed and a silent gloom pervaded the camp. Sometimes a cry of a bereaved mother, mourning for a starved child, wailed through the darkness. Siena's people, long used to starvation, did not suffer or grow weak so soon as the Crees. They were of hardier frame, and they were upheld by faith in their chief. When he would sicken it would be time for them to despair. But Siena walked erect as in the days of his freedom, nor did he stagger under the loads of firewood, and there was a light on his face. The Crees, knowing of Baroma's order that Siena should be the first to perish of starvation, gazed at the slave first in awe, then in fear. The last of the Sienas was succoured by the spirits.

But god-chosen though Siena deemed himself, he knew it was not by the spirits that he was fed in this time of famine. At night in the dead stillness, when no mourning of wolf came over the frozen wilderness, Siena lay in his brush tepee close and warm under his blanket. The wind was faint and low, yet still it brought the old familiar voices. And it bore another sound – the soft fall of a moccasin on the snow. A shadow passed between Siena's eyes and the pale light.

'Emihiyah comes,' whispered the shadow and knelt over him.

She tendered a slice of meat which she had stolen from Baroma's scant hoard as he muttered and growled in uneasy slumber. Every night since her father's order to starve Siena, Emihiyah had made this perilous errand.

And now her hand sought his and her dusky hair swept his brow. 'Emihiyah is faithful,' she breathed low.

'Siena only waits,' he replied.

She kissed him and stole away.

Cruel days fell upon the Crees before Baroma's pride was broken. Many children died and some of the mothers were beyond help. Siena's people kept their strength, and he himself showed no effect of hunger. Long ago the Cree women had deemed him superhuman, that the Great Spirit fed him from the happy hunting grounds.

At last Baroma went to Siena. 'Siena may save his people and the Crees.'

Siena regarded him long, then replied: 'Siena waits.'

'Let Baroma know. What does Siena wait for? While he waits we die.'

Siena smiled his slow, inscrutable smile and turned away.

Baroma sent for his daughter and ordered her to plead for her life.

Emihiyah came, fragile as a swaying reed, more beautiful than a rose choked in a tangled thicket, and she stood before Siena with doe eyes veiled. 'Emihiyah begs Siena to save her and the tribe of Crees.'

'Siena waits,' replied the slave.

Baroma roared in his fury and bade his braves lash the slave. But the blows fell from feeble arms and Siena laughed at his captors.

Then, like a wild lion unleashed from long thrall, he turned upon them: 'Starve! Cree dogs! Starve! When the Crees all fall like leaves in autumn, then Siena and his people will go back to the north.'

Baroma's arrogance left him then, and on another day, when Emihiyah lay weak and pallid in his wigwam and the pangs of hunger gnawed at his own vitals, he again sought Siena. 'Let Siena tell for what he waits.'

Siena rose to his lofty height and the leaping flame of the Northern Light gathered in his eyes. 'Freedom!' One word he spoke and it rolled away on the wind.

'Baroma yields,' replied the Cree, and hung his head.

'Send the squaws who can walk and the braves who can crawl out upon Siena's trail.'

Then Siena went to Baroma's lodge and took up the wonderful shooting stick and, loading it, he set out upon snowshoes into the white forest. He knew where to find the moose yards in the sheltered corners. He heard the bulls pounding the hard-packed snow and cracking their antlers on the trees. The wary beasts would not have allowed him to steal close, as a warrior armed with a bow must have done, but Siena fired into the herd at long range. And when they dashed off, sending the snow up like a spray, a huge black bull lay dead. Siena followed them as they floundered through the drifts, and whenever he came within range he shot again. When five mooses were killed he turned upon his trail to find almost the whole Cree tribe had followed him and were tearing the meat and crying out in a kind of crazy joy. That night the fires burned before the wigwams, the earthen pots steamed, and there was great rejoicing. Siena hunted the next day, and the next, and for ten days he went into the white forest with his wonderful shooting stick, and eighty moose fell to his unerring aim.

The famine was broken and the Crees were saved.

When the mad dances ended and the feasts were over, Siena appeared before Baroma's lodge. 'Siena will lead his people northward.'

Baroma, starving, was a different chief from Baroma well fed and in no pain. All his cunning had returned. 'Siena goes free. Baroma gave his word. But Siena's people remain slaves.'

'Siena demanded freedom for himself and people,' said the younger chief.

'Baroma heard no word of Siena's tribe. He would not have granted freedom for them. Siena's freedom was enough.'

'The Cree twists the truth. He knows Siena would not go without his people. Siena might have remembered Baroma's cunning. The Crees were ever liars.'

Baroma stalked before his fire with haughty presence. About him in the circle of light sat his medicine men, his braves and squaws. 'The Cree is kind. He gave his word. Siena is free. Let him take his wonderful shooting stick and go back to the north.'

Siena laid the shooting stick at Baroma's feet and likewise the powder horn and bullet pouch. Then he folded his arms, and his falcon eyes looked far beyond Baroma to the land of the changing lights and the old home on the green-white, rushing Athabasca, godforsaken river. 'Siena stays.'

Baroma started in amaze and anger. 'Siena makes Baroma's word idle. Begone!'

'Siena stays!'

The look of Siena, the pealing reply, for a moment held the chief mute. Slowly Baroma stretched wide his arms and lifted them, while from his face flashed a sullen wonder. 'Great Slave!' he thundered.

So was respect forced from the soul of the Cree, and the name thus wrung from his jealous heart was one to live forever in the lives and legends of Siena's people.

Baroma sought the silence of his lodge, and his medicine men and braves dispersed, leaving Siena standing in the circle, a magnificent statue facing the steely north.

From that day insult was never offered to Siena, nor word spoken to him by the Crees, nor work given. He was free to come and go where he willed, and he spent his time in lessening the tasks of his people.

The trails of the forest were always open to him, as were the streets of the Cree village. If a brave met him, it was to step aside; if a squaw met him, it was to bow her head; if a chief met him, it was to face him as warriors faced warriors.

One twilight Emihiyah crossed his path, and suddenly she stood as once before, like a frail reed about to break in the wind. But Siena passed on. The days went by and each one brought less labour to Siena's people, until that one came wherein there was no task save what they set themselves. Siena's tribe were slaves, yet not slaves.

The winter wore by and the spring and the autumn, and again Siena's fame went abroad on the four winds. The Chippewayans journeyed from afar to see the Great Slave, and likewise the Blackfeet and the Yellow Knives. Honour would have been added to fame; councils called; overtures made to the sombre Baroma on behalf of the Great Slave, but Siena passed to and fro among his people, silent and cold to all others, true to the place which his great foe had given him. Captive to a lesser chief, they said; the Great Slave who would yet free his tribe and gather to him a new and powerful nation.

Once in the late autumn Siena sat brooding in the twilight by Ema's tepee. That night all who came near him were silent. Again Siena was listening to voices on the wind, voices that had been still for long, which he had tried to forget. It was the north wind, and it whipped the spruces and moaned through the pines. In its cold breath it bore a message to Siena, a hint of coming winter and a call from Naza, far north of the green-white, thundering Athabasca, river without a spirit.

In the darkness when the camp slumbered Siena faced the steely north. As he looked a golden shaft, arrow-shaped and arrow-swift, shot to the zenith.

'Naza!' he whispered to the wind. 'Siena watches.'

Then the gleaming, changing Northern Lights painted a picture of gold and silver bars, of flushes pink as shell, of opal fire and sunset red; and it was a picture of Siena's life from the moment the rushing Athabasca rumbled his name, to the far distant time when he would say farewell to his great nation and pass forever to the retreat of the winds. God-chosen he was, and had power to read the story in the sky.

Seven nights Siena watched in the darkness; and on the seventh night, when the golden flare and silver shafts faded in the north, he passed from tepee to tepee, awakening his people. 'When Siena's people hear the sound of the shooting stick let them cry greatly: "Siena kills Baroma! Siena kills Baroma!" –'

With noiseless stride Siena went among the wigwams and along the lanes until he reached Baroma's lodge. Entering in the dark he groped with his hands upward to a moose's antlers and found the shooting stick. Outside he fired it into the air.

Like a lightning bolt the report ripped asunder the silence, and the echoes clapped and reclapped from the cliffs. Sharp on the dying echoes Siena bellowed his war whoop, and it was the second time in a hundred years for foes to hear that terrible, long-drawn cry.

Then followed the shrill yells of Siena's people: 'Siena kills Baroma . . . Siena kills Baroma . . . Siena kills Baroma!'

The slumber of the Crees awoke to a babel of many voices; it rose hoarsely on the night air, swelled hideously into a deafening roar that shook the earth.

In this din of confusion and terror when the Crees were lamenting the supposed death of Baroma and screaming in each other's ears, 'The Great Slave takes his freedom!' Siena ran to his people and, pointing to the north, drove them before him.

Single file, like a long line of flitting spectres, they passed out of the fields into the forest. Siena kept close on their trail, ever looking backward, and ready with the shooting stick.

SIENA WAITS

The roar of the stricken Crees softened in his ears and at last died away.

Under the black canopy of whispering leaves, over the grey, mist-shrouded muskeg flats, around the glimmering reed-bordered ponds, Siena drove his people.

All night Siena hurried them northward and with every stride his heart beat higher. Only he was troubled by a sound like the voice that came to him on the wind.

But the wind was now blowing in his face, and the sound appeared to be at his back. It followed on his trail as had the step of destiny. When he strained his ears he could not hear it, yet when he had gone on swiftly, persuaded it was only fancy, then the voice that was not a voice came haunting him.

In the grey dawn Siena halted on the far side of a grey flat and peered through the mists on his back trail. Something moved out among the shadows, a grey shape that crept slowly, uttering a mournful cry.

'Siena is trailed by a wolf,' muttered the chief.

Yet he waited, and saw that the wolf was an Indian. He raised the fatal shooting stick.

As the Indian staggered forward, Siena recognized the robe of silver fox and marten, his gift to Emihiyah. He laughed in mockery. It was a Cree trick. Tillimanqua had led the pursuit disguised in his sister's robe. Baroma would find his son dead on the Great Slave's trail.

'Siena!' came the strange, low cry.

It was the cry that had haunted him like the voice on the wind. He leaped as a bounding deer.

Out of the grey fog burned dusky eyes half-veiled by dusky hair, and little hands that he knew wavered as fluttering leaves. 'Emihiyah comes,' she said.

'Siena waits,' he replied.

Far to the northward he led his bride and his people, far beyond the old home on the green-white, thundering Athabasca, godforsaken river; and there, on the lonely shores of an inland sea, he fathered the Great Slave Tribe.

Zane Grey

Yaqui

I

SUNSET – it was the hour of Yaqui's watch. Chief of a driven remnant of the once mighty tribe, he trusted no sentinel so well as himself at the end of the day's march. While his braves unpacked the tired horses, and his women prepared the evening meal, and his bronze-skinned children played in the sand, Yaqui watched the bold desert horizon.

Long years of hatred had existed between the Yaquis of upland Sonora and the Mexicans from the east. Like eagles, the Indian tribe had lived for centuries in the mountain fastnesses of the Sierra Madre, free, happy, self-sufficient. But wandering prospectors had found gold in their country and that had been the end of their peace. At first the Yaquis, wanting only the wildness and loneliness of their homes, moved farther and farther back from the ever-encroaching advance of the gold diggers. At last, driven from the mountains into the desert, they realized that gold was the doom of their tribe and they began to fight for their land. Bitter and bloody were the battles; and from father to son this wild, free, proud race bequeathed a terrible hatred.

Yaqui was one of the last great chiefs of his once great tribe. All his life he remembered the words of his father and his grandfather – that the Yaquis must find an unknown and impenetrable hiding place or perish from the earth. When Mexican soldiers at the decree of their government made war upon this tribe, killing those who resisted and making slaves of the captured, Yaqui with his family and followers set out upon a last journey across the Sonoran wilderness. Hateful and fearful of the east, whence this blight of gold diggers and land robbers appeared to come, he had fled towards the setting sun into a waste of desert land unknown to his people – a desert of scorching heat and burning sand and tearing cactus and treacherous lava, where water and wood and grass seemed days apart. Some of the youngest children had died on the way and all except the strong braves were wearing out.

Alone, on a ridge of rising ground, Yaqui faced the back trail and watched with falcon eyes. Miles distant though that horizon was, those desert eyes could have made out horses against the clear sky. He did not gaze steadily, for the Indian method was to flash a look across the spaces, from near to far, and to fix the eye momentarily, to strain the vision and magnify all objects, then to avert the gaze from that direction and presently flash it back again.

Lonely, wild, and grand, the scene seemed one of lifelessness. Only the sun lived, still hot, as it burned red-gold far away on the rugged rim of this desert world. Nothing breathed in that vastness. To Yaqui's ear the silence was music. The red sun slipped down and the desert changed. The golden floor of sand and rock shaded cold to the horizon and above that the sky lost its rose, turning to intense luminous blue. In the far distance the peaks dimmed and vanished in purple. The fire of the western heavens paled and died, and over all the rock-ribbed, sand-encumbered plateau stole a wondrous grey shade. Yaqui watched until that grey changed to black and the horizon line was lost in night. Safe now from pursuers were he and his people until the dawn.

Then, guided by a speck of camp-fire light, he returned to his silent men and moaning women and a scant meal that he divided. Hunger was naught to Yaqui, nor thirst. Four days could he travel the desert without drink, an endurance most of his hardy tribe were trained to. And as for toil, the strength of his giant frame had never reached its limit. But strong chief that he was, when he listened to the moaning women and gazed at the silent, set faces of the children under the starlight he sagged to the sands and, bowing his head, prayed to his gods. He prayed for little – only life, freedom, loneliness, a hidden niche where his people would hear no steps and fear no spectres on their trail. Then with unquenchable faith he stretched his great length on the sands; and the night was as a moment.

In the grey of a dawn cold, pure, and silent, with the radiant morning star shining like a silver moon, the long file of Yaquis rode and tramped westward, on down the rugged bare slopes of this unknown desert.

And out of the relentless east, land of enemies, rose the glaring sun. Like magic the frost melted off the rocks and the cool freshness of morning changed to a fiery breath. The sun climbed, and the leagues were as long as the hours. Down into a broad region of lava toiled the fugitives. Travel over the jagged crusts and through the poison-spiked cholla lamed the horses and made walking imperative. Yaqui drove his people before him, and some of the weakest fell by the way.

Out of the hot lava and stinging cactus the Indians toiled and entered a region of bare stone, cut by wind and water into labyrinthine passages where, even if they had left tracks on the hard rocks, few pursuers could have followed them. Yaqui told this to his people, told them he saw sheep on the peaks above and smelled water, and thus urged them on and on league after league towards distant purple heights. Vast and hard as had been the desert behind them, this strange upflung desert before them seemed vaster and grimmer. The trackless way led ever upward by winding passages and gorges – a gloomy and weird region of coloured stone. And over all reigned the terrible merciless sun.

Yaqui sacrificed horses to the thirst and hunger of his people and abandoned the horror of toil under the sun to a slower progress by night. Blanched and magnified under the great stars, the iron-bound desert of riven rock, so unreal and weird, brought forth a chant from the lips of Yaqui's women. His braves, stoic like himself, endured and plodded on, lightening burdens of the weaker and eventually carrying the children. That night passed and a day of stupor in the shade of sun-heated rock; another night led the fugitives onward and upward through a maze of shattered cliffs, black and wild. Day dawned once more, showing Yaqui by the pitiless light that only his men could endure much more of this dragging on.

He made camp there and encouraged his people by a faith that had come to him during the night – a whisper from the spirit of his forefathers – to endure, to live, to go to a beautiful end his vision could not see. Then Yaqui stalked alone off into the fastnesses of the rocks and prayed to his gods for guidance. All about him were silence, desolation, a grey barren world of rock, a black barren world of lava. Far as his falcon eye could see to the north and east and south stretched the illimitable glaring desert, rough, peaked, spiked, riven, ghastly with yellow slopes, bleak with its bare belts, terrible with its fluted and upflung plateaus, stone faced by endless ramparts and fast bound to the fading distance. From the west, up over the dark and forlorn heights, Yaqui heard the whispers of his dead forefathers.

Another dawn found Yaqui on the great heights with the sunrise at his back and with another and more promising world at his feet.

'Land of our forefathers!' he cried out sonorously to his people, gazing mutely down into the promised land. A vast grey-green valley yawned at their feet. Leagues of grassy, rock-ribbed, and tree-dotted slopes led down to a gleaming white stream, winding like a silver ribbon down the valley, to lose itself far in the lower country, where the coloured desert merged into an immense and boundless void of hazy blue – the sea.

'Great Water, where the sun sleeps,' said Yaqui with long arm outstretched. 'Yaqui's father's father saw it.'

Yaqui carried the boy and led the way down from the heights. Mountain sheep and wild horses and deer and quail that had never before seen man showed no fear of this invasion of their wild home. And Yaqui's people, footsore and starved, gazed round them and, in the seeming safety of this desert-locked valley with its grass and water and wood and abundant game, they took hope again and saw their prayers answered and happiness once more possible. New life flushed their veins. The long slopes, ever greener as they descended, were welcome to aching eyes so tired of the glaring expanses of the desert.

For an encampment Yaqui chose the head of the valley. Wide and gently sloping, with a rock-walled spring that was the source of the stream, and large ironwood trees and pines and paloverdes, this lonely hidden spot satisfied the longing in Yaqui's heart. Almost his joy was complete. But never could he feel wholly secure again, even had he wings of an eagle. For Yaqui's keen eyes had seen gold in the sands of the stream; and gold spelled the doom of the Indian. Still Yaqui was grateful and content. Not soon indeed would his people be tracked to this fastness, and perhaps never. He cautioned his braves to save their scant gun ammunition, sending them out with bows and arrows to kill the tame deer and antelope. The weary squaws no longer chanted the melancholy songs of their woe. The long travel had ended. They unpacked their stores under the wide-spreading pines, made fires to roast the meat that would soon be brought, and attended to the ailments of the few children left to them. Soon the naked little ones, starved and cut and worn as they were, took to the clear cool water like goslings learning to swim.

Yaqui, carrying his rifle, stalked abroad to learn more of this wonderful valley. Stretching at length along the stream, he drank deeply, as an Indian who loved mountain water. The glint of gold in the wet sand did not please him as had the sweetness of the cold water. Grasping up a handful of sand and pebbles, he rubbed and washed it in his palm. Tiny grains of gold and little nuggets of gold! Somewhere up at the head of this valley lay the mother lode from which the gold had washed down.

Yaqui knew that here was the treasure for which the white men would spill blood and sell their souls. But to the Indians – the Papagos, the Yumas, the man-eating Seris, and especially to the Yaquis – gold was no more than rock or sand, except that they hated it for the curse of white hunters it lured to the desert. Yaqui had found many a rich vein and ledge and placer of gold. He had hated them, and now more than any other he hated this new discovery. It would be a constant peril to his people. In times of flood this mountain stream would carry grains of gold as far as it flowed down on the desert. Yaqui saw in it a menace. But there was hope in the fact that many treasures of the desert heights would never be seen by white men. His father had told him that. This grey valley was high, cradled in the rocky uplands, and it might be inaccessible from below.

Yaqui set out to see. His stride was that of the strongest and tallest of his tribe, and distance meant little to him. Hunger gnawed at his vitals, but the long march across the wastes and heights had not tired him. Yaqui had never known exhaustion. Before the sun stood straight overhead he had ascertained that this valley of promise was shut off from the west and that the stream failed in impassable desert. From north and east he had travelled, and therefore felt a grim security. But to the south he turned apprehensive eyes. Long he tramped and high he climbed, at last to see that the valley, this land of his forefathers, could be gained from the south. Range and ridge sloped gradually to a barren desolate land of sun and cacti, far as his desert eyes could see. That must be the land of the Seris, the man-eaters. But it was a waterless hell in summer. No fear from the south till the winter rains fell! Yaqui returned to his camp, reaching there at sunset. There was joy in the dusky welcoming eyes of his young wife as she placed fresh meat before him.

'Yaqui's only son will live,' she said, and pointed to the frail boy as he slept. The chief gazed sombrely at the little brown face of his son, the last of his race.

Days passed. With rest and food and water the gloomy spirit of the Yaquis underwent a gradual change. The wild valley was an Indian's happy hunting ground, encompassed by lofty heights known only to sheep and eagles. Like wild animals, all savages, in the peace and loneliness of a secluded region, soon forgot past trials and fears. Still, the chief Yaqui did not forget, but as time passed and nothing disturbed the serenity of this hiding place his vigilance slowly relaxed. The wind and the sun and the solitude and the presence of antelope and wild horses always within sight of camp – these factors of primitive nature had a healing effect upon his sore heart. In the canyons he found graves and bones of his progenitors.

Days passed into weeks. The scarlet blossoms flamed at the long ends of the *ocatilla*; one morning the pale vordes, which had been bare and shiny green, appeared to have burst into full bloom, a yellow flowering that absorbed the sunlight; cacti opened great buds of magenta; from the canyon walls, on inaccessible ledges, hung the exquisite and rare desert flowers, *lluvia d'oro*, shower of gold; and many beautiful flowers lifted their faces out of the tall grasses. This magic of spring did not last long. The flowers faded, died, and blew away on the dry wind; the tall grasses slowly yellowed and bleached. Summer came. The glaring sun blazed over the eastern ramparts, burned white down over the still solemn valley, and sank like a huge ball of fire into the distant hazy sea. With the torrid heat of desert Sonora came a sense of absolute security to the chief Yaqui. His new home was locked in the furnace of the sun-blasted waste land. The clear spring of mountain water sank lower and lower, yet it did not fail. The birds and beasts that visited the valley attested to the nature of the surrounding country. So the time came when Yaqui forgot the strange feeling of distant steps upon his trail.

YAQUI

When autumn came all the valley was dry and grey and withered, except the green line along the stream and the perennial freshness of the cactus plants and the everlasting green of the paloverdes. With the winter season came the rains, and a wave of ever-brightening green flushed the vast valley from its eastern height of slope to the far distant mouth, where it opened into the barren breaks of the desert.

Manifestly the god of the Yaquis had not forgotten them. As the months passed child after child was born to the women of the tribe. Yaqui's dusky-eyed wife bore him a healthy girl baby. As the chief balanced the tiny brown form in his great hand he remembered speech of his own father's: 'Son, let the Yaquis go back to the mountains of the setting sun – to a land free from white men and gold and fire water, to the desert valley where deer graze with horses. There let the Yaquis multiply into a great people or perish from the earth.'

Yaqui watched his girl baby with a gleam of troubled hope lighting in his face. His father had spoken prophecy. There waved the green grass of the broad valley, dotted with wild horses, antelope, and deer grazing among his stock. Here in his hand lay another child – a woman child – and he had believed his son to be the last of his race. It was not too late. The god of the Indian was good. His branch of the Yaquis would mother and father a great people. But even as he fondled his babe the toe of his moccasin stirred grains of gold in the sand.

Love of life lulled Yaqui back into his dreams. To live, to have his people round him, to see his dusky-eyed wife at her work, to watch the little naked children playing in the grass, to look out over that rolling, endless green valley, so wild, so lonely, so fertile – such a proof of god in the desert – to feel the hot sun and the sweet wind and the cool night, to linger on the heights watching, listening, feeling, to stalk the keen-eyed mountain sheep, to eat fresh meat and drink pure water, to rest through the solemn still noons and sleep away the silent melancholy nights, to enjoy the games of his forefathers – wild games of riding and running – to steal off alone into the desert and endure heat, thirst, cold, dust, starvation while he sought the Indian gods hidden in the rocks, to be free of the white man whom he recognized as a superior and a baser being – to live like the eagles – to live – Yaqui asked no more.

Yaqui laid the baby back in the cradle of its mother's breast and stalked out as a chief to inspire his people.

In that high altitude the morning air was cold, exhilarating, sweet to breathe and wonderful to send the blood racing. Some winter mornings there was just a touch of frost on the leaves. The sunshine was welcome, the day was short, the night was long. Yaqui's people reverted to their old order of happy primitive life before the white man had come with greed for gold and lust to kill.

The day dawned in which Yaqui took his son out and put him upon a horse. As horsemen the Yaquis excelled all other Indian tribes of the Southwest. Boys were given lessons at an early age and taught to ride bareback. Thus as youths they developed exceeding skill and strength.

Some of the braves had rounded up a band of wild horses and had driven them into a rough rock-walled triangle, a natural trap, the opening of which they had closed with a rude fence. On this morning the Yaquis all assembled to see the wild horses broken. Yaqui, as an inspiration to his little son and to the other boys of the tribe, chose the vicious leader of the band as the horse he would first ride and break. High on the rocky wall perched the black-eyed boys, eager and restless, excited and wondering, some of them naked and all of them stretching out tousled black heads with shining ragged hair flying in the wind. The women and girls of the tribe occupied another position along the outcropping of grey wall, their colourful garments lending contrast to the scene.

The enclosure was wide and long, containing both level and uneven ground, some of which was grass and some sand and rock. A few ironwood trees and one huge paloverde, under which Indians were lolling, afforded shade. At the edge of the highest slope began a line of pine trees that reached up to the bare grey heights.

Yaqui had his braves drive the vicious leader of the wild horses out into the open. It was a stallion, of ungainly shape and rusty colour, no longer young. With ugly head high, nostrils distended, mouth open and ears up, showing the white of vicious, fiery eyes, it pranced in the middle of the circle drawn by its captors.

Yaqui advanced with his long leather *riata*, and, once clear of the ring of horsemen enclosing the stallion, he waved them back. Then as the wild steed plunged to and fro, seeking for an opening in that circle, Yaqui swung the long noose. He missed twice. The third cast caught its mark, the snarling nose of this savage horse. Yaqui hauled the lasso taut. Then with snort of fright the stallion lunged and reared, pawing the air. Yaqui, hauling hand over hand, pulled him down and approached him at the same time. Shuddering all over, breathing with hard snorts, the stallion faced his captor one moment, as if ready to fight. But fear predominated. He leaped away. At the end of that leap, so powerful was the strain on him, he went down in the sand. Up he sprang, wilder than ever, and dashed forward, dragging the Indian, gaining yards of the lasso. But the mounted Yaquis blocked his passage; he had to swerve; and as he ran desperately in a circle once more the giant chief hauled hand over hand on the rope. Suddenly Yaqui bounded in and with a tremendous leap, like the leap of a huge panther, he gained the back of the stallion and seemed to become fixed there. He dropped the lasso, and with the first startled jump of the stallion the noose loosened and slipped off. Except for Yaqui's great, long brown legs, with their strung bands of muscle set like steel, the stallion was free.

The stallion bolted for the open. Only the rock wall checked his headlong flight. Then he wheeled and ran along the wall, bounding over rocks and ditches, stretching out until, with magnificent stride, he was running at his topmost speed. Along one wall and then the other he dashed, round and round and across, until the moment came when panic succeeded to fury, and then his tremendous energies were directed to the displacement of his rider. Wildly he pitched. With head down, legs stiff, feet together, he plunged over the sand, ploughing up the dust, and bounding straight up. But he could not unseat his inexorable rider. Yaqui's legs banded his belly and were as steel. Then the stallion, now lashed into white lather of sweat and froth, lunged high to paw the air and scream and plunge down to pitch again. His motions soon lost their energy, though not their fury. Then he reached back with eyes of fire and open mouth to bite. Yaqui's huge fist met him, first on the right, then, as he turned, on the left. Last he plunged to his knees and with rumbling heave of anger he fell on his side, meaning to roll over his rider. But the Yaqui's leg on that side flashed high while his hands twisted hard in the long mane. When the foiled horse rose again Yaqui rose with him, again fixed tight on his back. Another dash and burst of running, wild and blind this time and plainly losing speed, showed the weakening of the stallion. And the time arrived when, spent and beaten, he fell in the sand.

'Let Yaqui's son learn to ride like his father,' said the chief to his gleeful, worshipping son.

Then the chief again stalked forth, drawn irresistibly by something in the hour.

'Let Yaqui's son watch and remember to tell his son's son,' he said.

He scattered his riders to block the few passages out of the valley and he ordered his son and all the women of the tribe and their children again to climb high on the rocks, there to watch. The Indian gods said this day marked the rejuvenation of their tribe. Let his son, who would be chief some day, and his people, see the great runner of the Yaquis.

Naked except for his moccasins, the giant chief broke into a slow trot that was habitual with him when alone on a trail; and he crossed the stream and the plots of sand, and headed out into the grassy valley where deer grazed with the horses. Yaqui selected the one that appeared largest and strongest of the herd and to it he called in a loud voice, meant as well for the spirit of his forefathers and for his gods, watching and listening from the heights: 'Yaqui runs to kill!'

The sleek grey deer left off their grazing and stood at gaze, with long ears erect. Then they bounded off. Yaqui broke from his trot into a long, swinging lope and the length of his stride was such that he seemed to fly over the ground. Up the valley the deer scattered and Yaqui ran in the trail of the one to which he had called. Half a mile off it halted to look back. Then it grazed a little, but soon lifted its head to look again. Yaqui ran on at the same easy, distance-devouring stride. Presently the deer dashed away and kept on until it was a mere speck in Yaqui's eyes. It climbed a deer trail that led over the heights, to be turned back there by one of Yaqui's braves. Then it crossed the wide valley to be turned back by insurmountable cliffs. Yaqui kept it in sight and watched it trot and stop, run and walk and stop again, all the way up the long grassy slope towards the head of the valley.

Here among rocks and trees Yaqui lost sight of his quarry, but he trailed it with scarcely a slackening of his pace. At length, coming out upon a level open bench, he saw the deer he had chosen to run to death. It was looking back.

Down the grassy middle of the vast valley, clear to the mouth where the stream tumbled off into space, across the wide level from slope to slope, back under the beetling heights, Yaqui pursued the doomed deer.

Leagues and leagues of fleet running had availed the deer nothing. It could not shake off the man. More and more the distance between them lessened. Terror now added to the gradual exhaustion of the four-footed creature, designed by Nature to escape its foes. Yaqui, perfect in all the primal attributes of man, was its superior. The race was not to the swift but to the enduring.

Within sight of his people and his little son Yaqui overtook the staggering deer and broke its neck with his naked hands. Then for an instant he stood erect over his fallen quarry, tall gaunt giant, bathed in the weird afterglow of sunset; and he lifted a long arm to the heights, as if calling upon his spirits there to gaze down upon the victory of the red man.

II

IT was towards evening of another day, all the hours of which had haunted Yaqui with a nameless oppression. Like a deer that scented a faint strange taint on the pure air Yaqui pointed his sensitive nose towards the east, whence came the soft wind.

Suddenly his strong vision quivered to the movement of distant objects on the southern slope. Halting, he fixed his gaze. Long line of moving dots! Neither deer nor sheep nor antelope travelled in that formation. The objects were men. Yaqui's magnified sight caught the glint of sunset red on shining guns. Mexican soldiers! That nameless haunting fear of the south, long lulled, now had its fulfilment.

YAQUI

Yaqui leaped with gigantic bounds down the slope. Like an antelope he sprang over rocks and dips, and once on the grassy downs he ran the swiftest race of his life. His piercing yells warned his people in time to save them from being surprised by the soldiers. The first shots of combat were fired as he hurdled the several courses of the stream. Yaqui saw the running and crawling forms of men in dusty blue – saw them aim short carbines – saw spurts of flame and puffs of smoke.

Yaqui's last few bounds carried him into the stone-walled encampment, and the whistling bullets that missed him told how the line of soldiers were spreading to surround the place. Yaqui flung himself behind the wall and crawled to where his braves knelt with guns and bows ready. Some of them were shooting. The women and children were huddled somewhere out of sight. Steel-jacketed bullets cracked on the rocks and whined away. Yaqui knew how poor was the marksmanship of the Mexicans; nevertheless it seemed to him they were shooting high. The position of the Indians was open to fire from several angles.

During a lull in the firing a hoarse yell pealed out. Yaqui knew Spanish. 'Surrender, Yaquis!' was the command. The Yaquis answered by well-aimed bullets that brought sharp cries from the soldiers. Soon the encampment appeared entirely surrounded. Reports came from all sides and bullets whistled high, spatting into the trees. Then occurred another lull in the firing. Again a voice pealed out: 'Surrender, Yaquis, save your lives!'

The Indians recognized their doom. Each man had only a few shells for his gun. Many had only bows and arrows. They would be shot like wolves in a trap. But no Yaqui spoke a word.

Nevertheless, when darkness put an end to their shooting there were only a few who had a shell left. The Mexicans grasped the situation and grew bold. They built fires off under the trees. They crept down to the walls and threw stones into the encampment and yelled derisively: 'Yaqui dogs!' They kept up a desultory shooting from all sides as if to make known to the Indians that they were surrounded and vigilantly watched.

At dawn the Mexicans began another heavy volleying, firing into the encampment without aim but with deadly intent. Then, yelling their racial hatred of the Yaquis, they charged the camp. It was an unequal battle. Outnumbered and without ammunition the Yaquis fought a desperate but losing fight. One by one they were set upon by several, sometimes by half a dozen, Mexicans and killed or beaten into insensibility.

Yaqui formed the centre of several storms of conflict. With clubbed rifle he was like a giant fighting down a horde of little men.

'Kill the big devil!' cried a soldier.

From the thick of that mêlée sounded Spanish curses and maledictons and dull thuds and groans as well. The Yaqui was a match for all that could surround him. A Mexican fired a pistol. Then the officer came running to knock aside the weapon. He shouted to his men to capture the Yaqui chief. The Mexicans pressed closer, dodging the sweeping rifle, and one of them plunged at the heels of the Indian. Another did likewise and they tripped up the giant, who was then piled upon by a number of cursing soldiers. Like a mad bull Yaqui heaved and tossed, but to no avail. He was overpowered and bound with a lasso, and tied upright to the paloverde under which he had so often rested.

His capture ended the battle. And the Mexicans began to run about, searching. Daylight had come. From under a ledge of rock the Indian women and children were driven. One lithe, quick boy eluded the soldiers. He slipped out of their hands and ran. As he looked back over his shoulder his dark face shone wildly. It was Yaqui's son. Like a deer he ran, not heeding the stern calls to halt. 'Shoot!' ordered the officer. Then the soldiers levelled rifles and began to fire. Puffs of dust struck up behind, beside and beyond that flying form. But none hit him. They shot at him until he appeared to be out of range. And all eyes watched him flee. Then a last bullet struck its flying mark. The watchers heard a shrill cry of agony and saw the lad fall.

All the Indians were tied hand and foot and herded into a small space and guarded as if they had been wild cattle.

After several hours of resting and feasting and celebrating what manifestly was regarded as a great victory, the officer ordered the capture of horses and the burning of effects not transportable. Soon the beautiful encampment of the Yaquis was a scene of blackened and smoking ruin. Then, driving the Yaquis in a herd before them, the Mexicans, most of them now mounted on Indian horses, faced the ascent of the slope by which they had entered the valley.

Far down that ragged mountain slope the Mexicans halted at the camp they had left when they made their attack on the Yaquis. Mules and burros, packsaddles and camp duffel occupied a dusty bench upon which there grew a scant vegetation. All round were black slopes of ragged lava and patches of glistening white cholla.

The Yaquis received but little water and food, no blankets to sleep on, no rest from tight bonds, no bandaging of their fly-tormented wounds. But they bore their ills as if they had none.

Yaqui sat with his back to a stone and when unobserved by the guards he would whisper to those of his people nearest him. Impassively but with intent faces they listened. His words had some strange, powerful, sustaining effect. And all the time his inscrutable gaze swept down off the lava heights to the hazy blue gulf of the sea.

YAQUI

Dawn disclosed the fact that two of the Yaquis were badly wounded and could not be driven to make a start. Perhaps they meant to force the death that awaited them farther down the trail; perhaps they were absorbed in the morbid gloom of pain and departing strength. At last the officer, weary of his subordinate's failure to stir these men, dragged at them himself, kicked and beat them, cursing the while. 'Yaqui dogs! You go to the henequen fields!'

The older of these wounded Indians, a man of lofty stature and mien, suddenly arose. Swiftly his brown arm flashed. He grasped a billet of wood from a packsaddle and struck the officer down. The blow lacked force. It was evident that the Yaqui, for all his magnificent spirit, could scarcely stand. Excitedly the soldiers yelled, and some brandished weapons. The officer staggered to his feet, livid and furious, snarling like a dog, and ordering his men to hold back, he drew a pistol to kill the Yaqui. The scorn, the contempt, the serenity of the Indian, instead of rousing his respect, incurred a fury which demanded more than death.

'You shall walk the cholla torture!' he shrieked, waving his pistol.

In northwest Mexico, for longer than the oldest inhabitant could remember, there had been a notorious rumour of the cholla torture that the Yaquis meted out to their Mexican captives. This cholla torture consisted of ripping the skin off the soles of Mexicans' feet and driving them to walk upon the cactus beds until they died.

The two wounded Indians, with bleeding raw feet, were dragged to the cholla torture. They walked the white, glistening, needle-spiked beds of cholla blind to the cruel jeers and mute wonderment and vile maledictions of their hereditary foes. The giant Yaqui who had struck down the officer stalked unaided across the beds of dry cholla. The cones crackled like live bits of steel. They collected on the Yaqui's feet until he was lifting pads of cactus. He walked erect, with a quivering of all the muscles of his naked bronze body, and his dark face was set in a terrible hardness of scorn for his murderers.

Then when the mass of cactus cones adhering to the Yaqui's feet grew so heavy that he became anchored in his tracks the Mexican officer, with a fury that was not all hate, ordered his soldiers to dispatch these two Indians, who were beyond the reach of a torture hideous and appalling to all Mexicans. Yaqui, the chief, looked on inscrutably, towering above the bowed heads of his women.

This execution sobered the soldiers. Not only extermination did they mean to mete out to the Yaqui, but an extermination of horrible toil, by which the Mexicans were to profit.

Montes, a Brazilian, lolled in the shady spot on the dock. The hot sun of Yucatan was more then enough for him. The still air reeked with a hot pungent odour of henequen. Montes had learned to hate the smell. He was in Yucatan on a mission for the Brazilian government and also as an agent to study the sisal product – an advantageous business for him, to which he had devoted himself with enthusiasm and energy.

But two unforeseen circumstances had disturbed him of late and rendered less happy his devotion to his tasks. His vanity had been piqued, his pride had been hurt, his heart had been stormed by one of Mérida's coquettish beauties. And the plight of the poor Yaqui Indians, slaves in the henequen fields, had so roused his compassion that he had neglected his work.

So, as Montes idled there in the shade, with his legs dangling over the dock, a time came in his reflection when he was confronted with a choice between the longing to go home and a strange desire to stay. He gazed out into the gulf. The gunboat *Esperanza* had come to anchor in the roads off Progreso. She had a cargo of human freight – Yaqui Indian prisoners from the wild plateaus of Northern Sonora – more slaves to be broken in the terrible henequen fields. At that moment of Montes's indecision he espied Lieutenant Perez coming down the dock at the head of a file of *rurales*.

Gazing at Perez intently, the Brazilian experienced a slight cold shock of decision. He would prolong his stay in Yucatan. Strange was the nameless something that haunted him. Jealous curiosity, he called it, bitterly. Perez had the favour of the proud mother of Senorita Dolores Mendoza, the coquettish beauty who had smiled upon Montes. She cared no more for Perez than she cared for him or any of the young bloods of Mérida. But she would marry Perez.

Montes rose and stepped out of the shade. His commission in Yucatan put him on common ground with Perez, but he had always felt looked down upon by this little Yucatecan.

'Buenos dias, senor,' replied Perez to his greeting. 'More Yaquis.'

A barge was made fast to the end of the dock and the Yaquis driven off and held there in a closely guarded group.

The time came when Perez halted the loading of henequen long enough to allow the prisoners to march up the dock between files of *rurales*. They passed under the shadows of the huge warehouses, out into a glaring square where the bare sand radiated veils of heat.

At an order from Perez, soldiers began separating the Yaqui women and children from the men. They were formed in two lines. Then Perez went among them, pointing out one, then another.

Montes suddenly grasped the significance of this scene and it had strange effect upon him. Yaqui father and son – husband and wife – mother and child did not yet realize that here they were to be parted – that this separation was forever. Then one young woman, tall, with striking dark face, beautiful with the grace of some wild creature, instinctively divined the truth and she cried out hoarsely. The silence, the stoicism of these Indians seemed broken. This woman had a baby in her arms. Running across the aisle of sand, she faced a huge Yaqui and cried aloud in poignant broken speech. This giant was her husband and the father of that dusky-eyed baby. He spoke, laid a hand on her and stepped out. Perez, who had been at the other end of the aisle, saw the movement and strode towards them.

'Back, Yaqui dogs!' he yelled stridently, and he flashed his bright sword.

With tremendous stride the Yaqui reached Perez and towered over him.

'*Capitan*, let my wife and child go where Yaqui goes,' demanded the Indian in deep voice of sonorous dignity. His Spanish was well spoken. His bearing was that of a chief. He asked what seemed his right, even of a ruthless enemy.

But Perez saw nothing but affront to his authority. At his order the *rurales* clubbed Yaqui back into his squad. They would have done the same for the stricken wife, had she not backed away from their threatening advances. She had time for a long agonized look into the terrible face of her husband. Then she was driven away in one squad and he was left in the other.

Montes thought he would forever carry in memory the tragic face of that Yaqui's wife. Indians had hearts and souls the same as white people. It was a ridiculous and extraordinary and base thing to be callous to the truth. Montes had spent not a little time in the pampas among the Gauchos and for that bold race he had admiration and respect. Indeed, coming to think about it, the Gauchos resembled these Yaquis. Montes took the trouble to go among English and American acquaintances he had made in Progreso, and learned more about this oppressed tribe.

The vast plateau of northwestern Mexico, a desert and mountainous region rich in minerals, was the home of the Yaquis. For more than one hundred and sixty years there had been war between the Yaquis and the Mexicans. And recently, following a bloody raid credited to the Yaquis, the government that happened to be in power determined to exterminate them. To that end it was hunting the Indians down, killing those who resisted capture, and sending the rest to the torture of the henequen fields.

But more interesting was the new information that Montes gathered. The Yaquis were an extraordinary, able-bodied, and intelligent people. Most of them spoke Spanish. They had many aboriginal customs and beliefs, but some were Roman Catholics. The braves made better miners and labourers than white men. Moreover, they possessed singular mechanical gifts and quickly learned to operate machines more efficiently than most whites. They possessed wonderful physical development and a marvellous endurance. At sixty years Yaquis had perfectly sound white teeth and hair as black as night. These desert men could travel seventy miles on foot in one day with only a bag of pinole. Water they could do without for days. And it was said that some of the Yaqui runners performed feats of speed, strength, and endurance beyond credence. Montes, remembering the seven-foot stature of that Yaqui chief and the spread of shoulders and the wonder of his spare lithe limbs, thought that he could believe much.

The act of Perez in deliberately parting the chief from his loved ones was cruel and despicable; and it seemed to establish in Montes's mind an excuse for the disgust and hate he had come to feel for the tyrannical little officer. But, being frank with himself, Montes confessed that this act had only fixed a hate he already had acquired.

The Brazilian convinced himself that he had intuitively grasped a portent apparently lost on Perez. One of those silent, intent-faced Yaquis was going to kill this epauletted scion of a rich Yucatecan house. Montes had read it in these faces. He had lived among the blood-spilling Gauchos and he knew the menace of silent fierce savages. And he did not make any bones about the admission to himself that he hoped some Yaqui would kill the peacocked Mexican. Montes had Spanish in him, and something of the raw passion of the Gauchos he admired; and it suited him to absorb this morbid presentiment. The Yaqui chief fascinated him, impelled him. Montes determined to learn where this giant had been sent and to watch him, win his confidence, if such a thing was possible. *Quièn sabe?* Montes felt more reasons than one for his desire to get under the skin of this big Yaqui.

III

IN the interior of Yucatan there were vast barren areas of land fit only for the production of henequen. Nothing but jungle and henequen would grow there. It was a limestone country. The soil could not absorb water. It soaked through. Here and there, miles apart, were *cenotes*, underground caverns full of water, and usually these marked the location of a hacienda of one of the rich planters. The climate was hot, humid, and for any people used to high altitudes it spelled death.

The plantation of Don Sancho Perez, father of the young lieutenant, consisted of fifty thousand acres. It adjoined the hundred-thousand acre tract of Donna Isabel Mendoza. The old Don was ambitious to merge the plantations into one, so that he could dominate the fibre output of the region. To this end he had long sought to win for his son the hand of Donna Isabel's beautiful daughter.

YAQUI

The big Yaqui Indian who had been wantonly separated from his wife by young Perez was in the squad of prisoners that had been picked out by the young officer to work on his father's plantation.

They were manacled at night and herded like wild beasts into a pen and watched by armed guards. They were routed out at dawn and put to work in the fibre fields. For food they had, each of them, a single lump of coarse soggy bread – one lump once every day. When the weaker among them began to lag, to slow down, to sicken, they were whipped to their tasks.

Yaqui knew that never again would he see his wife and baby – never hear from them – never know what became of them. He was worked like a galley slave, all the harder because of his great strength and endurance. He would be driven until he broke down.

Yaqui's work consisted of cutting henequen fibre leaves. He had a curved machete and he walked down the endless aisles between the lines of great century plants and from each plant he cut the lower circle of leaves. Each plant gave him a heavy load and he carried it to the nearest one of the hand-car tracks that crossed the plantation. The work of other Indians was to push hand cars along these tracks and gather the loads.

It took Yaqui six days to cut along the length of one aisle. And as far as he could see stretched a vast, hot, green wilderness with its never-ending lines and lanes, its labyrinthine maze of intersecting aisles, its hazy, copper-hued horizons speared and spiked by the great bayonet-like leaves. He had been born and raised on the rugged mountain plateaus far to the north, where the clear, sweet, cold morning air stung and the midday sun was only warm to his back, where there were grass and water and flowers and trees, where the purple canyons yawned and the black peaks searched the sky. Here he was chained in the thick, hot, moist night, where the air was foul, and driven out in the long day under a fiery sun, where the henequen reeked and his breath clogged in his throat and his eyes were burning balls and his bare feet were like rotting hoofs.

The time came when Montes saw that the Yaqui looked no more towards that northland which he would never see again. He dreamed no more hopeless dreams. Somehow he knew when his wife and baby were no more a part of him on the earth. For something within him died and there were strange, silent voices at his elbow. He listened to them. And in the depths of his being there boiled a maelstrom of blood. He worked on and waited.

At night in the close-crowded filthy pen, with the dampness of tropical dews stealing in, and all about him the silent prostrate forms of his stricken people, he lay awake and waited enduringly through the long hours till a fitful sleep came to him. By day in the henequen fields, with the furnace blasts of wind swirling down the aisles, with the moans of his beaten and failing comrades full in his ears, he waited with a Yaqui's patience.

He saw his people beaten and scourged and starved. He saw them sicken and fail – wilt under the hot sun – die in the henequen aisles – and be thrown like dogs into ditches with quicklime. One by one they went and when they were nearly all gone another squad took their places. The Yaqui recognized Indians of other tribes of his race. But they did not know him. He had greatly changed. Only the shell of him was left. And that seemed unbreakable, deathless. He did not tell these newcomers to the fields what torture lay in store for them. He might have been dumb. He only waited, adding day by day, in the horror of the last throes of his old comrades, something more to the hell in his blood. He watched them die and then the beginning of the end for his new comrades. They were doomed. They were to be driven till they dropped. And others would be brought to fill their places, till at last there were no Yaquis left. The sun was setting for his race.

The Yaqui and his fellow toilers had one day of rest – the Sabbath. There was no freedom. And always there were guards and soldiers. Sunday was the day of bull fights in the great corral at the hacienda. And on these occasions Yaqui was given extra work. Montes knew the Indian looked forward to this day. The old Don's son, Lieutenant Perez, would come down from the city to attend the fight. Then surely Yaqui fed his dark soul with more cunning, more patience, more promise.

It was the Yaqui's work to help drag disembowelled and dying horses from the bull ring and to return with sand to cover up the gory spots in the arena. Often Montes saw him look up at the crowded circle of seats and at the box where the grey old Don and his people and friends watched the spectacle. There were handsome women with white lace over their heads and in whose dark and slumbrous eyes lurked something that Yaqui knew. It was something that was in the race. Lieutenant Perez was there leaning towards the proud senorita. The Indian watched her with strange intensity. She appeared indifferent to the efforts of the *picadores* and the *banderilleros*, those men in the arena whose duty it was to infuriate the bull for the artist with the sword – the matador. When he appeared the beautiful senorita wakened to interest. But not until there was blood on the bright blade did she show the fire and passion of her nature. It was sight of blood that quickened her. It was death, then, that she wanted to see.

And last the Yaqui let his gaze rivet on the dark, arrogant visage of young Perez. Did not the great chief then become superhuman, or was it only Montes's morbid fancy? When Yaqui turned away, did he not feel a promise of fulfilment in the red haze of the afternoon sun, in the red tinge of the stained sand, in the red and dripping tongue of the tortured bull? Montes knew the Yaqui only needed to live long enough and there would be something. And death seemed aloof from this Indian. The ferocity of the desert was in him and its incalculable force of life. In his eyes had burned a seared memory of the violent thrust with which Perez had driven his wife and baby forever from his sight.

Montes's changed attitude evidently found favour in the proud senorita's eyes. She had but trifled with an earnest and humble suitor; to the advances of a man, bold, ardent, strange, with something unfathomable in his wooing, she was not indifferent. The fact did not cool Montes's passion, but it changed him somehow. The Spanish in him was the part that so ardently loved and hated; his mother had been French, and from her he had inherited qualities that kept him eternally in conflict with his instincts.

Montes had his living quarters in Mérida, where all the rich henequen planters had town houses. It was not a long horseback ride out to the haciendas of the two families in which Montes had become most interested. His habit of late, after returning from a visit to the henequen fields, had been to choose the early warm hours of the afternoon to call upon Senorita Mendoza. There had been a time when his calls had been formally received by the Donna Isabel, but of late she had persisted in her siesta, leaving Montes to Dolores. Montes had grasped the significance of this – the future of Dolores had been settled and there no longer was risk in leaving her alone. But Montes had developed a theory that the future of any young woman was an uncertainty.

The Mendoza town house stood in the outskirts of fashionable Mérida. The streets were white, the houses were white, the native Mayan women wore white, and always it seemed to Montes as he took the familiar walk that the white sun blazed down on an immaculate city. But there were dark records against the purity of Mérida and the Yaqui slave driving was one of them. The Mendoza mansion had been built with money coming from the henequen fields. It stood high on a knoll, a stately white structure looking down upon a formal garden, where white pillars and statues gleamed among green palms and bowers of red roses. At the entrance, on each side of the wide flagstone walk, stood a huge henequen plant.

On this day the family was in town and Montes expected that the senorita would see him coming. He derived pleasure from the assurance that, compared with Perez, he was someone good to look at. Beside him the officer was a swarthy undersized youth. But Montes failed to see the white figure of the girl and suffered chagrin for his vanity.

The day was warm. As he climbed the high, wide stone steps his brow grew moist and an oppression weighed upon him. Only in the very early morning here in Yucatan did he ever have any energy. The climate was enervating. No wonder it was that servants and people slept away the warmer hours. Crossing the broad stone court and the spacious outside hall, Montes entered the dim, dark, musty parlours and passed through to the patio.

Here all was colourful luxuriance of grass and flower and palm, great still ferns and trailing vines. It was not cool, but shady and moist. Only a soft spray of falling water and a humming of bees disturbed the deep silence. The place seemed drowned in sweet fragrance, rich and subtle, thickening the air so that it was difficult to breathe. In a bower roofed by roses lay Senorita Mendoza, asleep in a hammock.

Softly Montes made his way to her side and stood looking down at her. As a picture, as something feminine, beautiful and young and soft and fresh and alluring, asleep and therefore sincere, she seemed all that was desirable. Dolores Mendoza was an unusual type for a Yucatecan of Spanish descent. She was blonde. Her hair was not golden, yet nearly so; she had a broad, low, beautiful brow, with level eyebrows, and the effect of her closed lids was fascinating with their promise; her nose was small, straight, piquant, with delicate nostrils that showed they could quiver and dilate; her mouth, the best feature of her beauty, was as red as the roses that drooped over her, and its short curved upper lip seemed full, sweet, sensuous. She had the oval face of her class, but fair, not olive-skinned, and her chin, though it did not detract from her charms, was far from being strong. Perhaps her greatest attraction, seen thus in the slumber of abandon, was her slender form, round-limbed and graceful.

Montes gazed at her until he felt a bitterness of revolt against the deceit of Nature. She gladdened all the senses of man. But somehow she seemed false to the effect she created. If he watched her long in this beautiful guise of sleep she would deaden his intelligence. She was not for him. So he pulled a red rose and pushed it against her lips, playfully tapping them until she awoke. Her eyes unclosed. They were a surprise. They should have been blue, but they were tawny. Sleepy, dreamy, wonderful cat eyes they were, clear and soft, windows of the truth of her nature. Montes suddenly felt safe again, sure of himself.

'Ah, Señor Montes,' she said. 'You found me asleep. How long have you been here?'

'A long time, I think,' he replied, as he seated himself on a bench near her hammock. 'Watching you asleep, I forgot time. But alas! time flies – and you awoke.'

Dolores laughed. She had perfect white teeth that looked made to bite and enjoy biting. Her smile added to her charm.

'Sir, one would think you like me best asleep.'

'I do. You are always beautiful, Dolores. But when you are asleep you seem sincere. Now you are – Dolores Mendoza.'

'Who is sincere? You are not,' she retorted. 'I don't know you any more. You seem to try to make me dissatisfied with myself.'

'So you ought to be.'

'Why? Because I cannot run away with you to Brazil?'

'No. Because you look like an angel but are not one. Because your beauty, your charm, your sweetness deceive men. You seem the incarnation of love and joy.'

'Ah,' she cried, stretching out her round arms and drawing a deep breath that swelled her white neck. 'You are jealous. But I am happy. I have what I want. I am young and I enjoy. I love to be admired. I love to be loved. I love jewels, gowns, all I have, pleasure, excitement, music, flowers. I love to eat. I love to be idle, lazy, dreamy. I love to sleep. And you, horrid man, awake me to make me think.'

'That is impossible, Dolores,' he replied. 'You cannot think.'

'My mind works pretty well. But I'll admit I'm a little animal – a tawny-eyed cat. So, Montes, you must stroke me the right way or I will scratch.'

'Well, I'd rather you scratched,' said Montes. 'A man likes a woman who loves him tenderly and passionately one moment and tears his hair out the next.'

'You know, of course, señor,' she replied mockingly. 'The little Alva girl, for instance. You admired her. Perhaps she –'

'She is adorable,' he returneed complacently. 'I go to her for consolation.'

Dolores made a sharp passionate gesture, a contrast to her usual languorous movements. Into the sleepy, tawny eyes shot a dilating fire.

'Have you made love to her?' she demanded.

'Dolores, do you imagine any man could resist that girl?' he rejoined.

'Have you?' she repeated with heaving breast.

Montes discarded his tantalizing lightness. 'No, Dolores, I have not. I have lived in a torment lately. My love for you seems turning to hate.'

'No!' she cried, extending her hands. She softened. Her lips parted. If there were depths in her, Montes had sounded them.

'Dolores, tell me the truth,' he said, taking her hands. 'You have never been true.'

'I am true to my family. They chose Perez for me to marry – before I ever knew you. It is settled. I shall marry him. But –'

'But! Dolores, you love me?'

She drooped her head. 'Yes, señor – lately it has come to that. Ah! Don't – don't! Montes, I beg of you! You forget – I'm engaged to Perez.'

Montes released her. In her confession and resistance there was proof of his injustice. She was no nobler than her class. She was a butterfly in her fancies, a little cat in her greedy joy of physical life. But in her agitation he saw a deeper spirit.

'Dolores, if I had come first – before Perez – would you have given yourself to me?' he asked.

'Ah, señor, with all my heart?' she replied softly.

'Dearest – I think I must ask you to forgive me for – for something I can't confess. And now tell me – this reception given tomorrow by your mother – is that to announce your engagement to Perez?'

'Yes and I will be free then till fall – when – when –'

'When you will be married?'

She bowed assent and hesitatingly slid a white hand toward him.

'Fall! It's a long time. Dolores, I must go back to Brazil.'

'Ah, señor, that will kill me! Stay!' she entreated.

'But it would be dangerous. Perez dislikes me. I hate him. Something terrible might come of it.'

'That is his risk. I have consented to marry him. I will do my duty before and after. But I see no reason why I may not have a little happiness – of my own – until that day comes. Life for me will not contain all I could wish. I told you; now I am happy. But you were included. Señor, if you love me you will remain.'

'Dolores, can you think we will not suffer more?' he asked.

'I know we will afterwards. But we shall not now.'

'Now is perilous to me. To realize you love me! I did not think you capable of it. Listen! something – something might prevent your marriage – or happen afterward. All – all is so uncertain.'

'*Quièn sabe?*' she whispered; and to the tawny, sleepy languor of her eyes there came a fancy, a dream, a mystic hope.

'Dolores, if Perez were lost to you – one way or another – would you marry me?' he broke out huskily. Not until then had he asked her hand in marriage.

'If such forlorn hope will make you stay – make you happy – yes, Señor Montes,' was her answer.

There came a time when Yaqui was needed in the factory where the henequen fibre was extracted from the leaves. He had come to be a valuable machine – an instrument of toil that did not run down or go wrong. One guard said to another: 'That big black peon takes a lot of killing!' and then ceased to watch him closely. He might have escaped. He might have crossed the miles and miles of henequen fields to the jungle, and under that dense cover had made his way northward to the coast. Yaqui had many a chance. But he never looked towards the north.

At first they put him to feeding henequen leaves into the maw of a crushing machine. The juicy, sticky, odorous substance of the big twenty-pound leaf was squeezed into a pulp, out of which came the white glistening threads of fibre. These fibres made sisal rope – rope second in quality only to the manila.

By and by he was promoted. They put him in the pressing room to work on the ponderous iron press which was used to make the henequen bales. This machine was a high, strange-looking object, oblong in shape, like a box, opening in the middle from the top down. It had several distinct movements, all operated by levers. Long bundles of henequen were carried in from the racks and laid in the press until it was half full. Then a lever was pulled, the machine closed on the fibre and opened again. This operation was repeated again and again. Then it was necessary for the operator to step from his platform upon the fibre in the machine and stamp it down and jump upon it and press it closely all round. When this had been done the last time the machine seemed wide open and stuffed so full that it would never close. But when the lever was pulled the ponderous steel jaws shut closer and closer and locked. Then the sides fell away, to disclose a great smooth bale of henequen ready for shipment.

The Yaqui learned to operate this press so skillfully that the work was left to him. When his carriers went out to the racks for more fibre he was left alone in the room.

Some strange relation sprang up between Yaqui and his fibre press. For him it never failed to operate. He knew to a strand just how much fibre made a perfect bale. And he became so accurate that his bales were never weighed. They came out glistening, white, perfect to the pound. There was a strange affinity between this massive steel-jawed engine and something that lived in the Yaqui's heart, implacable and immutable, appalling in its strength to wait, in its power to crush.

IV

THERE seemed no failing of the endurance of this primitive giant, but his great frame had wasted away until it was a mere hulk. Owing to his value now to the hacienda, Yaqui was given rations in lieu of the ball of soggy bread; they were not, however, what the Indian needed. Montes at last won Yaqui's gratitude.

'Señor, if Yaqui wanted to eat it would be meat he needed,' said the chief. Then Montes added meat to the wine, bread, and fruit he secretly brought to the Indian.

When Montes began covert kindnesses to the poor Yaqui slaves the chief showed gratitude and pathos: 'Señor Montes is good – but the sun of the Yaquis is setting.'

Perez in his triumphant arrogance evidently derived pleasure from being magnanimous to the man he instinctively knew was his rival.

One day at the hacienda when Montes rode up to meet Donna Isabel and Dolores he found them accompanied by Perez and his parents. Almost immediately the young officer suggested gayly:

'Señor, pray carry Dolores off somewhere. My father has something to plan with Donna Isabel. It must be a secret from Dolores. Take her a walk – talk to her, señor – keep her excited – make love to her!'

'I shall be happy to obey. Will you come, señorita?' said Montes.

If they expected Dolores to pout, they were mistaken. Her slow, sleepy glance left the face of her future husband as she turned away silently to accompany Montes. They walked along the palm-shaded road, out towards the huge, open, sunny space that was the henequen domain.

'I hate Perez,' she burst out suddenly. 'He meant to taunt you. He thinks I am his slave – a creature without mind or heart. Señor, make love to me!'

'You will be his slave – soon,' whispered Montes bitterly.

'Never!' she exclaimed passionately.

They reached the end of the shady road. The mill was silent. Montes saw the Indian standing motionless close at hand, in the shade of the henequen racks.

'Dolores, did you mean what you just said?' asked Montes eagerly.

'That I will never be Perez's slave?'

'No; the other thing you said.'

'Yes, I did,' she replied. Make love to me, señor. It was his wish. I must learn to obey.'

With sullen scorn she spoke, not looking at Montes, scarcely realizing the actual purport of her speech. But when Montes took her in his arms she started back with a cry. He held her. And suddenly clasping her tightly he bent his head to kiss the red lips she opened to protest.

'Let me go!' she begged wildly. 'Oh – I did not – mean – Montes, not so! Do not make me –'

'Kiss me!' whispered Montes hoarsely, 'or I'll never let you go. It was his wish. Come, I dare you – I beg you!'

One wild moment she responded to his kiss, and then she thrust him away.

'Ah, by the saints!' she murmured with hands over her face. 'Now I will love you more – my heart will break.'

'Dolores, I can't let Perez have you,' declared Montes miserably.

'Too late, my dear. I am to be his wife.'

'But you love me, Dolores?'

'Alas! too true. I do. Oh, I never knew how well!' she cried.

'Let us run away,' he implored eagerly.

Mournfully she shook her head, and looking up suddenly she espied the Yaqui. His great burning cavernous eyes, like black fire, were fixed upon her.

'Oh, that terrible Yaqui,' she whispered. 'It is he who watches us at the bull fights – Let us go, Montes – Oh, he saw us – he saw me – Come!'

Upon their return to the house the old Don greeted them effusively. He seemed radiant with happiness. He had united two of the first families of Yucatan, which unison would make the greatest henequen plantation. The beautiful señorita had other admirers. But this marriage had unusual advantages. The peculiar location and productiveness of the plantations and the obstacles to greater and quicker output that would be done away with, and the fact that Lieutenant Perez through his military influence could work the fields with peon labour – these facts had carried the balance in favour of the marriage. The old Don manifestly regarded the arrangement as a victory for him which he owed to the henequen, and he had decided to make the wedding day one on which the rich product of the plantation should play a most important part.

'But how to bring in the henequen!' he concluded in perplexity. 'I've racked my brain. Son, I leave it to you.'

Young Perez magnificently waved the question aside. Possessing himself of his fiancée's reluctant hand, he spoke in a whisper audible to Montes. 'We planned the wedding presents. That was the secret. But you shall not see – not know – until we are married!'

Montes dropped his eyes and his brow knit thoughtfully. Later, as a peon brought his horse, he called Perez aside.

'I've an idea,' he said confidentially. 'Have Yaqui select the most perfect henequen fibre to make the most beautiful and perfect bale of henequen ever pressed. Have Yaqui place the wedding presents inside the bale before the final pressing. Then sent it to Donna Isabel's house after the wedding and open it there.'

Young Perez clapped his hands in delight. What a capital plan! He complimented Montes and thanked him and asked him to keep secret the idea. Indeed, the young lieutenant waxed enthusiastic over the plan. It would be unique; it would be fitting to the occasion. Perez would have Yaqui pick over and select from the racks the most perfect fibres, to be laid aside. Perez would go himself to watch Yaqui at his work. He would have Yaqui practice the operation of pressing, so at the momentous hour there could be no hitch. And on the wedding day Perez would carry the presents himself. No hands but his own would be trusted with those jewels, especially the exquisite pearls that were his own particular gift.

At last the day arrived for the wedding. It was to be a holiday. Yaqui alone was not to lie idle. It was to fall to him to press that bale of henequen and to haul it to the bride's home.

But Perez did not receive all his gifts when he wanted them. Messengers arrived late and some were yet to come. He went to the mill, however, and put Yaqui to work at packing the henequen in the press and building it up. The Indian was bidden to go so far with the bale, leaving a great hole in the middle for the gifts and to have the rest of the fibre all ready to pack and press. Perez would not trust anyone else with his precious secret; he himself would hurry down with the gifts, and secretly, for the manner of presentation was to be a great surprise.

Blue was the sky, white gold the sun, and the breeze waved the palms. But for Montes an invisible shadow hovered over the stately Mendoza mansion where Dolores was to be made a bride. The shadow existed in his mind and took mystic shape – now a vast, copper-hazed, green-spiked plain of henequen, and then the spectral gigantic shape of a toiling man, gaunt, grim, and fire-eyed.

Montes hid his heavy heart behind smiling lips and the speech of a courtier. He steeled himself against a nameless and portending shock, waiting for it even when his mind scorned the delusion.

But the shock did not come at sight of Señorita Dolores, magnificently gowned in white, beautiful, serene, imperious, with her proud, tawny eyes and proud, red lips. Nor when those sleepy strange eyes met his. Nor when the priest ended the ceremony that made her a wife.

He noted when Lieutenant Perez laughingly fought his way out of the crowd and disappeared. Then the unrest of Montes became a haunting suspense.

By and by the guests were directed out to the shaded west terrace, where in the centre of the wide stoned space lay a huge white glistening bale of henequen. Beside it stood the giant Yaqui, dark, motionless, aloof. The guests clustered round.

When Montes saw the Yaqui like a statue beside the bale of henequen, he sustained the shock for which he had been waiting. He slipped to the front of the circle of guests.

'Ah!' exclaimed the old Don, eyeing the bale of henequen with great satisfaction. 'This is the surprise our son had in store for us. Here is the jewel case – here are the wedding presents!'

The guests laughed and murmured their compliments.

'Where is Señor Perez?' demanded the Don as he looked round.

'The boy is hiding,' replied Donna Isabel. 'He wants to watch his bride when she sees the gifts.'

'No – he would not be there,' declared the old Don in perplexity. Something strange edged into his gladness of the moment. Suddenly he wheeled to the Yaqui. But he never spoke the question on his lips. Slowly he seemed to be blasted by those great black-fired orbs, as piercing as if they had been lightning from hell.

'Hurry, open the bale,' cried the bride, her sweet voice trilling above the gay talk.

Yaqui appeared not to hear. Was he looking into the soul of the father of Lieutenant Perez? All about him betrayed almost a superhuman intensity.

'Open the bale,' ordered the bride.

Yaqui cut the wire. He did not look at her. The perfectly folded and pressed strands of fibre shook and swelled and moved apart as if in relief. And like a great white jewel case of glistening silken threads the bale of henequen opened.

It commanded a stilling of the gay murmur – a sudden silence that had a subtle effect upon all. The beautiful bride, leaning closer to look, seemed to lose the light of the tawny proud eyes. Her mother froze into a creature of stone. The old Don, in slow strange action, as if his mind had but feeble sway over his body, bent his grey head away from the gaunt and terrible Yaqui. Something showed blue down under the centre strands of the glistening fibre. With a swift flash of his huge black hand, with exceeding violence, Yaqui swept the strands aside. Then from his lips pealed an awful cry. Instead of the jewels, there, crushed and ghastly, lay the bridegroom Perez.

Zane Grey

Tappan's Burro

I

TAPPAN gazed down upon the newly-born little burro with something of pity and consternation. It was not a vigorous offspring of the redoubtable Jennie, champion of all the numberless burros he had driven in his desert-prospecting years. He could not leave it there to die. Surely it was not strong enough to follow its mother. And to kill it was beyond him.

'Poor little devil!' soliloquized Tappan. 'Reckon neither Jennie nor I wanted it to be born . . . I'll have to hold up in this camp a few days. You can never tell what a burro will do. It might fool us an' grow strong all of a sudden.'

Whereupon Tappan left Jennie and her tiny, grey lop-eared baby to themselves, and leisurely set about making permanent camp. The water at this oasis was not much to his liking, but it was drinkable, and he felt he must put up with it. For the rest the oasis was desirable enough as a camping site. Desert wanderers like Tappan favoured the lonely water holes. This one was up under the bold brow of the Chocolate Mountains, where rocky wall met the desert sand, and a green patch of *palo verdes* and mesquites proved the presence of water. It had a magnificent view down a many-leagued slope of desert growths, across the dark belt of green and the shining strip of red that marked the Rio Colorado, and on to the upflung Arizona land, range lifting to range until the saw-toothed peaks notched the blue sky.

Locked in the iron fastnesses of these desert mountains was gold. Tappan, if he had any calling, was a prospector. But the lure of gold did not bind him to this wandering life any more than the freedom of it. He had never made a rich strike. About the best he could ever do was to dig enough gold to grubstake himself for another prospecting trip into some remote corner of the American Desert. Tappan knew the arid South-west from San Diego to the Pecos River and from Picacho on the Colorado to the Tonto Basin. Few prospectors had the strength and endurance of Tappan. He was a giant in build, and at thirty-five had never yet reached the limit of his physical force.

With hammer and pick and magnifying glass Tappan scaled the bare ridges. He was not an expert in testing minerals. He knew he might easily pass by a rich vein of ore. But he did his best, sure at least that no prospector could get more than he out of the pursuit of gold. Tappan was more of a naturalist than a prospector, and more of a dreamer than either. Many were the idle moments that he sat staring down the vast reaches of the valleys, or watching some creature of the wasteland, or marvelling at the vivid hues of desert flowers.

Tappan waited two weeks at this oasis for Jennie's baby burro to grow strong enough to walk. And the very day that Tappan decided to break camp he found signs of gold at the head of a wash above the oasis. Quite by chance, as he was looking for his burros, he struck his pick into a place no different from a thousand others there, and hit into a pocket of gold. He cleaned out the pocket before sunset, the richer for several thousand dollars.

'You brought me luck,' said Tappan, to the little grey burro staggering round its mother. 'Your name is Jenet. You're Tappan's burro, an' I reckon he'll stick to you.'

Jenet belied the promise of her birth. Like a weed in fertile ground she grew. Winter and summer Tappan patrolled the sand beats from one trading post to another and his burros travelled with him. Jenet had an especially good training. Her mother had happened to be a remarkably good burro before Tappan had bought her. And Tappan had patience; he found leisure to do things, and he had something of pride in Jenet. Whenever he happened to drip into Ehrenberg or Yuma, or any freighting station, some prospector always tried to buy Jenet. She grew as large as a medium-sized mule, and a three-hundred-pound pack was no load to discommode her.

Tappan, in common with most lonely wanderers of the desert, talked to his burro. As the years passed this habit grew, until Tappan would talk to Jenet just to hear the sound of his voice. Perhaps that was all which kept him human.

'Jenet, you're worthy of a happier life,' Tappan would say, as he unpacked her after a long day's march over the barren land. 'You're a ship of the desert. Here we are, with grub an' water, a hundred miles from any camp. An' what but you could have fetched me here? No horse! No mule! No man! Nothin' but a camel, an' so I call you ship of the desert. But for you an' your kind, Jenet, there'd be no prospectors, and few gold mines. Reckon the desert would be still an unknown waste . . . You're a great beast of burden, Jenet, an' there's no one to sing your praise.'

And of a golden sunrise, when Jenet was packed and ready to face the cool, sweet fragrance of the desert, Tappan was wont to say:

'Go along with you, Jenet. The mornin's fine. Look at the mountains yonder callin' us. It's only a step down there. All purple an' violet! It's the life for us, my burro, an' Tappan's as rich as if all these sands were pearls.'

But sometimes, at sunset, when the way had been long and hot and rough, Tappan would bend his shaggy head over Jenet, and talk in different mood.

'Another day gone, Jenet, another journey ended – an' Tappan is only older, wearier, sicker. There's no reward for your faithfulness. I'm only a desert rat, livin' from hole to hole. No home! No face to see . . . Some sunset, Jenet, we'll reach the end of the trail. An' Tappan's bones will bleach in the sands. An' no one will know or care!'

When Jenet was two years old she would have taken the blue ribbon in competition with all the burros of the Southwest. She was unusually large and strong, perfectly proportioned, sound in every particular, and practically tireless. But these were not the only characteristics that made prospectors envious of Tappan. Jenet had the common virtues of all good burros magnified to an unbelievable degree. Moreover, she had sense and instinct that to Tappan bordered on the supernatural.

During these years Tappan's trail crisscrossed the mineral region of the Southwest. But, as always, the rich strike held aloof. It was like the pot of gold buried at the foot of the rainbow. Jenet knew the trails and the water holes better than Tappan. She could follow a trail obliterated by drifting sand or cut out by running water. She could scent at long distance a new spring on the desert or a strange water hole. She never wandered far from camp so that Tappan had to walk far in search of her. Wild burros, the bane of most prospectors, held no charm for Jenet. And she had never yet shown any especial liking for a tame burro. This was the strangest feature of Jenet's complex character. Burrows were noted for their habit of pairing off, and forming friendships for one or more comrades. These relations were permanent. But Jenet still remained fancy free.

Tappan scarcely realized how he relied upon this big, grey, serene beast of burden. Of course, when chance threw him among men of his calling he would brag about her. But he had never really appreciated Jenet. In his way Tappan was a brooding, plodding fellow, not conscious of sentiment. When he bragged about Jenet it was her good qualities upon which he dilated. But what he really liked best about her were the little things of every day.

During the earlier years of her training Jenet had been a thief. She would pretend to be asleep for hours, just to get a chance to steal something out of camp. Tappan had broken this habit in its incipiency. But he never quite trusted her. Jenet was a burro.

Jenet ate anything offered her. She could fare for herself or go without. Whatever Tappan had left from his own meals was certain to be rich dessert for Jenet. Every meal time she would stand near the camp fire, with one great long ear drooping, and the other standing erect. Her expression was one of meekness, of unending patience. She would lick a tin can until it shone resplendent. On long, hard, barren trails Jenet's deportment did not vary from that where the water holes and grassy patches were many. She did not need to have grass or grain. Brittle-bush and sage were good fare for her. She could eat greasewood, a desert plant that protected itself with a sap as sticky as varnish and far more dangerous to animals. She could eat cacti. Tappan had seen her break off leaves of the pricky pear cactus, and stamp upon them with her forefeet, mashing off the thorns, so that she could consume the succulent pulp. She liked mesquite beans, and leaves of willow, and all the trailing vines of the desert. And she could subsist in an arid waste land where a man would have died in short order.

No ascent or descent was too hard or dangerous for Jenet, provided it was possible of accomplishment. She would refuse a trail that was impassable. She seemed to have an uncanny instinct both for what she could do, and what was beyond a burro. Tappan had never known her to fail on something to which she stuck persistently. Swift streams of water, always bugbears for burros, did not stop Jenet. She hated quicksand, but could be trusted to navigate it, if that were possible. When she stopped gingerly, with little inch steps, out upon thin crust of ice or salty crust of desert sink hole, Tappan would know that it was safe, or she would turn back. Thunder and lightning, intense heat or bitter cold, the sirocco sand storm of the desert, the white dust of the alkali wastes – these were all the same to Jenet.

One August, the hottest and driest of his desert experience, Tappan found himself working a most promising claim in the lower reaches of the Panamint Mountains on the northern slope above Death Valley. It was a hard country at the most favourable season; in August it was terrible.

The Panamints were infested by various small gangs of desperadoes – outlaw claim jumpers where opportunity afforded – and out-and-out robbers, even murderers where they could not get the gold any other way.

Tappan had been warned not to go into this region alone. But he never heeded any warnings. And the idea that he would ever strike a claim or dig enough gold to make himself an attractive target for outlaws seemed preposterous and not worth considering. Tappan had become a wanderer now from the unbreakable habit of it. Much to his amaze he struck a rich ledge of free gold in a canyon on the Panamints; and he worked from daylight until dark. He forgot about the claim jumpers, until one day he saw Jenet's long ears go up in the manner habitual with her when she saw strange men. Tappan watched the rest of that day, but did not catch a glimpse of any living thing. It was a desolate place, shut in, red-walled, hazy with heat, and brooding with an eternal silence.

Not long after that Tappan discovered boot tracks of several men adjacent to his camp and in an out-of-the-way spot, which persuaded him that he was being watched. Claim jumpers who were not going to jump his claim in this torrid heat, but meant to let him dig the gold and then kill him. Tappan was not the kind of man to be afraid. He grew wrathful and stubborn. He had six small canvas bags of gold and did not mean to lose them. Still he was worried.

'Now, what's best to do?' he pondered. 'I mustn't give it away that I'm wise. Reckon I'd better act natural. But I can't stay here longer. My claim's about worked out. An' these jumpers are smart enough to know it . . . I've got to make a break at night. What to do?'

Tappan did not want to cache the gold, for in that case, of course, he would have to return for it. Still, he reluctantly admitted to himself that this was the best way to save it. Probably these robbers were watching him day and night. It would be most unwise to attempt escaping by travelling up over the Panamints.

'Reckon my only chance is goin' down into Death Valley,' soliloquized Tappan, grimly.

The alternative thus presented was not to his liking. Crossing Death Valley at this season was always perilous, and never attempted in the heat of day. And at this particular time of intense torridity, when the day heat was unendurable and the midnight furnace gales were blowing, it was an enterprise from which even Tappan shrank. Added to this were the facts that he was too far west of the narrow part of the valley, and even if he did get across he would find himself in the most forbidding and desolate region of the Funeral Mountains.

Thus thinking and planning, Tappan went about his mining and camp tasks, trying his best to act natural. But he did not succeed. It was impossible, while expecting a shot at any moment, to act as if there was nothing on his mind. His camp lay at the bottom of a rocky slope. A tiny spring of water made verdure of grass and mesquite, welcome green in all that stark iron nakedness. His camp site was out in the open, on the bench near the spring. The gold claim that Tappan was working was not visible from any vantage point either below or above. It lay back at the head of a break in the rocky wall. It had two virtues – one that the sun never got to it, and the other that it was well hidden. Once there, Tappen knew he could not be seen. This, however, did not diminish his growing uneasiness. The solemn stillness was a menace. The heat of the day appeared to be augmenting to a degree beyond his experience. Every few moments Tappan would slip back through a narrow defile in the rocks and peep from his covert down at the camp. On the last of these occasions he saw Jenet out in the open. She stood motionless. Her long ears were erect. In an instant Tappan became strung with thrilling excitement. His keen eyes searched every approach to his camp. And at last in the gully below to the right he discovered two men crawling along from rock to rock. Jenet had seen them enter that gully and was now watching for them to appear.

Tappan's excitement gave place to a grimmer emotion. These stealthy visitors were going to hide in ambush, and kill him as he returned to camp.

'Jenet, reckon what I owe you is a whole lot,' muttered Tappan. 'They'd have got me sure . . . But now –'

Tappan left his tools, and crawled out of his covert into the jumble of huge rocks toward the left of the slope. He had a six-shooter. His rifle he had left in camp. Tappan had seen only two men, but he knew there were more than that, if not actually near at hand at the moment, then surely not far away. And his chance was to worm his way like an Indian down to camp. With the rifle in his possession he would make short work on the present difficulty.

'Lucky Jenet's right in camp!' said Tappan, to himself. 'It beats hell how she does things!'

Tappan was already deciding to pack and hurry away. On the moment Death Valley did not daunt him. This matter of crawling and gliding along was work unsuited to his great stature. He was too big to hide behind a little shrub or a rock. And he was not used to stepping lightly. His hobnailed boots could not be placed noiselessly upon the stones. Moreover, he could not progress without displacing little bits of weathered rock. He was sure that keen ears not too far distant could have heard him. But he kept on, making good progress around that slope to the far side of the canyon. Fortunately, he headed the gully up which his ambushers were stealing. On the other hand, this far side of the canyon afforded but little cover. The sun had gone down back of the huge red mass of the mountain. It had left the rocks so hot Tappan could not touch them with his bare hands.

He was about to stride out from his last covert and make a run for it down the rest of the slope, when, surveying the whole amphitheatre below him, he espied the two men coming up out of the gully, headed toward his camp. They looked in his direction. Surely they had heard or seen him. But Tappan perceived at a glance that he was the closer to the camp. Without another moment of hesitation, he plunged from his hiding place, down the weathered slope. His giant strides set the loose rocks sliding and rattling. The men saw him. The foremost yelled to the one behind him. Then they both broke into a run. Tappan reached the level of the bench, and saw he could beat either of them into the camp. Unless he were disabled! He felt the wind of a heavy bullet before he heard it strike the rocks beyond. Then followed the boom of a Colt. One of his enemies had halted to shoot. This spurred Tappan to tremendous exertion. He flew over the rough ground, scarcely hearing the rapid shots. He could no longer see the man who was firing. But the first one was in plain sight, running hard, not yet seeing he was out of the race.

When he became aware of that he halted, and dropping on one knee, levelled his gun at the running Tappan. The distance was scarcely sixty yards. His first shot did not allow for Tappan's speed. His second kicked up the gravel in Tappan's face. Then followed three more shots in rapid succession. The man divined that Tappan had a rifle in camp. Then he steadied himself, waiting for the moment when Tappan had to slow down and halt. As Tappan reached his camp and dove for his rifle, the robber took his time for his last aim, evidently hoping to get a stationary target. But Tappan did not get up from behind his camp duffel. It had been a habit of his to pile his boxes of supplies and roll of bedding together, and cover them with a canvas. He poked his rifle over the top of this and shot the robber.

Then, heaving up, he ran forward to get sight of the second one. This man began to run along the edge of the gully. Tappan fired rapidly at him. The third shot knocked the fellow down. But he got up, and yelling, as if for succour, he ran off. Tappan got another shot before he disappeared.

'Ahuh!' grunted Tappan, grimly. His keen gaze came back to survey the fallen robber, and then went out over the bench, across the wide mouth of the canyon. Tappan thought he had better utilize time to pack instead of pursuing the fleeing man.

Reloading the rifle, he hurried out to find Jenet. She was coming in to camp.

'Shore you're a treasure, old girl!' ejaculated Tappan.

Never in his life had he packed Jenet, or any other burro, so quickly. His last act was to drink all he could hold, fill his two canteens, and make Jenet drink. Then, rifle in hand, he drove the burro out of camp, round the corner of the red wall, to the wide gateway that opened down into Death Valley.

Tappan looked back more than he looked ahead. And he had travelled down a mile or more before he began to breath more easily. He had escaped the claim jumpers. Even if they did show up in pursuit now, they could never catch him. Tappan believed he could travel faster and farther than any men of that ilk. But they did not appear.

Perhaps the crippled one had not been able to reach his comrades in time. More likely, however, the gang had no taste for a chase in that torrid heat.

Tappan slowed his stride. He was almost as wet with sweat as if he had fallen into the spring. The great beads rolled down his face. And there seemed to be little streams of fire trickling down his breast. But despite this, and his laboured panting for breath, not until he halted in the shade of a rocky wall did he realize the heat.

It was terrific. Instantly then he knew he was safe from pursuit. But he knew also that he faced a greater peril than that of robbers. He could fight evil men, but he could not fight this heat.

So he rested there, regaining his breath. Already thirst was acute. Jenet stood near by, watching him. Tappan, with his habit of humanizing the burro, imagined that Jenet looked serious. A moment's thought was enough for Tappan to appreciate the gravity of his situation. He was about to go down into the upper end of Death Valley – a part of that country unfamiliar to him. He must cross it, and also the Funeral Mountains, at a season when a prospector who knew the trails and water holes would have to be forced to undertake it. Tappan had no choice.

His rifle was too hot to hold, so he stuck it in Jenet's pack; and, burdened only by a canteen of water, he set out, driving the burro ahead. Once he looked back up the wide-mouthed canyon. It appeared to smoke with red heat veils. The silence was oppressive.

Presently he turned the last corner that obstructed sight of Death Valley. Tappan had never been appalled by any aspect of the desert, but it was certain that here he halted. Back in his mountain-walled camp the sun had passed behind the high domes, but here it still held most of the valley in its blazing grip. Death Valley looked a ghastly, glaring level of white, over which a strange dull leaden haze drooped like a blanket. Ghosts of mountain peaks appeared to show dim and vague. There was no movement of anything. No wind! The valley was dead. Desolation reigned supreme. Tappan could not see far toward either end of the valley. A few miles of white glare merged at last into a leaden pall. A strong odour, not unlike sulphur, seemed to add weight to the air.

Tappan strode on, mindful that Jenet had decided opinions of her own. She did not want to go straight ahead or to right or left, but back. That was the one direction impossible for Tappan. And he had to resort to a rare measure – that of beating her. But at last Jenet accepted the inevitable and headed down into the stark and naked plain. Soon Tappan reached the margin of the zone of shade cast by the mountain and was now exposed to the sun. The difference seemed tremendous.

He had been hot, oppressed, weighted. It was now as if he was burned through his clothes, and walked on red-hot sands.

When Tappan ceased to sweat and his skin became dry, he drank half a canteen of water, and slowed his stride. Inured to desert hardship as he was, he could not long stand this. Jenet did not exhibit any lessening of vigour. In truth what she showed now was an increasing nervousness. It was almost as if she scented an enemy. Tappan never before had such faith in her. Jenet was equal to this task.

With that blazing sun on his back, Tappan felt he was being pursued by a furnace. He was compelled to drink the remaining half of his first canteen of water. Sunset would save him. Two more hours of such insupportable heat would lay him prostrate.

The ghastly glare of the valley took on a reddish tinge. The heat was blinding Tappan. The time came when he walked beside Jenet with a hand on her pack, for his eyes could no longer endure the furnace glare. Even with them closed he knew when the sun sank behind the Panamints. That fire no longer followed him. And the red left his eyelids.

With the sinking of the sun the world of Death Valley changed. It smoked with heat veils. But the intolerable constant burn was gone. The change was so immense that it seemed to have brought coolness.

In the twilight – strange, ghostly, sombre, silent as death – Tappan followed Jenet off the sand, down upon the silt and borax level, to the crusty salt. Before dark Jenet halted at a sluggish belt of fluid – acid, it appeared to Tappan. It was not deep. And the bottom felt stable. but Jenet refused to cross. Tappan trusted her judgement more than his own. Jenet headed to the left and followed the course of the strange stream.

Night intervened. A night without stars or sky or sound, hot, breathless, charged with some intangible current! Tappan dreaded the midnight furnace winds of Death Valley. He had never encountered them. He had heard prospectors say that any man caught in Death Valley when these gales blew would never get out to tell the tale. And Jenet seemed to have something on her mind. She was no longer a leisurely, complacent burro. Tappan imagined Jenet seemed stern. Most assuredly she knew now which way she wanted to travel. It was not easy for Tappan to keep up with her, and ten paces beyond him she was out of sight.

At last Jenet headed the acid wash, and turned across the valley into a field of broken salt crust, like the roughened ice of a river that had broken and jammed, then frozen again. Impossible was it to make even a reasonable headway. It was a zone, however, that eventually gave way to Jenet's instinct for direction. Tappan had long ceased to try to keep his bearings. North, south, east, and west were all the same to him. The night was a blank – the darkness a wall – the silence a terrible menace flung at any living creature. Death Valley had endured them millions of years before living creatures had existed. It was no place for a man.

Tappan was now three hundred and more feet below sea level, in the aftermath of a day that had registered one hundred and forty-five degrees of heat. He knew, when he began to lose thought and balance – when only the primitive instincts directed his bodily machine. And he struggled with all his will power to keep hold of his sense of sight and feeling. He hoped to cross the lower level before the midnight gales began to blow.

Tappan's hope was vain. According to record, once in a long season of intense heat, there came a night when the furnace winds broke their schedule, and began early. The misfortune of Tappan was that he had struck this night.

Suddenly it seemed that the air, sodden with heat, began to move. It had weight. It moved soundlessly and ponderously. But it gathered momentum. Tappan realized what was happening. The blanket of heat generated by the day was yielding to outside pressure. Something had created a movement of the hotter air that must find its way upward, to give place for the cooler air that must find its way down.

Tappan heard the first, low, distant moan of wind and it struck terror to his heart: It did not have an earthly sound. Was that a knell for him? Nothing was surer than the fact that the desert must sooner or later claim him as a victim. Grim and strong, he rebelled against the conviction.

That moan was a forerunner of others, growing louder and longer until the weird sound became continuous. Then the movement of wind was accelerated and began to carry a fine dust. Dark as the night was, it did not hide the pale sheets of dust that moved along the level plain. Tappan's feet felt the slow rise in the floor of the valley. His nose recognized the zone of borax and alkali and nitre and sulphur. He had reached the pit of the valley at the time of the furnace winds.

The moan augmented to a roar, coming like a mighty storm through a forest. It was hellish – like the woeful tide of Acheron. It enveloped Tappan. And the gale bore down in tremendous volume, like a furnace blast. Tappan seemed to feel his body penetrated by a million needles of fire. He seemed to dry up. The blackness of night had a spectral, whitish cast; the gloom was a whirling medium; the valley floor was lost in a sheeted, fiercely seeping stream of silt. Deadly fumes swept by, not lingering long enough to suffocate Tappan. He would gasp and choke – then the posion gas was gone on the gale. But hardest to endure was the heavy body of moving heat. Tappan grew blind, so that he had to hold to Jenet, and stumble along. Every gasping breath was a tortured effort. He could not bear a scarf over his face. His lungs heaved like great leather bellows. His heart pumped like an engine short of fuel. This was the supreme test for his never proven endurance. And he was all but vanquished.

Tappan's sense of sight and smell and hearing failed him. There was left only the sense of touch – a feeling of rope and burro and ground – and an awful insulating pressure upon all his body. His feet marked a change from salty plain to sandy ascent and then to rocky slope. The pressure of wind gradually lessened: the difference in air made life possible; the feeling of being dragged endlessly by Jenet had ceased. Tappan went his limit and fell into oblivion.

When he came to, he was suffering bodily tortures. Sight was dim. But he saw walls of rocks, green growths of mesquite, tamarack, and grass. Jenet was lying down, with her pack flopped to one side. Tappan's dead ears recovered to a strange murmuring, babbling sound. Then he realized his deliverance. Jenet had led him across Death Valley, up into the mountain range, straight to a spring of running water.

Tappan crawled to the edge of the water and drank guardedly, a little at a time. He had to quell terrific craving to drink his fill. Then he crawled to Jenet, and loosening the ropes of her pack, freed her from its burden. Jenet got up, apparently none the worse for her ordeal. She gazed mildly at Tappan, as if to say: 'Well, I got you out of that hole.'

Tappan returned her gaze. Were they only man and beast, alone in the desert? She seemed magnified to Tappan, no longer a plodding, stupid burro.

'Jenet, you – saved – my life,' Tappan tried to enunciate. 'I'll never – forget.'

Tappan was struck then to a realization of Jenet's service. He was unutterably grateful. Yet the time came when he did forget.

II

TAPPAN had a weakness common to all prospectors: any tale of a lost gold mine would excite his interest; and well-known legends of lost mines always obsessed him.

Peg-leg Smith's lost gold mine had lured Tappan to no less than half a dozen trips into the terrible shifting-sand country of southern California. There was no water near the region said to hide this mine of fabulous wealth. Many prospectors had left their bones to bleach white in the sun, finally to be buried by the ever blowing sands. Upon the occasion of Tappan's last escape from this desolate and forbidding desert, he had promised Jenet never to undertake it again. It seemed Tappan promised the faithful burro a good many things. It had been a habit.

TAPPAN'S BURRO

When Tappan had a particularly hard experience or perilous adventure, he always took a dislike to the immediate country where it had befallen him. Jenet had dragged him across the Death Valley, through incredible heat and the midnight furnace winds of that strange place; and he had promised her he would never forget how she had saved his life. Nor would he ever go back to Death Valley! He made his way over the Funeral Mountains, worked down through Nevada, and crossed the Rio Colorado above Needles, and entered Arizona. He travelled leisurely, but he kept going, and headed southeast towards Globe. There he cashed one of his six bags of gold, and indulged in the luxury of a complete new outfit. Even Jenet appreciated this fact, for the old outfit would scarcely hold together.

Tappan had the other five bags of gold in his pack; and after hours of hesitation he decided he would not cash them and entrust the money to a bank. He would take care of them. For him the value of this gold amounted to a small fortune. Many plans suggested themselves to Tappan. But in the end he grew weary of them. What did he want with a ranch, or cattle, or an outfitting store, or any of the businesses he now had the means to buy? Towns soon palled on Tappan. People did not long please him. Selfish interest and greed seemed paramount everywhere. Besides, if he acquired a place to take up his time, what would become of Jenet? That question decided him. He packed the burro and once more took to the trails.

A dim, lofty, purple range called alluringly to Tappan. The Superstition Mountains! Somewhere in that purple mass hid the famous treasure called the Lost Dutchman gold mine. Tappan had heard the story often. A Dutch prospector struck gold in the Superstitions. He kept the location secret. When he ran short of money, he would disappear for a few weeks, and then return with bags of gold. Wherever his strike, it assuredly was a rich one. No one ever could trail him or get a word out of him. Time passed. A few years made him old. During this time he conceived a liking for a young man, and eventually confided to him that some day he would tell him the secret of his gold mine. He had drawn a map of the landmarks adjacent to his mine. But he was careful not to put on paper directions how to get there. It chanced that he suddenly fell ill and saw his end was near. Then he summoned the young man who had been so fortunate as to win his regard. Now this individual was a ne'er-do-well, and upon this occasion he was half drunk. The dying Dutchman produced his map, and gave it with verbal directions to the young man. Then he died. When the recipient of this fortune recovered from the effects of liquor, he could not remember all the Dutchman had told him. He tortured himself to remember names and places. But the mine was up in the Superstition Mountains. He never remembered. He never found the lost mine, though he spent his life and died trying. Thus the story passed into the legend of the Lost Dutchman.

Tappan now had his try at finding it. But for him the shifting sands of the southern California desert or even the barren and desolate Death Valley were preferable to this Superstition Range. It was a harder country than the Pinacate of Sonora. Tappan hated cactus, and the Superstitions were full of it. Everywhere stood up the huge *sahuaro*, the giant cacti of the Arizona plateaus, tall like branchless trees, fluted and columnar, beautiful and fascinating to gaze upon, but obnoxious to prospector and burro.

One day from a north slope Tappan saw afar a wonderful country of black timber, above which zigzagged for many miles a yellow, winding rampart of rock. This he took to be the rim of the Mogollon Mesa, one of Arizona's freaks of nature. Something called Tappan. He was forever victim to yearnings for the unattainable. He was tired of heat, glare, dust, bare rock, and thorny cactus. The Lost Dutchman gold mine was a myth. Besides, he did not need any more gold.

Next morning Tappan packed Jenet and worked down off the north slopes of the Superstition Range. That night about sunset he made camp on the bank of a clear brook, with grass and wood in abundance – such a camp site as a prospector dreamed of but seldom found.

Before dark Jenet's long ears told of the advent of strangers. A man and a woman rode down the trail into Tappan's camp. They had poor horses, and led a pack animal that appeared too old and weak to bear up under even the meagre pack he carried.

'Howdy,' said the man.

Tappan rose from his task to his lofty height and returned the greeting. The man was middle-aged, swarthy, and rugged, a mountaineer, with something about him that Tappan instinctively distrusted. The woman was under thirty, comely in a full-blown way, with rich brown skin and glossy dark hair. She had wide-open black eyes that bent a curious possession-taking gaze upon Tappan.

'Care if we camp with you?' she inquired, and she smiled.

That smile changed Tappan's habit and conviction of a lifetime.

'No indeed. Reckon I'd like a little company,' he said.

Very probably Jenet did not understand Tappan's words, but she dropped one ear, and walked out of camp to the green bank.

'Thanks, stranger,' replied the woman. 'That grub shore smells good.' She hesitated a moment, evidently waiting to catch her companion's eye, then she continued. 'My name's Madge Beam. He's my brother Jake . . . Who might you happen to be?'

'I'm Tappan, lone prospector, as you see,' replied Tappan.

'Tappan! What's your front handle?' she queried, curiously.

'Fact is, I don't remember,' replied Tappan, as he brushed a huge hand through his shaggy hair.

'Ahuh? Any name's good enough.'

When she dismounted, Tappan saw that she had a tall, lithe figure, garbed in rider's overalls and boots. She unsaddled her horse with the dexterity of long practice. The saddlebags she carried over to the spot the man Jake had selected to throw the pack.

Tappan heard them talking in low tones. It struck him as strange that he did not have his usual reaction to an invasion of his privacy and solitude. Tappan had thrilled under those black eyes. And now a queer sensation of the unusual rose in him. Bending over his camp-fire tasks he pondered this and that, but mostly the sense of the nearness of a woman. Like most desert men, Tappan knew little of the other sex. A few that he might have been drawn to went out of his wandering life as quickly as they had entered it. This Madge Beam took possession of his thoughts. An evidence of Tappan's preoccupation was the fact that he burned his first batch of biscuits. And Tappan felt proud of his culinary ability. He was on his knees, mixing more flour and water, when the woman spoke from right behind him.

'Tough luck you burned the first pan,' she said. 'But it's a good turn for your burro. That shore is a burro. Biggest I ever saw.'

She picked up the burned biscuits and tossed them over to Jenet. Then she came back to Tappan's side, rather embarrassingly close.

'Tappan, I know how I'll eat, so I ought to ask you to let me help,' she said, with a laugh.

'No, I don't need any,' replied Tappan. 'You sit down on my roll of beddin' there. Must be tired, aren't you?'

'Not so very,' she returned. 'That is I'm not tired of ridin'.' She spoke the second part of this reply in lower tone.

Tappan looked up from his task. The woman had washed her face, brushed her hair, and had put on a skirt – a singularly attractive change. Tappan thought her younger. She was the handsomest woman he had ever seen. The look of her made him clumsy. What eyes she had! They looked through him. Tappan returned to his task, wondering if he was right in his surmise that she wanted to be friendly.

'Jake an' I drove a bunch of cattle to Maricopa,' she volunteered. 'We sold 'em, an' Jake gambled away most of the money. I couldn't get what I wanted.'

'Too bad! So you're ranchers. Once thought I'd like that. Fact is, down here at Globe a few weeks ago I came near buyin' some rancher out an' tryin' the game.'

'You did?' Her query had a low, quick eagerness that somehow thrilled Tappan. But he did not look up.

'I'm a wanderer. I'd never do on a ranch.'

'But if you had a woman?' Her laugh was subtle and gay.

'A woman! For me? Oh, Lord, no!' ejaculated Tappan, in confusion.

'Why not? Are you a woman hater?'

'I can't say that,' replied Tappan, soberly. 'It's just – I guess – no woman would have me.'

'Faint heart never won fair lady.'

Tappan had no reply for that. He surely was making a mess of the second pan of biscuit dough. Manifestly the woman saw this, for with a laugh she plumped down on her knees in front of Tappan, and rolled her sleeves up over shapely brown arms.

'Poor man! Shore you need a woman. Let me show you,' she said, and put her hands right down upon Tappan's. The touch gave him a strange thrill. He had to pull his hands away, and as he wiped them with his scarf he looked at her. He seemed compelled to look. She was close to him now, smiling in good nature, a little scornful of man's encroachment upon the house-wifely duties of a woman. A subtle something emanated from her – a more than kindness or gaiety. Tappan grasped that it was just the woman of her. And it was going to his head.

'Very well, let's see you show me,' he replied, as he rose to his feet.

Just then the brother Jake strolled over, and he had a rather amused and derisive eye for his sister.

'Wal, Tappan, she's not overfond of work, but I reckon she can cook,' he said.

Tappan felt greatly relieved at the approach of this brother. And he fell into conversation with him, telling something of his prospecting since leaving Globe, and listening to the man's cattle talk. By and by the woman called, 'Come an' get it!' Then they sat down to eat, and, as usual with hungry wayfarers, they did not talk much until appetite was satisfied. Afterward, before the camp fire, they began to talk again, Jake being the most discursive. Tappan conceived the idea that the rancher was rather curious about him, and perhaps wanted to sell his ranch. The woman seemed more thoughtful, with her wide black eyes on the fire.

'Tappan, what way you travellin'? finally inquired Beam.

'Can't say. I just worked down out of the Superstitions. Haven't any place in mind. Where does this road go?'

'To the Tonto Basin. Ever heard of it?'

'Yes, the name isn't new. What's in this Basin?'

The man grunted. 'Tonto once was home for the Apache. It's now got a few sheep an' cattlemen, lots of rustlers. An' say, if you like to hunt bear an' deer, come along with us.'

'Thanks. I don't know as I can,' returned Tappan, irresolutely. He was not used to such possibilities as this suggested.

Then the woman spoke up. 'It's a pretty country. Wild an' different. We live up under the rim rock. There's mineral in the canyons.'

Was it that about mineral which decided Tappan or the look in her eyes?

Tappan's world of thought and feeling underwent as great a change as this Tonto Basin differed from the stark desert so long his home. The trail to the log cabin of the Beams climbed many a ridge and slope and foothill, all covered with manzanita, mescal, cedar, and juniper, at last to reach the canyons of the Rim, where lofty pines and spruces lorded it over the under forest of maples and oaks. Though the yellow Rim towered high over the site of the cabin, the altitude was still great, close to seven thousand feet above sea level.

Tappan had fallen in love with this wild wooded and canyoned country. So had Jenet. It was rather funny the way she hung around Tappan, mornings and evenings. She ate luxuriant grass and oak leaves until her sides bulged.

There did not appear to be any flat places in this landscape. Every bench was either up hill or down hill. The Beams had no garden or farm or ranch that Tappan could discover. They raised a few acres of sorghum and corn. Their log cabin was of the most primitive kind, and outfitted poorly. Madge Beam explained that this cabin was their winter abode, and that upon the Rim they had a good house and ranch. Tappan did not inquire closely into anything. If he had interrogated himself, he would have found out that the reason he did not inquire was because he feared something might remove him from the vicinity of Madge Beam. He had thought it strange the Beams avoided wayfarers they had met on the trail, and had gone round a little hamlet Tappan had espied from a hill. Madge Beam, with woman's intuition, had read his mind, and had said: 'Jake doesn't get along so well with some of the villagers. An' I've no hankerin' for gun play.' That explanation was sufficient for Tappan. He had lived long enough in his wandering years to appreciate that people could have reasons for being solitary.

This trip up into the Rim Rock country bade fair to become Tappan's one and only adventure of the heart. It was not alone the murmuring, clear brook of cold mountain water that enchanted him, nor the stately pines, nor the beautiful silver spruces, nor the wonder of the deep, yellow-walled canyons, so choked with verdure, and haunted by wild creatures. He dared not face his soul, and ask why this dark-eyed woman sought him more and more. Tappan lived in the moment.

He was aware that the few mountaineer neighbours who rode that way rather avoided contact with him. Tappan was not so dense that he did not perceive that the Beams preferred to keep him from outsiders. This perhaps was owing to their desire to sell Tappan the ranch and cattle. Jake offered to let it go at what he called a low figure. Tappan thought it just as well to go out into the forest and hide his bags of gold. He did not trust Jake Beam, and liked less the looks of the men who visited this wilderness ranch. Madge Beam might be related to a rustler, and the associate of rustlers, but that did not necessarily make her a bad woman. Tappan sensed that her attitude was changing, and she seemed to require his respect. At first, all she wanted was his admiration. Tappan's long unused deference for women returned to him, and when he saw that it was having some strange softening effect upon Madge Beam, he redoubled his attentions. They rode and climbed and hunted together. Tappan had pitched his camp not far from the cabin, on a shaded bank of the singing brook. Madge did not leave him much to himself. She was always coming up to his camp, on one pretext of another. Often she would bring two horses, and make Tappan ride with her. Some of these occasions, Tappan saw, occurred while visitors came to the cabin. In three weeks Madge Beam changed from the bold and careless woman who had ridden down into his camp that sunset, to a serious and appealing woman, growing more careful of her person and adornment, and manifestly bearing a burden on her mind.

October came. In the morning white frost glistened on the split-wood shingles of the cabin. The sun soon melted it, and grew warm. The afternoons were still and smoky, melancholy with the enchantment of Indian summer. Tappan hunted wild turkey and deer with Madge, and revived his boyish love of such pursuits. Madge appeared to be a woman of the woods, and had no mean skill with the rifle.

One day they were high on the Rim, with the great timbered basin at their feet. They had come up to hunt deer, but got no farther than the wonderful promontory where before they had lingered.

'Somethin' will happen to me today,' Madge Beam said, enigmatically.

Tappan never had been much of a talker. But he could listen. The woman unburdened herself this day. She wanted freedom, happiness, a home away from this lonely country, and all the heritage of woman. She confessed it broodingly, passionately. And Tappan recognized truth when he heard it. He was ready to do all in his power for this woman and believed she knew it. But words and acts of sentiment came hard to him.

'Are you goin' to buy Jake's ranch?' she asked.

'I don't know. Is there any hurry?' returned Tappan.

'I reckon not. But I think I'll settle that,' she said, decisively.

'How so?'

'Well, Jake hasn't got any ranch,' she answered. And added hastily, 'No clear title, I mean. He's only homesteaded one hundred an' sixty acres, an' hasn't proved up on it yet. But don't you say I told you.'

Was Jake aimin' to be crooked?

'I reckon . . . An' I was willin' at first. But not now.'

Tappan did not speak at once. He saw the woman was in one of her brooding moods. Besides, he wanted to weigh her words. How significant they were! Today more than ever she had let down. Humility and simplicity seemed to abide with her. And her brooding boded a storm. Tappan's heart swelled in his broad breast. Was life going to dawn rosy and bright for the lonely prospector? He had money to make a home for this woman. What lay in the balance of the hour? Tappan waited, slowly realizing the charged atmosphere.

Madge's sombre eyes gazed out over the great void. But, full of thought and passion as they were, they did not see the beauty of that scene. But Tappan saw it. And in some strange sense the colour and wildness and sublimity seemed the expression of a new state of his heart. Under him sheered down the ragged and cracked cliffs of the Rim, yellow and gold and grey, full of caves and crevices, ledges for eagles and niches for lions, a thousand feet down to the upward edge of the long green slopes and canyons, and so on down and down into the abyss of forested ravine and ridge, rolling league on league away to the encompassing barrier of purple mountain ranges.

The thickets in the canyons called Tappan's eye back to linger there. How different from the scenes that used to be perpetually in his sight! What riot of colour! The tips of the green pines, the crests of the silver spruces, waved about masses of vivid gold of aspen trees, and wonderful cerise and flaming red of maples, and crags of yellow rock, covered with the bronze of frostbitten sumach. Here was autumn and with it the colours of Tappan's favourite season. From below breathed up the low roar of plunging brook; an eagle screeched his wild call; an elk bugled his piercing blast. From the Rim wisps of pine needles blew away on the breeze and fell into the void. A wild country, colourful, beautiful, bountiful. Tappan imagined he could quell his wandering spirit here, with this dark-eyed woman by his side. Never before had Nature so called him. Here was not the cruelty of flinty hardness of the desert. The air was keen and sweet, cold in the shade, warm in the sun. A fragrance of balsam and spruce, spiced with pine, made his breathing a thing of difficulty and delight. How for so many years had he endured vast open spaces without such eye-soothing trees as these? Tappan's back rested against a huge pine that tipped the Rim, and had stood there, stronger than the storms, for many a hundred years. The rock of the promontory was covered with soft brown mats of pine needles. A juniper tree, with its bright green foliage and lilac-coloured berries, grew near the pine, and helped to form a secluded little nook, fragrant and somehow haunting. The woman's dark head was close to Tappan, as she sat with her elbows on her knees, gazing down into the basin. Tappan saw the strained tensity of her posture, the heaving of her full bosom. He wondered, while his own emotions, so long darkened roused to the suspense of that hour.

Suddenly she flung herself into Tappan's arms. The act amazed him. It seemed to have both the passion of a woman and the shame of a girl. Before she hid her face on Tappan's breast he saw how the rich brown had paled, and then flamed.

'Tappan! . . . Take me away . . . Take me away from here – from that life down there,' she cried, in smothered voice.

'Madge, you mean take you away – and marry you?' he replied.

'Oh, yes – yes – marry me, if you love me . . . I don't see how you can – but you do, don't you? – Say you do.'

'I reckon that's what ails me, Madge,' he replied, simply.

'*Say* so, then,' she burst out.

'All right, I do,' said Tappan, with heavy breath. 'Madge, words don't come easy for me . . . But I think you're wonderful, an' I want you. I haven't dared hope for that, till now. I'm only a wanderer. But it'd be heaven to have you – my wife – an' make a home for you.'

'Oh – Oh!' she returned, wildly, and lifted herself to cling round his neck, and to kiss him. 'You give me joy. Oh, Tappan, I love you. I never loved any man before. I know now . . . An' I'm not wonderful – or good. But I love you.'

The fire of her lips and the clasp of her arms worked havoc in Tappan. No woman had ever loved him, let alone embraced him. To awake suddenly to such rapture as this made him strong and rough in his response. Then all at once she seemed to collapse in his arms and to begin to weep. He feared he had offended or hurt her, and was clumsy in his contrition. Presently she replied:

'Pretty soon – I'll make you – beat me. It's your love – your honesty – that's shamed me. Tappan, I was party to a trick to – sell you a worthless ranch . . . I agreed to – try to make you love me – to fool you – cheat you . . . But I've fallen in love with you. – An' my God, I care more for your love – your respect – than for my life. I can't go on with it. I've double-crossed Jake, an' all of them . . . Now, am I worth lovin'? Am I worth havin'?'

'More than ever, dear,' he said.

'You will take me away?'

'Anywhere – any time, the sooner the better.'

She kissed him passionately, and then, disengaging herself from his arms, she knelt and gazed earnestly at him. 'I've not told all. I will some day. But I swear now on my soul – I'll be what you think me.'

'Madge, you needn't say all that. If you love me – it's enough. More than I ever dreamed of.'

'You're a man. Oh, why didn't I meet you when I was eighteen instead of now – twenty-eight, an' all that between . . . But enough. A new life begins here for me. We must plan.'

'You make the plans an' I'll act on them.'

For a moment she was tense and silent, head bowed, hands shut tight. Then she spoke:

'Tonight we'll slip away. You make a light pack, that'll go on your saddle. I'll do the same. We'll hide the horses out near where the trail crosses the brook. An' we'll run off – ride out of the country.'

Tappan in turn tried to think, but the whirl of his mind made any reason difficult. This dark-eyed, full-bosomed woman loved him, had surrendered herself, asked only his protection. The thing seemed marvellous. Yet she knelt there, those dark eyes on him, infinitely more appealing than ever, haunting with some mystery of sadness and fear he could not divine.

Suddenly Tappan remembered Jenet.

'I must take Jenet,' he said.

That startled her. 'Jenet – Who's she?'

'My burro.'

'Your burro. You can't travel fast with that pack beast. We'll be trailed, an' we'll have to go fast . . . You can't take the burro.'

Then Tappan was startled. 'What! Can't take Jenet? – Why, I – I couldn't get along without her.'

'Nonsense. What's a burro? We must ride fast – do you hear?'

'Madge, I'm afraid I – I must take Jenet with me,' he said, soberly.

'It's impossible. I can't go if you take her. I tell you I've got to get away. If you want *me* you'll have to leave your precious Jenet behind.'

Tappan bowed his head to the inevitable. After all, Jenet was only a beast of burden. She would run wild on the ridges and soon forget him and have no need of him. Something strained in Tappan's breast. He did not see clearly here. This woman was worth more than all else to him.

'I'm stupid, dear,' he said. 'You see I never before ran off with a beautiful woman . . . Of course my burro must be left behind.'

Elopement, if such it could be called, was easy for them. Tappan did not understand why Madge wanted to be so secret about it. Was she not free? But then, he reflected, he did not know the circumstances she feared. Besides, he did not care. Possession of the woman was enough.

Tappan made his small pack, the weight of which was considerable owing to his bags of gold. This he tied on his saddle. It bothered him to leave most of his new outfit scattered around his camp. What would Jenet think of that? He looked for her, but for once she did not come in at meal time. Tappan thought this was singular. He could not remember when Jenet had been far from his camp at sunset. Somehow Tappan was glad.

After he had his supper, he left his utensils and supplies as they happened to be, and strode away under the trees to the trysting-place where he was to meet Madge. To his surprise she came before dark, and, unused as he was to the complexity and emotional nature of a woman, he saw that she was strangely agitated. Her face was pale. Almost a fury burned in her black eyes. When she came up to Tappan, and embraced him, almost fiercely, he felt that he was about to learn more of the nature of womankind. She thrilled him to his depths.

'Lead out the horses an don't make any noise,' she whispered.

Tappan complied, and soon he was mounted, riding behind her on the trail. It surprised him that she headed down country, and travelled fast. Moreover, she kept to a trail that continually grew rougher. They came to a road, which she crossed, and kept on through darkness and brush so thick that Tappan could not see the least sign of a trail. And at length anyone could have seen that Madge had lost her bearings. She appeared to know the direction she wanted, but travelling upon it was impossible, owing to the increasingly cut-up and brushy ground. They had to turn back, and seemed to be hours finding the road. Once Tappan fancied he heard the thud of hoofs other than those made by their own horses. Here Madge acted strangely, and where she had been obsessed by desire to hurry she now seemed to have grown weary. She turned her horse south on the road. Tappan was thus enabled to ride beside her. But they talked very little. He was satisfied with the fact of being with her on the way out of the country. Some time in the night they reached an old log shack by the roadside. Here Tappan suggested they halt, and get some sleep before dawn. The morrow would mean a long hard day.

'Yes, tomorrow will be hard,' replied Madge, as she faced Tappan in the gloom. He could see her big dark eyes on him. Her tone was not one of a hopeful woman. Tappan pondered over this. But he could not understand, because he had no idea how a woman ought to act under such circumstances. Madge Bean was a creature of moods. Only the day before, on the ride down from the Rim, she had told him with a laugh that she was likely to love him madly one moment and scratch his eyes out the next. How could he know what to make of her? Still, an uneasy feeling began to stir in Tappan.

They dismounted, and unsaddled the horses. Tappan took his pack and put it aside. Something frightened the horses. They bolted down the road.

'Head them off,' cried the woman, hoarsely.

Even on the instant her voice sounded strained to Tappan, as if she were choked. But, realizing the absolute necessity of catching the horses, he set off down the road on a run. And he soon succeeded in heading off the animal he had ridden. The other one, however, was contrary and cunning. When Tappan would endeavour to get ahead, it would trot briskly on. Yet it did not go so fast but what Tappan felt sure he would soon catch it. Thus walking and running, he put some distance between him and the cabin before he realized that he could not head off the wary beast. Much perturbed in mind, Tappan hurried back.

Upon reaching the cabin Tappan called to Madge. No answer! He could not see her in the gloom nor the horse he had driven back. Only silence brooded there. Tappan called again. Still no answer! Perhaps Madge had succumbed to weariness and was asleep. A search of the cabin and vicinity failed to yield any sign of her. But it disclosed the fact that Tappan's pack was gone.

Suddenly he sat down, quite overcome. He had been duped. What a fierce pang tore his heart! But it was for loss of the woman – not the gold. He was stunned, and then sick with bitter misery. Only then did Tappan realize the meaning of love and what it had done to him. The night wore on, and he sat there in the dark and cold and stillness until the grey dawn told him of the coming of day.

The light showed his saddle where he had left it. Near by lay one of Madge's gloves. Tappan's keen eye sighted a bit of paper sticking out of the glove. He picked it up. It was a leaf out of a little book he had seen her carry, and upon it was written in lead pencil:

> 'I am Jake's wife, not his sister. I double-crossed him an' ran off with you an' would have gone to hell for you. But Jake an' his gang suspected me. They were close on our trail. I couldn't shake them. So here I chased off the horses an' sent you after them. It was the only way I could save your life.'

Tappan tracked the thieves to Globe. There he learned they had gone to Phoenix – three men and one woman. Tappan had money on his person. He bought horse and saddle, and, setting out for Phoenix, he let his passion to kill grow with the miles and hours. At Phoenix he learned Beam had cashed the gold – twelve thousand dollars. So much of a fortune! Tappan's fury grew. The gang separated here. Beam and his wife took stage for Tucson. Tappan had no trouble in trailing their movements.

Gambling dives and inns and freighting posts and stage drivers told the story of the Beams and their ill-gotten gold. They went on to California, down into Tappan's country, to Yuma, and El Cajon, and San Diego. Here Tappan lost track of the woman. He could not find that she had left San Diego, nor any trace of her there. But Jake Beam had killed a Mexican in a brawl and had fled across the line.

Tappan gave up for the time being the chase of Beam, and bent his efforts to find the woman. He had no resentment toward Madge. He only loved her. All that winter he searched San Diego. He made of himself a peddler as a ruse to visit houses. But he never found a trace of her. In the spring he wandered back to Yuma, raking over the old clues, and so on back to Tucson and Phoenix.

This year of dream and love and passion and despair and hate made Tappan old. His great strength and endurance were not yet impaired, but something of his spirit had died out of him.

One day he remembered Jenet. 'My burro!' he soliloquized. 'I had forgotten her . . . Jenet!'

Then it seemed a thousand impulses merged in one drove him to face the long road toward the Rim Rock country. To remember Jenet was to grow doubtful. Of course she would be gone. Stolen or dead or wandered off! But then who could tell what Jenet might do? Tappan was both called and driven. He was a poor wanderer again. His outfit was a pack he carried on his shoulder. But while he could walk he would keep on until he found that last camp where he had deserted Jenet.

October was colouring the canyon slopes when he reached the shadow of the great wall of yellow rock. The cabin where the Beams had lived – or had claimed they lived – was a fallen ruin, crushed by snow. Tappan saw other signs of a severe winter and heavy snowfall. No horse or cattle tracks showed in the trails.

To his amaze his camp was much as he had left it. The stone fireplace, the iron pots, appeared to be in the same places. The boxes that had held his supplies were lying here and there. And his canvas tarpaulin, little the worse for wear of the elements, lay on the ground under the pine where he had slept. If any man had visited this camp in a year he had left no sign of it.

Suddenly Tappan espied a hoof track in the dust. A small track – almost oval in shape – fresh! Tappan thrilled through all his being.

'Jenet's track, so help me God!' he murmured.

He found more of them, made that morning. And, keen now as never before on her trail, he set out to find her. The tracks led up the canyon. Tappan came out into a little grassy clearing, and there stood Jenet, as he had seen her thousands of times. She had both long ears up high. She seemed to stare out at that meek, grey face. And then one of the long ears flopped over and drooped. Such perhaps was the expression of her recognition.

Tappan strode up to her.

'Jenet – old girl – you hung round camp – waitin' for me, didn't you?' he said, huskily, and his big hands fondled her long ears.

Yes, she had waited. She, too, had grown old. She was grey. The winter of that year had been hard. What had she lived on when the snow lay so deep? There were lion scratches on her back, and scars on her legs. She had fought for her life.

'Jenet, a man can never always tell about a burro,' said Tappan. 'I trained you to hang round camp an' wait till I came back . . . "Tappan's burro", the desert rats used to say! An' they'd laugh when I bragged how you'd stick to me where most men would quit. But brag as I did, I never knew you, Jenet. An' I left you – an' forgot. Jenet, it takes a human bein' – a man – a woman – to be faithless. An' it takes a dog or a horse or a burro to be great . . . Beasts? I wonder now . . . Well, old pard, we're goin' down the trail together, an' from this day on Tappan begins to pay his debt.'

III

TAPPAN never again had the old *wanderlust* for the stark and naked desert. Something had transformed him. The green and fragrant forests, the brown-aisled, pine-matted woodlands, the craggy promontories and the great coloured canyons, the cold granite water springs of the Tonto seemed vastly preferable to the heat and dust and glare and the emptiness of the waste lands. But there was more. The ghost of his strange and only love kept pace with his wandering steps, a spirit that hovered with him as his shadow. Madge Beam, whatever she had been, had showed to him the power of love to refine and ennoble. Somehow he felt closer to her here in the cliff country where his passion had been born. Somehow she seemed nearer to him here than in all those places he had tracked her.

So from a prospector searching for gold Tappan became a hunter, seeking only the means to keep soul and body together. And all he cared for was his faithful burro Jenet, and the loneliness and silence of the forest land.

He was to learn that the Tonto was a hard country in many ways, and bitterly so in winter. Down in the brakes of the basin it was mild in winter, the snow did not lie long, and ice seldom formed. But up on the Rim, where Tappan always lingered as long as possible, the storm king of the north held full sway. Fifteen feet of snow and zero weather were the rule in dead of winter.

An old native once warned Tappan: 'See hyar, friend, I reckon you'd better not get caught up in the Rim Rock country in one of our big storms. Fer if you do you'll never get out.'

It was a way of Tappan's to follow his inclinations, regardless of advice. He had weathered the terrible midnight storm of hot wind in Death Valley. What were storm and cold to him? Late autumn on the Rim was the most perfect and beautiful of seasons. He had seen the forest land brown and darkly green one day, and the next burdened with white snow. What a transfiguration! Then when the sun loosened the white mantling on the pines, and they had shed their burdens in drifting dust of white, and rainbowed mists of melting snow, and avalanches sliding off the branches, there would be left only the wonderful white floor of the woodland. The great rugged brown tree trunks appeared mightier and statelier in the contrast; and the green of foliage, the russet of oak leaves, the gold of the aspens, turned the forest into a world enchanting to the desert-seared eyes of this wanderer.

With Tappan the years sped by. His mind grew old faster than his body. Every season saw him lonelier. He had a feeling, a vague illusive foreshadowing that his bones, instead of bleaching on the desert sands, would mingle with the pine mats and the soft fragrant moss of the forest. The idea was pleasant to Tappan.

One afternoon he was camped in Pine Canyon, a timber-sloped gorge far back from the Rim. November was well on. The fall had been singularly open and fair, with not a single storm. A few natives happening across Tappan had remarked casually that such autumns sometimes were not to be trusted.

This late afternoon was one of Indian summer beauty and warmth. The blue haze in the canyon was not all the blue smoke from Tappan's camp-fire. In a narrow park of grass not far from camp Jenet grazed peacefully with elk and deer. Wild turkeys lingered there, loth to seek their winter quarters down in the basin. Grey squirrels and red squirrels barked and frisked, and dropped the pine and spruce cones, with thud and thump, on all the slopes.

Before dark a stranger strode into Tappan's camp, a big man of middle age, whose magnificent physique impressed even Tappan. He was a rugged, bearded giant, wide-eyed and of pleasant face. He had no outfit, no horse, not even a gun.

'Lucky for me I smelled your smoke,' he said. 'Two days for me without grub.'

'Howdy, Stranger,' was Tappan's greeting. 'Are you lost?'

'Yes an' no. I could find my way out down over the Rim, but it's not healthy down there for me. So I'm hittin' north.'

'Where's your horse an' pack?'

'I reckon they're with the gang thet took more of a fancy to them than me.'

'Ahuh! You're welcome here, stranger,' replied Tappan. 'I'm Tappan.'

'Ha! Heard of you. I'm Jess Blade, of anywhere. An' I'll say, Tappan, I was an honest man till I hit the Tonto.'

His laugh was frank, for all its note of grimness. Tappan liked the man, and sensed one who would be a good friend and bad foe.

'Come an' eat. My supplies are peterin' out, but there's plenty of meat.'

Blade ate, indeed, as a man starved, and did not seem to care if Tappan's supplies were low. He did not talk. After the meal he craved a pipe and tobacco. Then he smoked in silence, in a slow realizing content. The morrow had no fears for him. The flickering ruddy light from the camp fire shone on his strong face. Tappan saw in him the drifter, the drinker, the brawler, a man with good in him, but over whom evil passion or temper dominated. Presently he smoked the pipe out, and with reluctant hand knocked out the ashes and returned it to Tappan.

'I reckon I've some news thet'd interest you,' he said.

'You have?' queried Tappan.

'Yes, if you're the Tappan who tried to run off with Jake Beam's wife.'

'Well, I'm that Tappan. But I'd like to say I didn't know she was married.'

'Shore, I know thet. So does everybody in the Tonto. You were just meat for thet Beam gang. They had played the trick before. But accordin' to what I hear thet trick was the last fer Madge Beam. She never came back to this country. An' Jake Beam, when he was drunk, owned up thet she'd left him in California. Some hint at worse. Fer Jake Beam came back a harder man. Even his gang said thet.'

'Is he in the Tonto now?' queried Tappan, with a thrill of fire along his veins.

'Yep, thar fer keeps,' replied Blade, grimly. 'Somebody shot him.'

'Ahuh!' exclaimed Tappan with a deep breath of relief. There came a sudden cooling of the heat of his blood.

After that there was a long silence. Tappan dreamed of the woman who had loved him. Blade brooded over the camp fire. The wind moaned fitfully in the lofty pines on the slope. A wolf mourned as if in hunger. The stars appeared to obscure their radiance in haze.

'Reckon thet wind sounds like storm,' observed Blade, presently.

'I've heard it for weeks now,' replied Tappan.

'Are you a woodsman?'

'No, I'm a desert man.'

'Wal, you take my hunch an' hit the trail fer low country.'

This was well meant, and probably sound advice, but it alienated Tappan. He had really liked this hearty-voiced stranger. Tappan thought moodily of his slowly ingrowing mind, of the narrowness of his soul. He was past interest in his fellow men. He lived with a dream. The only living creature he loved was a lop-eared, lazy burro, growing old in contentment. Nevertheless that night Tappan shared one of his two blankets.

In the morning the grey dawn broke, and the sun rose without its brightness of gold. There was a haze over the blue sky. Thin, swift-moving clouds scudded up out of the southwest. The wind was chill, the forest shaggy and dark, the birds and squirrels were silent.

'Wal, you'll break camp today,' asserted Blade.

'Nope. I'll stick it out yet a while,' returned Tappan.

'But, man, you might get snowed in, an' up hyar thet's serious.'

'Ahuh! Well, it won't bother me. An' there's nothin' holdin' you.'

'Tappan, it's four days' walk down out of this woods. If a big snow set in, how'd I make it?'

'Then you'd better go out over the Rim,' suggested Tappan.

'No. I'll take my chance the other way. But are you meanin' you'd rather not have me with you? Fer you can't stay hyar.'

Tappan was in a quandary.

Some instinct bade him tell the man to go. Not empty-handed, but to go. But this was selfish, and entirely unlike Tappan as he remembered himself of old. Finally he spoke:

'You're welcome to half my outfit – go or stay.'

'Thet's mighty square of you, Tappan,' responded the other, feelingly. 'Have you a burro you'll give me?'

'No, I've only one.'

'Ha! Then I'll have to stick with you till you leave.'

No more was said. They had breakfast in a strange silence. The wind brooded its secret in the tree tops. Tappan's burro strolled into camp, and caught the stranger's eye.

'Wal, thet's shore a fine burro,' he observed. 'Never saw the like.'

Tappan performed his camp tasks. And then there was nothing to do but sit around the fire. Blade evidently waited for the increasing menace of storm to rouse Tappan to decision. But the greying over of sky and the increase of wind did not affect Tappan. What did he wait for? The truth of his thoughts was that he did not like the way Jenet remained in camp. She was waiting to be packed. She knew they ought to go. Tappan yielded to a perverse devil of stubbornness. The wind brought a cold mist, then a flurry of wet snow. Tappan gathered firewood, a large quantity. Blade saw this and gave voice to earnest fears. But Tappan paid no heed. By nightfall sleet and snow began to fall steadily. The men fashioned a rude shack of spruce boughs, ate their supper, and went to bed early.

It worried Tappan that Jenet stayed right in camp. He lay awake a long time. The wind rose, and moaned through the forest. The sleet failed, and a soft, steady downfall of snow gradually set in. Tappan fell asleep. When he awoke it was to see a forest of white. The trees were mantled with blankets of wet snow, the ground covered two feet on a level. But the clouds appeared to be gone, the sky, was blue, the storm over. The sun came up warm and bright.

'It'll all go in a day,' said Tappan.

'If this was early October I'd agree with you,' replied Blade. 'But it's only makin' fer another storm. Can't you hear thet wind?'

Tappan only heard the whispers of his dreams. By now the snow was melting off the pines, and rainbows shone everywhere. Little patches of snow began to drop off the south branches of the pines and spruces, and then larger patches, until by mid-afternoon white streams and avalanches were falling everywhere. All of the snow, except in shaded places on the north sides of trees, went that day, and half of that on the ground. Next day it thinned out more, until Jenet was finding the grass and moss again. That afternoon the telltale thin clouds raced up out of the southwest and the wind moaned its menace.

'Tappan, let's pack an' hit it out of hyar,' appealed Blade, anxiously. 'I know this country. Mebbe I'm wrong, of course, but it feels like storm. Winter's comin' shore.'

'Let her come,' replied Tappan, imperturbably.

'Say, do you want to get snowed in?' demanded Blade, out of patience.

'I might like a little spell of it, seein' it'd be new to me,' replied Tappan.

'But man, if you ever get snowed in hyar you can't get out.'

'That burro of mine could get me out.'

'You're crazy. Thet burro couldn't go a hundred feet. What's more, you'd have to kill her an' eat her.'

Tappan bent a strange gaze upon his companion, but made no reply. Blade began to pace up and down the small bare patch of ground before the camp fire. Manifestly, he was in a serious predicament. That day he seemed subtly to change, as did Tappan. Both answered to their peculiar instincts, Blade to that of self-preservation, and Tappan, to something like indifference. Tappan held fate in defiance. What more could happen to him?

Blade broke out again, in eloquent persuasion, giving proof of their peril, and from that he passed to amaze and then to strident anger. He cursed Tappan for a nature-loving idiot.

'An' I'll tell you what,' he ended. 'When mornin' comes I'll take some of your grub an' hit it out of hyar, storm or no storm.'

But long before dawn broke that resolution of Blade's had become impracticable. Both men were awakened by a roar of storm through the forest, no longer a moan, but a marching roar, with now a crash and then a shriek of gale! By the light of the smouldering camp fire Tappan saw a whirling pall of snow, great flakes as large as feathers.

Morning disclosed the setting in of a fierce mountain storm, with two feet of snow already on the ground, and the forest lost in a blur of white.

'I was wrong,' called Tappan to his companion. 'What's best to do now?'

'You damned fool!' yelled Blade. 'We've got to keep from freezin' an' starvin' till the storm ends an' a crust comes on the snow.'

For three days and three nights the blizzard continued, unabated in its fury. It took the men hours to keep a space cleared for their camp site, which Jenet shared with them. On the fourth day the storm ceased, the clouds broke away, the sun came out. And the temperature dropped to zero. Snow on the level just topped Tappan's lofty stature, and in drifts it was ten and fifteen feet deep. Winter had set in without compromise. The forest became a solemn, still, white world. But now Tappan had no time to dream. Dry firewood was hard to find under the snow. It was possible to cut down one of the dead trees on the slope, but impossible to pack sufficient wood to the camp. They had to burn green wood. Then the fashioning of snowshoes took much time. Tappan had no knowledge of such footgear. He could only help Blade. The men were encouraged by the piercing cold forming a crust on the snow. But just as they were about to pack and venture forth, the weather moderated, the crust refused to hold their weight, and another foot of snow fell.

'Why in hell didn't you kill an elk?' demanded Blake, sullenly. He had become darkly sinister. He knew the peril and he loved life. 'Now we'll have to kill an' eat your precious Jenet. An' mebbe she won't furnish meat enough to last till this snow weather stops an' a good freeze'll make travellin' possible.'

'Blade, you shut up about killin' an' eatin' my burro Jenet,' returned Tappan, in a voice that silenced the other.

Thus instinctively these men became enemies. Blade thought only of himself. Tappan had forced upon him a menace to the life of his burro. For himself Tappan had not one thought.

Tappan's supplies ran low. All the bacon and coffee were gone. There was only a small haunch of venison, a bag of beans, a sack of flour, and a small quantity of salt left.

'If a crust freezes on the snow an' we can pack that flour, we'll get out alive,' said Blade. 'But we can't take the burro.'

Another day of bright sunshine softened the snow on the southern exposures, and a night of piercing cold froze a crust that would bear a quick step of man.

'It's our only chance – an' damn slim at thet,' declared Blade.

Tappan allowed Blade to choose the time and method, and supplies for the start to get out of the forest. They cooked all the beans and divided them in two sacks. Then they baked about five pounds of biscuits for each of them. Blade showed his cunning when he chose the small bag of salt for himself and let Tappan take the tobacco. This quantity of food and a blanket for each Blade declared to be all they could pack. They argued over the guns, and in the end Blade compromised on the rifle, agreeing to let Tappan carry that on a possible chance of killing a deer or elk. When this matter had been decided, Blade significantly began putting on his rude snowshoes, that had been constructed from pieces of Tappan's boxes and straps and burlap sacks.

'Reckon they won't last long,' muttered Blade.

Meanwhile Tappan fed Jenet some biscuits and then began to strap a tarpaulin on her back.

'What you doin'?' queried Blade, suddenly.

'Gettin' Jenet ready,' replied Tappan.

'Ready! For what?'

'Why, to go with us.'

'Hell!' shouted Blade, and he threw up his hands in helpless rage.

Tappan felt a depth stirred within him. He lost his late taciturnity and silent aloofness fell away from him. Blade seemed on the moment no longer an enemy. He loomed as an aid to the saving of Jenet. Tappan burst into speech.

'I can't go without her. It'd never enter my head. Jenet's mother was a good faithful burro. I saw Jenet born way down there on the Rio Colorado. She wasn't strong. An' I had to wait for her to be able to walk. An' she grew up. Her mother died, an' Jenet an' me packed it alone. She wasn't no ordinary burro. She learned all I taught her. She was different. But I treated her same as any burro. An' she grew with the years. Desert men said there never was such a burro as Jenet. Called her Tappan's burro, an' tried to borrow an' buy an' steal her . . . How many times in ten years Jenet has done me a good turn I can't remember. But she saved my life. She dragged me out of Death Valley . . . An' then I forgot my debt. I ran off with a woman an' left Jenet to wait as she had been trained to wait . . . Well, I got back in time . . . An' now I'll not leave her. It may be strange to you, Blade, me carin' this way. Jenet's only a burro. But I won't leave her.'

'Man, you talk like thet lazy lop-eared burro was a woman,' declared Blade, in disgusted astonishment.

'I don't know women, but I reckon Jenet's more faithful than most of them.'

'Wal, of all the stark, starin' fools I ever run into you're the worst.'

'Fool or not, I know what I'll do,' retorted Tappan. The softer mood left him swiftly.

'Haven't you sense enough to see thet we can't travel with your burro?' queried Blade, patiently controlling his temper. 'She has little hoofs, sharp as knives. She'll cut through the crust. She'll break through in places. An' we'll have to stop to haul her out – mebbe break through ourselves. Thet would make us longer gettin' out.'

'Long or short we'll take her.'

Then Blade confronted Tappan as if suddenly unmasking his true meaning. His patient explanation meant nothing. Under no circumstances would he ever have consented to an attempt to take Jenet out of that snow-bound wilderness. His eyes gleamed.

'We've a hard pull to get out alive. An' hard-workin' men in winter must have meat to eat.'

Tappan slowly straightened up to look at the speaker.

'What do you mean?'

For answer Blade jerked his hand backward and downward, and when it swung into sight it held Tappan's worn and shining rifle. Then Blade, with deliberate force, that showed the nature of the man, worked the lever and threw a shell into the magazine. All the while his eyes were fastened on Tappan. His face seemed that of another man, evil, relentless, inevitable in his spirit to preserve his own life at any cost.

'I mean to kill your burro,' he said, in voice that suited his look and manner.

'No!' cried Tappan, shocked into an instant of appeal.

'Yes, I am, an' I'll bet, by God, before we get out of hyar you'll be glad to eat some of her meat!'

That roused the slow-gathering might of Tappan's wrath.

'I'd starve to death before I'd – I'd kill that burro, let alone eat her.'

'Starve an' be damned!' shouted Blade, yielding to rage.

Jenet stood right behind Tappan, in her posture of contented repose, with one long ear hanging down over her grey meek face.

'You'll have to kill me first,' answered Tappan, sharply.

'I'm good fer anythin' – if you push me,' returned Blade, stridently.

As he stepped aside, evidently so he could have unobstructed aim at Jenet, Tappan leaped forward and knocked up the rifle as it was discharged. The bullet sped harmlessly over Jenet. Tappan heard it thud into a tree. Blade uttered a curse. And as he lowered the rifle in suddenly deadly intent, Tappan grasped the barrel with his left hand. Then, clenching his right, he struck Blade a sodden blow in the face. Only Blade's hold on the rifle prevented him from falling. Blood streamed from his nose and mouth. He bellowed in hoarse fury,

'I'll kill you – fer thet!'

Tappan opened his clenched teeth: 'No, Blade – you're not man enough.'

Then began a terrific struggle for possession of the rifle. Tappan beat at Blade's face with his sledge-hammer fist. But the strength of the other made it imperative that he use both hands to keep his hold on the rifle. Wrestling and pulling and jerking, the men tore round the snowy camp, scattering the camp fire, knocking down the brush shelter. Blade had surrendered to a wild frenzy. He hissed his maledictions. His was the brute lust to kill an enemy that thwarted him. But Tappan was grim and terrible in his restraint. His battle was to save Jenet. Nevertheless, there mounted in him the hot physical sensations of the savage. The contact of flesh, the smell and sight of Blade's blood, the violent action, the beastly mien of his foe, changed the fight to one for its own sake. To conquer this foe, to rend him and beat him and beat him down, blow on blow!

Tappan felt instinctively that he was the stronger. Suddenly he exerted all his muscular force into one tremendous wrench. The rifle broke, leaving the steel barrel in his hands, the wooden stock in Blade's. And it was the quicker-witted Blade who used his weapon first to advantage. One swift blow knocked Tappan down. As he was about to follow it up with another, Tappan kicked his opponent's feet from under him. Blade sprawled in the snow, but was up again as quickly as Tappan. They made at each other, Tappan waiting to strike, and Blade raining blows on Tappan. These were heavy blows aimed at his head, but which he contrived to receive on his arms and the rifle barrel he brandished. For a few moments Tappan stood up under a beating that would have felled a lesser man. His own blood blinded him. Then he swung his heavy weapon. The blow broke Blade's left arm. Like a wild beast, he screamed in pain; and then, without guard, rushed in, too furious for further caution. Tappan met the terrible onslaught as before, and watching his chance, again swung the rifle barrel. This time, so supreme was the force, it battered down Blade's arm and crushed his skull. He died on his feet – ghastly and horrible change! – and swaying backward, he fell into the upbanked wall of snow, and went out of sight, except for his boots, one of which still held the crude snowshoe.

Tappan stared, slowly realizing.

'Ahuh, stranger Blade!' he ejaculated, gazing at the hole in the snow bank where his foe had disappeared. 'You were goin' to – kill an' eat – Tappan's burro!'

Then he sighted the bloody rifle barrel, and cast it from him. He became conscious of injuries which needed attention. But he could do little more than wash off the blood and bind up his head. Both arms and hands were badly bruised, and beginning to swell. But fortunately no bones had been broken.

Tappan finished strapping the tarpaulin upon the burro; and, taking up both his and Blade's supply of food, he called out, 'Come on, Jenet.'

Which way to go! Indeed, there was no more choice for him than there had been for Blade. Towards the Rim the snowdrift would be deeper and impassable. Tappan realized that the only possible chance for him was down hill. So he led Jenet out of camp without looking back once. What was it that had happened? He did not seem to be the same Tappan that had dreamily tramped into this woodland.

A deep furrow in the snow had been made by the men packing firewood into camp. At the end of this furrow the wall of snow stood higher than Tappan's head. To get out on top without breaking the crust presented a problem. He lifted Jenet up, and was relieved to see that the snow held her. But he found a different task in his own case. Returning to camp, he gathered up several of the long branches of spruce that had been part of the shelter, and carrying them out he laid them against the slant of snow he had to surmount, and by their aid he got on top. The crust held him.

Elated and with revived hope, he took up Jenet's halter and started off. Walking with his rude snowshoes was awkward. He had to go slowly, and slide them along the crust. But he progressed. Jenet's little steps kept her even with him. Now and then one of her sharp hoofs cut through, but not to hinder her particularly. Right at the start Tappan observed a singular something about Jenet. Never until now had she been dependent upon him. She knew it. Her intelligence apparently told her that if she got out of this snow-bound wilderness it would be owing to the strength and reason of her master.

Tappan kept to the north side of the canyon, where the snow crust was strongest. What he must do was to work up to the top of the canyon slope, and then keeping to the ridge travel north along it, and so down out of the forest.

Travel was slow. He soon found he had to pick his way. Jenet appeared to be absolutely unable to sense either danger or safety. Her experience had been of the rock confines and the drifting sands of the desert. She walked where Tappan led her. And it seemed to Tappan that her trust in him, her reliance upon him, were pathetic.

'Well, old girl,' said Tappan to her, 'it's a horse of another colour now – hey?'

At length he came to a wide part of the canyon, where a bench of land led to a long gradual slope, thickly studded with small pines. This appeared to be fortunate, and turned out to be so, for when Jenet broke through the crust Tappan had trees and branches to hold to while he hauled her out. The labour of climbing that slope was such that Tappan began to appreciate Blade's absolute refusal to attempt getting Jenet out. Dusk was shadowing the white aisles of the forest when Tappan ascended to a level. He had not travelled far from camp, and the fact struck a chill upon his heart.

To go on in the dark was foolhardy. So Tappan selected a thick spruce, under which there was a considerable depression in the snow, and here made preparations to spend the night. Unstrapping the tarpaulin, he spread it on the snow. All the lower branches of this giant of the forest were dead and dry. Tappan broke off many and soon had a fire. Jenet nibbled at the moss on the trunk of the spruce tree. Tappan's meal consisted of beans, biscuits, and a ball of snow, that he held over the fire to soften. He saw to it that Jenet fared as well as he. Night soon fell, strange and weirdly white in the forest, and piercingly cold. Tappan needed the fire. Gradually it melted the snow and made a hole, down to the ground. Tappan rolled up in the tarpaulin and soon fell asleep.

In three days Tappan travelled about fifteen miles, gradually descending, until the snow crust began to fail to hold Jenet. Then whatever had been his difficulties before, they were now magnified a hundredfold. As soon as the sun was up, somewhat softening the snow, Jenet began to break through. And often when Tappan began hauling her out he broke through himself. This exertion was killing even to a man of Tappan's physical prowess. The endurance to resist heat and flying dust and dragging sand seemed another kind from that needed to toil on in this snow. The endless snow-bound forest began to be hideous to Tappan. Cold, lonely, dreary, white, mournful – the kind of ghastly and ghostly winter land that had been the terror of Tappan's boyish dreams! He loved the sun – the open. This forest had deceived him. It was a wall of ice. As he toiled on, the state of his mind gradually and subtly changed in all except the fixed and absolute will to save Jenet. In some places he carried her.

The fourth night found him dangerously near the end of his stock of food. He had been generous with Jenet. But now, considering that he had to do more work than she, he diminished her share. On the fifth day Jenet broke through the snow crust so often that Tappan realized how utterly impossible it was for her to get out of the woods by her own efforts. Therefore Tappan hit upon the plan of making her lie on the tarpaulin, so that he could drag her. The tarpaulin doubled once did not bake a bad sled. All the rest of that day Tappan hauled her. And so all the rest of the next day he toiled on, hands behind him, clutching the canvas, head and shoulders bent, plodding and methodical, like a man who could not be defeated. That night he was too weary to build a fire, and too worried to eat the last of his food.

Next day Tappan was not unalive to the changing character of the forest. He had worked down out of the zone of the spruce trees; the pines had thinned out and decreased in size; oak trees began to show prominently. All these signs meant that he was getting down out of the mountain heights. But the fact, hopeful as it was, had drawbacks. The snow was still four feet deep on a level and the crust held Tappan only about half the time. Moreover, the lay of the land operated against Tappan's progress. The long, slowly descending ridge had failed. There were no more canyons, but ravines and swales were numerous. Tappan dragged on, stern, indomitable, bent to his toil.

When the crust let him down, he hung his snowshoes over Jenet's back, and wallowed through, making a lane for her to follow. Two days of such heart-breaking toil, without food or fire, broke Tappan's magnificent endurance. But not his spirit! He hauled Jenet over the snow, and through the snow, down the hills, and up the slopes, through the thickets, knowing that over the next ridge, perhaps, was deliverance. Deer and elk tracks began to be numerous. Cedar and juniper trees now predominated. An occasional pine showed here and there. He was getting out of the forest land. Only such mighty and justifiable hope as that could have kept him on his feet.

He fell often, and it grew harder to rise and go on. The hour came when the crust failed altogether to hold Tappan, and he had to abandon hauling Jenet. It was necessary to make a road for her. How weary, cold, horrible, the white reaches! Yard by yard Tappan made his way. He no longer sweated. He had no feeling in his feet or legs. Hunger ceased to gnaw at his vitals. His thirst he quenched with snow – soft snow now, that did not have to be crunched like ice. The pangs in his breast were terrible – cramps, constrictions, the piercing pains in his lungs, the dull ache of his overtaxed heart.

Tappan came to an opening in the cedar forest from which he could see afar. A long slope fronted him. It led down and down to open country. His desert eyes, keen as those of an eagle, made out flat country, sparsely covered with snow, and black dots that were cattle. The last slope! The last pull! Three feet of snow, except in drifts; down and down he plunged, making way for Jenet! All that day he toiled and fell and rolled down this league-long slope, wearing towards sunset to the end of his task, and likewise to the end of his will.

Now he seemed up and now down. There was no sense of cold or weariness. Only direction! Tappan still saw! The last of his horror at the monotony of white faded from his mind. Jenet was there, beginning to be able to travel for herself. The solemn close of endless day found Tappan arriving at the edge of the timbered country, where wind-bared patches of ground showed long, bleached grass. Jenet took to grazing.

As for Tappan, he fell with the tarpaulin, under a thick cedar, and with strengthless hands plucked and plucked at the canvas to spread it, so that he could cover himself. He looked again for Jenet. She was there, somehow a fading image, strangely blurred. She was grazing.

Tappan lay down, and stretched out, and slowly drew the tarpaulin over him.

A piercing cold night wind swept down from the snowy heights. It wailed in the edge of the cedars and moaned out towards the open country. Yet the night seemed silent. The stars shone white in a deep blue sky – passionless, cold, watchful eyes, looking down without pity or hope or censure. They were the eyes of Nature. Winter had locked the heights in its snowy grip. All night that winter wind blew down, colder and colder. Then dawn broke, steely, grey, with a flare in the east.

Jenet came back where she had left her master. Camp! As she had returned thousands of dawns in the long years of her service. She had grazed all night. Her sides that had been flat were now full. Jenet had weathered another vicissitude of her life. She stood for a while, in a doze, with one long ear down over her meek face. Jenet was waiting for Tappan.

But he did not stir from under the long roll of canvas. Jenet waited. The winter sun rose in cold yellow flare. The snow glistened as with a crusting of diamonds. Somewhere in the distance sounded a long-drawn, discordant bray. Jenet's ears shot up. She listened. She recognized the call of one of her kind. Instinct always prompted Jenet. Sometimes she did bray. Lifting her grey head she sent forth a clarion: '*Hee-haw hee-haw-haw – hee-haw how-e-e-e!*'

That stentorian call started the echoes. They pealed down the slope and rolled out over the open country, clear as a bugle blast, yet hideous in their discordance. But this morning Tappan did not awaken.

Frank C. Robertson

Three Little Calves

THE sharp clatter of iron-shod hoofs ringing on the hard rocks brought Stan Gordon out of his saddle doze and made him aware of his surroundings. Somebody, he thought, was in a great hurry.

Then he heard a volley of spluttering oaths in a boy's shrill voice mingled with the hoarse bellow of an enraged man. A minute later he could see the participants of the quarrel in a wide, rocky, and now almost dry creek bottom.

There were three people instead of two, though one man appeared to be an interested spectator. Things were happening rapidly between the other two. The big man whom the boy was cursing was striking out viciously with a quirt at the boy. Then his horse became frantic at the menacing quirt and lunged wildly forward against the boy's small pony, knocking it clear off its feet. The man's horse recovered itself enough to leap clear across the pony, and a moment later the pony scrambled to its feet.

Stan could not tell whether the boy had been trampled on or not, but for one horrifying second the lad's foot was caught in the stirrup. It came loose and the pony dashed into the brush and disappeared, while the boy covered his face with his hands and writhed in agony.

Stan noticed that whichever way the boy turned, his left foot remained in the same position. His leg had been broken somewhere between the knee and ankle.

Almost before the pony had got under way, Stan had leaped to the ground beside the injured boy. Neither of the other men made a move to dismount and help. Stan straightened out the leg into a more natural position. The boy gave a sharp cry of pain, and then bit his lip with a fierce determination to suppress his groans.

'I'll git you fer this, Skinner Butler,' he ground out as he flinched away from Stan. The latter saw that his eyes were tightly closed to keep back the tears.

'This ain't Butler, kid,' Stan said kindly. 'This is a white man.' Then he got to his feet and regarded the two men balefully.

They were both big men, but there their similarity ceased. The one who had caused the accident was dark and square built, and might not have been bad looking except for a wide, flat nose that gave his face a vicious and domineering expression. Now his thick lips were drawn back from strong, yellow teeth, and this manner was certainly not contrite.

The other man was younger, and though of about the same height and weight he was more inclined to fat. His broad face was liberally sprinkled with feckles, and he seemed stupid rather than brutal. But the inaction of the men in the face of the boy's painful predicament made Stan see red. His hand moved slowly to the handle of his gun.

'Are you fellows goin' to help me with this kid, or are yuh goin' to set there all day like knots on a log?' he demanded savagely. 'If yuh ain't gonna help, rattle yore hocks outa here, an' yuh'd better hit a zig-zag course while you're doin' it.'

'Help him, Speck,' the man called Butler said tersely. Then turning his horse he rode close to where Stan waited. His face was livid with passion.

'Lissen to me, young feller,' he snarled. 'Don't yuh ever make the mistake again o' tellin' me what to do or not do. I'm cock o' the walk hereabouts, an' if yuh make any moves with that gun I'll come back an' cram it down yore throat.' He wheeled his horse and rode on down the creek on a walk.

Stan decided that he could do the boy more good by helping him to a house than by fighting with the man who had caused the accident.

The other man now dismounted and came forward with an unashamed grin on his freckled face. He gave Stan a brief but not unfriendly nod.

'It's sure tough, Bobby,' he said soothingly. 'Butler sure didn't mean to bowl yore pony over. It was just one o' them things that happen. Grit yore teeth an' bear it.'

'He didn't care what he done when he was hittin' at me with his quirt,' the boy gritted.

'Yeah, but the things yuh called him had him crazy mad,' the other argued mildly. 'He'll be sorry when he has time to cool off.'

'Yo're damn right he'll be sorry,' the boy said bitterly.

'Forgit that stuff, Bobby,' the cowboy said impatiently. 'Nobody ever got anywhere by startin' a fight with Butler. No matter how far yuh go he'll go yuh one better.'

'Cut out the argument, an' let's talk about gittin' this kid home,' Stan interrupted sharply. 'Where does he live an' how are we goin' to git him there?'

'It's only 'bout half a mile to the house, an' I reckon we'd better carry him,' Speck said.

Stan got his pack horse and pulled his axe out from under the pack ropes. Chopping a couple of light poles, they constructed a fairly serviceable stretcher out of lass ropes and blankets. Then with Speck bearing the front end and leading the way, and Stan bearing the rear end and leading the horses they started for the house.

The house was located at the junction of two creeks, each of which was bordered by a fringe of willows. There was a large corral just across one of the creeks from the house, but there were no outbuildings to speak of. In fact, it looked more like a summer camp than a home. It was in the heart of the range, and certainly could never be used for farming purposes.

As they came in sight, a woman and a girl dressed in overalls left the house and came running toward them.

'Here's your mother an' Madge,' Speck informed the moaning boy. 'What'll we tell 'em?'

'Tell 'em my horse fell with me,' the boy gritted between gasps of pain. 'That's enough for 'em to know. I don't want Madge shootin' at that skunk till I get well. He's *my* meat, an' I want him.'

The women arrived white and breathless and ranged themselves on either side of the stretcher. Bobby managed a smile of reassurance, and Speck essayed an explanation.

Mrs Bronson wrung her hands helplessly and started to cry, but the black-eyed girl of seventeen showed no inclination toward tears. There was a stormy look in her eyes as she gazed at Speck, and her strong little chin came up pugnaciously.

'Lucky you two just happened along – when yuh did,' she said, and Stan thought there was a subtle inflection in her words.

The two men carried the boy into the two-room shack and laid him on a bed. Then they left him with the women and returned to the outdoors, where over a cigarette they swapped a few words of conversation. Then Mrs Bronson appeared at the door.

'I wish one of you boys would ride to town and get a doctor for Bobby,' she said timidly.

'I'll go, yuh bet your life,' Speck answered promptly. 'This feller here says he'll stick around an' help with the chores till yuh can git somebody else.'

'Oh, thank you so much,' the woman said, tearful with gratitude. 'I don't know what we'd have ever done if you boys hadn't happened along, an' Madge never could have tended to things alone. It was just all her an' Bobby both could do.'

In the face of such gratitude Stan could not have left them had he wanted to; he went back into the house.

'This brockle-faced neighbour o' yours has took it on himself to hire me out, so if there's anything special yuh want done let me know,' he said to the girl.

'I'm shore glad to hear that, stranger,' Bobby said earnestly. 'I don't know whether yo're any good or not, but yuh can help Madge some, an' them thirty cows has to be milked whether school keeps or not.'

Stan was utterly stricken at the mention of milk cows. Like every cowboy he had always considered it far beneath his dignity to milk cows. Now he knew why Speck had been so anxious to go for the doctor.

It was long past dark, and the doctor had come and gone, before the last cow was milked. There were only twenty-five giving milk, but that was more than plenty. Of the twenty-five Stan had milked seven. During the milking Stan tried to get some information out of the girl.

He had taken it for granted that Mrs Bronson was a widow. But no widow would have the nerve to bring a herd of dairy cows right out in the heart of the cattle range and expect to get away with it. Already Stan had guessed the reason for Skinner Butler's enmity. This was Butler's stock range, and naturally he resented having anyone camp down in the middle of it and eat his grass.

'Is your father livin'?' Stan asked abruptly.

'Yes.' Madge bent over a milk can and dragged it a few inches in the direction of the house.

'Where is he?' Stan persisted.

'He – he's away.'

'He is? Really!' Stan said mockingly, but the girl offered no further explanation.

They carried the milk to the house, after which the milk had to be separated and a hungry horde of dogey calves fed. Stan turned in at midnight completely worn out.

At the breakfast table next day, Stan casually mentioned the absent Bronson, but the family shut up like clams. He gave it up and returned to work. As he passed the calf pasture he paused to observe the condition of the calves, and idly counted them. To his surprise he counted more calves than there were cows giving milk, and he knew that there were others in the brush besides.

Quite a number of them were old enough to make their own way, and fully half of them were thoroughly weaned from their mothers. But none of them were branded. Stan resolved to correct that oversight at the first opportunity.

He was still leaning on the fence when he saw Speck approaching.

'Well, stranger, how's the dairy business?' Speck grinned.

'Worse.' Stan grunted. 'Are you stickin' around now to help pail these cows?'

'Nope, I'm too brutal.'

'Well, if yuh're so damn brutal, suppose yuh take a coupla hours off an' help me brand these calves.'

'Sure, I'll help yuh do that,' Speck agreed readily. 'Git your brandin' irons while I build a fire.'

It was slow, tedious work for just the two of them, but they finished up just before noon.

'That's the biggest calf crop I ever branded,' Stan commented as he put out the fire and gathered up the irons. 'Where'd they all come from?'

'Oh, the kids picked 'em up here an' there,' Speck answered carelessly. 'The poison was purty bad around here last spring an' a lot o' cows died. Madge an' Bobby used to pick up the orphan calves an' then raise 'em on a bucket.'

'Good for the kids, an' good for the calves,' Stan said.

'Yeah, but hard on the old man,' Speck drawled. 'He's in the jailhouse now.'

'What?' Stan demanded, startled.

'Yeah, for stealin' calves,' Speck nodded.

'Ah, hell, they can't put a man in jail because his kids kept a few dogey calves from starvin' to death,' Stan argued.

'I know they can't! but he's in there just the same – an' with the prospect of remaining' for quite some time. Yuh see, it don't offen happen, but once in a while a calf gits poison an' the cow escapes. Prob'ly that's what makes some range cows come a-bawlin' around this here corral, but some people don't think so,' Speck said dryly.

'So Skinner Butler had Bronson arrested, huh?' Stan supplemented.

'However did yuh guess it?' Speck grinned.

'I wasn't guessin',' Stan said curtly. 'I've met the animal, an' that's the kind of stunt I'd expect him to pull. But even if Bronson was goin' out on the range an' takin' calves from perfectly healthy cows, there's no way to prove it. The calves wasn't branded.'

'Well, there's a lot more calves than he's got cows, an' anyhow they're branded now,' Speck said with a grin.

'What the hell are you tryin' to pull?' Stan rasped. 'Is this a frame-up? You work for Butler, don't yuh? Why didn't yuh tell me these calves were disputed property?'

'Well, yuh never asked me,' Speck retorted. 'I don't wonta go blattin' other people's affairs to every stranger that comes along. Yuh asked me to help yuh brand 'em, an' I did. I s'posed yuh knew what yuh were doin'.'

'I think I git yuh, Speck,' Stan said balefully. 'You just happen to be one of those unfortunates who can't resist the chance to let other people git themselves into trouble. Yuh like trouble, but yuh ain't got the guts to git into it yourself. If trouble comes of this yuh'll assume just as much responsibility as I do, an' the Bronsons won't have none. Otherwise you an' me will mix.'

A sudden commotion interrupted any retort Speck might have been going to make. A bunch of range cattle had come out on the edge of the meadow and were heading for the salt troughs by the corral, when Madge came out with the two big and rather savage ranch dogs and set them on the cattle. In less than a minute the cattle were out of sight and headed down the canyon in a wild stampede, with the dogs at their heels while Madge shrilly urged them on.

'Now d'ye see why the Bronsons ain't pop'lar up here?' Speck demanded angrily. 'Now it'll take me half a day gittin' them cattle back up where the feed's good, an' look at the fat that'll be run off 'em.'

Stan was no less angry. He felt that it was an uncalled-for thing to do. Somebody could have saddled a horse and drove the cattle back up the range where they belonged.

He turned to Speck to volunteer his services in helping get the cattle back when he saw that worthy moving hurriedly toward his horse.

'See you again,' Speck grunted, and then angled away at a trot, skirting the calf pasture in a way that would enable him to enter the timber between two parallel trails, either of which would have been a more direct route. Then Stan saw a horseman loping down the meadow, and knew that Speck was manoeuvring to keep out of the newcomer's sight.

A moment later Stan recognized Skinner Butler. Butler was in a towering rage. He was headed straight for the house, but when he saw Stan he changed his course. He checked his horse a dozen paces away and dismounted. 'Yuh damn cow-chaser!' he said, and rushed straight at Stan.

Explanations were not required. Butler was too angry for speech and he was determined to vent his spleen upon the first object that came handy. Stan was glad that he happened to be there. Stan stepped forward to meet the cattleman's assault.

Stan ducked just in time to avoid a terrific swing aimed at his head, and countered with one of his own. It was a straight right jab and had every ounce of his strength behind it, and it landed flush on the bridge of Butler's nose. The man staggered back, but Stan was hurt fully as bad. He had forgotten his hands, sprained and swollen from unaccustomed milking, and the pain was intolerable. He realized then that he had to win the fight early or not at all, and he waded in with a staggering left that again rocked Butler. But he could not put the man down. And so far as hitting was concerned, Stan knew that he was through.

Before Butler could recover his balance, Stan rushed in and, lifting his bulky antagonist clear of the ground, slammed him down upon his back. Thus far the fight had been in his favour, but the advantage could not last. For a minute he managed to stay on top by a somewhat disconcerting use of his elbows, but he quickly found himself being turned underneath.

He took two stunning blows on the side of his head, but managed to protect his face. Then out of the corner of his eye he saw a stick descending with considerable force. It landed with a full thud somewhere above him, and was followed by a startled oath from Butler.

Again and again the stick rose and fell, and as Stan felt no more blows being rained upon him, he turned to look.

Butler was still seated astride his chest, but he was far too busy to deal out punishment. One arm was crooked protectingly over his head, and the other hand was making futile grabs at the club which Madge was wielding with such joyful abandon.

The stick was not heavy enough to knock the man out, but the way Butler was twisting his arm about in an effort to take each succeeding blow in a fresh place was evidence that the blows were painful.

Then, suddenly, the two dogs took a hand in the mêlée. Stan heard their menacing growls as they returned from their chase after the cattle, and then with a yell Butler sprang to his feet. For a moment pandemonium reigned supreme. Butler's horse had taken fright at the fury of the dogs and was racing away up the meadow. Madge had thrown away her club and was jumping up and down delightedly and urging the dogs on to the fray. Butler also was gyrating wildly, but not joyfully. One dog had fastened its fangs into the fleshy part of his hip, and was grimly hanging on, while the other was viciously snapping at the rancher's face and hands. This one made no effort to hang on, but already blood was dripping from half a dozen wounds on the man's arms and his shirt was being torn to ribbons.

Stan leaped to his feet and yelled at the dogs, but with Madge urging them on they would pay no attention to him. He made a lunge at the leaping dog and caught it by the tail as it missed Butler's nose by an inch. The dog turned upon him, but he yelled at Butler to climb the fence, and managed to hold the animal while he got on top of the corral.

Even there Butler's position was precarious. The fence was not very high and in order to keep out of the way of the still aggressive dogs he had to stand on the top pole, and maintain his balance by stooping over and grasping the top of a post which extended less than a foot above the top pole. His position was less dignified than it was secure.

'We licked him, I guess,' Madge announced with a sigh of great achievement.

Stan was as angry at the girl as he was at Butler or Speck, but as he looked at her he had to grin in spite of himself.

'Yeah, we've licked him all right, but what are we gonna do with him?' he queried.

'Poke him off the fence an' let the dogs have him,' the girl answered dispassionately. 'We don't want him.' She picked up a long pole and seemed about to carry out her judgement.

'No, yuh don't,' Stan said, and took the pole away from her. 'You saved me from a hell of a lickin' an' evidently had a good time doin' it but it was all caused by yuh settin' them dogs on the cattle. If I stick around here, that's got to stop. Them cattle will lose all the weight they've put on all summer on account o' that. I don't like Butler a bit better than you do, but I sure can't blame him fer bein' sore about that.'

'I will not stop,' the girl stated defiantly. 'Old Skinner brought it all on himself. We started out to drive the range cattle back but he wouldn't stand for it. My dad homesteaded this land an' Butler tried to keep us from usin' any range outside of it, an' we've got just as good a right to open range as he has. He said we didn't have any right to drive cattle on the open range an' threatened to have us all arrested. When we have to turn Butler's cows loose that way they're back in fifteen minutes, but when they git headed downhill with the dogs behind 'em they don't come back for a while.'

Again Stan saw the justice of the girl's case, even though he might not approve of her methods. The hoggish, arrogant Butler was altogether at fault.

'Yuh're pretty comtemptible, ain't yuh, Butler?' he addressed the man on the fence. 'Just for that, I'm goin' to let yuh roost right there on the fence till the dogs git tired o' watchin' yuh. An' yuh might as well git this straight, we're gonna hold enough range for these milk cows. We'll shoot square if you will, but these bulldozin' tactics o' yours have gotta stop.'

'Wait till I ketch you away from the damn girl an' her dogs,' Butler gritted. He tried to straighten up to make his threat emphatic, almost lost his balance, and swung his arms wildly to catch the post again as one of the dogs leaped at him.

'You look just like a treed cat when you're humped over like that,' Madge told the cattleman. An outburst of violent profanity followed, but apparently Madge was used to strong language, and the more Butler cursed the better she liked it.

Remembering Bobby's broken leg and the other persecutions the Bronson family had endured from the bully, Stan hadn't the heart to rob the girl of her revenge. He knew that dinner was ready, and he decided to let the cattleman cool his heels until the meal was over.

But before they had started to eat they saw Speck ride up to the corral, and after a few unsuccessful attempts succeed in getting his horse close enough to the fence to enable his boss to transfer from his ungraceful perch to the back of Speck's saddle. They rode away in the direction from which Speck had approached that morning, and the folks in the shack could see that Speck was laughing heartily, and that his employer's temper was not being improved by the puncher's unseemly mirth.

Just at dusk, when Stan and Madge were doing the separating, a sudden commotion on the part of the dogs warned them of the approach of another visitor. The dogs paid little or no attention to Speck for he had been around the place enough for them to know him. The uproar they had made now convinced both Stan and Madge that the visitor was Butler.

It was too dark for them to discern more than the bare outline of the horse and rider, but as the dogs went charging out they saw the horse spin around and break back down the trail with the dogs in hot pursuit, while Stan yelled frantically, but without avail for them to come back.

For a couple of hundred yards the yapping, snarling dogs kept up the pursuit; then the man got his horse under control and wheeled it about. At the same time came the report of a gun, and an orange streak stabbed downward. The voice of one dog was abruptly silenced, and with a woof of terror the other dog turned tail and fled back toward the house, but the horseman had now turned pursuer. Three times more the gun spurted flame, and then the horseman turned and disappeared in the brush.

Madge was already running toward where the dogs had last been heard, and Stan followed as soon as he could without spilling a lot of milk. But he was not surprised at Madge's dull pronouncement when he reached her.

'They're both dead. Butler – killed 'em.'

Stan said nothing. He blamed himself for not having thought to tie the dogs up. He might have known that Butler would kill them sooner or later. Butler was a most obstinate man, and he had only acted according to his nature.

Two more quiet days passed. Bobby was improving, and after Stan had insisted upon having a heart to heart talk with the family about Bronson he was able to cheer them up considerably. Bronson had been unable to raise bail, but his trial was only ten days distant, and Stan was quite certain that Butler could not bring enough real evidence to convict.

And then Stan got up one morning to find the calves all out. Investigation revealed that somebody had neatly cut a hole through the fence at the bottom of the pasture. While the dogs were alive it could not have been done, and there could be little doubt as to who had done it.

By the time the milking was done perhaps half of the calves had returned for their usual nourishment, but the rest seemed to have scattered in all directions. Stan spent the remainder of the day hunting for them.

When milking time came, he was still short of a number of calves. He was out early the next morning, and he congratulated himself that he had had the forethought to brand them, as otherwise many of them would surely have been lost. Then in the middle of the forenoon he made a discovery that robbed him of all his previous self-satisfaction. In the little open park a couple of miles from the ranch he came upon three calves bearing Bronson's brand, but they were sucking cows which were undubitably the property of Skinner Butler.

He scrutinized the branded calves closely. They looked very much like some of the calves he had branded, and it was evident that the same branding iron had been used; nevertheless he was quite convinced that those calves had never seen the inside of Bronson's corral. They did not have the appearance of ever having been separated from their mothers.

Stan did not doubt that Butler himself had put Bronson's brand on his own calves. And when he got back and discovered that the branding irons were in a slightly different place from where he had left them, it became near certainty. And with the evidence of those Bronson branded calves sucking Butler cows, Bronson would surely be convicted.

Stan hated to tell Madge, but if Butler was to be foiled then he would have to have to have some help, and the girl was the only help available.

That night a full moon was just rising to the south when Stan and Madge mounted their horses and rode away. It was three hours later when they returned.

'If there ain't no more than them three calves, I reckon your dad will soon be back here milkin' his cows, an' I for one won't be sorry,' Stan told the girl as they unsaddled.

The next day Stan was not greatly surprised to see Skinner Butler, Speck, and a mean-looking puncher called Slim Carl, riding up to the house. He was only surprised that they did not have a sheriff with them. As usual Speck was wearing a grin, but the other two showed nothing but cold hostility. Stan and Madge were near the corral, but with the exception of Speck, who greeted them with a nod and a smile, they were ignored, and the Butler trio rode on to the house.

'Hey, Mrs Bronson, come out here,' Butler called arrogantly.

'Yes? What do you want?' Mrs Bronson asked timidly as she came to the door.

'I want yore husband's brandin' irons,' Butler said curtly. 'Some o' the calves you people branded are back with their mothers now, an' I want them irons fer evidence. I got the goods on yore man this time. Where are they??

Mrs Bronson was too frightened to speak.

'You go to yore mother an' keep yore jib outa this,' Stan commanded Madge sternly. 'I'll do the talkin'.' Something in his tone made the girl obey rather hurriedly, nor did she venture to speak a word – a most unusual procedure for her.

'Just what d'ye want them irons for, Butler?' Stan asked.

'It's none o' yore business, but I'm turnin' 'em over to the prosecutin' attorney. If you know where they're at yuh'd better trot 'em out,' Butler said arrogantly.

'All right, I'll git 'em,' Stan said meekly, and walked down to where he had been sleeping. He rummaged in his warbag until he found his gun, and buckled it around his waist. Then he got the branding irons – there were two of them, for Bronson branded with a 37 – mounted his horse, and returned to where the men waited.

'Here's the irons, Brother Butler,' he said. 'An' here's another one to see that you don't monkey with 'em none.' He slapped the gun on his hip suggestively.

'What's the big idee?' Butler demanded, his eyes widening.

'Just this: if these brandin' irons are goin' to the prosecutin' attorney, I'm goin' along with 'em.' Stan had tied the branding irons behind his saddle, and it would obviously be dangerous to attempt to take them.

'You fellers collect them cows an' calves an' have 'em here by the middle o' the afternoon when I git back with the sheriff an' the prosecutin' attorney,' Butler directed his two men. 'Come on, feller,' he added grimly to Stan. 'An' don't try running' off with them irons, because I pack one myself.'

Bútler set a fast pace, and Stan was not loath to keep up with him. Two hours later they drew up in front of the courthouse. A veranda-like porch stretched along one side of the building about six feet above a cement walk, and here half a dozen lazy office holders were taking their comfort. The sheriff and two deputies were easily recognizable by their badges, but Butler addressed himself to another man, who proved to be the county attorney.

'I've got the final evidence in that Bronson case, Mr Madsen,' Butler said as he strode up on the porch, closely followed by Stan.

'Glad to hear it, Mr Butler,' the attorney said with a mild display of interest. But the sheriff and his deputies brought their back-tilted chairs down with a thump. 'What is it?' queried Madsen.

'Just this: I've found three o' my calves wearin' Bronson's brand.'

'You can prove they are your property?'

'They're sucking' my cows, if that's any evidence,' Butler grinned.

'It ought to be,' Madsen said. 'But you told me Bronson hadn't any of the calves until they were thoroughly weaned.'

'That's been his game, but Bronson has been down here in jail where he couldn't play his game. His kid got his leg broke a week ago, an' the old lady hired a tramp cowpuncher to help the girl do the work. An' what does this bum puncher do but git ambitious an' brand all them calves Bronson's been stealin'.'

Butler paused, scowled at Stan, and then continued triumphantly.

'Well, that's what I been waitin' for, so I slipped down in the night an' turned the whole calf bunch out. This puncher got out after 'em, but before he got 'em back three o' the youngest ones had got with their mothers. They're wearin' Bronson's brand plain as print, an' I made that crazy cowhand bring the irons down here so there couldn't be no substitution. That's them on his saddle, an' this is the man,' Butler ended triumphantly.

Stan found all eyes directed his way.

'Is that right?' Madsen asked him.

'Approximate,' Stan said laconically.

'Did you know the ownership of those calves was disputed when you branded them?'

'I did not. I supposed they belonged to Mrs Bronson. In fact, I didn't know then there was such a person as Bronson.'

'And when did you find it out?'

'Right after I finished brandin'. Yuh see, one o' Butler's riders helped me do it, an' when we was through he sprung it on me.'

'My man was only tryin' to help me collect evidence,' Butler put in.

'Of course,' Madsen replied. 'Now, cowboy, when you were hunting for those calves after they got out, did you see any of them running with Butler's cows?'

'I seen three calves follerin' Butler's cows an' wearin' Bronson's brand, but they wasn't the ones I branded. I got every one o' my calves back,' Stan said quietly.

'Then how do you account for it?' the attorney demanded sharply. The others listened breathlessly.

'It's easy,' Stan said mildly. 'Butler put that 37 on with a runnin' iron himself, him an' his punchers, just to frame Bronson up. He broke Bobby Bronson's leg, an' killed Madge's dogs, so I know there was nothin' too underhanded an' cowardly fer him to tackle.'

Butler's face went livid with rage, and he sprang forward with outthrust hands to grasp Stan by the throat. For an instant he was wide open, evidently expecting Stan to try to elude his wild rush. Instead, the puncher stepped forward and threw his fist with all the power of his hundred and seventy pounds behind it, flush to the point of Butler's unprotected chin.

Butler was stopped abruptly and sent staggering back the other way. He struck the railing around the porch, and unable to check himself turned backward over it and crashed first upon the cement walk and then rolled over and over in agony. He was a horrible sight. His nose had been flattened out and broken, several front teeth knocked out, and his lower lip torn and mangled.

'My Gosh, he shore walked into one then!' exclaimed the sheriff to nobody in particular, and leaped over the railing to the cattleman's assistance.

It was half an hour before Butler could be fixed up. Then, with a bandage from his chin to his mouth, another across his nose, and still another going clear around his head to hold the others in place he looked what he was, a badly injured man. When he attempted to talk his words were an indistinguishable jumble.

'Butler made one little mistake when he was tellin' about me,' Stan informed the attorney and the sheriff. 'He said he made me bring them irons down. He couldn't keep me from bringin' 'em. I figger it was just an excuse to git to hide 'em. I don't believe any man could run a brand with a runnin' iron just exactly like the brand from a stamp-iron. But if the stamp-iron itself ain't around, they might look the same. I'm bettin' that them three calves' brands won't fit these stamp irons.'

'An' I bet shay do. Zey're out zere an' we'll shee,' Butler mumbled.

'Fair enough,' Stan said. 'He's tryin' to say that his two calf thieves will have the three cows an' their calves at Mrs Bronson's corral. We'll go an' see if these irons fit all the brands, but I want a brand inspector along.'

'That's me,' said one of the men who had been sitting on the porch.

'Well, you take Butler's horse back with you an' we'll bring Butler up in my car after a while,' the sheriff directed Stan. 'But I don't believe for a minute that Butler branded those calves.'

'There is no question of Bronson's guilt in my mind,' Madsen said, 'but we'll look into this matter.'

Both Speck and Slim Carl were at Bronson's when Stan returned, and the three cows and their calves were close at hand. Stan had taken a short cut and arrived before the sheriff and the others, but their car could be heard labouring up the steep grade. The two Butler men rode over to speak to Stan, and even Speck showed some agitation.

'Where's Butler?' Slim Carl demanded. 'What're you doin' with his horse?'

'Butler wanted to fight, so they're bringin' him home in an ambulance,' Stan laughed.

Mrs Bronson and Madge came hurriedly out, but at that moment the sheriff's car poked its nose into the clearing, and the cowboys turned their startled gaze upon the swaddled head of their employer.

'There's the cows an' calves, sheriff,' Stan said quietly. 'Do yuh want 'em in the corral where we can examine 'em?'

'Yes, we want 'em where we can compare the brands with the others,' the sheriff replied.

'Those brands all look alike to me,' Mr Madsen said, after the calves had been examined.

'Hell, o' course they're alike,' Slim Carl spoke up. 'Who said they wasn't?'

Jackson, the brand inspector, made reply. 'They're all branded with the 37 – all right, but I'm not at all sure these three were stamped with the same iron that branded the others.'

'I know damn well they were,' Carl said hotly.

'How do you know that?' Madsen asked, perhaps more through his habit of cross-examining witnesses than because he entertained doubts. The Butler cowpuncher looked slightly nonplussed, and turned to his employer. Butler mumbled something, but Carl could not tell what it was.

'The only way to make sure is to get the iron and compare them with the brands,' the inspector said. Stan had the irons ready, and a moment later he hung his rope on one of the three disputed calves and with the willing aid of the men on foot it was thrown to the ground.

The brand inspector took the irons, one after the other, and fitted them over the fresh scars. The horizontal part of the 7 extended fully half an inch beyond the end of the iron, and the middle prong of the 3 was about the same distance too long.

'They don't fit,' the inspector said crisply. 'This calf wasn't branded with either of these irons.'

'Mebbe the irons slipped a little,' the sheriff said.

'No chance,' the inspector replied. 'If it had, the vertical part of the 7 would be blotched, and the same thing applies to the 3. But catch the others, boys, we'll try 'em all.'

The brands on the other two calves were found to be just the same as the first one. Butler's eyes had turned beady, but he had to let Slim Carl be his spokesman.

'I know damn well this crook has switched the irons,' the latter snarled furiously. 'These won't fit these other calves either.'

'Try 'em,' Stan drawled.

A dozen or more of the bucket-fed dogies were caught and thrown, but both irons fitted every brand exactly.

'There's no question but this is a deliberate frame-up, Mr Madsen,' the brand inspector spoke up evenly. 'No doubt Butler is reponsible, but my guess is that Slim Carl here used the runnin' iron. I've been watching for a certain artist in that line that's been working around this country, and I think I've got him.'

There was no question but that the shot had told. Slim Carl licked his lips feverishly. 'You're all wrong, Jackson,' he said nervously. 'Them brands were stamped on. I knew they was.'

'Well, prove it,' Attorney Madsen snapped.

Slim Carl turned abruptly on Speck. 'Damn yore awkward soul, you git me outa this!' he gritted with sudden fierce hysteria.

A rumbling bellow came from the bandages on Skinner Butler's face, but nobody paid any attention. Everybody was looking at Speck, whose jaw had dropped stupidly.

'What about it, Speck?' Madsen demanded ominously. 'If you know anything about this, it'll be better for you if you come clean.'

'They – they was stamped all right,' Speck gulped. 'I – I – stamped 'em myself.'

Skinner Butler started forward, but stopped abruptly as he found the sheriff's gun digging him in the ribs.'

'Go on an' spill it, Speck,' Stan said softly. 'Yo're among friends now, but if these *hombres* git loose yore life won't be worth a tinker's dam.'

'I – I – only done what Butler told me to,' Speck stammered. 'It was none o' my business what brand he wanted put on his calves. They had me use the irons because I'd helped this puncher here brand Bronson's calves an' knew just where the irons went. But Butler an' Carl was both there an' held the calves.'

'Is that true, Carl?' the sheriff asked.

'Absolutely,' the puncher sneered. 'But you ain't got nothin' on me. As Speck just said, it didn't make any difference to me what brand Butler put on his own calves. Speck stole the irons from this corral an' put 'em back again. It'd 'a worked, too, if Speck hadn't been so damned clumsy an' mussed up the brands some way. But it's him an' Butler for it. Yuh can't prove anything against me.'

'I'd sure like to,' the brand inspector said regretfully.

Suddenly Butler began to mumble again. For a minute they could not understand him. Then it dawned upon them that he was accusing Slim Carl of running brands on other people's cattle.

'Damn if he'z gonna git out o' thish clear,' the enraged cattleman mumbled through his thickened lips. 'He's been runnin' bran's fer years, an' I can proof it!'

'Better put the manacles on both Butler an' Carl, sheriff,' the inspector said with a satisfied grin. And yet the brand inspector seemed reluctant to leave the corral, even after the sheriff was ready to start to town with his prisoners.

'I can't understand it,' he commented to the assembly at large. 'The frame-up against Bronson is admitted, but I still claim that those brands were not stamped with the same iron, even if Speck does admit it. I'd give a dollar to know.'

'Pay me,' Stan grinned. 'But hold yore prisoners, sheriff. This is goin' to be quite a shock to 'em. They did brand with the same irons I used – but I changed 'em after I used 'em. I thought they was low-down enough to try this, so I set a trap for 'em.'

For a while the only sound was the hard and angry breathing of the prisoners.

'Well, if you're that handy with a running iron, I'll have to keep my eye on you,' remarked the inspector. But he was smiling, and he handed over a silver dollar which Stan promptly dropped into his pocket.

'You can look for your husband home tomorrow, Mrs Bronson,' the prosecuting attorney said. 'And I don't think you'll be bothered any more after this.'

After they had gone Stan stood leaning thoughtfully over the corral fence. Suddenly he became aware of Madge pulling at his sleeve, and she was looking worshipfully up into his face.

'Gee, but I'd like to 'a' been there when yuh busted Butler!' she said.

Will Jenkins

Thief!

HONEST Dan Coupland stood up abruptly from the sizzling pan of bacon over the camp fire. Suddenly alert, yet with a faintly whimsical smile upon his lips, he listened to distant, muted, futile little 'pop-pops' born to his ears by the wind. Two shots, a third, then silence.

With a certain calm celerity, marvellously swift of results, he trampled out the fire, kicked enough dust over the ashes to smother any remaining spark, and gathered up his coffee pot in one hand. He abandoned the bacon. In any event, it had been buried in the swirl of dust with which he had overwhelmed his fire.

In another instant he had seized the bridle of his horse and the pair, man and animal, had vanished in the brushwood. Then there was silence. The wind blew swiftly up from the plains and wandered in among the hills. The sage trembled and whispered, leaf upon leaf, but there was no sign or sound to indicate that any man lay hidden near by. Dan, himself, had settled down peacefully. He surveyed a little spot of ground, kicked aside a sharp-pointed stone, and spoke to his horse.

'Get down, ol' scout, an' lie quiet. I'm darned if I'll let 'em do me out of my coffee.'

So it was that he placidly drank of the strong, black brew while the prairie breeze blew over his head and his horse lay prone and quiet, gazing at him through liquid, trustful brown eyes. He drank the stuff in quietness, smiling a little, though his ears were alert for more of the sounds that at first had caused his hiding.

They came – a shot no more than a hundred yards distant, then the desperate clattering of a horse's hoofs. Answering shots from farther behind. Honest Dan Coupland looked out discreetly, chirruped to his horse and flung himself on the animal's back as it sprang erect. A moment later he was plunging out of his hiding place and had joined the fleeing man.

'Trouble, Gus?' he inquired mildly.

The other man cursed.

'Th' whole dam' county's up an' chasin' me.' He swore again. 'We gotta ride ahead o' us.'

Dan rode for a moment or so, meditative.

'What'd yuh do, Gus?' he asked. 'It's all Greek to me'

Their pursuers topped a rise a quarter of a mile to their rear and a sputter of angry and entirely useless shots told of the hysterical rage that possessed the posse. Dan ignored them.

'Shootin', an' then some,' snarled Gus, sinking his spurs needlessly deep into his labouring horse. 'Damn!'

The horse had stumbled and nearly fell. Dan reined in until his companion had caught up with him again.

'Y'orter stick to rustlin' like I do,' he commented. 'But stric'ly speakin', what rustlin' I do ain't stealin'. Duck 'em at th' stream ahead?'

Gus nodded. Both men rode recklessly down a steep and rocky incline and into the foaming, rippling waters of a brook that had carved out a bed untold centuries past. Without a word, they turned upstream, the water hissing and gurgling about the horses' fetlocks.

'Here,' said Dan suddenly.

He swerved his horse back in the direction from which they had come. There was a narrow little gully emptying down just there, barely wide enough for a single rider, but providentially not too steep for a horse to climb. They made it to the top, and found themselves screened from the riders who were following.

'Now what?' demanded Gus.

'Set still,' advised Dan, fishing for a pipe. 'They'll see our tracks leadin' to th' stream. They won't see 'em on the other side. What'll they do? They'll cross the stream an' scatter, lookin' for th' place we clumb out. An' while they're doin' that, we'll be wendin' our way to other an' more peaceful scenes.'

He dismounted and scratched a match. When his pipe was lighted, he stood by his horse's head, calmly smoking. He heard the sound of the pursuing horsemen as they rushed down to the creek. Then there was a shout and a murmur as of many curses. Then the posse did exactly what Dan had foretold. It crossed the creek, split into two parties, and they spread out to look for tracks where the fugitives had emerged. So closely did the posse follow those who fled that there would not yet have been time for the hoofprints from the stream to dry, even had the pair elected to clamber out over rocky ground which would show no ordinary tracks.

'Lucky it's a clear stream,' observed Dan calmly as the riders went clattering by. 'If we'd stirred up any mud, they'd ha' seen it.'

They rattled and clinked into the distance and he counted again. Gus essayed to mount and his horse shied away from him. He struck at it, cursing as he did so. Dan's voice, with a sudden edge on it, halted him.

'Looka here, Gus,' he was saying coldly, 'quit abusin' that horse. You spurred him just now when there weren't no need of it. You done me a good turn once, but y'know I sorter like horses.'

Gus whirled, and Dan's hand flitted lightly to his belt. For an instant they faced each other, then Gus sullenly turned back and climbed into his saddle. Dan sat imperturbable.

'Reckon we better split, Gus,' he said quietly. 'I may be a rustler, an' all that, but I don't usual do no shootin' unless I have to, an' I shore don't beat up my horses. I'm goin' to meander off by myself. You oughter slip th' sheriff an' them easy enough.'

He touched the reins and his animal obediently started off. Dan turned in his saddle to remark softly:

'I'd like t' mention, Gus, that I ain't asked you just what happened. You said shootin', but I know yuh pretty well. Shootin', with you, means in th' back or somethin'. That's th' real reason I'm quittin' yuh, now that you're pretty safe. Me, I'm an honest rustler.'

He rode off. Gus, behind him, gazed lustfully at the broad target his back presented. But a shot, even now, would bring the posse like a hive of angry bees, and Gus had reasons of his own for wishing to avoid notice. He let Dan escape, precisely as Dan had figured, and presently rode slowly and cautiously off in another direction.

Sunset found Dan seated on a huge boulder that jutted out just where the mountains sloped downward into the plains. His horse waited patiently behind him. He was a lonely figure seated there, with his chin cupped in one palm, and his eyes were tired as he stared down at the broad expanse of green below him. Far in the distance, to his left, was a toy ranch house in a little grove of cottonwood trees. There was a tiny speck of a pool there, and the massed, blurred figures of cattle.

Dan watched them sombrely.

'Walton's feedin' most of 'em on the southern line,' he commented to his horse. 'We could cut off twenty or thirty, or maybe more, if we put our mind to it. I don't just feel like it, Buck. I'm gettin' sort of tired of havin' to steal what's mine. Look at that there ranch, will yuh? It's ours, Buck, all ours, 'an them cattle we got cached in that there little canyon are ours by right, only we stole 'em. Ain't it a shame, ol' scout?'

The horse nickered softly. For a long time there was silence. In the west the sun was sinking. Great clouds of scarlet and gold hung in the sky. The dim peaks of a second range of hills were upthrust against the light. Gradually dusk was settling in the valley between, and a delicate purple haze softened and made obscure all the gently rolling grazing land, and the ranch buildings, and blotted out completely the bare, whitewashed buildings of Glover, the little town that could barely be made out at midday.

Sitting there in the falling dusk, Honest Dan seemed to be lost in thought. The last crimson rays of the sun beat upon his motionless figure and turned him to bronze. It seemed as if he were going over the past, slowly in his mind.

It was not a past to be ashamed of. Cowboy, small owner, rancher with many broad acres. And now cattle thief. He had owned the ranch whose tiny buildings were fading by imperceptible degrees into the darkness of the valley. He had sold, as he thought, a part of his holding, and the deed had read for the whole. He had accepted what he considered a fair but high price for one half his tract, and had failed to read the document he had signed. Walton, to whom he had made his sale, had the law on his side. Undoubtedly the deed was valid, but Honest Dan Coupland was not one to submit to injustice without a fight. Refusing the aid of his own men, he had ridden into Glover, looking for Walton. They had met in the single dusty street. Pistols had flashed.

Dan was now an outlaw, with a perverse regret that he had only wounded the man who had swindled him. He rustled cattle from his former ranch with a stout assertion that they belonged to him. He scrupulously refused to steal from any other herds. A dozen times he had made forays. Back in the hills there were eight hundred head of cattle in a tiny canyon that none but himself knew of. There were many men among the hills who had helped him, honest men and outlaws alike. The countryside rather liked Dan, though Walton had offered five hundred dollars reward for his arrest. Only, it was indubitable that Dan did associate with men less desirable than himself. He had had them help him in his own forays, which he classed as crusades rather than raids or thefts, and the countryside as a whole viewed him with misgiving, mingled with a sympathetic tolerance.

Slowly the sunlight faded away, and the shadows crept up from the lowlands, surrounding him as he sat deep in thought. The higher peaks still glowed faintly when he shook himself a little and rose. The air was cold, with the sun gone from it.

He made his way rather stiffly toward his waiting horse. And he suddenly heard a sound which made him instantly alert. The cautious clatter of a pony's hoofs moving toward him. Dan listened keenly, looking swiftly about him, and melted into the landscape. For a long time there was no sound.

And then a tired pony, head drooping, came slowly up to the place he had left. It was a small pony, and even a rather fat one. It had been curried and cared for and ridden lightly until it had lost something of the wiriness of your plain and mountain horse. The rider was small, too, and as tired as his mount. A very tiny rifle was slanted across the pommel of his saddle. He gazed about him wearily.

'I thought I saw somebody here,' said the small boy bravely to his pony. 'I sure did think I saw somebody here. I guess we'll have to camp by ourselves. It's – it's sort of lonesome up here, ain't it?'

Honest Dan Coupland materialized from the gloom.

'Hello there, son,' he said gravely. 'How's tricks?'

The tiny rifle was levelled instantly.

'Put 'em up,' said the boyish voice sternly. 'Put 'em up an' let me look at you.'

Honest Dan grinned. The rifle would fire a bullet almost the size of a pea. He obligingly elevated his arms and stepped forward, his horse following him over the loose stones.

A very tired little boy surveyed him and dropped the rifle.

'I – I thought you were Gus Hill,' he said, relief coming into his voice despite himself. 'I'm lookin' for him.'

Honest Dan nodded gravely.

'You got separated from th' posse?' he inquired casually, though his eyes were twinkling.

'They – they wouldn't let me go with them,' the boy informed him. 'So I started off by myself. I'm awful tired. Have you got a – a house up here?'

Dan shook his head.

'Nope,' he admitted. 'I'm aimin' to make camp a little ways away. Would you care about sittin' by my fire?'

The boy nodded.

'I sure would like to,' he admitted. 'Y'see, I wasn't thinkin' about bein' out all night by myself, and I didn't bring along much chuck.'

'I got plenty for two,' Dan assured him. 'Come along.'

He rode slowly away, chuckling to himself. He did not know much about children, but he knew that the little boy would have fiercely resented any offer to carry him. The tiny pony followed with a tiny rider struggling to conceal the fatigue that threatened to topple him from the saddle.

Coffee and beans are not the most digestible of foods, but the small boy ate voraciously, while his lids drooped from sheer weariness. Dan treated him in all respects as he would an adult, though a smile was never far from his lips. The idea of a nine-year-old starting out alone in quest of an outlaw was not laughable in itself; rather it pleased him in a curious fashion for which a smile was the only possible expression. Dan's demeanour to his guest was that of the West, where no one asks questions of a passer-by.

'Gosh, this is good,' said the boy blissfully, keeping himself awake only to eat. 'I ate some berries this afternoon, but they weren't very nice. I was thinking of the Arabs, you know. They live on dates.'

Dan agreed, and put another generous helping of beans upon the tin plate the boy had emptied.

'Dad's goin' to be mad,' said the youthful one sleepily. 'He's th' sheriff, you know. He says he don't want me mixin' with any outlaws just yet a while, but when I grow up it's another matter. Then he grins. I'll show him.'

Gradually the torpor of a full stomach added itself to the weariness of fatigue and he slumbered, with a half-filled plate in his hand.

Smiling, Honest Dan took away the dish and rolled the boy in his own and only blanket. He unsaddled the pony the boy had ridden and hobbled it. His own horse, Buck, would not stray far. Then he heaped fresh fuel upon the camp fire and settled down with a pipe, to review many old memories and make fresh plans.

They had camped in a little grove not far from an infinitesimal stream. The trees, overhead, whispered in deep tones as the wind of the heights pressed upon them. It was a curious scene. The flickering camp fire, pouring its ruddy light upon Dan's weather-beaten features. The boy deep in the dreamless sleep of childhood, only his sunburned little features showing out of the enveloping blanket. Dan, sprawled upon the ground with his back against a saddle, pipe in mouth, staring now and then at the fire, only to lift his eyes to the sheriff's son.

Odd! The sheriff and Dan had been good friends before Dan took to the hills. Even now, Dan was sure, there was more than a little good feeling on both sides, though the sheriff, as sheriff, would most certainly do his best to capture Dan if he saw the ghost of a chance. In the morning, he would show the boy the posse's camp, or their trail. He could certainly find his way to them then. But in the meantime –

His eyes wandered again and again to the small head projecting from the blanket. Lucky man, the sheriff.

Dan knocked out his pipe and tried to sleep himself, but the night was a little bit biting. He wasn't as young as he had been. Six or seven years, now, of hiding. Now and then a jaunt to the border and a taste of civilization, but always back again to where he could look over the ranch that had once been his, and to plan new forays upon its herds.

They belonged to him. He had money in the bank, too, at Glover. It was the money he had been paid for half the ranch. Some day he'd have to go down and hold up the bank to get it. He couldn't draw on it, as an outlaw. Then, too, it was appropriate that he had left it untouched, in token of his refusal to recognize the doctored deed Walton had sprung on him. He'd pulled out quite a lot of cattle, all told. Fifty head here, a hundred there. Once he'd taken five hundred at a clip. They were his cattle.

He waked from a slight doze with that curious, catlike faculty of instant alertness that was second nature. The boy was moaning a little in his sleep, and as Dan took his hand away from his lip, a trifle ashamed, the youngster opened his eyes. For a moment they were clouded and sleepy, then something made him grimace and twist. He set his teeth, and saw Dan looking at him.

'I – I guess I'm sick,' he said bravely. 'I feel – awful, inside.'

Dan was on his feet.

'Pain?' he demanded.

'Aw-awful one,' said the boy, grimacing again. His face was a little pale, even in the ruddy firelight. In daylight it would have been paler still.

Dan felt singularly helpless. Confronted with any normal emergency, he would have been at ease, but this was a matter outside his ken. He hesitated.

'Say, what does your mother do when you get sick like this?' he asked suddenly.

'Never was – sick this way – before.' The little fellow was doing his best to be brave, but he was a very sick boy. 'I – I wonder if it was those berries?'

A little yelp was wrenched from him, and despite himself, tears began to ooze from his eyes. Dan jumped.

Berries! There were very many berries that were unwholesome in the extreme for human beings to eat. Some of them were actively poisonous. Suppose the boy had eaten – Dan's forehead felt cold from a sudden sweat. He was a good fifteen miles from a town or a doctor. There was only one ranch house in less than ten, three hours away, in the dark, and downhill, and that was Walton's ranch, where he would be shot down on sight, without a chance to get any help for the boy. There remained only the posse. The boy's father was there.

Dan whistled shrilly, and his horse plunged toward him. In a matter of seconds he had flung on his saddle and cinched it. It did not occur to him that he was riding straight into captivity he had dodged for years when he picked up the blanket-wrapped bundle, paused to kick out his fire, and swung up with the boy in his arms.

He rode away through the utter blackness, forced to let his horse pick its way, but urging it on whenever he dared. He was on fire with anxiety.

The ride was terribly long, longer to Dan than to the sick boy in his arms. The boy had to give up the struggle after a little, and lay sobbing in his bundle, deathly sick and frightened.

Up and down hills, through thickets of young trees, now with a canopy of stars overhead, now winding along a narrow canyon with a small and singing stream in its centre, Dan rode. Always he held his bundle close. After a long time a little hand struggled out of the envoloping blankets and crept into his own.

'It – it don't hurt so much when I can hold on.' A paroxysm of nausea cut off the speech, and Dan urged on his horse again.

The three fires glowed out at last, a long distance away. The horse had to pick his way down a steep hillside, and Dan felt as if he would never reach the bottom, though he did not dare to try for better speed, lest a stumble spoil the boy's chances for life. Dan already felt that they were slim.

Then on over the softer grass, at a trot. Up to the bivouac. A call.

'Hey, by the camp fire!'

A dozen faces turned to him as he rode into the circle of light, and a dozen hands dropped to as many holsters. Dan paid no attention. He rode up to the very edge of a fire and swung out of the saddle.

'Here's the sheriff's kid,' he announced anxiously. 'He's sick. Is Doc Burnly with yuh?'

The sheriff took the bundle.

'H-hello, dad.' It was a weak, but brave little voice. 'I'm – I'm sorter sick.'

The sheriff took him in his arms, cast a curious look at Dan, and went quickly to one of the other fires. His voice came back.

'Keep Dan here a minute.' The tone was curious, too. Dan stiffened.

He stood there, growing gradually a little more ominous and more grim as a dozen men watched him. His hands hung easily at his sides, not far from his holster. A dozen pairs of more than half hostile eyes were upon him. Every man present knew him, Honest Dan Coupland, rustler, with five hundred dollars on his head, offered by the man from whose ranch – once his own – alone he stole cattle.

It was a long five minutes before the sheriff came back.

'Indigestion,' he said curtly to Dan. 'Coffee and beans, on top of an all-day ride. He's packed full of baking-soda now, and he'll be all right in half an hour. Thanks.'

'I'm awful glad,' said Dan in tones of sheer relief. 'He had me scared. I'll leave his pony where you-all'll pick him up on th' way back.'

He made a movement as if to go.

'Wait a minute,' said the sheriff sharply. His eyes were glowing strangely. 'Where are you going?'

Dan faced him, and grew a trifle pale, though with anger rather than fear.

'I was figurin' on goin' away,' he said softly. 'Were you thinkin' of stoppin' me?'

His right hand, the gun hand, twitched a little. The sheriff wavered between two emotions.

'I'm grateful t'you for bringing my boy back,' he said harshly, 'but you were with Gus Hill to-day.'

'Sure I was,' admitted Dan with a trace of amusement. 'He done me a favour once. I owed him a good turn. I got him loose from you-all.'

Sheer rage came into the sheriff's face. There was a simultaneous movement among the listeners.

'An' you call yourself a man!' raged the sheriff. 'Damn yuh!'

'I'm waitin' for you to draw,' said Den evenly. 'Somebody's goin' to get shot up – I reckon me among 'em,' he added softly.

For an instant lives hung upon a split second. If any man among the dozen or more had moved as much as a finger, death would have rushed from blued-steel muzzles.

The sheriff spoke suddenly, as if the words were forced from his lips.

'You know what Gus Hill did?'

'Nope,' admitted Dan coolly. 'He said some shootin'. We split up right after we lost you all.'

The sheriff told him, his features twisted with the rage that possessed him. And when he had finished, Dan's own lips were tight-compressed.

'Why – why, I knew 'em,' he said uncertainly. 'I – I – Gawd, Harry, I'd ha' shot him myself! I owed him a good turn, so I helped him get away. He's hidin', same as me, and I'd ha' helped anybody you were lookin' for. But that – why, I knew li'l Sally when she weren't no more'n knee-high.'

He rubbed his hand across his forehead, dazed. Then a sudden thought struck him, and he dropped his arm to look squarely at the sheriff.

'Just why'd you tell me, Harry?' he asked quietly. 'You ain't thinkin' I'd lead you'all to his hidin' place, are you?'

'We'll forget you're an outlaw, Dan,' said the sheriff. 'While you're with us. We'll let you get away. Just help us find that one man.'

Dan's lips flickered into a tiny smile.

'You might forget I'm outlawed, Harry, but it ain't so easy for me. Y'see, th' only friends I've had for a long time have been them fellers. It wouldn't do for me to help you catch one of 'em. They sorter trust me.'

'We'll let you go clear away.'

Dan's smile vanished.

'Y'ain't stoppin' me – yet.'

He very calmly mounted, and looked down at the sheriff.

'I'm goin' t' ride outer yore camp, Harry, just like I come in. Anybody that wants to'make a few pennies by disputin' th' path is welcome to his chance.' He eyed the assemblage grimly. 'But if yuh want t'leave that there badge o' yours behind, an' take a ride with me, I might show yuh some fun.'

A moment's hesitation, and the badge was ripped off. The sheriff picked up a saddle.

'I'm with you,' he said briefly.

The two horsemen rode away from the encampment and into the blackness of the mountain night. They rode at the hillside and clambered among its loosened stones until the three camp fires were left far below. Then the foremost reined in for an instant.

'Now jus' remember, Harry, that th' majesty of th' law is lef' behind. I'm takin' you places as my friend. Th' sheriff don't know what happens back here – an' you don't try t'make any arrests.'

The second figure nodded grimly.

'I'm after Gus Hill. Sally's dead by now. She was dying when we left. Her husband never moved after Gus shot him.'

Dan, in the darkness, did not reply. He merely set his horse in a given direction and jogged along through the darkness.

Sunrise. A glory of gold and red and ochre and yellow among the cliffs and canyons. A splendour of green upon the not too precipitous hillsides. Cloudlings rising from the beds on which they seemed to have rested during the night. A long, white mass of vapour disentangling itself from a forest upon a slope. Vapours from the valleys writhing into nothingness as the chill rays of the morning sun grew warm and warmer. The morning wind sweeping across the open spaces, humming softly.

Two infinitesimal figures crossing a grassy knoll, men on horseback. They passed over the green space and began to descend a long slope of naked earth, too steeply slanting for grass to gain a foothold before erosion tore loose its support. Small rocks and stones slid from beneath the horses' feet, to go bouncing and clanking down into the valley below.

Mid-morning. A weary horse patiently breasting a rise in the ground, followed by another, as weary as the first. Two men, iron men, riding easily after nearly thirty-six hours in the saddle. They came to a stop atop the rise, and Dan surveyed the ground before him. Hills and valleys in a chaos of elevations and depressions, spread in every direction. He looked, exhaustively, and nodded.

'Over there,' he said with an air of satisfaction. 'That ought to be Gus's place yonder.'

It was merely a gash in the earth, a quarter of a mile wide and two long. The sheriff squinted.

'Right,' he said quietly. 'Thanks, Dan.'

Dan looked at him curiously.

'What's th' idea?' he asked. 'Figurin' on goin' after him alone?'

The sheriff looked down at his saddle-bow.

'You said you were a rustler, and wouldn't give him up. It wouldn't be wise for you. Your friends wouldn't overlook your helping me take him.'

Dan went white beneath his tan.

'You're figurin' on keepin' my help secret, Harry?' he queried. 'So's I won't be potted at by rustlers an' honest men alike?'

The sheriff hesitated, and nodded.

'I'm runnin' this,' said Dan, utterly pale. 'I used t'know li'l' Sally. You ride to th' head of th' canyon. I'll take th' mouth. We'll close in together. I'll go slow t'give you a start.'

Without a word, the sheriff started off. Dan stared after him, and touched the reins. His horse moved away.

'Figurin' me like that,' Dan muttered. 'Thinkin' I'd turn over a outlaw like me. My Gawd!'

He dipped beneath a little hillock and was lost to sight.

The canyon was a veritable pocket. Sheer, rocky walls on either side hemmed in the rider. Only at the mouth and at the upper end was there a trace of an entrance way. The mouth was wide and level. The head sloped down just enough to make it possible for a rider to come down safely. For a long time it was empty. Far over, at one side, there was a flash of brown, which resolved itself into an unsaddled horse grazing among the bushes. There was a tiny, squat cabin half hidden beneath a cliff. From its chimney a little wisp of smoke was curling up. Dan rode briskly up the centre of the canyon and to the cabin. He dismounted and went within, leaving his mount standing patiently, wearily, at the door. Then stillness.

In the far distance, the sheriff appeared. He began to pick his way down the slope, a microscopic figure. He reached the canyon floor and urged his animal to a trot. Coming over the long, soft grass, he saw the little hut with its curling smoke, sure sign of occupancy. Then his eyes fastened upon the horse before the door. He recognized it as Dan's.

His lips tightened, and his hand went to his holster, assuring him that it was cleared and his pistol ready for use. His eyes narrowed a trifle.

'Both of 'em,' he grunted, 'and under cover. An' Dan could've shot me himself any time durin' th' night.'

He neared the cabin, coming grimly. Irrelevantly, he wished he had not shed his badge before leaving camp. Dan was expert with the pistol in a land of experts. Gus Hill was by no means a bad shot. And both of them were sheltered by a house, while he was in the open.

The brooding stillness of the little canyon seemed suddenly ominous. Only the sound of his horse's hoofs on the soft ground. Then the infinitely faint sound of a movement where the unsaddled horse shouldered aside the brushwood in quest of a daintier morsel.

The sheriff was within three hundred yards of the cabin. He drew his revolver and cantered on.

Then a shot, two shots, so close together that they seemed as one. Silence again.

The sheriff came cautiously closer to the house. At a hundred yards there was no sound. At fifty, no movement. The sheriff suddenly sprinted and flung himself inside the door, revolver ready.

One man lay sprawling upon the floor, a little red stain gathering beneath him. Honest Dan Coupland was leaning against the wall, thoughtfully blowing the last traces of smoke from the muzzle of his weapon. He looked up with a faint smile as the sheriff hurtled into the single room.

'I'm a rustler, Harry,' he said quietly. 'I couldn't give him up, or help you get him, because th' fellers in th' hills, they sorter trust me. But seein' what he did yesterday, I could call him a blanky-blank yeller-livered skunk. An' I did.'

Only then did the sheriff see a spreading dark blotch on his shirt. He sprang forward as Dan wavered and helped him to a chair.

'Pinked me,' said Dan dizzily. 'Maybe, after all, you'll have t' take me in. But I warn yuh, I'm goin' t' escape or somethin'.'

'Dan!' cried the sheriff desperately. 'Buck up! Let me look at that wound!'

With frantic haste, he stripped off the shirt and worked like a madman to staunch the all too copious flow of blood.

It was a long time later that he laughed shakily.

'My God! I thought he'd done for you. Now listen, Dan. I'm going to tell you something. Walton skipped out day before yesterday. He's been playing too much poker, and got in a bad way. The bank in Glover has a mortgage on his ranch, and they're going to foreclose it. And I've got in interest in the bank. You've got a big deposit there. You remember? Here's what you're going to do. You're going to give me a cheque, and I'm going to buy in that ranch for you. It's going to belong to you again, and you're going to have to prosecute yourself for stealing cattle from your own herds. Hear me?'

'Sure,' said Dan weakly. He stirred feebly. 'Durn it, why didn't you tell me before?'

'Would you have told a man you thought was helping you catch one of his friends?' asked the sheriff directly. 'Even if he'd done what Gus there did?'

'Don't know as I would,' admitted Dan, faintly. 'Sure about that there ranch, Harry?'

'Sure.'

Dan lay quiet for an instant.

'I'll be able t'ride in a day or so,' he said presently, though his voice was weak. 'I want t'get back to th' ranch in a hurry. All th' herds are down by th' southern line. I want t'shift 'em. It's dangerous. A darn' rustler could run off a hundred or two head 'thout any trouble, an' all rustlers ain't honest like I am.'

Harry Sinclair Drago

Ghost of the Cimarron

FROM across the open prairie they approached the main-travelled road into Pawnee. The hour was late and the moonlit Kansas night was very still. Protected by the shoulder of a little knoll, they pulled up their ponies.

'We'll wait here for him,' said one. 'He ought to be along in fifteen, twenty minutes.'

The tall, gaunt man who had spoken was Luke Coffey. The others did not question his judgement. Silent, alert eyes fastened on the road, they waited. They were several hundred yards from it, but in the moonlight they could see it uncoiling over the rolling treeless plain like a silvery ribbon.

The minutes dragged by and only the champing of their ponies broke the stillness of the night. Finally Luke glanced at his watch. 'Almost midnight,' he observed quietly.

The others nodded. One said: 'We couldn't have missed him, Luke?'

'No. The road is deep in dust. It'll muffle the sound of a team. We'll see him before we hear him.'

His observation satisfied them. Even among these hard-bitten men, with whom he rode tonight, Luke Coffey was accounted a man of parts, a tried and true hand at this business which engaged them. His lean, stony-eyed face, sharpened with an unrecognized tension, was an imperturbable mask.

But that was true of the others, too. There were six of them: Flint Tanner, who once had ridden with Butch Cassidy and the Wild Bunch; like Patrick and Dutch George, left-overs from Bill Doolin's long-riders; Reb Sontag, the last of the Sontag gang; Luke Coffey and the Kiowa Kid, a smiling, blue-eyed man, with an unruly shock of flaxen hair.

In point of years, the Kid was the baby of this outfit; he was also a newcomer to it. But the law already had grudges enough against him to recommend him to the men with whom he was riding now. His forays into outlawry had been uniformly disastrous, however; a fact which kept recurring to Luke and one or two others. They didn't dislike the Kid; he had a crooked smile that was hard to resist. Neither could they forget that his record was against him; that he was either a reckless fool or a hoodoo; and one was as dangerous as the other in their eyes.

Having expressed themselves frankly, the Kiowa Kid knew exactly where he stood with them. He had continued to smile and he smiled tonight, though they were over a hundred miles north of the Oklahoma line and had two railroads between them and the security of the jungle-like brakes of the Cimarron. To-morrow, they were to rob a bank. The fact seemed to rest very lightly on him. He rolled a cigarette deftly and reached for a match. Luke was watching him. 'If you got to smoke, Kid, climb down out of that saddle and hug the ground before you strike a light,' he said sharply. 'We're a long ways from home.'

The Kid grinned. 'Sure enough,' he agreed. He slid down effortlessly and cupped his hat over the match before he struck it. Without seeming to, Luke continued to regard him. He couldn't figure the Kid out. No matter how sharply you brought him up he never seemed to resent it. It passed belief in Luke's mind.

Dark-visaged Reb Sontag edged his pony up beside Coffey. He was leading a saddled horse, a long-legged sorrel. The stirrups had been dropped over the horn to keep them from flapping against the animal's sides if they had to get away in a hurry. A canvas bag hung from the horn, too. Reb had a similar bag on his own saddle. It was filled with cartridges for their rifles. The canvas bag on the led horse appeared to contain nothing more ominous than a lightning rod.

'Sunthin's happened to him,' Reb jerked out. 'It ain't Doc's way to stall along like this. I'm for ridin' back to that last town and locatin' him.'

'Take it easy,' Luke advised. 'Someone comin' now. It'll be Doc, like as not.'

They waited three or four minutes as the two-horse team approached. It was hitched to a light rig, such as Doc had said he'd get.

'It's Doc, all right,' Ike Patrick declared. 'I'll give him the call.' Cupping a hand over his mouth he produced an excellent imitation of the sand crane's long-drawn cry. As it floated across the still night air the man in the rig raised his whip over his shoulder. It was the signal they had agreed on.

'It's Doc, sure enough,' Luke announced. Unconsciously, there was a note of relief in his voice. 'We can ride down to the road.'

The little man in the buggy saw them coming and he let the team amble along at an even pace. He was sixty if he was a day; and that's old for an outlaw. Of course, he had not been outside the law all those years. That was just as true of the men he led; at one time or another, all had been cowboys. For five years, though, he had been darting out of the wild, uninhabited Cherokee Strip to stick up trains and hoist banks in Kansas, Oklahoma and, on rare occasions, in New Mexico and the Texas Panhandle.

Heck Short, the United States Marshal for Northern Oklahoma, had first dubbed him The Ghost of the Cimarron. It was no mean compliment, coming from a man-hunter of Heck's recognized ability. Running Doc Johnson to earth had kept him and his deputies busy for several years now. Four or five times they had had him trapped apparently; somehow he had eluded them.

If the truth must be told, little Doc, with his puckered brown eyes and slow, whimsical smile, had come to enjoy this tilting with the law, beyond all other things in his life. It still thrilled him to be able to ride into a town in broad daylight and cow it by the very fact of his presence, sometimes without firing a shot, simply because he was Doc Johnson, the notorious outlaw; the allegiance of such men as Luke Coffey, Reb Sontag, Flint Tanner, had not ceased to warm something in him; the excitement of sticking up a train, of robbing a bank, had not palled on him; the thrill in the endless hide-and-go-seek with the law.

He had been an outlaw too long to have any illusions left about how it would end. Neither was he fooling himself that there was any profit to be winnowed from this business. At best, it was a game of wits, and he accepted it as such.

For two weeks he had planned this raid into Kansas. So far, he had not made a mistake. He had brought his men to within a few miles of Pawnee without man or woman catching sight of them. He had crossed railroads, avoided a score of towns, crept by farmhouses and ranches. It had meant travelling by night and seeking cover by day. But those were only the preliminaries; the hours that lay ahead should test his resourcefulness. He looked forward to them with quiet confidence.

Earlier this evening he had walked into the little hamlet of Arcola and purchased a team and rig. He would need it in Pawnee. The big sorrel that Reb Sontag led belonged to him. The bag that hung on the saddle horn contained not only several samples of lightning rods, but catalogues, order blanks and the other advertising matter that a pedlar of lightning rods – common enough in that country in that day – would have in his possession. It was in such guise that he intended to drive into Pawnee and size up the bank. He had even thought to equip himself with a pair of gold-rimmed spectacles, and, back in Arcola, he had bought himself a black Derby hat and a green carpet bag. Strange equipment for an outlaw.

Glasses and hat, plus a fresh shave, had produced a change in him that Luke and the others found little short of amazing.

'You look almost like a preacher,' Flint Tanner declared with a chuckle.

'You said it!' the Kid laughed. 'Heck Short himself wouldn't know you in that get-up, Doc.'

The little man cut the merriment short.

'Did you git here without bein' seen?' he asked.

'Yeh,' Luke answered. 'Didn't come close to runnin' into anyone . . . The Kid says we're about five miles south of Pawnee.'

'So I judge, from what I learned in Arcola,' Doc observed. He turned to the Kiowa Kid. 'You're still sure we can find cover between here and town? I'm depending on you; you know this country.'

It was not often that he had to put himself in another man's hands in a matter as delicate as this. But he liked the Kid; trusted him. Otherwise, Kiowa would never have ridden with them.

'I'm as sure as I ever was; and that's positive,' the Kid answered. 'You stick to the road; the rest of us will get back on the prairie. Go about two miles; you'll see the place then, an abandoned house burned down years ago. You turn in; you'll see the old barn then, back some distance from the road. We can put the horses in there and lie out in the brush.'

There was confidence in the Kid's tone. His story was exactly the one he had told several times before when Doc was making his plans.

The little man said: 'All right. Toss that bag into the back of the rig, Reb, and let me have my rifle. You can git along then. You'll be there ahead of me. Just be awful sure you got that barn to yourselves when you ride up to it. You see to that, Luke; don't take anythin' for granted. If you find things okay, one of you come back to the road and hail me as I drive by.'

In a few minutes the night had swallowed them. Doc picked up the reins and drove on, his rifle on the seat beside him.

He had the road to himself. He let the horses make their own gait. Twenty minutes later he began to scan the country off to the right of the road for sight of the barn. The prairie was treeless, and he had no difficulty locating the building. Once abreast the old farm he could see the ruins of the house, just as the Kid had described them. The road that led into it was high in weeds.

He was almost upon it before he heard himself called. He recognized Luke Coffey's voice.

'It's all right,' said Luke.

Doc pulled up the team and handed his rifle to him. 'I'll go right along,' he declared. 'I don't want to drive into town too late.' He bent down and opened the carpet bag, exposing a pair of .45s. He left the bag open, so that he could get to his guns in a hurry if he needed them.

'When do you suppose we'll be seein' you?' Luke asked.

'About noon, I'd say. I want to look things over awful careful. I'll go to the hotel and git a room when I git in. I'll be up early. If things work out, we'll walk into the bank about half-past two. I want to make it as late as I can so we won't have so long to go until dark.'

Luke nodded. 'Better locate this Cass Chilton, the sheriff of this county. There's no bluff about him, Doc.'

'Don't worry; I'll tend to all that,' the little man observed drily. He picked up the reins. 'By the way, Luke, if I ain't back by one o'clock don't wait no longer; I won't be comin' back. You understand?'

'Yeh,' Luke muttered woodenly. They had been together a long time. In all his turbulent life the tall man had never liked anyone so well as he did little Doc Johnson. 'So long,' he said.

'So long,' Doc called back as he drove on. The moment had a strange drag for him, too.

In Pawnee, he put his team in the hotel barn and walked into the office. He signed himself as John Black, of Emporia, and was shown to his room.

Ten minutes later, a ruddy-cheeked man walked into the hotel and glanced at the register.

'You're up late, Cass,' the clerk said.

'Just getting ready to turn in,' was the easy answer.

'A lightning rod salesman,' the clerk explained as he saw the sheriff glance at the signature of the late arrival. 'You acquainted with him?'

'No,' Chilton laughed. 'You can't know all these lightning rod fellers.'

He went out presently, but he did not go home. Frank Ross, his chief deputy, was asleep in a chair in the sheriff's office. Chilton awakened him.

'Well, he's here, Frank,' he said. 'Got in a few minutes ago.' Ross rubbed the sleep out of his eyes.

He said: 'We better grab him, Cass. Why take a chance of waiting?'

'We'll wait,' Chilton said grimly. 'We'll grab the whole bunch tomorrow.'

II

'Don't do that!' Reb Sontag rasped as Luke snapped his watch open for the tenth time within an hour. 'Do you have to look at that timepiece every five minutes? . . . We got hours to go yet!'

Luke glared at him angrily and turned away muttering to himself.

Reb was known to be nerveless in a pinch; he had proved it on a score of occasions when his life hung in the balance. Now the snapping of a watch case was enough to startle him. It was indicative of the tension that gripped them. The Kiowa Kid's smile had not deserted him, however. He seemed the least troubled of all. It was strange, considering that he was a tenderfoot compared with Luke and the others. They had been through similar hours of waiting, of dreadful expectancy, often enough to have become used to them, it seemed. But, of course, there are some things men never get used to when they have a price on their heads.

It was after ten now. All morning, farmers had been driving by, on their way into Pawnee. Their passing pulled the six men to sharp attention. Luke had punched a hole in the rotting front door of the barn, and he watched the road with never-ending suspicion.

He heard a wagon approaching now. He hurried across the barn floor and with his eyes to the hole watched the wagon until it was gone. Turning, he found the Kid standing beside him. Through slitted eyes he regarded Kiowa coldly. 'What's on your mind?' he asked.

His unfriendliness was wasted on the Kid. 'That swell to the north, Luke – you could see almost all the way into Pawnee. A man could crawl through the brush and reach it easy enough.'

Luke shook his head emphatically. 'We're stickin' right here!' he said. 'Don't make any mistake about that, Kid!'

'All right,' the other grinned. 'It was just an idea.'

Together they walked back into the brush at the rear of the barn where a blanket had been spread. Dutch, Ike Patrick and the others were sprawled out around it. On the blanket itself lay their rifles and the bag of ammunition. Earlier, they had played cards. The game had died for lack of interest. There was nothing to do but wait now, and the minutes were crawling like hours.

Eleven o'clock came. Finally it was noon. There was no sign of Doc. Flint Tanner jerked himself to his feet and began to pace back and forth, his lean, hard face corded with anxiety.

'Flint, will you stop it?' Reb growled at him. 'Pull yourself together! There ain't nothin' to worry about. Doc said he wouldn't be back until noon . . . You drive a man nuts!'

'It's noon, and he ain't here,' Flint muttered. 'I don't like it. I got a hunch there's somethin' wrong. I can feel it.'

'You've had that hunch ever since we left the Strip,' the Kid chided. 'If you'd had your way, we would've passed up this chance to get our hands on some real money.'

'You bet we would've passed it up!' Flint blazed back at him. "And that goes for the rest of us, too! You sold Doc this damn-fool idea; it's on your account we're here!'

Kiowa refused to get angry. 'Things have worked out as I said they would, ain't they?' he inquired without raising his voice.

'I don't know whether they have or not!' Flint muttered fiercely. 'I'll tell you better when I see Doc ridin' in . . . And I won't be sure even then.'

There was an insinuation here that the Kid could not ignore. The others were listening, faces shadowed with their thinking.

'Why not call your shots, if you've got somethin' on your mind?' the Kid queried, a thin smile on his lips.

Flint Tanner glowered at him murderously. 'I'll call my shots with you – any time! I'm tellin' you now that I'm damn sick and tired of your smilin', grinnin' mug. You can't mesmerize me like you have Doc. I know what we're facin'. If we're lucky enough to ride out of Pawnee without a shot bein' fired, we'll still be in the soup up to our necks . . . Railroads, telegraph wires, a hundred miles of open country! You can't beat a combination like that! Some of us have taken our last look at the Strip.'

'Doc's got all that figgered out,' said Luke. 'Don't worry about the getaway. Doc never overplays his hand, Flint.'

'You're right; he's always got a trick up his sleeve,' Ike Patrick agreed. Dutch George nodded. Reb grumbled sceptically to himself and got up. Giving his gun belt a hitch, he walked to the barn, his step nervous, hurried. He was back in a minute.

'Don't see nothin' of him yet,' he complained. 'Minutes clickin' away, too . . . Good God, look at your watch, Luke!' he burst out violently. 'What time is it?'

'Eleven minutes past twelve,' said Luke. He didn't try to hide his concern. 'He should have been here by now.'

'You bet he should!' Flint rasped. 'I been tellin' you that for an hour! It don't take him all mornin' to size up a bank –'

'You wait here,' Luke interrupted. 'I'm goin' up the road and have a look.'

He was gone only three or four minutes when they saw him runnin' back. They stiffened in their tracks.

'It's okay,' he told them; 'I see him comin'. He's takin' his time. Ever'thin' must be all right.'

They sighed their relief. The Kiowa Kid dared to laugh.

He said: 'I told you this would work out, Flint.'

'You just be sure it does work out!' Tanner shot back at him. It sobered the Kid in a flash.

'What do you mean?' he demanded, the blood draining away from his face.

'You asked for it, so here it is,' Flint answered stonily: 'Things have a habit of goin' wrong when you're around. I can give you the names of half-a-dozen men, all under the sod today, who were connected with you.'

'Yeh?' Kiowa muttered thinly. 'Accidents happen –'

'Don't let one happen today,' Flint warned. 'I'll be keepin' my eye on you, Kid. One phoney move out of you and it will be your last.'

The Kid stood transfixed for a moment, a steely glitter in his blue eyes. He was quick with a gun, but the odds were all against him here. A flash of sense cut through the red curtain of his rage. 'Hell,' he muttered, with a tight little laugh, 'I ain't goin' to let you burn me up now. This thing will keep.'

'Both of you shut up!' Luke ordered. 'This ain't no time for flyin' off the handle.'

Doc drove in a few minutes later. There was a twinkle in his eyes, proof enough that everything was all right. Accordingly Luke started to scold him.

'You sure took your time,' he said. 'You got any idea of what we been goin' through here, wonderin' what had happened to you?'

'Well, business is business,' the little man declared without the vestige of a smile. 'I sold four orders of rods . . . Mighty neighbourly people round about Pawnee –'

'Come on, Doc, let's have it!' Flint cut in. 'How do things look?'

'They couldn't be better,' the little man declared, with sudden gravity. 'The Kid had everything sized up just as I found it.' He gave Kiowa an approving nod. 'This bank is wide open for a touch. Plenty of money there, too. It didn't take me long to git everythin' located.'

'Why were you so late then?' Flint demanded.

The man's impatience was thoroughly understandable to Doc. 'Well, I heard that the sheriff was goin' over to Argenta on the noon train,' he explained. 'I hung around to see if he would go. He did, and two of his deputies went with him. They can't git back before evenin' . . . That makes it just about perfect for us, don't it?'

Even Flint had no fault to find now. Doc had brought out some food. He got it from the buggy and they sat down around the blanket and ate.

His presence, plus the promise of action, unloosened their snarled nerves. Doc himself seemed as imperturbable as ever. Secretly, he studied the Kid. He knew how the others would stand up, once they reached town. Kiowa had recovered his poise. Still, he had less to say than usual.

'There won't be any difficulty about this, Kid,' Doc observed encouragingly. 'We won't be in Pawnee more than ten minutes. Just keep a cool head and do what you're told. I figger there's a chance we can hoist this bank without firing a shot. That's the way I want it if it can be accomplished.'

'You won't have to be doin' any worryin' about me,' Kiowa assured him.

'There won't be any time for worryin',' the little man reminded pointedly.

'You goin' to leave the team and ride in with us?' the Kid asked.

'No, I'm goin' to drive back.' Doc had his plans all worked out. He called them around him. 'I'll go back in the rig,' he said. 'We'll put the rifles in the buggy and cover them up with this blanket. There's a hitch-rack at the side of the bank. I'll leave the team there. You boys will be behind me all the time. If you're careful, you can ride up to the rack a few seconds after I get there.'

'It's takin' a chance, puttin' all the rifles in the buggy,' Luke objected. 'If anythin' happened –'

'We won't let nothin' happen,' Doc declared grimly. 'And it's worth somethin' to us if we can git into town without our guns showin'.'

He got out an old envelope and, splitting it, drew a map of the bank corner.

'This is the road as it enters town,' he explained. 'We cross the railroad tracks, and the bank is on the next corner, right here. Dutch will lead my hoss. When we get to the rack, he'll gather up the reins of all of 'em and stay right there . . . You got that, Dutch?'

'Yah, I unerstan',' Dutch George nodded.

'There ain't a window on the side of the bank,' Doc went on, 'but there's a back door . . . Ike, you'll keep that back door covered. Just stand at the corner of the alley. Don't let no one come out. That plain?'

'Sure,' Ike muttered. 'Nobody gits out the back door.'

'Right! Now look here,' Doc continued, and his pencil travelled along the side of the bank to the corner; 'Luke and me are goin' into the bank. Reb will make his stand at the front door; Flint, you take the corner; Kid, you'll go on across the street and sit down on the hotel porch. You'll have a grandstand seat. Don't let no one come out. If we get into a jam, you drop back to the back corner.' He looked them over at length. 'Is that all clear to everyone?'

Luke was ready with a question.

He asked: 'That makes five of us who'll be walkin' to the corner. Are we walkin' up together?'

'No,' Doc told him. 'The Kid will start first; he's got the farthest to go. You and me will follow him. Reb and Flint will be behind us. You'll take your rifles out of the buggy as soon as you hand your hosses over to Dutch. Flint can git my rifle and shove it in my saddle boot . . . Anythin' else?'

There were other questions. Doc had a ready answer for each. He told them how they were to close in after Luke and he came out of the bank; how they were to leave town. No detail seemed to have escaped him. He went over everything several times, and when it seemed that they could not possibly have failed to grasp what he expected of them, he drilled them once more.

'Remember,' he cautioned them, 'don't use your guns unless there's no other way out. If we can knock this bank over without any bloodshed it will dull the edge of any pursuit that's organized to run us down. Stealin' money from a bank is one thing; killin' innocent citizens is another.'

It was two o'clock when he told them to put their rifles in the rig. He went into the barn then and looked the horses over carefully. They were going to play an awfully important part in the hours to come.

'Guess you can throw your saddles on 'em, boys,' he said. The Kiowa Kid was the last to enter the barn. Doc gave him an encouraging slap on the back. 'This ain't nothin', Kid,' he protested. 'Let's hear you laugh once.'

A mirthless, perfunctory grin was the best the Kid could manage. 'I'll do my laughin' tomorrow,' he muttered, his blue eyes flinty as he hurried on.

There was something vaguely forbidding in his tone that pulled Doc up. He stared after him for a moment wondering whether to call him back or not. He decided to let it go. 'Nerves,' he told himself. 'He'll snap out of it when he gits movin'.'

He climbed into the rig. He was still wearing the Derby and the glasses. He took the hat off and was about to toss it into the brush when he changed his mind. 'Better wear it,' he told himself. 'I hate the damn thing.'

Luke came out of the barn, leading his horse.

'Luke, you hold your watch on me,' Doc said. 'Give me five minutes, then you boys pull put, two at a time. Don't be more than a hundred yards behind me when I cross the railroad tracks.'

He had no more to say. Raising a hand to Luke, he drove away.

First making sure that there was no one on the road, he turned into it and let the team jog along. The carpet bag that held his .45s rested on the floor of the buggy. He opened it, and unbuttoning his coat, shoved the guns into his belt.

He had time now to go over his plans and all that had been said. He could find nothing he would have changed. Only that remark of the Kid's came back to trouble him. He tried to dismiss it, but it stuck in his mind.

'Funny, he should have said it just that way,' he thought. 'I wonder what he had in his mind.'

III

Though Pawnee was rapidly putting its cow town days behind it and becoming a thriving farm centre, it was still no unusual sight to see three or four cowboys riding into town from the ranches to the southwest.

Doc was counting on that to help him get his men to the bank before the real reason for their presence was discovered. Every second that suspicion could be delayed was precious.

The railroad was just ahead. He glanced back. Luke and Ike were not more than a hundred and fifty yards behind him. The others were only a short distance in the rear. They couldn't have timed themselves better.

'Workin' out nice,' he told himself.

Once across the tracks, he did not look back again: his attention was all on the street ahead of him now. Something queer about it struck him; something that narrowed his eyes to even sharper attention. When he had ridden out of Pawnee that noon the street had been lined with teams. The hitch-racks were deserted now. Only a handful of people were on the sidewalks; all of them men.

'Strange,' he thought. 'Maybe it don't mean a thing, but it looks queer. They couldn't have cleared out any cleaner if they was expectin' us.' But that was preposterous. 'Why, shucks, there can't be nothin' to that,' he argued. 'I been too careful.'

He drove on, every inch of him keyed up to a piercing alertness. Reaching the bank corner, he turned the team into the side street and headed into the hitch-rack. He hadn't been there ten seconds when Luke and Ike Patrick rode up beside him. Their faces were tense, pinched.

'Did you notice that street?' Luke demanded in a breath. 'Somethin' wrong!'

'There can't be,' Doc insisted. 'We're goin' through with this play.'

He was out of the buggy as the others rode up. Their faces were sharp with sudden suspicion of trouble. Flint Tanner was watching the Kid like a hawk.

'Get movin'!' Doc ordered before they could voice what was in their minds. 'Everythin' will be all right!'

The Kid had grabbed his rifle and was walking back to the corner. Dutch had gathered up the reins. Ike was heading for the alley at the rear of the bank. Luke fell in beside Doc as he walked briskly back to the main street. Reb and Flint were only a few feet behind them.

The very air had suddenly become charged with an electric tension. A stillness that was not unlike the hush that precedes a storm had settled on Pawnee.

The Kid had reached the hotel porch opposite the bank by the time Doc and Luke arrived at the corner. Their attention was not on him, but Flint Tanner was following every move he made. He saw Kiowa start to take a chair beside the hotel door. With cat-like quickness then, the Kid leaped through the door.

'Doc, he's gone!' Flint cried. 'He's got inside! The rat has sold us out!'

Doc stopped in his tracks. Before he could speak, Ike Patrick came running back from the alley. His grizzled face was damp with excitement.

'There's a posse down that alley, Doc!' he burst out. 'Seven, eight men! For God's sake don't stand here! We'll be shot down like sheep!'

The little man needed to hear no more. 'Git back to the hosses!' he jerked out. 'We'll follow this side road out! Make it quick!'

They had not taken two steps before the muzzles of three or four rifles were thrust through the open window of the hotel. Instantly, they spurted flame. The four men leaped to the protection of the bank wall. Reb Sontag was a little too slow. Without a sound he swung around on his heels and let his gun fall. Luke tried to grab him, but Reb fell forward on his face, dead when he hit the sidewalk.

'He's gone!' Ike yelled as he saw Doc start to bend down. 'You can't do nuthin' for him! That bunch in the alley will be at us in a second!'

The horses were rearing. The firing from the hotel grew more violent. The four men swung up into their saddles with difficulty. Doc Johnson reached down and untied the team. Flint and Ike had their rifles to their shoulders and were banging away at the snipers in the hotel.

'What do you want of the team?' Luke shouted at Doc.

The little man didn't stop to answer. He grabbed the off horse by the bridle and pulled the team in motion.

'Come on!' he cried to Luke and the others. Reaching the alley, he turned the team into it and sent them crashing into the posse that was dashing toward the street.

The alley was narrow. The possemen, seeing themselves bottled up, flung up their guns and fired. Somehow, Doc weathered the first blast, but before he could wheel his horse a slug crashed into his knee, shattering the bone.

Suddenly weak with excruciating pain, he grabbed his saddle horn, and as he did, a man opened the rear door of the bank and shoved out a gun. It was Cass Chilton, the sheriff, who should have been in Argenta, forty miles away.

'Throw up your hands, Doc! I got you!' Chilton cried.

The words were no more than off his tongue when Flint shot the gun out of his hand. The sheriff leaped back to safety.

'Hang on, Doc!' Luke shouted. 'We got to get outa here!'

'Let go my hoss! I can make it!' the little man flung back. 'Up this road and across the tracks when we git out of town!'

His knee was a grinding torture, but his head was clearing. He threw his big sorrel into a gallop.

Crossing the mouth of the alley, another hail of lead met them. The snipers who had been firing from the hotel had run out into the street. Their slugs were kicking up the dust all around the fleeing men. Ike and Flint turned in their saddles and pumped their rifles as fast as they could work the bolts.

Flint had been hit. The bullet had carried away his hat. Blood smeared his face. Ike had fared even worse. The whole front of him was a gory mess.

Dutch still led the horses that Reb and the Kid had ridden into Pawnee. It slowed him up. Luke grabbed one of the ponies. They couldn't afford to turn the extra mounts adrift until they were out of town. If one of their ponies went down, an extra horse would be priceless.

They were taking it at a dead run now. Open country beckoned them on. Little Doc swung to the south, across the railroad. The others were at his heels. Looking back they could see no sign of a posse; but they would be pursued; that was inevitable. By telegraph, no matter how roundabout the way, the country ahead of them would be warned of their coming. Wanted men, they knew they were riding for their lives.

They cursed the Kiowa Kid as they raked their ponies with the spurs. It was plain enough how he had sold them out to Cass Chilton. The deal had evidently been made before the Kid showed up in the Strip and won Doc's confidence. Just to live and be able to square their accounts with him was all they asked now.

They, at least, had always regarded the Kid with suspicion; Doc had trusted him. That made this black hour of treachery even harder for him to bear. He understood now what was in Kiowa's mind when he had said he would do his laughing to-morrow. Indeed, a hundred little things came back to him with new understanding. No wonder the Kid had been so untroubled on the long ride up from the Strip; he knew where he was going; that they could have ridden down the main street of the towns they avoided and had no hand raised to stop them. Undoubtedly, Chilton had tipped off his brother peace officers to look the other way and wait for him to get the Ghost of the Cimarron and his gang dead-to-rights.

Doc glanced at Ike. The man's face was as grey as ashes. He had seen men die before, and he knew that Ike didn't have long to go. His own body was wracked with agony. From the hip down he had lost all use of his right leg. He could hear the blood sucking up and down in his boot. It made him wonder what his chances were. Flint Tanner's wound was trifling. Luke and Dutch didn't have a mark on them. But this was only the beginning.

They were half a mile out of Pawnee before they saw any sign of the expected pursuit.

'Bunch of 'em comin'!' Luke called.

Doc nodded. 'Let 'em come. They'll think twice about it before they try to close in on us in this open country . . . It's shoot to kill now, boys. Some of us have got to come through this mess. You know why.'

'You bet we know why!' Flint rasped. 'I hope I'm the one lucky enough to meet up with him!'

The road they had followed into town lay before them. They crossed it and struck into the barren, rolling prairie to the west of it.

Doc kept glancing at Ike. The man rode slouched over in his saddle, hands grasping the horn.

'Ike – are you good for another hour?' the little man asked anxiously. 'We're goin' to pull up when we reach that hill where I left you boys when I went in to buy the team.'

'I can make it – and that's about all,' Ike got out with an effort. 'Don't let me slow you up, Doc. It's keno for me this time.'

'You hang on; we'll fix you up,' Doc lied valiantly. He raised his voice. 'Boys, don't push the hosses so hard! Let's see if that bunch wants to close in on us!'

It became apparent in a few minutes that the posse was content to keep them in sight and stay out of range.

'I thought so,' Doc explained. 'They figger they can make us run our ponies into the ground and that they'll git fresh mounts, and maybe some help toward evenin', and have us where they want us . . . We'll play it smarter than that. When we reach the hill we'll hole up until dark. We can stand off fifty men from there.'

There were no counter suggestions; if anyone could get them back to the Strip, he could. They knew he was badly wounded. It encouraged them to find him so full of fight.

In that land of few hills they could not miss the one they sought. With the posse always in sight, though not a shot was exchanged, they approached it. They started to swing around it, only to suddenly send their ponies up the slope.

Cass Chilton was a shrewd man. He sensed the move they were making and he and his men opened fire in a vain attempt to cut them down. In a minute or two the tables were turned and the posse had to drop back.

There was a slight depression on the crest of the hill. It was deep enough to protect the horses. Both Ike and Doc had to be lifted down from their saddles. Luke tore up a shirt and bound the little man's knee. There was nothing they could do for Ike. Flint Tanner refused attention. In his bitterness he had a snarl for all of them.

Doc said: 'I know how you feel, Flint. This is all my fault and I ain't denyin' it. I didn't think a man could fool me; but the Kid got under my skin; I liked him – trusted him.'

'You don't hear me kickin,' Ike Patrick murmured. 'You thought you was right. If we didn't like the set-up we could have pulled out before we left the Strip. You gave us the chance.'

'I ain't blamin' no one but myself,' Flint growled. 'I had the hunch, and I didn't do nothin' about it. That's what burns me!'

They didn't have a drop of water. It was hot on the hilltop. As the sun began to drop toward the horizon, Ike begged for a drink. At times, he was delirious.

'He won't last till dark,' Luke whispered to Doc. The little man could only agree. And yet, when night fell, Ike was still alive. The cool, evening breeze seemed to revive him.

'The moon will be up early,' Flint declared woodenly. 'How much longer are we waitin' here?'

Ike overheard the question and he took it on himself to answer. 'You better go purty soon,' he said. 'It won't git no darker. When you're ready, put me on my horse. Tie my legs so I won't fall off. I'll take the extra horses and ride down the hill and pump my gun as long as I'm able. That'll give the rest of you a chance to get away.'

'No; we can't do that, Ike,' Doc protested. 'You're goin' with us.'

The others objected just as strenuously. Ike only smiled wanly. 'Don't be fools,' he murmured weakly. 'I'm at the end of my string, and I'm goin' out trying' to do somethin' for my pals. You can't deny me that favour, boys. Just git the Kid some day. That'll square everythin' for me and Reb.'

In the end, he had his way. When they had tied him in his saddle, Luke put a rifle in his hands. Ike fumbled with his fingers as he tried to find the trigger.

'There it is,' he muttered. 'I got her now.'

Doc edged his horse up beside him. The others were mounted and waiting. 'Ike – I ain't goin' to say so long er anythin',' he murmured heavily. 'I'd trade places with you in a second if it made any sense –'

'But it don't,' Ike replied. 'You'll lose that leg perhaps, but you'll get by; I can't. Just git these horses movin' for me, and pull your freight.'

Luke Coffey's face was grim in the darkness as he slapped the led horses into a gallop. Over the crest and down the slope they dashed. They carried Ike's pony along with them. His gun began to spit flame.

'Come on,' Doc jerked out harshly, 'and don't forget what happened here.'

IV

Los Alamitos was just a little 'dobe mining town, nestling in a cup of the barren, tawny hills of Old Mexico, two hundred miles south of the Rio Grande.

In the blinding white sunshine of mid-day it was squalid, unlovely, as only Mexican towns can be. But there was always an hour or two in the evening, after the sun had dropped behind the San Jacinto peaks, when a great peace seemed to settle on it; the hills lost their harshness and the town itself seemed to lose its ugliness. To little Doc Johnson it was the pleasantest time of the day.

He and Luke had been in Los Alamitos for almost three years. They had bought a claim above town and built themselves a comfortable shack. If their mine had not begun to pay dividends, it was perfectly all right with them. At least, it gave them an excuse for their presence, and that was enough.

They were situated high enough to give them a commanding view of the valley. Doc liked to sit out in front of the house and watch the purple shadows deepen as evening came on. He was out there this evening, after supper, his pipe going and his wooden leg propped up on a bench of his own making.

He was only a shadow of the wiry man he once had been. Pain had dimmed the reckless light that had burned so brightly in his eyes. For years he had been packing a slug wound around in his back. The old wound, plus the loss of his leg, was dragging him down now. He never complained, though he knew he was riding a down-hill trail; and as the weeks slipped by he talked more and more of going home. Not to Oklahoma; but to the land of his boyhood. In his time, he had roamed over all of the West. Not even to Luke did he indicate which particular part of it was really home to him.

With the supper dishes out of the way Luke joined him this evening. For an hour they sat and smoked, with hardly a word passing between them. Twilight faded into night. Below them the lights of Los Alamitos began to prick the darkness. Doc watched them for a long time.

'A man ought to be contented here,' he murmured quietly, 'we're safe; this mine will make a living if it's worked right; the climate's fine. Don't seem like a person should be wantin' to be somewhere else all the time.'

'It's better than bein' in the pen,' Luke observed bluntly. Through old Texas newspapers they knew that Flint and Dutch had run foul of the law. 'If I was you, I'd think that over considerable before I made up my mind to go back to the States.'

'I've given it a lot of thought, Luke. I don't want to die in prison. The law's got a number of grudges against me, but somehow I figger I won't be picked up. I've never been photographed. That'll be in my favour. I've changed some, too; and I've lost a leg since the law had its last look at me.'

'Don't talk nonsense,' Luke grumbled. 'Men like Heck Short would know you at a glance. Course, I know you ain't thinkin' of going back to Oklahoma; but I don't care where you go, they'll have your description, and they'll pick you up.'

Luke was not as convinced of the soundness of his prophecy as he pretended, though he had voiced it from the moment Doc had first intimated he was thinking of returning to the States. But he did not want to be left alone in Mexico, and he was ready to take any stand that would keep the little man there with him.

'I don't know that you're right,' Doc argued. 'I been away from my home range for seventeen years . . . That's a long time. There can't be so many left who used to know me. As for any printed description of me that's been sent out – well, I'll take my chance on it. I'm goin' back the first of the month, Luke.'

Luke was silent for several minutes, his face grey in the moonlight. 'You always was stubborn,' he muttered. An idea occurred to him that pulled him up in his chair. 'Doc, is all this talk about goin' home only a stall? Are you really aimin' to git back so you can pick up the Kid's trail?'

The little man shook his head thoughtfully. 'No, I'm afraid that's somethin' that never can be squared now. I know Flint and Dutch wouldn't be where they are today if they hadn't tried to run him down. I figgered at first that we might bump into him down here.'

'So did I,' Luke monotoned. 'But he ain't in Mexico; we'd have been tipped off by now, if he was, after the money we offered for word of him. It's a cinch he didn't only square himself with the law but had a piece of change handed him, too. It takes money for a man to drop out of sight as neat as he did.'

'There's never been any argument about that,' said Doc. 'And the money didn't come from Chilton; the railroads or banks put it up, and I reckon the federal marshals had a finger in it.' He shook his head sadly. 'How long ago that all seems!'

Luke studied him for a moment. 'What'll you do if you happen to run into the Kid?'

'What I've always said I'd do,' Doc answered, without turning his head. 'Time don't dim that a bit . . . But about you, Luke. The mine is yours. You can git somebody up here to help you work it. The vein looks purty good.'

'I'll sell the mine first chance I git,' Luke muttered. 'I couldn't stand bein' here alone.'

'I know,' the little man murmured. 'I know exactly how you feel. I don't like to leave you; but I don't give myself over a year. I'd rather go this way; in a few months I won't be able to git around much . . . You've got a lot of livin' ahead of you yet. Maybe that's why you can't understand this feelin' that's draggin' me home –'

'Oh, I want you to go,' Luke exclaimed. 'Your mind is set on it; don't think I'd try to keep you. And don't worry about me; I'll git along all right; I'll drift down to Guaymas or Mazatlán and find somebody that talks my lingo.'

He got to his feet, his hard-bitten face emotionless.

'Night's turnin' cold,' he said; 'you better be comin' in.' His tone was sharp, petulant. Doc understood.

'I'll be in as soon as I finish my pipe,' he told him. His pipe had been out for fifteen minutes. It hurt him to see Luke take his going this way. He could hear him shuffling around in the kitchen, his step leaden. He wanted to say something, but he was strangely without words for such a moment as this. And yet, he was deeply touched. They had been together a long time, and whatever else they were, they had been brave men. Between them there had always been unselfishness, loyalty, gruff kindliness and a faith in each other that few ever know.

The first of the month was only four days away. They were a long time passing. Doc had few things there that he wanted to take with him. When it came time for him to go, he was ready in a few minutes. There was a stage down the mountains to Hermosillo, where he could catch a train for the border. Several hours before the stage was due to leave, Luke and he appeared in Los Alamitos and repaired to their favourite cantina.

After the third round of tequila the world took on a rosier hue, and by stage-time both were beyond remembering why they were in town this evening, which was exactly what they wanted. The driver of the stage had presence of mind enough, however, to round up his prospective passengers. When he came for Doc, the little man did not protest; neither did Luke. In fact, the night was gone and the following day well along before either realized that half the length of Sonora lay between them.

From Arizona, Doc's way lay west. Days later, he stood on a station platform, gazing with fond remembrance at Tularosa, the little Nevada town he had not seen in seventeen years.

'It sure looks good!' he told himself. 'I could find my way around with my eyes shut!'

V

Opposite the depot, where the old Nevada House had stood, he could see the blackened stumps of the foundation. A fire had levelled the place. Nothing else had changed much. The courthouse, with the sheriff's office and the jail at the rear, still stood on a little square of its own, five or six feet above the level of the street. Farther along, he could see familiar signs on the buildings. Even the old Index Saloon was still doing business.

'It sure looks good,' he repeated, his gaze wandering to the coalyard beyond the station. The sign still read: C. P. Haskins, Coal and Ice. There was a man at the scales, but it wasn't C. P.

He started down the street, peering here and there as he clumped along. It was only two blocks to the Index. Only once or twice did he see a face that looked familiar. It rubbed some of the eagerness out of his eyes. But there was Espinosa, the saddle maker, still working at his bench, turning out as fine a saddle as man ever made. It heartened him, and he turned into the Index with head up. A bartender slid a bottle of rye towards him. The man was a stranger.

Doc dashed off his drink before he spoke. 'Billy Krinkle still run the Index?' he asked.

'Krinkle?' the bartender laughed. 'Billy's been laid away ten years or more. Sam Kelting runs the place now . . . You a stranger here, eh?'

'I used to live here years ago,' Doc said as he poured himself a second drink and invited the barman to join him. 'Punched cattle all over this country.'

He asked after four or five old acquaintances. The man had heard the names before, but they were no longer around Tularosa. Vic Rossman still owned the bank; Mose Eberhardt still had the big store. But they had never been buddies of his; it was the boys who had stormed into Tularosa at the steer-shipping, or at the end of the month, pockets bulging with uneasy wages, and turned the town inside out in their frantic haste to catch up with pleasures long denied, that he had come a-seeking.

There was one for whom he had not inquired yet. Dreading the worst, he had held that name back. With unconcealed trepidation, he was about to voice a question concerning him, when a tall, broad-shouldered man pushed back the swinging doors of the saloon and looked in. There was a star on his vest, and he had the indefinable something about him that told the returned prodigal that he was face to face with the sheriff of the county.

He found something vaguely familiar about him. That he was there, seeking him so soon, Doc doubted. But now he saw the sheriff eye him with sudden interest; interest that deepened to frank surprise.

The sheriff let the doors bang behind him as he strode into the Index. The years had greyed his hair; his long moustache was streaked with silver. His eyes had not changed, however, and they wrinkled into a smile now that the little man at the bar would have recognized in China.

'Kim! Kim Younger!' he cried. 'It's you as sure as shootin'.'

The sheriff grabbed his hand and started to pump it. 'Drew Johnson!' he grinned. 'After all these years! Why, you dang little runt, where you been? And what's the meaning of this wooden leg?'

Little Doc – or Drew, to give him his real name – had foreseen these questions, and he had his answers ready. He had been in South America, mining; he had lost his leg in a blast.

'I was almost afraid to ask about you, Kim,' he said; 'the others all seem to be gone.'

'Oh, they ain't all gone. Some of them have moved away, but I hear from them now and then.'

'And your boy, Billy?' Doc asked.

'Big as I am!' Kim declared proudly. 'He'll be twenty this birthday. Wait till he learns you're here! He's never forgot you, Drew.'

Little Doc shook his head. 'A man – and to think I used to ride him on my knee.'

They had too much to talk about to tell it all there. Arm in arm they went up the street to the sheriff's office, and Doc, who had been looking askance at jails and peace officers for a number of years, overcame his uneasiness and settled down in solid comfort.

According to his story, he had made money and lost it several times. He was back in Tularosa to stay now; he had enough to keep him in comfort and wanted to get a little cabin, somewhere on the edge of town, so that he could keep a horse.

Kim knew just the place for him. Before noon came, Doc was settled. The sheriff had been a widower for many years. That evening the two had supper together, with Kim doing the cooking – the first of many meals they were to share. If from that first evening together Doc carried home anything to worry him, it was the fact that Kim was now serving his third term of office, a period covering the years in which the law had marked him as a wanted man.

'But there ain't a trace of suspicion in his mind,' Doc told himself. 'I'd feel it if there was.'

The following day he had Espinosa fix up a saddle for him, with a stirrup made to accommodate his peg leg. Before the saddle was finished he had acquired a roan gelding. He could get around now, and it became the usual thing to see him riding into town from his cabin and hitching his pony in front of the sheriff's office. Often the animal stood there all day, while its owner lounged in one of Kim's comfortable chairs.

Even though he had not been told, Doc would have known before he had been back in Tularosa twenty-four hours that the life of the town had changed. Once it had depended solely on cattle and sheep. Sheep were still important, but the big cow outfits belonged to the past. Sheep had crowded them out. The range had changed; the grass was gone.

But of even greater moment to Tularosa had been the discovery of rich veins of gold ore in the Santa Rosita Mountains, forty miles to the north. It was rich compensation for the passing of the cattle era. A small army of men had taken to the hills, and from the big National mine, the Charleston and a score of others, Tularosa reaped a harvest.

There was not a draw or canyon in those hills with which Doc was not familiar. Untold times he had rolled up in his blanket for the night at the base of the very dike where the National strike had been made.

This mining activity had brought problems of its own to Kim Younger. There had once been a time when he knew just about who was out in the hills. But that was beyond him now; too many new men had drifted in. There had been several robberies already; payrolls on their way to the mines. An attempt had even been made to rob a bullion wagon.

These tales had a peculiar interest for Doc Johnson. Where there were robberies the law became active, and that was a menace to his safety, for if suspicion ever caught him in its web he could not hope to hide his past. Cautiously, he drew the sheriff out on what he knew about the bandits.

'Two of 'em,' Kim told him; 'both masked. They seem to know when the money is going up to the National. I tried to trap 'em last month; laid out in Singer Canyon with my deputies all night; they crossed me and grabbed the payroll down below at Cottonwood Creek Crossing.'

'Likely place for a stickup,' Doc mused. 'Coon Flat is another.'

'No, the Flat's too near the mine,' Kim argued. 'If a man was fool enough to stage a robbery there, where would he go to get away? Over the summit and across the Owyhee Desert?' Younger shook his head confidently. 'I don't believe it; the going would be too hard, and a stranger would get lost.'

Doc let it go at that. In his days of outlawry he had always done the unexpected, and the Owyhee would have served him in this instance.

Kim expected his boy in over the week-end, but Saturday and Sunday passed and young Billy did not put in an appearance. Kim was as disappointed as Doc.

'He'll surely be in next week,' Younger insisted. 'I'll get word to him if I hear of anyone going over towards Antelope Springs.'

Antelope Springs was across the Santa Rosita range, at the edge of the Owyhee. Doc said it was too far to bring the boy in just for a visit. 'No hurry,' he insisted; 'a week or two more don't matter.'

Kim puffed his cigar for a moment. 'I wish I could get him to give up this wild horse idea,' he declared soberly. 'He's been at it all summer and hasn't made a cent. I could get him a job at the National; but that don't appeal to him; he wants to be out in the open, he says.'

'I don't blame him for that,' Doc observed. 'He comes by it natural, Kim, bein' your son.'

'Maybe,' Younger murmured thoughtfully. 'I guess I was wild at his age, too; but I picked my friends a little more careful. I didn't want him to throw in with this fellow Williams, who put this idea of running broomtails into his head. If you want to make anything out of wild horses it takes a big outfit – five or six men – and even then, when you divide up it don't leave anything more than poor wages.'

Tex Williams' name had come into their conversation before. Kim had always spoken disparagingly of him. Doc asked a question or two about him now.

'No, I won't say he's a bad egg,' the sheriff answered. 'You can't help liking him; but he's shiftless, Drew. He's been around here two years or more, and I never knew him to have a job. Billy thinks he's the salt of the earth . . . I can't understand it.'

'Well, he must have had some money to get the old Quigg place at the Springs,' said the little man.

'He didn't put up a cent,' Kim told him. 'The Springs failed completely two years running, and Quigg gave up the place. There's a little water there this year, but the trees are all dead; nothing but sand and sage-brush as far as you can see.'

Doc thought no more about it as the days passed. The following Saturday morning Kim and he were sitting in the shade in front of the office when two horsemen turned the corner and rode towards them.

'Here's Billy now!' Kim exclaimed. And then, with sudden loss of enthusiasm; 'Tex Williams is with him.'

Billy was in the lead. Doc searched his face in vain for some familiar feature. In this lean, bronzed six-footer there was nothing left to remind him of the little lad he had known.

Kim read his thought. He said: 'You wouldn't know him, eh, Drew? . . . And, of course, he'll only remember your name, nothing more.'

The two men slid out of their saddles and Billy turned the ponies over to his friend, who stopped to tie them. Doc's attention was focused only on the boy.

'Billy, I got a surprise for you,' said his father. 'You see this little runt here. Know who he is?'

There was only blank question in the boy's eyes.

'It's Drew Johnson,' said Jim.

The name unlocked some vague but treasured memories in Billy Younger. He shook Doc's hand warmly. 'Pop and I have always wondered what became of you – and here you are back in Tularosa. Where have you been all this time?'

'Oh, South America – Mexico –'

'You have?' Billy beamed. 'That's swell! My pal, Tex Williams, has been down there. I've heard all about it.' He turned to call to Williams. 'Tex, come here! I want you to meet an old friend of mine!'

Tex Williams turned and started towards them, a smile on his lips and his step jaunty. Suddenly his face seemed to go grey, and he half turned, as though about to run. Whatever his hidden impulse, he overcame it, and walked up to them, his good-looking face an expressionless mask.

Unnoticed by Kim and his son, Doc's expression had changed, too. For a split second his eyes had narrowed with a lethal hatred. He had himself in hand now. He was face to face with the Kiowa Kid.

He had sworn to kill him on sight. He had a gun on him; here was the target he had sought; but the Kid was safe for the moment. The little man had put two and two together in a hurry. Many things were plain to him now that Kim Younger had not been able to fathom . . . Robbery – two masked men – a boy with a wild streak in him led astray by a human wolf – a strange knowledge of when money was being sent to the National; of where the sheriff and his deputies would be waiting.

It was very simple, Doc told himself.

'Tex, this is Drew Johnson, one of the best friends I ever had,' young Billy was saying. 'He's been away about seventeen years. Been down in your country. Shake hands with him.'

The Kiowa Kid hesitated, but Doc stuck out his hand. It took nerve to do that, loathing the Kid as he did.

'Glad to meet you,' the Kid muttered.

'Glad to meet anybody who is a friend of Billy's,' said Doc. 'I understand you been in South America.'

'Yeh –' the Kid nodded.

'Then we ought to have somethin' to talk about,' Doc said evenly. 'Look me up . . . I'll be expectin' you.'

VI

It was almost noon before Doc mounted his pony and rode down Tularosa's main street. Instead of going to his cabin, he struck off across the sage-brush flats; he wanted time to think things over before he settled down to wait for the Kid to come.

He knew that Kiowa would come, sooner or later, the time depending on how long it took him to convince himself that he was in no immediate danger of being shot down in his tracks. Doc even dared to believe he knew the line of reasoning the Kid would follow in arriving at such a decision.

'He knows I'll kill him for the rat he is, if I ever git the chance to do it and keep myself in the clear,' he thought; 'but he'll also be smart enough to figger that he's got so much on me that I'll be mighty careful about startin' anythin'. Then it'll occur to him that he can use Billy to tie my hands; and that's just about the truth. If he's got anythin' on the boy, he'll use it as a club on me.'

The thought was enough to whip him into a cursing fury for a minute. With unseeing eyes he stared at the brown Humboldt that flowed along silent and treacherous on its twisting course down the valley.

'It would kill Kim if he ever learned that the boy was mixed up in those robberies,' he muttered fiercely. 'The Kid will think of that, too, damn him! He heard enough this mornin' to know I'll never let that happen if I can prevent it.'

And yet, he had only to think of Reb Sontag, of Ike, of Dutch and Flint Tanner, grinding out their lives in prison, to gaze at the wooden stump that served him for a leg and realize how numbered were his own days, to promise himself that the Kid should die for his treachery.

Before he headed back to town he had resolved on his course. He'd give the Kid a few days to break with Billy. Then he and Kiowa would leave Tularosa together. In some lonely canyon, death would catch up with the latter.

Arrived at home, he left the door open and took a seat inside that permitted him to watch the approach from town. The afternoon wore on without bringing the Kid.

'He'll come,' Doc muttered imperturbably.

Towards evening he saw a rider turn off the main street and strike across the vacant lot towards the cabin. It was the Kid.

'Come in!' Doc called out stonily as the other pulled up at the door.

Kiowa dropped his reins over his pony's head, and taking off his gun-belt, draped it over his saddle horn. Unarmed he strode into the cabin.

Seconds passed as they stared at each other. Doc was in no hurry to speak, and the Kid was silent, too.

'Kid – you know where you stand with me,' the little man said finally.

'Skip it,' Kiowa muttered. 'We got other things to talk about. Before you open up, get this: I ain't afraid of you, Doc. I wouldn't be here if I was. I've got a card up my sleeve, and you know it. You won't start any gunplay with me; and you'll do no talkin'.'

'You got it all figgered out, eh?' Doc inquired flatly. A thin, contemptuous smile hovered over his mouth. 'You ain't afraid, but you was awful careful to leave your guns outside.'

'My way of being smart,' the Kid flung back, with a sickly grin. He couldn't forget that he was standing up to The Ghost of the Cimarron – an experience that had put fear in the hearts of better men than he.

'The same kind of smartness that makes you think you can save your rotten carcass by hidin' behind Billy Younger,' the little man ground out forbiddingly. 'You're goin' to warn me that I can't touch you without smearin' him.'

The Kid found himself beaten to the punch, and it disconcerted him momentarily.

'You figger it will stop me cold,' Doc drove on; 'that to keep Kim Younger from learnin' the truth I'll let you back me into a corner!'

'It'll stop you,' the Kid blurted out viciously.

'No, it won't stop me, Kid! I wouldn't draw the line at letten' you have it right where you stand, unarmed or not. You wrote your ticket when you sold us out in Pawnee. You may figger I'd have some explainin' to do that I couldn't git away with . . . Well, you can forgit that part of it. I came back here to die; it don't matter much to me whether I go now or a few months from now. But I'd like to keep this town's good opinion of me; and I aim to do it. I'm goin' to give you three days to break with Billy. I don't care what excuse you give him. When the three days are up you and me are leavin' this country together.'

'That's what you think,' the Kid jeered. 'Let me tell you somethin'; I'm stickin' right here! I've got things fixed. If anythin' happens to me, Younger and Dan Strickling, the superintendent of the National, will know in twenty-four hours who it was that got those payrolls.'

Wooden-faced, Doc glared at him for a moment. He said.

'Kid, you're lyin'; you ain't that clever!'

From somewhere the Kid found courage to meet him eye to eye. 'If you think I'm lyin', make the most of it!'

He didn't wait to say more.

'Three days!' Doc called out as Kiowa swung up into the saddle.

'You'll wait a long while,' the Kid sneered, riding away.

Doc had not bothered to come to the door. For the better part of an hour he sat in his chair, pursuing his thoughts. He had issued an ultimatum, and he knew in his soul that he never could make it stick. Undoubtedly, the Kid was bluffing about having arranged things so that Kim and Strickling would discover the truth about Billy . . . Undoubtedly; but that wasn't being sure; and Doc realized he was helpless until he could be sure.

'And that'll be never,' he brooded. 'The only way to find out is to step into the trap, and then it'll be too late to do anythin' about it.'

He considered other plans of action, but always young Billy was left open to suspicion. Any thought of speaking plainly to the boy met his prompt veto. There was more to this than just covering up Billy's mistakes; he wanted to see the boy put back on the right trail.

Doc was down town that evening. There was nothing about his manner to suggest that anything was amiss. On the street, he encountered Kim. They walked back to the office together. Kim volunteered the information that Billy and Williams were down the street.

'What do you think of the man?' the sheriff asked.

'Oh, I don't dislike him,' Doc declared casually. 'Little hair-brained, of course.'

'He was out to see you, eh?'

'Yeh. Had quite a talk. I wouldn't try to turn the boy against him if I was you, Kim. This fellow Williams is a rolling stone; he'll pull out of this country without warning some day, and that'll be the end of it.'

'I hope he goes soon,' the sheriff muttered. 'I don't like him. He's dug up a little money from somewhere; he and Billy are spending it.'

'We did the same thing a thousand times,' Doc laughed. 'We never minded being broke.'

'I know we didn't,' Kim grumbled. 'It don't mean a dang thing when you see your boy making the same mistakes you made. I want to see him buckle down and get ahead, amount to something, Drew. I swear I'd rather see him in his grave than to turn out as worthless as some of the boys around town . . . You know he's all I got.'

Doc nodded. He thought he understood fully what was in Kim's mind. His face was grim in the shadows where he sat, outside the office. 'I wouldn't worry about him,' he murmured quietly. 'He's a fine lad, and he'll make a man you'll be proud of. Take my word.'

He sat around with Kim until almost midnight, without seeing anything more of the Kid or Billy.

'You have Sunday dinner with us,' the sheriff invited as Doc was leaving. 'There'll be just the three of us. I'll arrange that.'

Back at his cabin, Doc did not turn in at once. He placed a great significance on the fact that the Kid was beginning to spend money.

'He won't keep that up very long before somebody will be askin' questions,' he said to himself. 'Whatever it is that I do, it can't be put off very long.'

He thought of things that Younger had said that evening. It fortified him in his resolve to close the Kid's mouth forever, as speedily as he could find a way. Kim had been the best friend he had ever had. That alone would have been warrant enough for what he proposed to do.

'I've done a lot of things in my time that was wrong,' he muttered. 'This will be one thing that was right. Maybe it'll help to balance my slate and take a load off my mind as well.'

Kim Younger's cottage was only a block from the office. Doc had just turned the courthouse corner the following noon when Billy overtook him. They walked to the house together.

Kim was in the kitchen. He was really an excellent cook. 'You and Billy sit down and talk for a few minutes,' he said. 'Dinner's about ready.'

'Sure,' Doc answered; 'take your time.'

Without seeming to, he studied the boy as they sat on the porch, and the feeling grew on him that under his calm surface Billy's nerves were tight as a drum; that a tense preoccupation gripped him. Several times Doc had to repeat a question. When asked about their plans for the wild horse round-up, the boy's answers were vague, perfunctory.

Doc knew what was worrying him. It was something that only a man who had lived outside the law could appreciate. The little man found his own conversation drying up, and he was glad when Kim called them to eat.

Before dinner was finished the sheriff made an announcement that pulled Doc up sharply. 'Don Strickling is in town,' Kim said. 'The payroll is going out Tuesday. Dan figures by sending it along a little early it will be safer.'

Doc flashed a glance at Billy. The boy had not looked up from his plate. And now Billy said:

'I wondered why Strickling didn't try something like that. But chances are he won't be stuck up again in a year.'

'I'm going to make sure he won't this time,' Kim declared. 'I'm going to lay out at Cottonwood Creek Crossing and I'll have two or three deputies planted in Singer Canyon. We'll slip out of town tomorrow afternoon and get ourselves fixed before daylight.'

'That ought to do the trick,' Billy remarked, reaching for his coffee. The cup tipped over. 'Damn it!' he snapped irritably. 'Look at that mess!'

Kim passed it off with a laugh. Doc's eyes were empty as he buttered a slice of bread. It was all very plain to him.

'I'd watch Coon Flat,' he said guilelessly, eyeing the boy. He saw the pulse in Billy's neck beat faster; knew he was hanging on his father's answer.

'That's foolish,' Kim said. 'I've told you so before. If you could look at this as a bandit would – and that's the way to look at it – you'd agree with me. The first thing they figure on is a way out . . . No sir, I'll divide my men between the Crossing and Singer Canyon!'

Doc didn't press the point. Billy's relief was evident to him, and that was what he had been angling for. To a certainty he knew that the Kiowa Kid and the boy would be in Coon Flat to hold up Strickling.

The little man told himself he wanted to be alone to decide what he was to do; but twenty-four hours passed and he was still as far as ever from finding a course that would accomplish his ends.

Early Monday afternoon he was at the sheriff's office. He had spent a sleepless night. Stepping into the office he found Kim and Tiny Albers, his chief deputy, with their heads together.

'I didn't know you was busy,' he apologized, starting for the door.

'Come in,' Kim insisted; 'no secrets from you.' He leaned back in his chair and laughed quietly. 'Dan Strickling was just here, Drew. I mentioned your hunch about Coon Flat to him, and he thinks enough of it to send a man out to the mine with word to have four or five of the boys planted down there by daylight tomorrow morning.'

'He does, eh?' Doc queried, as he sought a chair. In his casual tone there was nothing to suggest what this bit of information meant to him.

'I told him to go ahead,' Kim went on. 'I couldn't miss a chance like that to put you in your place, Drew.'

Doc pretended to find it amusing. He asked about Billy, and learned that the boy and the Kid had left Tularosa an hour ago for Antelope Springs.

'No!' Doc exclaimed tensely. 'That's too bad –' His concern was genuine enough, though it did not spring from the reason that Kim Younger supplied.

'Frank Stock has been wantin' me to spend a day or two at the ranch,' the little man went on. 'I figgered I'd ride out with Billy and his friend . . . I suppose they're goin' around by way of the South Fork.'

'They always do,' said Kim. 'If you're ready to go you can overtake 'em; they'll waste an hour at the Willow Point stage station.'

'Well, if that's the case, I think I will tag after 'em. I'll see you in a day or two, Kim . . . So long, Tiny!'

Once he had reached his cabin, he tarried only long enough to get his guns. He set a course across the sage-brush then that would take him into the hills several miles west of Willow Point. It was not in his mind to meet up with the Kid and Billy. By striking through the mountains he could reach Antelope Springs well ahead of them. That was what he proposed to do.

'A shame I can't let the Kid ride into this and git his carcass pumped full of lead,' he brooded. 'But I got to think of Billy; I got to put him in the clear. And I can't wait now. No matter what comes of it, I've got to call the Kid's bluff.'

VII

Twilight was turning the grim, grey Owyhee into an undulating purple sea by the time Doc got his first glimpse of the dead poplars that stood like sentinels around the tumble-down house at Antelope Springs.

Leaving his horse out in the brush, several hundred yards from the house, he approached it warily. The long ride had been an ordeal for him. It made him realize how fast he was slipping.

He convinced himself in a few minutes that he had arrived ahead of Billy and the Kid. The door was not locked. He walked in and looked the place over. Save for a table, a couple of chairs and the bunks, it was bare. In the gloom, he found a lantern on the wall, above the table. He knew they would make a light as soon as they arrived. That meant they would come in the door and go directly to the table. Taking that into consideration, he explored an unused bedroom. Dragging one of the chairs into it, he half closed the door and settled down to await their coming.

The better part of an hour passed before he heard horses approaching. Voices drifted in to him, and he knew it was the boy and the Kiowa Kid. They were at odds about something, their tones sharp, acrimonious.

'You'll go through with this, Billy,' the Kid said flatly as they pulled up at the door. 'It'll give us about ten thousand, altogether. You can do what you please with your end of it; me, I'm goin' to drift.'

Doc saw them enter, black against the door. The Kid was in the lead. He went to the table and took down the lantern. A match flared in his hand. Presently, he had the lantern going. He started to straighten up.

'Stand where you are – both of you,' Doc called out. There was a dreadful finality in his voice. Billy's eyes went round with surprise. The Kid sucked in his breath noisily.

'Now up with your hands,' the little man commanded.

Slowly they obeyed.

Stepping into the room, Doc said: 'Billy, your friend knows I'll bust him without battin' an eyelash. Don't you make the mistake of thinkin' there's any nonsense about this. The two of you turn your faces around now; I want to get your guns.'

When he had disarmed them he told them to sit down on the bunk. The smoke-blackened lantern cast its flickering light on them. The Kid's face was murderous; Billy could only stare his amazement.

'We're goin' to have a little talk, boys,' Doc said. 'I know you're due at Coon Flat in a few hours. You needn't worry about it; we'll take care of that little stickup.'

Billy didn't protest his innocence nor pretend not to understand this talk of stickup at Coon Flat. Doc liked him better for it.

'I warned you not to start anythin' with me!' the Kid whipped out. 'That still goes!'

'It goes in the discard with me,' Doc got out tonelessly. 'Bluff or not, I'm callin' your hand tonight. And just so Billy will understand what we're talkin' about, we'll start from scratch. We'll put all the cards on the table.' He broke off to gaze at the boy for a moment. 'Billy,' he said softly, 'have you ever heard of Doc Johnson, the outlaw – sometimes called The Ghost of the Cimarron?'

'I've read about him in the papers,' the boy acknowledged. His face was bloodless in the flickering light.

'Well, you're lookin' at him,' the little man monotoned. 'I'm Doc Johnson – '

'Oh, don't take that way of handing it to me,' Billy burst out desperately. 'I know you've got me, Drew. You don't have to invent any story –'

'I'm Doc Johnson,' the other went on, ignoring the interruption, 'and this skunk, that you call your friend, used to ride with my bunch. His name wasn't Tex Williams in those days. We called him the Kiowa Kid –'

Incredulity began to fade out of the boy's eyes, and as Doc went on relating step by step the tragedy and treachery of that day in Pawnee, the dead level tone rising to a horrible hammer beat, he knew he was hearing the truth. It seemed to put a spell on him, and, speechless, his gaze went from Doc to the Kid and back again in pathetic amazement.

As for the Kid, his eyes were as venomous as an adder's as he sat muttering and cursing to himself.

Doc brought his story up to his return to Tularosa and his talk with Kiowa.

'Drew, will you believe me, when I tell you I got mixed up in that first holdup before I knew what I was doing?' Billy burst out. 'I got information from Pop that this rat wanted. I passed it along to him, and then he threatened to give me away if I didn't go through with the job . . . After that he had plenty on me.'

'And I got plenty on you now!' the Kid ground out. 'You'll be awful careful that nothin' happens to me.'

Doc said: 'Shut up! Nothin' you can say will change this play a bit.' He addressed himself to the boy again. 'You know what it'll do to your father if he finds out.'

Billy nodded miserably. 'Been driving me mad,' he murmured.

'Well, I figger he won't know. If I'm wrong, it won't help this rattler none . . . Where is the stuff you got off Strickling?'

Billy jerked his head at the Kid. 'He buried it.'

'Where?'

'Under the horse trough.'

The Kid ripped out an oath. 'I suppose you're goin' to return it,' he sneered. 'That's rich; Doc Johnson handin' over a bunch of jack like that!'

'Stranger things have happened,' the little man droned. He told them about Strickling's altered plans; of the trap that awaited them at Coon Flat. 'I wish I could have let you ride into that, Kid. But no matter; I've got somethin' better fixed up for you.' He turned to the boy. 'Now rip up that bedtick, Billy; I'm going to tie up both of you. I'll leave you here. Me and the Kid are goin' to stick up Strickling tomorrow mornin'.'

'No, Drew!' Billy protested. 'You'll be killed!'

'Not both of us,' said Doc. 'You get the tick ripped up. And git this; it's your story: I been around here, under cover, for three months. You never was sure about it until tonight. You been passin' information on to the Kid. It hit you all at once this evenin' what you had been doin'. You tried to stop us, and we knocked you cold and left you here . . . You just stick to that. It will work out okay.'

Billy tried to object, but in the end he did as he had been told.

'Now you stretch out on the floor, Kid,' Doc ordered. 'Be damn sure you lie still.'

'If you want me on the floor you'll have to put me there!' the Kid growled defiantly.

Doc raised his gun an inch or two. A slug burned the Kid's cheek. 'Will you git down as I asked?' he demanded without inflection.

Slowly the Kid obeyed. His hands were bound behind him. Doc then bound the boy hand and foot and pushed him over on the bunk. 'I got to mess you up a little,' he said flatly. He made a thorough job of it.

After picking up the Kid's guns he told the latter to get to his feet. 'Git outside now and git on your horse. One wrong move out of you and it'll be all over.'

The Kid mounted.

'Head for the little arroyo beyond the corral,' Doc ordered. 'My pony is there.'

Ten minutes later they were moving into the hills. Doc looked back once. He could no longer see the light that burned in the house. 'Kid,' he muttered dismally, 'I hope Reb and Ike are watchin'. They been waitin' a long time for this.'

The Kid had no words in him.

Daylight found them stretched out on a rocky shelf, about fifteen feet above the trail Strickling must take on his way up to the National. A spur of the Santa Rositas, dwindling away to ragged little hills, had brought them to where they lay. In a narrow ravine, to the rear of them, they had hidden their ponies.

In the lemon yellow dawn little Doc scanned the ountry round about. A mile or more below him he could see the fringe of trees at Cottonwood Creek Crossing. Kim and one or two men would be there, scanning the trail even as he was. To the north, Tiny Albers and his companions would be watching from their ambush in Singer Canyon. Presently, Dan Strickling would come riding by, and then the final scene in this little play would hold the stage for a brief and bitter moment.

Doc's gaze returned to the Kid stretched out five or six feet away. They had not spoken in hours. There was nothing to be said. When a man stands on the scaffold, the noose about his neck and the black cap drawn down over his face, the world about him standing still, waiting, he knows it is too late for words.

It was like that with the Kiowa Kid. He was all bad, and he had a wide streak of yellow in him, but he did not whine nor beg. Not because he was above whining; he knew it was too late for that; that it had been too late ever since that afternoon in Pawnee.

If the Kid's mouth twitched; if his eyes were wide, staring, it was not strange; he had a taste in his mouth that was like ashes; he was gazing at something beyond the understanding of man.

The yellow sky warmed to rose, and the dawn wind sprang up. Somewhere off in the malpais a coyote bayed his obeisance to the wonder of the new day; and then a little speck came bobbing along the trail. It was Dan Strickling, a rifle across his saddle bow and four thousand dollars in coin in his saddle bags.

It does not take a man long to cover a mile when he is astride a good horse. The Kid heard the patter of the pony, and he looked. For ten seconds he looked, and he marvelled at how fast the man came. And then the Kiowa Kid put his face in the dust and groaned.

And now Dan Strickling was riding by.

'Kid,' Doc whispered, 'this is where you git it.'

The little man's hand was steady, and his aim was true.

A shudder or two, and the Kid lay still. But Doc was not watching. He was pumping his guns in the direction of Dan Strickling. If he failed to score a hit it was no accident.

The superintendent of the National flung his rifle to his shoulder and fired several times. Then he used his spurs, just as Doc had known he would.

The little man watched him go. Then he removed the Kid's bonds and put a gun in the stiffening fingers. All he had to do now was to get back to his horse and hope he could win across the Owyhee. Kim would find the Kid. How reasonable it would be to suppose that one of Dan Strickling's shots had killed him.

Time was precious; the shooting would have been heard at the Crossing. Doc began to run, his wooden stump banging on the rocks. He had gone only a few yards when he fell. He scrambled up, but before he could take a step a gun roared. Clutching his stomach, he tumbled forward.

It was Kim and his deputies, trying to keep abreast of Strickling. The sheriff had found a fresh trail, and it had led him to the two ponies.

Ten hours later Doc opened his eyes. He was in the little hospital in Tularosa. Men who have been shot in the stomach with a 30-30 rifle do not get better.

The nurse stepped out of the room and a man entered. It was Kim Younger. He sat down beside the bed. For a long time he and Doc gazed at each other. There was great understanding in that steadfast meeting of the eyes. In itself it made all things right between them. But Kim had been waiting there for hours, hoping he might be able to say a word or two.

'Drew,' he murmured softly, 'I want you to know I appreciate what you did. I know all . . . Billy told me.'

Doc shook his head weakly. 'Why did he have to do that?' he murmured. 'I didn't want you to know, Kim –'

'He couldn't keep the truth back. I went to the springs and found him trussed up, just as you'd left him. He showed me where the money was.' Kim sighed heavily. 'It's broken me all up, Drew – finding this out. I never dreamed the boy was mixed up in these robberies –'

Doc's eyes were sharp again for a moment. 'Anyone else know?'

'No – only me.'

'That's good . . . No one must ever know.'

Kim shook his head grimly. 'They've got to know! I've got to tell 'em, Drew! I couldn't let them go on thinking that you were a thief. It would be different if you had ever had a black mark against you.'

Little Doc studied him with veiled eyes. Kim had said he knew all, but it was plain enough that he was mistaken; that Billy's story had not disclosed the fact that Drew Johnson and The Ghost of the Cimarron were one. It silenced the little man for a minute or two; he wanted to be awfully sure that he said the right thing now.

'Kim,' he said at last, 'an hour or two is all I've got left . . . Oh, that's all right,' he insisted as the other would have denied the obvious. 'I ain't kickin' a bit; but you can't deny me the last favour I'll ever ask. What people think of me after I'm gone don't matter. You know I tried to cover up for the boy. I don't want to kick off knowin' it was all in vain . . . You've got to let folks think that holdup was on the level.'

Unnoticed, Billy had entered the room. His eyes were bleak as he approached the bed.

'Drew, I heard what you just said,' his voice seemed to stick in his throat. 'I can't let you cover up for me. I made a mistake, and I'm ready to pay for it –'

Doc's fingers searched for his hand. A ghost of a smile softened his chalk-like face. 'It's all right, my boy; you've begun to pay for it already; and you'll keep on payin' as long as you're on the level with yourself . . . I gave you a story to tell your father. You could have stuck to it and no one would ever have questioned you. But you wouldn't take that way out; you admitted your mistake; and if there was one thing I had to know about you to prove that the wild streak in you ain't a bad streak, it was that.'

'I had to play it that way,' Billy got out brokenly, unashamed of his misting eyes, 'I had to tell Pop . . . I hope you aren't sore about it, Drew –'

Little Doc shook his head faintly. 'I ain't sore about nothin' now, Billy. For the first time in years everythin' is all right with me . . . I'm restin' easy.'

George Brydges Rodney

The Killers

TWENTY-TWO LE GRAND, official lion-hunter for the Huisache District, buying cartridges in Jolter's Emporium in Elkhorn, flinched under a heavy-handed slap on his shoulder. He faced to see big Frank Gaines, the sheriff of Vargas County.

'I've been waitin' for you, Twenty-two,' quoth Gaines. 'I got some dam' bad news fer you.'

Twenty-two blinked at him wordlessly. He was nearly seventy years old and did not weigh more than a hundred and twenty. He was as thin as an elk's sinew but as strong as 'whang'. Twenty-two Le Grand was an institution in the land. He drew Government pay as an official lion-hunter plus a county bonus on the scalps. For thirty years he had worked at his trade. At first men had scoffed at killing lions with a twenty-two calibre rifle, but the laughter died as men saw old Twenty-two, with a light rifle and a fox terrier, rid the range of the pests. For five years Twenty-two had, with his partner Scotty Barnes, sporadically worked a gold claim in the Secaturas till a dynamite blast, exploding prematurely, left Scotty blind and wholly dependent on Twenty-two. The curious affection that work breeds between men stood the strain. Twenty-two, grim, grey and silent, ranged the hills while blind Scotty, equally silent, learned to keep house.

'What's the matter?' asked Twenty-two.

'Ben Timmins came in a bit ago,' said Gaines. 'Damn it all, Twenty-two, I'm no good at beatin' about the bush. You been home lately?'

'Not fer three days. I been up in the Hand o' God hills after lions.'

'Whitey Morgan got loose from the La Salle jail yesterday,' said Gaines. 'He drifted down past your place last night. He found poor ol' Scotty by his-self. He killed Scotty an' looted the house an' –'

Twenty-two clawed at the counter and for a moment the world seemed black. 'Tell me all you know,' he said.

'Ben didn't see smoke so he went in the house. Scotty was lyin' on the floor. He had his gun in his hand and an axe was layin' by him . . .'

'How'd Ben know it was Morgan?' demanded Twenty-two.

'They found his footprints at your spring. They was the prints o' boots with M on 'em in nails. Sheriff Oakes from La Salle says that's Morgan. But there's more to it 'n that. Lee here, who keeps the Bon Ton garage, says that last night he seen a man standin' around but paid no attention to him till he seen him signal Jim Pender fer a lift. Lee says that Jim picked the man up and, as he climbed in the car, he seen then it was Morgan. Lee says the whole thing was so open that he thought Morgan must have been pardoned or somethin' like that. Anyhow, that's how things stand. Morgan killed Scotty and got Jim Pender to give him a lift. I had to tell you, ol' timer. Did you see Wilson o' the Bar O? He was lookin' fer you. You know that old lion they call Stub-tail?'

Twenty-two nodded wordlessly, his mind on his other affairs.

'Wilson says he turned loose a two-thousand-dollar thoroughbred stallion,' said Gaines, 'an' that lion, ol' Stub-tail, killed him. His neck was tore out and he was all cat-clawed. Morez, Wilson's man, seen the lion runnin' off at daylight after the killin'. There's a five-hundred-dollar reward fer that cat. You git the cat an' we all 'll git Morgan. Wilson told me to tell you to come out to the Bar O fixed to stay till you git that cat.'

Twenty-two pondered the matter. He did not think quickly. In any case Gaines was right. Morgan's capture was a matter for the officers of the law. His own business first was to do the work he was paid for doing. When he had done that he could assist Gaines. He turned to the big sheriff.

'All right,' he said, 'I'll get on out to the Bar O, but I'll be back an' help you git Morgan. I'll get him if it takes all my life.'

He picked up his cartridges, whistled Nip, his fox terrier, and drifted out of the store with the noiseless step of the mountain man.

He knew that his quest would be difficult. He had had many trials of intelligence with the great lion and had always come off second-best. This time, he determined, should be the last so that he could return and devote his time to running down Morgan, who had killed old Scotty. Head bent and eyes on his feet, he walked slowly over to the one little drug store, where Ed Juston, the proprietor, greeted him pleasantly and went on with his work.

'Ne' mind me, Ed . . .' Twenty-two passed behind the counter and busied himself at a bottle-filled shelf. 'I only want ten cents wuth o' this.'

Juston looked, laughed and filled a bottle.

'You must be fixin' to go to a dance an' git throwed out,' he said.

Twenty-two stowed his purchase in his pocket, swung into the saddle and headed his ancient pony, Red, for the Jawbone Pass, letting him pick his own gait.

Far over to the left a dust-devil danced athwart the plain till a cross-current of hot air cut it down. A shimmering blue mirage rose above the mesquite tops and prairie dogs yip-yapping at him drove Nip frantic. Twenty-two saw all subconsciously. He was seeking the answer to a problem. He and that tan devil, Stub-tail, had clashed in battle and so far the cat had won. In the midst of his planning he spied on the soft sand of the desert floor a mark that had not been made by man or beast. It was just a sort of broad smear across the sand as though a great broom had been passed over the sands. Twenty-two scrutinized it carefully.

'What the devil has done that? What fer kind of a thing makes a trail six foot wide? I'm a-goin' to find out.'

That trail led straight across the flat heading for the distant foothills, and he followed it for hour after hour. Finally he stopped by a huge pinnacle of red rock, drank some warm water from his canteen and swabbed out his pony's mouth; then he swung again into the saddle and urged the tired pony across the shifting sands.

'Hey there! What's that?'

He drew Red to a sudden halt as a huge buzzard rose from a clump of greasewood and soared ponderously. Twenty-two caught the rush of air from his wings as he settled close at hand. Then another buzzard dropped from the central blue. Twenty-two urged Red to a real walk. Then suddenly he uttered a sharp oath and drove both spurs into the rowel-seats and clattered down the slope with his pack jangling. There before him a small, dilapidated automobile, dusty and sun-scarred, lay on its side. It had ploughed up the sand as a plough turns a furrow and twenty-two eyed it critically as he rode up to it. He noted the absence of licence plates, then he saw something else: a rope had been tied to the axle, the other end of that rope was fast to a great bundle of brush wrapped in some old ore-sacks. The cause of that curious trail was plain to his desert-trained eyes. The driver of that car had sought to wipe out all signs of his tyre-marks.

A harsh croak and the flutter of heavy wings made him glance up and he saw three great buzzards hopping about among the greasewood clumps. He flung out of the saddle and covered twenty yards to a dark clump of brush that half-hid a long dark object. His first glance told him what it was – the body of a man. The body lay on its face, a hat by it and a great piece of ore-bearing rock, dark and stained with blood, lay close by. He picked up the rock, examined it and laid it aside. Then he leaned over the body.

'Huh,' he muttered. 'It's Jim Pender. The back of his head's been beat in. That's what comes o' pickin' up a stranger fer a ride.'

He picked up the rock and almost at first glance the matter became clear. There is no rock on the desert. That rock came from the hills and his knowledge of ore and the sight of a filled ore-sack in the car told him that Pender's head had been beaten in with a piece of rock from his own prospect that he happened to have in his car when he picked up Morgan, not knowing who he was. Then Morgan had tied the brush behind the car to brush out all trail sign. The inference was plain.

'Morgan's got this far, anyhow,' muttered Twenty-two. 'I'll get over to the Bar O an' have Wilson telephone Gaines to get his posse over in this direction.'

When Wilson, at the Bar O, learned what Twenty-two had found, his wrath overflowed.

'I'll git Gaines at once,' he snapped. 'You never mind him. We all 'll git Morgan. He can't git away. You git that lion. That's what you're paid for. We'll git Morgan.'

Twenty-two nodded wordlessly, ate his supper and bedded down under a huge alamo cottonwood. Sun-up found him heading for the blue foot-hills where rumour said the big lion had last been seen.

Twenty-two knew lions as well as any man can know them; that is, he knew that nothing can be certainly foretold of them. He found the valley and located the bones of the dead stallion that had been picked clean by coyotes. He studied the locality. The lion, of course, had killed far from his lair and he would certainly seek water after his kill. Twenty-two mounted Red and headed for the nearest water-hole, a placid pool of brown water under some stunted juniper trees. Tangled scrub overhung three sides of the pond and on the fourth side a deep-trodden cattle-trail led between two huge boulders to the water's edge. Twenty-two unslung his canteen, left Red at the open end of the trail, and, kneeling at the water's edge, sank his canteen to fill it. In that moment it happened.

A mountain seemed to fall from the hot, blue sky above him. He was flattened out like a frog on a rock. His grey old face was ground into the shallow water and he was nearly drowned as he fought for breath. Then his arms were almost twisted from their sockets he was dimly aware of hands clawing at his wind-pipe; then being dragged feet-first from the pool and flung upon his back.

When consciousness returned, he was lying on his back under a mesquite bush, his hands were tied behind his back and his mouth was filled with blood and sand. Deadly nausea overcame him. He turned on his side and was violently sick. As he sat up he was aware of a man squatting under a bush malevolently regarding his every movement. He had seen that man once before and he knew him at once. It was Whitey Morgan, the Killer.

The man was as huge as a gorilla. His bowed shoulders were inhuman in their spread and his shaven head was set on his frame without any semblance of a neck. Bestial power was there. The man was a hold-over from the Stone Age.

'Well,' snarled Morgan. 'You know me, huh? What the hell was you follerin' me fer?'

'I wasn't follerin' you,' said Twenty-two. 'I come up here to track a mountain lion that killed a two-thousand-dollar stallion fer the Bar O ranch.'

'Like hell you did. Think I don't know? Well, you got yourself into one hell of a mess. What you got on that cayuse? I need supplies.' He walked over and examined the pack on Red. 'Grub, huh? That's good. I need grub. What else you got?'

He went through Twenty-two's pockets and laid the result on a rock.

'Matches . . . tobacco an' this damned bottle, huh? What's this?' He sniffed at the purchase Twenty-two had made at Juston's drug store. 'What in hell's this stinkin' stuff?'

Twenty-two made no reply. His mind was on other things. He knew that Morgan would not stop at another killing. If he could not manage to escape, his fate was sealed.

The roan pony chose that particular moment to roll with his pack. With a little grunt, he sank on his off side and with a jangle of his equipment rolled over, and the sack of flour burst. Morgan flung himself at the pony with a crackling oath.

'Up, you damned fool,' he shouted, and kicked viciously.

That fierce kick went home on the slender foreleg, and with a little grunt Red tried to move. But the leg had broken like a pipe-stem. Twenty-two let go a sharp oath as Morgan, after one look at his handiwork, raised his rifle and fired. Red crumpled up like a wet hide, kicked once and lay still, and Morgan turned on his prisoner.

'I was aimin' to kill you right here,' he snarled, 'but now the pony's dead I'll pack you instead o' him. By God, I'll pack you like a burro.'

He jerked the helpless Twenty-two to his feet and, making as small a pack as he could of flour, coffee and bacon, he fastened the pack to Twenty-two's shoulders with the latigo cut from the saddle.

'You're my burro,' he snarled. 'Break down an' you git a bullet 'tween the ears like the horse did. Hit the trail.'

Twenty-two took a few steps and almost fell. He snatched at a mesquite bush and recovered his balance. The pack weighed nearly fifty pounds and to pack it along a mid-Arizona trail on an August afternoon was plain hell. Morgan's jeering comments passed unheeded. From time to time Morgan tried to kill Nip with the rifle but Nip was wary.

'For God's sake gi' me water,' sobbed Twenty-two finally, as they stopped for breath at the top of a steep rise.

Morgan gave him a small swallow of water and drank some himself.

'Pour some on my wrists,' said Twenty-two. 'They're chafed raw.'

Morgan splashed a few drops on the chafed wrists and laughed at the sight of the caked blood. A moment later he kicked Twenty-two to his feet and prodded him into the trail with the muzzle of his cocked rifle. He had slung Twenty-two's light rifle across his shoulders.

He made camp that night upon Wolf Mesa that is edged with a rim-rock that stands thirty feet sheer above the flat lands. The flat mesa is covered with mesquite and madrono and the land below the rim-rock is a universal tangle of cats-claw and mesquite and wild gourd vines. Morgan snatched the lariat from the pack and lashed Twenty-two's feet with it; then he set to work to make a fire.

The sun was bedding in a belt of blue-black clouds and a cold wind was blowing in fitful gusts, sure precursor of a wind-storm. Suddenly, out of that blue and sulphur-coloured sky, under the dark veil of the junipers, a shrill scream echoed and re-echoed. There was about that scream a note so eerie and soul-searching that Morgan, who was city-bred, felt his blood chill. He dropped an armful of fuel and straightened up.

'What – what the hell is that?' he asked quaveringly.

'Mountain lion,' grunted Twenty-two. 'A big one. It's smelt us. You'd better git a lot o' wood. I never heerd one yell like that less'n he meant fight – listen to that, will you.'

Another yell shrilled out above the fitful booming of the wind in the juniper bush.

'By God!' Twenty-two's voice changed. 'There's a second one . . . An' a third too. A whole bunch o' lions has got together. They do that sometimes.'

Shrill screams tore the sun-set with a threatening note. In all the desert there is no sound like that scream. For complete and utter loneliness, for desolateness and weird grief that scream stands alone. It is like the hopeless scream of a crazy woman and it makes the hearer realize the depth of human woe. As that cry echoed among the canyons below the rim-rock Morgan picked up his rifle and drew closer to the fire.

'Three of 'em huh? Do they ever attack man?'

'When two er three git together they've been knowed to,' said Twenty-two. 'You'd better git a lot o' wood. I wouldn't go out among the brush after dark. Not tonight. You'll need a big fire tonight.'

If Twenty-two had asked to be released, Morgan would have suspected a plan. As it was he cast an apprehensive glance at the dark ring of the juniper brush and set to work to gather wood. The moment he passed into the heavy scrub, Twenty-two came to life. That request to have water poured on his wrists had been made for a purpose. When wet, raw-hide will stretch like rubber, a fact that Morgan either did not know or had forgotten. Twenty-two hitched his body away from the fire till he felt his sore wrists strike a ledge of sharp-edged rock. The stone was soft from weather but he sawed and rubbed his wrists along it. From time to time a sharp edge cut his flesh and won a curse but he sawed steadily for he knew he had no time to lose. Finally the raw-hide gave a little then it fell apart, chafed in two and his hands were freed.

Morgan coming back to the fire with a load of wood, dropped his wood and picked up his rifle. He needed more fuel but he dared not go far from the protecting fire with those yells and screams ringing in his ears. He glanced at Twenty-two. The old man lay like a graven image. Satisfied, Morgan went for more wood while Twenty-two worked and twisted his hands behind his back to restore his circulation. The moment Morgan was hidden by the brush, Twenty-two fumbled a knife from a pocket, cut his feet free and snatched the twenty-two rifle that gave him his name. Softly and quickly he worked the lever and saw that the magazine was full. He knew that he could not oppose a light rifle to Morgan's heavy gun.

'I got to whittle him down to my size,' he muttered. 'I'll fix him so he can't shoot.'

He lay motionless as Morgan returned and threw an armful of wood on the fire. A sudden gust of wind drove the black greasy smoke into the killer's face and he was still cursing and wiping his weeping eyes when Twenty-two fired.

The crack of the rifle sounded like a field gun in the stillness. Then a blistering curse broke from Morgan as his right hand dropped to his side with a bullet through the wrist. The blood spurted out in great jets and the hand hung as from a leather hinge. He strove to swing his rifle to the front but Twenty-two was too quick for him.

'Drop that gun or I'll kill you,' he snapped.

The gun-muzzle was not ten feet from Morgan's belly. His hands went up. With a sweep of his foot Twenty-two sent the rifle beyond Morgan's reach. It hit a rock and the stock broke.

'Drop your right hand,' said Twenty-two. 'Move your left hand and I'll kill you.'

He swiftly retrieved the lariat and cast the loop about Morgan's left hand. He jerked that hand down and circled the body with a quick twist of the rope and lashed the arm fast to the body. Morgan cursed and begged.

'I'm bleedin' to death,' he whined. 'You le' me go an' I'll –'

'Shut up,' snarled Twenty-two. 'Save your breath. You'll need it.'

Then he caught the wounded right hand, jerked it down and lashed it to the other and tied a bit of 'whang' about the wrist to check the blood flow.

'Now we'll hit the trail,' he said. 'With them three lions on the prod, I ain't spendin' a night here. We'll head fer the rim-rock.' He prodded Morgan in the back with the muzzle of his cocked rifle and they headed for the rim-rock.

That rock dropped twenty feet sheer and its edge was fringed with juniper trees. Twenty-two drove Morgan close to a juniper not ten feet from the cliff edge.

'I'll fix you to stay put while I git wood,' he said. 'Put your arms around that 'ere tree.'

In mortal terror of that rifle, Morgan obeyed. The next moment a rope was passed about his neck and he was lashed with his face to the rough tree-bole; then his hands were drawn together on the far side of the tree and were tightly lashed. His wounded wrist was bleeding afresh and his whole arm ached.

'Now I reckon you'll stay where I put you,' muttered Twenty-two. He paused as a whiff of stench came to him from Morgan. 'Where's that bottle you took outen my pocket?' he asked. Without waiting for an answer he thrust a hand into Morgan's coat pocket and drew it out wet. 'Whew!' He smelled his hand and was almost sick. 'If you admire that stink you kin have my share of it. That's Valerian. Them cats'll travel miles to git it. Same as a dog with carrion –'

A sudden sharp, blood-curdling scream made even Twenty-two jump.

'Huh. When you broke that bottle you most likely drawed all the cats in ten miles. If that's so, I'll likely have to set up all night.'

He set to work gathering wood and night had come when he got back with his last load. Afar in the brush he saw two points of greenish light. Seeing them, Nip made a quick rush into the scrub and came back whimpering as a long yell rose in the scrub. Twenty-two flung an armful of fuel on the fire and turned to his prisoner.

'Why'd you kill old Scotty Barnes?' he asked. 'He was my partner. He was blind and never hurt anybody in his life. Why'd you kill him? eh?'

'You go to hell,' said Morgan. 'How'd I know he was blind? I seen him go fer his gun an' I plugged him. You listen to me – you turn me loose an' I'll square it all right with you. See if I don't –'

Twenty-two paid no attention to him. His thoughts were with his dead partner. He rose to search for his pipe and in rising made his great mistake. He stepped too close to Morgan.

As the wizened body brushed against him, Morgan the Killer saw his chance. He saw one last chance for his revenge and he took it without a thought of what lay beyond. His booted foot, shod with heavy leather reinforced with steel shot out like a huge piston and the heel caught twenty-two full in the groin. The impact sent him backward, staggering to a fall. Nip started up with a growl and rushed at his master who staggered back and back. He snatched at madrono and grease-wood but they stripped in his grip as his heels struck the edge of the rim-rock and he toppled over into the gorge below. Nip made a wild dash at his vanishing figure and with a little whimper hurled himself into space to follow the master he loved. The scuffle of Twenty-two's feet on the shaly scarp was followed by the tinkle of falling stones. Then came silence.

For a long five minutes Whitey Morgan did not realize what he had done. His one-track mind was filled with rejoicing that he had killed his foe for no ordinary man could live after a fall like that. He pulled and wrenched at his bound wrists but that whang that tied them did not give.

His heart sank almost with a thud. He could not get loose. Yet – to stay here was to die miserably in his bonds. To die of hunger and thirst. Thirst! When he could hear the cluck and gurgle of a running stream in the canyon below him. Even if men should rescue him, his fate was sealed. He would certainly he hanged. In killing old Twenty-two he had only made his own fate more certain.

He pulled and tugged at his bonds that gave a little as the sweat from his aching wrists wet the raw-hide. But they did not give enough to release his hands. Old Twenty-two had tied him too securely for that. Also some sand got on the 'whang' and worked into the raw flesh and, with salty sweat and chafing his wrists burned like fire. A dull ache like the ache of a raging tooth ran up both arms to the elbows and his back and shoulders felt as though he had been beaten for hours. He moved restlessly a few inches and a groan burst from his parched lips. But even yet he did not realize his predicament.

The fire crashed into a bed of embers and a cloud of grey ash rose in a smoky spiral. The heavy stinking reek of valerian rose and sickened him. He had never known it before. Now he only found it the worst stench that he had ever known. Then, suddenly, those words of Twenty-two recurred to him.

'That stink'll draw cats for twenty miles,' he had said.

He turned his head from the tree to get fresh air and he gave a sudden gasp as his eyes focused on two points of green fire low down in the brush across the fire from him. He gave a sudden yell. The lights shifted and went out as lamps are blown out in a high wind. Then they lit again – closer!

Frenziedly the thoroughly alarmed man tugged and strained at his wounded wrists. The tough raw-hide slid along the sweaty flesh and brought fresh blood but no release. The mingled smell of blood and sweat and wood-smoke and valerian drove in a gust toward those gleaming points of light but the raw-hide did not give. He kicked wildly and his scuffling feet sent a shower of stones and gravel across the dying fire. A jet of sparks rose and those green lights again went out. They lit again a little to the right then. Morgan's heart leaped into his throat at the sight – a great, tawny, slinking shape crouched for a second in full view in the open. A long slinking shape, its cat-like head dropped, its great tail moving gently from side to side.

The fire died lower. A burning branch fell apart with a little crash and the lion leaped five feet back; then it gathered itself and again came on. Suddenly the beast raised its head, its throat pulsed in the fire-light and Whitey Morgan, the Killer, heard the most terrible cry that he had ever heard; the wild, soul-shaking 'Cou-ga . . .a . . .a' that gives the beast one of its many names. Inch by inch the great beast passed to the left of the tree and its padding feet made no sound as it passed from point to point like a shadow in some evil dream. It knew by instinct where to find the jugular vein.

The frantic man shouted again and again. His voice broke into a scream of terror and the lion leaped straight in the air. Then it caught a whiff of the valerian, closed in a little and studied the man at the tree. Then suddenly without any warning the tawny body seemed to draw together. The great feet spread under its weight and the steadily swishing tail stiffened like a bar of iron.

Then the cat leaped.

Nip, far down in the ca;xtnon, lying on Twenty-two's breast licking at his master's unconscious face, whimpered at a yell that came to him; a yell that was the embodiment of fear and terror so great that it shouted of a human soul being torn loose from its harbourage. Then came silence. Nip licked and whimpered till a slight quiver in the inert body set him almost wild with delight. But it was hours before the grey little man sat up and dazedly rubbed his head as the first rays of the sun ran up the sky.

'That was sure one hell of a tumble, Ol' Timer,' said Twenty-two. His old eyes scanned the rim-rock and he examined his arms and legs and grinned painfully. 'Nothin' busted. That rifle fallin' under me saved me even if it did bruise me a bit. That fall was meant to kill me all right. Well! One thing's sure. Mr Morgan sure spent one hell of a night tied to that 'ere tree. If I know my knots, he's tied fer keeps. What the hell ails you Nip?' he asked sharply as Nip, barking shrilly dashed through the brush heading for the Gonsalvo trail below them. Twenty-two listened carefully till he heard the metallic tinkle of iron on rock, then he scooped up his rifle, tested bolt and follower and headed through the tangled thicket. He halted at the sight of a lean horse's head thrusting through the cat's-claw and wild gourd. Then he saw a face he knew and hailed.

'Hey there, Winder,' he shouted. 'I'm sure glad to see you. I'm in one hell of a fix.'

'Hello there Twenty-two.' Winder checked his horse and swung out of the saddle. 'The Bar O told me you was after ol' Stub-tail. What luck?'

'Right funny kind o' luck,' quoth Twenty-two. 'I come out to git ol' Stub-tail an' I be dogged if I didn't git Whitey Morgan. That killer.'

'You got –' Winder eyed him for a moment and burst into incredulous laughter. 'You always was a practical joker,' he said, wiping his eyes. 'If you've got Morgan, where's he at?'

'I tied him fast to a tree on the rim-rock,' said Twenty-two. 'That was last night. I stepped too close to him an' he kicked me over the aidge o' the rock. Aimed to kill me I reckon. I ought to be all busted up but I ain't.'

Winder eyed him in disbelief. 'Where's your camp?' he asked.

'Camp hell. I just told you. Morgan killed Persons and Jim Pender an' my partner Scotty Barnes. I tell you, I've got Morgan tied to a tree up on the mesa. Most likely he's half froze by this time.'

'You're sure playin' in luck,' said Winder. 'There's five hundred dollars reward fer ol' Stub-tail. There's a thousand fer Morgan dead or alive. If you're tellin' the truth, Twenty-two, you've got a thousand dollars. I bet you kin use that.'

'I could have when old Scotty was alive,' said Twenty-two soberly. 'If I had the money to git him to hospital I might have saved his sight. I'm clearin' up old Scotty's score, Joe.'

'Aye. I *sabe*,' Winder nodded. 'An' you git a thousand dollars fer doin' it. Come on Old Timer, I'll give you a hand with Morgan. Let's get up on the mesa where he is.'

They tried a dozen trails before they climbed the steep ascent. Finally Winder clawed his way up a narrow, deep, water-channel and dropped his lariat back for Twenty-two and, clinging almost by their teeth, they reached the lip of the rim-rock, Winder ahead. The moment he raised his head above the rim-rock he almost fell back in his astonishment and he motioned frantically for Twenty-two to pass him the rifle. But Twenty-two shook his head and silently worked his way up along side him.

'Quiet you damned li'l fool,' hissed Winder. 'Look, will you! God! I never seen such a thing.'

Twenty-two raised a cautious head above the rock, behind a tuft of curly mesquite grass that gave perfect cover and looked. Not thirty yards away stood the tree to which Morgan had been tied. No body stood lashed to the trunk but he knew Morgan could never have got loose. He held the grass-stems aside and looked again.

At the foot of the tree, his arms circling the trunk, lay an inert mass that had been Whitey Morgan and over it, both paws dabbled in half-congealed blood, patting the body with its great paws, then dropping his great head to lick his paws, Twenty-two saw the biggest lion that he had ever seen. One quick glance at the switching tail showed him that that tail did not end in a finely graduated point. It had at some time been cut off almost square either by a trap or an axe. There was no question about it. That was Stub-tail. Twenty-two dared detection by whispering to Winder.

'That's ol' Stub-tail,' he said. 'That's him –'

'Five hundred dollars reward,' breathed Winder behind his hand. 'He's killed Morgan. A thousand dollars too fer Morgan. Oh you, Jay Gould! Shoot.'

Twenty-two's hands trembled like aspen leaves as he raised his rifle and nested his chin in the curve of the stock. His eye drew the ivory bead of the front sight down into its notch and brought it in line with the little tuft of hair at the base of the lion's throat. A perfect target at less that forty yards. He knew now how they had got so close undetected. The stench of that valerian had killed all lesser smells. He could hit a dime at that distance in that light.

Winder held his breath as he watched the gnarled old hand close gently on the trigger but he missed the equally delicate pressure of the left hand that supported the rifle barrel. Nip howled once at the whip-like crack and a tiny jet of yellow dust sprang from the heart of a mesquite clump three feet to the left of the tawny head. Followed a sudden flurry, the lightning-like rush of a yellow body and the cat was gone!

The next moment Winder, cursing and breathless, was clawing wildly at Twenty-two as he ran towards the tree.

'You . . . you . . . you damned ol' butter-fingers,' sobbed Winder, set to gibbering by the steep climb and the run. 'I could ha' hit him with a rock an' you miss him with a rifle at thirty yards. He was worth five hundred dollars to you. One comfort is – you won't get it.'

Twenty-two said not a word as they went forward to the tree.

'I don't *sabe* it at all,' growled Winder. 'I thought cats never attacked man.'

'He never would have rushed Morgan but fer that valerian,' quoth Twenty-two. 'Beside that – it was Morgan's pay-day –' He glanced at Winder but Winder did not laugh. 'Morgan killed Scotty Barnes. Me an' old Scotty was partners for more'n twenty years, Joe. Knowin' what I knowed when I seen that cat over the body, I wouldn't have shot that cat fer a million dollars.'

Winder let go a great breath. 'You got a thousand dollars anyhow,' he said.

But Twenty-two shook his head. 'No,' he said. 'Nobody cleans up on Morgan. His killer goes free. Morgan stays here on Wolf Mesa where the lion pulled him down.'

'You damned old fool,' snapped Winder, losing all his patience. 'You surely don't mean that you'll not claim the reward. Is that what you mean?'

'Hell, man,' said Twenty-two Le Grand sharply. 'Am I a hangman to take pay for a killin'? Justice is justice. I take no money for the lion that killed Morgan. I take no blood money for the death of the man who killed my partner.'

'Anyhow,' said Winder. 'You're a fool. You've lost fifteen hundred dollars.'

'You'd better go to school and study vulgar fractions,' said Twenty-two Le Grand. 'I've only lost five hundred dollars. The price of a lion's scalp. Let's go.'

Max Brand

Battle's End

THREADING a needle with gloves on is a hard job. But I would rather try to thread a needle than handle a rifle with the sort of mittens that one wears in the Arctic. In the first place, it is hard to work the forefinger inside of the trigger guard, and I worked and worked at my own pair until I had managed to construct a finger cover that was smaller without being thin enough to allow the finger to grow cold. Furthermore, I got Jerry Payson, who used to be a blacksmith, to make a much larger guard. It looked like nothing much, that guard, when it was finished, but it was roomy and comfortable, and exactly what I wanted for the occasion. I had Jerry make two pairs, because I wanted one for my own rifle and an extra one for Massey's, in case he should regain his eyesight.

After Jerry finished the guards and put them on the rifles, I took mine outside of Circle City to do some practising. I had just finished a hard freighting trip to Forty Mile, and now I had some time out while we waited to get a new job. Even with the bigger guard, I found the rifle wonderfully clumsy. It seemed to slip and give, and it would not fit snugly against the shoulder, because of the thickness of the coat that I had on. Well, no matter for inconveniences, a fellow will put up with them when he feels that his life is going to depend upon the makeshift, one day!

I had drilled away six times at a willow at fifty yards before I hit the trunk fairly, and the shock of the bullet whizzing through dislodged a chunk of snow frozen into an upper fork of the little tree. When that lump fell, what do you think? A snow shoe rabbit jumped up and skidded for safer country!

That rabbit had been lying low there all the time I put the *whiz* of five bullets over his head! But, as Massey used to say, a rabbit is such a fool that it is almost a genius.

I swung the gun around and tried for that rabbit, but he did a spry hop just as I pulled the trigger. I tried again, and though he swerved as I fired, the bullet was going faster than his tricky legs, and he rolled head over heels – a good fresh meal for Massey and me, I hoped.

I was about to start for that jack, when a voice said behind me: 'Wasting ammunition this far north, Joe May?'

I turned around short and saw Doctor Hector Forman right behind me. He must have sneaked up while I was shooting, but for that matter, he was so small and light that it was no wonder he could get across the snow without making much noise.

I looked at him with an odd feeling, as I always had since he began to take care of Massey. Partly, I respected and liked him for the time he was spending on Massey – probably for nothing. Partly, I was afraid and suspicious of him. For he looked like a red fox, all sharp nose and bright eyes. He never could keep from smiling as he talked, as though he knew all about what went on inside one's mind and found it ridiculous. He was the most unpleasant fellow I ever knew, in lots of ways, but he was a bang-up doctor. Charitable, too, and the good he had done in Circle City you hardly would believe.

For that matter, most doctors are apt to be a little hard boiled. They have to see men and women in their worst moments, and they're likely to grow cynical.

'I was just having a little fun,' said I.

He nodded at me. He was always nodding, no matter what anyone said, as though he understood what you said and what you had back in your mind.

'Pretty far north for that kind of fun,' says he.

I kicked at the snow and said nothing. What was there to say?

'Ammunition makes heavy luggage,' said he, 'and at a dollar a pound for freight, I don't see how you can afford to bring in so much of it.'

'Aw, I don't bring in much,' said I.

'I've seen you out here a dozen times if I've seen you once,' said he, 'and every time you've shot off enough powder and lead to keep a whole tribe in caribou meat for the winter.'

'Well, I gotta have my fun,' said I.

He nodded at me again. 'A man ought to live near water,' says he, 'if he expects his house to catch on fire.'

He waited for me to say something. I could only scowl and wish that I'd never met him. He went on, asking questions mostly. That was his way. He made everyone who talked to him feel like a patient.

'You've just come in from a trip?' says he.

'Yes,' said I.

'Good pay?'

'Pretty good.'

'And all the profits to be spent on Massey again, I suppose?'

I shrugged my shoulders and was silent.

'What did Massey ever do for you?' says the doctor.

'Aw, he just took me in when I was starving. That's all,' said I. For it made me mad, this hard, critical, probing way of Forman's.

'How old are you?' says he.

'Twenty,' said I, and looked him in the eye.

But it was no good. He knew that I was lying, and he merely grinned at me.

'Twenty,' said he, and nodded once more. 'But pretty soon you'll hear from the girl, and she'll send up enough money to get Massey out of Alaska.'

'What girl?' said I.

'Why, Massey's girl,' says he.

I scowled at him, blacker than ever. 'I don't know nothing about that,' I answered.

'No, you wouldn't,' said Forman, dry as a chip. He shrugged his shoulders to settle the furs closer to his skinny, shivering body.

'You come out here to see me about something?' I asked.

'Me? No, I just wanted to see the shooting,' said he.

He smiled, to let me see openly that he did not mean what he said. But I knew that already.

'This all started about a dog, I believe?' said he.

'A dog?' I asked him, dodging as well as I could.

'You don't know anything about that either, do you?' said he.

I stared at him.

'Isn't it a fact,' said he, 'that Calmont and Massey were once great friends?'

I said nothing. Of course, all Alaska knew that.

'And that they spent a winter out from Nome, and that one of Calmont's dogs in the team had a litter, and that Alec the Great was one of the puppies.'

'I don't know nothing about that,' said I.

'The rest of the country does, though,' said he.

'That's none of my business,' said I.

'Murder is every man's business, my boy,' he barked at me suddenly.

I winced. It was an ugly word, but it fitted the case.

'That dog grew attached to Massey, not to Calmont,' went on the doctor, hard and sharp as ever. 'They fought about Alec, finally, and Calmont laid him out, and tied him on the floor of the igloo, and went off to leave him to starve or die of cold. Is that wrong? No, it's not wrong! And then the dog broke away from Calmont and got back to Massey, and, somehow, Massey managed to get free of the cords, though I don't believe what people say when they tell that Alec chewed the cords away to set the man free. Do you?'

I stared at him again. 'Well,' said I, 'you don't know Alec as well as I do.'

'All right,' went on the doctor. 'The fact is that Massey got back to Nome with the dog, which Calmont claimed, but the jury in Nome awarded the dog to the man it loved, eh? Touching idea, that!'

He gave a cackling laugh and clapped his hands together.

'Now, what's the rest of the story, my lad?' said he.

'Well, I don't know,' said I.

'I'll tell you, then,' said he. 'A girl shows up in Nome in a desperate need of money, and sells herself to the highest bidder. To be the wife of the man able to bid her in, eh? Now, then, Calmont is the man who gets her, for eleven thousand dollars. A high-priced wife, even this far north! Can't eat wives – or diamonds either, for that matter. And after the girl's sold, you and Massey steal her away and cart her south, and Massey's hope is that Calmont will overtake them and the two of them can fight it out. But, on the way, he takes a few practice shots, and with one of them he burns his eyes with a back fire. Is that right?'

'Massey can tell you better than I can,' said I.

'Then Calmont does overtake you. He finds Massey blinded. He won't take the girl in spite of the way she's double-crossed him. He won't take a woman who loves another man, eh?'

I only shrugged again. It was pretty clear that he knew nearly everything. I suppose that he had ways of finding out part of it, and the rest he guessed. He had a brain in his head, no matter what I felt about him.

'But he does take that dog, Alec the Great, and you and Massey and the girl come on here. She goes south the first chance she gets, to rake together money and send it in to you two for the trip out. You stay here to take care of Massey. And the Massey sits still and eats his heart out because of Alec the Great. Am I still correct?'

'I got nothing to say,' said I.

'Now, then,' went on Forman, 'if I succeed in my work, and if Massey sees again, the first thing that he will do will be to take the trail of Calmont. There'll be a fight. And most likely the pair of them will be killed. They're too tough to die easily. Very well, that's the reason that you're out here practising with your rifle. You have an idea that you'll be travelling on that trail with Massey, before long.'

I sighed at this. It was perfectly true.

'Well,' said I, 'is he going to be able to see?'

Forman puckered up his face, and swayed his head from side to side.

'If I let him see, I'll practically be responsible for the lives of two men – to say nothing of a boy or two thrown in for full measure. I imagine that there wouldn't be much left of you, if you were tangled up in a battle between that couple, eh?'

I shuddered. It was exactly my own idea.

'Well,' said Forman, 'I don't think that there's much wrong with his eyes, after all. It was a shallow burn. At any rate, I'm taking the bandages off in about five minutes, if you care to come along and see the result.'

Care to come along? I ran at Forman and caught him by the arm.

'D'you mean that Hugh Massey has a good chance?' I shouted at him.

He grinned sourly down at me. 'Considering what's likely to follow, do you think that you'd be glad of it?' said he.

That stopped me. He was right. I hardly knew whether to be glad or sorry.

We went back into that silent town, the doctor slipping clumsily on his snowshoes. I wonder whatever could have brought him up here into the bitter, long winter of Alaska, he was so unfit for the life.

He had only one quality of the frontiersman, a bitter, hard temper that never gave way. But as for strength, vitality of body, youth, he had none of these things at all. Nevertheless, he was an exceptional man, as he had just proved by reading to me almost the entire strange story of Calmont and Massey. Of course, some of the headlines, as one might say, of that story, had been known to everyone for a long time – that is, such features as that they had once been great friends and that they had afterward become great enemies and that only the blinding of Massey had prevented the final battle between them.

There were some people who swore that the only reason Massey remained in Alaska was not that he couldn't get out, but because he wanted to be close to Calmont and his chance for revenge. Well, I suppose I knew Massey about as well as anyone in the world did – outside of Calmont himself – but Massey was not a talking man, and he never had made a confidant of me. I don't think that he ever would have paid much attention to me, if it had not been for the fact that I once helped Alec the Great from a mob of hungry huskies.

So, as we went along, I kept giving this doctor side glances for I half felt that he was more fiend than man.

As we passed Don Lurcher's house, we heard them shouting and singing inside. They had their own supply of alcohol in that place, and the amount of noise that they squeezed out of themselves through the entire winter was a thing to hear, but not to believe. Everything else was cold, white, and still, for the soft snow ate up the sound of the footfall, except for the little metallic squeaks and crunchings, now and again.

We got to our shack.

It was a fairly comfortable one, with very thick walls of logs that had been rafted down the Yukon. On the outside of the logs, there was a thick layer of sod, which helped to turn the edge of the wind.

Inside, everything was fixed up pretty well. There were two comfortable bunks, and a stove that was not big, but it heated that little place as well as the sun ever heated the earth on a spring morning, say. Yes, we were pretty comfortable – for Circle City.

But there was one figure in the shack that was not at all comfortable to see. I had looked at him every day for months – except when I was making a freighting trip – and I never could get used to the sight.

I mean Massey.

The grim, enduring look that pinched the corners of his mouth never had altered since the first day of his blindness. Of course, he could not read, so I often read aloud to him. And he had only one occupation all the day long. That was to keep himself fit, and how he did it!

Once, he had been more tiger than man. He was not very big, but I never saw more concentrated essence of sheer power than he showed. Calmont, perhaps, was stronger in his hands, but then Calmont was a good deal bigger. When the pair of them were together as friends in the old days, there was a saying in Skagway – when Skagway was toughest – that the two of them were equal to any four in the world in a rough and tumble. And I believe the legend.

Now, Massey spent hours every day doing calisthenics, and we had rigged a bar across one corner of the room on which he performed all the antics of a monkey on the branch of a tree.

That was to keep himself right and in trim, and why? Well, he never spoke about it, but I knew. Massey felt that he had one chance in ten of getting back his eyesight. And if ever that returned, he did not want to find himself soft. He wanted to start immediately on the trail of Calmont!

He was fit as a fiddle, therefore, physically, and I've always thought that this good training kept him from going despondent as he sat there through his long night.

This day the doctor said as he went in: 'Well, Massey, how are things going?'

Massey lifted his head and nodded. 'I can't complain,' said he.

'Complaints never cured a wound, though tears may have washed a few,' says the doctor in his harsh voice. 'I'm going to take the bandage off you, now. Boy, close that door, and put a blanket over the window. Too much light might be a torment to him, if he's going to see!'

Massey said not a word. I went to do as I was told, trembling with excitement, and that confounded Forman was whistling idly as he laid out his things on the deal table in the centre of the room. He had no more soul than a snake, was the thought that ran through my head.

With the door closed, and the window veiled, there was no more light in that room than the red streaks that showed around the stove, and one glowing spot where the handle of the damper fitted into the thin chimney.

Then I stood by, waiting, while the doctor worked at the bandages. He said: 'Keep your eyes closed while I take the bandage off. Then open your eyes very slowly.'

I saw a movement of the dull shadows, as the doctor did something with his hands and then stepped back. And suddenly Massey stood up.

Neither of them spoke for a long moment. My heart got so big that I thought it would break.

'Hugh!' I screamed out suddenly. 'Can you see? Can you see anything?'

Now, imagine that man having sat there through the dull, endless hours of every day, looking at the empty thought of his young, ruined life, with no more hope for the future than a drowning man where help is not in sight – imagine that, and then conceive of the iron grip that he kept on himself.

He answered in the calmest voice in the world:

'I can see perfectly, Forman. Thank you.'

'Take the blanket off the window, boy,' said Forman.

I did.

And now I could see the unveiled eyes of Hugh Massey for the first time, with recognition in them as he looked at me. Even this dim twilight through the window, however, was almost too much for him, and he shaded his eyes as he looked at me.

I have never seen anything so exciting. The Yukon breaking up in the summer was nothing compared to the making of this man whole again. I ran to him and shook his hand. I threw my arms around him and hugged him. I laughed. I shouted. Tears of pure joy ran down my face, and in general I played the fool.

But Massey was as calm as steel.

When he talked, it was to the doctor. He said that he realized he owed a great debt to the doctor, and that it would not be forgotten.

'Massey,' said the doctor, with such a changed voice that I should not have recognized the sound of it, 'up there in Nome, one evening, old "Doctor" Borg, as they called him, made you and Calmont swear that you never would attack one another. What about it now?'

'Attack him, Forman?' said Massey very gently. 'Why, I never would think of breaking my word – unless he attacks me. Of course, a man is allowed to defend himself. Am I right?'

'Do you think Calmont will come hunting you?'

'Do I think? Oh, I know! Besides, I'll probably not be hard to find.'

'You mean what?'

'Why, man, I simply mean that Calmont has a dog of mine! Keeping it for me, as you might say. Of course, I'll have to go to get the dog back. Calmont's over on Birch Creek, I believe?'

The doctor said nothing. He got on his coat and went to the door, which he jerked open. As he stood there in the entrance, he half-turned, and he snapped over his shoulder:

'If there's murder in this business, I, for one, wash my hands. They're clean of it!'

A staggering thing, in a way, to hear from him. I mean to say, all at once I realized that under his hard exterior the doctor was a law-abiding man, and that he actually was interested in something higher and stronger than human law, at that.

Massey, when the door closed, went over to the stove and took off the lid. Shading his eyes and squinting, he looked down into the red heart of the fire. Then, as though this satisfied him in a way that I could not understand, he replaced the lid and returned to his bunk, where he sat down.

I said nothing, this while. I was somewhere between joy in the moment and fear for what was to come.

At last he said to me: 'Well, old son, we're together again, at last!'

As though we had been apart all these weeks and months! But I knew what he meant. Whole mountain ranges of misery had grown up between him and the rest of the world, even including me.

'I can't really wish,' said he, 'for you to get into the state that I've been in, but, otherwise, I don't think that I can ever repay you, Joe.'

It was the first time that he ever had said so much as 'thank you'. I had almost thought, at times, that he was taking everything for granted. But that hardly mattered, because I had owed my life to him, that horrible day, long ago, in Nome.

But this gratitude, from a man of iron, affected me a good deal more than I can explain. I merely said:

'It's all right, Hugh. There doesn't have to be any talk about repaying – not between you and me!'

He considered this for a moment in his deliberate way. Then he answered:

'No, I never could repay. I've been helpless in your hands. You've had to nurse me, feed me by hand, shave me, dress me, partly. There never can be any repaying. Except with bloodshed!' he added in an odd inflection. 'Except with bloodshed, Joe, old fellow!'

The tears were in my eyes, listening to him. I knew exactly what he meant. And I knew that he was a man to be believed. And it's not a light thing to hear such a man as Massey say that he's ready to die for you – almost anxious to!

'We're only even,' said I. 'I don't forget that day in Tucker's boarding-house in Nome. I'll never forget that!'

At this he laughed a little. 'All right,' said he. 'We'll talk no more about it.'

And, from that day, we never did.

Of course, Circle City knew all about the affairs of Massey and Calmont, or enough, at least, to expect the sparks to fly so soon as ever the pair of them met, and the expectation got high and drawn. But, in the meantime, Massey was as calm and deliberate as you please.

There were several things that he wanted to do. He used to talk matters over with me, and I would sit listening with my eyes popping.

In the first place, he wanted to get his eyes accustomed to light, and his hands accustomed to a gun.

In the second place, he wished to wait until the Yukon was frozen, which would make distance travelling a lot easier. Already the ice was forming and floating in blocks and jams down the river, like white logs. Hardly an hour went by without giving us the vibration and the thunder of a shoal of ice, grounding against an island. The cold got greater and greater, and Massey went out into the pinch of it regularly, giving himself larger and larger doses, so that he would become inured.

In the third place, he said to me: 'Even a rattlesnake gives you a warning, and so I'll give one to poor Arnie.'

He had a fiendish way of giving pet names and speaking gently about Calmont. He used to smile with a very peculiar sweetness when he talked about Calmont, and I hated to face him or to hear him, at such times. This warning he sent in due time.

He wrote out a letter and spent a lot of time composing it, and making the copy neat. He showed it to me with anxiety, hoping that I would point out anything that might be wrong about it.

This is the way it ran:

'DEAR ARNIE,

'It's a long time since I've seen you, and I haven't had a chance to thank you for the good care that you've been giving to Alec all this time. He must have grown, but I hope that he'll remember me.

'However, now I can see again, and I may be of use to Alec, and he to me. If you are coming in to Circle City, let me know. Otherwise, I'll come out there to call on you and to get my dog.

'Please figure out your bill. I have an idea as to how much I owe you, but I would like to know exactly what you think on the same point.

'Always thinking of you,
'HUGH MASSEY.'

This letter gave me a chill. It sounded so friendly, I mean, and there was such purring malice between the lines. Why, that letter would have fooled any outsider, I suppose, but of course it would not fool Calmont. He knew that the one comfort that Massey could have had in his blindness would have been the dog. And he knew that all Massey owed him was a perfect and gigantic hatred. However, this note was sent off to Birch Creek by a man who was just starting out in that direction.

We waited for word to come back. Calmont probably would not overlook this warning. He would come in or else he would ask Massey to go out.

Gun practice went on every day outside of the town, with Massey using a revolver or a rifle like a master. I was a clumsy hand with any gun, compared with him. He had a natural talent for weapons, and he had cultivated his gifts.

Even when he was back in the shack, he used to do knife tricks, throwing a heavy hunting-knife across the width of the room into the trunk of a sapling not two inches thick. I almost began to think that the knife would be his best weapon at close quarters.

His spirits were rising all this while. The prospect of the fight that was coming was like a secret joy constantly being whispered into his ears.

He told me that I was to leave him. I could have half of the dog team and wait there in Circle City, in case he had to go out and find Calmont. That was what I wanted to do; but I pointed out that Calmont had a new partner up on Birch Creek, and that the odds would be two to two, no matter how the fight came off. He admitted this, but he swore that he would never let me get into action on his behalf.

This problem haunted me.

To go on the trail of Calmont was a nightmare to me in prospect, but I did not see how I could let Massey go out there by himself to fight two men. Two pairs of eyes are a lot better than one, and so are two guns, even though young hands are gripping one of them. It was my duty, according to the code, to go with Massey when the pinch came.

The code I mean is the law of the frontier, where the fellow who leaves his bunkie in the lurch is branded for all his life. A year before this, I would still have been young enough to escape from too much blame. But now I was seventeen, and pretty well hardened and bronzed by that last year of Northern life, so that I looked older than the fact. I was treated like a man. I had been doing a man's work in freighting, and I would be expected to act like a man in the extreme pinch.

Well, duty is as cold a judge as Judge Colt. It held me up, but it made me mighty queer in the pit of the stomach.

Finally, I said to him one evening: 'Look here, Hugh. Suppose you were standing in my boots. What would you do? Would you let yourself be left behind? What would people think of me? They know that Calmont has a partner.'

'Oh, dang what people think!' said Massey.

But he said this without conviction, and after that he talked very little on the subject.

I found a couple of men in Circle City who knew Calmont's partner, however, and from them I got a good description of the man who was to be my half of the fight. A tough bit of meat for any man's eating was what he sounded to me.

Sam Burr was his name. Down around the Big Bend country they still remember him. He had a reputation there so bad that there was a time when any decent man could have taken a shot at Sam Burr without being so much as arrested for a killing that everybody thought was needed. The truth is that Sam was not quite right in the head, to my way of thinking. He was a mental defective. The only thing that gave him any real pleasure was fighting. And his idea about fighting was that of an Indian of the true old school. A bullet through the back was better than a bullet through the forehead. To stalk a man like a beast gave him the joy of a beast. As a matter of fact, there was Indian blood in him, and, like a good many half-breeds, he had the bad qualities of both bloods.

I asked why Calmont ever had hitched himself up to a man of that calibre.

'I guess,' said the fellow who was telling me, 'that Calmont needed some excitement, when there was no Massey on his trail. He picked up Sam Burr, and Sam will sure be a hypodermic for him!'

They said that he was a thin, stringy man, a great runner and packer, and a natural-born gun fighter.

So from that moment, I had nightmares, and day horrors, with a thin-faced, dark-eyed fellow always playing the part of the fiend to toast me on the coals of my imagination.

The Yukon was well frozen over, when surprising word came in from Birch Creek that Calmont was no longer there. It made a sensation in Circle City. Calmont had pulled out some time before, and rumour said that he had trekked for the Klondike, and that he and Sam Burr had staked out a claim, not on Bonanza Creek, but on another run of water not far away.

I was the one who brought word of this rumour to Massey, and I saw his features contract and a perfectly fiendish hate and malice come into his eyes.

I knew his thought. He was wondering whether or not Calmont had heard of his cure, and had purposely cleared out of our neck of the woods; but a moment of reflection was enough to clear away that doubt. Calmont would not run a mere couple of hundred miles or so. He would go two thousand, at least, if he wanted to get rid of Massey permanently.

Massey said nothing at the time. He only took a couple of turns through the shack, and went to bed early that evening. I did the same, after getting my pack together, because I guessed that we would be making an early start.

We were, as a matter of fact. We got out after about five hours' sleep, and I started catching up the dogs. Massey wanted to stop me.

He said: 'Old son, what kind of a man would I be if I let you go along on this little job and get your head shot off?'

'What sort of a man would I be,' said I, 'if I let you go, with both Calmont and Sam Burr ahead of you?'

'Oh, Sam is no job at all, Joe,' said he. 'He won't trouble me at all.'

'Then he'll be easy for me,' said I. 'If you stop me, Hugh, I'll follow along after you without dogs.'

'Well,' said he, 'Dawson will be a better place to argue this.'

Afterwards, I found out what he meant by this. At the time, I really thought that he spoke only words.

We hit the river ice. It was new and slick and smooth, but pretty dangerous in spots. But we had six dogs in our team, two having died, and those six were as fast and strong a lot as I ever saw. Then we had a leader who was a marvel, and could read the mind of the ice, not like an Alec the Great, but about as well as any other dog I ever saw.

Day by day, as the trip progressed, the ice got stronger and safer. We marched ourselves into high spirits, too.

The weather was good; the dogs were well and strong; we had good camps, plenty of tea and flour and bacon, and under circumstances like those, conditions were about as good as a man could ask for. It doesn't take much to make a man happy, when he's been used to the Arctic. It's the absence of misery rather than the presence of comforts that counts.

As we got along up the river, on excellent going and with the ice growing thicker every moment, Massey was so happy that I found him with a contented smile on his face, more than once. Besides, he was often humming. And it's rare when you catch an Alaska dog-puncher in such a frame of mind, or ready to waste any energy on music making. For my part, I just closed my eyes to tomorrow and took every moment as it came.

At last we got up to sight of Dawson itself, a glad thing to Massey, and a horrible one to me. That huddle of houses dwindled in my eyes and I half expected that a gigantic form would stride out from it, wearing the wolfish face of that fellow Calmont.

We passed the mouth of the Klondike. It was fully a hundred yards from bank to bank and it rushed its currents along so fast that there was only a thin sheathing of ice across the top though the Yukon was well crusted over. But the Klondike was only beginning to freeze, the black ice covering it with a sort of white dust. There were distinct sled tracks up this creek, and the tracks went out at a big irregular break. There was no need to ask what had happened to some poor puncher, sled, dogs and all!

That was our welcome, you might say, to Dawson.

At this time, Dawson was running pretty wild. It was not as bad as Nome, because Dawson lies in Canada, and the Mounted Police had their eye on the place. There are police and police, but the North West Mounted were always all by themselves. Three of them were worth thirty of any other kind, unless it were the Texas Rangers, in their palmy days. Still, Dawson was so full of pep, and people, and money, that it was hard even for the Mounted to keep the town in order.

Imagine what had happened.

Men who had starved and toiled on Birch Creek and thanked Heaven for twenty-five-cent pans, were now up there on the Klondike washing five and six hundred dollars to a pan. They had their smudgy fires going to thaw out the soil down to bed pan, and there they literally scooped out the treasure. Money came in so fast that the men did not know what to do with it.

We got into Dawson when everything was in full blast. The strange thing was that there was so little talk about claims and gold. Gold was everywhere. It was like dirt under the feet. But imagine dirt that is dynamite, and that men will sell their souls for!

People talked about 'outside', and the news they had got out of papers two months old, and which was the prettiest girl in such and such a dance hall, and whose dog would pull the heaviest load, and which dog was the smartest leader, but there was not so much talk about gold. If you heard a man talking at the bar about the richness of such and such a claim, you could put it down that he was trying to sell that claim and that it was probably a blank.

Not always.

Right after we got to Dawson we went into the Imperial bar and got some food and bought a drink. Not that Massey was a drinking man, but because that was the only way to enter into talk, and it was gossip about big Calmont that he wanted to hear.

Just after we had lined up at the bar, a fellow came in whom the barman knew.

Their talk went something like this:

'Hellow, Jack,' says the barman.

'Hullo, Monte,' said the miner.

His face was covered with six inches of hair. His furs were worn through at the elbows and patched with sackcloth. He was the toughest, most miserable-looking man that I ever saw.

'How's things?' said the barman.

'Fair to middling,' said Jack. 'How's things?'

'Busy,' said Monte. 'Down for a rest?'

'Down to quit,' said Jack.

'Got through the gold dirt?'

'Naw, it's panning faster'n ever. But I'm tired.'

'Of what?'

'Gold,' said Jack.

I gaped at him. But nobody else seemed to notice. Imagine a man being tired of gold! And such a man – looking like a second-hand clothes dealer.

'What you taken out?' says Monte.

'About fifty thousand dollars,' said Jack. 'Gimme another and have one with me.'

'I ain't drinking. But here's yours. Is fifty thousand your pile?'

'Yeah, that's about right.'

'Couldn't use no more?'

'No, no more than that. Fifty thousand is just my size. Twenty thousand for the ranch that I want down there in Colorado, and thirty thousand to blow thawing out the ice that's been froze into me up here in Bonanza Creek.'

'Gunna sell the claim?'

'Yeah, I reckon.'

'What's the price?'

'I dunno. Whatever I can get for it.'

Well, I heard afterwards that Jack sold his claim for fifteen thousand dollars, but he did not leave Dawson with his money. He was not robbed, either. But he got too much bad whisky aboard and gambled his whole sixty-five thousand dollars away in a week. The people that bought the claim for fifteen thousand on straight hearsay, cleaned up another fifty thousand in a few weeks out of it, while Jack went up the creek and located again. This time he stayed for three months, and came out with a hundred thousand flat. He was lucky, of course. But there were a good many stories like this floating around when I was in the Klondike. People got so that gold, as I said before, was not really interesting. You have to translate the metal into houses, acres, clothes, jewels and such things, before it grows exciting, and it was hard to visualize home comforts when in Dawson.

This yarn of Jack's about his profits made my eyes pop, but my interest did not last, for I knew that there was something else that meant a lot more to me.

It was the news about big Calmont. Out of that same barman we got it.

'Partner,' says Massey in his gentle, persuasive voice, 'know anybody around here by the name of Calmont?'

The bar-tender was spinning out a row of eight glasses down the bar, and the way he gave those glasses a flip and made them walk into place was a caution. Then he fished out two glasses and rocked them down the bar in the same way. He was proud of his art and too busy to pay much attention to Massey.

'Partner,' says Massey again, 'I just asked you a question about Arnie Calmont. D'you know him?'

'Busy!' barks Monte.

Massey reached a hand across the bar and taps the other on the shoulder.

The fellow jumped as though a gun had been nudged against his tender flesh.

'Hey, what's the matter?' said he.

'I was asking for a little conversation,' says Massey.

Monte gave him a look, and gave me a look, too. What he saw in me did not matter. There was a certain air about Massey that was enough for him.

'Calmont's up the creek,' said he.

'Where?'

'Not on Bonanza. Off in the back country. I dunno where. Sam Burr could tell you that.'

'Where's Sam Burr? With Calmont?'

'No, he's over at Parson's boarding-house.'

Massey did not stop to thank Monte or to finish the whisky. He turned on his heel and strode from the room, with me at his heels.

We found Parson's boarding-house, a low, dingy dive, and asked for Burr. He was there, all right.

'Are you doctors?' asks the fellow who meets us at the door.

We said that we were not, but that we wanted a friendly word with Burr.

'Calmont ain't sent you?'

'No, we sent ourselves.'

With that, he took us into a small room where I had my first sight of Sam Burr. He was all that I had expected to find him. He was simply a lean, greasy, good-for-nothing half-breed, with poison in his eye. When I had a look at the yellow whites of his eyes, I was glad that I was not apt to have to stand up against him with a gun, a knife, or even empty hands. He looked tricky enough to lick Jim Jeffries just then, and that was when Jeff was knocking them cold.

However, he was not apt to be doing any fighting for a time. He lay in his bunk with some dingy blankets wrapped around him. There was a bandage around his head and a settled look about him that told he had been badly hurt.

This fellow lay back in the bunk, as I've said, and looked us over at this leisure. He had been reading a dog-eared old magazine, which he lowered and stared at us curiously. He was like a savage dog that stands in its own front yard and wonders whether you'll come close enough to have your throat cut. That was the calm, grim way that he drifted his glance over us.

'Hullo,' says Massey.

Sam Burr made a slight movement with his hand that could have been taken to mean anything – and it was clear that he didn't care how we interpreted it.

'You're not with Calmont,' said Massey.

'Unless he's under the bunk,' says Burr.

He was one of those cool, sneering fellows. I hated him at first glance, and hated him twice over the moment that he spoke.

Massey went closer to him.

'Do you know me, Burr?' said he.

'No,' said Burr. 'I ain't got that – pleasure.'

Why, he had to sneer and scowl at everything! Whatever he touched had to be made sticky with his tarry innuendoes.

'My name is Massey,' said Hugh.

This jolted Burr in the right place. He let out a grunt and blinked up at us.

'You're Massey? You're the fellow!' said he.

'You busted with Calmont?' asked Massey.

'I'm gunna finish him,' declared Sam Burr. 'I'm gunna get even with him. He jumped me!'

'Is he here in Dawson?'

'Ah,' says Burr, staring at Massey thoughtfully, 'you want him all right, but I dunno that you'll get him. He's a hard case, that fellow Calmont.'

Massey dismissed the idea of difficulty. His nerves were as tight as strings on a drum. He showed it. Have you ever seen a hound trembling against the leash?

'Well, he ain't here,' said Burr at last.

'Where is he, then?'

'Up the creek.'

'Can you tell me where?'

'Yeah. I can tell you where. I reckon that I will, too.'

'Good,' said Massey, and sat down.

He seemed more at ease now, and spared time to ask: 'What was the trouble?'

'Why, you wouldn't believe!' answered Sam Burr. 'There we was getting along pretty good. He's a grouch, but so am I. We done fine together. But he exploded all account of a dang dog that he has along with him, or that he used to have. Alec the Great is what I mean.'

Massey rose up from his chair as though some hand were pulling him by the hair of the head.

'Used to have?' says he.

'Yeah,' said Burr, not noticing the excitement. 'He set a fool lot on that dog, and it was the meanest, sulkiest brute that I ever seen. Had to be muzzled. Would've took Calmont's heart out as quick as a wink. I took him out on the lead one day, and the beast whirled and tried for my throat. Nacherally I let the lead strap loose, and off he went. When Calmont heard of that, he near went crazy. He jumped me when I wasn't looking.'

Then he saw Massey's face and paused.

Well, he had the best sort of a reason for stopping. I had seen Massey excited and angry before, but never so white and still, with his eyes burning in his face. Of course, Burr could not understand, but I did. There were three purposes in Massey's mind.

One was to marry Marjorie, when he got out of the country to the south.

One was to kill Calmont.

And the third was to get back Alec the Great.

Of the three, there was no doubt as to which stood at the head of the list. It was Alec the Great.

That doesn't talk down about his hatred of Calmont, either, or his love for Marjorie. Both those things were real, but Alec was something unique. He loved that dog like a friend, like a child, and like a dog, all in one. They had been through trouble together, of course. Not so many men can say honestly that they owe their lives to the brains and the teeth of a dog, but Massey could say that. Besides, he had a natural talent for animals, and I've seen him hold a long conversation with Alec, and Alec understanding most of the words.

Much as he wanted the life of Calmont, he wanted Alec the Great still more. Now he stood there white and still, looking down at Sam Burr, until the half-breed gaped up at him.

'Where is Calmont now?' asked Massey through his teeth.

'Why, up on the claim, I guess – unless he's gone off through the woods trying to find that dang murdering dog?'

'Where's the claim?'

'Up on Pension Creek.'

'Where on the creek?'

'It's the only one on Pension Creek, and you can't miss it.'

'Thanks,' said Massey, and started for the door.

'Mind you,' sang out Sam Burr, 'I've been saving that gent for myself! But if you're gunna try to help yourself first to him, leave a little for me. And go careful. He's kept in good gun practice!'

Massey gave no reply to this, but went off through the doorway, with me fairly treading on his heels. He led the way back to the sheds, and there he said:

'We'll not go on together, son. We'll make an even split right here, and you wait for me here with your half. Wait for ten days, and if I'm not back by that time, I'll never be back, I reckon.'

I argued that I would have to stay with him, but he was like a stone, at first, and went on dividing up everything until we had two equal loads and two dog teams, instead of the one. It gave me a mighty feeling of loneliness, I can tell you, to see him doing these things. Finally I said:

'I can't stay behind, Hugh.'

He answered:

'What sort of a man would I be if I went in with a helper to fight against one man?'

I saw that I could not answer this with words, so I did not argue any more. We went off to get a meal, and then rented a small, damp, cold room, where we turned in.

I remember that Massey sat for a time on the edge of his bed with his chin in his hand.

'How far would Alec go?' he said over and over to himself. 'How far would Alec go?'

'Clear back to nature,' said I. 'There was always about sixty per cent wolf in him.'

At this suggestion he jerked back his head and groaned, but a moment later he wrapped himself in his blankets and went to sleep.

I was still dead tired from the trail when something waked me. I had heard nothing, but I had a definite feeling that I was alone in the room. A ghastly feeling in the Arctic, and a thing that haunts many men on the trail – the dread that companions may leave them during the night.

I sat up with a jerk, and, looking across the room, I could see by the dingy twilight that seeped through the little window that Massey had actually gone!

He had gone for Pension Creek, of course, to get there and do his work before I arrived.

I jumped into my boots, and rolled my pack, and lighted out after him. I already had my sled in good order, after the division of the load. And the three dogs that Massey had left for me were the better half of the pack. He was not the sort ever to give a friend the worst of anything.

In the cold bleakness of that morning I got under way and headed out on to the Klondike. A low mist was hanging over the ice, over the town, over the trees. Breathing was difficult. I hated and dreaded the work before me and the goal to which I was driving, but I went on. I had been so long with Massey, thinking of his problems, and studying his welfare, and taking care of him, that I had no ability to attach myself to a lonely life and a goal of my own.

So I headed out there on to the ice.

It was very thin. Two or three times in the first mile I could feel it bending under me, and I increased the speed of the dogs for the sake of putting a less steady pressure upon any spot of the surface.

In this way I went over the first mile, taking a zigzag course until I picked up the sign of sled and dogs.

I studied the marks of the dogs' feet, where the surface was soft enough to keep a clear print of them, and presently I came to the wide-spreading, three-toed impression of Bosh, the big sled dog. I knew that print well, and there was no doubt in my mind that it was Bosh, all right.

Then I noted the very marks that the sled left, and a certain slight tendency it had to side-slip toward the right. By this I was confirmed in all that I had felt before. It was without mistake the lead sled of our outfit, and that was the team of Hugh Massey.

After this, I settled down to a rapid pace, pressing the dogs a little. They went extremely well, for they were not overloaded, and they seemed to know that they were heading after an old human friend and many dog companions.

The mist finally lifted and the way became brighter and easier. Finally, I could see Massey going along ahead of me, his dogs strung out and pulling hard. I smiled to myself as I watched the rhythm of his marching shoulders, for this was a place where a lightweight was better than a strong body. He had to go with consummate care over the frozen stream which had eaten up one life so recently, and as he wove from side to side, picking the secure going, and as his leader studied the ice as a good dog should, he was losing ground and time. I could march straight ahead without danger, and well my wise leader knew it.

I could afford to slow up our pace. The steel runners cut and gritted away at the cold road. The ice began to glow with brilliant reflections, and sometimes we went over places where the surface water had been frozen so suddenly and strongly that it seemed to have been arrested in mid-leap – for it was still clear and translucent, and every moment I expected to fall through the crust.

I stuck there in place behind my friend for several hours, and still, to my amazement, he never turned his head. Usually he was as wary as a wild Indian, and could not go a mile without sweeping everything round him with a glance.

But now it was a different matter. There was only one point in the compass that had any meaning for him, and this was the point toward which lay the claim of his enemy Calmont. As a matter of fact I kept there behind him, unnoticed, until he turned off the river to camp for the night, and then I pulled up beside him.

You never could tell what Massey would do in such a pinch as this. If he had ordered me furiously back to Dawson or berated me coldly for being a fool, or turned a cold shoulder on me and said nothing at all, I should not have been surprised.

Instead, he acted as though we had been marching together all the day long, and merely told me, quietly, what I was to do in the work of preparing the camp.

We had about as cheerful a camp that night as we ever had made. Of course, there was plenty of fuel, and a whipping hail storm, followed by a fall of snow and then a gale of wind, was nothing to us. We ate a good big dinner, turned in and slept just like rocks. At least, I can answer for my part.

In the morning we resumed our march under a grey sky.

The wind had died before the snow stopped falling; the result was that the trees were streaked and piled with white along every branch, and now and then some unperceived touch of breeze would shake down a little shower, and make whispers of surprise in the forest. This snowfall dusted over the ice and gave a better grip for the dogs, and, besides, it made the runners go more sweetly. For steel does not love ice, but bites hard upon it like a dog on a bone.

Our mileage was exceptionally good this day, and we plugged along with a will. That night Massey spoke for the first and last time about this new business I had taken in hand.

'I've tried to keep you out of this,' said he, 'and it seemed that I couldn't do it. Well, every man has to run his own business, and if you think that you belong here with me, perhaps you're right. You know, of course, that you're not to pull a gun on Calmont. I don't think that there'd be any need of it, anyway.'

'Hugh,' said I, 'tell me how you feel about Calmont, really. Don't you sometimes remember that he was your old partner and bunkie?'

He looked thoughtfully aside at me, nodding his head at his own thought, and not at me.

'Sometimes at night,' said Massey, 'I dream of the old days. Yes, sometimes at night I remember him the way he used to be before he went mad. Why d'you ask?'

'Well, of course, I haven't been through what you were through with him. Only, seeing that he was your old partner, I can't help wondering how –'

'How I could want to kill him?'

'Yes, that's it.'

'It's horrible to you, I suppose?' said he.

'Yes, it's pretty horrible to me.'

He nodded again and even whistled a little, until I thought that his mind had wandered far away and left me. But at length he merely remarked:

'Yes, I suppose it would seem that way to you.'

This invitation of mine to have him talk a bit was not rewarded at all. But that good-natured calm of his reply, and the emotionless manner in which he received my suggestion of a conscience at work, meant more to me than if he had raved and gnashed his teeth and fallen into a stamping fury.

'Have you any doubt, Hugh?' I could not help going on.

'Doubt about what?' said he.

'About what will happen when you meet him? Are you sure that you can handle Calmont?'

He just looked me straight in the eye and smiled.

'Just enough doubt, Joe,' said he, 'to make the business a lark.'

When we reached Pension Creek all the country was frozen as still as ice. The trees were like leaden clouds chained to the sides of the hills and frosted cold to the touch. It seemed that fire could never thaw and heat the iron hardness of that frozen wood. The axe edge used to bound back from it in my numb, weak fingers. The wind was iced into stillness also, and for that we thanked our stars, because it was bitter weather even without a breeze to drive the invisible knife-blades into us.

Never have I seen such evidences of cold, though I have no doubt that I have been in places where the thermometer sank lower. But here it was perhaps the dampness of the air which made every breath lodge, as it were, near the heart. The water seemed to have been checked in mid-flow, for instead of finding a solid, glassy surface, there were partial strata extending from the banks, turned to stone as they poured out on the main face of the water. This made very bumpy going. Besides, the stream was narrow, crooked, and had many cascades where we had to put all the dogs on one sled and heave with our shoulders to get it up.

It was a strange thing, that Pension Creek. Perhaps it was because we were drawing close to the claim where the battle was to be fought out, but it seemed to me that I never had seen a stream that wound in such a dark and secret snake trail through the woods.

We crawled with difficulty and pain up to the place where Pension Creek dwindled to a runlet.

'We should have taken the left fork,' said Massey. 'We've left the main stream.'

I thought the same thing, but as we were about to check the dogs, we turned a bend of the ice road and saw the shack before us. It was the usual thing – just a low log wall, with the look of crouching to avoid the cold. Close to the edge of the creek we saw the smudge of the thawing fire, and smoke was climbing out of the chimney at the end of the roof and walking up into the still air in a solid spiral. We stopped the team, then, swinging them close under the bank so that we could not be seen from the house.

Massey motioned to me to remain behind.

I wanted to. I had not the heart to see that battle, but, on the other hand, I could not remain there shivering with the dogs, looking down at their heaving sides, when my friend was in that house fighting for his life. I wondered what it would be – a single crash and echo of an exploding gun, or a prolonged turmoil, a floundering struggle, perhaps someone yelling out, finally, as a knife or a bullet went home – perhaps only that awful noise which a choking man makes. I had heard that once during a rough-and-tumble fight in a Nome bar-room. Well, as Massey climbed up the bank, I climbed after him.

He was half-way toward the house when he knew that I was coming. He paused and, glancing over his shoulder, shook his head and waved his hand to warn me back. But I would not be warned. He could not delay to argue the point. He went straight on, soft as a shadow, and I moved as silently as I could behind him.

This was as dreadful as anything that I ever have seen or heard of. I mean to say that stealthy, gliding motion with which Massey went toward the house, stalking a man.

He turned around the shoulder of the house just as the door squeaked in opening, and big Calmont walked out and fairly put his breast against the muzzle of Massey's revolver.

Massey was still crouching like a beast of prey. I looked to hear the shot and see Calmont fall dead, but the calm of that big fellow was wonderful to see. He merely looked down at the gun and then leisurely turned his gaze upon Massey.

'Well, you got me,' said he.

'Yes,' said Massey. 'I got you – boy!'

No cursing or berating, you see. It was worse than cursing, however; the deep satisfaction in Massey's voice. I can still hear it.

'Come in and sit down,' said Calmont.

'Don't mind if I do,' said Massey.

Calmont went in before us. He had fixed that door so that it closed with a spring, and it was an odd sight to watch him enter and hold the door open – as if he feared that the back-swing of the door might unsettle Massey's aim.

I pressed in behind them, and we sat down on three home-made stools, near the stove.

It was the sort of interior you would expect to find. Just naked usefulness and damp and misery. But this was made up for by the sight of some leather sacks in the corner of the room, lying unguarded on the floor. Two were plump. One was about half full.

'You've had luck,' said Massey, and turned his head and nodded toward the pile of little sacks.

No doubt, in his mind was a hope that Calmont would be tempted by this turning of his head to pull a gun, if he wore one. And he did wear one. We learned afterwards that even when he was sure that Massey would be blind for ever, he could not live without a Colt constantly in his clothes or under his hand. No surety was enough to put Massey out of his mind and his fear.

However, this temptation was a little too patent and open, Calmont made no move toward drawing a weapon, but he answered: 'Yes, I've struck it rich.'

'That's good,' answered Massey.

'Yeah. About thirty thousand dollars, if the stuff is seventeen an ounce.'

'You've taken out near two thousand ounces?'

'Yeah. You see Sam Burr?'

'We saw him.'

'How's Sam?'

'He's getting better. He's still a mite nervous.'

'Yeah,' said Calmont; 'I reckon he might be. Never had nerves that were any good, Sam didn't.'

He said to me: 'There's some coffee in that pot, kid. Go fetch it and fill some cups. Honest coffee is what is there! There's some bacon yonder, too, and –'

I got up.

'Sit still,' ordered Massey. 'We don't eat and we don't drink with Arnie Calmont.'

The glance of Calmont a second time flickered from the gun up to the face of his old companion, and I knew what was in his mind. It was a clever move, too. The smell of that simmering coffee filled the room. My very heart ached for a long, hot draft of it; but, of course, when you eat and drink with a man in the North, you're bound to him as a guest, as he is to you as a host. This, among certain classes of men, is a sacred obligation. I could see at a glance where Calmont and Massey belonged in the category.

'Sam told you the way up?' said Calmont, not pressing his hospitality upon us.

'No, he didn't,' lied Massey.

Naturally he did not want to draw the blame on to the head of any other man, or involve another in his own quarrel.

'Nobody but Burr knew,' said Calmont. 'If they did, they'd be up here in a crowd – but Burr still hopes that he'll get out and manage to come up here and clean me out – and the rich surface deposits, too.'

'You've gone and lost Alec,' said Massey.

'Burr lost him,' said Calmont.

'After you stole him,' replied Massey.

'He's my dog,' stated Calmont.

'He was judged to me.'

'By that old fool, Borg.'

'You swallowed his judgement.'

'I swallowed nothing. A man has gotta back down when there's a dozen hired guns ready for him. But what Borg decided didn't make no difference to me.'

'You agreed to it,' said Massey.

'And what if I did? I never meant agreeing in my heart.'

'No, that's your way,' admitted Massey.

There was a good deal of sting in their words, but so far they had kept their voices gentle. This did not greatly surprise me in Massey. I knew him and the iron grip he kept on his nerve at all times. But it did surprise me in Calmont, there was so much brute in him.

He looked more the wolf than ever now. His beard and whiskers had been unshaved for a long time, and so his face was covered almost to the eyes with a dense growth clipped off roughly and fairly short. Through this tangle his lips were a red line, and his eyes glittered.

This hair of Calmont's did not grow straight and orderly as the hair of ordinary men grows, but it snarled and twisted a good deal like the coat of an Airedale, and increased his beast look a thousandfold. That, and the bright animal look in his little eyes.

I had only had, before, two good looks at him in all my life, but they had been on such occasions that the face of this man had been burned into my mind – a thing to dream of.

Now I looked at him partly as a human and partly as a nightmare come true.

He did not pay much attention to me. Only now and then his glance wandered aside and touched on me. And I would rather have had vitriol trickled across my face. It was almost like having his big hands jump at my throat.

'That's my way,' said Calmont, 'and it's the right way. If ever there was a court of real law, what chance would you have agin' me, to claim Alec the Great?'

'The Alaska way is a good enough way for me,' said Massey.

'Yeah? Well, we'll see.'

'Very quick we'll see, too. This is gunna be decided for ever, and right now!'

'All right,' said Calmont, 'it'll have to be decided, then.'

To my amazement he smiled a little, and this shocked me so much that I glanced quickly over my shoulder toward the door. It was closed, however. No silent partner of Calmont was standing there to give him an unsuspected advantage. But, from the look on the man's face you would have said that he had the upper hand, and that we were helpless before him.

'Are you wearing a gun?' said Massey.

'No,' said Calmont.

'You lie,' retorted Massey.

'Do I?'

'Yes. But we're going to see how long your lie will last. First of all, I want to chat with you a few minutes.'

'About sore eyes?' asked Calmont curiously.

At that temptation I suspected that Massey would lose his self-control and murder the man straight off, but his shoulder merely twitched a little.

'About Alec,' said he.

The lip of Calmont lifted like the disdainful lip of a wolf.

'I'll tell you nothin' about him!' said he.

After this, Massey waited for a moment. Just how this odd duel between them was going to turn out I could not guess.

'Put some wood into the stove,' said Massey to me.

I did as he directed me, stepping around carefully so that I should not come between them. I put some wood into the stove and moved the damper so that the draft began to pull and hum up the chimney. Then I moved back where I could watch them both from the side. They were as different as could be. Calmont still with his snarling look, and Massey fixed and intent and staring. Wolf and bull-terrier, one might say.

'You've lost Alec and you want him to stay lost?' queried Massey.

'That's my business,' answered Calmont, 'I'll gather him in when I want him. He's out to pasture.'

'You know where he is, eh?'

'I know where he is,' nodded Calmont.

Massey drew in a quick little gasping breath.

'Arnie,' said he, 'I've got you here in the hollow of my hand. But I'll give you another chance. I'll give you a free break for your gun. I'll put up this Colt and give you an equal break to get out yours.'

'And how do I pay for the chance?' asked Calmont.

'It's free as can be. Tell me where to find Alec. Where he's running, I mean,' answered Massey.

Calmont looked deliberately up to the ceiling, and then back at Massey. He was wearing the most disagreeable of sneers as usual.

'I dunno that I'll do that,' he said.

'What good would Alec be to you?' asked Massey calmly. 'No matter if you know where he is. If he's running wild, you'll never catch him. He's too wise to be trapped. He's too fast to be caught by huskies; and he's too strong to be stopped by hounds. He's gone, as far as you're concerned.'

'I'll take my chances,' said Calmont sullenly.

'Even when you had him with you, what good was he to you, Arnie?'

'A dog don't have to do parlour tricks for me,' answered Calmont in anger.

'You had to keep him muzzled. He hates you. What good is he to you, man?'

'The good of keeping him away from you,' answered Calmont. 'You thief!'

'I'm a thief, am I?'

'Aye, and a rotten low one!'

'I've stolen what?'

'Alec, first. Then the girl. Then you sneaked away your own life through my hands, when I should've had you, and found you blind!'

His voice rose. He roared out the last words.

'I understand you,' said Massey. 'You're complaining of the way I've treated you. Did I ever try to murder you? Did I ever strike foul in a fight, as you did? Did I ever tie you hand and foot and leave you to starve or freeze without so much as a match near by to make a fire?'

'D'you think that I regret that?' answered Calmont. 'No, I only wish that I'd been able to do what I wanted with you and leave you there to turn to ice.'

'You were a fool,' said Massey. 'When the spring brought in the prospectors they would have been sure to find my body, and that would have meant hanging for you!'

'Would it? I'd be glad to hang, Massey, if I could send you out of life half a step ahead of me!'

I think that he meant what he said, there was such a brutal loathing in his face as he stared at Massey. Evil always seems more formidable than good, and I wondered that Massey dared to sit there and offer to fight Calmont on even terms.

'Let's get away from ourselves,' said Massey, 'and talk about the dog. Alec – what earthly purpose have you in wanting that dog, man? He hates you. He has hated you nearly from the first.'

'You tricked him into it!' declared Calmont.

'I? You had a fair chance at him out there in that igloo. You know that you had a fair shot at him, Calmont!'

'You lie!' said Calmont with the uttermost bitterness. 'You'd put your hands and your words on to him. How'd I have a chance? I couldn't talk dog talk, the way that you can! You tricked me out of my right in him!'

'You've had time since. What have you managed to do with him?'

'You think I've done nothin', eh?'

'Not a thing, I'd put my bet.'

'Then you're a fool!' said Calmont. 'It takes time. Time is all that I need with him. He's my dog, and down in his heart he knows that he's mine. He's like a sulky kid, that's all. But I can see through him. I know that he's mine at bottom and will be all mine, in a little time.'

'He never so much as licked your hand!' said Massey.

'You lie!' shouted Calmont, in one of his furious rages. 'He did when he was a pup even.'

'Before he was old enough to know better!'

'I tell you,' shouted Calmont, 'that if it hadn't been for that fool of a Sam Burr, I would have had that dog talking my talk. I had to wait to let the rot you'd talked to him get out of his mind. But he was comin' my way. He was gunna be my dog ag'in. I tell you what, he ate out of my hand the very mornin' of the last day that he was here!'

He cried this last out in a triumph. He was greatly excited. His eyes shone, and his smile was like the smile of a child. All at a stroke, half of my fear and loathing of this man turned to pity. He had induced the dog actually to eat out of his hand, and this triumph still put a fire in his eye! Yes, poor Calmont! He was simply not like other men.

'Tell me where he is,' said Massey, 'and you'll have an even break to polish me off. I'll put my gun on the ground. Then you can tell me!'

I saw Calmont measure the distance from the ground to Massey's hanging hand.

Then he shook his head.

'You're a trickster. You're a sleight-of-hander! Bah, Massey. D'you think that I've lived with you so long and don't know your ways?'

Massey waited, and watched him. Then, slowly and deliberately he raised his revolver and covered the forehead of Calmont.

'I should have done it long ago,' he said. 'It's not a crime. It's a good thing to put a cur like you out of the world. You're a fiend. You're a cold-blooded snake, Calmont. You tried to murder me. Now I'm going to do justice on you.'

'Hugh! Hugh!' I shouted. 'It's murder!'

'Shut up and keep away from me!' said Massey, as cold as steel.

Calmont, in the meantime, did not beg for his life, did not flinch. I hope never to see such a thing again. He merely leaned a bit forward and looked with his usual sneering smile into the eye of the revolver, exactly like a man staring at a camera when his picture is about to be taken. His colour did not alter. There was no fear in Arnold Calmont when he looked death in the face, and that is a thing worth remembering.

I saw the forefinger of Massey tighten on the trigger. He was actually beginning to squeeze it, with the slowness of a man who wants to prolong a pleasure as much as possible, and this time I ran in front of the gun.

It was a wild thing for me to do, but I was so excited that I forgot the gun might go off any second. I simply could not stand by and see such a frightful thing done. Yet I don't remember that there was a look of evil in the face of Massey. His attitude was that of an executioner. He detested Calmont so much that I think it was something like a holy rite – the slaughter of that wolf-faced man.

At any rate, I got in there between them on the jump and yelled out: 'You'll never find Alec if you shoot him! Alec will be gone for good, Hugh! Will you listen?'

I saw him wince. He snarled at me to get out of the way. But a moment later he stood up – it had been one of the chief horrors that these fellows were seated all through that talk making the affair so utterly casual. Then he said: 'You're right! Why should I throw away my chances at Alec for the sake of butchering this animal? Step away, son. I won't pull the trigger.'

He dropped the gun to his side as he spoke, and I side-stepped gladly from between them.

What immediately followed I only vaguely know, because the instant the excitement was over, my knees fairly sagged under me. I had a violent sense of nausea, and dropping down on a stool, I held my head in both hands. There is shock from a punch or a fall; there is a worse shock from mere horror, and every nerve in me felt this one.

I remember that Massey finally said: 'Calmont, there's no good throwing away a great thing because we hate each other. We both want that dog. If you won't tell me where he is, come along with me and we'll hunt him together. The man who gets him, turns him into the fund, so to speak, and then we'll fight it out for that. You don't think you're quite my size with a gun. Then we'll have it out with bare hands if you want. How does that sound to you?'

I groaned a little as I thought of this possibility. The two of them, I mean, turned into beasts and tearing and beating at one another.

'We hunt for Alec first, and when we've got him, we fight for him? Is that it?' asked Calmont, with a new ring in his voice.

'Aye, that's it.'

'Massey,' said the wolf-man, 'there's something in you after all. You got brains. I'll shake with you on that!'

'I'd rather handle a rattler,' said Massey.

'Dang you!' burst out Calmont. 'I'll choke better words than that out of you before the end!'

They glared at each other like wild animals for a moment, but there were bars between them now – that is to say, they were kept from murder on the spot by the knowledge that they needed one another.

There was such a gigantic will in each of them that I felt thin and light as an autumn leaf, helped up in the air by the pressure of adverse winds.

'Cut some bacon,' said Massey to me.

I went to do it. My knees were still sagging under me, and my hand shook when it grasped the knife, but I was eager to have this accomplished. I got the bacon sliced into the pan in short order, and when it was cooked and the flapjacks frying afterward, then I laid it out on tin plates and served coffee.

They each picked up some bacon and a cup of the coffee at the same time, and at the same instant they were about to drink, when I saw their eyes meet and their hands lower. Each had the same thought, I suppose, that if they ate and drank together in this manner, then it would be necessary for them religiously to respect the truce until Alec was taken.

Then they drank at the same instant, watching each other fiercely above the rims of the cups.

For my part I made a prayer that Alec should never be caught!

It is by no means an unusual thing for men to fall out in the North and still to continue in a form of partnership, for the mere good reason that manpower is worth something up there in the frozen land. You will see partners together who really hate one another for everything except muscle worth. But that was very different from the way of Calmont and Massey, now that they were together.

Their hatred was so uniquely perfect that sometimes I had to rub my eyes and stare at them. I could not realize that they were there before me, one of them making trail, and one of them driving the dogs, and working the gee pole. But one thing I found out at once – that they travelled like the wind.

Calmont had no dogs at all. They had been either run off or killed by the wolves, he said; and when he admitted this, Massey had grown suddenly thoughtful.

'Your dogs were all run off before Alec left?' he asked.

'No. After,' said Calmont.

'And what about the wolves?'

'I know what you mean,' said Calmont gloomily.

'Well, d'you think that it's right?'

'He's gone wild,' said Calmont. 'There ain't any doubt of that. I know that he's gone wild and that it'll be the very dickens to get him back. There's a lot of wolf blood in him, Hugh. You know that. His ma was mighty treacherous before him.'

'You think that he's gone back to some wolf tribe, Arnie?'

'I reckon he has. Or else he's leadin' those four huskies of mine, and getting them back to the wild. Any way you figure it, he's gone.'

'What makes you think you know where to find him?'

'There come in an Injun here one day, and he talks to me a little while he eats my chow. He's seen a white wolf, he tells me.'

'Alec?'

'Alec sure!'

'Where did he see him?'

'A good long march over the ridge.'

'And how did he see him?'

'He was out with a pair of dogs, and goin' along pretty good one day when he come to dark woods and, while he was in the thick of the shadow of 'em, out comes a rush of wolves, with a big white one in the front, and those murderin' brutes they killed and half ate his dogs right under his eyes.'

'That doesn't sound like Alec!'

'He ain't the same!' said the other. 'When Alec was with you, he was only a pup. But now he's grown up, and he's growed bad – in spots. The wolf in him has come out a good deal lately!'

He suddenly saw that this, in a very definite sense, was a criticism of himself, and he bit his lip. Wherever Alec was concerned he was as thin-skinned as a girl, though in all other matters he was armoured like a rhinoceros.

'Did this white wolf have Alec's marking?'

'He had black ears.'

'No black on his muzzle and tail-tip?'

'His muzzle was red, by the time that Injun got a fair look at it, and I reckon that Alec was moving so fast that his tail-tip couldn't be seen very clearly.'

'There've been white wolves before, and even white wolves with black ears. What makes you think that this was Alec?'

'Well, I'll tell you that, too. The Injun said that one of the wolves behind the white leader had a long strip of grey down its right shoulder, and squarish head for a wolf, and by the rest of that description I made out a pretty good picture of Bluff, my sled dog. So I figured that the band of wolves that jumped that outfit was simply Alec and my team behind him, runnin' wild.'

Massey, at this, considered for a moment.

'And you're heading now for the place where those wolves were seen?'

'No, I sent that Injun back on good, fat pay, to trail that pack and find out what he could about it. He went off with his one-dog sled, and he came back without it. He said after he got over the ridge, he had been tackled in the middle of the night by the same pack, and that he himself had seen the white leader cut the throat of his one dog as if with a knife. He was pretty excited, that Injun, when he came back here.

He wanted most of the world to pay him back for that sled and the dog that he had lost.'

'You gave him some cash, I suppose?' said Massey.

'Yeah, I give him some cash to square himself, for one thing.'

Suddenly Massey grinned.

'And you gave him a licking for the rest of what he wanted?'

Calmont grinned in turn.

'You know me pretty good, Hugh,' said he.

I saw them smiling at one another with a perfect though mute understanding, and for the first time since I had met Massey, and heard of Calmont, I saw how these two men might have been companions and bunkies for years together, as everyone knew that they had been.

Massey turned off this familiar and friendly strain to say:

'Look here, Calmont. Maybe they're five hundred miles from where you saw them.'

'You know wolves, do you?' asked Calmont, in his usual snarling voice.

'Pretty well.'

'You don't know a dang thing about 'em! A wolf don't usually run on more than a forty-mile range. And likely even the winter starving time won't make him wander more than a hundred or so. They gotta have the knowledge of the country that they run in, or they're nigh afraid even to hunt. Like Eskimo, you might say.'

'Why like Eskimo?'

'Well, I recollect bein' up north on the borders of the Smith Bay, I think it was, and I had some Eskimos along with me, and we was winterin' there, and I told 'em to put out their fish nets and try to catch something. But they said that there wasn't no fish in them waters, and that there wasn't any use in wastin' time on them. And then along comes a bunch of the native tribe that knows that shore, and they put out their nets and catch a ton of fish, and we all ate them. After that, my Eskimos wanted to stay there for ever, but I had to move. Well, wild animals are the same way. They hunt in the country that they know.'

'But Alec never knew any wild country.'

'He'll learn to, then. And within a coupla days' marches of where that Injun found him and the dog-team that he swiped, we'll have a pretty fair shot to find him, too.'

Massey, after a time, admitted that this was true, and that was the reason that we kept on toward the place.

Of course, it would seem madness to most people, but not to me. I had seen Alec. This amount of trouble, no dog was really worth; but Alec was not a dog. A wolf, then, you ask? No, not a wolf either. But he had learned so much from Massey that, when I saw him, he was almost half-human.

To see that dog bringing his master matches, or gun, or slippers, or parka, well, it was worth a good deal! To see him walk a tight-rope was a caution, and to see a thousand other ways that he had of acting up was a caution too. The only way that Massey punished him was, when he had been really bad, to leave him outside of the tent at night. And there Alec would sit and cry like a baby and mourn like a wolf until finally he was let in.

Outside of that I never had seen Massey so much as speak rough to him, far less strike him with hand or whip. They were partners, as surely as ever man and man were partners. Why, for my own part, I never had much influence with Alec. I was not what you would call an intimate acquaintance, but still it gripped my heart like a strong hand when I thought of him being lost to us and condemned to the wilderness, where no man would ever again see his bright, fierce, wise, affectionate eyes.

Yes, in my own way I loved Alec, though it is hard for a boy to give his heart as freely as a man does. Boys are more selfish, more impulsive, more womanish than grown men. They make a fuss about an animal, or a person. But here were two grown men – the hardest I ever have known – who were willing to die for the sake of getting that dog back in traces!

This taught me a good deal. I used to watch the pair of them, day after day. The wonder of this situation never left me, but all the while I was saying to myself that they were labouring together like brothers for a goal which, when they reached it, would make them kill one another.

It was the strangest thing I ever saw. It was the strangest thing that ever was imagined. But they needed one another. Calmont cold not catch the dog without the help of Massey, and Massey could not find the region where Alec was ranging without the help of Calmont. They were loathing one another, but tied to each other by a common need.

I can tell you two strange things that happened on that out-trail.

The third day out we came to a place where the surface ice suddenly thinned – I don't know why, on that little mangy stream – but Massey, who was making trail, suddenly broke through and disappeared before our eyes.

I say that he disappeared. I mean that he almost did, but while one of his hands was still reaching for the edge of the ice and breaking it away, Calmont, with a yell, threw himself forward and skidded along on hands and legs, like a seal – to keep the weight over a bigger surface – until he got to the edge of the hole in a moment, and caught the hand of Massey just as it was taking its last hold.

When he tried to pull Massey out the ice gave way in great sections, and I think that they would have gone down together if I hadn't swerved the team away from the place and thrown Calmont a line.

By the aid of that and the dogs, and I pulling like sixty, we got them both out on the ice, and I started a huge fire, and they were soon thawing out.

But the wonderful part was not so much the speed with which Calmont had gone to the rescue, as it was his bulldog persistence in sticking to the rescue work in spite of the fact that every instant it looked as though the powerful current would pull down both the drowning man and the would-be rescuer.

This amazed them both, also, I have no doubt. But the point of the matter was that no thanks were given or expected. They growled at each other more than ever, and seemed ashamed.

The very next day we were going up a steep, icy slope, the dogs pulling only one sled, when Calmont, ahead of us, slipped and fell like a stone. I got out of the way with a yell of fear, but Massey stood there on a ledge of frozen, slippery rock, with a fifty-foot drop just behind him. To see the last of Calmont, he only needed to step out of the way, but he wouldn't. He tackled that spinning, falling body. The shock of it dragged them both to the trembling brink of the drop, but there they luckily lodged, two inches from death for them both.

They simply got up and shook themselves like dogs, and went on with the day's march.

That same night, when we camped, I watched the pair of them carefully, for I had high hopes that murder might no longer be in the air. There is no greater thing a man may do than lay down his life for a friend. And if that is true, what is to be said of him who has offered to lay down his life?

Well, each of these men had done exactly that for the other. But instead of a thawing of that cold ice of hatred which encased them both they looked on one another, so far as I could tell, with an increased aversion. It was perfectly clear to me that what they had done was simply for the sake of forwarding the march; for the sake of Alec the Great, you might say. And that seemed more and more true as I stared at them.

They never spoke to one another if they could avoid it. Often when something had to be said, one of them would speak to me, so that he could make his mind clear on a subject. This may seem childish, but it did not strike me that way. There was too much danger in the air.

The night settled down on us damp and thick with cold. A really deadly mist poured into the hollows and rose among the trees until we could see only the ones near at hand. And even these looked like ghosts waiting around us. So we built up a whacking big fire to drive away the cold, and in this way we made ourselves fairly comfortable, though comfort is only a comparative thing in that far north. Sometimes I found myself wishing for the fireless camps of the open tundra in preference to this choking mist which lay heavy on the lungs with every breath that we drew.

I tried to make a little talk as we sat around the fire, getting the ache of the march out of our legs, but they stared at the flames, or at one another, and they would not answer me except with grunts. They were thinking about the future, and Alec, and the fight that was to come, no doubt, and they could not be bothered by the chatter of a youngster like me.

We all turned in, with a fire built up on each side, and a tunnel of warmth in between. That is an extravagant way of camping, because it takes so much wood chopping, but we had three pairs of hands for all work and we could afford to waste wood and a little labour.

In the middle of the night I sat up straight, with my heart beating and terror gripping me, for I had just had a dream in which Calmont had leaned over me with his wolfish face and, opening his mouth, showed me a set of real wolf's fangs to tear my throat.

Naturally I stared across at him, and there I saw him, sitting up as I was, and his face more wolfish than ever in that reddish half-light. For the fire had died down, throwing up a good deal of heat, but only enough light to stain the deathly mist that had crept in close about the camp. Through this fog, I saw Calmont watching me, and the shock was even worse than the nightmare, as you can imagine.

He lifted his head as though listening to something. Then, far away, I heard the cry of wolves upon a blood trail. At least, so it sounded to me, for I always feel that I can recognize the wolf's hunting cry. And certainly the sound was travelling rapidly across the hills, dipping dimly into valleys and rising loud on the ridges. Massey jumped up at that moment. The sight of him was as good as a warm sunrise to me. He made my blood run smoothly again.

'That may be the pack we're after,' said Massey.

We threw on the fire enough wood to scare away wild animals, and then we struck out on a line that promised to cut the path of the wolves, if they held upon a straight course.

A few paces from the fire the mist closed thickly over us; but when we got to the first ridge, a wind struck the fog away, or sent it in tangles through the trees. We had been stumbling blindly before, but now we had a much better light.

Calmont held up a hand to order a halt, and listened. In such moments he was the natural master, for he was a good woodsman. Massey looked to him and mutely accepted his leadership.

'The hill!' said Calmont, and started down the slope at a great speed, nursing his rifle under the pit of his arm.

We crossed the hollow, slipping on the ice that crusted the frozen stream there, and toiled up the farther slope to the next crest. There Calmount put us in hiding in the brush, at a point where we could look down on a considerable prospect.

Ice encased the naked branches and the slender stems of the brush. The cold of it brushed through my clothes and set me shivering, while we listened to the pack as it swung over a height, dropped into a vagueness in a hollow, and again boomed loudly just before us.

We were about to see something worth seeing, and perhaps it was the ghostliness of the night, the strange arctic light, the still stranger mist in the trees, that made me feel very hollow and homesick, so that with a great pang I wished myself back among the Arizona sands, and the smoky herbage of the desert. This scene was too unearthly for my taste.

'They're running fast,' said Massey, canting his ear to the noise.

'Shut up!' answered Calmont in his usual growl.

And Massey was still. In the woods he always acknowledged Calmont's leadership.

Over the ridge before us now broke the silhouette of a great bull moose, and he came down the slope with enormous strides. He looked like a mountain of meat, loftier than the stunted trees, and streaking behind him, gaining at his heels, was a white wolf.

All snow-white he looked in that light, a beautiful thing to watch as he galloped.

'Alec!' said Massey under his breath.

And suddenly I knew that he was right. Yes, and now I could see, I thought, the black ears and tail tip, and the dark of Alec's muzzle. But he looked twice as big as when I last had seen him.

How my heart leaped then! Not only to see him, but to realize that this was the goal toward which we had travelled so far, and that for the sake of Alec even such enemies as Calmont and Massey had sworn a truce. To avoid the battle that would surely come after his capture, suddenly I wish that the big hoofs of the moose would split the skull of Alec to the brain. I mean that I almost wished this, but not quite; for to wish for Alec's death was almost like wishing for the death of a man, he had such brains and spirit, and a sort of human, resolute courage.

Behind Alec, over the rim of the ridge, pitched four more running, and Calmont immediately exclaimed: 'My team! Mine and maybe the Injun's dog!'

Well, they looked wolfish enough, except that one had a white breastplate that no wolf was apt to show. They seemed half dead with running, but they kept on, with Alec showing them the way to hold on to a trail.

In the flat of the hollow the moose hit a streak of ice, floundered and almost fell. He recovered himself, but the effort seemed to take the last of his wind and strength, for instead of bolting straightway, he whirled about and struck at Alec with a fore-hoof. It was like the reach of a long straight left, and it would have punched Alec into kingdom come if it should have landed.

Well, it did not land. I suppose that at such a time the training Alec had had in dodging whip strokes stood him in good stead. Even the lightning stroke of a bull moose is not so fast as the flick of a whip-lash.

The moose was well at bay now as Alec swerved from the blow. The other huskies came up with a rush, but they did not charge home. They knew perfectly well that there was death in any stroke from that towering brute. So they sat down in the snow and hung out their tongues. They moved, however, to different points of the compass. No one could have taught them much about moose hunting. But here was where the wolf blood, in which they were rich, came to their help. They manoeuvred so that they could threaten the moose from any side; and he, with constant turnings of his head, marked them down with his little bright eyes.

While the four sat down at the four points of the compass, as it were, Alec stalked around as chief inspector and director of attack.

Calmont pulled his rifle to his shoulder.

But Massey jerked it down.

'He'll brain Alec!' protested Calmont.

'Never in the world!' declared Massey. 'That dog can take care of himself against anything but a thunderbolt, and even a lightning flash would have to be a real bull's eye to hit that dodging youngster. No, no, Arnie! We've got to use this chance to work down close to him. Move softly. They've got something on their hands now that'll make their ears slow to hear, but anything is likely to put them on the run. They've gone wild, Arnie. They've gone wild, and Heaven knows whether or not Alec is too wild ever to be tamed again! Let's sneak down on them, man. I want to get close enough so that he can hear my voice well enough to know it. That's our one chance, I take it!'

Calmont did not protest. What Massey said seemed too thoroughly right to be argued against, and therefore we all began to work down the slope through the verge of the brush.

Mind you, this was a frightfully slow business. The frozen twigs of the bushes were as brittle as glass and as likely to snap. And, as Massey had said, the least alarm might send these wild ones scampering. We had to mind every step, everything against which we brushed, putting back the little branches as cautiously as though they were made of diamonds.

What I saw of the scene in the hollow was somewhat veiled, naturally, by the branches that came between me and the moving figures, but nothing of importance escaped me, because I was breathlessly hanging on the scene.

That moose looked as big as an elephant, and the wolves shrank into insignificance in comparison. However, the man-trained dog, Alec, went calmly about, prospecting. It looked exactly as though he were laying out a plan of attack, and a moment later we could see what was in his mind. I suppose that animals can only communicate with one another in a vague way, but it appeared exactly as though Alec had done some talking.

The next moment the attack was neatly made. All the wolves rose to their feet at the same moment – wolves, I say, for wolves they were now! – and as the moose jumped a bit with excitement Alec made straight for his head.

It was only a feint. He merely made a pretence of driving in for the throat, though he came so close in this daring work that he had to squat, as the moose hit like a flash over his head. Then, as he leaped back, the second half of the attack went home. For a big husky sprang at the moose from behind and tried for the hamstring with gaping mouth.

He had delayed too long. He had not quite timed his attack with the feint of his boss. The result was that the moose had time to meet the second half of the battle with a hard-driven kick.

The wolf sailed far off through the air with a death shriek that rang terribly through the hollow, and so ended the first phase of the contest.

We were down a bit nearer, when the second part of the battle actually began.

After the death of the first husky, the others showed a strong mind to go on their way; this mountain of meat suddenly smelled rank in their nostrils, for they had made a clever attack, and they had gained nothing but a dead companion.

Calmont was very angry. They had looked on while one of his dogs was killed, and the thing rubbed him the wrong way.

However, Massey convinced him that he would have to be more patient, and we were. We went on working our way closer and closer down the slope, keeping well into our screen of brush. For the dogs, after all, did not draw off. They had only four altogether by this time, and four looked a small number to beat that wise and dangerous old fighter, the moose.

Alec, however, continued to walk around his circle, and he seemed to force his friends to get in closer – up to the firing line, as you might say, from which a quick rush and leap would get them to the enemy.

I suppose the moose felt the game was in his hands by this time, but he maintained a perfect watch and ward.

I noticed everything that followed very closely, for I was in an excellent position, and the detailed manoeuvring was as follows:

One of the huskies worked around until he was exactly in front of the head of the big quarry. Two others took positions on the sides. Alec, in the meantime, in one of his slow circles, came just behind the heels of the moose.

This was the time agreed upon. You would have thought that having failed in these tactics the first time Alec would not try them again. There are other ways of bothering a moose, but perhaps Alec felt that there was none so good as this. On this occasion the husky in front made the feint at the head. He was not so sure of himself as Alec had been. Or perhaps he was discouraged by the poor success of the first venture. At any rate, he only made a feeble feint, which caused the moose to lift a fore-foot, without striking.

However, the rear attack was in better hands – or perhaps I should say feet and teeth. At the precise moment when the husky made his clumsy and half-hearted feint, Alec sprang in like a white flash. I saw the gleam of his big fangs, and I could almost hear the shock of the stroke as his teeth struck the hamstring full and fair, as it seemed to me.

Then he dropped flat to the ground, and the moose, with the uninjured leg, kicked twice, like lightning, above the head of Alec. After that the dog jumped back like a good boxer who has made his point and lets the judge note it.

The stroke had gone home, but it had not cut the cord in two. The big beast was still standing without a sign of failing on any leg, and though he shook his head, he seemed as formidable and unhurt as ever.

That touch of the spur at least made him restless. While Alec licked his red-stained lips and the other dogs stood up trembling with fresh hope and fresh hunger, the quarry wheeled and fled with his long-striding trot. After him went the pack, but not far. For though the stroke of Alec had not quite severed the cord, it must have been hanging together by a mere thread. I could almost swear that I heard a distinct sound of something parting under high tension, and the moose slipped down on his haunches, sliding on the icy crust of the snow and knocking up a shower of it before him.

That slip was the last of him, and again Alec was the operator – or swordsman. He whipped around under the head of that big fighter and cut his throat for him as well as any butcher could have done. Then back he jumped.

The moose tried to rise. He floundered and fell again with a dog hanging to either flank, tearing, and Alec's teeth again slashed his throat. That was almost the finishing stroke.

My hair stood up on my head. There was something unbelievably horrible about this. It was like seeing three or four kindergarten children put down a gigantic athlete and pommel him to death! All in a moment the moose was down, and dead, and the pack was eating.

But then I saw the explanation, and the horror left me. It was brains that had won. Alec, like a general overlooking a battlefield, stood up with his fore-feet on the head of the moose and looked over his friends and their feasting with a red laugh of triumph – a silent laugh, of course, but one whose meaning you could not mistake.

He was the fellow with the brains. He was steel against stone; powder against bow and arrows; science against brute power. The very fact that he restrained his appetite now was the proof that he had a will and a power of forethought.

I had seen him before a great deal. He had shown me more favour than anyone outside of his master, Massey. But, nevertheless, I never before had guessed what a great animal he was, and why two men were willing to risk their lives to get him. I knew now fully, as I watched him standing over the head of his kill.

He had broadened and strengthened in appearance. I had last seen him as half a puppy; but now he was the finished product, and this life in the open, I could guess, and the starvation periods, and the interminable trails, and the hard battles, were the things which had tempered and hardened his fine metal to just the cutting edge.

I heard Calmont muttering softly to himself. His eyes blazed; his face was working. I suppose he would have given almost anything in the world to possess Alec, just then. Massey, however, to whom the dog meant still more, said not a word to anyone, but continued to work softly, delicately, through the brush.

We were not the only creatures who were stealing up on the feasting huskies, however. Alec the Great had not yet tasted the first reward of his victory, when out of the brush on the farther side of the hollow streamed five timber wolves.

You could tell the difference instantly between them and the huskies. They were tall, but slighter. Their tails were more bushy. There was more spring in their stride, and by the flat look in their sides and the movement of the loose robe over their shoulders, it was fairly certain that they were burned out with starvation. A dog as thin as that would hardly have been able to walk. It would have lain down to let the cold finish what starvation had almost ended. But a wolf keeps its strength and endurance almost as long as it can stand.

These five came on with a rush, forming a flying wedge, with the big grey leader in front. Calmont would have unhesitatingly used his gun at once, and I was of the same mould, but again Massey protested.

'You'll see something,' said he, 'if those dogs have rubbed off the man smell in the woods and the snow.'

Afterwards, I understood what he meant.

At the first sound behind them, Alec gave the snarl that was the danger signal, and at the sound of it, as he whirled about, the three who followed his orders leaped up beside him and presented a solid front to the foe.

They looked big enough and strong enough to do the trick, but I knew that they could not. There's only about one dog in a thousand that can fight a wolf single-handed. Even a half-bred husky, bigger, stronger in every other way, lacks the jaw power which is the wolf's distinguishing virtue. The house dog has no chance at all. Back in Arizona, I had seen a single lobo, and not a big one at that, fight three powerful dogs. He killed one of them with a single stroke. And he was slashing the others to bits when I managed to get a lump of lead into his wise and savage brain.

Alec was a different matter. He was man-trained before he ever began to learn the lessons of the wilderness, and after seeing what he had done to the moose, I should not have been surprised if he could take care of himself with a single wolf of average powers. However, I did not think that his company would last long against that savage assault. It would be soon over, and the wild wolves would sweep on to the moose meat that waited before them.

That was why I stared at Massey who was dragging down Calmont's rifle for the second time.

Then I saw Alec do a strange thing that took my breath.

He left the moose; he left his three companions, and walked a few stiff-legged steps straight out to meet the enemy.

I thought at first that he meant to take the whole first brunt on himself, which would have meant a quick death.

That was not the meaning of it, however. The finesse of arctic etiquette, at least among wolves, was not yet familiar to me.

As soon as Alec went out there by himself, the rush of the wolf pack was stayed. Four of them finally stopped short and stood in a loose semi-circle, their red tongues hanging out, and their little eyes fiery bright. Their whole charge from the brush had had a queer effect which I am not able to describe. It was as though some of the mist tangles in the trees had taken on solid weight and life, and had come out there with feet and teeth.

This was a serious matter. I wondered how far those dogs and wolves would have to travel before they would find another meat mountain like that moose. It was as though a small crew of buccaneers had captured a towering galleon laden with gold and spices, and had been surprised while plundering by a greater crew of pirates.

Now that the wolves had halted in their charge, I began to see how the thing might work out.

The leader, after giving a glance to right and left at his rank and file, stalked out by himself toward Alec. They came straight on toward one another until they were no more than six steps apart. There they paused, in different attitudes.

The wolf dropped his head; his hair bristled along his back; his hanging brush almost touched the ground; and his face had the most wicked expression. Alec, on the other hand, kept his head up, and there was no sign of bristling fur. He was on watch, I would have said; and he needed to be, for that timber wolf went at him in a moment like the jump of an unfastened spring.

'Watch!' said Massey.

It was worth watching. Since then, I've seen a burly prize-fighter rush wildly at a smaller foe and be knocked kicking at the first blow. Alec was not so tall, but he was heavier than this wild brute, and he had man-trained brains. Wolf fighting is leap, stroke, shoulder blow or shoulder parry, and always a play to knock the other off his feet.

Well, Alec stood up there like a foolish statue while that grey bolt flew at him across the snow, silent and terrible. At the very moment of impact, Alexander the Great dropped flat to the ground and reached for the other's throat with his long jaws. They spun over and over, but at the end of the last gyration, the wolf leader lay on his back, and Alec stood over him, slowly and comfortably crushing the life out at his throat!

No fight to the death is a pretty thing to watch. The way Alec set his teeth, like a bulldog, while the grey leader kicked and choked and lolled his red tongue, made me more than a bit sick. However, the other wolves and the rest of the dogs did nothing about it. They had not moved from their places, which made a rough circle, except for an old wolf bitch who ran up while the struggle was going on and trotted around and around the two warriors, sometimes whining, once sitting down on her haunches, and howling at the sky.

I wondered whether she were the wife or the mother of the big grey wolf. Certainly he seemed to mean something to her, but she did not bare a tooth to help him in this pinch. A mysterious law of the wilderness made her keep hands off religiously during the battle.

It was over in just a minute. Alec stood back from the dead body of his enemy and, crouched a bit, with his back fur rising, he sent up a howl that filled me full of cold pins and needles. Even Massey groaned faintly as we heard this yell.

The ghoulish howl of triumph ended before any of the huskies or the wolves stirred; but when it was over the whole gang threw themselves on the moose and made a red riot of that good flesh. Alec went in to get his share now, also, and in less time than one could imagine, those powerful brutes were gorging in the vitals of the big carcass.

'He's run amuck,' said Massey through his teeth, very softly. But he was so close to me that I heard every word. 'He's gone back to his wild blood! I'll never get him now!'

That was exactly how I felt about it, too. It looked as though big Alec were the purest wolf in the world, and one of the biggest. He had seemed to loom among the huskies, but he looked still bigger compared with the wild beasts. He was in magnificent condition. Even in that dim light there was a sheen in his long, silky coat, and that is a sure sign of health in a dog.

Well, I watched Alec in there getting his meal and told myself that there was mighty little similarity between him and the dog I had known. The colour and markings were the same, and that was all. The whole air of him was different. This wild, grim Alexander the Great looked up to his name, more than ever, but I was sure that I wanted nothing to do with him, until I had been properly introduced to him all over again by Massey.

Massey himself had led the way down to the edge of the brush which was closest to the kill and the feasters. Then he turned his head to us and warned us with a gesture to keep back out of sight and to make no noise. The look with which he accompanied that silent warning was something to remember for a long time, it was so frightened, and so tense. A man might look like that just before he asked the lady of his heart to marry him.

Then out into the open stepped Massey.

At the sight of him, the old female who had made the fuss about the fight, leaped right straight up into the air with a warning yip. Her back had been turned fairly on us, but she was apparently one of those old she-wolves who have eyes wherever they have nerves. This warning of hers whipped the rest of the lot away from the moose. They scattered like dead leaves in a wind, for a short distance, and then swirled about and faced us.

Only Alec stood his ground in the grandest style, facing Massey, with his forepaws on the shoulder of the moose, and his muzzle and breast crimsoned. There he waited, wrinkling his lips in rage and hatred as he saw the man step out from the brush. A good picture he made just then – a good picture to scare a tiger with!

Massey walked out slowly, but not stealthily. He held out one hand and said in a perfectly natural voice – or perhaps there was just a shade of quiver in it – 'Hello, Alec, old boy!'

Alec went up in the air as the old wolf had done before him. You would have thought that there was dynamite in the words of his master. He landed a bit back from the head of the moose, while the other huskies and the wolves took this for a signal, and scattered into the shadows and mists of the opposite line of brush.

'Alec!' called Massey again, walking straight on with his hand extended.

Alexander the Great spun around and bolted for the brush, with his ears flattened and his tail tucked between his legs!

Great Scott, how my heart beat! There was the end, I thought, of Alec the Great, the thinking dog, the king of his kind. He would be a king of the woods now, in exchange for his former position. I didn't suppose that the change could be called a step down, from his own view-point.

'Alec, Alec!' called Massey, in a sort of agony.

But Alec went out of sight among the brush with a rush of speed.

Massey ran forward, stumbling, so that it was pretty certain he was more than half blind. Poor Massey! He called again and again.

But I heard big Calmont gritting his teeth, and I felt also that it was a lost cause, when, out of the shadows popped that white beauty in the black mask and stood not twenty steps from Massey.

'Thank God!' I distinctly heard Massey say.

Then he went toward Alec carefully, hand out in the usual, time-honoured gesture. And finally Alec made a definite response.

He did not bolt this time. Instead, he dropped to his belly, and looked for all the world as though he were on the verge of charging straight at the man. He had all the aspects of a dog enraged and ready for battle, not for flight.

He looked more evil than he had when he was at the torn body of the moose, warning the man away.

However, when he rose it was not to charge.

He got up slowly, and I saw that the ruff of stiffened mane no longer stood out around his neck and shoulders. He stopped the snarling which had been rumbling in the hollow of his body like a furious and distant thunder. A sort of intimate thunder, one might say. And strung out straight and still, like a setter on a point, he poked his nose out at Massey and seemed to be studying the man.

It was as though he were half statue and half enchanted.

'He's gunna win,' said Calmont through his teeth. 'He's got him charmed like a snake charms a bird!'

He was glad to see Massey show such a power over the dog, of course; but just the same, he could not help hating the man for the very strength which he showed. I believe that Calmont, in his heart, was profoundly convinced that Massey possessed the evil eye which masters beast and man.

In the meantime, Massey stopped advancing, and continued to talk gently and steadily to the dog. Alec lost his frozen pose and came up to his master, one halting step after another, exactly as though he were being pulled on a rope. Calmont began to swear softly under his breath.

Alec was about to stride towards the outstretched hand of his man, and I looked to see him ours in another instant, but then a very odd trick of fate turned up. In the woods, close at hand, a wolf howled sharp and thin. I don't know why, but I was instantly convinced that it was the old female wolf.

At her call, Alec twitched around and was gone in a gleaming streak across the clearing and into the wood toward the voice.

So the victory was snatched out of the very finger-tips of Massey! And that wolf cry out of the mist of the forest was the most uncanny part of a very uncanny night.

Massey did not wait there any longer. He turned about and called us out, for he said that Alec would not come back again that night.

'Or any other night!' said Calmont. 'He's gone for good!'

Massey did not answer, except with a look that cut as deep as a knife stroke.

We set about cutting up the moose, slashing away the parts which the wolves and dogs had mangled, and finding, of course, a vast plenty that had not been spoiled. Everything would be good, either for us or for our team! It was a mountain of meat, for sure.

I was sent back to the camp to hitch up the team to an empty sled and bring it back, so that the meat could be loaded on board, since there was far more than three back loads in the heap, naturally. So I went off, with the howling of the wolves, as it seemed to me, floating out at me everywhere, from the horizon of the circling hills.

When I got near the site of our camp, I rubbed my eyes, amazed. For there was no sign of the tent. It had vanished!

Yet it was certainly our site. For presently I recognized the cutting which we had done for firewood in the adjacent grove, and then, hurrying on closer, I saw the explanation. The tent was there, but it had been knocked flat to the ground, while the snow all about was trampled and scuffed a lot.

Just before the tent lay the body of Muley, one of the poorer dogs in the team of Massey. He had had his throat cut for him neatly, after the wolf style, and somehow I could not but suspect that Alec the Great had done the job. It looked his style of thing, I must say.

The other five dogs were gone, and I knew where. It was pretty plain to me that Alec was an organizing genius. The way he had mastered both half-wild huskies and all the wild timber wolves was a caution, and I could swear that he had stormed along on our back trail until he found our camp; and then, after corrupting the minds of the dog team with a few insidious whispers about the pleasures of the jolly green woods, he had led them away, except for poor Muley. Muley must have resisted. Perhaps he was the opposition speaker and got the knife for his brave stand.

The camp was a frightful wreck. Not only were the dogs gone, but everything had been messed up. Every package that could be slashed open with teeth was spilled. The very tent cloth was badly ripped and chewed. So were sleeping bags, etcetera.

I took stock of the extent of the disaster and then listed details of it. Then I turned about and ran as fast as I could back to the place of the moose.

I found that Massey and Calmont had finished their butchering. Massey sat resting, puffing away at a pipe, while Calmont had his chin propped on his clenched fist, in dark thought. When I told them what I had discovered, Calmont cursed loudly.

'The whole thing is bust!' he shouted. 'I'm sick of it.'

'Go home then,' said Massey, after taking a few more puffs on his pipe. 'For my part, I'm going to stay here until I get him or until he dies!'

Most men, when they talk about doing or dying, are bluffing, of course. Well, Massey was not. There was no bluff in his whole system. He was simply steel, inside and out.

He had had a number of checks in this business. He had lost the best dog team that I ever saw in the Northland. He had spent a vast amount of valuable time. He had risked his life over and over again. But now he was settled to the work. Partly, I suppose, the very opposition of hard luck served to make him all the more determined to push through the business. Partly it must have been that he loved Alec the Great in a way that we could not quite understand.

I wondered what Calmont would do, and expected to see him trudge back across the country to his shack and resume mining operations. But that was not Calmont's kind. He could stick to disagreeable or hopeless work as long as the next one; and besides, I think he was biding his time and licking his lips for the moment when the dog might be taken by some lucky trick, and the long-postponed fight could take place.

At any rate, though he made no declaration of policy, he stayed on. The first thing we did was to build ourselves a fairly comfortable shelter with the sewed-up remnants of the tent and a lot of logs which we felled in a choice bit of woods. In the clearing that we made before the shack, we put up a meat platform, which was so high that not even a lynx or a fisher could jump to the edge of it. On this we stacked up the frozen moose meat, which made prime eating, I can tell you.

My special job was the light but mean one of stopping the chinks and holes among the log walls of our house with moss, and I was at work for days, doing my clumsy caulking. However, we got the place in fairly good shape, and prepared for a long stay.

Even Massey seemed to have no good plans. When Calmont asked him, he simply replied: 'I'm trusting to luck and patience, and that's all. Goodness knows how to go about this. Starvation is the only hope I know of that may be long enough to catch Alec!'

This needed explaining, but Massey pointed out, with a good deal of sense, that wolves and dogs will nearly always establish a regular beat through the woods or over the hills and stick to the particular field which they have outlined. Probably in hard times the range is extended a good deal, but it is nearly always run inside of quite distinct limits.

Well, these were hard times for the wolves. We ourselves found little game, but enough to keep our larder well stocked, chiefly because Massey marched for many hours and many miles every day, studying the range of Alec's band, and also shooting everything that he could find. Everything, he said, that he added to our cache on the meat platform was a possibility removed from the teeth and the starved stomachs of Alec and his forces. In fact, he hoped that by sharpening Alec's hunger, he could eventually draw him close to the shack. As a last resort, he was willing to try traps to catch him, at the risk of taking him with a broken leg. But he wanted to wait until the last moment before he did this.

The position which we had selected was, according to Massey's explorations, about the centre of the wolf range, and, therefore, we were in fairly close striking distance of all their operations.

In the meantime, poor Alec, by his Napoleonic stroke of running off his old companions, the dog team of Massey, had simply loaded himself down with doubled responsibilities. There were now twelve hungry mouths following him, and though we constantly heard the voices of the pack on the blood trail, we guessed that they got little for their trouble, and I've no doubt that rabbits and such lean fare made up most of their meals, such as they were.

Several times we saw them in the distance, and in the glasses of Massey they began to look very tucked-up and gaunt. If there was anything to be hoped for from a partnership with starvation, it looked as though we had it working already.

In the meantime, we sat back at ease and ate our moose meat and simply guarded against wolverines, those expert thieves being the only robbers we had to fear in that part of the woods. The attitude of Massey and Calmont toward one another had not altered. They were simply coldly polite and reserved; and each had an icy look of hatred with which he contemplated the other in unobserved moments. However,

I was pretty willing to stack my money on Alec remaining a free dog. And so long as he ran at large, I saw no chance of the battle taking place. Instinctively, silently, I was praying all day and every day that the fight might not become a fact.

For the more I knew of this pair, the more closely they seemed matched. Massey had the speed of hand, the dauntless spirit, the high courage and the coldly, settled heart of a fighting man. But Calmont balanced these qualities with his enormous strength and a certain brutal savagery which was liable to show him a way to win simply because it would never have occurred to a fair mind like Massey's.

If they fought I was reasonably sure that Calmont would bring it about that the battle should be hand to hand, and there all his natural advantages of weight and superior height would be sure to tell. That nightmare of expectancy never left me for a moment, night or day.

We had been out there in the woods for about two weeks, eating well and keeping ourselves snug by burning a vast quantity of fuel; and then Alec the Great struck a counter-blow, most unexpectedly.

One night I was wakened from sound sleep by muffled noises from the front of the house, though there was enough of a wind whistling to cover any ordinary disturbance. Whatever made these noises it was not the wind, so I got up and went to the door. This I pushed open and looked on to one of the queerest pictures that any man ever can have seen.

Up there on top of our meat platform was the fine white figure of Alec the Great, and he was dragging great chunks of meat to the edge of the platform and letting them fall into the throats of his followers. This was almost literally true, for the instant that a bit of meat fell it seemed to be devoured before it had a chance to touch the ground.

It was not so amazing that he had got to the top of the platform. Calmont carelessly had left the ladder standing against it, the evening before, forgetful of Alec's ability to climb such things. What startled me was that he should be pulling that meat off the platform and letting it fall to his mates. I dare say that any other animal would have filled his own belly and disregarded its companions. At least, not many outside of the mothers of litters would have had the wit or the impulse to give away fine provisions.

Well, there was Alec up there doing the very thing I have described. It took my breath so that I stared for a moment, incapable of movement. Then I slipped back to Massey and shook him by the shoulder. He waked with a start and grabbed me so hard that he almost broke me in two.

'It's only Joe,' I told him. 'Alec's outside with his gang. Up on the meat platform. Maybe you can do something about –'

He was at the door before I had finished saying this. On the way he caught down from the wall a leather rope which he had been making during the past few days, and using as a lariat, in practice. And if he could get out there close enough to the platform, I was reasonably sure that he would be able to pop the rope on to Alec, and then perhaps have that white treasure for good!

Calmont was up now. The three of us looked out on the destruction of our provisions with no care about them, but only the hope that we could evolve out of this loss a way of capturing the great dog.

Massey decided that he would go out through the back wall, and that is what he did, pulling up some of the flooring boughs which we used to keep us off the frozen ground, and then burrowing out through the drifted snow beyond.

The other pair of us, still waiting breathlessly inside the doorway, presently made out Massey stalking through the gloom of the woods at the side of the meat cache.

It looked to me like the end of the chase, and perhaps it might have been, except for a strange thing.

Alec was still pulling the supplies to the edge and letting them topple to the ground, the rest of the pack were gathered below, snarling softly now and then, but enjoying that rain of food with burning eyes. One, however, had withdrawn with a prize to the edge of the shrubbery, and this one now started up with a loud, frightened yell.

Once more I could have sworn that it was the old female of whom I've spoken before.

She had spotted Massey, in spite of his Indian-like care. And, at that alarm, that wolf-dog pack hit the grit for the shadows as fast as they could scamper.

Alexander the Great, however, delayed a fraction of a second. He picked up a chunk of frozen meat, jumped into the snow with it, and ran after the rest of his boys, carrying his lunch-basket with him, as one might say.

This was an exhibition of good, cool nerve. It was like seeing a man come out of a burning building reading a newspaper on the way, and stopping on the front porch to admire a headline.

Calmont laughed aloud, and I could not help grinning, but poor Massey came in with a desperate face. He actually sat by the fire with his head in his hands, after this, and he said to me that the job was hopeless. They never would capture Alec.

I dared not say that I hoped they wouldn't!

This adventure made him feel that he would have to resort to the traps after all. We had some along with us, carted in from Calmont's shack, and these we oiled up and Calmont himself set them, because he knew the ways of wild animals very well, and had done a good deal of trapping here and there in his day.

Several days after the affair of the meat platform, when we judged that the pack would have empty bellies and eager teeth once more, the traps were placed in well-selected spots, and baited.

The next morning we followed along from trap to trap and found that every one of them had been exposed by scratching in the snow around them.

After this, the wolves had apparently gone on, leaving the traps exposed to ridicule and the open light of the day. Calmont scratched his head and swore that he would try again and again, and again we made the experiment. But it was nearly always with the same result.

Then we saw that the footprints around the traps were always the well-known sign of Alec. The scoundrel was doing all of this detective work which made us feel so helpless and foolish! Presently we began to feel as though Alec were quietly laughing at us, and heartily scorning our foolish efforts to capture him in his own domain. For my part I had given up the idea entirely.

Then came the great blizzard.

For ten days the wind hardly stopped blowing for a moment. At times we had a sixty-mile wind, and zero weather, which is the coldest thing in the world, so far as I know. There was a great deal of snow that fell during this storm, and at the end of the time, when the gale stopped, we went out into a white world in which Alec was to write a new chapter.

We were a little low in wood for burning, and I went out that morning to get a bit of exercise and also to chop down some trees and work them into the right lengths. I picked out some of about the right diameter and soon the axe strokes were going home, while the air filled with the white smoke of the dislodged snow that puffed out from the branches. There was enough wind, now and then, to pick up light whirls of the snow from the ground also, or from the tips of branches, and the air was constantly filled with a dazzling bright mist. Such an atmospheric condition often brings on snow blindness, I believe. And after working for a time, I was fairly dizzy with the shifting lights and with the surge of blood into my head from the swinging of the axe.

I stepped back finally, when I had got together a good pile of fuel; and it was then that I saw the rabbit which was eventually to lead on to that adventure.

It looked like a mere puff of snow at first. Then I saw the dull gleam of its eyes and threw the axe at it.

It hopped a few short bounds away and crouched again. It acted as though it were altogether too weak to move very far.

So I suddenly ran after it, picking up the axe, and the rabbit bobbed up and down, keeping just a little ahead of me, and going with a stagger. It was certainly either sick or exhausted from hunger. Hunger I guessed, because one of the prolonged arctic storms is apt to starve even rabbits.

I went over the top of the next hill and down into the hollow, when, out of the whirling snow mist, leaped a white fox and caught up that rabbit at my very feet!

He carried it off to a very short distance and there actually stopped and began to eat in full view of me. This amazed me more than ever. They say that animals can tell, sometimes, when men have guns with them and when their hands are empty. Mine were not quite empty. I had the light axe, but the fox seemed to know perfectly well that it was a rather silly weapon for distance work.

He went on eating while I walked slowly toward him.

Two or three times he retreated with the remains of his dinner. But he was reluctant, and he gave me a snaky look and a couple of silent snarls when I walked up on him.

He was about gone with exhaustion and hunger, I could guess. His belly cleaved to his backbone. He was bent like a bow with emptiness and with cold, and looked brittle and stiff.

The way he put himself outside that rabbit was worth seeing, and when he had finished it he did not skulk off, but licked his red chops and began to eye me!

I tried to laugh at the impudence of him, but I found that I was getting the creeps. A fox is not a very big creature, and, minus its beautiful coat, it is usually a poor little starveling. But that fox seemed to grow bigger and bigger.

Finally, I again threw my axe at it.

The beast let the axe fly over its head without so much as budging, and, staring at me, it licked its red lips again. I was to it what a moose would be to a man – a mountain of meat, and somehow I knew that that beast was coveting the lord of creation as represented by me.

I stepped back. The fox came a step after me. I turned back on it. The little brute snarled at me with the utmost hate and would not budge.

This angered me so much that I shouted, and ran forward, after which my fox shrank a little to the side, and remained there, snarling, its snaky bright eyes on my throat. I was almost afraid to pick up my axe, for fear I would be rushed as I bent forward; but when I had the axe in my hand I decided that I would waste no more time out here getting myself frozen, but go back toward the house, in the hope of luring this vengeful fox after me.

But the matter of the fox was taken off my hands exactly as the matter of the rabbit had been. Out of the snow mist, shining and thick, a stream of gaunt, grey forms came streaking with a shining white body in the fore-front. The fox whirled about and started to scamper, but he had waited too long in his interest in me.

Before he could get into his running stride, Alec the Great struck him down before my eyes, and the poor fox screamed for one half-second as the grey flood closed over him.

I dare say that between the time the meat was stolen from the platform and the time this fox was pulled down that pack had not touched food of any kind. At least, they looked it, with their hollowed stomachs and arched backs, and their eyes were stains of red, glaring frightfully.

'Alec!' I shouted loudly. 'Alec, Alec!'

At my voice, that wave of grey parted from above the bones of the fox and then closed together once more over it. They, also, seemed to know pretty well that even if I were a man, yet I had no gun with me. I whirled the axe and shouted again, without getting any more response than if I had shouted at the arctic trees in their winter silence.

This frightened me suddenly.

There are stories about hungry wolves and over-confident men. You will hear those stories occasionally in camp, when the beasts are howling far away on a blood trail. They make bad yarns and haunt one at night.

Well, I backed away from that gang and then turned and started for the house. I had barely got started when I heard a rushing sound behind me, something like that of a gust of wind through trees. I looked back over my shoulder. It was no wind. It was the noise of the loose, dry snow, whipped up by the running legs of thirteen dogs and wolves, for that whole pack was coming for me, and Alec the Great was in the lead, with the ugly wolf bitch at his side.

Fear did not numb me, luckily. There was a patch of trees standing in a huddle to one side of me, and I got to those trees as fast as a greyhound could have jumped the distance. They would guard my back if only I could fight off the enemy from the front! I shouted with all my might, but – perhaps it was the sight of the snow fog in the air – I was sure that my voice would never reach to the ears of my friends in the house.

If only the wolves would howl!

But they did not. They sat down in a semicircle before me, while Alec the Great, according to his usual tactics, marched up and down along the line, marshalling his forces, planning his wicked devices.

I say wolves, though most of them were merely huskies, but they looked all wolf now and they certainly acted all wolf, as well! Their red eyes had evil in them, and there was more evil in Alec, our former pet, than in any of the rest of the lot.

Suddenly I said: 'Alec, old boy, you ought to remember me. Yonder in Nome I got you out of as bad a mess as this, when the dog team was about to mob you!'

Now, when I said this, I give you my word that that beautiful white brute stopped his slinking walk and turned his head toward me, with ears so pricked and with eyes so bright that I could have sworn that he understood every syllable that I was speaking.

He waited there, with a fore-paw raised, and smiling a red, wolfish smile. I was understood by him he seemed to be saying; but he was not at all convinced that he intended to return good for good.

While I was talking to Alec, the real mischief started. The old bitch had worked herself close to me through the snow, wriggling like a seal, and unnoticed by me until she rose from the ground at my very feet and tried for my throat. She would have got it, too, except that I jerked down the axe from my shoulder with an instinctive, not an aimed, blow, that went straight home between her eyes. It split her skull. She struck me heavily on the chest, knocking me back against the trees, and then fell dead at my feet, while I, gasping, and shouting louder than ever for help, swung the axe again and prepared to meet the rush.

It came.

One of the wolves, a big, strong male, rushed in on me, as though trying to take advantage of any confusion I might be in after repulsing the attack of the bitch. I made a half turn and gave it to him alongside the head. It did not kill him. It merely slashed him badly, and made him spring for my throat.

Then they settled down in their semicircle again, and once more they waited.

Alec set the example of patience by lying prone on his belly in the snow and commencing to bite out the ice from between his toes. Only the wolf which had been wounded stood stiffly in place, his eyes red and green by turns, like lights on a railway, except that green was the danger signal here.

All that scene is burnt into my mind, though I thought at the time that I would never remember anything except the wolfish eyes. Fear and horror came over me in waves. Sometimes I thought that I might faint. The dread of this kept me strung taut. And I remember how a puff of wind opened the snow mist before me and gave me a sight of the whole hollow, and the dark forest beyond, while a hope leaped up for an instant in my breast, and was gone again as the mist closed in once more.

I saved up my voice, as it were, and shouted very high, and then lower, wondering if any sound might come to the cabin where two strong men and rifles were ready to scatter ten times as many wolves as these like nothing at all!

As I shouted, I remembered that the wolves and dogs would cant their heads a little and listen like connoisseurs of music. If it came to making a noise, I was an amateur compared to these musicians of the wilderness. This comparison struck me at the time and almost made me smile, which shows how oddly we can detach ourselves from ourselves.

Well, Alec was the one who brought me down.

The treacherous dog must have been planning it carefully in his almost human brain. He was lying there licking his forelegs one instant, and the next moment he was in at me like a flash. I suppose he had gathered his hind legs carefully beneath him for the spring, while he maintained that sham in front to deceive me. And deceive me he did, and most perfectly.

The first thing I knew, that white flash was on me.

He did not go for the throat. Instead, he used the trick that Massey had taught him with such care in the days of his puppyhood. He simply gave me his shoulder at the knees, and the force of that blow laid me flat with a jolt that almost winded me.

I jerked my arms across my face and throat, instead of striking out. I heard a deep, moaning growl which I supposed was the joy note from those hungry vandals.

Well, it makes me blush to relate that I closed my eyes and simply waited that frightful split second for my murder to commence, knowing that something was standing over me, snarling frightfully. Teeth clashed. Something tugged at my clothes.

And then I opened my cowardly eyes and saw that Alec the Great was standing over me, not trying for my throat, but keeping back the wolf pack with his bared teeth!

People have tried to explain all this to me. They have said that, of course, scent is the keenest sense in a dog or a wolf, and that it was not until he was close to me, this cold, blowing day, that Alec the Great was able to note my scent and record me in his memory as an old friend. Some people have even said that it was all a game on his part. But then, they were not there to see the look in his eyes before he jumped in at me. However, I never have been convinced by any of these attempted explanations. They may be all correct, but I suppose I prefer to keep the thing a miracle.

When I looked up and saw how the battle was going, you can imagine that I got to my feet in double-quick time. I scooped up the axe which had fallen from my hand into the deep snow, only the end of the haft sticking out above the surface.

My troubles were not over. The pack had yielded ground for a moment at the strange spectacle of its leader going over to the enemy, but hunger was more eloquent than their respect for the teeth of Alec the Great.

They came bundling in toward us in a tumult. And Alec?

Why, he fought them off like a master, with my help. I kept my axe swinging as hard and as fast as I could, and as the wolves swerved this way and that from the blade – a tooth which they learned quickly to respect – Alec flashed out at them like a sword from its scabbard and cutting right and left was back again in the shallow shelter which I made for him.

That dog moved as quickly as a striking snake. Even the real wild wolves were slow compared with him. And this again, of course, was the result of man training, plus native ability and brains. He seemed to think out things in a human manner. In parrying those attacks, for instance, he gave almost all his attention to the big grey wolf which already had been slashed by the axe blade. That fellow was the champion of the old brigade, one might say, and he led the way for the rest, feinting in very cleverly, and always trying to get at me, as though he understood perfectly well that what made the strength of Alec and me was our partnership, and that I was the weaker of the two. Half a dozen times his long fangs were not an inch from my face, for he was always trying for my throat.

And Alec, making this his chief enemy, finally found a chance to rip that timber wolf right across the belly as he was jumping up and in.

The wounded beast hit the ground and went off to a little distance before it lay down on the snow.

Then it got up, leaving a pool of red where it had lain, and went off with small, slow steps. I guessed that it was bleeding to death rapidly and wanted to get into the dark of the forest before its fellows found out its bad condition.

Well, it had no luck. It was leaving a broad trail behind it, and famine and the bad luck they were having with Alec and me, made the rest of the pack swerve away from us and head after their wounded companion.

When he saw them coming, I saw him quicken his pace into a wretched, short-striding gallop. He got to the shadow of the woods a bit before the others, but I knew that they must have been on him in a swarming crowd a moment later. Yet there was no sound to tell of it. Hunger shut their throats. Just as they had swarmed silently around me, so they must have swarmed silently around that wounded comrade, tearing him to bits.

For my part, I cared not a whit what became of them and all the rest of the wolves and huskies in the world, for I was down on my knees in the snow with my arms around Alec the Great hugging him against my breast like a long-lost brother.

His reaction to this was very odd.

First, he shuddered and snarled, and I could feel and see his hair bristling along his back. But, after a moment, Alec became a different creature.

He had had a long contact with the wilderness, of course, and I suppose his long association with Calmont had given humanity a black eye with him for the time being. But as I talked to Alec and caressed him, finally his tail began to wag. He kissed my face, and, sitting down in the snow before me, he laughed in my face, with his wise head canted a little to one side, exactly as he used to carry it in the old days, when he was asking what he should do next.

This delighted me wonderfully, and I began to laugh until the tears stung my face.

However, I had to get home quickly.

Half a dozen times, the cutting fangs of those desperadoes had touched my clothes, and with the next grip huge rents and tears appeared. These let in the cold on me, like water through a sieve, and I was shuddering from head to foot.

So I headed up the hill, my heart very high, you may be sure, and my head turned to watch Alec.

Well, he came right up after me until we reached the ridge of the hill, with the cabin in full view on its side. There Alec the Great sat down and would not budge for a long moment.

He stared at the house, then he turned his head and looked toward the woods, and if ever a strong brain turned two ideas back and forth visibly, it was Alec there on the hill, looking down, as I felt, at all humanity, all civilization, and calmly asking himself if the penalties were worth the pleasures compared with the wild, free life of a king of the woods. I called him. I coaxed him. Finally, he jumped up as though he had known what to do all the time, but had merely been resting. And with Alec at my heels, I went on to the cabin and thrust open the clumsy door which we had made to seal the entrance.

It seemed dim inside, and the air was rank with great swirls of pipe smoke, and the reeking fumes of frying bacon. It was very close, and the air was bad, but it was warm. However, no conqueror ever walked into a castle in a conquered city with a greater feeling of pride than I had as I stalked in with Alec at my heels.

Calmont saw us first, and groaned out an oath which held all his amazement in it. He stood back against the wall, still gasping and muttering, while Alec crouched on the threshold and snarled in reply. Those green eyes of his plainly told what he thought of Calmont and all of Calmont's kind!

Massey, when he saw what I had with me, made no remark at all. But he looked at me like a fellow seeing a ghost. It was a moment before Alec spotted him, and then he crawled across the floor, dragging himself almost on his belly, until he was close. Once in range, he leaped fairly at Massey, and in another moment they were wrestling all over the floor of that cabin, and threatening to wreck the place.

It was just one of their little games, but since they last played it together, Alec had about doubled his strength. He was a handful, I can tell you!

At this game I looked on with a wide grin, but Calmont saw nothing jolly about it at all. It meant that the dog was back, and that he was still as much of an outcast as ever. It was again Calmont against the world of Massey, Alec the Great, and me.

Poor Calmont! Looking back at him as he was then, I can look a little deeper into his nature than I thought I could at that time. That reunion of Massey with the dog was a grand thing to watch, I thought, and I laughed rather drunkenly – with a mug of coffee steaming in one hand, and a chunk of meat in the other, while Calmont turned his back on the dog and the man, and paid his attention to me.

He found some cuts and tied them up for me. I wished then that there had been twice as many cuts, for Calmont put his great hand on my shoulder and said: 'Kid, you're a good game one! A right good game one!'

It was the very first kind word that he ever had spoken to me. It was almost the first time that he had so much as taken notice of my existence, and I was puffed up so big that I would have floated at a touch.

I felt that I was a man now, and a mighty important man too, having done myself what the pair of them had been unable to accomplish. It didn't occur to me that the whole affair had been accident. Boys never think out the discreditable chance parts of an adventure. In a way, I think that the young are apt to live on the impressions which they give older people. I had made a great impression this day, and it brimmed my cup with happiness.

When things settled down, Massey, sitting on the floor with big Alec laughing silently beside him, asked me for the whole story. I pretended to be reluctant to speak, but I let them drag the yarn out of me, speaking short and carelessly, but all the while almost bursting with my pride; and so I went from the rabbit to the fox, and from the fox to the wolves. And Massey listened and nodded with shining eyes.

He did not commend me openly. But then he was not the man to do that before a comparative stranger like Calmont. Whatever I did that was worth doing, I knew that Massey took as much joy in it as I did myself. He was that kind of a man, but he spoke his praise in one or two short words, quietly, when I was alone with him. It was one of the qualities that made me love him.

When I got on to the end of the story, and how Alec had hesitated on the top of the hill, Massey simply said, 'Well, he'll never hesitate again.' Afterwards, he added, 'I make out that you left one wolf dead there on the snow, old son?'

I said that the bitch had been stretched dead there.

'But, lad,' said Massey, 'that means that you just walked off and left a perfectly good wolf skin behind you?'

I said that was it. I was not interested in skinning wolves just then.

'Trot off there and get it, then,' said Massey. 'You'll want to keep that skin, with the slit in the skull and all. It'll give a point to the telling of this story, one day, for your friends and your children, and all such! Trot off and get that and start in hoping right now that the pack hasn't returned to dine off that dead body!'

The idea seemed perfectly clear to me. I jumped up without a word, and without another thought, and tore out of that shack like mad, to get to the place before the wolves came back.

I got across the hill, and breathed more easily when I saw the body stretched there, dark against the snow, and the wind riffling in the long fur.

I had my knife out as I got up to the body, but when I turned the wolf on her back and was about to make the first cut, I remembered suddenly, the other half of what was to come.

Calmont and Massey, and the agreement they had made!

Then I saw, with blinding clearness, that it was simply a trick of that clever Massey to get me out of the way. I was to be shunted to one side, and while I collected my foolish wolf skin, they were back there fighting life and death – and the ownership of Alec!

As fast as I could leg it, I hurried back toward the cabin. The wind had dropped to nothing, but the snow was falling very fast, filling the air with a white, thick dust. There was one comfort – that I heard not a sound from the direction of the cabin, and this I took to be a great and sure sign, because when two such giants met, I could not help feeling that there would be an uproar which could be heard for tens of miles away.

Quite winded, I reached the upper rim of the hill and saw the dull outlines of the cabin looming before me through the shimmer of the mist of snowfall. All seemed peaceful to me, and I stopped for an instant to draw breath; and all at once I wished that I had not left the wolf, but that I had done my work before I came back to the cabin, carrying the wolf skin for which I had been sent.

I was embarrassed, ill at ease, and shifting from one foot to the other. As people do, in such a state of mind, I shifted my glance to the side, and there I saw in the bottom of the hollow what looked to me like two giants breathing and tossing about a white vapour.

I looked again, and then all the dreamlike quality of this scene vanished, for I knew that it was Calmont and Massey fighting for their lives – and Alec!

Where was Alexander the Great?

I saw him then, on a short chain fastened outside the cabin, and at the same time I heard him bark twice or thrice in a mournful, inquiring tone. As if he asked what those two men were doing at the lower end of the hollow.

It struck me at the time as rather a ghastly thing that the two of them should have decided to fight it out with the dog there to look on. But while I thought of this, I began to run toward the pair of them, not really hoping that I could stop their battle, but because I could not remain at a distance. For it suddenly came home to me that, though I loved Massey, I could not look on the death of Calmont with equanimity. I remembered then, and never was to forget, how he had put his heavy hand on my shoulder and said, 'You're game!'

Other men in my life have occasionally said pleasant things to me, but not even from Massey did I ever receive such an accolade.

So I lunged down the hollow with my heart in my mouth.

I could distinguish them at once, partly by the superior size of Calmont and partly by the superior speed of Massey. He was like a cat on his feet, and even the thickness of the snow could not altogether mask his celerity. The snow, too, was kicked up in light, fluffy clouds around the site of the struggle, and yet through this glimmering, white mist I followed every act of the two battlers.

I saw Calmont run in, like a bull, head down, terrible in his force and weight; and I saw Massey leap aside like a light-footed wolf. Oh, that gave me hope for Massey! Like a wolf in speed, like a wolf in action, and like a wolf, also, in the ability to hurt terribly when the opportunity came.

It came at that very moment.

I could not see the strokes which he delivered, but distinctly through the mist I saw Calmont turn and strive to come in again, and saw him checked and wavering before what he met.

Of course his plan was clear. He was a great wrestler, equipped for the game by his gigantic muscles, and what he wanted was to close with his old bunkie, and, gripping him close, get a stranglehold.

It seemed to me that I could tell the whole argument – how Massey had held out for knife or gun, and how Calmont had insisted grimly that it should be hand to hand, where his weight and superior strength would tell.

Well, I knew the fiery disposition of Massey too well to doubt what the outcome of such an argument would be even before I saw the actual result of it. He could not decline a dare. He had to fight, if a fight were offered, no matter what the odds.

So there they were, meeting each other according to Calmont's desire.

Yet it was not going, apparently, as Calmont would have wished. He was baffled before those educated fists of Massey.

I saw him rush again, and again I saw him go back from Massey, and I knew that blows were propelling him.

At this, I tried to cry out, and either my excitement or my breathlessness stopped my voice before it could issue from my lips.

Running down at full speed, I was much closer when I saw Massey, in turn, take the aggressive.

It was a beautiful thing to see him dart in, wavering like a windblown leaf, but hitting, I have no doubt, like the stroke of sledgehammers, for that monstrous Calmont reeled before him again, and suddenly there was no Calmont any longer!

He was down, I saw next. He was more than half buried in the loose snow which they had kicked up into a dense cloud about them.

And now would Massey leap in to take advantage of a fallen enemy?

No, there was something knightly about Massey. Such a thing was simply out of his mind, and he kept his distance while Calmont struggled clumsily to his feet.

I should say that he was not actually on his feet, but only on his knees as I came hurtling down the hill toward them. I ran straight between them, and as I did so, I saw that Calmont had pulled out from beneath his clothes that revolver whose possession he had denied. He pulled it out, and through the snow mist I saw him levelling it at Massey, and I saw the red-stained face of Calmont there behind the gun.

I shouted at him: 'Calmont! Calmont! Fight fair!'

I shouted at him, I say, just as I came between him and his enemy, and made it so that at that moment he pulled the trigger.

At this time I don't remember hearing the gun at all. I only saw the flash of the powder – and a heavy impact struck me in the body.

That I remember, and with sickening distinctness the knowledge that I had been shot. The force of the blow whirled me half around. I staggered and was about to fall when I saw Calmont, through a haze of terror and of snow mist, leap upward from the ground and throw the revolver he had used far away, and come rushing in to me with his arms thrown out.

He caught me up. It was like being seized in the noose of steel cables. That man was a gorilla and did not know his strength compared with the frailty of ordinary human flesh and bone.

He caught me up, and I looked to his face and saw it through the swirling darkness that comes at fainting.

When I next saw with any distinctness, there was a frightful, burning pain in my side, and I remember that my throat was hard and aching, as if I had been screaming. And I suppose that was exactly what I was doing.

I looked up, and saw Calmont's face above me, contorted like a fiend's. I thought, in my agony, that Calmont was a demon, appointed by fate to torment me.

At that moment, I heard him cry out: 'I'll hold him, Hugh, and you do the thing. I can't bear it!'

Then I saw that Hugh Massey was holding me, and that he was transferring me to Calmont's arms.

I remember feeling that everything would have to turn out all right, in spite of pain and torment, so long as Massey was there. He was not the sort to deny an old friend and companion. He would rather die than do such a thing, but there was a profound wonder that the pair of them could have been working over one cause, and that cause myself!

This blackness into which I had dropped thinned again, later on, and I found myself looking up toward the ceiling of the room of the cabin. There was a vast weakness which, like a tangible thing, was floating back and forth inside me.

And then I heard the voice of Calmont, low, and hard, and strained, as he said: 'Massey, I want you to hear something.'

To this Massey said: 'I've heard enough from you. I most certainly wish that I could even forget the thought of you!'

'Aye,' said Calmont, 'and so do I. I wish that I could forget, but I can't. I've been a mean one and a low one. I was being fair licked, today, and I took an underhand way of pulling myself even with you. You've been licking me twice, Massey, when I've tried an extra trick, outside of the game. And if we fought again, I couldn't promise that I'd still be fair. But I want to say this to you –'

'I've heard enough of your sayings,' said Hugh Massey.

'You've heard enough, and I'm tired of my own voice,' said Calmont, 'but what I want to say is this: everything is yours. You've beaten me in everything, I dunno how. But it's because you're the better man, I reckon. Strong hands is one thing, but goodness is another, too.

'I've missed that out of my figgering!' said Calmont, continuing. 'I've figgered that I could take as much as I could grab – and carry. But I've been wrong. You're a smaller man, but you've got Marjorie, and you have got Alec, and the kid there loves you like a brother. A good, game kid,' said Calmont.

I half closed my eyes, for it was a sweet thing to hear. I hardly cared whether I lived or died. I was too sick to care much. And that is the consolation of sickness, to be sure! The fellow who is about to die is generally more than half numb and does not suffer as much as he seems to.

'Shut up,' said Massey. 'You'll be waking the kid.'

'Aye,' said Calmont softly, 'I'll shut up. Only – I wanted to say something –'

'I'm not interested in your sayings,' said Massey.

A little strength came back to me at this. I managed to call out: 'Hugh!'

There was simply a swish of wind, he came so fast. He stood above me and looked down at me with a sort of a smile that a man generally is ashamed to show to a man. He keeps it for children and women.

'Aye, partner,' says he.

I closed my eyes and let the echo of that go kindly through me. 'Partner,' he had called me, and no other man in the world, I knew, ever had been called by that name by Massey, except Arnie Calmont himself, in the old days that never would come again.

'Hugh,' said I, 'will you give me your hand?'

He grabbed my hand. His grip was terrible to feel.

'Are you feeling bad?' he says to me. 'Oh, Calmont, you'll pay for this!'

Suddenly there was the terrible, wolfish face of Calmont on the other side of me, leaning above. Except that he didn't look wolfish then, only mightily strained and sick.

'I'll pay on earth and hereafter!' said Calmont.

'Calmont – Hugh!' said I.

I stared up at them. I felt that I was dying, but I wanted only the strength to say to them what was in my mind.

They both leaned close. Massey suddenly slumped to his knees with a loud bang, and gently slid an arm under my head.

'Hold hard, old boy,' he says to me.

'I'm holding – hard,' said I. 'Will you listen?'

'Aye,' says he, 'I'll listen.'

'Yes,' says Calmont, 'and more than that!'

Calmont had hold of one of my hands. Hugh had hold of the other. I pulled my two hands together. For I saw then, that nothing in the world could stop them from killing one another. Most of the bitterness had been on Calmont's part, before this. But, afterwards, it would be Massey who would never rest until he had squared accounts.

Alec, who always knew when something important was being said, came and laid his head on my shoulder in a strange way.

'Calmont – Massey,' I panted. 'Don't let me go black again before I've told you –'

'Don't tell us anything,' said Calmont. 'Close your eyes. Rest up. You're going to be fine. I'll make you fine. You hear me? You're right as can be, kid!'

I closed my eyes, as he said, because it seemed to rest me and to save my strength.

'Partners,' said I, 'it looks to me as though you two would have to team together. You started together. You stayed fast together, till Alec budged you apart. Together, you could beat a hundred, but apart you'll only serve to kill each other. I'm sort of fading out. But before I finish, I'd like to see you shake hands and see that you're friends again.'

'I'll see him danged,' said Massey in a terrible voice. 'I'll see him danged before I'll take his hand. I'll sooner take his throat!'

Well he meant it. He was that kind of a man.

I looked up at them, but I was dumb, and black was floating and then whirling before my eyes.

Calmont held out his hand.

'Aye, Hugh,' said he, 'whatever you please, afterward. But this is for the kid.'

At that, I saw Massey grip the hand of Calmont in both of his. They stared at each other. Never were there two such men again in the world as that pair who stood over me there in the cabin, with Alec whining pitifully at my ear.

'Maybe the kid's right, and we've both been wrong,' said Massey suddenly. 'Maybe we've always needed each other! Here's my hand for good and all, Arnie, and dang me if I ever go back on my word!'

'Your word,' said Calmont, 'is a pile better than gold, to me. And this is the best minute I've ever seen. Mind the kid – mind –'

The last of this, however, came dimly to me. I felt a vast happiness coming over me, but the darkness increased, and a sudden pain in the side stabbed inward until it reached my heart, and then the rest of the world was completely lost.

But I think that if I had died then I would have died happily, so far as happy deaths are possible, with a feeling that I had managed a great thing before the end of me.

At any rate, the world vanished from before my senses and did not come back to me until I saw, over my head, the cold, bright faces of the stars, and heard Hugh Massey giving brief, low-voiced orders to dogs.

'How is he?' asked Massey from a distance.

'His heart is going still – but dead slow,' said the voice of Calmont just above me. 'Go on, and go fast, and Heaven help us!'

Sometimes I think, when I remember that ride through the winter cold and through the ice of the wind, that it could not be, and that no man – or boy – could have lived through what flowed through me, at that time; but the facts are there for men to know, in spite of the way the doctor cursed and opened his eyes when he looked at me in Dawson.

What had happened, I learned afterwards from Massey, was that Alec, being left free to run as he would while Calmont and Hugh struggled to keep a spark of life in me during those first days, had gradually hunted through the woods until he called back to him with his hunting song the lost members of the team of Calmont, and the fragments of Massey's own string. They came back, and they settled in around the house as if they never had been away. That was the influence of Alec, who had driven them wild and who was able, in this manner, to tame them again.

I never could say whether he was more man than dog, or more dog than man, or more wizard than either.

At any rate, the time came when Calmont and Massey decided that they could not keep the failing life in me with their own meagre resources, and so they took the great chance, and the only chance, of taking me off to Dawson.

I wish that I had had consciousness enough to have seen and appreciated that ride down to Dawson. It passed to me like a frightfully bad dream, for I was tormented with pain, and I know that I must have cried out in delirium many a time, and wakened, setting my teeth over another yell.

But how much I should have liked to see Calmont herding that team forward, and Massey breaking the trail, or Calmont driving, and Massey beside me.

They were men. They were hard men. They were the very hardest men that I ever saw in all that cold, hard country. But they treated me as if each of them were my blood brother.

When they got me down to Dawson and took me into the doctor's office, I came to for fair, and I wish that I hadn't, for I had to endure the probing of the wound, with both Calmont and Massey looking on.

If they had not been there, I could have yelled my head off, which would have been a relief; but both of them were standing by, and I had to grip my jaws hard together and endure the misery, and a mighty sick business that was.

I remember that Calmont assured the doctor that if I died, there would be one doctor fewer in Dawson; and I remember that Massey told him that if I got well there would be a certain number of pounds of gold –

But the doctor danged them both – which is a way that doctors have, and assured them that he cared not a rap for the pair of them multiplied by ten.

Well, I was put away in a bed, and gradually life began to come back to me, though the doctor himself assured me that there was not the slightest good reason for me coming back to the land of the living, and that according to all the books I should have died. He even made a chart to show me all the vital parts that the bullet had gone through.

However, here I am to write the end of this story.

I write it, however, not in Alaska's blues and whites, but among Arizona's own twilight purples, with the voice of Marjorie Massey singing in the kitchen, and the voice of Hugh sounding in the corral, where he's breaking a three-year-old and I can hear the yipping of Alexander the Great.

I get up to look out of the window, and see Alec perched on top of the fence, laughing a red laugh at the world, of which he knows that he is the master, the undisputed king of the road, boss of the ranch dogs for fifty miles around, slayer of coyotes, foxes, and even the tall timber wolves. He goes where he pleases. He opens doors to go and come. He thinks nothing of waking the entire household in the middle of the night. He knows that for him there is not in the world a stick, a stone, a whip, or a harsh word.

I think of this as I see the big rascal standing on the fence and then go back to my chair and take from my pocket a yellow paper. It is fraying at the creases as I unfold it and read in a heavy scrawl what Calmont left behind him when he departed one night from among us, after coming all the way back from the white North to stand behind Hugh at his wedding as best man:

'God be good to all of you, but you'll be better off without me.'

D. M. Johnson

A Man Called Horse

HE was a young man of good family, as the phrase went in the New England of a hundred-odd years ago, and the reasons for his bitter discontent were unclear, even to himself. He grew up in the gracious old Boston home under his grandmother's care, for his mother had died in giving him birth; and all his life he had known every comfort and privilege his father's wealth could provide.

But still there was the discontent, which puzzled him because he could not even define it. He wanted to live among his equals – people who were no better than he and no worse either. That was as close as he could come to describing the source of his unhappiness in Boston and his restless desire to go somewhere else.

In the year 1845 he left home and went out West, far beyond the country's creeping frontier, where he hoped to find his equals. He had the idea that in Indian country, where there was danger, all white men were kings, and he wanted to be one of them. But he found, in the West as in Boston, that the men he respected were still his superiors, even if they could not read, and those he did not respect weren't worth talking to.

He did have money, however, and he could hire the men he respected. He hired four of them, to cook and hunt and guide and be his companions, but he found them not friendly.

They were apart from him and and he was still alone. He still brooded about his status in the world, longing for his equals.

On a day in June, he learned what it was to have no status at all. He became a captive of a small raiding party of Crow Indians.

He heard gunfire and the brief shouts of his companions around the bend of the creek just before they died, but he never saw their bodies. He had no chance to fight, because he was naked and unarmed, bathing in the creek, when a Crow warrior seized and held him.

His captor let him go at last, let him run. Then the lot of them rode him down for sport, striking him with their coup sticks. They carried the dripping scalps of his companions, and one had skinned off Baptiste's black beard as well, for a trophy.

They took him along in a matter-of-fact way, as they took the captured horses. He was unshod and naked as the horses were, and like them he had a rawhide thong around his neck. So long as he didn't fall down, the Crows ignored him.

On the second day they gave him his breeches. His feet were too swollen for his boots, but one of the Indians threw him a pair of moccasins that had belonged to the half-breed, Henry, who was dead back at the creek. The captive wore the moccasins gratefully. The third day they let him ride one of the spare horses so the party could move faster, and on that day they came in sight of their camp.

He thought of trying to escape, hoping he might be killed in flight rather than by slow torture in the camp, but he never had a chance to try. They were more familiar with escape than he was and, knowing what to expect, they forestalled it. The only other time he had tried to escape from anyone he had succeeded. When he had left his home in Boston, his father had raged and his grandmother had cried, but they could not talk him out of his intention.

The men of the Crow raiding party didn't bother with talk.

Before riding into camp they stopped and dressed in their regalia, and parts of their victims' clothing; they painted their faces black. Then, leading the white man by the rawhide around his neck as though he were a horse, they rode down towards the tepee circle, shouting and singing, brandishing their weapons. He was unconscious when they got there; he fell and was dragged.

He lay dazed and battered near a tepee while the noisy life of the camp swarmed around him and Indians came to stare. Thirst consumed him, and when it rained he lapped rainwater from the ground like a dog. A scrawny, shrieking, eternally busy old woman with ragged greying hair threw a chunk of meat on the grass, and he fought the dogs for it.

When his head had cleared, he was angry, although anger was an emotion he knew he could not afford.

It was better when I was a horse, he thought – when they led me by the rawhide around my neck. I won't be a dog, no matter what!

The hag gave him stinking, rancid grease and let him figure out what it was for. He applied it gingerly to his bruised and sun-seared body.

Now, he thought, I smell like the rest of them.

While he was healing, he considered coldly the advantages of being a horse. A man would be humiliated, and sooner or later he would strike back and that would be the end of him. But a horse had only to be docile. Very well, he would learn to do without pride.

He understood that he was the property of the screaming old woman, a fine gift from her son, one that she liked to show off. She did more yelling at him than at anyone else, probably to impress the neighbours so they would not forget what a great and generous man her son was. She was bossy and proud, a dreadful sag of skin and bones, and she was a devilish hard worker.

The white man, who now thought of himself as a horse, forgot sometimes to worry about his danger. He kept making mental notes of things to tell his own people in Boston about this hideous adventure. He would go back a hero and he would say, 'Grandmother, let me fetch your shawl. I've been accustomed to doing little errands for another lady about your age.'

Two girls lived in the tepee with the old hag and her warrior son. One of them, the white man concluded, was his captor's wife and the other was his little sister. The daughter-in-law was smug and spoiled. Being beloved, she did not have to be useful. The younger girl had bright, wandering eyes. Often enough they wandered to the white man who was pretending to be a horse.

The two girls worked when the old woman put them at it, but they were always running off to do something they enjoyed more. There were games and noisy contests, and there was much laughter. But not for the white man. He was finding out what loneliness could be.

That was a rich summer on the plains, with plenty of buffalo for meat and clothing and the making of tepees. The Crows were wealthy in horses, prosperous and contented. If their men had not been so avid for glory, the white man thought, there would have been a lot more of them. But they went out of their way to court death, and when one of them met it, the whole camp mourned extravagantly and cried to their God for vengeance.

The captive was a horse all summer, a docile bearer of burdens, careful and patient. He kept reminding himself that he had to be better-natured than other horses, because he could not lash out with hoofs or teeth. Helping the old woman load up the horses for travel, he yanked at a pack and said, 'Whoa, brother. It goes easier when you don't fight.'

The horse gave him a big-eyed stare as if it understood his language – a comforting thought, because nobody else did. But even among the horses he felt unequal. They were able to look out for themselves if they escaped. He would simply starve. He was envious still, even among the horses.

Humbly he fetched and carried. Sometimes he even offered to help, but he had not the skill for the endless work of the women, and he was not trusted to hunt with the men, the providers.

When the camp moved, he carried a pack trudging with the women. Even the dogs worked then, pulling small burdens on travois of sticks.

The Indian who had captured him lived like a lord, as he had a right to do. He hunted with his peers, attended long ceremonial meetings with much chanting and dancing, and lounged in the shade with his smug bride. He had only two responsibilities: to kill buffalo and to gain glory. The white man was so far beneath him in status that the Indian did not even think of envy.

One day several things happened that made the captive think he might some time become a man again. That was the day when he began to understand their language. For four months he had heard it, day and night, the joy and the mourning, the ritual chanting and sung prayers, the squabbles and the deliberation. None of it meant anything to him at all.

But on that important day in early fall the two young women set out for the river, and one of them called over her shoulder to the old woman. The white man was startled. She had said she was going to bathe. His understanding was so sudden that he felt as if his ears had come unstopped. Listening to the racket of the camp, he heard fragments of meaning instead of gabble.

On that same important day the old woman brought a pair of new moccasins out of the tepee and tossed them on the ground before him. He could not believe she would do anything for him because of kindness, but giving him moccasins was one way of looking after her property.

In thanking her, he dared greatly. He picked a little handful of fading fall flowers and took them to her as she squatted in front of her tepee, scraping a buffalo hide with a tool made from a piece of iron tied to a bone. Her hands were hideous – most of the fingers had the first joint missing. He bowed solemnly and offered the flowers.

She glared at him from beneath the short ragged tangle of her hair. She stared at the flowers, knocked them out of his hand and went running to the next tepee, squalling the story. He heard her and the other women screaming with laughter.

The white man squared his shoulders and walked boldly over to watch three small boys shooting arrows at a target. He said in English, 'Show me how to do that, will you?'

They frowned, but he held out his hand as if there could be no doubt. One of them gave him a bow and one arrow, and they snickered when he missed.

The people were easily amused, except when they were angry. They were amused, at him, playing with the little boys. A few days later he asked the hag, with gestures, for a bow that her son had just discarded, a man-size bow of horn. He scavenged for old arrows. The old woman cackled at his marksmanship and called her neighbours to enjoy the fun.

When he could understand words, he could identify his people by their names. The old woman was Greasy Hand, and her daughter was

Pretty Calf. The other young woman's name was not clear to him, for the words were not in his vocabulary. The man who had captured him was Yellow Robe.

Once he could understand, he could begin to talk a little, and then he was less lonely. Nobody had been able to see any reason for talking to him, since he would not understand anyway. He asked the old woman, 'What is my name?' Until he knew it, he was incomplete. She shrugged to let him know he had none.

He told her in the Crow language, 'My name is Horse.' He repeated it, and she nodded. After that they called him Horse when they called him anything. Nobody cared except the white man himself.

They trusted him enough to let him stray out of camp, so that he might have got away and, by unimaginable good luck, might have reached a trading post or a fort, but winter was too close. He did not dare without a horse, he needed clothing and a better hunting weapon than he had, and more certain skill in using it. He did not dare steal, for then they would surely have pursued him, and just as certainly they would have caught him. Remembering the warmth of the home that was waiting in Boston, he settled down for the winter.

On a cold night he crept into the tepee after the others had gone to bed. Even a horse might try to find shelter from the wind. The old woman grumbled, but without conviction. She did not put him out.

They tolerated him, back in the shadows, so long as he did not get in the way.

He began to understand how the family that owned him differed from the others. Fate had been cruel to them. In a short, sharp argument among the old women, one of them derided Greasy Hand by sneering 'You have no relatives,' and Greasy Hand raved for minutes of the deeds of her father and uncles and brothers. And she had had four sons, she reminded her detractor – who answered with scorn, 'Where are they?'

Later the white man found her moaning and whimpering to herself, rocking back and forth on her haunches, staring at her mutilated hands. By that time he understood. A mourner often chopped off a finger joint. Old Greasy Hand had mourned often. For the first time he felt a twinge of pity, but he put it aside as another emotion, like anger, that he could not afford. He thought: What tales I will tell when I get home.

He wrinkled his nose in disdain. The camp stank of animals and meat and rancid grease. He looked down at his naked, shivering legs and was startled, remembering that he was still only a horse.

He could not trust the old woman. She fed him only because a starved slave would die and not be worth boasting about. Just how fitful her temper was he saw on the day when she got tired of stumbling over one of the hundred dogs that infested the camp. This was one of her own dogs, a large, strong one that pulled a baggage travois when the tribe moved camp.

Countless times he had seen her kick at the beast as it lay sleeping in front of the tepee, in her way. The dog always moved, with a yelp, but it always got in the way again. One day she gave the dog its usual kick and then stood scolding at it while the animal rolled its eyes sleepily. The old woman suddenly picked up her axe and and cut the dog's head half off with one blow. Looking well satisfied with herself, she beckoned her slave to remove the body.

It could have been me, he thought, if I were a dog. I'm a horse.

His hope of life lay with the girl, Pretty Calf. He set about courting her, realizing how desperately poor he was both in property and honour. He owned no horse, no weapon but the old bow and the battered arrows. He had nothing to give away, and he needed gifts, because he did not dare seduce the girl.

One of the customs of courtship involved sending a gift of horses to a girl's older brother and bestowing much buffalo meat upon her mother. The white man could not wait for some far-off time when he might have either horses or meat to give away. And his courtship had to be secret. It was not for him to stroll past the groups of watchful girls, blowing a flute made of an eagle's wing bone, as the flirtatious young bucks did.

He could not ride past Pretty Calf's tepee, painted and bedizened, he had no horses, no finery.

Back home, he remembered, I could marry just about any girl I'd want to. But he wasted little time thinking about that. A future was something to be earned.

The most he dared do was wink at Pretty Calf now and then, or state his admiration, while she giggled and hid her face. The least he dared do to win his bride was to elope with her, but he had to give her a horse to put the seal of tribal approval on that. And he had no horse until he killed a man to get one . . .

His opportunity came in early spring. He was casually accepted by that time. He did not belong, but he was amusing to the Crows, like a strange pet, or they would not have fed him through the winter.

His chance came when he was hunting small game with three young boys who were his guards as well as his scornful companions. Rabbits and birds were of no account in a camp well fed on buffalo meat, but they made good targets.

His party walked far that day. All of them at once saw the two horses in the sheltered coulee. The boys and the man crawled forward on their bellies, and then they saw an Indian who lay on the ground, moaning, a lone traveller. From the way the boys inched eagerly forward, Horse knew the man was fair prey – a member of some enemy tribe.

This is the way the captive white man acquired wealth and honour to win a bride and save his life: he shot an arrow into the sick man, a split second ahead of one of his small companions, and dashed forward to strike the still groaning man with his bow, to count first coup. Then he seized the hobbled horses.

By the time he had the horses secure, and with them his hope for freedom, the boys had followed, counting coup with gestures and shrieks they had practised since boyhood, and one of them had the scalp. The white man was grimly amused to see the boy double up with sudden nausea when he had the thing in his hand's . . .

There was a hubbub in the camp when they rode in that evening, two of them on each horse. The captive was noticed. Indians who had ignored him as a slave stared at the brave man who had struck first coup and had stolen horses.

The hubbub lasted all night, as fathers boasted loudly of their young sons' exploits. The white man was called upon to settle an argument between two fierce boys as to which of them had struck second coup and which must be satisfied with third. After much talk that went over his head, he solemnly pointed at the nearest boy. He didn't know which boy it was and didn't care, but the boy did.

The white man had watched warriors in their triumph. He knew what to do. Modesty about achievements had no place among the Crow people. When a man did something big, he told about it.

The white man smeared his face with grease and charcoal. He walked inside the tepee circle, chanting and singing. He used his own language.

'You heathens, you savages,' he shouted. 'I'm going to get out of here some day! I am going to get away!' The Crow people listened respectfully. In the Crow tongue he shouted 'Horse! I am Horse!' and they nodded.

He had a right to boast, and he had two horses. Before dawn, the white man and his bride sheltered beyond a far hill, and he was telling her, 'I love you, little lady. I love you.'

She looked at him with her great dark eyes, and he thought she understood English words – or as much as she needed to understand.

'You are my treasure,' he said, 'more precious than jewels, better than fine gold. I am going to call you Freedom.'

When they returned to camp two days later, he was bold but worried. His ace, he suspected, might not be high enough in the game he was playing without being sure of the rules. But it served.

Old Greasy Hand raged – but not at him. She complained loudly that her daughther had let herself go too cheap. But the marriage was as good as any Crow marriage. He had paid a horse.

He learned the langauge faster after that, from Pretty Calf, whom he sometimes called Freedom. He learned that his attentive, adoring bride was fourteen years old.

One thing he had not guessed was the difference that being Pretty Calf's husband would make in his relationship to her mother and brother. He had hoped only to make his position a little safer, but he had not expected to be treated with dignity. Greasy Hand no longer spoke to him at all. When the white man spoke to her, his bride murmured in dismay, explaining at great length that he must never do that. There could be no conversation between a man and his mother-in-law. He could not even mention a word that was part of her name.

Having improved his status so magnificently, he felt no need for hurry in getting away. Now that he had a woman, he had as good a chance to be rich as any man. Pretty Calf waited on him; she seldom ran off to play games with other young girls, but took pride in learning from her mother the many women's skills of tanning hides and making clothing and preparing food.

He was no more a horse but a kind of man, a half-Indian, still poor and unskilled but laden with honours, clinging to the buckskin fringes of Crow society.

Escape would wait until he could manage it in comfort, with fit clothing and a good horse, with hunting weapons. Escape could wait until the camp moved near some trading post. He did not plan how he would get home. He dreamed of being there all at once, and of telling stories nobody would believe. There was no hurry.

Pretty Calf delighted in educating him. He began to understand tribal arrangements, customs and why things were as they were. They were that way because they had always been so. His young wife giggled when she told him, in his ignorance, things she had always known. But she did not laugh when her brother's wife was taken by another warrior. She explained that solemnly with words and signs.

Yellow Robe belonged to a society called the Big Dogs. The wife stealer, Cut Neck, belonged to the Foxes. They were fellow-tribesmen; they hunted together and fought side by side, but men of one society could take away wives from the other society if they wished, subject to certain limitations.

When Cut Neck rode up to the tepee, laughing and singing, and called to Yellow Robe's wife, 'Come out! Come out!' she did as ordered, looking smug as usual, meek and entirely willing. Thereafter she rode beside him in ceremonial processions and carried his coup stick, while his other wife pretended not to care.

'But why?' the white demanded of his wife, his Freedom. 'Why did our brother let his woman go? He sits and smokes and does not speak.'

Pretty Calf was shocked at the suggestion. Her brother could not possibly reclaim his woman, she explained. He could not even let her come back if she wanted to – and she probably would want to when Cut Neck tired of her. Yellow Robe would not even admit that his heart was sick. That was the way things were. Deviation meant dishonour.

The woman could have hidden from Cut Neck, she said. She could even have refused to go with him if she had been *ba–wurokee* – a really virtuous woman. But she had been his woman before, for a little while on a berrying expedition, and he had a right to claim her.

There was no sense in it, the white man insisted. He glared at his young wife. 'If you go, I will bring you back!' he promised.

She laughed and buried her head against his shoulder. 'I will not have to go,' she said. 'Horse is my first man. There is no hole in my moccasin.'

He stroked her hair and said, '*Ba-wurokee.*'

With great daring, she murmured '*Hay-ha*', and when he did not answer, because he did not know what she meant, she drew away hurt.

'A woman calls her man that if she thinks he will not leave her. Am I wrong?'

The white man held her closer and lied. 'Pretty Calf is not wrong. Horse will not leave her. Horse will not take another woman, either.' No, he certainly would not. Parting from this one was going to be harder than getting her had been. '*Hay-ha*,' he murmured. 'Freedom.'

His conscience irked him, but not very much. Pretty Calf could get another man easily enough when he was gone, and a better provider. His hunting skill was improving, but he was still awkward.

There was no hurry about leaving. He was used to most of the Crow ways and could stand the rest. He was becoming prosperous. He owned five horses. His place in the life of the tribe was secure, such as it was. Three or four young women, including the one who had belonged to Yellow Robe, made advances to him. Pretty Calf took pride in the fact that her man was so attractive.

By the time he had what he needed for a secret journey, the grass grew yellow on the plains and the long cold was close. He was enslaved by the girl he called Freedom and, before the winter ended, by the knowledge that she was carrying his child . . .

The Big Dog society held a long ceremony in the spring. The white man strolled with his woman along the creek bank, thinking: When I get home I will tell them about the chants and the drumming. Some time. Some time.

Pretty Calf would not go to bed when they went back to the tepee.

'Wait and find out about my brother,' she urged. 'Something may happen.'

So far as Horse could figure out, the Big Dogs were having some kind of election. He pampered his wife by staying up with her by the fire. Even the old woman, who was a great one for getting sleep when she was not working, prowled around restlessly.

The white man was yawning by the time the noise of the ceremony died down. When Yellow Robe strode in, garish and heathen in his paint and feathers and furs, the women cried out. There was conversation, too fast for Horse to follow, and the old woman wailed once, but her son silenced her with a gruff command.

When the white man went to sleep, he thought his wife was weeping beside him.

'He wears the bearskin belt. Now he can never retreat in battle. He will always be in danger. He will die.'

Maybe he wouldn't, the white man tried to convince her. Pretty Calf recalled that some few men had been honoured by the bearskin belt, vowed to the highest daring, and had not died. If they lived through the summer, then they were free of it.

'My brother wants to die,' she mourned. 'His heart is bitter.'

Yellow Robe lived through half a dozen clashes with small parties of raiders from hostile tribes. His honours were many. He captured horses in an enemy camp, led two successful raids, counted first coup and snatched a gun from the hand of an enemy tribesman. He wore wolf tails on his moccasins and ermine skins on his shirt, and he fringed his leggings with scalps in token of his glory.

When his mother ventured to suggest, as she did many times, 'My son should take a new wife, I need another woman to help me,' he ignored her. He spent much time in prayer, alone in the hills or in conference with a medicine man. He fasted and made vows and kept them. And before he could be free of the heavy honour of the bearskin belt, he went on his last raid.

The warriors were returning from the north just as the white man and two other hunters approached from the south, with buffalo and elk meat dripping from the bloody hides tied on their restive ponies. One of the hunters grunted, and they stopped to watch a rider on the hill north of the tepee circle.

The rider dismounted, held up a blanket and dropped it. He repeated the gesture.

The hunters murmured dismay. 'Two! Two men dead!' They rode fast into the camp where there was already wailing.

A messenger came down from the war party on the hill. The rest of the party delayed to paint their faces for mourning and for victory. One of the two dead men was Yellow Robe. They had put his body in a cave and walled it in with rocks. The other man died later, and his body was in a tree.

There was blood on the ground before the tepee to which Yellow Robe would return no more. His mother, with her hair chopped short, sat in the doorway, rocking back and forth on her haunches, wailing her heartbreak. She cradled one mutilated hand in the other. She had cut off another finger joint.

Pretty Calf had cut off chunks of her long hair and was crying as she gashed her arms with a knife. The white man tried to take the knife away, but she protested so piteously that he let her do as she wished. He was sickened with the lot of them.

Savages! he thought. Now I will go back! I'll go hunting alone, and I'll keep going.

But he did not go just yet, because he was the only hunter in the lodge of the two grieving women, one of them old and the other pregnant with his child.

In their mourning, they made him a pauper again. Everything that meant comfort, wealth and safety they sacrificed to the spirits because of the death of Yellow Robe. The tepee, made of seventeen fine buffalo hides, the furs that should have kept them warm, the white deerskin dress, trimmed with elk teeth, that Pretty Calf loved so well, even their tools and Yellow Robe's weapons – everything but his sacred medicine objects – they left there on the prairie, and the whole camp moved away. Two of his best horses were killed as a sacrifice, and the women gave away the rest. They had no shelter. They would have no tepee of their own for two months at least of mourning, and the women would have to tan hides to make it. Meanwhile they could live in huts made of willows, covered with skins given them in pity by their friends. They could have lived with relatives, but Yellow Robe's women had no relatives.

The white man had not realized until then how terrible a thing it was for a Crow to have no kinfolk. No wonder old Greasy Hand had only stumps for fingers. She had mourned, from one year to the next, for everyone she had ever loved. She had no one left but her daughter, Pretty Calf.

Horse was furious at their foolishness. It had been bad enough for him, a captive, to be naked as a horse and poor as a slave, but that was because his captors had stripped him. These women had voluntarily given up everything they needed.

He was too angry at them to sleep in the willow hut. He lay under a sheltering tree. And on the third night of the mourning he made his plans. He had a knife and a bow. He would go after meat, taking two horses. And he would not come back. There were, he realized, many things he was not going to tell when he got back home.

In the willow hut, Pretty Calf cried out. He heard rustling there, and the old woman's querulous voice.

Some twenty hours later his son was born, two months early, in the tepee of a skilled medicine woman. The child was born without breath, and the mother died before the sun went down.

The white man was too shocked to think whether he should mourn, or how he should mourn. The old woman screamed until she was voiceless. Piteously she approached him, bent and trembling, blind with grief. She held out her knife and he took it.

She spread out her hands and shook her head. If she cut off any more finger joints, she could do no more work. She could not afford any more lasting signs of grief.

The white man said, 'All right! All right!' betweeen his teeth. He hacked his arms with the knife and stood watching the blood run down. It was little enough to do for Pretty Calf, for little Freedom. Now there is nothing to keep me, he realized. When I get home, I must not let them see the scars.

He looked at Greasy Hand, hideous in her grief-burdened age, and thought: I really am free now. When a wife dies, her husband has no more duty towards her family. Pretty Calf had told him so, long ago, when he wondered why a certain man moved out of one tepee and into another.

The old woman, of course, would be a scavenger. There was one other with the tribe, an ancient crone who had no relatives, towards whom no one felt any responsibility. She lived on food thrown away by the more fortunate. She slept in shelters that she built with her own knotted hands. She plodded wearily at the end of the procession when the camp moved. When she stumbled nobody cared. When she died, nobody would miss her.

Tomorrow morning, the white man decided, I will go.

His mother-in-law's sunken mouth quivered. She said one word, questioningly. She said, '*Eero-oshay?*' She said, 'Son?'

Blinking, he remembered. When a wife died, her husband was free. But her mother, who had ignored him with dignity, might if she wished ask him to stay. She invited him by calling him Son, and he accepted by answering Mother.

Greasy Hand stood before him, bowed with years, withered with unceasing labour, loveless and childless, scarred with grief. But with all her burdens, she still loved life enough to beg it from him, the only person she had any right to ask. She was stripping herself of all she had left, her pride.

He looked eastward across the prairie. Two thousand miles away was home. The old woman would not live for ever. He could afford to wait, for he was young. He could afford to be magnanimous, for he knew he was a man. He gave her the answer. '*Eegya*,' he said. 'Mother'.

He went home three years later. He explained no more than to say, 'I lived with Crows for a while. It was some time before I could leave. They called me horse.'

He did not find it necessary either to apologize or to boast, because he was the equal of any man on earth.

John O'Reilly

The Sound of Gunfire

HE rode into town on a sunless day with the sky as grey as the streaks in his hair, and he swung out of the saddle where a group of rannies were talking in front of the saloon. He wasn't much over thirty-five, despite the grey hair, and he had a tanned, bony face, slightly haggard, and strange-looking eyes. They were grey, too, and completely blank and expressionless, and they didn't waver or move when he sidestepped the other men and walked through the batwings.

'I'm looking for McCord,' he told the barkeep. 'This his place?'

There was a big sign outside the saloon which said *McCord's*, and a couple of *No Credit* notices signed with McCord's name behind the bar. The keep stared at the grey-haired man for a moment, then guffawed and slammed a dirty hand on the bar.

'No education, huh?' He jerked a thumb at the signs. 'Can't you read, pard?'

The man reached forward, took hold of the bartender's shirtfront, and pulled him across the bar. His expressionless eyes stared straight ahead. 'You can't read when you're blind, mister. Get McCord.'

He released the keep and listened to his footsteps move down the length of the saloon. A minute later he heard two pairs of feet returning, and one of them moved into position next to him.

'Nice to meet you, McCord,' he said softly.

The man next to him had a deep, harsh voice, 'How do you know I'm McCord?'

'Easy,' the grey-eyed man said. 'You fit your description. Tall, maybe six-four, heavy, smooth-shaven.'

'The keep told me you were blind.'

'I've been blind for years,' the stranger said. 'Enough years so it doesn't matter . . .

'When I talked to the barkeep, I smelled his stinking rotgut breath right in my nose, which makes him slightly taller than I am – say six-three. His head didn't touch the drape when he walked into your room in the back but I heard the drape rustle up high when you walked out – so you're taller. Heavy, too – easy to tell that by the way your feet hit the floor. And smooth-shaven – you rubbed your jaw a minute ago, and I heard a rasping sound instead of the soft one you get when you stroke hair.'

'You're guessing,' the other man said.

'I don't guess about things like that,' the blind man said. 'A schoolteacher I used to know told me it's called the law of compensation – nature providin' that when a man loses one sense another gets twice as strong. That's the way it is with me – I can hear things no one else can hear. That's why I know you're rolling a smoke on heavy brown paper. White paper has a softer sound.'

McCord shook his head. 'Very interesting, mister,' he said. 'Very interesting. You learn something every day.' He paused. 'But what I want to know is, what's it got to do with me?'

'I'm just statin' my qualifications, McCord. Fact is, I rode into town to do a job for you.'

'What kind of job?'

The blind man leaned forward. 'I hear tell,' he said, 'that you want Johnny Hale dead.'

McCord's hand jerked, and his whisky glass tumbled to the floor. It shattered loudly, and there was silence for a minute. Then McCord said: 'You're crazy.'

'Sane as any gunfighter,' the blind man said. 'My price, McCord, is one thousand dollars.'

'I tell you you're crazy,' McCord said hoarsely. 'And even if I did want somebody killed, what kind of hired gun would *you* make? A blind man – you wouldn't even know where to shoot.'

The grey-eyed man laughed, a laugh as unhumorous and unemotional as his eyes. 'McCord,' he said, 'I've been listening to your clock on the wall there ever since I came into this place. You've probably never noticed it, but the pendulum makes one sound when it swings to the right, and another when it swings to the left.' His gun flashed in his hand, and a bullet tore the pendulum neatly off its mount. 'It was swinging right that time.'

He laughed again. 'How about it, McCord?'

There was another dead silence. Then McCord said, chokingly, 'Out. Get out, don't come into this place again.'

Smiling gently, the blind man walked out of the saloon.

Johnny Hale's office was an airless little room just beyond the schoolhouse, a desk and two chairs in back of a rusty-hinged door with *Sheriff* scrawled on it in crude black letters. The blind man went there directly, his nostrils twitching slightly as he approached the desk. 'Hale around?'

'Me,' the man behind the desk said. He didn't sound like much more than a button, maybe a few years over voting age. It was the way the blind man had figured he would sound, from his description: unruly sandy hair, kid's face with a couple of freckles on the bridge of his nose, wide grin. 'What can I do for you?'

'Nothing much,' the blind man said. His long fingers found the empty chair and sat down. 'I just thought we ought to meet, seein' I've been volunteerin' to kill you.'

Hale's breath whooshed out in a rush. 'Say that again.'

The blind man smiled. 'I've just been down to McCord's saloon, tellin' McCord my price to put a bullet in you is a thousand dollars. Cheap, too, considerin' the prices some hired guns draw.'

Hale jumped to his feet and came around the desk. He thrust his face close to the blind man's. 'What is this, mister – some kind of joke?'

'No joke a-tall,' the grey-eyed man said casually. 'Word's pretty general all around this territory that McCord is out to get you, and I just sorta thought I'd get *my* bid in. Honest shootin' work is scarce these days, Johnny.' He paused. 'Want to make a counter-offer on McCord's gizzard, son?'

He could feel Hale staring hard at him. 'I'll counter-offer you right into the hoosegow in a minute,' the Sheriff said slowly. 'I don't need any hired gunnies to do my work for me. I'll get McCord before he gets me – but I'll do it legal.'

'Got grounds, Johnny?'

'None of your business,' Hale snapped. He paused. 'Well, maybe it is, if you're with McCord.' His hands slapped the leather of his holsters. 'Mister, I'm so close to pinnin' cattle-stealin' on McCord that you'd better make your play right now, if you're going to make it at all. Couple more days, and you'll have to take your pay out of McCord's pocket while he's hangin' from the end of a rope.'

The blind man grinned. 'Easy, son, easy – don't get your temper up. Right now everything's still in what you might call the negotiation stage.' He got to his feet, his hands away from his sides. 'I'm sure glad you're close to the proof, Johnny. Your ideas on the subject are no secret around town, you know, and it would be kind of embarrassin' if you were accusin' the wrong guy.'

Hale swore. 'McCord's behind all the cattle-rustlin' in the last couple of months, all right; I'm not the kind of hombre who talks without reason.'

The blind man smiled again, and walked to the door. 'That's what I kinda figgered,' he said. Then he turned.

'Guess you've noticed by now that I'm a sort a nosy bird,' he said. 'One more question, son: you happen to have your own ranch?'

Hale stared at him. 'Huh? Me? No, course not – sheriffin's my full-time job. It's all I can do hangin' around town keepin' things orderly.'

'That's what I figgered, too,' the blind man said. His blank eyes stared at the Sheriff for a moment. 'Well, so long, son – maybe I'll be seeing you again soon . . .'

He thought it would come the moment he passed the schoolhouse, which was still lighted, but the pressure against his eyes lessened and he knew the light had gone out just as he reached it. Then he stopped. The light footsteps he had heard leaving the schoolhouse were running toward him, and when he heard a girl's voice say, 'Bill! Bill Reynolds!' – the same voice, grown-up now, but with the familiar quality of sweetness – he knew it was Lorna Stone.

He turned and said, 'Been a long time, hasn't it?'

She was in his arms and her lips touched his before she answered. 'Almost eight years,' she said. 'Eight years – but you came right away.'

'Us blind fellers ain't kept too busy, Lorna,' he said softly. 'Anyway, I wanted to know if you grew up the way I figgered . . .'

He heard the swift intake of her breath. 'Your – your eyes, Bill. How can you . . .?'

'Lots of ways, Lorna,' he said. 'That perfume, for instance – not the strong, smelly stuff some gals wear – but soft and gentle and just right. And the fact that you're at the schoolhouse – takes courage to take a job as unpopular as book-learnin' out here.' He reached out and touched her hair. 'And your hair's long and soft, and probably just as red as when – I used to be able to see it. You're a beautiful girl, Lorna.'

Her voice was strained when she answered. 'Johnny – Johnny Hale, the boy I'm going to marry – he says I am.'

The blind man's face lost its smile. 'I've just been talkin' to him, Lorna – and I'm afraid your letter was right. That boy *is* usin' his mouth too much . . .'

'Then you think '

'That McCord *isn't* behind the rustling?' he finished for her. 'No Lorna, I think Hale's right about that. But he's still talkin' too much.' He paused. 'Lorna, there's something I've got to tell you . . .'

There was a sudden sharp crackling sound in the brush down the road. He said rapidly, 'I'll have to save it. Lorna, honey, get into that schoolhouse and stay there until I come for you, Quick!'

She started to protest. 'Bill –' she said.

'Inside. You wrote that I was the only friend you could turn to. Inside, before you don't have any at all.'

When she entered the schoolhouse, he started to walk forward. Might as well get under way, and over.

The shot came just when he knew it would – the moment he stepped away from the darkened schoolhouse into the area which pressure on his eyes told him was lighted. For a moment he felt wild, muscle-stiffening fear, the way he had felt as a kid when owlhoots killed his mother and dad and fired the bullet which left him alive but blind, and then it passed away. He fell on to his stomach, and his gun leaped forward in his hand.

He fired twice rapidly in the direction of the sound, and heard footsteps running. Then another shot snapped back at him, close, and he knew the other had found cover and was trying to finish his work. He grinned crookedly and laped back into the darkness.

We're on even ground now, he thought – *maybe not so even, at that. Any fool ought to know better than to tangle with a blind man in the dark, but he won't.*

He waited until another shot came, hitting not so close. Then calmly, methodically, the way a man does a thing he has done often before, he fired again – and heard the familiar coughing, gasping shout. The sound of a dying man, choking off into silence.

Casually, the blind men reached out and felt along the ground until he found a fist-sized rock. He flipped it into the air and listened to it land in the soft earth a few feet away.

A bullet whanged metallically against the rock.

So it wasn't over. He fired carefully at the sound, and heard another body drop.

There was a long silence, and he realized that the men across the road were beginning to understand that a gun battle in pitch darkness with a blind man was suicidal. They were firing by guess-work; he was right at home. The blind man heard soft, rapid whispers – three voices – and they began to run toward him. They came from different directions.

He caught one of them with a bullet in the stomach, and then the other two were upon him. He brought his knife into play.

It was the colour of silver and had a long razor-sharp blade, and it came from the blind man's sleeve and moved upward with a tearing movement into the body of the nearest man. The man started to curse and then bubbles of blood cut off his voice, and he made a sound deep in his stomach and rolled over on one side.

The other man twisted out of the way of the knife, and his back fell against the blind man's right hand. The blind man stiffened the hand and pulled it upwards. He rabbit-punched twice, and the man slumped to the ground without a sound.

Calmly, the blind man got to his feet and shot him three times through the chest.

He took a deep breath. 'I never do fight fair with killers,' he said, and bent down beside the man he'd shot. The man was still alive; thick gasps gurgled through his lips.

'McCord?' the blind man asked.

The dying man didn't answer for a minute. Then his voice, McCord's voice, said, spitting the words out: 'Go to hell.'

'Not me,' the grey-eyed man said. 'That's where you're going, McCord, any minute now.' He paused. 'Why'd you jump me tonight?'

The thick gasps continued; no answer.

'McCord,' the blind man said again. 'You're checking out soon. Why don't you tell me?' And then he stopped: McCord wouldn't be answering anyone again.

The blind man sighed and reloaded his gun and cleaned his knife and put them away. Nobody had come at the sound of gunfire. This was on the edge of town, and it wasn't surprising about anybody else – but Johnny Hale should have shown better sense.

Some hombres aren't as smart as a weak-minded cayuse, the blind man thought sadly, and he opened the schoolhouse door and called Lorna. 'I was going to tell you about this,' he said, 'but maybe I'd better show you.'

Johnny Hale was at the little cook-stove in the room adjoining his office when Lorna and the grey-eyed blind man entered, and he whirled and let the pan clatter to the floor.

'Don't you ever investigate shooting, Johnny?' the blind man asked.

'Shooting?' the Sheriff said, 'I – didn't hear any shooting.'

'Son,' the blind man said, 'your ears would have to be as useless as my eyes to keep you from hearing the shooting that just went on.'

'Your eyes?' Hale said. 'What's wrong with . . .'

'Now let's not act damn silly, son,' the grey-eyed man said, gently. 'It doesn't take much to spot a blind man. I was kind of curious when you didn't say anything when I felt around for a chair, but that, I know now, was because one of McCord's boys beat me to your place and told you about me.' He sighed. 'You know, it sure would have been more convincing for you to have come running out just before – but I guess you were too sure things would go right to bother.'

He heard Hale slump heavily in a chair. 'I won't even try to figger out what you're talkin' about.'

'Ain't hard to figger, Johnny,' the blind man said. 'Puttin' it in black and white, there's just two things I don't like: outlaws, and people who try to kill me or get me killed.' He rolled a smoke with his left hand and kept his right close to his holster. 'It just looks to me like you fit in both those classes.'

Hale's answer came in a harsh, bitter voice. 'I kind of figured you were a mite loco when you first came in here. Now I'm beginning to think it's a lot more than a mite.'

The blind man shook his head sadly. 'Aw, now, Johnny,' he said, 'You shouldn't go calling people names when you know it isn't so. Listen, son, and tell me if I'm shootin' close to the target.

'I first began to figure somethin' was funny when Lorna wrote and told me she was scared of trouble bacause you'd been tellin' everybody around town that McCord was behind the rustlin', and McCord was tellin' everyone around town he was going to get you. Hell, Johnny, that wasn't as smart a scheme as you thought.'

'You're still talkin' loco,' Hale said.

'It'll make sense soon. Your scheme wasn't so smart because, in a wide-open town like this one, a feller like McCord doesn't go around threatenin' things for months without doin' something about it – and a sheriff doesn't accuse a man of rustlin' unless he's got plenty of proof.

' 'Course, you and I know why you started that talk. You figgered if everybody thought you and McCord was enemies, nobody'd ever connect you together on the cattle-stealin'. Later on, I guess, when there wasn't too much left to rustle, you planned to say you found you were wrong, and apologize.' He spat. 'Sure must've been awkward when a professional gun like I said I was come up to McCord and offered to do a job on you . . .'

'Lorna,' Hale cut in, his voice suddenly thin and high. 'You brought this crazy man here. Tell him he's wrong; tell him he'll get in trouble spreading stuff like this . . .'

The blind man felt Lorna's fingers pressing more tightly on his arm. 'No, Johnny,' she said, slowly, 'I'm afraid I can't. I think he's right. I think now that I've known it from the start . . .'

'All right,' Hale said. His words were coming faster now, feverishly, hysteria in them. 'If you want to stick with your blind boy-friend there, go ahead – but I tell you he's crazy. Everything he's said is guesswork . . .'

And then the blind man stepped closer. 'It's not guesswork, Johnny,' he said. 'If you want to fool a man who can't see and has to rely on other senses, you better take baths more often. You told me before that you stay round town and haven't a ranch of your own – but the stink of cattle is all over you.

'Where did you get it if you haven't been rustling with McCord?' . . .

Young Hale was fast, the blind man knew that the moment he heard the slap of hand against leather. He pulled his own gun and, fanning his shots, jerked the trigger three times. He heard his bullets thud into flesh before Hale's first came, awry and heading for the side wall, and he knew Hale would be dead before he hit the floor.

He turned to the red-headed girl. Her body was warm and trembling against him.

'I'm sorry, Lorna,' he said. 'It would have happened to him sooner or later, anyway.'

He put his arm gently around her waist. 'I'll take you home,' he said. 'You'll feel better later on . . .'

'No,' she said. 'Not home. There's nothing for me here. I'm going back with you.'

They walked out into the clear night air, farther and farther away from the echoes of the sound of gunfire – and he wanted to tell her that he could not let her come, that he could not let her saddle herself with a blind man. But then she kissed him and he forgot all about it, and somehow the subject never came up after that.

J. V. Olsen

The Man We Called Jones

THE gun? The .45 hanging over the mantel? Why, sure; look at it. Look at it, but don't handle the belt, son. It's old, over sixty years old. Leather's brittle, hasn't been worked. Like to fall apart.

Why do I keep it there? I can tell you a story about it if you want. Really a story about the man who owned it. The bravest and best man I ever knew . . .

It was way back, the summer of 1890. This same valley. I was seventeen that year. You weren't yet a twinkle in your pappy's eye, so it'll take a sight of doing for you to see it as it was then. You made your way by team, by horseback, or walked. Roads were mud, mud, mud.

The valley was all big ranches, or rather most one big ranch. That'd be Kurt Gavin's Anchor. Gavin came into the country early after the last tide of gold-seekers was drifting out, drove his stakes deep and far, and being a little bigger and a little tougher than most others, he made it stick.

By '90 with the Cheyennes long pacified and the territory opened to homesteading, Gavin was the biggest man in the valley, nigh the biggest in the territory. Even his swelling herds couldn't graze the whole of the open range he laid claim to. Least, that's what the homestead farmers figured. Or sodbusters, as the cattlemen called 'em – the *damned* sod-busters who came in with their ploughs and chewed up the good graze.

Which is what we did in Gavin's eyes to the range he called his, because Uncle Jace and me were among the first. We'd had strong ties back in Ohio, but my ma had been dead a good many years. Typhoid-pneumonia had taken Pa in '89. Uncle Jace and Pa had been mighty close brothers. They'd run the farm together for years, and the old home held too many memories for Uncle Jace. He hadn't any family or close kin left, 'cept for me, and nothing to hold him from pulling stakes for the West, which he'd always wanted.

A year after Pa's death saw me and Uncle Jace running a shoestring outfit on Gavin's east range. Gavin give word to his riders to hooraw us off, and I tell you the high-spirited lads made our lives some miser-able what with cutting our barbed wire and riding shortcuts through our fields, or riding past the house of a midnight after a drunk in town, screeching, shooting at the sky.

You could call Uncle Jace a peaceable man, but he was that stubborn he wouldn't budge off what was his by law. And when Gavin's crew pulled down a whole section of fence by roping the posts and dragging it away with the ponies, Unc's temper busted. Him and me were out scouting boundary that morning when we found the fence down and some Anchor cows foraging in the young corn. They'd even left one rope on the fence to make their sign plain.

Unc was mad clean through, though not so's you could see it – 'less you knew Unc. Me helping, he hazed the cows out cool as you please, and we got tools and repaired the fence, Uncle Jace giving brief, jerky orders in as few words as needed.

Afterward, grimy and soaked with sweat, he turned to me. 'Get on your horse, Howie. I'm going to see Gavin.'

We cut across the Anchor land on a beeline for the ranch headquarters, Uncle Jace riding ahead. He was a huge-framed man, though so leaned-down with hard work, the clothes hung on him like tattered cast-offs on a scarecrow. Even so, with the big back of him erect and high in his wrath, I could almost hear his rage crackle across the space between us.

Unc didn't pack a sidearm. He had his old Union issue Spencer .54 in the saddle boot under his leg, and I'd seen him drive nailheads with it, and I was some squirrelly, I tell you.

It must have been ten minutes later when we sighted the little knot of horsemen off to our left, and Unc quartered his bronc around so we were heading for them. I caught his thought then – that these were the jiggers who pulled the fence down and ran that Anchor beef through the break.

Coming near up, we saw all five of them were mounted but not moving, and then we saw why. They were grouped under one of the big old iron-woods you don't see anymore, and there was a rope tied to a spreading bough. The end of the rope was noosed around the neck of one of them, a little fella with his hands tied at his back. They were all of them motionless, waiting on our approach.

The little one I'd never seen, but the other four all were all Anchor crewmen I recognized – one of them Gavin's tough ramrod, Tod Carradine. He was a tall, pale-eyed Texan with ice in his smile, cocky, sure of himself. The others were ordinary punchers with the look of men ready for a dirty job they didn't relish, but held to be necessary.

'Howdy, Tod,' Uncle Jace said in a voice easy-neutral without being friendly. 'Hemp cravat for the man?'

'Why yes, Devereux,' said Carradine in a voice amused, also without being friendly. 'You ever see this little man before?'

Unc shook his head without taking his eyes off Carradine. He wasn't worried about the others.

Carradine pointed lazily at the hip of the horse the little fella sat. It bore an Anchor brand. 'We found him hypering off our range on this bronc.' Carradine smiled, altogether pleasant. 'Suit you, Devereux?' he then asked in a voice suggesting he didn't give a damn how Unc was suited.

It was open and shut, far as I could see. A stranger had been caught riding off Anchor range on an Anchor horse. The answer for that was one no Westerner would argue. That's why I was surprised when Uncle Jace's glance shuttled to the little fella.

'Friend,' Unc said quietly, 'speak out your say. It's your right. How'd it happen?'

The little man looked up slowly. His head had been bent and I hadn't seen his face full till now. It was shocking, pitiful, ravaged somehow in a way I couldn't explain. He gave a bare tilt of his head toward Carradine, murmured, 'However he says,' and looked down again.

Carradine smiled fully at Unc. He repeated: 'Suit you, Devereux?'

'Not quite,' Uncle Jace frowned, looking back at the Anchor foreman.

Carradine was still smiling, uncertainly. It had only come to him then what this was building to. He was the only Anchor man packing a gun, and I saw the instant impulse chase through his mind.

Uncle Jace didn't waste time. He never wasted time, or words either. Somehow the old Spencer cavalry carbine was ready to his hand, and he laid it light across the pommel. 'Don't even think about it, Tod,' Unc advised mildly. 'Howie, cut the gent loose. Give him a hand down. Tod, take what's yours and keep your dogs off my fence-line. Or I'll larrup you out of this valley at the end of a horsewhip.'

Carradine's hands hung loosely, his eyes hot and wild – wicked. He said, 'I'll mind this, Devereux!'

'Do that. I'd kind of deplore having to remind you,' Unc said mildly.

We silently watched the four Anchor men out of sight. I found my voice. 'Unc, we going to see Gavin?'

'We won't have to. He'll hear about this.'

Uncle Jace got off his horse, only now taking a close look at the raggedy drifter, and his eyes went quick with a pitying kindness as his hand went out. 'I'm Jace Devereux. My nephew, Howie. We homestead over east.'

The little horse-thief looked at Unc in a grave, considering way. He said in a bass deep, startling in such an undersize man, 'My name is Jones. I'd admire to work for you. For nothin'.'

Unc looked at the hand in his own, seeing it crossed with rope-scars. 'Well, now, as a cowman, ain't you afraid of some farm stink wearing off on you?'

'I'd admire to work for you,' Jones repeated, adding, 'for nothin'.'

I knew a kind of warm surge for this runty, spooky-looking gent with his sad and faded eyes looking up from the shadow of his Stetson at Unc's great height. And glancing at Uncle Jace, I saw he felt the same.

He said in his rich big voice, 'Come along, and hang up your hat, Jones.'

That was the way of it, and Jones settled into the workaday routine of the farm, as natural a part of it as the buildings themselves, already dry and grey and weatherbeaten. Jones was all of those, too. He was that colourless he might have been anywhere from thirty-five to fifty-five. He fitted to the new work like an old hand, so quiet you'd hardly know he was there but for the new-improving ways the farm began to shape up.

He stayed, and we called him Jones, just Jones. He never gave another name and we never asked. I reckoned Unc had been shamed into hiring him. Shamed by the little fella's offering his services for nothing, though the main reason he'd saved Jones was to retaliate on Anchor and show what he thought of all its power. Jones must have known that. How could life kick a man into such a corner he could be so beggar-grateful? It was as though no one'd done him even a half-intended kindness till now.

I saw him right off as a man a boy could tie to. He worked alongside Uncle Jace, who was twice his size and three times his power, and he let Unc set the pace. He'd be so tired he could barely stand, and never a whimper. Watching him hump alongside Uncle Jace in the fields, he cut a comical earnest figure that made you want to laugh and cry all at once. It might be that I'd laugh, and sometimes, if you laughed too hard, he had a way of looking at you that made you feel you'd need a ladder to reach a snake's belly.

But there was another special way he could look, a way that made you feel two feet taller, like the wry grin of him when I'd lick him in our nightly games in the kitchen. He was mighty proud of his checker game, was Jones. It was the one little vanity he had, yet he was the best loser ever I saw.

We got close, the two of us. Mind, I was just seventeen, a hard time of growing up. You get that age, you'll know what I mean. A lot of things are confusing to a fellow. In the one month he was with us, it was Jones helped me see my way to the end of more than one bad time. He had a way of looking at things, of talking them out so they'd seem a lot clearer. Fact, he was as much pa as I ever knew after my own pa died. He sort of took up that empty place in one boy's life that Uncle

Jace, for all he was as big a man inside him as outside, couldn't quite fill.

Jones would go into the settlement of Ogallala now and then to get supplies, and Gavin's riders hoorawed him every time, and sent him packing out of town. They never hazed him if Unc or I was along, so I never seen it. Heard plenty, though. Neighbours saw to that. Folks would snicker behind their hands watching Jace Devereux's new man go out of his way to walk around trouble. Never carried a gun, either. Not even a rifle on his saddle.

Never spoke of his past, did Jones. But he had one behind the face he showed the world. Remember, he'd come to us a reprieved horse-thief. And strange how Uncle Jace in taking him on hadn't thought, being a middling cautious man, that he might be getting a pig in a poke. But seemed like it hadn't even occurred to Unc.

Uncle Jace was right that Gavin had heard his warning to leave us be. His riders hauled off their war of nerves, at least on Unc and me and our fences and crops, and rode herd on the homesteaders – and, of course, Jones. Gavin had soft-pedaled on us, but we only wondered what he had up his sleeve.

We found out about a month after Jones came to the farm. Gavin himself, sided by Tod Carradine, came riding into the yard one night after supper, as Uncle Jace and Jones and me was sitting on the front steps, breaking in some new cob pipes.

Gavin's hardness was a legend in the territory, and it was easy to see that age hadn't softened him. He was a blocky, well-fed man in the slightly dust-soiled dignity of a black suit, and his habit of authority sat him like a heavy fist. There was even a touch of arrogance to the way he bent the hand holding his cigar.

Uncle Jace got off the step, knocking out his pipe. 'Light down a spell, Gavin. You too, Tod.'

'I'll speak my piece from here,' Gavin said. 'Your tracks are big, Devereux. Big enough so I respect 'em.' He paused, and Unc didn't speak, wondering, like me, where this was leading to.

Gavin said it then: 'I need men like you, Devereux. Sign on with me for double wages. The boy, too.'

Unc said, 'No,' instantly, as I knew he would. We Devereuxs aren't that way we work for other people. And even if Unc was, it wouldn't be he'd work for the likes of Gavin.

The rancher didn't look mad, not even greatly concerned. He'd had his own way for too many years. There was only a faint irritation in his voice. 'You go, Devereux. You go this week – or next week you'll crawl out of this valley on your belly.' He turned his horse in a violent way and rode out of the yard.

Carradine's soft drawling chuckle slid into the quiet like a gliding rattler. 'I always suspicioned you was a Sunday man, Devereux. Now we'll see.'

'A Sunday man?'

'A man who's a man one day – when he talks big. I don't think you'll back up what you said when you saved that horse-stealer.' Carradine smiled with full insolence. 'I don't think you can.'

'You tell me that with Anchor behind you,' Uncle Jace said, the snap of an icicle in his voice, 'which by my lights makes you a yellow dog, Tod.'

Carradine smiled, ever so gentle. 'I'll be in town tomorrow afternoon – in front of Red Mike's. You be there, and we'll see if you're man enough to call me that again. Or send your big bad hired man . . .'

So the issue was in the open now.

When the sound of Carradine riding off had died on the still evening air, I turned to Unc. 'He's a mean one, Uncle Jace. With a gun. There's stories followed him from Texas.'

'And I offer there's something to 'em,' Jones said softly, his voice startling us. He could kind of fade back so you forgot he was there. 'It's why he needled you. I reckon you'd better not take him up, Jace.'

'And I reckon I had,' Unc said grimly.

Jones only nodded. 'I figured so,' he said, and walked around back. I wanted to say more to Uncle Jace, but a look in his face warned me, and in a minute I followed Jones around back where he was working with the axe on some stovewood. He had his shirt off against the heat, and the scrawny, knobbly upper body of him gleaming with sweat made him look like a plucked chicken.

Jones paused, leaned on the axe and mopped his face with his shirt. 'Why has Gavin got his sights primed for your unc, Howie? There's other farmers squattin' on his land, and more comin'.'

'Squatting' was the word a *cattleman* would use for a legal government homestead. It was Jones saying it, though, so I let it ride. You didn't get mad at Jones.

'The others got no heart to 'em,' I said with contempt. 'Unc's got more gall than a government mule, and the homesteaders know it as well as Gavin. If he can stampede Unc, the others'll follow suit.'

'Hum,' said Jones, and went back to his work. I got the other axe and helped. But a couple times I caught him leaning on his axe and looking off toward the hills with that air like a considerable thought was riling him.

I didn't sleep much that night, thinking about the next day, with Carradine waiting in front of Red Mike's bar and Unc dead set on meeting him. Uncle Jace was no gunman. He knew it, I knew it. Even Jones knew it.

So I was near relieved when about noon of the next day Jones came into the kitchen where I was fixing some grub and quietly told me that Uncle Jace's leg had got broken. They'd been heisting the massive ridgepole timber of the barn Unc had finally got to building, raising it into place, and it fell . . .

Between the two of us we splinted up Unc's leg and got him into bed. His face was white and drawn, and his eyes near starting from his head with the pain.

Jones said in his gentle voice, 'I reckon this is in the way of a lifesaver for you, Jace.'

'But won't they say Unc ran away from it?' I asked.

'They'll say more,' Uncle Jace said bitterly between set teeth. 'They'll say I got stove up a-purpose to get out of meeting Tod. And it'll be a spell before I can call any of 'em a liar and back it. By that time the farmers will be out, and Gavin'll swallow up their homesteads.'

Jones and I looked at each other. Unc was right; he was the backbone of the homesteaders. With him broken, they'd cut and run.

'That leg'll need a sawbones,' Jones said, unruffled. 'I'm going into town, and I'll send one.'

There was a note in Jones's voice that left me curious, and after a while, when Uncle Jace was resting more easy, I followed Jones out to the harness shed where he'd rigged his bunk. I came to stand in the doorway as I saw him, and I almost fell over. Jones didn't see me. He was facing a shard of mirror he had nailed on the wall over an old packing crate which held his possibles – and there was a gun in his hand.

For thirty seconds I stood and watched as he drew and fixed a mock bead on his own reflection, the hammer falling on an empty chamber each time. I tell you, he made that fine-balanced gun do tricks.

The truth all rushed down on me at once, I'd had it figured how Jones's hell-born past was that of any rabbity little gent who couldn't hold up his head in a world of big men. But the man who could make a cutter do his will like this one – why, he was head and shoulders over the biggest man.

It was the gun – that was the hell in Jones's life. That's why he'd never packed it, why he walked soft and gave Gavin's loudmouths a wide berth. It wasn't them he was afraid of, it was himself. His own skill, his deadly skill. That was the real truth and tragedy of his backtrail. While the rest of us, rancher and homesteader, talked war and primed ourselves for it, Jones was already fighting his own private battle, a harder one than any of us would ever know.

Now he'd lost his war. Lost it in the way a real man would – by facing out the enemy of the only one who ever befriended him . . .

He'd loaded the gun while my thoughts raced. Like magic, that gun it was in the fine-tooled holster, and then he swung toward the door and saw me.

For a full five seconds he didn't speak. 'I'm going to see Carradine, Howie. You won't try to stop me.' There was the thinnest undercore of steel to his voice, and I wouldn't have tried even if I'd been of a mind to.

But I was going with him, and I said so. He didn't comment, and it was that way the whole ride. Neither of us spoke a word till we'd nearly reached Ogallala.

'Jones,' I said. He grunted. 'Jones, I wouldn't be surprised you let that beam slip on purpose to keep Uncle Jace from going out.'

'You talk too much,' he said mildly, and that was all. I didn't care, I was that sure he'd saved Unc's life.

Ogallala was drowsing in the westering sun. One horse stood hipshot at the tie rail in front of Red Mike's: Carradine's blazeface sorrel.

Jones hauled up across the street, stepping down and throwing his reins. His gaze fixed Red Mike's as he said to me, 'You get in the store and stay there.' I didn't, but I got back on the walk out of the way, and he didn't even look at me.

'Carradine!' That was Jones's silence-shattering voice. A big voice for a little man. Maybe as big as the real Jones.

After a little, the batwing doors parted and Tod Carradine stood tall in the shadow of the weather-beaten false-front. Stepping off the walk, bareheaded, the sun caught on his face, showing it red with heat and whisky. He'd been drinking, but he wasn't drunk.

When he saw who it was hailed him, he looked ready to laugh. Almost. He peered sharp at Jones, and something seemed to shut it off in his throat before it started.

'Carradine,' Jones said. 'Carradine, you brag something fierce. Back it.'

Carradine began to smile, understanding, his teeth showing very white. He cut a mighty handsome figure in the sun. 'All right, bravo,' he said. 'All right, bravo.'

But I watched Jones. And I watched it happen.

Carradine was fast. Mighty fast. But Jones was the man. The last of a dying breed. Not one of your patent-leather movie cowboys with their gun-fanning foolery and their two fast-blazing sixguns. The man Jones knew you couldn't hit a barn fanning. He got his gun out right fast, but then took his time as you had to when it was a heavy single-action Colt you were handling. Carradine got two fast shots off before Jones's one bullet buckled him in the middle and smashed him into the walk on his back . . .

He didn't touch Jones; the other fellow did. The one in the alley between the store and the feed-barn, at our back – stationed there in case this happened. I heard this dirty son's gun from the alley and I saw Jones's scrawny body flung forward off balance. Before the shot sound died, I saw Jones haul around, his gun blasting, and this bushwhacker, hard-hit, fling out away from the alley with his gun going off in the hot blue face of the sky. He went down and moved no more.

Jones was sinking to his knees, the light going from his eyes and a funny little smile on his face. It was the first and the last time I saw him smile with all a smile should mean.

When I reached him and caught him as he slipped down, he looked up, recognizing me, and said, 'Tell your unc – you tell him to keep that peg dusted, Howie. My hat won't be on it . . .' The smile was gone as he lifted his head to stare at me with a fierce intensity. 'Howie, mind what I say. If you forget everything else about me, never forget what I learned – the hard way. You can't run from what you made of yourself. You can't run that far . . .'

The voice trailed, and the eyes looked on, not at me . . . or at anything.

I eased down the meager body of the man we called Jones, and wanted to cover his face from the prying, question-rattling crowd. I remember I had to do that, and there was only my ragged pocket bandana. When I'd finished and looked up, there was someone standing over me I didn't at first recognize for the wet blurring in my eyes. But then I blinked and saw it was Gavin.

He was holding his cigar in his arrogant way, frowning around at his two dead hirelings and at Jones, and not believing it. I went up and after him with my fists doubled. Then a big man with a close-clipped Vandyke threw a beefy arm across my chest.

'Hold it, son. I have a word for Mr Gavin.'

Gavin fixed his cold stare on the newcomer. 'Who the hell are you?'

'Baines, special agent for the U.S. Land Office. Washington has been getting notices about your terrorizing government homesteaders. And I've seen enough to validate it. You and I'll discuss that shortly.' The big man turned back to me and nodded down to Jones. 'He a friend of yours, son?'

I managed to find words. 'Jones was the best.'

'Jones?' Baines eyed me closely. 'I reckon you didn't know him very well. Suggest you write to the sheriff at Cheyenne. He'll give you particulars. So can a lot of others.'

That's about all. Within weeks, a new flood of homesteaders filled the valley. I saw Gavin a few times after, a broken old man. I don't know what Baines told him, but the hand of the government can be right heavy.

About Jones?

Yes, I could've written to Cheyenne and found out. But I didn't. I never wanted to find out.

All I can tell you is what he was to me – friend of the Devereuxs, the bravest and best man I ever knew. The man we called Jones.

Jack Schaefer

One Man's Honour

THIS happened out where distance ran past vision and only clumped silver-green of sagebrush and blunt bare rising ridges of rock broke the red-brown reaches of sand and sun-baked silt. No highways or railroads sliced it into measurable stretches. Only a lone rutted trace snaked through, following the lower levels, worn by freighters who crawled at long intervals with their clumsy wagons from the last meager town far southward on the river to the rolling cattle ranges far northward on the more fertile uplands. Yet here and there, off the trace, widely separated and hidden between the ridges where slow short-season streams made narrow areas of green before dying in the sand, the first settlers had come. They would increase and windmills would rise to draw upon the sub-surface water and in time a network of roads would fan out and wheels would grind dust for hot winds to whirl. Now they were few and far, lost in the immensity of distance and red-brown desolation under the limitless depth of sky.

Late afternoon sun slanted over one of the higher ridges and shone on the sparse beginnings of a homestead claim. Clear and hot in the clean air, it shone on a long strip of shallow-ploughed ground that followed the gradual curve of an almost-dry stream bed where a few brackish pools lingered and on a sagging pole corral where an old milk cow and two stocky ungainly draught horses drooped in motionless rest and beside this on the shelter, half dugout cut into the rise of a small ground swell, half timbered with scrub logs from the stunted cottonwoods that straggled along the other side of the stream bed. Trimmed branches corded together and plastered over with clay formed the roof and a rusting stovepipe rose from it. On the split-log doorstep sat a little girl. Her short scratched sunburned legs barely reached the ground. Her light brown hair, sun-bleached in lighter streaks, curled softly down to frame a round snub-nosed face whose dark eyes, unmasked by the light lashes, were wide and bright. A twenty-foot length of rope was tied around her waist and fastened to a staple driven into the doorjamb. She was small and serious and very quiet and she smoothed the skirt of her small flour-sacking dress down over her bare knees and poked, earnest and intent, one small moccasined foot at an ant scurrying in the dooryard dust.

Behind her, in the dim recess of the one-windowed shelter, a tall flat-bodied man stooped over a rumpled bed against the rear wall and laid a moistened cloth across the forehead of a woman lying there. His voice was low and harsh with irritation but the touch of his hand was gentle. 'What's got into ye?' he said.

The woman stared up at him, apology plain on her thin flushed face. 'I don't know,' she whispered. 'It just came on me sudden-like.' Her thin body under the patched gingham of dress shook with slight tremors as with a chill yet drops of sweat streaked her cheeks. Her voice came faint and wavering. 'You'll have to do the food. There's soup in the kettle.'

The man brushed one hand impatiently at the flies hovering over the bed. 'Ye'll be better in the morning,' he said. Abruptly he turned and went to the stove set against the right wall. The woman watched him. She tried to speak and could not. She lay still a moment and summoned strength to rise on her elbows and send her voice across the room to him. 'Wait,' she said. 'Wait. You'll have to do the game with her. It's her fun. It helps her learn.'

The man swung his head to look at the doorway. The little girl sat still, her back to him, her head bent forward as she peered at something by her feet. The last sun slanting over the ridge filtered through the tangled curls along her neck. Slowly the lines of worry and irritation faded from the man's face and the tightness around his mouth eased. He went to the doorway and leaned low to untie the rope around her waist. She stood up, small and soft beside his hard height, and stretched back her head to look up at him. She raised one small hand and reached to put it in one of his big calloused hands. Together they went along the front of the shelter towards the corral.

Near the corner the man stopped. He slapped his free hand on the side of the shelter. 'This,' he said.

Gravely the little girl regarded the shelter. A triumphant smile crinkled her small face. 'Hello, house,' she said.

'Right,' the man said. They moved on and stopped by an old wagon pulled in close alongside the shelter. The man reached under and pulled out an empty milk pail and held it up. Gravely the little girl regarded it. Her small eyebrows drew down in a frown. She looked up at the man in doubt and back at the object in his hand. 'Hello,' she said slowly, 'hello, buck-et.'

'That's it!' The man grinned down at her and reached to put the pail back under the wagon. They moved on to the sagging poles of the corral. The man pointed over the poles at the cow and the little girl peered through them beside him. She spoke at once, quick and proud. 'Hello, cow.'

'What's the cow's name?'

'Bess-ie.'

'Mighty smart ye're getting to be,' the man said. He pointed over the poles at the draft horses standing together in a corner.

The little girl tossed her head. 'Hello, horse.'

'No,' the man said. 'There's two of them. More than one. Horses.'

The little girl looked up at him, small and earnest and intent. She looked back through the poles across the corral. 'Hello, hor-ses.'

Forty-three miles to the south and five miles west of the meager town on the river, where the ground dipped in a hollow some ten feet below the level expanse around, a saddled horse stood alone, ground-reined, patiently waiting. A wide-brimmed weather-worn hat hung on the saddle horn. Several hundred yards away the river road followed the bank, a dust track running west into fading distance and east towards the low hills hiding the town. Close by the roadside two small rocks jutted out of the ground, butted against each other. Together they were little more than three feet wide, irregular in shape, no more than eighteen inches high at the highest point. The late afternoon sun slanted down on them and they made a small lengthening patch of shade. Beside them, stretched out, head and shoulders into the shade, a man lay flat, belly down, pressed against the ground. Beside him lay a rifle. Its barrel had been rubbed with dirt to remove all shine. He was a short man, short and thick, with a head that seemed small, out of proportion to the thick body, set too close into the hunched shoulders. His hair was a dirty black, close-cropped with the rough scissor slashes of his own cutting plainly marked, and it merged with no visible break into the dark unshaven stubble down his cheeks and around his narrow tight-lipped mouth.

He raised his head higher to sight along the road to the west through the cleft where the tops of the two rocks joined. Pushing with his toes in beaten scarred old knee-length boots, he hitched his body a few inches to the left so that it lay almost exactly parallel to the road, invisible to anyone approaching in the distance from the west. As he moved, the hammer of the revolver in a holster at his side made a tiny groove in the ground and he reached to test the firmness of its seat in the holster and free it of any clinging dirt. His voice was a low murmur lost in the vast empty reaches of space, the flat inflectionless voice of a man accustomed to being along and to talking to himself. 'Last place they'd be expecting trouble,' he said.

He lay flat, his head relaxed on its side with one ear against the ground, and the sun dropped slowly down the sky and the patch of shade of the rocks spread down his back and reached the brass-studded cartridge belt around his waist and far out along the road to the west a tiny puff of dust appeared and crept closer, barely seeming to move only to grow imperceptibly larger in the angled foreshortening of distance. Faint tremors in the ground came to the man's ear. He raised his head and sighted through the rock cleft. He rolled on his side and pulled the tattered old bandanna tied loosely around his neck up over his face, up to the bridge of his nose so that only his eyes and forehead showed over it. He rolled back into position and took the rifle and eased the barrel forward through the cleft. Propped on his elbows with the curved butt of the rifle against his right shoulder and his right cheek under the bandanna against the stock, he watched the puff of dust far out along the road.

It was no longer just a puff of dust. Emerging from it yet never escaping and always emerging as the dust rose under the hoofs was a light fast freight wagon drawn by two stout horses at a steady trot. Two men sat on the board-backed seat, the driver and another man with a shotgun between his knees, the butt on the floorboard, the barrel pointing at the sky.

The man behind the rocks waited. He waited until the wagon was little more than one hundred feet away and in a few seconds he would begin to be visible over the top of the rocks and his finger tightened on the trigger of the rifle and with the crash of the shot the man with the shotgun jolted hard against the back of the wagon seat and the horses reared, beating upward with their front hoofs and trying to swing away, and the man with the shotgun dropped it clattering on the floorboard and struggled to stand on the swaying platform and toppled sideways into the road dust and lay still.

The man behind the rocks let the rifle stock fall to the ground and leaped up and in the leaping took the revolver from the holster at his side. He moved out and around the rocks and closer to the wagon and watched the driver fighting with the horses to quiet them. He watched the driver pull them to quivering stillness and become aware of him and the gun in his hand and stiffen in a tight silence. 'That's right,' he said. 'Keep your hands on those reins where I can see them.' He moved closer and to the right side of the wagon and with his left hand took the shotgun from the floorboard and tossed it back from the road. He moved out and around the horses to the left side of the wagon and took the driver's revolver from its holster and threw it towards the river. He stepped back, away from the wagon. 'Now,' he said. 'Take it slow. Wrap the reins around that brake. Put your hands up behind your head.' The driver hesitated. His lips were pale, pressed tight together, and a slow flush crept up his cheeks. He reached slowly and looped the reins over the brake handle and raised his hands and clasped them together at the back of his head.

The man with the gun stepped up by the body of the wagon. He was careful to stand facing part way forward so that the driver was always within his angle of vision. With his left hand he unfastened the rope lashed over the wagon and pulled away the light canvas dust cover. Four square boxes and several small crates and a half-dozen sacks of potatoes were exposed to view. He chuckled, a strange harsh sound in the wide silence. 'Mighty little load to be packing a guard,' he said. He swung his head for a quick check of the load and back to look straight at the driver. His voice was suddenly sharp and biting. 'Where is it? I know you're carrying it.' The driver had pivoted his body at the hips to watch him and stared at him and said nothing.

The man with the gun grunted and reached with his left hand to yank aside one of the sacks of potatoes. He reached again and heaved to move aside the one that had been beneath the first. He plunged the hand into the hole opened to the bed of the wagon and felt around and pulled out a small metal box. He stepped back and again his strange harsh chuckle sounded in the silence.

The voice of the driver broke through the tight line of his lips. 'You'll never get away with it, Kemp. I'd know that gunbelt anywhere.'

The man with the gun let the metal box fall from his left hand and lifted the hand and pulled the bandanna down from his face. 'Too bad,' he said. He raised his right hand and the gun in it bucked with the shot and the driver rose upright off the seat arching his back in sudden agony and fell sideways over the footboard to strike on the wagon tongue and bounce to the ground between the harness tugs and with the roar of the shot the horses were rearing and they plunged ahead and the wheels crunched over the driver's body as they rolled forward along the road.

The man with the gun took one leap after the wagon and stopped. He raised the gun again and in almost aimless haste fired the four remaining bullets in it at the plunging horses. The horses drove forward, goaded by several flesh wounds, and the reins ripped off the brake handle and the wagon careened after them and swerved to the left and the left front wheel struck against the rocks behind which the man had been hiding. The wagon bounced upward as the wheel cracked and the harness tugs snapped and the horses, freed of the weight, surged in frantic gallop along the road.

The man threw the empty revolver to the ground. He raced to the wagon and around it to the rocks and leaped over them and grabbed the rifle. He dropped to his right knee and braced his left elbow on his left knee to steady his aim and fired and one of the horses staggered and fell and the other, pulled sideways by the falling weight, lashed frantically with its hoofs and the harness parted and the horse galloped ahead alone along the road. Already it was a far shape, dwindling into distance, and the man fired again and again until the magazine of the rifle was emptied and the bullets kicked small spurts of dust and the horse galloped on unhit into the low hills. The man threw down the rifle and stood erect. He was shaking with a tense fury. He stood still, forcing himself to quiet, driving the shaking out of his body. He drew a long breath. 'That'll tell 'em too damn soon,' he said. Quickly he took up the rifle and opened the breech and blew through the barrel and loaded the magazine with bullets from the pocket of his faded old shirt. He hurried back where he had dropped the metal box. The two bodies lay near in the road dust and already the flies were gathering and he paid no attention to them. He picked up the revolver and loaded it with bullets from the brass-studded belt around his waist. He reached down and blasted the lock of the metal box with a single shot and ripped the top open and took out two small plump leather bags and a sheaf of bills and jammed these into the pockets of his old patched pants. At a steady run he moved away from the road, across the level expanse, to the hollow several hundred yards away and the waiting horse. With swift sure gestures he slapped the hat on his head and pushed the rifle into its saddle scabbard and transferred the two small bags and the bills to the saddlebag. He swung up and yanked the horse around, lifting it into a fast lope, and headed north through the red-brown reaches of distance.

Early morning sun slanted in from the east on the homestead shelter. It made a narrow triangular patch of brightness on the packed dirt floor through the open doorway and pushed a soft glow farther into the room. On the edge of a low short trundle cot against the back wall by the foot of the big bed the little girl sat, her body bent forward, her small face puckered in a frown as she concentrated on the problem of putting the right little moccasin on the right foot. On the bed itself the woman lay thin and motionless. Her eyes were closed. At intervals the eyelids twitched and flickered and were still. Her mouth was partly open and her breath drew through it in long slow straining gasps. On the floor beside the bed, stretched on an old quilt folded over, the man lay asleep, fully dressed except for his short thick boots.

The little girl finished with the moccasins. She slid to the floor and turned and tried to smooth the old blanket on her cot. She took hold of the cot and tugged at it to pull it a few inches out from the wall. She went to the end of it away from the bed and turned her small back to it and against it and pushed with her feet to move it along the floor and slide it under the bed.

The scratching sound of the cot runners scraping on the hard dirt floor roused the man. He bent his body at the waist to sit up and wavered and fell back. He pushed against the floor with both hands and was up to sitting position. He looked around, his eyes glassy and staring, and saw the boots and his attention focused on them and he reached for them and struggled to get them on. He heaved himself over on one hip and pushed against the floor and stood swaying on his feet. Sweat streamed down his face and his body shook as with a chill. He took a step and staggered and fell towards the wall and clutched at it for support. He moved along it to the head of the bed. Leaning his weight on one hand on the bed, he reached with the other to the woman's shoulder and gently shook her. Her head wobbled limply at the pressure and her eyes remained closed. He straightened against the wall. Slowly he wiped one hand down over his damp face and let it fall to his side.

The little girl stood by the foot of the bed and looked up at him. Slowly his attention focused on her. He stared at her for a long moment and she looked up at him and a small smile of greeting touched her face and was gone. He drew a long slow sobbing breath and by sheer effort of will pushed out from the wall. His feet dragged and he moved in a strange lurching walk. He took the old quilt from the floor and reached under the bed to take the old blanket from the cot and pulled a pile of empty flour sacks down from a shelf. With these in his arms he staggered to the doorway and out and along the front of the shelter to the old wagon beside it. He heaved his load into the body of the wagon and leaned panting on the side to reach in and spread out the sacks and put the blanket and quilt over them. Weakness took him and he swayed against one of the wagon wheels and hung over it while sweat dripped in tiny glistening beads from his chin to the ground below. He pushed out from the wheel and veered to the shelter wall and hitched his way along towards the door. The little girl was in the doorway and she backed away inside and he held to the doorjamb and pulled himself around and in and a short way along the inside wall and reached for the team harness hanging on two wooden pegs and in the reaching suddenly sagged in a limp helplessness and collapsed doubling forward to bump against the wall and slide to the floor. His body stretched out and rolled over and his unseeing eyes stared upward a few seconds and the lids dropped and no motion stirred in him except the long slow heaving of his chest.

The little girl stared at the man lying still and silent and her eyebrows drew together in a frown. She looked at the woman on the bed and back at the man on the floor. She turned away and went to the table under the one window in the right wall and climbed on the chair beside it and then onto the table. Standing on tiptoe and leaning out she reached one hand into an earthenware jar on the shelf by the window and took it out with a cracker clutched in her fingers. She climbed down to the chair and sat on it with her short sunburned legs swinging over the edge. Gravely she regarded the object in her hand. 'Hello, cracker,' she said in a soft hushed voice. Gravely she bit off a corner and began to chew it.

A mile and a half to the southeast the early morning sun sent long shadows streaming out from a man and a horse climbing the rough slope of a twisting boulder-strewn ridge. The man rode with his short thick body hunched forward and the sun glinted on the brass studdings of the cartridge belt around his waist. The horse was sweat-streaked, tired, taking the slope in short spurts as the man kicked it forward.

They topped the ridge and dropped a short way down the near side and stopped. The man swung to the ground. He took off his weather-worn hat and slapped at himself with it to knock some of the dust off his clothes and hung it on the saddle horn. He turned back to the top of the ridge and lay flat on the blunt bare rock to peer over. No motion anywhere disturbed the empty distance. He turned his head to look at the horse standing with braced legs apart, head hanging, grateful for the rest. He settled himself more comfortably on the rock and watched over the ridge top. The shadows of the boulders down the slope shrank slightly as the sun crept upward and far out along his back trail around a swelling shoulder of wind-piled sand a straggling line of seven tiny figures crawled into view. 'Damn funny,' he said in a flat inflectionless voice. 'Can't shake 'em.'

The seven tiny figures crawled closer, increasing in size, seeming to increase in pace as the distance dwindled, and they were seven men on horseback, six in a ragged relatively compact group and one alone in the lead.

The man on the ridge top shaded his eyes against the slant sun and studied the figure in the lead, distinguishable now across the dwindling distance, a lean long-armed figure wearing a buckskin shirt, slim and straight in the saddle on a tall grey horse. He wore no hat and his hair, iron-grey and long, caught the sun clearly in the bobbing rhythm of riding. He rode at a fast trot and at intervals pulled his horse to a brief walk and leaned in the saddle to check the ground beside and ahead.

The man on the ridge top smacked a clenched fist on the rock. 'That's it,' he said. 'Thought he'd left for the mines.' He licked his dry lips and spat out the dust-dirty saliva. 'Can't just keep running,' he said. 'Not with him after.' He crawled down from the ridge top a few feet and turned squatting on his heels to look down the near slope. Down where it slipped into level expanse of red-brown ground and sparse silver-green of sagebrush, a few-score feet out from the base, a stony dry stream bed followed the twisting formation of the ridge. To the right, swinging in along the level from round a curving twist of the ridge and cutting across the dry stream bed to push in a long arc towards a far break in the next ridge, ran the wagon trace. Plain in the sand dust of the trace, visible from the height, were the day-old unending ribbon ruts of wheel tracks and the hoofprints of many horses heading north.

The man's eyes brightened. He leaped down the slope to his horse and took the rifle from the saddle scabbard and was back on his belly at the ridge top. The seven figures, suddenly larger, made grotesque in the clear clean brightness of sun by the long shadows streaming sideways from them, were little more than half a mile away. Deliberately, in slow succession, careless of exact aim at the range, he fired once at the figure in the lead and twice at the group behind and a strange harsh chuckle came from him as he saw them scatter and swing their horses and gallop back and cluster again in a jumble around the lean man on the grey horse. 'That'll do it,' he said. 'They'll take time working up this hill.' He pulled back from the ridge top and ran to the horse and jammed the rifle into the scabbard and slammed the hat on his head and swung into the saddle. At a hard run he drove the horse angling down the slope, across the first few-score feet of level stretch, across the dry stream bed and angling on across the level to the wagon trace.

He rode along the trace thirty feet, forty, and eased the horse to a slow stop. Holding it steady, headed north, he backed it along the trace, back to where he had angled in and past, back to the crossing of the dry stream bed. Gripping the reins short and pulling up hard on the horse's head so that it rose on its hind legs, front hoofs pawing the air, he yanked its head savagely to the left and slammed the heels of his heavy old boots into its flanks and it leaped, twisting sideways, and was off the trace on the dry stones on the stream bed and he clamped down hard on the reins to hold it from breaking into a surging gallop. Head bent to one side, peering down in steady concentration, he walked the horse along the stream bed, picking his way, holding to the side where the rolled loose stone lay thickest.

He turned his head to look back and up at the ridge top where he had been. Faintly, over the high rock, came the sound of a shot and then another. He looked ahead where the stream bed, following the ridge, curved left with it and disappeared from sight. He urged the horse into a trot and he was around the bend, out of sight of the wagon trace behind. He pulled the horse to the right and out of the stream bed and on the easier sand-silt ground he pushed it into a lope, moving west as the ground rose and swinging northwestward as it dropped again.

The morning sun, higher now, shone clear and hot on the homestead shelter and beat slanting against the high ridge behind and beyond. A quarter of a mile away, up past the long shallow-ploughed strip by the almost dry stream bed, close in by the base of the ridge, a man sat, short and thick and hunched in the saddle, on a tired sweat-streaked horse. He held the wide brim of his weather-worn hat low over his eyes with one hand as he studied the whole scene before him. Not a sound that he could hear disturbed the empty silence. Not a living thing moved anywhere in sight except the two horses and the old cow in the corral twitching in patient endurance at the flies. He dropped the hand from his hat and reached to take the rifle from its scabbard and hold it ready across the saddle in front of him. He urged the horse into a slow walk, along the base of the ridge and swinging to come to the shelter from the rear.

Fifty feet from the low blank rear wall of the shelter he stopped the horse and dismounted. Quietly he slipped the rifle back into the scabbard and took off his hat and hung it on the saddle horn and in the same gesture flowing onward took the revolver from the holster at his side. Quietly he walked to the rear wall of the shelter. He moved along the rear wall to the right corner and leaned to peer around and then to look across the short space at the corral. He saw that the horses were heavy draft animals and he shook his head in disgust and he saw the swelling udders of the cow, and a puzzled frown showed through the dark stubble on his face and the cow, sighting him, pressed against the poles of the corral and lowed with a soft sighing moan. At the sound he leaped back, close against the rear wall, and the empty silence regained and held and he relaxed and moved again, forward and around the corner.

He was moving past the wagon drawn in by the side of the shelter when he stopped and dropped below the wagon level and listened. Faint, from inside the shelter, he heard a slow creaking sound, then again and yet again and continuing in slow steady rhythm. He waited. The sound stopped and in the silence there was another sound, not heard, below hearing, sensed or felt, and the slow creaking began again and continued, deliberate, unhurried. Cautiously he moved, forward, around the front corner, along the blank wall towards the open doorway. Half crouched, gun raised and ready, he swung swiftly around the door-jamb and into the doorway and there, halfway across the room and confronting him, perched on the seat edge of an old rocking chair and swinging her small body to make the chair roll on its rockers, was a little girl. Caught, rigid in a kind of frantic immobility, he stared at her and her eyes widened at the sight of him and her small body stiffened, swaying gently to the dying motion of the chair. Gravely she regarded him. Her lips lifted slightly in a suggestion of a smile. 'Hello, man,' she said.

Slowly he straightened. He turned his head and saw the woman motionless on the bed and the man limp on the floor and heard the other sound, audible now inside the room, the long slow unconscious gaspings for breath. He looked back at the little girl and suddenly he was aware of the gun in his hand and he turned his body sidewise to her and as he turned, his head remained towards her swivelling on his short thick neck and with a quick furtive motion he slid the gun into its holster. He stood still a long moment, his head fixed in its sidelong tipped slant over his shoulder, and looked down at her and gravely she watched him and he seemed unable to look away. Abruptly he jerked his head around straight, swinging his eyes to inspect the room. He went to the shelf by the one window and took a nearly empty flour sack from the floor beneath and laid this on the table. He reached to the shelf and snatched the few cans there and dropped them into the sack.

He stopped, silent and tense, his jaws clenched together, the cords in his neck standing out in strain. He swung around and leaned against the table and jutted his head forward and down at her. His voice struck at her with an angry intensity. 'There'll be people coming! They'll untangle my trail! The;'ll get here sometime!' She stared at him, understanding or not understanding unknown on her face, and he pulled himself around and scooped the bag off the table. He strode to the doorway and out and along the front wall of the shelter and around and back to his horse. He jammed the old hat on his head and fumbled in the saddlebag until he found a short piece of cord and with this tied the flour sack close up to the saddle horn. He mounted and the horse, stronger for the rest, responded as he pulled it around and headed off northwestward, angling towards the high ridge.

He rode slowly, head down, hunched in the saddle, letting the horse find its own pace. There was no urging along the reins, no drumming of heels on its flanks, and the horse stopped. The man sat still in the saddle. He drew a long breath and let it out with a sighing sound. His voice came, flat, inflectionless. 'Maybe they won't,' he said. Suddenly an explosive fury seemed to burst inside him and strike outward into action. Viciously he yanked the horse around to the right and kicked it into headlong gallop, heading northeastward towards a far lowering of the ridge.

The fury in him dwindled with the wind of movement and a quietness came over him. He was aware of the horse straining under him, of its heavy breathing. He pulled it to a steady jogging.

He rode on, a short thick man on a tired horse, dirty, unshaven, dingy in old stained clothes except for the glintings of brass on the cartridge belt around his waist. He rode on, a small moving blot in the vast red-brown reaches of distance, and he passed over the far lowering of the ridge and down the long gradual slope beyond and up a wide ground swell of shifting sand and before him, stretching out of distance into distance, was the wagon trace and a third of a mile away, headed north along it, moving away from him, were seven men on horseback. The lean man on the grey horse and another man were in the lead, one on each side of the trace, bent in their saddles, studying the ground as they moved ahead, and the other five followed.

The man on the ground swell of shifting sand stopped his horse and took the rifle from its scabbard. A strange harsh chuckle sounded in the sun-hot silence and was cut short by the shot and he saw the spurt of dust beside the lean man's horse and all of them halt with sudden startled jerks and swing in their saddles to look towards him. He jammed the rifle back into its scabbard and lifted his horse rearing to wheel it around and drove it at a fast gallop back down the ground swell of sand the way he had come. He was well up the long gradual slope towards the lowering of the ridge when he looked back and saw them coming over the ground swell and lining out in full gallop behind him. Savagely he beat at the horse and it surged up and over the lowering of the ridge and as it raced down the other side towards the long level stretch to the homestead shelter he felt the first falterings in its stride, the slight warning stumblings and recoveries, and he took hold of the sack tied to the saddle horn and snapped the cord with a lurch of his weight in the saddle and let the sack fall. The horse drove on, frantic in lessening rushes of strength, and again he looked back. They were coming steadily, no closer than before, coming with steady intensity of purpose. He saw them pull sliding to a bunched brief stop by the sack and one swing down and grab it and shake out the contents in a flurry of flour and in the stopping he increased his lead. The shelter was just ahead now and he yanked the horse to a skidding stop in front of it and whipped the revolver from the holster at his side and fired two shots towards the doorway, low, into the doorstep. He caught a flashing glimpse of the little girl inside shrinking back from the roar of the shots and he was beating the horse forward again, past the corral, across the shallow-ploughed strip, angling back towards the high ridge.

He reached the base and started up and the horse, faltering often now, laboured into the climb. It stopped, legs braced and quivering, ribs heaving, a bloody froth bubbling in its nostrils. He pivoted to the right in the saddle and looked back. Riderless horses stood in front of the shelter and the lean man in the buckskin shirt near them directing the others. One man ran towards the closest brackish pool in the almost dry stream bed with a bucket in his hand. Another strode towards the corral with the team harness over his shoulder. Another heaved at the tongue of the old wagon to swing it out from the side wall of the shelter. And yet another mounted one of the saddled horses and swung off southeastward.

The man on the ridge slope checked each in the one swift sliding glance and stared intently at the blank walls of the shelter as if trying to force vision through them. Suddenly, as thought and bodily awareness coincided, he pivoted around and to the left in the saddle. Two of them had not stopped by the shelter, had galloped on past and swept in a wide arc towards him. They were little more than three hundred yards away. One of them was still approaching and the other had stopped and was raising a rifle to his shoulder. The man on the ridge yanked upward on his reins trying to lift the horse into motion and even before he heard the shot he felt the horse leap shuddering and its forelegs doubled under and he jumped free as it collapsed forward and sideways on the slope. He leaned down and jerked the rifle free and crouched behind the still quivering body of the horse and sent a single shot crashing down towards the level and saw the two men circle back to a safer distance and turn their horses sideways towards him and dismount to stand behind them with the barrels of rifles resting over the saddles.

He reached with one hand into the pocket of his old shirt and with fumbling fingers counted the rifle bullets there. He turned his head to study the slope rising behind him. Bare rock climbed with scant crevices and small pockets of dirt where a few scraggly bushes clung. Fifty feet higher the slope levelled in a small ledge that had caught several large stones in age-gone descent. At intervals above were other small ledges. He looked back over the body of the horse and sent another shot crashing down and leaped up crouching and scrambled towards the first ledge above and a barrage of shots battered from the two men below and out and a bullet smashed into his left shoulder and spun him falling and he rolled back behind the body of the horse and hitched himself around to hold the rifle with his right hand over it. The sun beat clean and hot upon him and the two men below and out watched over their saddles and he lay quiet watching them.

Down and across the level expanse the lean man in the buckskin shirt stepped out from the doorway of the shelter and around the corner for a clear view of the ridge and the body of the horse, small at the distance yet distinct against the rock. His eyes narrowed as he peered intently and he made out the dull dirtied deadliness of the rifle barrel pointing over the body. He walked to the tall grey horse ground-reined in front of the shelter and took his rifle from its saddle scabbard. Quietly, paying no attention to the harnessing of the draft horses to the old wagon, he walked around the other side of the shelter and started back towards the ridge directly behind. He came on tracks, hoofprints in the loose dirt heading southwestward into distance towards the far lowering of the ridge. He stopped and looked down at these a long moment and moved on and came to the base of the ridge and climbed until he was almost parallel on it to the man behind the body of the horse not quite a half mile away. He lay flat on a slight levelling of the slope and adjusted the sights on his rifle and pushed the barrel out in front of him and settled into position and waited. Several shots came from the two men out on the level expanse and the man behind the body of the horse hunched himself forward and up to reply to them and the man in the buckskin shirt tightened his finger on his trigger in a slow steady squeeze. He saw the man behind the body of the horse jerk convulsively and try to rise and fall forward over the body of the horse and lie still. He saw the two men out on the level mount and start towards the ridge. Quietly he stood up and walked back towards the shelter.

The wagon was ready. Two of the saddled horses were tied behind it and a blanket had been rigged over the wagon body for shade. Under it lay the still forms of the man and the woman from inside the shelter. The little girl, small and shrinking and silent, sat on the seat between two of the other men.

'Take it easy but aimin' for time,' the man in the buckskin shirt said. 'Hit for the trace then towards town. Maybe the doc'll meet you part way.'

The draft team, fresh and strong, leaned into the harness and the tugs tightened and the wagon moved away. The man in the buckskin shirt turned to watch the two men who had ridden to the ridge approach leading their horses. An old battered saddle and a bridle hung bouncing from the saddle horn of one of the horses. The body of a man, short and thick with a brass-studded cartridge belt around its waist, hung limply over the saddle of the other horse.

'Did you get it?' said the man in the buckskin shirt.

'Yes,' said one of the men. 'In the saddle bag there.'

The man in the buckskin shirt stepped forward and bent to slip a shoulder close against the saddle up under the body of the man in the brass-studded belt and lifted it away and went and heaved it over the saddle of the tall grey horse. He stepped into the shelter and came out carrying a spade in one hand. He took the reins of the tall grey horse with the other hand and led it away. Head low, staring at the ground before him, he led it, past the corral, across the almost dry stream bed, and stopped at last by the straggling row of stunted cottonwoods. He looked up. The other men had followed him.

'Don't be a fool,' one of the other men said. 'Drag him out somewheres and let the buzzards and coyotes have him. He wasn't no more'n an animal himself.'

'No,' the man in the buckskin shirt said. He looked back past the shelter, on into the vast empty distance where the trail of a tired horse led northeastward towards the far lowering of the ridge and returned. 'He was a murderin' thievin' son-of-a-bitch. But he was a man.' Quietly, bending to the hot task in the clean sun, the man in the buckskin shirt struck the spade into the red-brown earth.

Jack Schaefer

Sergeant Houck

SERGEANT HOUCK stopped his horse just below the top of the ridge ahead. The upper part of his body was silhouetted against the sky line as he rose in his stirrups to peer over the crest. He urged the horse on up and the two of them, the man and the horse, were sharp and distinct against the copper sky. After a moment he turned and rode down to the small troop waiting. He reined beside Lieutenant Imler.

'It's there, sir. Alongside a creek in the next hollow. Maybe a third of a mile.'

Lieutenant Imler looked at him coldly. 'You took your time, Sergeant. Smack on the top, too.'

'Couldn't see plain, sir. Sun was in my eyes.'

'Wanted them to spot you, eh, Sergeant?'

'No, sir. Sun was bothering me. I don't think –'

'Forget it, Sergeant. I don't like this either.'

Lieutenant Imler was in no hurry. He led the troop slowly up the hill. The real fuss was fifty-some miles away. Captain McKay was hogging the honours there. Here he was, tied to this sideline detail. Twenty men. Ten would have been enough. Ten and an old hand like Sergeant Houck.

With his drawn sabre pointing forward, Lieutenant Imler led the charge up and over the crest and down the long slope to the Indian village. There were some scattered shots from bushes by the creek, ragged pops indicating poor powder and poorer weapons, probably fired by the last of the old men left behind when the young braves departed in war paint ten days before. The village was silent and deserted.

Lieutenant Imler surveyed the ground they'd taken. 'Spectacular achievement,' he muttered to himself. He beckoned Sergeant Houck to him.

'Your redskin friend was right, Sergeant. This is it.'

'Knew he could be trusted, sir.'

'Our orders are to destroy the village. Send a squad out to round up any stock. There might be some horses around. We're to take them in.' Lieutenant Imler waved an arm at the thirty-odd skin-and-pole huts. 'Set the others to pulling those down. Burn what you can and smash everything else.'

'Right, sir.'

Lieutenant Imler rode into the slight shade of the cottonwoods along the creek. He wiped the dust from his face and set his campaign hat at a fresh angle to ease the crease the band had made on his forehead. Here he was, hot and tired and way out at the end of nowhere with another long ride ahead, while Captain McKay was having it out at last with Grey Otter and his renegade warriors somewhere between the Turkey Foot and the Washakie. He relaxed to wait in the saddle, beginning to frame his report in his mind.

'Pardon, sir.'

Lieutenant Imler looked around. Sergeant Houck was standing nearby with something in his arms, something that squirmed and seemed to have dozens of legs and arms.

'What the devil is that, Sergeant?'

'A baby, sir. Or rather, a boy. Two years old, sir.'

'How the devil do you know? By his teeth?'

'His mother told me, sir.'

'His mother?'

'Certainly, sir. She's right here.'

Lieutenant Imler saw her then, standing beside a neighbouring tree, shrinking into the shadow and staring at Sergeant Houck and the squirming child. He leaned to look closer. She wore a shapeless, sack-like covering with slits for her arms and head. She was sun-and-wind-burned, dark yet not as dark as he expected. And there was no mistaking the colour of her hair. It was light brown and long and coiled in a bun on her neck.

'Sergeant! It's a white woman!'

'Right, sir. Her name's Cora Sutliff. The wagon train she was with was wiped out by a raiding party. She and another woman were taken along. The other woman died. She didn't. The village bought her. She's been in Grey Otter's lodge.' Sergeant Houck smacked the squirming boy briskly and tucked him under one arm. He looked straight at Lieutenant Imler. 'That was three years ago, sir.'

'Three years? Then that boy –'

'That's right, sir.'

Captain McKay looked up from his desk to see Sergeant Houck stiff at attention before him. It always gave him a feeling of satisfaction to see this great, granite man. The replacements they were sending these days, raw and unseasoned, were enough to shake his faith in the service. But as long as there remained a sprinkling of these case-hardened old-time regulars, the Army would still be the Army.

'At ease, Sergeant.'

'Thank you, sir.'

Captain McKay drummed his fingers on the desk. This was a ridiculous situation and the solid, impassive bulk of Sergeant Houck made it seem even more so.

'That woman, sergeant. She's married. The husband's alive – wasn't with the train when it was attacked. He's been located. Has a place about twenty miles out of Laramie. The name's right and everything checks. You're to take her there and turn her over with the troop's compliments.'

'Me, sir?'

'She asked for you. The big man who found her. Lieutenant Imler says that's you.'

Sergeant Houck considered this expressionlessly. 'And about the boy, sir?'

'He goes with her.' Captain McKay drummed on the desk again. 'Speaking frankly, Sergeant, I think she's making a mistake. I suggested she let us see that the boy got back to the tribe. Grey Otter's dead and after that affair two weeks ago there's not many of the men left. But they'll be on the reservation now and he'd be taken care of. She wouldn't hear of it; said if he had to go she would, too.' Captain McKay felt his former indignation rising again. 'I say she's playing the fool. You agree with me, of course.'

'No, sir. I don't.'

'And why the devil not?'

'He's her son, sir.'

'But he's – Well, that's neither here nor there, Sergeant. It's not our affair. We deliver her and there's an end to it. You'll draw expense money and start within the hour.'

'Right, sir.' The sergeant straightened and made for the door.

'Houck.'

'Yes, sir.'

'Take good care of her – and that damn' kid.'

'Right, sir.'

Captain McKay stood by the window and watched the small cavalcade go past toward the post gateway. Lucky that his wife had come with him to this god-forsaken station lost in the prairie wasteland. Without her they would have been in a fix with the woman. As it was, the woman looked like a woman now. And why shouldn't she, wearing his wife's third-best crinoline dress? It was a bit large, but it gave her a proper feminine appearance. His wife had enjoyed fitting her, from the skin out, everything except shoes. Those were too small. The woman seemed to prefer her worn moccasins anyway. And she was uncomfortable in the clothes. But she was decently grateful for them, insisting she would have them returned or would pay for them somehow. She was riding past the window, sidesaddle on his wife's horse, still with that strange shrinking air about her, not so much frightened as remote, as if she could not quite connect with what was happening to her, what was going on around her.

Behind her was Private Lakin, neat and spruce in his uniform, with the boy in front of him on the horse. The boy's legs stuck out on each side of the small, improvised pillow tied to the forward arch of the saddle to give him a better seat. He looked like a weird, dark-haired doll bobbing with the movements of the horse.

And there beside the woman, shadowing her in the mid-morning, was that extra incongruous touch, the great hulk of Sergeant Houck, straight in his saddle, taking this as he took everything, with no excitement and no show of any emotion, a job to be done.

They went past and Captain McKay watched them ride out through the gateway. It was not quite so incongruous after all. As he had discovered on many a tight occasion, there was something comforting in the presence of that big man. Nothing ever shook him. You might never know exactly what went on inside his close-cropped skull, but you could be certain that what needed to be done he would do.

They were scarcely out of sight of the post when the boy began squirming. Private Lakin clamped him to the pillow with a capable right hand. The squirming persisted. The boy seemed determined to escape from what he regarded as an alien captor. Silent, intent, he writhed on the pillow. Private Lakin's hand and arm grew weary. He tickled his horse forward with his heels until he was close behind the others.

'Beg pardon, sir.'

Sergeant Houck shifted in his saddle and looked around. 'Yes?'

'He's trying to get away, sir. It'd be easier if I tied him down. Could I use my belt, sir?'

Sergeant Houck held in his horse to drop back alongside Private Lakin. 'Kids don't need tying,' he said. He reached out and plucked the boy from in front of Private Lakin and laid him, face down, across the withers of his own horse and smacked him sharply. Then he set him back on the pillow. The boy sat still, very still. Sergeant Houck pushed his left hand into his left side pocket and pulled out a fistful of small hard biscuits. He passed these to Private Lakin. 'Stick one of these in his mouth when he gets restless.'

Sergeant Houck urged his horse forward until he was beside the woman once more. She had turned her head to watch and she stared sidewise at him for a long moment, then looked straight forward again.

They came to the settlement in the same order: the woman and Sergeant Houck side by side in the lead, Private Lakin and the boy tagging behind at a respectful distance. Sergeant Houck dismounted and helped the woman down and handed the boy to her. He saw Private Lakin looking wistfully at the painted front of the settlement's one saloon and tapped him on one knee. 'Scat,' he said and watched Private Lakin turn his horse and ride off, leading the other two horses.

Then he led the woman into the squat frame building that served as general store and post office and stage stop. He settled the woman and her child on a preserved-goods box and went to the counter to arrange for their fares. When he came back to sit on another box near her, the entire permanent male population of the settlement was assembled just inside the door, all eleven of them staring at the woman.

'. . . that's the one . . .'

'. . . an Indian had her . . .'

'. . . shows in the kid . . .'

Sergeant Houck looked at the woman. She was staring at the floor and the blood was leaving her face. He started to rise and felt her hand on his arm. She had leaned over quickly and clutched his sleeve.

'Please,' she said. 'Don't make trouble on account of me.'

'Trouble?' said Sergeant Houck. 'No trouble.' He stood up and confronted the fidgeting men by the door. 'I've seen kids around this place. Some of them small. This one needs decent clothes and the store here doesn't stock them.'

The men stared at him, startled, and then at the wide-eyed boy in his clean but patched skimpy cloth covering. Five or six of them went out through the door and disappeared in various directions. The others scattered through the store. Sergeant Houck stood sentinel, relaxed and quiet by his box, and those who had gone out straggled back, several embarrassed and empty-handed, the rest proud with their offerings. Sergeant Houck took the boy from the woman's lap and stood him on his box. He measured the offerings against the small body and chose a small red checked shirt and a small pair of overalls. He set the one pair of small scuffed shoes aside. 'Kids don't need shoes,' he said. 'Only in winter.'

When the coach rolled in, it was empty and they had it to themselves for the first hours. Dust drifted steadily through the windows and the silence inside was a persistent thing. The woman did not want to talk. She had lost all liking for it and would speak only when necessary. And Sergeant Houck used words with a natural economy, for the sole simple purpose of conveying or obtaining information that he regarded as pertinent to the business immediately in hand. Only once did he speak during these hours and then only to set a fact straight in his mind. He kept his eyes fixed on the scenery outside as he spoke.

'Did he treat you all right?'

The woman made no pretence of misunderstanding him. 'Yes,' she said.

The coach rolled on and the dust drifted. 'He beat me once,' she said and four full minutes passed before she finished the thought. 'Maybe it was right. I wouldn't work.'

They stopped for a quick meal at a lonely ranch house and ate in silence while the man there helped the driver change horses. It was two mail stops later, at the next change, that another passenger climbed in and plopped his battered suitcase and himself on the front seat opposite them. He was of medium height and plump. He wore city clothes and had quick eyes and features that seemed small in the plumpness of his face. He took out a handkerchief and wiped his face and took off his hat to wipe all the way up his forehead. He laid the hat on top of the suitcase and moved restlessly on the seat, trying to find a comfortable position.

'You three together?'

'Yes,' said Sergeant Houck.

'Your wife then?'

'No,' said Sergeant Houck. He looked out the window on his side and studied the far horizon.

The coach rolled on and the man's quick eyes examined the three of them and came to rest on the woman's feet.

'Begging your pardon, lady, but why do you wear those things? Moccasins, aren't they? They more comfortable?'

She shrank back further in the seat and the blood began to leave her face.

'No offence, lady,' said the man. 'I just wondered –' He stopped. Sergeant Houck was looking at him.

'Dust's bad,' said Sergeant Houck. 'And the flies this time of year. Best to keep your mouth closed.' He looked out the window again, and the only sounds were the running beat of the hoofs and the creakings of the old coach.

A front wheel struck a stone and the coach jolted up at an angle and lurched sideways and the boy gave a small whimper. The woman pulled him on to her lap.

'Say,' said the man. 'Where'd you ever pick up that kid? Looks like –' He stopped. Sergeant Houck was reaching up and rapping against the top of the coach. The driver's voice could be heard shouting at the horses and the coach stopped. One of the doors opened and the driver peered in. Instinctively he picked Sergeant Houck.

'What's the trouble, soldier?'

'No trouble,' said Sergeant Houck. 'Our friend here wants to ride up with you.' He looked a' the plump man. 'Less dust up there. It's healthy and gives a good view.'

'Now, wait a minute,' said the man. 'Where'd you get the idea –'

'Healthy,' said Sergeant Houck.

The driver looked at the bleak, impassive hardness of Sergeant Houck and at the twitching softness of the plump man. 'Reckon it would be,' he said. 'Come along. I'll boost you up.'

The coach rolled along the false-fronted one street of a mushroom town and stopped before a frame building tagged Hotel. One of the coach doors opened and the plump man retrieved his hat and suitcase and scuttled into the building. The driver appeared at the coach door. 'Last meal here before the night run,' he said.

When they came out, the shadows were long and fresh horses had been harnessed. As they settled themselves again, a new driver, whip in hand, climbed up to the high seat and gathered the reins into his left hand. The whip cracked and the coach lurched forward and a young man ran out of the low building across the street carrying a saddle. He ran alongside and heaved the saddle up on the roof inside the guardrail. He pulled at the door and managed to scramble in as the coach picked up speed. He dropped on to the front seat, puffing deeply. 'Evening, ma'am,' he said between puffs. 'And you, general.' He leaned forward to slap the boy gently along the jaw. 'And you too, bub.'

Sergeant Houck looked at the lean young man, at the faded Levis tucked into high-heeled boots, the plaid shirt, the amiable competent young face. He grunted a greeting, unintelligible but a pleasant sound.

'A man's legs ain't made for running,' said the young man. 'Just to fork a horse. That last drink was near too long.'

'The Army'd put some starch in those legs,' said Sergeant Houck.

'Maybe. Maybe that's why I ain't in the Army.' The young man sat quietly, relaxed to the jolting of the coach. 'Is there some other topic of genteel conversation you folk'd want to worry some?'

'No,' said Sergeant Houck.

'Then maybe you'll pardon me,' said the young man. 'I hoofed it a lot of miles to-day.' He worked hard at his boots and at last got them off and tucked them out of the way on the floor. He hitched himself up and over on the seat until he was resting on one hip. He put an arm on the window sill and cradled his head on it. His head dropped down and he was asleep.

Sergeant Houck felt a small bump on his left side. The boy had toppled against him. Sergeant Houck set the small body across his lap with head nestled into the crook of his right arm. He leaned his head down and heard the soft little last sigh as drowsiness overcame the boy. He looked sidewise at the woman and dimly made out the outline of her head falling forward and jerking back up and he reached his left arm along the top of the seat until his hand touched her far shoulder. He felt her shoulder stiffen and then relax as she moved closer and leaned toward him. He slipped down lower in the seat so that her head could reach his shoulder and he felt the gentle touch of her brown hair on his neck above his shirt collar. He waited patiently and at last he could tell by her steady deep breathing that all fright had left her and all her thoughts were stilled.

The coach reached a rutted stretch and began to sway and the young man stirred and began to slide on the smooth leather of his seat. Sergeant Houck put up a foot and braced it against the seat edge and the young man's body rested against it. Sergeant Houck leaned his head back on the top of the seat. The stars came out in the clear sky and the running beat of the hoofs had the rhythm of a cavalry squad at a steady trot and gradually Sergeant Houck softened slightly into sleep.

Sergeant Houck awoke, as always, all at once and aware. The coach had stopped. From the sounds outside, fresh horses were being buckled into the traces. The first light of dawn was creeping into the coach. He raised his head and he realized that he was stiff.

The young man was awake. He was inspecting the vast leather sole of Sergeant Houck's shoe. His eyes flicked up and met Sergeant Houck's eyes and he grinned.

'That's impressive footwear,' he whispered. 'You'd need starch in the legs with hoofs like that.' He sat up and stretched, long and reaching, like a lazy young animal. 'Hell,' he whispered again. 'You must be stiff as a branding iron.' He took hold of Sergeant Houck's leg at the knee and hoisted it slightly so that Sergeant Houck could bend it and ease the foot down to the floor without disturbing the sleeping woman leaning against him. He stretched out both hands and gently lifted the sleeping boy from Sergeant Houck's lap and sat back with the boy in his arms. The young man studied the boy's face. 'Can't be yours,' he whispered.

'No,' whispered Sergeant Houck.

'Must have some Indian strain.'

'Yes.'

The young man whispered down at the sleeping boy. 'You can't help that, can you, bub?'

'No,' said Sergeant Houck suddenly, out loud. 'He can't.'

The woman jerked upright and pulled over to the window on her side, rubbing at her eyes. The boy woke up, wide awake on the instant and saw the unfamiliar face above him and began to squirm violently. The young man clamped his arms tighter. 'Morning, ma'am,' he said. 'Looks like I ain't such a good nursemaid.'

Sergeant Houck reached out a hand and picked up the boy by a grip on the small overalls and deposited him in a sitting position on the seat beside the young man. The boy sat very still.

The sun climbed into plain view and now the coach was stirring the dust of a well-worn road. It stopped where another road crossed and the young man inside pulled on his boots. He bobbed his head in the direction of a group of low buildings up the side road. 'Think I'll try it there. They'll be peeling broncs about now and the foreman knows I can sit a saddle.' He opened a door and jumped to the ground and turned to poke his head in. 'Hope you make it right,' he said. 'Wherever you're heading.' The door closed and he could be heard scrambling up the back of the coach to get his saddle. There was a thump as he and the saddle hit the ground and then voices began outside, rising in tone.

Sergeant Houck pushed his head through the window beside him. The young man and the driver were facing each other over the saddle. The young man was pulling the pockets of his Levis inside out. 'Lookahere, Will,' he said. 'You know I'll kick in soon as I have some cash. Hell, I've hooked rides with you before.'

'Not now no more,' said the driver. 'The company's sore. They hear of this they'd have my job. I'll have to hold the saddle.'

'You touch that saddle and they'll pick you up in pieces from here to breakfast.'

Sergeant Houck fumbled for his inside jacket pocket. He whistled. The two men turned. He looked hard at the young man. 'There's something on the seat in here. Must have slipped out of your pocket.'

The young man leaned in and saw the two silver dollars on the hard seat and looked up at Sergeant Houck. 'You've been in spots yourself,' he said.

'Yes,' said Sergeant Houck.

The young man grinned. He picked up the coins in one hand and swung the other to slap Sergeant Houck's leg, sharp, stinging and grateful. 'Age ain't hurting you any, general,' he said.

The coach started up and the woman looked at Sergeant Houck. The minutes passed and still she looked at him.

'If I'd had brains enough to get married,' he said, 'might be I'd have had a son. Might have been one like that.'

The woman looked away, out of her window. She reached up to pat at her hair and the firm line of her lips softened in the tiny imperceptible beginnings of a smile. The minutes passed and Sergeant Houck stirred again. 'It's the upbringing that counts,' he said and settled into silent immobility, watching the miles go by.

It was near noon when they stopped in Laramie and Sergeant Houck handed the woman out and tucked the boy under one arm and led the way to the waiting room. He settled the woman and the boy in two chairs and left them. He was back soon, driving a light buckboard wagon drawn by a pair of deep-barrelled chestnuts. The wagon bed was well padded with layers of empty burlap bags. He went into the waiting room and picked up the boy and beckoned to the woman to follow. He put the boy down on the burlap bags and helped the woman up on the driving seat.

'Straight out the road, they tell me,' he said. 'About fifteen miles. Then right along the creek. Can't miss it.'

He stood by the wagon, staring along the road. The woman leaned from the seat and clutched at his shoulder. Her voice was high and frightened. 'You're going with me?' Her fingers clung to his service jacket. 'Please! You've got to!'

Sergeant Houck put a hand over hers on his shoulder and released her fingers. 'Yes. I'm going.' He put the child in her lap and stepped to the seat and took the reins. The wagon moved forward.

'You're afraid,' he said.

'They haven't told him,' she said, 'about the boy.'

Sergeant Houck's hands tightened on the reins and the horses slowed to a walk. He clucked sharply to them and slapped the reins on their backs and they quickened again into a trot. The wagon topped a slight rise and the road sloped downward for a long stretch to where the green of trees and tall bushes showed in the distance. A jack rabbit started from the scrub growth by the roadside and leaped high and levelled out, a grey-brown streak. The horses shied and broke rhythm and quieted to a walk under the firm pressure of the reins. Sergeant Houck kept them at a walk, easing the heat out of their muscles, down the long slope to the trees. He let them step into the creek up to their knees and dip their muzzles in the clear running water. The front wheels of the wagon were in the creek and he reached behind him to find a tin dipper tucked among the burlap bags and leaned far out to dip up water for the woman, the boy and himself. He backed the team out of the creek and swung them into the ruts leading along the bank to the right.

The creek was on their left and the sun was behind them, warm on their backs, and the shadows of the horses pushed ahead. The shadows were longer, stretching farther ahead, when they rounded a bend along the creek and the buildings came in sight, the two-room cabin and the several lean-to sheds and the rickety pole corral. A man was standing by one of the sheds and when Sergeant Houck halted the team he came toward them and stopped about twenty feet away. He was not young, perhaps in his middle thirties, but with the young look of a man on whom the years have made no mark except that of the simple passing of time. He was tall, soft and loose-jointed in build, and indecisive in manner and movement. His eyes wavered as he looked at the woman, and the fingers of his hands hanging limp at his sides twitched as he waited for her to speak.

She climbed down her side of the wagon and faced him. She stood straight and the sun behind her shone on her hair. 'Well, Fred,' she said. 'I'm here.'

'Cora,' he said. 'It's been a long time, Cora. I didn't know you'd come so soon.'

'Why didn't you come get me? Why didn't you, Fred?'

'I didn't rightly know what to do, Cora. It was all so mixed up. Thinking you were dead. Then hearing about you. And what happened. I had to think about things. And I couldn't get away easy. I was going to try maybe next week.'

'I hoped you'd come. Right away when you heard.'

His body twisted uneasily while his feet remained flat and motionless on the ground. 'Your hair's still pretty,' he said. 'The way it used to be.'

Something like a sob caught in her throat and she started toward him. Sergeant Houck stepped down on the other side of the wagon and walked off to the creek and kneeled to bend and wash the dust from his face. He stood drying his face with a handkerchief and watching the little eddies of the current around several stones in the creek. He heard the voices behind him.

'Wait, Fred. There's something you have to know.'

'That kid? What's it doing here with you?'

'It's mine, Fred.'

'Yours? Where'd you get it?'

'It's my child. Mine.'

There was silence and then the man's voice, bewildered, hurt. 'So it's really true what they said. About that Indian.'

'Yes. He bought me. By their rules I belonged to him. I wouldn't be alive and here now, any other way. I didn't have any say about it.'

There was silence again and then the man spoke, self-pity creeping into his tone. 'I didn't count on anything like this.'

Sergeant Houck walked back to the wagon. The woman seemed relieved at the interruption. 'This is Sergeant Houck,' she said. 'He brought me all the way.'

The man nodded his head and raised a hand to shove back the sandy hair that kept falling forward on his forehead. 'I suppose I ought to thank you, soldier. All that trouble.'

'No trouble,' said Sergeant Houck.

The man pushed at the ground in front of him with one shoe, poking the toe into the dirt and studying it. 'I suppose we ought to go inside.

It's near suppertime. I guess you'll be taking a meal here, soldier, before you start back to town.'

'Right,' said Sergeant Houck. 'And I'm tired. I'll stay the night, too. Start in the morning. Sleep in one of those sheds.'

The man pushed at the ground more vigorously. The little pile of dirt in front of his shoe seemed to interest him a great deal. 'All right, soldier. Sorry there's no quarters inside.' He turned quickly and started for the cabin.

The woman took the boy from the wagon and followed him. Sergeant Houck unharnessed the horses and led them to the creek for a drink and to the corral and let them through the gate. He walked quietly to the cabin doorway and stopped just outside.

'For God's sake, Cora,' the man was saying, 'I don't see why you had to bring that kid with you. You could have told me about it. I didn't have to see him.'

'What do you mean?'

'Why, now we've got the problem of how to get rid of him. Have to find a mission or some place that'll take him. Why didn't you leave him where he came from?'

'No! He's mine!'

'Good God, Cora! Are you crazy? Think you can foist off a thing like that on me?'

Sergeant Houck stepped through the doorway. 'Thought I heard something about supper,' he said. He looked around the small room, then let his eyes rest on the man. 'I see the makings on those shelves. Come along, Mr Sutliff. A woman doesn't want men cluttering about when she's getting a meal. Show me your place before it gets dark.'

He stood, waiting, and the man scraped at the floor with one foot and slowly stood up and went with him.

They were well beyond earshot of the cabin when Sergeant Houck spoke again. 'How long were you married? Before it happened?'

'Six years,' said the man. 'No, seven. It was seven when we lost the last place and headed this way with the train.'

'Seven years,' said Sergeant Houck. 'And no child.'

'It just didn't happen. I don't know why.' The man stopped and looked sharply at Sergeant Houck. 'Oh. So that's the way you're looking at it.'

'Yes,' said Sergeant Houck. 'Now you've got one. A son.' 'Not mine,' said the man. 'You can talk. It's not *your* wife. It's bad enough thinking of taking an Indian's leavings.' He wiped his lips on his sleeve and spat in disgust. 'I'll be damned if I'll take his kid.'

'Not his any more. He's dead.'

'Look, man. Look how it'd be. A damned little halfbreed. Around all the time to make me remember what she did. A reminder of things I'd want to forget.'

'Could be a reminder that she had some mighty hard going. And maybe come through the better for it.'

'*She* had hard going! What about me? Thinking she was dead. Getting used to that. Maybe thinking of another woman. Then she comes back – and an Indian kid with her. What does that make me?'

'Could make you a man,' said Sergeant Houck. 'Think it over.' He turned away and went to the corral and leaned on the rail, watching the horses roll the sweat-itches out on the dry sod. The man went slowly down by the creek and stood on the bank, pushing at the dirt with one shoe and kicking small pebbles into the water. The sun, holding to the horizon rim, dropped suddenly out of sight and dusk came swiftly to blur the outlines of the buildings. The woman appeared in the doorway and called and they went in. There was simple food on the table and the woman stood beside it. 'I've already fed him,' she said and moved her head toward the door to the inner room.

Sergeant Houck ate steadily and reached to refill his plate. The man picked briefly at the food before him and stopped, and the woman ate nothing at all. The man put his hands on the table edge and pushed back and stood up. He went to a side shelf and took a bottle and two thick cups and set them by his plate. He filled the cups a third full from the bottle and shoved one along the table boards toward Sergeant Houck. He lifted the other. His voice was bitter. 'Happy homecoming,' he said. He waited and Sergeant Houck took the other cup and they drank. The man lifted the bottle and poured himself another drink.

The woman looked quickly at him and away.

'Please, Fred.'

The man paid no attention. He reached with the bottle toward the other cup.

'No,' said Sergeant Houck.

The man shrugged. 'You can think better on whisky. Sharpens the mind.' He set the bottle down and took his cup and drained it. Sergeant Houck fumbled in his right side pocket and found a short straight straw there and pulled it out and put one end in his mouth and chewed slowly on it. The man and the woman sat still, opposite each other at the table, and seemed to forget his quiet presence. They stared everywhere except at each other. Yet their attention was plainly concentrated on each other. The man spoke first. His voice was restrained, carrying conscious patience.

'Look, Cora. You wouldn't want to do that to me. You can't mean what you said before.'

Her voice was determined. 'He's mine.'

'Now, Cora. You don't want to push it too far. A man can take just so much. I didn't know what to do after I heard about you. But I was all ready to forgive you. And now you –'

'Forgive me!' She knocked against her chair rising to her feet. Hurt and bewilderment made her voice ragged as she repeated the words. 'Forgive me?' She turned and ran into the inner room. The handleless door banged shut behind her.

The man stared after her and shook his head and reached again for the bottle.

'Enough's enough,' said Sergeant Houck.

The man shrugged in quick irritation. 'For you maybe,' he said and poured himself another drink. 'Is there any reason you should be noseying in on this?'

'My orders,' said Sergeant Houck, 'were to deliver them safely. Both of them.'

'You've done that,' said the man. He lifted the cup and drained it and set it down carefully. 'They're here.'

'Yes,' said Sergeant Houck. 'They're here.' He stood up and stepped to the outside door and looked into the night. He waited a moment until his eyes were accustomed to the darkness and could distinguish objects faintly in the starlight. He stepped out and went to the pile of straw behind one of the sheds and took an armload and carried it back by the cabin and dropped it at the foot of a tree by one corner. He sat on it, his legs stretched out, his shoulders against the tree, and broke off a straw stem and chewed slowly on it. After a while his jaws stopped their slow slight movement and his head sank forward and his eyes closed.

Sergeant Houck woke up abruptly. He was on his feet in a moment, and listening. He heard the faint sound of voices in the cabin, indistinct but rising as the tension rose in them. He went toward the doorway and stopped just short of the rectangle of light from the lamp.

'You're not going to have anything to do with me!' The woman's voice was harsh with stubborn anger. 'Not until this has been settled right!'

'Aw, come on, Cora.' The man's voice was fuzzy, slow-paced. 'We'll talk about that in the morning.'

'No!'

'All right!' Sudden fury made the man's voice shake. 'You want it settled now. Well, it's settled! We're getting rid of that damn' kid first thing to-morrow!'

'No!'

'What gave you the idea you've got any say around here after what you did? I'm the one to say what's to be done. You don't be careful, maybe I won't take you back.'

'Maybe I don't want you to!'

'So damn' finicky all of a sudden! After being with that Indian and maybe a lot more!'

Sergeant Houck stepped through the doorway. The man's back was to him, and he spun him around and his right hand smacked against the side of the man's face and sent him staggering against the wall.

'Forgetting your manners won't help,' said Sergeant Houck. He looked around, and the woman had disappeared into the inner room. The man leaned against the wall, rubbing his cheek, and she came out, the boy in her arms, and ran toward the other door.

'Cora!' the man shouted. 'Cora!'

She stopped, a brief hesitation in flight. 'I don't belong to you,' she said and was gone through the doorway. The man pushed out from the wall and started after her and the great bulk of Sergeant Houck blocked the way.

'You heard her,' said Sergeant Houck. 'She doesn't belong to anybody now. Nobody but that boy.'

The man stared at him and some of the fury went out of his eyes and he stumbled to his chair at the table and reached for the bottle. Sergeant Houck watched him a moment, then turned and quietly went outside. He walked toward the corral, and as he passed the second shed she came out of the darker shadows and her voice, low and intense, whispered at him: 'I've got to go. I can't stay here.'

Sergeant Houck nodded and went on to the corral. He harnessed the horses quickly and with a minimum of sound. He finished buckling the traces and stood straight and looked toward the cabin. He walked to the doorway and stepped inside. The man was leaning forward in his chair, his elbows on the table, staring at the empty bottle.

'It's finished,' said Sergeant Houck. 'She's leaving now.'

The man shook his head and pushed at the bottle with one forefinger. 'She can't do that.' He looked up at Sergeant Houck and sudden rage began to show in his eyes. 'She can't do that! She's my wife!'

'Not any more,' said Sergeant Houck. 'Best forget she ever came back.' He started toward the door and heard the sharp sound of the chair scraping on the floor behind him. The man's voice rose, shrilling up almost into a shriek.

'Stop!' The man rushed to the wall rack and grabbed the rifle there and held it low and aimed it at Sergeant Houck. 'Stop!' He was breathing deeply and he fought for control of his voice. 'You're not going to take her away!'

Sergeant Houck turned slowly. He stood still, a motionless granite shape in the lamplight.

'Threatening an Army man,' said Sergeant Houck. 'And with an empty gun.'

The man wavered and his eyes flicked down at the rifle. In the second of indecision Sergeant Houck plunged toward him and one huge hand grasped the gun barrel and pushed it aside and the shot thudded harmlessly into the cabin wall. He wrenched the gun from the man's grasp and his other hand took the man by the shirt front and pushed him down into the chair.

'No more of that,' said Sergeant Houck. 'Best sit quiet.' He looked around the room and found the box of cartridges on a shelf and he took this with the rifle and went to the door. 'Look around in the morning and you'll find these.' He went outside and tossed the gun up on the roof of one of the sheds and dropped the little box by the pile of straw and kicked some straw over it. He went to the wagon and stood by it and the woman came out of the darkness, carrying the boy.

The wagon wheels rolled silently. The small creakings of the wagon body and the thudding rhythm of the horses' hoofs were distinct, isolated sounds in the night. The creek was on their right and they followed the road back the way they had come. The woman moved on the seat, shifting the boy's weight from one arm to the other, until Sergeant Houck took him by the overalls and lifted him and reached behind to lay him on the burlap bags. 'A good boy,' he said. 'Has the Indian way of taking things without yapping. A good way.'

The thin new tracks in the dust unwound endlessly under the wheels and the waning moon climbed through the scattered bushes and trees along the creek.

'I have relatives in Missouri,' said the woman. 'I could go there.'

Sergeant Houck fumbled in his side pocket and found a straw and put this in his mouth and chewed slowly on it. 'Is that what you want?'

'No.'

They came to the main-road crossing and swung left and the dust thickened under the horses' hoofs. The lean dark shape of a coyote slipped from the brush on one side and bounded along the road and disappeared on the other side.

'I'm forty-seven,' said Sergeant Houck. 'Nearly thirty of that in the Army. Makes a man rough.'

The woman looked straight ahead and a small smile showed in the corners of her mouth.

'Four months,' said Sergeant Houck, 'and this last hitch's done. I'm thinking of homesteading on out in the Territory.' He chewed on the straw and took it between a thumb and forefinger and flipped it away. 'You could get a room at the settlement.'

'I could,' said the woman. The horses slowed to a walk, breathing deeply, and he let them hold the steady, plodding pace. Far off a coyote howled and others caught the signal and the sounds echoed back and forth in the distance and died away into the night silence.

'Four months,' said Sergeant Houck. 'That's not so long.'

'No,' said the woman. 'Not too long.'

A breeze stirred across the brush and she put out a hand and touched his shoulder. Her fingers moved down along his upper arm and curved over the big muscles there and the warmth of them sank through the cloth of his worn service jacket. She dropped her hand in her lap again and looked ahead along the ribbon of the road. He clucked to the horses and urged them again into a trot and the small creakings of the wagon body and the dulled rhythm of the hoofs were gentle sounds in the night.

The late moon climbed and its pale light shone slantwise down on the moving wagon, on the sleeping boy and the woman looking straight ahead, and on the great solid figure of Sergeant Houck.

ACKNOWLEDGEMENTS

The Publishers wish to thank the following for permission to reprint previously published material. Every effort has been made to locate all persons having any rights in the stories appearing in this book but appropriate acknowledgement has been omitted in some cases through lack of information. Such omissions will be corrected in future printings of the book upon written notification to the Publishers.

Dr Loren Grey for 'Siena Waits'; 'Yaqui'; and 'Tappan's Burro' by Zane Grey.

Dodd, Mead and Company Inc. for 'Battle's End' by Max Brand.

McIntosh and Otis Inc. for 'A Man Called Horse' by Dorothy M. Johnson. Copyright © 1949. Copyright © renewed 1977 by Dorothy M. Johnson.

Don Congdon Associates Inc. and André Deutsch Ltd for 'One Man's Honor' and 'Sergeant Houck' by Jack Schaefer. Copyright © 1959 by Jack Schaefer; renewed 1987 by Jack Schaefer and copyright © 1951; renewed 1971 by Jack Schaefer respectively.